Penguin Books

THE NANCY MITFORD OMNIBUS

Nancy Mitford was born in 1904. Her childhood in a large remote country house with five sisters and one brother is described in the early chapters of *The Pursuit of Love*, which, said Miss Mitford, are largely auto-biographical. She was, she said, uneducated except for being taught to ride and to speak French. She lived in Paris and she periodically contributed articles on life there to the *Sunday Times*. In 1956 she edited *Noblesse Oblige*, a collection of essays on U-usage.

Nancy Mitford wrote several novels and edited two books of Victorian letters, *The Ladies of Alderley* and *The Stanleys of Alderley*. She also translated into English Madame de La Fayette's classic novel *La Princesse de Clèves*, and wrote four biographies, *Madame de Pompadour*, *Voltaire in Love*, *The Sun King* and *Frederick the Great*. Her adaptation of a play by André Roussin ran for years in London under the title *The Little Hut*. She was awarded the C.B.E. in 1972 and died in 1973.

The Nancy Mitford Omnibus

The Pursuit of Love
Love in a Cold Climate
The Blessing
Don't Tell Alfred

Penguin Books
in association with Hamish Hamilton

Penguin Books Ltd, Harmondsworth, Middlesex, England
Viking Penguin Inc., 40 West 23rd Street, New York, New York 10010, U.S.A.
Penguin Books Australia Ltd, Ringwood, Victoria, Australia
Penguin Books Canada Limited, 2801 John Street, Markham, Ontario, Canada L3R 1B4
Penguin Books (N.Z.) Ltd, 182–190 Wairau Road, Auckland 10, New Zealand

The Pursuit of Love published 1945
Published in Penguin Books 1949

Love in a Cold Climate first published 1949
Published in Penguin Books 1954

The Blessing first published 1951
Published in Penguin Books 1957
Copyright 1951 by Nancy Mitford
All rights reserved

Don't Tell Alfred first published 1960
Published in Penguin Books 1963
Copyright © Nancy Mitford, 1960
All rights reserved

This combined volume first published as *The Best Novels of
Nancy Mitford* Hamish Hamilton Ltd 1974
Published in Penguin Books 1986
Reprinted 1987

Copyright © Nancy Mitford, 1974
All rights reserved

Printed and bound in Great Britain by
Cox & Wyman Ltd, Reading
Typeset in Baskerville

CONTENTS

THE PURSUIT OF LOVE

TO
GASTON PALEWSKI

CHAPTER I

THERE is a photograph in existence of Aunt Sadie and her six children sitting round the tea-table at Alconleigh. The table is situated, as it was, is now, and ever shall be, in the hall, in front of a huge open fire of logs. Over the chimney-piece plainly visible in the photograph, hangs an entrenching tool, with which, in 1915, Uncle Matthew had whacked to death eight Germans one by one as they crawled out of a dug-out. It is still covered with blood and hairs, an object of fascination to us as children. In the photograph Aunt Sadie's face, always beautiful, appears strangely round, her hair strangely fluffy, and her clothes strangely dowdy, but it is unmistakably she who sits there with Robin, in oceans of lace, lolling on her knee. She seems uncertain what to do with his head, and the presence of Nanny waiting to take him away is felt though not seen. The other children, between Louisa's eleven and Matt's two years, sit round the table in party dresses or frilly bibs, holding cups or mugs according to age, all of them gazing at the camera with large eyes opened wide by the flash, and all looking as if butter would not melt in their round pursed-up mouths. There they are, held like flies in the amber of that moment—click goes the camera and on goes life; the minutes, the days, the years, the decades, taking them further and further from the happiness and promise of youth, from the hopes Aunt Sadie must have had for them, and from the dreams they dreamed for themselves. I often think there is nothing quite so poignantly sad as old family groups.

When a child I spent my Christmas holidays at Alconleigh; it was a regular feature of my life, and, while some of them slipped by with nothing much to remember, others were distinguished by violent occurrences and had a definite character of their own. There was the time, for example, when the servants' wing caught fire, the time when my pony lay on me in the brook and nearly drowned me (not very nearly, he was soon dragged off, but meanwhile bubbles were said to have been observed). There was drama when Linda, aged ten, attempted suicide in order to rejoin an old smelly Border Terrier which Uncle Matthew had had put down. She collected and ate a basketful of yew-berries, was discovered by Nanny and given mustard and water to make her sick. She was then 'spoken to' by Aunt Sadie, clipped over the ear by Uncle Matthew, put to bed for two days and given a Labrador puppy, which soon took the place of the old Border in her affections. There was much worse drama when Linda, aged twelve, told the daughters of neighbours, who had come to tea, what are supposed to be the facts of life. Linda's presentation of the 'facts' had been so gruesome that the children left Alconleigh howling dismally, their nerves permanently impaired, their future chances of a sane and happy sex life much reduced. This resulted in a series of dreadful punishments, from a real beating, administered by Uncle Matthew, to luncheon up-stairs for a week. There was the unforgettable holiday when Uncle Matthew and Aunt Sadie went to Canada. The Radlett children would rush for the newspapers every day hoping to see that their parents' ship had gone down with all aboard; they yearned to be total orphans —especially Linda, who saw herself as Katie in *What Katie Did*, the reins of the household gathered into small but capable hands. The ship met with no iceberg and weathered the Atlantic storms, but meanwhile we had a wonderful holiday, free from rules.

But the Christmas I remember most clearly of all was when I was fourteen and Aunt Emily became engaged. Aunt Emily was Aunt Sadie's sister, and she had brought me up from babyhood, my own mother, their youngest sister, having felt herself too beautiful and too gay to be burdened with a child at the age of nineteen. She left my father when I was a month old, and subsequently ran away so often, and with so many different people, that she became known to her family and friends as the Bolter; while my father's second, and pre-sently his third, fourth and fifth wives, very naturally had no great wish to look after me. Occasionally one of these impetuous parents would appear like a rocket, casting an unnatural glow upon my hori-zon. They had great glamour, and I longed to be caught up in their fiery trails and be carried away, though in my heart I knew how lucky I was to have Aunt Emily. By degrees, as I grew up, they lost all charm for me; the cold grey rocket cases mouldered where they had happened to fall, my mother with a major in the South of France, my father, his estates sold up to pay his debts, with an old Rumanian countess in the Bahamas. Even before I was grown up much of the glamour with which they had been surrounded had faded, and finally there was nothing left, no foundation of childish memories to make them seem any different from other middle-aged people. Aunt Emily was never glamorous but she was always my mother, and I loved her.

At the time of which I write, however, I was at an age when the least imaginative child supposes itself to be a changeling, a Princess of Indian blood, Joan of Arc, or the future Empress of Russia. I hankered after my parents, put on an idiotic face which was intended to convey mingled suffering and pride when their names were mentioned, and thought of them as engulfed in deep, romantic, deadly sin.

Linda and I were very much preoccupied with sin, and our great hero was Oscar Wilde.

'But what did he *do*?'

'I asked Fa once and he roared at me—goodness, it was terrifying. He said: "If you mention that sewer's name again in this house I'll thrash you, do you hear, damn you?" So I asked Sadie and she looked awfully vague and said : "Oh, duck, I never really quite knew, but whatever it was was worse than mùrder, fearfully bad. And, darling, don't talk about him at meals, will you?" '

'We must find out.'

'Bob says he will, when he goes to Eton.'

'Oh, good! Do you think he was worse than Mummy and Daddy?'

'Surely he couldn't be. Oh, you are so lucky, to have wicked parents.'

This Christmas-time, aged fourteen, I stumbled into the hall at Alconleigh blinded by the light after a six-mile drive from Merlinford station. It was always the same every year; I always came down by the same train, arriving at tea-time, and always found Aunt Sadie and the children round the table underneath the entrenching tool, just as they were in the photograph. It was always the same table and the same tea-things; the china with large roses on it, the tea-kettle and the silver dish for scones simmering over little flames—the human beings of course were getting imperceptibly older, the babies were becoming children, the children were growing up, and there had been an addition in the shape of Victoria, now aged two. She was waddling about with a chocolate biscuit clenched in her fist, her face was smothered in chocolate and was a horrible sight, but through the sticky mask shone unmistakably the blue of two steady Radlett eyes.

There was a tremendous scraping of chairs as I came in, and a pack of Radletts hurled themselves upon me with the intensity and almost the ferocity of a pack of hounds hurling itself upon a fox. All except Linda. She was the most pleased to see me, but determined not to show it. When the din had quieted down and I was seated before a scone and a cup of tea, she said :

'Where's Brenda?' Brenda was my white mouse.

'She got a sore back and died,' I said. Aunt Sadie looked anxiously at Linda.

'Had you been riding her?' said Louisa, facetiously. Matt, who had recently come under the care of a French nursery governess, said in a high-pitched imitation of her voice: "C'était, comme d'habitude, les voies urinaires.'

'Oh, dear,' said Aunt Sadie, under her breath.

Enormous tears were pouring into Linda's plate. Nobody cried so much or so often as she; anything, but especially anything sad about animals, would set her off, and, once begun, it was a job to stop her. She was a delicate, as well as a highly nervous child, and even Aunt Sadie, who lived in a dream as far as the health of her children was concerned, was aware that too much crying kept her awake at night, put her off her food, and did her harm. The other children, and especially Louisa and Bob, who loved to tease, went as far as they dared with her, and were periodically punished for making her cry. *Black Beauty, Owd Bob, The Story of a Red Deer,* and all the Seton Thompson books were on the nursery index because of Linda, who, at one time or another, had been prostrated by them. They had to be hidden away, as, if they were left lying about, she could not be trusted not to indulge in an orgy of self-torture.

Wicked Louisa had invented a poem which never failed to induce rivers of tears:

'A little, houseless match, it has no roof, no thatch,
It lies alone, it makes no moan, that little, houseless match.'

When Aunt Sadie was not around the children would chant this in a gloomy chorus. In certain moods one had only to glance at a match-box to dissolve poor Linda; when, however, she was feeling stronger, more fit to cope with life, this sort of teasing would force out of her very stomach an unwilling guffaw. Linda was not only my favourite cousin, but, then and for many years, my favourite human being. I adored all my cousins, and Linda distilled, mentally and physically, the very essence of the Radlett family. Her straight features, straight brown hair and large blue eyes were a theme upon which the faces of the others were a variation; all pretty, but none so absolutely distinctive as hers. There was something furious about her, even when she laughed, which she did a great deal, and always as if forced to against her will. Something reminiscent of pictures of Napoleon in youth, a sort of scowling intensity.

I could see that she was really minding much more about Brenda than I did. The truth was that my honeymoon days with the mouse were long since over; we had settled down to an uninspiring relationship, a form, as it were, of married blight, and, when she had developed a disgusting sore patch on her back, it had been all I could do to behave decently and treat her with common humanity. Apart from the shock it always is to find somebody stiff and cold in their cage in the morning, it had been a very great relief to me when Brenda's sufferings finally came to an end.

'Where is she buried?' Linda muttered furiously, looking at her plate.

'Beside the robin. She's got a dear little cross and her coffin was lined with pink satin.'

'Now, Linda darling,' said Aunt Sadie, 'if Fanny has finished her tea why don't you show her your toad?'

'He's upstairs asleep,' said Linda. But she stopped crying.

'Have some nice hot toast, then?'

'Can I have Gentleman's Relish on it?' she said, quick to make capital out of Aunt Sadie's mood, for Gentleman's Relish was kept strictly for Uncle Matthew, and supposed not to be good for children. The others made a great show of exchanging significant looks. These were intercepted, as they were meant to be, by Linda, who gave a tremendous bellowing boo-hoo and rushed upstairs.

'I wish you children wouldn't tease Linda,' said Aunt Sadie, irritated out of her usual gentleness, and followed her.

The staircase led out of the hall. When Aunt Sadie was beyond earshot, Louisa said: 'If wishes were horses beggars would ride. Child hunt tomorrow, Fanny.'

'Yes, Josh told me. He was in the car—been to see the vet.'

My Uncle Matthew had four magnificent bloodhounds, with which he used to hunt his children. Two of us would go off with a good start to lay the trail, and Uncle Matthew and the rest would follow the hounds on horseback. It was great fun. Once he came to my home and hunted Linda and me over Shenley Common. This caused the most tremendous stir locally, the Kentish week-enders on their way to church were appalled by the sight of four great hounds in full cry after two little girls. My uncle seemed to them like a wicked lord of fiction, and I became more than ever surrounded with an aura of madness, badness, and dangerousness for their children to know.

The child hunt on the first day of this Christmas visit was a great success. Louisa and I were chosen as hares. We ran across country, the beautiful bleak Cotswold uplands, starting soon after breakfast when the sun was still a red globe, hardly over the horizon, and the trees were etched in dark blue against a pale blue, mauve and pinkish sky. The sun rose as we stumbled on, longing for our second wind; it shone, and there dawned a beautiful day, more like late autumn in its feeling than Christmas-time.

We managed to check the bloodhounds once by running through a flock of sheep, but Uncle Matthew soon got them on the scent again, and, after about two hours of hard running on our part, when we were only half a mile from home, the baying slavering creatures caught up with us, to be rewarded with lumps of meat and many caresses. Uncle Matthew was in a radiantly good temper, he got off his horse and walked home with us, chatting agreeably. What was most unusual, he was even quite affable to me.

'I hear Brenda has died,' he said, 'no great loss I should say. That mouse stank like merry hell. I expect you kept her cage too near the radiator. I always told you it was unhealthy, or did she die of old age?'

'She was only two,' I said, timidly.

Uncle Matthew's charm, when he chose to turn it on, was considerable, but at that time I was always mortally afraid of him, and made the mistake of letting him see that I was.

'You ought to have a dormouse, Fanny, or a rat. They are much more interesting than white mice—though I must frankly say, of all the mice I ever knew, Brenda was the most utterly dismal.'

'She was dull,' I said, sycophantically.

'When I go to London after Christmas, I'll get you a dormouse. Saw one the other day at the Army & Navy.'

'Oh Fa, it *is* unfair,' said Linda, who was walking her pony along beside us. 'You know how I've always longed for a dormouse.'

'It is unfair' was a perpetual cry of the Radletts when young. The great advantage of living in a large family is that early lesson of life's essential unfairness. With them I must say it nearly always operated in favour of Linda, who was the adored of Uncle Matthew.

Today, however, my uncle was angry with her, and I saw in a flash that this affability to me, this genial chat about mice, was simply designed as a tease for her.

'You've got enough animals, miss,' he said, sharply. 'You can't control the ones you have got. And don't forget what I told you—that dog of yours goes straight to the kennel when we get back, and stays there.'

Linda's face crumpled, tears poured, she kicked her pony into a canter and made for home. It seemed that her dog Labby had been sick in Uncle Matthew's business-room after breakfast. Uncle Matthew was unable to bear dirtiness in dogs, he flew into a rage, and, in his rage, had made a rule that never again was Labby to set foot in the house. This was always happening, for one reason or another, to one animal or another, and, Uncle Matthew's bark being invariably much worse than his bite, the ban seldom lasted more than a day or two, after which would begin what he called the Thin End of the Wedge.

'Can I bring him in just while I fetch my gloves?'

'I'm so tired—I can't go to the stables—do let him stay just till after tea.'

'Oh, I see—the thin end of the wedge. All right, this time he can stay, but if he makes another mess—or I catch him on your bed—or he chews up the good furniture (according to whichever crime it was that had resulted in banishment), I'll have him destroyed, and don't say I didn't warn you.'

All the same, every time sentence of banishment was pronounced, the owner of the condemned would envisage her beloved moping his life away in the solitary confinement of a cold and gloomy kennel.

'Even if I take him out for three hours every day, and go and chat to him for another hour, that leaves twenty hours for him all alone with nothing to do. Oh, why can't dogs read?'

The Radlett children, it will be observed, took a highly anthropomorphic view of their pets.

Today, however, Uncle Matthew was in a wonderfully good temper, and, as we left the stables, he said to Linda, who was sitting crying with Labby in his kennel:

'Are you going to leave that poor brute of yours in there all day?'

Her tears forgotten as if they had never been, Linda rushed into the house with Labby at her heels. The Radletts were always either on a peak of happiness or drowning in black waters of despair; their emotions were on no ordinary plane, they loved or they loathed, they laughed or they cried, they lived in a world of superlatives. Their life with Uncle Matthew was a sort of perpetual Tom Tiddler's ground. They went as far as they dared, sometimes very far indeed, while sometimes, for no apparent reason, he would pounce almost before they had crossed the boundary. Had they been poor children they would probably have been removed from their roaring, raging, whacking papa and sent to an approved home, or, indeed, he himself would have been removed from them and sent to prison for refusing to educate them. Nature, however, provides her own remedies, and no doubt the Radletts had enough of Uncle Matthew in them to enable them to weather storms in which ordinary children like me would have lost their nerve completely.

CHAPTER II

IT was an accepted fact at Alconleigh that Uncle Matthew loathed me. This violent, uncontrolled man, like his children, knew no middle course, he either loved or he hated, and generally, it must be said, he hated. His reason for hating me was that he hated my father; they were old Eton enemies. When it became obvious, and obvious it was from the hour of my conception, that my parents intended to doorstep me, Aunt Sadie had wanted to bring me up with Linda. We were the same age, and it had seemed a sensible plan. Uncle Matthew had categorically refused. He hated my father, he said, he hated me, but, above all, he hated children, it was bad enough to have two of his own. (He evidently had not envisaged so soon having seven, and indeed both he and Aunt Sadie lived in a perpetual state of surprise at having filled so many cradles, about the future of whose occupants they seemed to have no particular policy.) So dear Aunt Emily, whose heart had once been broken by some wicked dallying monster, and who intended on this account never to marry, took me on and made a life's work of me, and I am very thankful that she did. For she believed passionately in the education of women, she took immense pains to have me properly taught, even going to live at Shenley on purpose to be near a good day school. The Radlett daughters did practically no lessons. They were taught by Lucille, the French nursery governess, to read and write, they were obliged, though utterly unmusical, to 'practise' in the freezing ballroom for one hour a day each, when, their eyes glued to the clock, they would thump out the 'Merry Peasant' and a few scales, they were made to go for a French walk with Lucille on all except hunting days, and that was the extent of their education. Uncle Matthew loathed clever females, but he considered that gentlewomen ought, as well as being able to ride, to know French and play the piano. Although as a child I rather naturally envied them their freedom from thrall and bondage, from sums and science, I felt, nevertheless, a priggish satisfaction that I was not growing up unlettered, as they were.

Aunt Emily did not often come with me to Alconleigh. Perhaps she had an idea that it was more fun for me to be there on my own, and no doubt it was a change for her to get away and spend Christmas with the friends of her youth, and leave for a bit the responsibilities of her old age. Aunt Emily at this time was forty, and we children had long ago renounced on her behalf the world, the flesh, and the devil. This year, however, she had gone away from Shenley before the holidays began, saying that she would see me at Alconleigh in January.

On the afternoon of the child hunt Linda called a meeting of the Hons. The Hons was the Radlett secret society, anybody who was not a friend to the Hons was a Counter-Hon, and their battle-cry was 'Death to the horrible Counter-Hons'. I was a Hon, since my father, like theirs, was a lord.

There were also, however, many honorary Hons; it was not necessary to have been born a Hon in order to be one. As Linda once remarked: 'Kind hearts are more than coronets, and simple faith than Norman blood.' I'm not sure how much we really believed this, we were wicked snobs in those days, but we subscribed to the general idea. Head of the hon. Hons was Josh, the groom, who was greatly beloved by us all and worth buckets of Norman blood; chief of the horrible Counter-Hons was Craven, the gamekeeper, against whom a perpetual war to the knife was waged. The Hons would creep into the woods and hide Craven's steel traps, let out the chaffinches which, in wire cages without food or water, he used as bait for hawks, give decent burial to the victims of his gamekeeper's larder, and, before a meet of the hounds, unblock the earths which Craven had so carefully stopped.

The poor Hons were tormented by the cruelties of the countryside, while, to me, holidays at Alconleigh were a perfect revelation of beast-liness. Aunt Emily's little house was in a village; it was a Queen Anne box; red brick, white panelling, a magnolia tree and a delicious fresh smell. Between it and the country were a neat little garden, an iron-work fence, a village green and a village. The country one then came to was very different from Gloucestershire, it was emasculated, sheltered, over-cultivated, almost a suburban garden. At Alconleigh the cruel woods crept right up to the house; it was not unusual to be awoken by the screams of a rabbit running in horrified circles round a stoat, by the strange and awful cry of the dog-fox, or to see from one's bedroom window a live hen being carried away in the mouth of a vixen; while the roosting pheasant and the waking owl filled every night with wild primeval noise. In the winter, when snow covered the ground, we could trace the footprints of many creatures. These often ended in a pool of blood, a mass of fur or feathers, bearing witness to successful hunting by the carnivores.

On the other side of the house, within a stone's throw, was the Home Farm. Here the slaughtering of poultry and pigs, the castration of lambs and the branding of cattle, took place as a matter of course, out in the open for whoever might be passing by to see. Even dear old Josh made nothing of firing, with red-hot irons, a favourite horse after the hunting season.

'You can only do two legs at a time,' he would say, hissing through his teeth as though one were a horse and he grooming one, 'otherwise they can't stand the pain.'

Linda and I were bad at standing pain ourselves, and found it intolerable that animals should have to lead such tormented lives and tortured deaths. (I still do mind, very much indeed, but in those days at Alconleigh it was an absolute obsession with us all.)

The humanitarian activities of the Hons were forbidden, on pain of punishment, by Uncle Matthew, who was always and entirely on the side of Craven, his favourite servant. Pheasants and partridges must be preserved, vermin must be put down rigorously, all except the fox, for whom a more exciting death was in store. Many and many a whacking did the poor Hons suffer, week after week their pocket-money was stopped, they were sent to bed early, given extra practising to do; nevertheless they bravely persisted with their discouraged and discouraging activities. Huge cases full of new steel traps would arrive periodically from the Army & Navy Stores, and lie stacked until required round Craven's hut in the middle of the wood (an old railway carriage was his headquarters, situated, most inappropriately, among the primroses and blackberry bushes of a charming little glade); hundreds of traps, making one feel the futility of burying, at great risk to life and property, a paltry three or four. Sometimes we would find a screaming animal held in one; it would take all our reserves of courage to go up to it and let it out, to see it run away with three legs and a dangling mangled horror. We knew that it then probably died of blood-poisoning in its lair; Uncle Matthew would rub in this fact, sparing no agonizing detail of the long-drawn-out ordeal, but, though we knew it would be kinder, we could never bring ourselves to kill them; it was asking too much. Often, as it was, we had to go away and be sick after these episodes.

The Hons' meeting-place was a disused linen cupboard at the top of the house, small, dark, and intensely hot. As in so many country houses, the central-heating apparatus at Alconleigh had been installed in the early days of the invention, at enormous expense, and was now thoroughly out of date. In spite of a boiler which would not have been too large for an Atlantic liner, in spite of the tons of coke which it consumed daily, the temperature of the living-rooms was hardly affected, and all the heat there was seemed to concentrate in the Hons' cupboard, which was always stifling. Here we would sit, huddled up on the slatted shelves, and talk for hours about life and death.

Last holidays our great obsession had been childbirth, on which entrancing subject we were informed remarkably late, having supposed for a long time that a mother's stomach swelled up for nine months and then burst open like a ripe pumpkin, shooting out the infant. When the real truth dawned upon us it seemed rather an anticlimax, until Linda produced, from some novel, and read out loud in ghoulish tones, the description of a woman in labour.

'Her breath comes in great gulps—sweat pours down her brow like water—screams as of a tortured animal rend the air—and can this face, twisted with agony, be that of my darling Rhona—can this torture-chamber really be our bedroom, this rack our marriage-bed? "Doctor, doctor," I cried, "do something"—I rushed out into the night——' and so on.

We were rather disturbed by this, realizing that too probably we in our turn would have to endure these fearful agonies. Aunt Sadie, who had only just finished having her seven children, when appealed to, was not very reassuring.

'Yes,' she said, vaguely. 'It is the worst pain in the world. But the funny thing is, you always forget in between what it's like. Each time, when it began, I felt like saying, "Oh, now I can remember, stop it, stop it." And, of course, by then it was nine months too late to stop it.'

At this point Linda began to cry, saying how dreadful it must be for cows, which brought the conversation to an end.

It was difficult to talk to Aunt Sadie about sex; something always seemed to prevent one; babies were the nearest we ever got to it. She and Aunt Emily, feeling at one moment that we ought to know more, and being, I suspect, too embarrassed to enlighten us themselves, gave us a modern text-book on the subject.

We got hold of some curious ideas.

'Jassy,' said Linda one day, scornfully, 'is obsessed, poor thing, with sex.'

'Obsessed with sex!' said Jassy, 'there's nobody so obsessed as you, Linda. Why if I so much as look at a picture you say I'm a pygma-lionist.'

In the end we got far more information out of a book called *Ducks and Duck Breeding*.

'Ducks can only copulate,' said Linda, after studying this for a while, 'in running water. Good luck to them.'

This Christmas Eve we all packed into the Hons' meeting-place to hear what Linda had to say—Louisa, Jassy, Bob, Matt and I.

'Talk about back-to-the-womb,' said Jassy.

'Poor Aunt Sadie,' I said. 'I shouldn't think she'd want you all back in hers.'

'You never know. Now rabbits eat their children—somebody ought to explain to them how it's only a complex.'

'How can one *explain* to *rabbits*? That's what is so worrying about animals, they simply don't understand when they're spoken to, poor angels. I'll tell you what about Sadie though, she'd like to be back in one herself, she's got a thing for boxes and that always shows. Who else —Fanny, what about you?'

'I don't think I would, but then I imagine the one I was in wasn't very comfortable at the time you know, and nobody else has ever been allowed to stay there.'

'Abortions?' said Linda with interest.

'Well, tremendous jumpings and hot baths anyway.'

'How *do* you know?'

'I once heard Aunt Emily and Aunt Sadie talking about it when I was very little, and afterwards I remembered. Aunt Sadie said: "How does she manage it?" and Aunt Emily said: "Skiing, or hunting, or just jumping off the kitchen table." '

'You are so lucky, having wicked parents.'

This was the perpetual refrain of the Radletts, and, indeed, my wicked parents constituted my chief interest in their eyes—I was really a very dull little girl in other respects.

'The news I have for the Hons today,' said Linda, clearing her throat like a grown-up person, 'while of considerable Hon interest generally, particularly concerns Fanny. I won't ask you to guess, because it's nearly tea-time and you never could, so I'll tell straight out. Aunt Emily is engaged.'

There was a gasp from the Hons in chorus.

'Linda,' I said, furiously, 'you've made it up.' But I knew she couldn't have.

Linda brought a piece of paper out of her pocket. It was a half-sheet of writing-paper, evidently the end of a letter, covered with Aunt Emily's large babyish handwriting, and I looked over Linda's shoulder as she read it out:

'. . . not tell the children we're engaged, what d'you think darling, just at first? But then suppose Fanny takes a dislike to him, though I don't see how she could, but children are so funny, won't it be more of a shock? Oh, dear, I can't decide. Anyway, do what you think best, darling, we'll arrive on Thursday, and I'll telephone on Wednesday evening and see what's happened. All love from Emily.'

Sensation in the Hons' cupboard.

CHAPTER III

'But why?' I said, for the hundredth time.

Linda, Louisa and I were packed into Louisa's bed, with Bob sitting on the end of it, chatting in whispers. These midnight talks were most strictly forbidden, but it was safer, at Alconleigh, to disobey rules during the early part of the night than at any other time in the twenty-four hours. Uncle Matthew fell asleep practically at the dinner-table. He would then doze in his business-room for an hour or so before dragging himself, in a somnambulist trance, to bed, where he slept the profound sleep of one who has been out of doors all day until cockcrow the following morning, when he became very much awake. This was the time for his never-ending warfare with the housemaids over wood-ash. The rooms at Alconleigh were heated by wood fires, and Uncle Matthew maintained, rightly, that if these were to function properly, all the ash ought to be left in the fireplaces in a great hot smouldering heap. Every housemaid, however, for some reason (an early training with coal fires probably) was bent on removing this ash altogether. When shakings, imprecations, and being pounced out at by Uncle Matthew in his paisley dressing-gown at six a.m., had convinced them that this was really not feasible, they became absolutely determined to remove, by hook or by crook, just a little, a shovelful or so, every morning. I can only suppose they felt that like this they were asserting their personalities.

The result was guerrilla warfare at its most exciting. Housemaids are notoriously early risers, and can usually count upon three clear hours when a house belongs to them alone. But not at Alconleigh. Uncle Matthew was always, winter and summer alike, out of his bed by five a.m., and it was then his habit to wander about, looking like Great Agrippa in his dressing-gown, and drinking endless cups of tea out of a thermos flask, until about seven, when he would have his bath. Breakfast for my uncle, my aunt, family and guests alike, was sharp at eight, and unpunctuality was not tolerated. Uncle Matthew was no respecter of other people's early morning sleep, and after five o'clock one could not count on any, for he raged round the house, clanking cups of tea, shouting at his dogs, roaring at the housemaids, cracking the stock whips which he had brought back from Canada on the lawn with a noise greater than gun-fire, and all to the accompaniment of Galli Curci on his gramophone, an abnormally loud one with an enormous horn, through which would be shrieked 'Una voce poco fa'—'The Mad Song' from *Lucia*—'Lo, here the gen-tel lar-ha-hark'—and so on, played at top speed, thus rendering them even higher and more screeching than they ought to be.

Nothing reminds me of my childhood days at Alconleigh so much as those songs. Uncle Matthew played them incessantly for years, until the spell was broken when he went all the way to Liverpool to hear Galli Curci in person. The disillusionment caused by her appearance was so great that the records remained ever after silent, and were replaced by the deepest bass voices that money could buy.

'Fearful the death of the diver must be,

Walking alone in the de-he-he-he-he-epths of the sea' or 'Drake is going West, lads'.

These were, on the whole, welcomed by the family, as rather less piercing at early dawn.

'Why should she want to be married?'

'It's not as though she could be in love. She's forty.'

Like all the very young we took it for granted that making love is child's play.

'How old do you suppose he is?'

'Fifty or sixty I guess. Perhaps she thinks it would be nice to be a widow. Weeds, you know.'

'Perhaps she thinks Fanny ought to have a man's influence.'

'Man's influence!' said Louisa. 'I foresee trouble. Supposing he falls in love with Fanny, that'll be a pretty kettle of fish, like Somerset and Princess Elizabeth—he'll be playing rough games and pinching you in bed, see if he doesn't.'

'Surely not, at his age.'

'Old men love little girls.'

'And little boys,' said Bob.

'It looks as if Aunt Sadie isn't going to say anything about it before they come,' I said.

'There's nearly a week to go—she may be deciding. She'll talk it over with Fa. Might be worth listening next time she has a bath. You can, Bob.'

Christmas Day was spent, as usual at Alconleigh, between alternate bursts of sunshine and showers. I put, as children can, the disturbing news about Aunt Emily out of my mind, and concentrated upon enjoyment. At about six o'clock Linda and I unstuck our sleepy eyes and started on our stockings. Our real presents came later, at breakfast and on the tree, but the stockings were a wonderful *hors d'œuvre* and full of treasures. Presently Jassy came in and started selling us things out of hers. Jassy only cared about money because she was saving up to run away—she carried her post office book about with her everywhere, and always knew to a farthing what she had got. This was then translated by a miracle of determination, as Jassy was very bad at sums, into so many days in a bed-sitting-room.

'How are you getting on, Jassy?'

'My fare to London and a month and two days and an hour and a half in a bed-sitter, with basin and breakfast.'

Where the other meals would come from was left to the imagination. Jassy studied advertisements of bed-sitters in *The Times* every morning. The cheapest she had found so far was in Clapham. So eager was she for the cash that would transform her dream into reality, that one could be certain of picking up a few bargains round about Christmas and her birthday. Jassy at this time was aged eight.

I must admit that my wicked parents turned up trumps at Christmas, and my presents from them were always the envy of the entire household. This year my mother, who was in Paris, sent a gilded bird-cage full of stuffed humming-birds which, when wound up, twittered and hopped about and drank at a fountain. She also sent a fur hat and a gold and topaz bracelet, whose glamour was enhanced by the fact that Aunt Sadie considered them unsuitable for a child, and said so. My father sent a pony and cart, a very smart and beautiful little outfit, which had arrived some days before, and been secreted by Josh in the stables.

'So typical of that damned fool Edward to send it here,' Uncle Matthew said, 'and give us all the trouble of getting it to Shenley. And I bet poor old Emily won't be too pleased. Who on earth is going to look after it?'

Linda cried with envy. 'It *is* unfair,' she kept saying, 'that you should have wicked parents and not me.'

We persuaded Josh to take us for a drive after luncheon. The pony was an angel and the whole thing easily managed by a child, even the harnessing. Linda wore my hat and drove the pony. We got back late for the Tree—the house was already full of tenants and their children; Uncle Matthew, who was struggling into his Father Christmas clothes, roared at us so violently that Linda had to go and cry upstairs, and was not there to collect her own present from him. Uncle Matthew had taken some trouble to get her a longed-for dormouse and was greatly put out by this; he roared at everybody in turns, and ground his dentures. There was a legend in the family that he had already ground away four pairs in his rages.

The evening came to a climax of violence when Matt produced a box of fireworks which my mother had sent him from Paris. On the box they were called *pétards*. Somebody said to Matt: 'What do they do?'

to which he replied: '*Bien, ça pète, quoi?*' This remark, overheard by
Uncle Matthew, was rewarded with a first-class hiding, which was
actually most unfair, as poor Matt was only repeating what Lucille had
said to him earlier in the day. Matt, however, regarded hidings as a
sort of natural phenomenon, unconnected with any actions of his own,
and submitted to them philosophically enough. I have often wondered
since how it was that Aunt Sadie could have chosen Lucille, who was
the very acme of vulgarity, to look after her children. We all loved her,
she was gay and spirited and read aloud to us without cease, but her
language really was extraordinary, and provided dreadful pitfalls for
the unwary.

'*Qu'est-ce que c'est ce custard, qu'on fout partout?*'

I shall never forget Matt quite innocently making this remark in
Fullers at Oxford, where Uncle Matthew had taken us for a treat. The
consequences were awful.

It never seemed to occur to Uncle Matthew that Matt could not
know these words by nature, and that it would really have been more
fair to check them at their source.

CHAPTER IV

I NATURALLY awaited the arrival of Aunt Emily and her future
intended with some agitation. She was, after all, my real mother, and,
greatly as I might hanker after that glittering evil person who bore me,
it was to Aunt Emily that I turned for the solid, sustaining, though on
the face of it uninteresting, relationship that is provided by motherhood
at its best. Our little household at Shenley was calm and happy and
afforded an absolute contrast to the agitations and tearing emotions of
Alconleigh. It may have been dull, but it was a sheltering harbour, and
I was always glad to get back to it. I think I was beginning dimly to
realize how much it all centred upon me; the very timetable, with its
early luncheon and high tea, was arranged to fit in with my lessons and
bedtime. Only during those holidays when I went to Alconleigh did
Aunt Emily have any life of her own, and even these breaks were infrequent, as she had an idea that Uncle Matthew and the whole stormy
set-up there were bad for my nerves. I may not have been consciously
aware of the extent to which Aunt Emily had regulated her existence
round mine, but I saw, only too clearly, that the addition of a man to
our establishment was going to change everything. Hardly knowing
any men outside the family, I imagined them all to be modelled on the
lines of Uncle Matthew, or of my own seldom seen, violently emotional
papa, either of whom, plunging about in that neat little house, would

have been sadly out of place. I was filled with apprehension, almost with horror, and, greatly assisted by the workings of Louisa's and Linda's vivid imaginations, had got myself into a real state of nerves. Louisa was now teasing me with the *Constant Nymph*. She read aloud the last chapters, and soon I was dying at a Brussels boarding-house, in the arms of Aunt Emily's husband.

On Wednesday Aunt Emily rang up Aunt Sadie, and they talked for ages. The telephone at Alconleigh was, in those days, situated in a glass cupboard halfway down the brilliantly lighted back passage; there was no extension, and eavesdropping was thus rendered impossible. (In later years it was moved to Uncle Matthew's business-room, with an extension, after which all privacy was at an end.) When Aunt Sadie returned to the drawing-room she said nothing except: 'Emily is coming tomorrow on the three-five. She sends you her love, Fanny.'

The next day we all went out hunting. The Radletts loved animals, they loved foxes, they risked dreadful beatings in order to unstop their earths, they read and cried and rejoiced over Reynard the Fox, in summer they got up at four to go and see the cubs playing in the pale-green light of the woods; nevertheless, more than anything in the world, they loved hunting. It was in their blood and bones and in my blood and bones, and nothing could eradicate it, though we knew it for a kind of original sin. For three hours that day I forgot everything except my body and my pony's body; the rushing, the scrambling, the splashing, struggling up the hills, sliding down them again, the tugging, the bucketing, the earth and the sky. I forgot everything, I could hardly have told you my name. That must be the great hold that hunting has over people, especially stupid people; it enforces an absolute concentration, both mental and physical.

After three hours Josh took me home. I was never allowed to stay out long or I got tired and would be sick all night. Josh was out on Uncle Matthew's second horse; at about two o'clock they changed over, and he started home on the lathered, sweating first horse, taking me with him. I came out of my trance, and saw that the day, which had begun with brilliant sunshine, was now cold and dark, threatening rain.

'And where's her ladyship hunting this year?' said Josh, as we started on a ten-mile jog along the Merlinford road, a sort of hog's back, more cruelly exposed than any road I have ever known, without a scrap of shelter or windscreen the whole of its fifteen miles. Uncle Matthew would never allow motor cars, either to take us to the meet or to fetch us home; he regarded this habit as despicably soft.

I knew that Josh meant my mother. He had been with my grandfather when she and her sisters were girls, and my mother was his heroine, he adored her.

'She's in Paris, Josh.'

'In Paris—what for?'

'I suppose she likes it.'

'Ho,' said Josh, furiously, and we rode for about half a mile in silence. The rain had begun, a thin cold rain, sweeping over the wide views on each side of the road; we trotted along, the weather in our faces. My back was not strong, and trotting on a side-saddle for any length of time was agony to me. I edged my pony on to the grass, and cantered for a bit, but I knew how much Josh disapproved of this, it was supposed to bring the horses back too hot; walking, on the other hand, chilled them. It had to be jog, jog, back-breaking jog, all the way.

'It's my opinion,' said Josh at last, 'that her ladyship is wasted, downright wasted, every minute of her life that she's not on a 'oss.'

'She's a wonderful rider, isn't she?'

I had had all this before from Josh, many times, and could never have enough of it.

'There's no human being like her, that I've ever seen,' said Josh, hissing through his teeth. 'Hands like velvet, but strong like iron, and her seat——! Now look at you, jostling about on that saddle, first here, then there—we shall have a sore back tonight, that's one thing certain we shall.'

'Oh, Josh—trotting. And I'm so tired.'

'Never saw her tired. I've seen 'er change 'osses after a ten-mile point, get on to a fresh young five-year-old what hadn't been out for a week— up like a bird—never know you had 'er foot in your hand, pick up the reins in a jiffy, catch up its head, and off and over a post and rails and bucking over the ridge and furrow, sitting like a rock. Now his lordship (he meant Uncle Matthew) he can ride, I don't say the contrary, but look how he sends the 'osses home, so darned tired they can't drink their gruel. He can ride all right, but he doesn't study his 'oss. I never knew your mother bring them home like this, she'd know when they'd had enough, and then heads for home and no looking back. Mind you, his lordship's a great big man, I don't say the contrary, rides every bit of sixteen stone, but he has great big 'osses and half kills them, and then who has to stop with them all night? Me!'

The rain was pouring down by now. An icy trickle was feeling its way past my left shoulder, and my right boot was slowly filling with water, the pain in my back was like a knife. I felt that I couldn't bear another moment of this misery, and yet I knew I must bear another five miles, another forty minutes. Josh gave me scornful looks as my back bent more and more double; I could see that he was wondering how it was that I could be my mother's child.

'Miss Linda,' he said, 'takes after her ladyship something wonderful.'

At last, at last, we were off the Merlinford road, coming down the valley into Alconleigh village, turning up the hill to Alconleigh house, through the lodge gates, up the drive, and into the stable yard. I got stiffly down, gave the pony to one of Josh's stable boys, and stumped away, walking like an old man. I was nearly at the front door before I remembered, with a sudden leap of my heart, that Aunt Emily would have arrived by now, with HIM. It was quite a minute before I could summon up enough courage to open the front door.

Sure enough, standing with their backs to the hall fire, were Aunt Sadie, Aunt Emily, and a small, fair, and apparently young man. My immediate impression was that he did not seem at all like a husband. He looked kind and gentle.

'Here is Fanny,' said my aunts in chorus.

'Darling,' said Aunt Sadie, 'can I introduce Captain Warbeck?'

I shook hands with the abrupt graceless way of little girls of fourteen, and thought that he did not seem at all like a captain either.

'Oh, darling, how wet you are. I suppose the others won't be back for ages—where have you come from?'

'I left them drawing the spinney by the Old Rose.'

Then I remembered, being after all a female in the presence of a male, how dreadful I always looked when I got home from hunting, splashed from head to foot, my bowler all askew, my hair a bird's nest, my stock a flapping flag, and, muttering something, I made for the back stairs, towards my bath and my rest. After hunting we were kept in bed for at least two hours. Soon Linda returned, even wetter than I had been, and got into bed with me. She, too, had seen the Captain, and agreed that he looked neither like a marrying nor like a military man.

'Can't see him killing Germans with an entrenching tool,' she said, scornfully.

Much as we feared, much as we disapproved of, passionately as we sometimes hated Uncle Matthew, he still remained for us a sort of criterion of English manhood; there seemed something not quite right about any man who greatly differed from him.

'I bet Uncle Matthew gives him rat week,' I said, apprehensive for Aunt Emily's sake.

'Poor Aunt Emily, perhaps he'll make her keep him in the stables,' said Linda with a gust of giggles.

'Still, he looks rather nice you know, and, considering her age, I should think she's lucky to get anybody.'

'I can't wait to see him with Fa.'

However, our expectations of blood and thunder were disappointed, for it was evident at once that Uncle Matthew had taken an enormous fancy to Captain Warbeck. As he never altered his first opinion of people, and as his few favourites could commit nameless crimes without doing wrong in his eyes, Captain Warbeck was, henceforward, on a good wicket with Uncle Matthew.

'He's such a frightfully clever cove, literary you know, you wouldn't believe the things he does. He writes books, and criticizes pictures, and whacks hell out of the piano, though the pieces he plays aren't up to much. Still, you can see what it would be like, if he learnt some of the tunes out of the *Country Girl*, for instance. Nothing would be too difficult for him, you can see that.'

At dinner Captain Warbeck sitting next to Aunt Sadie, and Aunt Emily next to Uncle Matthew, were separated from each other, not only by four of us children (Bob was allowed to dine down, as he was going to Eton next half), but also by pools of darkness. The dining-room table was lit by three electric bulbs hanging in a bunch from the ceiling, and screened by a curtain of dark-red jap silk with a gold fringe. One spot of brilliant light was thus cast into the middle of the table, while the diners themselves, and their plates, sat outside it in total gloom. We all, naturally, had our eyes fixed upon the shadowy figure of the fiancé, and found a great deal in his behaviour to interest us. He talked to Aunt Sadie at first about gardens, plants and flowering shrubs, a topic which was unknown at Alconleigh. The gardener saw to the garden, and that was that. It was quite half a mile from the house, and nobody went near it, except as a little walk sometimes in the summer. It seemed strange that a man who lived in London should know the names, the habits, and the medicinal properties of so many plants. Aunt Sadie politely tried to keep up with him, but could not altogether conceal her ignorance, though she partly veiled it in a mist of absent-mindedness.

'And what is your soil here?' asked Captain Warbeck.

Aunt Sadie came down from the clouds with a happy smile, and said, triumphantly, for here was something she did know, 'Clay.'

'Ah, yes,' said the Captain.

He produced a little jewelled box, took from it an enormous pill, swallowed it, to our amazement, without one sip to help it down, and said, as though to himself, but quite distinctly,

'Then the water here will be madly binding.'

When Logan, the butler, offered him shepherd's pie (the food at Alconleigh was always good and plentiful, but of the homely school-room description) he said, again so that one did not quite know whether he meant to be overheard or not,

'No, thank you, no twice-cooked meat. I am a wretched invalid, I must be careful, or I pay.'

Aunt Sadie, who so much disliked hearing about health that people often took her for a Christian Scientist, which, indeed, she might have become had she not disliked hearing about religion even more, took absolutely no notice, but Bob asked with interest, what it was that twice-cooked meat did to one.

'Oh, it imposes a most fearful strain on the juices, you might as well eat leather,' replied Captain Warbeck, faintly, heaping on to his plate the whole of the salad. He said, again in that withdrawn voice:

'Raw lettuce, anti-scorbutic,' and, opening another box of even larger pills, he took two, murmuring, 'Protein.'

'How delicious your bread is,' he said to Aunt Sadie, as though to make up for his rudeness in refusing the twice-cooked meat. 'I'm sure it has the germ.'

'What?' said Aunt Sadie, turning from a whispered confabulation with Logan ('ask Mrs. Crabbe if she could quickly make some more salad').

'I was saying that I feel sure your delicious bread is made of stone-ground flour, containing a high proportion of the germ. In my bedroom at home I have a picture of a grain of wheat (magnified, naturally) which shows the germ. As you know, in white bread the germ, with its wonderful health-giving properties, is eliminated—extracted, I should say—and put into chicken food. As a result the human race is becoming enfeebled, while hens grow larger and stronger with every generation.'

'So in the end,' said Linda, listening all agog, unlike Aunt Sadie, who had retired into a cloud of boredom, 'Hens will be Hons and Hons will be Hens. Oh, how I should love to live in a dear little Hon-house.'

'You wouldn't like your work,' said Bob, 'I once saw a hen laying an egg, and she had a most terrible expression on her face.'

'Only about like going to the lav,' said Linda.

'Now, Linda,' said Aunt Sadie sharply, 'that's quite unnecessary. Get on with your supper and don't talk so much.'

Vague as she was, Aunt Sadie could not always be counted on to ignore everything that was happening around her.

'What were you telling me, Captain Warbeck, something about germs?'

'Oh, not germs—the germ——'

At this point I became aware that, in the shadows at the other end of the table, Uncle Matthew and Aunt Emily were having one of their usual set-tos, and that it concerned me. Whenever Aunt Emily came to Alconleigh these tussles with Uncle Matthew would occur, but, all the same, one could see that he was fond of her. He always liked people who stood up to him, and also he probably saw in her a reflection of Aunt Sadie, whom he adored. Aunt Emily was more positive than Aunt Sadie, she had more character and less beauty, and she was not worn out with childbirth, but they were very much sisters. My mother was utterly different in every respect, but then she, poor thing, was, as Linda would have said, obsessed with sex.

Uncle Matthew and Aunt Emily were now engaged upon an argument we had all heard many times before. It concerned the education of females.

Uncle Matthew: 'I hope poor Fanny's school (the word school pronounced in tones of withering scorn) is doing her all the good you think it is. Certainly she picks up some dreadful expressions there.'

Aunt Emily, calmly, but on the defensive: 'Very likely she does. She also picks up a good deal of education.'

Uncle Matthew: 'Education! I was always led to suppose that no educated person ever spoke of notepaper, and yet I hear poor Fanny asking Sadie for notepaper. What is this education? Fanny talks about mirrors and mantelpieces, handbags and perfume, she takes sugar in her coffee, has a tassel on her umbrella, and I have no doubt that, if she is ever fortunate enough to catch a husband, she will call his father and mother Father and Mother. Will the wonderful education she is getting make up to the unhappy brute for all these endless pinpricks? Fancy hearing one's wife talk about notepaper—the irritation!'

Aunt Emily: 'A lot of men would find it more irritating to have a wife who had never heard of George III. (All the same, Fanny darling, it is called writing-paper you know—don't let's hear any more about note, please.) That is where you and I come in you see, Matthew, home influence is admitted to be a most important part of education.'

Uncle Matthew: 'There you are——'

Aunt Emily: 'A most important, but not by any means the most important.'

Uncle Matthew: 'You don't have to go to some awful middle-class establishment in order to know who George III was. Anyway, who was he, Fanny?'

Alas, I always failed to shine on these occasions. My wits scattered to the four winds by my terror of Uncle Matthew, I said, scarlet in the face:

'He was king. He went mad.'

'Most original, full of information,' said Uncle Matthew, sarcastically. 'Well worth losing every ounce of feminine charm to find that out, I must say. Legs like gateposts from playing hockey, and the worst seat on a horse of any woman I ever knew. Give a horse a sore back as soon as look at it. Linda, you're uneducated, thank God, what have you got to say about George III?'

'Well,' said Linda, her mouth full, 'he was the son of poor Fred and the father of Beau Brummel's fat friend, and he was one of those vacillators you know. "I am his Highness's dog at Kew, pray tell me, sir, whose dog are you?"' she added, inconsequently. 'Oh, how sweet!'

Uncle Matthew shot a look of cruel triumph at Aunt Emily. I saw that I had let down the side and began to cry, inspiring Uncle Matthew to fresh bouts of beastliness.

'It's a lucky thing that Fanny will have £15,000 a year of her own,' he said, 'not to speak of any settlements the Bolter may have picked up in the course of her career. She'll get a husband all right, even if she does talk about lunch, and envelope, and put the milk in first. I'm not afraid of that, I only say she'll drive the poor devil to drink when she has hooked him.'

Aunt Emily gave Uncle Matthew a furious frown. She had always tried to conceal from me the fact that I was an heiress, and, indeed, I only was one until such time as my father, hale and hearty and in the prime of life, should marry somebody of an age to bear children. It so happened that, like the Hanoverian family, he only cared for women when they were over forty; after my mother had left him he had embarked upon a succession of middle-aged wives whom even the miracles of modern science were unable to render fruitful. It was also believed, wrongly, by the grown-ups that we children were ignorant of the fact that my mamma was called the Bolter.

'All this,' said Aunt Emily, 'is quite beside the point. Fanny may possibly, in the far future, have a little money of her own (though it is ludicrous to talk of £15,000). Whether she does, or does not, the man she marries may be able to support her—on the other hand, the modern world being what it is, she may have to earn her own living. In any case she will be a more mature, a happier, a more interested and interesting person if she——'

'If she knows that George III was a king and went mad.'

All the same, my aunt was right, and I knew it and she knew it. The Radlett children read enormously by fits and starts in the library at Alconleigh, a good representative nineteenth-century library, which had been made by their grandfather, a most cultivated man. But, while they picked up a great deal of heterogeneous information, and gilded it with their own originality, while they bridged gulfs of ignorance with their charm and high spirits, they never acquired any habit of concentration, they were incapable of solid hard work. One result, in later life, was that they could not stand boredom. Storms and difficulties left them unmoved, but day after day of ordinary existence produced an unbearable torture of ennui, because they completely lacked any form of mental discipline.

As we trailed out of the dining-room after dinner, we heard Captain Warbeck say:

'No port, no, thank you. Such a delicious drink, but I must refuse. It's the acid from port that makes one so delicate now.'

'Ah—you've been a great port drinker, have you?' said Uncle Matthew.

'Oh, not me, I've never touched it. My ancestors——'

Presently, when they joined us in the drawing-room, Aunt Sadie said: 'The children know the news now.'

'I suppose they think it's a great joke,' said Davey Warbeck, 'old people like us being married.'

'Oh, no, of course not,' we said, politely, blushing.

'He's an extraordinary fella,' said Uncle Matthew, 'knows everything. He says those Charles II sugar casters are only a Georgian imitation of Charles II, just fancy, not valuable at all. Tomorrow we'll go round the house and I'll show you all our things and you can tell us what's what. Quite useful to have a fella like you in the family, I must say.'

'That will be very nice,' said Davey faintly, 'and now I think, if you don't mind, I'll go to bed. Yes, please, early morning tea—so necessary to replace the evaporation of the night.'

He shook hands with us all, and hurried from the room, saying to himself: 'Wooing, so tiring.'

'Davey Warbeck is a Hon,' said Bob as we were all coming down to breakfast next day.

'Yes, he seems a terrific Hon,' said Linda sleepily.

'No, I mean he's a real one. Look, there's a letter for him, The Hon. David Warbeck. I've looked him up, and it's true.'

Bob's favourite book at this time was Debrett, his nose was never out of it. As a result of his researches he was once heard informing Lucille that *'les origines de la famille Radlett sont perdues dans les brumes de l'antiquité'*.

'He's only a second son, and the eldest has got an heir, so I'm afraid Aunt Emily won't be a lady. And his father's only the second Baron, created 1860, and they only start in 1720, before that it's the female line.' Bob's voice was trailing off. 'Still——' he said.

We heard Davey Warbeck, as he was coming down the stairs, say to Uncle Matthew:

'Oh no, that couldn't be a Reynolds. Prince Hoare, at his very worst, if you're lucky.'

'Pig's thinkers, Davey?' Uncle Matthew lifted the lid of a hot dish.

'Oh, yes please, Matthew, if you mean brains. So digestible.'

'And after breakfast I'm going to show you our collection of minerals in the north passage. I bet you'll agree we've got something worth having there, it's supposed to be the finest collection in England—left me by an old uncle, who spent his life making it. Meanwhile, what'd you think of my eagle?'

'Ah, if that were Chinese now, it would be a treasure. But Jap I'm afraid, not worth the bronze it's cast in. Cooper's Oxford, please, Linda.'

After breakfast we all flocked to the north passage, where there were hundreds of stones in glass-fronted cupboards. Petrified this and fossilized that, blue-john and lapis were the most exciting, large flints which looked as if they had been picked up by the side of the road, the least. Valuable, unique, they were a family legend. 'The minerals in the north passage are good enough for a museum.' We children revered them. Davey looked at them carefully, taking some over to the window and peering into them. Finally, he heaved a great sigh and said:

'What a beautiful collection. I suppose you know they're all diseased?'

'Diseased?'

'Badly, and too far gone for treatment. In a year or two they'll all be dead—you might as well throw the whole lot away.'

Uncle Matthew was delighted.

'Damned fella,' he said, 'nothing's right for him, I never saw such a fella. Even the minerals have got foot-and-mouth, according to him.'

CHAPTER V

THE year which followed Aunt Emily's marriage transformed Linda and me from children, young for our ages, into lounging adolescents waiting for love. One result of the marriage was that I now spent nearly all my holidays at Alconleigh. Davey, like all Uncle Matthew's favourites, simply could not see that he was in the least bit frightening, and scouted Aunt Emily's theory that to be too much with him was bad for my nerves.

'You're just a lot of little crybabies,' he said scornfully, 'if you allow yourselves to be upset by that old cardboard ogre.'

Davey had given up his flat in London and lived with us at Shenley, where, during term-time, he made but little difference to our life, except in so far as a male presence in a female household is always salutary (the curtains, the covers, and Aunt Emily's clothes underwent an enormous change for the better), but, in the holidays, he liked to carry her off, to his own relations or on trips abroad, and I was parked at Alconleigh. Aunt Emily probably felt that, if she had to choose between her husband's wishes and my nervous system, the former should win the day. In spite of her being forty they were, I believe, very much in love: it must have been a perfect bore having me about at all, and it speaks volumes for their characters that never, for one moment, did they allow me to be aware of this. Davey, in fact was, and has been ever since, a perfect stepfather to me, affectionate, understanding, never in any way interfering. He accepted me at once as belonging to Aunt Emily, and never questioned the inevitability of my presence in his household.

By the Christmas holidays Louisa was officially 'out', and going to hunt balls, a source of bitter envy to us, though Linda said scornfully that she did not appear to have many suitors. We were not coming out for another two years—it seemed an eternity, and especially to Linda, who was paralysed by her longing for love, and had no lessons or work to do which could take her mind off it. In fact, she had no other interest now except hunting, even the animals seemed to have lost all charm for her. She and I did nothing on non-hunting days but sit about, too

large for our tweed suits, whose hooks and eyes were always popping off
at the waist, and play endless games of patience; or we lolled in the
Hons' cupboard, and 'measured'. We had a tape-measure and com-
peted as to the largeness of our eyes, the smallness of wrists, ankles, waist
and neck, length of legs and fingers, and so on. Linda always won.
When we had finished 'measuring' we talked of romance. These were
most innocent talks, for to us, at that time, love and marriage were
synonymous, we knew that they lasted for ever, to the grave and far,
far beyond. Our preoccupation with sin was finished; Bob, back from
Eton, had been able to tell us all about Oscar Wilde, and, now that his
crime was no longer a mystery, it seemed dull, unromantic, and incomprehensible.

We were, of course, both in love, but with people we had never met,
Linda with the Prince of Wales, and I with a fat, red-faced, middle-
aged farmer, whom I sometimes saw riding through Shenley. These
loves were strong, and painfully delicious; they occupied all our
thoughts, but I think we half realized that they would be superseded in
time by real people. They were to keep the house warm, so to speak, for
its eventual occupant. What we never would admit was the possibility
of lovers after marriage. We were looking for real love, and that could
only come once in a lifetime; it hurried to consecration, and thereafter
never wavered. Husbands, we knew, were not always faithful, this we
must be prepared for, we must understand and forgive. 'I have been
faithful to thee, Cynara, in my fashion' seemed to explain it beautifully.
But women—that was different; only the lowest of the sex could love or
give themselves more than once. I do not quite know how I reconciled
these sentiments with the great hero-worship I still had for my mother,
that adulterous doll. I suppose I put her in an entirely different
category, in the face that launched a thousand ships class. A few historical characters must be allowed to have belonged to this, but Linda
and I were perfectionists where love was concerned, and did not ourselves aspire to that kind of fame.

This winter Uncle Matthew had a new tune on his gramophone,
called 'Thora'. 'I live in a land of roses,' boomed a deep male voice,
'but dream of a land of snow. Speak, speak, SPEAK to me, Thora.' He
played it morning, noon and night; it suited our mood exactly, and
Thora seemed the most poignantly beautiful of names.

Aunt Sadie was giving a ball for Louisa soon after Christmas, and to
this we pinned great hopes. True, neither the Prince of Wales nor my
farmer was invited, but, as Linda said, you never could tell in the
country. Somebody might bring them. The Prince might break down in
his motor-car, perhaps on his way to Badminton; what could be more
natural than that he should while away the time by looking in on the
revelry?

'Pray, who is that beautiful young lady?'

'My daughter Louisa, sir.'

'Ah, yes, very charming, but I really meant the one in white taffeta.'

'That is my younger daughter Linda, Your Royal Highness.'

'Please present her to me.'

They would then whirl away in a waltz so accomplished that the other dancers would stand aside to admire. When they could dance no more they would sit for the rest of the evening absorbed in witty conversation.

The following day an A.D.C. asking for her hand——

'But she is so young!'

'His Royal Highness is prepared to wait a year. He reminds you that Her Majesty the Empress Elizabeth of Austria was married at sixteen. Meanwhile, he sends this jewel.'

A golden casket, a pink white cushion, a diamond rose.

My daydreams were less exalted, equally improbable, and quite as real to me. I imagined my farmer carrying me away from Alconleigh, like young Lochinvar, on a pillion behind him to the nearest smith, who then declared us man and wife. Linda kindly said that we could have one of the royal farms, but I thought this would be a great bore, and that it would be much more fun to have one of our own.

Meanwhile, preparations for the ball went forward, occupying every single member of the household. Linda's and my dresses, white taffeta with floating panels and embroidered bead belts, were being made by Mrs. Josh, whose cottage was besieged at all hours to see how they were getting on. Louisa's came from Reville, it was silver lamé in tiny frills, each frill edged with blue net. Dangling on the left shoulder, and strangely unrelated to the dress, was a large pink silk overblown rose. Aunt Sadie, shaken out of her accustomed languor, was in a state of exaggerated preoccupation and worry over the whole thing; we had never seen her like this before. For the first time, too, that any of us could remember, she found herself in opposition to Uncle Matthew. It was over the following question: The nearest neighbour to Alconleigh was Lord Merlin; his estate marched with that of my uncle, and his house at Merlinford was about five miles away. Uncle Matthew loathed him, while, as for Lord Merlin, not for nothing was his telegraphic address Neighbourtease. There had, however, been no open breach between them; the fact that they never saw each other meant nothing, for Lord Merlin neither hunted, shot, nor fished, while Uncle Matthew had never in his life been known to eat a meal in anybody else's house. 'Perfectly good food at home,' he would say, and people had long ago stopped asking him. The two men, and indeed their two houses and estates, afforded an absolute contrast. Alconleigh was a large, ugly, north-facing, Georgian house, built with only one intention, that of sheltering, when the weather was too bad to be out of doors, a succession of bucolic squires, their wives, their enormous families, their dogs, their horses, their father's relict, and their unmarried sisters. There was no attempt at decoration, at softening the lines, no apology for a façade, it was all as grim and as bare as a barracks, stuck up on the high hillside. Within, the keynote, the theme, was death. Not death of maidens, not death romantically accoutred with urns and weeping willows, cypresses and valedictory odes, but the death of warriors and of animals, stark, real. On the walls halberds and pikes and ancient muskets were arranged in crude patterns with the heads of beasts slaughtered in many lands, with the flags and uniforms of bygone Radletts. Glass-topped cases contained, not miniatures of ladies, but miniatures of the medals of their lords, badges, penholders made of tiger's teeth, the hoof of a favourite horse, telegrams announcing casualties in battle and commissions written out on parchment scrolls, all lying together in a timeless jumble.

Merlinford nestled in a valley of south-west aspect, among orchards and old mellow farmhouses. It was a villa, built at about the same time as Alconleigh, but by a very different architect, and with a very different end in view. It was a house to live in, not to rush out from all day to kill enemies and animals. It was suitable for a bachelor, or a married couple with one, or at most two, beautiful, clever, delicate children. It had Angelica Kauffman ceilings, a Chippendale staircase, furniture by Sheraton and Hepplewhite; in the hall there hung two Watteaus; there was no entrenching tool to be seen, nor the head of any animal.

Lord Merlin added continually to its beauties. He was a great collector, and not only Merlinford, but also his houses in London and Rome flowed over with treasures. Indeed, a well-known antique dealer from St. James's had found it worth his while to open a branch in the little town of Merlinford, to tempt his lordship with choice objects during his morning walk, and was soon followed there by a Bond Street jeweller. Lord Merlin loved jewels; his two black whippets wore diamond necklaces designed for whiter, but not slimmer or more graceful necks than theirs. This was a neighbour-tease of long standing; there was a feeling among the local gentry that it incited the good burghers of Merlinford to dishonesty. The neighbours were doubly teased, when year after year went by and the brilliants still sparkled on those furry necks intact.

His taste was by no means confined to antiques; he was an artist and a musician himself, and the patron of all the young. Modern music streamed perpetually from Merlinford, and he had built a small but exquisite playhouse in the garden, where his astonished neighbours were sometimes invited to attend such puzzlers as Cocteau plays, the opera 'Mahagonny', or the latest Dada extravagances from Paris. As Lord Merlin was a famous practical joker, it was sometimes difficult to know where jokes ended and culture began. I think he was not always perfectly certain himself.

A marble folly on a nearby hill was topped with a gold angel which blew a trumpet every evening at the hour of Lord Merlin's birth (that this happened to be 9.20 p.m., just too late to remind one of the B.B.C. news, was to be a great local grievance in years to come). The folly glittered by day with semi-precious stones, by night a powerful blue beam was trained upon it.

Such a man was bound to become a sort of legend to the bluff Cotswold squires among whom he lived. But, although they could not approve of an existence which left out of account the killing, though by no means the eating, of delicious game, and though they were puzzled beyond words by the aestheticism and the teases, they accepted him without question as one of themselves. Their families had always known his family, and his father, many years ago, had been a most popular M.F.H.; he was no upstart, no new rich, but simply a sport of all that was most normal in English country life. Indeed, the very folly itself, while considered absolutely hideous, was welcomed as a landmark by those lost on their way home from hunting.

The difference between Aunt Sadie and Uncle Matthew was not as to whether Lord Merlin should or should not be asked to the ball (that question did not arise, since all neighbours were automatically invited), but whether he should be asked to bring a house party. Aunt Sadie thought he should. Since her marriage the least worldly of women, she had known the world as a girl, and she knew that Lord Merlin's house party, if he consented to bring one, would have great decorative value. She also knew that, apart from this, the general note of her ball would be utter and unrelieved dowdiness, and she became aware of a longing to look once more upon young women with well brushed hair, London complexions, and Paris clothes. Uncle Matthew said: 'If we ask that brute Merlin to bring his friends, we shall get a lot of aesthetes, sewers from Oxford, and I wouldn't put it past him to bring some foreigners. I hear he sometimes has Frogs and even Wops to stay with him. I will not have my house filled with Wops.'

In the end, however, as usual, Aunt Sadie had her way, and sat down to write:

'Dear Lord Merlin,
    We are having a little dance for Louisa, etc. . . .'

while Uncle Matthew went gloomily off, having said his piece, and put on 'Thora'.

Lord Merlin accepted, and said he would bring a party of twelve people, whose names he would presently submit to Aunt Sadie. Very correct, perfectly normal behaviour. Aunt Sadie was quite agreeably surprised that his letter, when opened, did not contain some clockwork

joke to hit her in the eye. The writing-paper did actually have a picture
of his house on it, and this she concealed from Uncle Matthew. It was
the kind of thing he despised.

A few days later there was another surprise. Lord Merlin wrote
another letter, still jokeless, still polite, asking Uncle Matthew, Aunt
Sadie and Louisa to dine with him for the Merlinford Cottage Hospital
Ball. Uncle Matthew naturally could not be persuaded, but Aunt Sadie
and Louisa went. They came back with their eyes popping out of their
heads. The house, they said, had been boiling hot, so hot that one
never felt cold for a single moment, not even getting out of one's coat
in the hall. They had arrived very early, long before anyone else was
down, as it was the custom at Alconleigh always to leave a quarter of an
hour too soon when motoring, in case there should be a puncture. This
gave them the opportunity to have a good look round. The house was
full of spring flowers, and smelt wonderful. The hot-houses at Alconleigh were full of spring flowers, too, but somehow they never found
their way into the house, and certainly would have died of cold if they
had. The whippets did wear diamond necklaces, far grander ones than
Aunt Sadie's, she said, and she was forced to admit that they looked
very beautiful in them. Birds of paradise flew about the house, quite
tame, and one of the young men told Louisa that, if she came in the
daytime, she would see a flock of multi-coloured pigeons tumbling
about like a cloud of confetti in the sky.

'Merlin dyes them every year, and they are dried in the linen cupboard.'

'But isn't that frightfully cruel?' said Louisa, horrified.

'Oh, no, they love it. It makes their husbands and wives look so
pretty when they come out.'

'What about their poor eyes?'

'Oh, they soon learn to shut them.'

The house party, when they finally appeared (some of them shock-
ingly late) from their bedrooms, smelt even more delicious than the
flowers, and looked even more exotic than the birds of paradise. Everybody had been very nice, very kind to Louisa. She sat between two
beautiful young men at dinner, and turned upon them the usual
gambit:

'Where do you hunt?'

'We don't,' they said.

'Oh, then why do you wear pink coats?'

'Because we think they are so pretty.'

We all thought this dazzlingly funny, but agreed that Uncle Matthew
must never hear of it, or he might easily, even now, forbid the Merlinford party his ball.

After dinner the girls had taken Louisa upstairs. She was rather
startled at first to see printed notices in the guest rooms:

OWING TO AN UNIDENTIFIED CORPSE IN THE CISTERN VISITORS ARE
REQUESTED NOT TO DRINK THE BATH WATER.

VISITORS ARE REQUESTED NOT TO LET OFF FIREARMS, BLOW BUGLES,
SCREAM OR HOOT, BETWEEN THE HOURS OF MIDNIGHT AND SIX A.M.

and, on one bedroom door:

MANGLING DONE HERE

But it was soon explained to her that these were jokes.

The girls had offered to lend her powder and lipstick, but Louisa
had not quite dared to accept, for fear Aunt Sadie would notice. She
said it made the others look simply too lovely.

As the great day of the Alconleigh ball approached, it became obvious that Aunt Sadie had something on her mind. Everything appeared to be going smoothly, the champagne had arrived, the band,
Clifford Essex's third string, had been ordered, and would spend the
few hours of its rest in Mrs. Craven's cottage. Mrs. Crabbe, in conjunction with the Home Farm, Craven, and three women from the village
who were coming in to help, was planning a supper to end all suppers.
Uncle Matthew had been persuaded to get twenty oil-stoves, with
which to emulate the caressing warmth of Merlinford, and the gardener
was prepared to transfer to the house every pot-plant that he could lay
his hands on. ('You'll be dyeing the White Leghorns next,' said Uncle
Matthew, scornfully.)

But, in spite of the fact that the preparations seemed to be going forward without a single hitch, Aunt Sadie's brow was still furrowed with
anxiety, because she had collected a large house-party of girls and their
mammas, but not one single young man. The fact was that those of her
own contemporaries who had daughters were glad to bring them, but
sons were another matter. Dancing partners, sated with invitations at
this time of year, knew better than to go all the way down to Gloucestershire to a house as yet untried, where they were by no means certain of
finding the warmth, the luxury and fine wines which they looked upon
as their due, where there was no known female charmer to tempt them,
where they had not been offered a mount, and where no mention had
been made of a shoot, not even a day with the cocks.

Uncle Matthew had far too much respect for his horses and his
pheasants to offer them up to be messed about by any callow unknown
boy.

So here was a horrible situation. Ten females, four mothers and six
girls, were advancing from various parts of England, to arrive at a
household consisting of four more females (not that Linda and I
counted, still we wore skirts and not trousers, and were really too old

to be kept all the time in the schoolroom) and only two males, one of whom was not yet in tails.

The telephone now became red-hot, telegrams flew in every direction. Aunt Sadie abandoned all pride, all pretence that things were as they should be, that people were asked for themselves alone, and launched a series of desperate appeals. Mr. Wills, the vicar, consented to leave Mrs. Wills at home, and dine, *en garçon*, at Alconleigh. It would be the first time they had been separated for forty years. Mrs. Aster, the agent's wife, also made the same sacrifice, and Master Aster, the agent's son, aged not quite seventeen, was hurried off to Oxford to get himself a ready-made dress suit.

Davey Warbeck was ordered to leave Aunt Emily and come. He said he would, but unwillingly, and only after the full extent of the crisis had been divulged. Elderly cousins, and uncles who had been for many years forgotten as ghosts, were recalled from oblivion and urged to materialize. They nearly all refused, some of them quite rudely—they had, nearly all, at one time or another, been so deeply and bitterly insulted by Uncle Matthew that forgiveness was impossible.

At last Uncle Matthew saw that the situation would have to be taken in hand. He did not care two hoots about the ball, he felt no particular responsibility for the amusement of his guests, whom he seemed to regard as an onrushing horde of barbarians who could not be kept out, rather than as a group of delightful friends summoned for mutual entertainment and joyous revelry. But he did care for Aunt Sadie's peace of mind, he could not bear to see her looking so worried, and he decided to take steps. He went up to London and attended the last sitting of the House of Lords before the recess. His journey was entirely fruitful.

'Stromboli, Paddington, Fort William and Curtley have accepted,' he told Aunt Sadie, with the air of a conjurer producing four wonderful fat rabbits out of one small wine-glass.

'But I had to promise them a shoot—Bob, go and tell Craven I want to see him in the morning.'

By these complicated devices the numbers at the dinner-table would now be even, and Aunt Sadie was infinitely relieved, though inclined to be giggly over Uncle Matthew's rabbits. Lord Stromboli, Lord Fort William and the Duke of Paddington were old dancing partners of her own, Sir Archibald Curtley, Librarian of the House, was a well-known diner-out in the smart intellectual world, he was over seventy and very arthritic. After dinner, of course, the dance would be another matter. Mr. Wills would then be joined by Mrs. Wills, Captain Aster by Mrs. Aster, Uncle Matthew and Bob could hardly be counted as partners, while the House of Lords contingent were more likely to head for the bridge table than for the dancing floor.

'I fear it will be sink or swim for the girls,' said Aunt Sadie, dreamily.

In one way, however, it was all to the good. These old boys were Uncle Matthew's own choice, his own friends, and he would probably be polite to them; in any case they would know what he was like before they came. To have filled the house with strange young men would, she knew, have been taking a great risk. Uncle Matthew hated strangers, he hated the young, and he hated the idea of possible suitors for his daughters; Aunt Sadie saw rocks ahead, but this time they had been circumnavigated.

This then is a ball. This is life, what we have been waiting for all these years, here we are and here it is, a ball, actually going on now, actually in progress round us. How extraordinary it feels, such unreality, like a dream. But, alas, so utterly different from what one had imagined and expected; it must be admitted, not a good dream. The men so small and ugly, the women so frowsty, their clothes so messy and their faces so red, the oil-stoves so smelly, and not really very warm, but, above all, the men, either so old or so ugly. And when they ask one to dance (pushed to it, one cannot but suspect, by kind Davey, who is trying to see that we have a good time at our first party), it is not at all like floating away into a delicious cloud, pressed by a manly arm to a manly bosom, but stumble, stumble, kick, kick. They balance, like King Stork, on one leg, while, with the other, they come down, like King Log, on to one's toe. As for witty conversation, it is wonderful if any conversation, even of the most banal and jerky description, lasts through a whole dance and the sitting out. It is mostly: 'Oh, sorry—oh, my fault,' though Linda did get as far as taking one of her partners to see the diseased stones.

We had never learnt to dance, and, for some reason, we had supposed it to be a thing which everybody could do quite easily and naturally. I think Linda realized there and then what it took me years to learn, that the behaviour of civilized man really has nothing to do with nature, that all is artificiality and art more or less perfected.

The evening was saved from being an utter disillusionment by the Merlinford house party. They came immensely late, we had all forgotten about them in fact, but, when they had said how do you do to Aunt Sadie and taken the floor, they seemed at once to give the party a new atmosphere. They flourished and shone with jewels, lovely clothes, brilliant hair and dazzling complexions; when they danced they really did seem to float, except when it was the Charleston, and that, though angular, was so accomplished that it made us gasp with admiration. Their conversation was quite evidently both daring and witty, one could see it ran like a river, splashing, dashing and glittering in the sun. Linda was entranced by them, and decided then and there that she would become one of these brilliant beings and live in their world, even if it took her a lifetime to accomplish. I did not aspire to this. I saw that they were admirable, but they were far removed from me and my orbit, belonging more to that of my parents; my back had been towards them from the day Aunt Emily had taken me home, and there was no return—nor did I wish for it. All the same, I found them fascinating as a spectacle, and, whether I sat out with Linda or stumped round the room with kind Davey, who, unable to persuade any more young men to take us on, gave us an occasional turn himself, my eyes were glued to them. Davey seemed to know them all quite well, and was evidently great friends with Lord Merlin. When he was not being kind to Linda and me, he attached himself to them, and joined in their accomplished chatter. He even offered to introduce us to them, but, alas, the floating panels of taffeta, which had seemed so original and pretty in Mrs. Josh's cottage, looked queerly stiff beside their printed chiffons, so soft and supple; also, our experiences earlier in the evening had made us feel inferior, and we begged him not to.

That night in bed, I thought more than ever of the safe sheltering arms of my Shenley farmer. The next morning Linda told me that she had renounced the Prince of Wales.

'I have come to the conclusion,' she said, 'that Court circles would be rather dull. Lady Dorothy is a lady-in-waiting and look at her.'

CHAPTER VI

THE ball had a very unexpected sequel. Lord Fort William's mother invited Aunt Sadie and Louisa to stay at their place in Sussex for a hunt ball, and, shortly afterwards, his married sister asked them to a shoot and an Infirmary Ball. During this visit, Lord Fort William proposed to Louisa and was accepted. She came back to Alconleigh a fiancée, to find herself the centre of attention there for the first time since the birth of Linda had put her nose for ever out of joint. This was indeed an excitement, and tremendous chats took place in the Hons' cupboard, both with and without Louisa. She had a nice little diamond ring on her fourth finger, but was not as communicative as we could have wished on the subject of Lord (John now to us, but how could we remember that?) Fort William's love-making, retiring, with many blushes, behind the smoke-screen of such things being too sacred to speak of. He soon appeared again in person, and we were able to observe him as an individual, instead of part, with Lord Stromboli and the Duke of Paddington, of a venerable trinity. Linda pronounced the summing-up. 'Poor old thing, I suppose she likes him, but, I must say, if he was one's dog one would have him put down.' Lord Fort William was thirty-nine, but he certainly looked much more. His hair seemed to be slipping off backwards, like an eiderdown in the night, Linda said, and he had a generally uncared-for middle-aged appearance. Louisa, however, loved him, and was happy for the first time in her life. She had always been more frightened of Uncle Matthew than any of the others, and with good reason; he thought she was a fool and was never at all nice to her, and she was in heaven at the prospect of getting away from Alconleigh for ever.

I think Linda, in spite of the poor old dog and the eiderdown, was really very jealous. She went off for long rides by herself, and spun more and more fantastic daydreams; her longing for love had become an obsession. Two whole years would have to be made away with somehow before she would come out in the world, but oh the days went dragging by. Linda would flop about in the drawing-room, playing (or beginning and then not finishing) endless games of patience, sometimes by herself, sometimes with Jassy, whom she had infected with her own restlessness.

'What's the time, darling?'

'Guess.'

'A quarter to six?'

'Better than that.'

'Six!'

'Not quite so good.'

'Five to?'

'Yes.'

'If this comes out I shall marry the man I love. If this comes out I shall marry at eighteen.'

If this comes out—shuffle—if this comes out—deal. A queen at the bottom of the pack, it can't come out, begin again.

Louisa was married in the spring. Her wedding dress, of tulle frills and sprays of orange blossom, was short to the knee and had a train, as was the hideous fashion then. Jassy got very worked up about it.

'So unsuitable.'

'Why, Jassy?'

'To be buried in, I mean. Women are always buried in their wedding dresses, aren't they? Think of your poor old dead legs sticking out.'

'Oh, Jassy, don't be such a ghoul. I'll wrap them up in my train.'

'Not very nice for the undertakers.'

Louisa refused to have bridesmaids. I think she felt that it would be agreeable, for once in her life, to be more looked at than Linda.

'You can't think how stupid you'll look from behind,' Linda said, 'without any. Still, have it your own way. I'm sure we don't want to be guyed up in blue chiffon, I'm only thinking what would be kinder for you.'

On Louisa's birthday John Fort William, an ardent antiquarian, gave her a replica of King Alfred's jewel. Linda, whose disagreeableness at this time knew no bounds, said that it simply looked like a chicken's mess. 'Same shape, same size, same colour. Not my idea of a jewel.'

'I think it's lovely,' said Aunt Sadie, but Linda's words had left their sting all the same.

Aunt Sadie had a canary then, which sang all day, rivalling even Galli-Curci in the pureness and loudness of its trills. Whenever I hear a canary sing so immoderately it recalls that happy visit, the endless flow of wedding presents, unpacking them, arranging them in the ballroom with shrieks of admiration or of horror, the hustle, the bustle, and Uncle Matthew's good temper, which went on, as fine weather sometimes does, day after unbelievable day.

Louisa was to have two houses, one in London, Connaught Square, and one in Scotland. Her dress allowance would be three hundred a year, she would possess a diamond tiara, a pearl necklace, a motor-car of her own and a fur cape. In fact, granted that she could bear John Fort William, her lot was an enviable one. He was terribly dull.

The wedding day was fine and balmy, and, when we went in the morning to see how Mrs. Wills and Mrs. Josh were getting on with the decorations, we found the light little church bunchy with spring flowers. Later, its well-known outlines blurred with a most unaccustomed throng of human beings, it looked quite different. I thought that I personally should have liked better to be married in it when it was so empty and flowery and full of the Holy Ghost.

Neither Linda nor I had ever been to a wedding before, as Aunt Emily, most unfairly we thought at the time, had been married privately in the chapel at Davey's home in the North of England, and we were hardly prepared for the sudden transformation on this day of dear old Louisa, of terribly dull John, into eternal types of Bride and Bridegroom, Heroine and Hero of romance.

From the moment when we left Louisa alone at Alconleigh with Uncle Matthew, to follow us in the Daimler in exactly eleven minutes, the atmosphere became positively dramatic. Louisa, enveloped from head to knee in tulle, sat gingerly on the edge of a chair, while Uncle Matthew, watch in hand, strode up and down the hall. We walked, as we always did, to the church, and arranged ourselves in the family pew at the back of it, from which vantage point we were able to observe with fascination, the unusual appearance of our neighbours, all tricked out in their best. The only person in the whole congregation who looked exactly as usual was Lord Merlin.

Suddenly there was a stir. John and his best man, Lord Stromboli, appearing like two jacks-in-the-box from nowhere, stood beside the altar steps. In their morning coats, their hair heavily brilliantined, they looked quite glamorous, but we hardly had time to notice this fact before Mrs. Wills struck up 'Here comes the Bride', with all the stops out, and Louisa, her veil over her face, was being dragged up the aisle at double quick time by Uncle Matthew. At this moment I think Linda would gladly have changed places with Louisa, even at the cost—the heavy cost—of being happy for ever after with John Fort William. In what seemed no time at all Louisa was being dragged down the aisle again by John, with her veil back, while Mrs. Wills nearly broke the windows, so loud and so triumphant was her 'Wedding March'.

Everything had gone like clockwork, and there was only one small incident. Davey slipped out of the family pew almost unobserved, in the middle of 'As pants the hart' (Louisa's favourite hymn) and went straight to London, making one of the wedding cars take him to Merlinford station. That evening he telephoned to say that he had twisted his tonsil, singing, and had thought it better to go immediately to Sir Andrew Macpherson, the nose, throat and ear man, who was keeping him in bed for a week. The most extraordinary accidents always seemed to overtake poor Davey.

When Louisa had gone away and the wedding guests had left Alconleigh, a sense of flatness descended upon the house, as always happens on these occasions. Linda then became plunged into such despairing gloom that even Aunt Sadie was alarmed. Linda told me afterwards that she thought a great deal about killing herself, and would most likely have done so had the material difficulties not been so great.

'You know what it is,' she said, 'trying to kill rabbits. Well, think of *oneself*!'

Two years seemed an absolute eternity, not worth ploughing through even with the prospect (which she never doubted, just as a religious person does not doubt the existence of heaven) of blissful love at the end of it. Of course, this was the time when Linda should have been made to work, as I was, all day and hard, with no time for silly dreaming except the few minutes before one went to sleep at night. I think Aunt Sadie dimly perceived this fact, she urged her to learn cooking, to occupy herself in the garden, to be prepared for confirmation. Linda furiously refused, nor would she do jobs in the village, nor help Aunt Sadie in the hundred and one chores which fall to the lot of a country squire's wife. She was, in fact, and Uncle Matthew told her so countless times every day, glaring at her with angry blue eyes, thoroughly bloody-minded.

Lord Merlin came to her rescue. He had taken a fancy to her at Louisa's wedding, and asked Aunt Sadie to bring her over to Merlinford some time. A few days later he rang up. Uncle Matthew answered the telephone, and shouted to Aunt Sadie, without taking his mouth away from the receiver:

'That hog Merlin wants to speak to you.'

Lord Merlin, who must have heard, was quite unmoved by this. He was an eccentric himself, and had a fellow feeling for the idiosyncrasies of others. Poor Aunt Sadie, however, was very much flustered, and, as a result, she accepted an invitation which she would otherwise most probably have refused, to take Linda over to Merlinford for luncheon.

Lord Merlin seemed to become immediately aware of Linda's state of mind, was really shocked to discover that she was doing no lessons at all, and did what he could to provide some interests for her. He showed her his pictures, explained them to her, talked at length about art and literature, and gave her books to read. He let fall the suggestion, which was taken up by Aunt Sadie, that she and Linda should attend a course of lectures in Oxford, and he also mentioned that the Shakespeare Festival was now in progress at Stratford-on-Avon.

Outings of this kind, which Aunt Sadie herself very much enjoyed, soon became a regular feature of life at Alconleigh. Uncle Matthew scoffed a bit, but he never interfered with anything Aunt Sadie wanted to do; besides, it was not so much education that he dreaded for his daughters, as the vulgarizing effect that a boarding-school might have upon them. As for governesses, they had been tried, but none had ever been able to endure for more than a few days the terror of Uncle Matthew's grinding dentures, the piercing, furious blue flash of his eyes, the stock whips cracking under their bedroom windows at dawn. Their nerves, they said, and made for the station, often before they had had time to unpack enormous trunks, heavy as though full of stones, by which they were always accompanied.

Uncle Matthew went with Aunt Sadie and Linda on one occasion to a Shakespeare play, *Romeo and Juliet*. It was not a success. He cried copiously, and went into a furious rage because it ended badly. 'All the fault of that damned padre,' he kept saying on the way home, still wiping his eyes. 'That fella, what's 'is name, Romeo, might have known a blasted papist would mess up the whole thing. Silly old fool of a nurse too, I bet she was an R.C., dismal old bitch.'

So Linda's life, instead of being on one flat level plain of tedium, was now, to some extent, filled with outside interests. She perceived that the world she wanted to be in, the witty, sparkling world of Lord Merlin and his friends, was interested in things of the mind, and that she would only be able to shine in it if she became in some sort educated. The futile games of patience were abandoned, and she sat all day hunched up in a corner of the library sofa, reading until her eyes gave out. She often rode over to Merlinford, and, unbeknownst to her parents, who never would have allowed her to go there, or indeed anywhere, alone, left Josh in the stable yard where he had congenial friends, and chatted for hours with Lord Merlin on all sorts of subjects. He knew that she had an intensely romantic character, he foresaw much trouble ahead, and he continually urged upon her the necessity for an intellectual background.

CHAPTER VII

WHAT could possibly have induced Linda to marry Anthony Kroesig? During the nine years of their life together people asked this question with irritating regularity, almost every time their names were mentioned. What was she after, surely she could never possibly have been in love with him, what was the idea, how could it have happened? He was admittedly very rich, but so were others and surely the fascinating Linda had only to choose? The answer was, of course, that, quite simply, she was in love with him. Linda was far too romantic to marry without love and indeed I, who was present at their first meeting and during most of their courtship, always understood why it had happened. Tony, in those days, and to unsophisticated country girls like us, seemed a glorious and glamorous creature. When we first saw him, at Linda's and my coming-out ball, he was in his last year at Oxford, a member of Bullingdon, a splendid young man with a Rolls Royce, plenty of beautiful horses, exquisite clothes, and large luxurious rooms, where he entertained on a lavish scale. In person he was tall and fair, on the heavy side, but with a well-proportioned figure; he had already a faint touch of pomposity, a thing which Linda had never come across before, and which she found not unattractive. She took him, in short, at his own valuation.

What immediately gave him great prestige in her eyes was that he came to the ball with Lord Merlin. It was really most unlucky, especially as it happened that he had only been asked at the eleventh hour, as a stopgap.

Linda's ball was not nearly such a fiasco as Louisa's had been. Louisa, a married London lady now, produced a lot of young men for Aunt Sadie's house-party, dull, fair Scotch boys mostly, with nice manners; nothing to which Uncle Matthew could possibly take exception. They got on quite well with the various dull dark girls invited by Aunt Sadie, and the house-party seemed to 'go' very nicely, though Linda had her head in the air, saying they were all too impossibly dreary for words. Uncle Matthew had been implored by Aunt Sadie for weeks past to be kind to the young and not to shout at anybody, and he was quite subdued, almost pathetic in his wish to please, creeping about as though there were an invalid upstairs and straw in the street.

Davey and Aunt Emily were staying in the house to see me come out (Aunt Sadie had offered to bring me out with Linda and give us a London season together, an offer which was most gratefully accepted by Aunt Emily) and Davey constituted himself a sort of bodyguard to

Uncle Matthew, hoping to stand as much as possible between him and the more unbearable forms of irritation.

'I'll be simply wonderful to everybody, but I won't have the sewers in my business-room, that's all,' Uncle Matthew had said, after one of Aunt Sadie's prolonged exhortations, and, indeed, spent most of the week-end (the ball was on a Friday and the house-party stayed on until Monday) locked into it, playing '1812' and the 'Haunted Ballroom' on the gramophone. He was rather off the human voice this year.

'What a pity,' said Linda, as we struggled into our ball dresses (proper London ones this time, with no floating panels), 'that we are dressing up like this, and looking so pretty, and all for those terrible productions of Louisa's. Waste, I call it.'

'You never know in the country,' I said, 'somebody may bring the Prince of Wales.'

Linda shot me a furious look under her eyelashes.

'Actually,' she said, 'I am pinning great hopes on Lord Merlin's party. I'm sure he'll bring some really interesting people.'

Lord Merlin's party arrived, as before, very late, and in very high spirits. Linda immediately noticed a large, blond young man in a beautiful pink coat. He was dancing with a girl who often stayed at Merlinford called Baby Fairweather, and she introduced him to Linda. He asked her to dance the next, and she abandoned one of Louisa's Scotch boys, to whom she had promised it, and strutted off with him in a quick one-step. Linda and I had both been having dancing lessons, and, if we did not exactly float round the room, our progress was by no means so embarrassing as it had been before.

Tony was in a happy mood, induced by Lord Merlin's excellent brandy, and Linda was pleased to find how well and easily she was getting on with this member of the Merlinford set. Everything she said seemed to make him laugh; presently they went to sit out, she chattered away, and Tony roared with laughter. This was the royal road to Linda's good books; she liked people who laughed easily more than anything; it naturally did not occur to her that Tony was a bit drunk. They sat out the next dance together. This was immediately noticed by Uncle Matthew, who began to walk up and down in front of them, giving them furious looks, until Davey, observing this danger signal, came up and hurried him away, saying that one of the oil-stoves in the hall was smoking.

'Who is that sewer with Linda?"

'Kroesig, Governor of the Bank of England, you know; his son.'

'Good God, I never expected to harbour a full-blooded Hun in this house—who on earth asked him?'

'Now, Matthew dear, don't get excited. The Kroesigs aren't Huns, they've been over here for generations, they are a very highly respectable family of English bankers.'

'Once a Hun always a Hun,' said Uncle Matthew, 'and I'm not too set on bankers myself. Besides, the fella must be a gate-crasher.'

'No, he's not. He came with Merlin.'

'I knew that bloody Merlin would start bringing foreigners here sooner or later. I always said he would, but I didn't think even he would land one with a German.'

'Don't you think it's time somebody took some champagne to the band?' said Davey.

But Uncle Matthew stumped down to the boiler room, where he had a long soothing talk with Timb, the odd man, about coke.

Tony, meanwhile, thought Linda ravishingly pretty, and great fun, which indeed she was. He told her so, and danced with her again and again, until Lord Merlin, quite as much put out as Uncle Matthew by what was happening, firmly and very early took his party home.

'See you at the meet tomorrow,' said Tony, winding a white silk scarf round his neck.

Linda was silent and preoccupied for the rest of the evening.

'You're not to go hunting, Linda,' said Aunt Sadie the next day, when Linda came downstairs in her riding-habit, 'it's too rude, you must stay and look after your guests. You can't leave them like that.'

'Darling, darling Mummie,' said Linda, 'the meet's at Cock's Barn, and you know how one can't resist. And Flora hasn't been out for a week, she'll go mad. Be a love and take them to see the Roman villa or something, and I swear to come back early. And they've got Fanny and Louisa after all.'

It was this unlucky hunt that clinched matters as far as Linda was concerned. The first person she saw at the meet was Tony, on a splendid chestnut horse. Linda herself was always beautifully mounted. Uncle Matthew was proud of her horsemanship, and had given her two pretty, lively little horses. They found at once, and there was a short, sharp run, during which Linda and Tony, both in a somewhat showing-off mood, rode side by side over the stone walls. Presently, on a village green, they checked. One or two hounds put up a hare, which lost its head, jumped into a duckpond, and began to swim about in a hopeless sort of way. Linda's eyes filled with tears.

'Oh, the poor hare!'

Tony got off his horse, and plunged into the pond. He rescued the hare, waded out again, his fine white breeches covered with green muck, and put it, wet and gasping, into Linda's lap. It was the one romantic gesture of his life.

At the end of the day Linda left hounds to take a short cut home across country. Tony opened a gate for her, took off his hat, and said:

'You are a most beautiful rider, you know. Good night, when I'm back in Oxford I'll ring you up.'

When Linda got home she rushed me off to the Hons' cupboard and told me all this. She was in love.

Given Linda's frame of mind during the past two endless years, she was obviously destined to fall in love with the first young man who came along. It could hardly have been otherwise; she need not, however, have married him. This was made inevitable by the behaviour of Uncle Matthew. Most unfortunately Lord Merlin, the one person who might perhaps have been able to make Linda see that Tony was not all she thought him, went to Rome the week after the ball, and remained abroad for a year.

Tony went back to Oxford when he left Merlinford, and Linda sat about waiting, waiting, waiting for the telephone bell. Patience again. If this comes out he is thinking of me now this very minute—if this comes out he'll ring up tomorrow—if this comes out he'll be at the meet. But Tony hunted with the Bicester, and never appeared on our side of the country. Three weeks passed, and Linda began to feel in despair. Then one evening, after dinner, the telephone bell rang; by a lucky chance Uncle Matthew had gone down to the stables to see Josh, about a horse that had colic, the business-room was empty, and Linda answered the telephone herself. It was Tony. Her heart was choking her, she could scarcely speak.

'Hullo, is that Linda? It's Tony Kroesig here. Will you come to lunch next Thursday?'

'Oh! But I should never be allowed to.'

'Oh, rot,' very impatiently, 'several other girls are coming down from London—bring your cousin if you like.'

'All right, that will be lovely.'

'See you then—about one—7 King Edward Street, I expect you know the rooms. Altringham had them when he was up.'

Linda came away from the telephone trembling, and whispered to me to come quick to the Hons' cupboard. We were absolutely forbidden to see young men at any hour unchaperoned, and other girls did not count as chaperons. We knew quite well, though such a remote eventuality had never even been mooted at Alconleigh, that we would not be allowed to have luncheon with a young man in his lodgings with any chaperon at all, short of Aunt Sadie herself. The Alconleigh standards of chaperonage were medieval; they did not vary in the slightest degree from those applied to Uncle Matthew's sister, and to Aunt Sadie in youth. The principle was that one never saw any young man alone, under any circumstances, until one was engaged to him. The only people who could be counted on to enforce this rule were one's mother or one's aunts, therefore one must not be allowed beyond the reach of their ever-watchful eyes. The argument, often put forward by Linda, that young men were not very likely to propose to girls they hardly knew, was brushed aside as nonsense. Uncle Matthew had proposed, had he not? to Aunt Sadie, the very first time he ever saw her, by the cage of a two-headed nightingale at an Exhibition at the White City. 'They respect you all the more.' It never seemed to dawn upon the Alconleighs that respect is not an attitude of mind indulged in by modern young men who look for other qualities in their wives than respectability. Aunt Emily, under the enlightened influence of Davey, was far more reasonable, but, of course, when staying with the Radletts, I had to obey the same rules.

In the Hons' cupboard we talked and talked. There was no question in our minds but that we must go, not to do so would be death for Linda, she would never get over it. But how to escape? There was only one way that we could devise, and it was full of risk. A very dull girl of exactly our age called Lavender Davis lived with her very dull parents about five miles away, and once in a blue moon, Linda, complaining vociferously, was sent over to luncheon with them, driving herself in Aunt Sadie's little car. We must pretend that we were going to do that, hoping that Aunt Sadie would not see Mrs. Davis, that pillar of the Women's Institute, for months and months, hoping also that Perkins, the chauffeur, would not remark on the fact that we had driven sixty miles and not ten.

As we were going upstairs to bed, Linda said to Aunt Sadie, in what she hoped was an offhand voice, but one which seemed to me vibrant with guilt :

'That was Lavender ringing up. She wants Fanny and me to lunch there on Thursday.'

'Oh, duck,' said Aunt Sadie, 'you can't have my car, I'm afraid.'

Linda became very white, and leant against the wall.

'Oh, please, Mummy, oh please do let me, I do so terribly want to go.'

'To the Davises,' said Aunt Sadie in astonishment, 'but, darling, last time you said you'd never go again as long as you lived—great haunches of cod you said, don't you remember? Anyhow, I'm sure they'll have you another day, you know.'

'Oh, Mummy, you don't understand. The whole point is a man is coming who brought up a baby badger, and I do so want to meet him.'

It was known to be one of Linda's greatest ambitions, to bring up a baby badger.

'Yes, I see. Well, couldn't you ride over?'

'Staggers and ringworm,' said Linda, her large blue eyes slowly filling with tears.

'What did you say, darling?'

'In their stables—staggers and ringworm. You wouldn't want me to expose poor Flora to that.'

'Are you sure? Their horses always look so wonderful.'

'Ask Josh.'

'Well, I'll see. Perhaps I can borrow Fa's Morris, and, if not, perhaps Perkins can take me in the Daimler. It's a meeting I must go to, though.'

'Oh, you are kind, you are kind. Oh, do try. I do so long for a badger.'

'If we go to London for the season you'll be far too busy to think of a badger. Good night then, ducks.'

'We must get hold of some powder.'

'And rouge.'

These commodities were utterly forbidden by Uncle Matthew, who liked to see female complexions in a state of nature, and often pronounced that paint was for whores and not for his daughters.

'I once read in a book that you can use geranium juice for rouge.'

'Geraniums aren't out at this time of year, silly.'

'We can blue our eyelids out of Jassy's paint-box.'

'And sleep in curlers.'

'I'll get the verbena soap out of Mummy's bathroom. If we let it melt in the bath, and soak for hours in it, we shall smell delicious.'

'I thought you loathed Lavender Davis.'

'Oh, shut up, Jassy.'

'Last time you went you said she was a horrible Counter-Hon, and you would like to bash in her silly face with the Hons' mallet.'

'I never said so. Don't invent lies.'

'Why have you got your London suit on for Lavender Davis?'

'Do go away, Matt.'

'Why are you starting already, you'll be hours too early.'

'We're going to see the badger before luncheon.'

'How red your face is, Linda. Oh, oh you do look so funny!'

'If you don't shut up and go away, Jassy, I swear I'll put your newt back in the pond.'

Persecution, however, continued until we were in the car and out of the garage yard.

'Why don't you bring Lavender back for a nice long cosy visit?' was Jassy's parting shot.

'Not very Honnish of them,' said Linda, 'do you think they can possibly have guessed?'

We left our car in the Clarendon yard, and, as we were very early, having allowed half an hour in case of two punctures, we made for Elliston & Cavell's ladies-room, and gazed at ourselves, with a tiny feeling of uncertainty, in the looking-glasses there. Our cheeks had round scarlet patches, our lips were the same colour, but only at the edges, inside it had already worn off, and our eyelids were blue, all out of Jassy's paint-box. Our noses were white, Nanny having produced some powder with which, years ago, she used to dust Robin's bottom. In short, we looked like a couple of Dutch dolls.

'We must keep our ends up,' said Linda uncertainly.

'Oh, dear,' I said, 'the thing about me is, I always feel so much happier with my end down.'

We gazed and gazed, hoping thus, in some magical way, to make ourselves feel less peculiar. Presently we did a little work with damp handkerchiefs, and toned our faces down a bit. We then sallied forth into the street, looking at ourselves in every shop window that we passed. (I have often noticed that when women look at themselves in every reflection, and take furtive peeps into their hand looking-glasses, it is hardly ever, as is generally supposed, from vanity, but much more often from a feeling that all is not quite as it should be.)

Now that we had actually achieved our objective, we were beginning to feel horribly nervous, not only wicked, guilty and frightened, but also filled with social terrors. I think we would both gladly have got back into the car and made for home.

On the stroke of one o'clock we arrived in Tony's room. He was alone, but evidently a large party was expected, the table, a square one with a coarse white linen cloth, seemed to have a great many places. We refused sherry and cigarettes, and an awkward silence fell.

'Been hunting at all?' he asked Linda.

'Oh, yes, we were out yesterday.'

'Good day?'

'Yes, very. We found at once, and had a five-mile point and then——' Linda suddenly remembered that Lord Merlin had once said to her: 'Hunt as much as you like, but never talk about it, it's the most boring subject in the world.'

'But that's marvellous, a five-mile point. I must come out with the Heythrop again soon, they are doing awfully well this season, I hear. We had a good day yesterday, too.'

He embarked on a detailed account of every minute of it, where they found, where they ran to, how his first horse had gone lame, how, luckily, he had then come upon his second horse, and so on. I saw just what Lord Merlin meant. Linda, however, hung upon his words with breathless interest.

At last noises were heard in the street, and he went to the window.

'Good,' he said, 'here are the others.'

The others had come down from London in a huge Daimler, and poured, chattering, into the room. Four pretty girls and a young man. Presently some undergraduates appeared, and completed the party. It was not really very enjoyable from our point of view, they all knew each other too well. They gossiped away, roared with laughter at private jokes, and showed off; still, we felt that this was Life, and would have been quite happy just looking on had it not been for that ghastly feeling of guilt, which was now beginning to give us a pain rather like indigestion. Linda turned quite pale every time the door opened, I think she really felt that Uncle Matthew might appear at any moment, cracking a whip. As soon as we decently could, which was not very soon, because nobody moved from the table until after Tom had struck four, we said good-bye, and fled for home.

The miserable Matt and Jassy were swinging on the garage gate.

'So how was Lavender? Did she roar at your eyelids? Better go and wash before Fa sees you. You have been hours. Was it cod? Did you see the badger?'

Linda burst into tears.

'Leave me alone, you horrible Counter-Hons,' she cried, and rushed upstairs to her bedroom.

Love had increased threefold in one short day.

On Saturday the blow fell.

'Linda and Fanny, Fa wants you in the business-room. And sooner you than me by the look of him,' said Jassy, meeting us in the drive as we came in from riding. Our hearts plunged into our boots. We looked at each other with apprehension.

'Better get it over,' said Linda, and we hurried to the business-room, where we saw at once that the worst had occurred.

Aunt Sadie, looking unhappy, and Uncle Matthew, grinding his teeth, confronted us with our crime. The room was full of blue lightning flashing from his eyes, and Jove's thunder was not more awful than what he now roared at us:

'Do you realize,' he said, 'that, if you were married women, your husbands could divorce you for doing this?'

Linda began to say no they couldn't. She knew the laws of divorce from having read the whole of the Russell case off newspaper with which the fires in the spare bedrooms were laid.

'Don't interrupt your father,' said Aunt Sadie, with a warning look.

Uncle Matthew, however, did not even notice. He was in the full flood and violence of his storm.

'Now we know you can't be trusted to behave yourselves, we shall have to take certain steps. Fanny can go straight home tomorrow, and I never want you here again, do you understand? Emily will have to control you in future, if she can, but you'll go the same way as your mother, sure as eggs is eggs. As for you, miss, there's no more question of a London season now—we shall have to watch you in future every minute of the day—not very agreeable, to have a child one can't trust—and there would be too many opportunities in London for slipping off. You can stew in your own juice here. And no more hunting this year. You're damned lucky not to be thrashed; most fathers would give you a good hiding, do you hear? Now you can both go to bed, and you're not to speak to each other before Fanny leaves. I'm sending her over in the car tomorrow.'

It was months before we knew how they found out. It seemed like magic, but the explanation was simple. Somebody had left a scarf in Tony Kroesig's rooms, and he had rung up to ask whether it belonged to either of us.

CHAPTER VIII

As always, Uncle Matthew's bark was worse than his bite, though, while it lasted, it was the most terrible row within living memory at Alconleigh. I was sent back to Aunt Emily the next day, Linda waving and crying out of her bedroom window: 'Oh, you *are* lucky, not to be me' (most unlike her, her usual cry being: 'Isn't it lovely to be lovely *me*'); and she was stopped from hunting once or twice. Then relaxation began, the thin edge of the wedge, and gradually things returned to normal, though it was reckoned in the family that Uncle Matthew had got through a pair of dentures in record time.

Plans for the London season went on being made, and went on including me. I heard afterwards that both Davey and John Fort William took it upon themselves to tell Aunt Sadie and Uncle Matthew (especially Uncle Matthew) that, according to modern ideas, what we had done was absolutely normal, though, of course, they were obliged to own that it was very wrong of us to have told so many and such shameless lies.

We both said we were very sorry, and promised faithfully that we would never act in such an underhand way again, but always ask Aunt Sadie if there was something we specially wanted to do.

'Only then, of course, it will always be no,' as Linda said, giving me a hopeless look.

Aunt Sadie took a furnished house for the summer near Belgrave Square. It was a house with so little character that I can remember absolutely nothing about it, except that my bedroom had a view over chimney-pots, and that on hot summer evenings I used to sit and watch the swallows, always in pairs, and wish sentimentally that I too could be a pair with somebody.

We really had great fun, although I don't think it was dancing that we enjoyed so much as the fact of being grown up and in London. At the dances the great bar to enjoyment was what Linda called the chaps. They were terribly dull, all on the lines of the ones Louisa had brought to Alconleigh; Linda, still in her dream of love for Tony, could not distinguish between them, and never even knew their names. I looked about hopefully for a possible life-partner, but, though I honestly tried to see the best in them, nothing remotely approximating to my requirements turned up.

Tony was at Oxford for his last term, and did not come to London until quite the end of the season.

We were chaperoned, as was to be expected, with Victorian severity. Aunt Sadie or Uncle Matthew literally never let us out of the sight of one or the other; as Aunt Sadie liked to rest in the afternoon, Uncle Matthew would solemnly take us off to the House of Lords, park us in the Peeresses' Gallery, and take his own forty winks on a back bench opposite. When he was awake in the house, which was not often, he was a perfect nuisance to the Whips, never voting with the same party twice running; nor were the workings of his mind too easy to follow. He voted, for instance, in favour of steel traps, of blood sports and of steeplechasing, but against vivisection and the exporting of old horses to Belgium. No doubt he had his reasons, as Aunt Sadie would remark, with finality, when we commented on this inconsistency. I rather liked those drowsy afternoons in the dark Gothic chamber, fascinated by the mutterings and antics that went on the whole time, and besides, the occasional speech one was able to hear was generally rather interesting. Linda liked it too, she was far away, thinking her own thoughts. Uncle Matthew would wake up at tea-time, conduct us to the Peers' dining-room for tea and buttered buns, and then take us home to rest and dress for the dance.

Saturday to Monday was spent by the Radlett family at Alconleigh; they rolled down in their huge, rather sick-making Daimler; and by me at Shenley, where Aunt Emily and Davey were always longing to hear every detail of our week.

Clothes were probably our chief preoccupation at this time. Once Linda had been to a few dress shows, and got her eye in, she had all hers made by Mrs. Josh, and, somehow, they had a sort of originality and prettiness that I never achieved, although mine, which were bought at expensive shops, cost about five times as much. This showed, said Davey, who used to come and see us whenever he was in London, that either you get your clothes in Paris or it is a toss-up. Linda had one particularly ravishing ball-dress made of masses of pale grey tulle down to her feet. Most of the dresses were still short that summer, and Linda made a sensation whenever she appeared in her yards of tulle, very much disapproved of by Uncle Matthew, on the grounds that he had known three women burnt to death in tulle ball-dresses.

She was wearing this dress when Tony proposed to her in the Berkeley Square summer-house at six o'clock on a fine July morning. He had been down from Oxford about a fortnight, and it was soon obvious that he had eyes for nobody but her. He went to all the same dances, and, after stumping round with a few other girls, would take Linda to supper, and thereafter spend the evening glued to her side.

Aunt Sadie seemed to notice nothing, but to the whole rest of the debutante world the outcome was a foregone conclusion, the only question being when and where Tony would propose.

The ball from which they had emerged (it was in a lovely old house on the east side of Berkeley Square, since demolished) was only just alive, the band sleepily thump-thumped its tunes through the nearly empty rooms; poor Aunt Sadie sat on a little gold chair trying to keep her eyes open and passionately longing for bed, with me beside her, dead tired and very cold, my partners all gone home. It was broad daylight. Linda had been away for hours, nobody seemed to have set eyes on her since supper-time, and Aunt Sadie, though dominated by her fearful sleepiness, was apprehensive, and rather angry. She was beginning to wonder whether Linda had not committed the unforgivable sin, and gone off to a night club.

Suddenly the band perked up and began to play 'John Peel' as a prelude to 'God Save the King'; Linda, in a grey cloud, was galloping up and down the room with Tony; one look at her face told all. We climbed into a taxi behind Aunt Sadie (she never would keep a chauffeur up at night), we splashed away past the great hoses that were washing the streets, we climbed the stairs to our rooms, without a word being spoken by any of us. A thin oblique sunlight was striking the chimney-pots as I opened my window. I was too tired to think, I fell into bed.

We were allowed to be late after dances, though Aunt Sadie was always up and seeing to the household arrangements by nine o'clock. As Linda came sleepily downstairs the next morning, Uncle Matthew shouted furiously at her from the hall:

'That bloody Hun Kroesig has just telephoned, he wanted to speak to you. I told him to get to hell out of it. I don't want you mixed up with any Germans, do you understand?'

'Well, I am mixed up,' said Linda, in an offhand, would-be casual voice, 'as it happens I'm engaged to him.'

At this point Aunt Sadie dashed out of her little morning-room on the ground floor, took Uncle Matthew by the arm, and led him away. Linda locked herself into her bedroom and cried for an hour, while Jassy, Matt, Robin, and I speculated upon future developments in the nursery.

There was a great deal of opposition to the engagement, not only from Uncle Matthew, who was beside himself with disappointment and disgust at Linda's choice, but also quite as much from Sir Leicester Kroesig. He did not want Tony to marry at all until he was well settled in his career in the City, and then he had hoped for an alliance with one of the other big banking families. He despised the landed gentry, whom he regarded as feckless, finished and done with in the modern world, he also knew that the vast, the enviable capital sums which such families undoubtedly still possessed, and of which they made so foolishly little use, were always entailed upon the eldest son, and that very small provision, if any, was made for the dowries of daughters. Sir Leicester and Uncle Matthew met, disliked each other on sight, and were at one in their determination to stop the marriage. Tony was sent off to America, to work in a bank house in New York, and poor Linda, the season now being at an end, was taken home to eat her heart out at Alconleigh.

'Oh, Jassy, darling Jassy, lend me your running-away money to go to New York with.'

'No, Linda. I've saved and scraped for five years, ever since I was seven, I simply can't begin all over again now. Besides I shall want it for when I run away myself.'

'But, darling, I'll give it you back, Tony will, when we're married.'

'I know men,' said Jassy darkly.

She was adamant.

'If only Lord Merlin were here,' Linda wailed. 'He would help me.' But Lord Merlin was still in Rome.

She had 15s. 6d. in the world, and was obliged to content herself with writing immense screeds to Tony every day. She carried about in her pocket a quantity of short, dull letters in an immature handwriting and with a New York postmark.

After a few months Tony came back, and told his father that he could not settle down to business or banking, or think about his future career at all, until the date for his marriage had been fixed. This was quite the proper line to take with Sir Leicester. Anything that interfered with making money must be regulated at once. If Tony, who was a sensible fellow, and had never given his father one moment's anxiety in his life, assured him that he could only be serious about banking after marriage, then married he must be, the sooner the better. Sir Leicester explained at length what he considered the disadvantage of the union. Tony agreed in principle, but said that Linda was young, intelligent, energetic, that he had great influence with her, and did not doubt that she could be made into a tremendous asset. Sir Leicester finally gave his consent.

'It might have been worse,' he said, 'after all, she is a lady.'

Lady Kroesig opened negotiations with Aunt Sadie. As Linda had virtually worked herself into a decline, and was poisoning the lives of all around her by her intense disagreeableness, Aunt Sadie, secretly much relieved by the turn things had taken, persuaded Uncle Matthew that the marriage, though by no means ideal, was inevitable, and that, if he did not wish to alienate for ever his favourite child, he had better put a good face on it.

'I suppose it might have been worse,' Uncle Matthew said doubtfully, 'at least the fella's not a Roman Catholic.'

CHAPTER IX

THE engagement was duly announced in *The Times*. The Kroesigs now invited the Alconleighs to spend a Saturday to Monday at their house near Guildford. Lady Kroesig, in her letter to Aunt Sadie, called it a week-end, and said it would be nice to get to know each other better. Uncle Matthew flew into a furious temper. It was one of his idiosyncrasies that, not only did he never stay in other people's houses (except, very occasionally, with relations), but he regarded it as a positive insult that he should be invited to do so. He despised the expression 'week-end', and gave a sarcastic snort at the idea that it would be nice to know the Kroesigs better. When Aunt Sadie had calmed him down a bit, she put forward the suggestion that the Kroesig family, father, mother, daughter Marjorie and Tony, should be asked instead if they would spend Saturday to Monday at Alconleigh. Poor Uncle Matthew, having swallowed the great evil of Linda's engagement, had, to do him justice, resolved to put the best face he could on it, and had no wish to make trouble for her with her future in-laws. He had at heart a great respect for family connections, and once, when Bob and Jassy were slanging a cousin whom the whole family, including Uncle Matthew himself, very much disliked, he had turned upon them, knocked their heads together sharply, and said:

'In the first place he's a relation, and in the second place he's a clergyman, so shut up.'

It had become a classical saying with the Radletts.

So the Kroesigs were duly invited. They accepted, and the date was fixed. Aunt Sadie then got into a panic, and summoned Aunt Emily and Davey. (I was staying at Alconleigh anyhow, for a few weeks' hunting.) Louisa was feeding her second baby in Scotland, but hoped to come south for the wedding later on.

The arrival at Alconleigh of the four Kroesigs was not auspicious. As the car which had met them at the station was heard humming up the drive, every single light in the whole house fused—Davey had brought a new ultra-violet lamp with him, which had done the trick. The guests had to be led into the hall in pitch darkness, while Logan fumbled about in the pantry for a candle, and Uncle Matthew rushed off to the fuse box. Lady Kroesig and Aunt Sadie chatted politely about this and that, Linda and Tony giggled in the corner, and Sir Leicester hit his gouty foot on the edge of a refectory table, while the voice of an invisible Davey could be heard, apologizing in a high wail, from the top of the staircase. It was really very embarrassing.

At last the lights went up, and the Kroesigs were revealed. Sir

Leicester was a tall fair man with grey hair, whose undeniable good looks were marred by a sort of silliness in his face; his wife and daughter were two dumpy little fluffy females. Tony evidently took after his father, and Marjorie after her mother. Aunt Sadie, thrown out of her stride by the sudden transformation of what had been mere voices in the dark into flesh and blood, and feeling herself unable to produce more topics of conversation, hurried them upstairs to rest, and dress for dinner. It was always considered at Alconleigh that the journey from London was an experience involving great exhaustion, and people were supposed to be in need of rest after it.

'What is this lamp?' Uncle Matthew asked Davey, who was still saying how sorry he was, still clad in the exiguous dressing-gown which he had put on for his sun-bath.

'Well, you know how one never can digest anything in the winter months.'

'I can, damn you,' said Uncle Matthew. This, addressed to Davey, could be interpreted as a term of endearment.

'You think you can, but you can't really. Now this lamp pours its rays into the system, your glands begin to work, and your food does you good again.'

'Well, don't pour any more rays until we have had the voltage altered. When the house is full of bloody Huns one wants to be able to see what the hell they're up to.'

For dinner, Linda wore a white chintz dress with an enormous skirt, and a black lace scarf. She looked entirely ravishing, and it was obvious that Sir Leicester was much taken with her appearance—Lady Kroesig and Miss Marjorie, in bits of georgette and lace, seemed not to notice it. Marjorie was an intensely dreary girl, a few years older than Tony, who had failed so far to marry, and seemed to have no biological reason for existing.

'Have you read *Brothers*?' Lady Kroesig asked Uncle Matthew, conversationally, as they settled down to their soup.

'What's that?'

'The new Ursula Langdok—*Brothers*—it's about two brothers. You ought to read it.'

'My dear Lady Kroesig, I have only ever read one book in my life, and that is *White Fang*. It's so frightfully good I've never bothered to read another. But Davey here reads books—you've read *Brothers*, Davey, I bet.'

'Indeed, I have not,' said Davey petulantly.

'I'll lend it to you,' said Lady Kroesig, 'I have it with me, and I finished it in the train.'

'You shouldn't,' said Davey, 'read in trains, ever. It's madly wearing to the optic nerve centres, it imposes a most fearful strain. May I see the menu, please? I must explain that I'm on a new diet, one meal white, one meal red. It's doing me so much good. Oh, dear, what a pity. Sadie—oh, she's not listening,—Logan, could I ask for an egg, very lightly boiled, you know. This is my white meal, and we are having saddle of mutton, I see.'

'Well, Davey, have your red meal now and your white meal for breakfast,' said Uncle Matthew. 'I've opened some Mouton Rothschild, and I know how much you like that—I opened it specially for you.'

'Oh, it is too bad,' said Davey, 'because I happen to know that there are kippers for breakfast, and I do so love them. What a ghastly decision. No! it must be an egg now, with a little hock. I could never forgo the kippers, so delicious, so digestible, but, above all, so full of proteins.'

'Kippers,' said Bob, 'are brown.'

'Brown counts as red. Surely you can see that.'

But when a chocolate cream, in generous supply, but never quite enough when the boys were at home, came round, it was seen to count as white. The Radletts often had cause to observe that you could never entirely rely upon Davey to refuse food, however unwholesome, if it was really delicious.

Aunt Sadie was making heavy weather with Sir Leicester. He was full of boring herbaceous enthusiasms, and took it for granted that she was too.

'What a lot you London people always know about gardens,' she said. 'You must talk to Davey, he is a great gardener.'

'I am not really a London person,' said Sir Leicester, reproachfully. 'I work in London, but my home is in Surrey.'

'I count that,' Aunt Sadie said, gently but firmly, 'as the same.'

The evening seemed endless. The Kroesigs obviously longed for bridge, and did not seem to care so much for racing demon when it was offered as a substitute. Sir Leicester said he had had a tiring week, and really should go to bed early.

'Don't know how you chaps can stand it,' said Uncle Matthew, sympathetically. 'I was saying to the bank manager at Merlinford only yesterday, it must be the hell of a life fussing about with other blokes' money all day, indoors.'

Linda went to ring up Lord Merlin, who had just returned from abroad. Tony followed her, they were gone a long time, and came back looking flushed and rather self-conscious.

The next morning, as we were hanging about in the hall waiting for the kippers, which had already announced themselves with a heavenly smell, two breakfast trays were seen going upstairs, for Sir Leicester and Lady Kroesig.

'No, really, that beats everything, dammit,' said Uncle Matthew. 'I never heard of a *man* having breakfast in bed before.' And he looked wistfully at his entrenching tool.

He was slightly mollified, however, when they came downstairs, just before eleven, all ready to go to church. Uncle Matthew was a great pillar of the church, read the lessons, chose the hymns, and took round the bag, and he liked his household to attend. Alas, the Kroesigs turned out to be blasted idolaters, as was proved when they turned sharply to the east during the creed. In short, they were of the company of those who could do no right, and sighs of relief echoed through the house when they decided to catch an evening train back to London.

'Tony is Bottom to Linda, isn't he?' I said sadly.

Davey and I were walking together through Hen's Grove the next day. Davey always knew what you meant, it was one of the nice things about him.

'Bottom,' he said sadly. He adored Linda.

'And nothing will wake her up?'

'Not before it's too late, I fear. Poor Linda, she has an intensely romantic character, which is fatal for a woman. Fortunately for them, and for all of us, most women are madly *terre à terre*, otherwise the world could hardly carry on.'

Lord Merlin was braver than the rest of us, and said right out what he thought. Linda went over to see him and asked him.

'Are you pleased about my engagement?' to which he replied:

'No, of course not. Why are you doing it?'

'I'm in love,' said Linda proudly.

'What makes you think so?'

'One doesn't think, one knows,' she said.

'Fiddlesticks.'

'Oh, you evidently don't understand about love, so what's the use of talking to you.'

Lord Merlin got very cross, and said that neither did immature little girls understand about love.

'Love,' he said, 'is for grown-up people, as you will discover one day. You will also discover that it has nothing to do with marriage. I'm all in favour of you marrying soon, in a year or two, but for God's sake, and all of our sakes, don't go and marry a bore like Tony Kroesig.'

'If he's such a bore, why did you ask him to stay?'

'I didn't ask him. Baby brought him, because Cecil had 'flu and couldn't come. Besides, I can't guess you'll go and marry every stopgap I have in my house.'

'You ought to be more careful. Anyhow, I can't think why you say Tony's a bore, he knows everything.'

'Yes, that's exactly it, he does. And what about Sir Leicester? And have you seen Lady Kroesig?'

But the Kroesig family was illuminated for Linda by the great glow of perfection which shone around Tony, and she would hear nothing against them. She parted rather coldly from Lord Merlin, came home, and abused him roundly. As for him, he waited to see what Sir Leicester was giving her for a wedding present. It was a pigskin dressing-case with dark tortoiseshell fittings and her initials on them in gold. Lord Merlin sent her a morocco one double the size, fitted with blonde tortoiseshell, and instead of initials, LINDA in diamonds.

He had embarked upon an elaborate series of Kroesig-teases of which this was to be the first.

The arrangements for the wedding did not go smoothly. There was trouble without end over settlements. Uncle Matthew, whose estate provided a certain sum of money for younger children, to be allocated by him as he thought best, very naturally did not wish to settle anything on Linda, at the expense of the others, in view of the fact that she was marrying the son of a millionaire. Sir Leicester, however, refused to settle a penny unless Uncle Matthew did—he had no great wish to make a settlement in any case, saying that it was against the policy of his family to tie up capital sums. In the end, by sheer persistence, Uncle Matthew got a beggarly amount for Linda. The whole thing worried and upset him very much, and confirmed him, if need be, in his hatred of the Teutonic race.

Tony and his parents wanted a London wedding, Uncle Matthew said he had never heard of anything so common and vulgar in his life. Women were married from their homes; he thought fashionable weddings the height of degradation, and refused to lead one of his daughters up the aisle of St. Margaret's through a crowd of gaping strangers. The Kroesigs explained to Linda that, if she had a country wedding, she would only get half the amount of wedding presents, and also that the important, influential people, who would be of use, later, to Tony, would never come down to Gloucestershire in the depth of winter. All these arguments were lost on Linda. Since the days when she was planning to marry the Prince of Wales she had had a mental picture of what her wedding would be like, that is, as much like a wedding in a panto-mime as possible, in a large church, with crowds both outside and in, with photographers, arum lilies, tulle, bridesmaids, and an enormous choir singing her favourite tune, 'The Lost Chord'. So she sided with the Kroesigs against poor Uncle Matthew, and, when fate tipped the scales in their favour by putting out of action the heating in Alconleigh church, Aunt Sadie took a London house, and the wedding was duly celebrated with every circumstance of publicized vulgarity at St. Margaret's.

What with one thing and another, by the time Linda was married, her parents and her parents-in-law were no longer on speaking terms. Uncle Matthew cried without restraint all through the ceremony; Sir Leicester seemed to be beyond tears.

CHAPTER X

I THINK Linda's marriage was a failure almost from the beginning, but I really never knew much about it. Nobody did. She had married in the face of a good deal of opposition; the opposition proved to have been entirely well founded, and, Linda being what she was, maintained, for as long as possible, a perfect shop-front.

They were married in February, had a hunting honeymoon from a house they took at Melton, and settled down for good in Bryanston Square after Easter. Tony then started work in his father's old bank, and prepared to step into a safe Conservative seat in the House of Commons, an ambition which was very soon realized.

Closer acquaintance with their new in-laws did not make either the Radlett or the Kroesig families change their minds about each other. The Kroesigs thought Linda eccentric, affected, and extravagant. Worst of all, she was supposed not to be useful to Tony in his career. The Radletts considered that Tony was a first-class bore. He had a habit of choosing a subject, and then droning round and round it like an inaccurate bomb-aimer round his target, ever unable to hit; he knew vast quantities of utterly dreary facts, of which he did not hesitate to inform his companions, at great length and in great detail, whether they appeared to be interested or not. He was infinitely serious, he no longer laughed at Linda's jokes, and the high spirits which, when she first knew him, he had seemed to possess, must have been due to youth, drink, and good health. Now that he was grown up and married he put all three resolutely behind him, spending his days in the bank house and his evenings at Westminster, never having any fun or breathing fresh air: his true self emerged, and he was revealed as a pompous, money-grubbing ass, more like his father every day.

He did not succeed in making an asset out of Linda. Poor Linda was incapable of understanding the Kroesig point of view; try as she might (and in the beginning she tried very hard, having an infinite desire to please) it remained mysterious to her. The fact is that, for the first time in her life, she found herself face to face with the bourgeois attitude of mind; and the fate often foreseen for me by Uncle Matthew as a result of my middle-class education had actually befallen her. The outward and visible signs which he so deprecated were all there—the Kroesigs said notepaper, perfume, mirror and mantelpiece, they even invited her to call them Father and Mother, which, in the first flush of love, she did, only to spend the rest of her married life trying to get out of it by addressing them to their faces as 'you', and communicating with them by postcard or telegram. Inwardly their spirit was utterly commercial, everything was seen by them in terms of money. It was their barrier, their defence, their hope for the future, their support for the present, it raised them above their fellowmen, and with it they warded off evil. The only mental qualities that they respected were those which produced money in substantial quantities, it was their one criterion of success, it was power and it was glory. To say that a man was poor was to label him a rotter, bad at his job, idle, feckless, immoral. If it was somebody whom they really rather liked, in spite of this cancer, they could add that he had been unlucky. They had taken care to insure against this deadly evil in many ways. That it should not overwhelm them through such cataclysms beyond their control as war or revolution they had placed huge sums of money in a dozen different countries; they owned ranches, and estancias, and South African farms, an hotel in Switzerland, a plantation in Malaya, and they possessed many fine diamonds, not sparkling round Linda's lovely neck to be sure, but lying in banks, stone by stone, easily portable.

Linda's upbringing had made all this incomprehensible to her; for money was a subject that was absolutely never mentioned at Alconleigh. Uncle Matthew had no doubt a large income, but it was derived from, tied up in, and a good percentage of it went back into, his land. His land was to him something sacred, and, sacred above that, was England. Should evil befall his country he would stay and share it, or die, never would the notion have entered his head that he might save himself, and leave old England in any sort of lurch. He, his family and his estates were part of her and she was part of him, for ever and ever. Later on, when war appeared to be looming upon the horizon, Tony tried to persuade him to send some money to America.

'What for?' said Uncle Matthew.

'You might be glad to go there yourself, or send the children. It's always a good thing to have——'

'I may be old, but I can still shoot,' said Uncle Matthew, furiously, 'and I haven't got any children—for the purposes of fighting they are all grown up.'

'Victoria——'

'Victoria is thirteen. She would do her duty. I hope, if any bloody foreigners ever got here, that every man, woman and child would go on fighting them until one side or the other was wiped out. Anyhow, I loathe abroad, nothing would induce me to live there, I'd rather live in the gamekeeper's hut in Hen's Grove, and, as for foreigners, they are all the same, and they all make me sick,' he said pointedly, glowering at Tony, who took no notice, but went droning on about how clever he had been in transferring various funds to various places. He had always remained perfectly unaware of Uncle Matthew's dislike for him, and, indeed, such was my uncle's eccentricity of behaviour, that it was not very easy for somebody as thick-skinned as Tony to differentiate between Uncle Matthew's behaviour towards those he loved and those he did not.

On the first birthday she had after her marriage, Sir Leicester gave Linda a cheque for £1,000. Linda was delighted and spent it that very day on a necklace of large half pearls surrounded by rubies, which she had been admiring for some time in a Bond Street shop. The Kroesigs had a small family dinner party for her, Tony was to meet her there, having been kept late at his office. Linda arrived, wearing a very plain white satin dress cut very low, and her necklace, went straight up to Sir Leicester, and said: 'Oh, you were kind to give me such a wonderful present—look——'

Sir Leicester was stupefied.

'Did it cost all I sent you?' he said.

'Yes,' said Linda. 'I thought you would like me to buy one thing with it, and always remember it was you who gave it to me.'

'No, dear. That wasn't at all what I intended. £1,000 is what you might call a capital sum, that means something on which you expect a return. You should not just spend it on a trinket which you wear three or four times a year, and which is most unlikely to appreciate in value. (And, by the way, if you buy jewels, let it always be diamonds—rubies and pearls are too easy to copy, they won't keep their price.) But, as I was saying, one hopes for a return. So you could either have asked Tony to invest it for you, or, which is what I really intended, you could have spent it on entertaining important people who would be of use to Tony in his career.'

These important people were a continual thorn in poor Linda's side. She was always supposed by the Kroesigs to be a great hindrance to Tony, both in politics and in the City, because, try as she might, she could not disguise how tedious they seemed to her. Like Aunt Sadie, she was apt to retire into a cloud of boredom on the smallest provocation, a vague look would come into her eyes, and her spirit would absent itself. Important people did not like this; they were not accustomed to it; they liked to be listened and attended to by the young with concentrated deference when they were so kind as to bestow their company. What with Linda's yawns, and Tony informing them how many harbour-masters there were in the British Isles, important people were inclined to eschew the young Kroesigs. The old Kroesigs deeply deplored this state of affairs, for which they blamed Linda. They saw that she did not take the slightest interest in Tony's work. She tried to at first but it was beyond her; she simply could not understand how somebody who already had plenty of money could go and shut himself away from God's fresh air and blue skies, from the spring, the summer, the autumn, the winter, letting them merge into each other unaware that they were passing, simply in order to make more. She was far too young to be interested in politics, which were anyhow, in those days before Hitler came along to brighten them up, a very esoteric amusement.

'Your father was cross,' she said to Tony, as they walked home after dinner. Sir Leicester lived in Hyde Park Gardens, it was a beautiful night, and they walked.

'I don't wonder,' said Tony shortly.

'But look, darling, how pretty it is. Don't you see how one couldn't resist it?'

'You are so affected. Do try and behave like an adult, won't you?'

The autumn after Linda's marriage Aunt Emily took a little house in St. Leonard's Terrace, where she, Davey and I installed ourselves. She had been rather unwell, and Davey thought it would be a good thing to get her away from all her country duties and to make her rest, as no woman ever can at home. His novel, *The Abrasive Tube*, had just appeared, and was having a great success in intellectual circles. It was a psychological and physiological study of a South Polar explorer, snowed up in a hut where he knows he must eventually die, with enough rations to keep him going for a few months. In the end he dies. Davey was fascinated by Polar expeditions; he liked to observe, from a safe distance, how far the body can go when driven upon thoroughly indigestible foodstuffs deficient in vitamins.

'Pemmican,' he would say, gleefully falling upon the delicious food for which Aunt Emily's cook was renowned, 'must have been so bad for them.'

Aunt Emily, shaken out of the routine of her life at Shenley, took up with old friends again, entertained for us, and enjoyed herself so much that she talked of living half the year in London. As for me, I have never, before or since, been happier. The London season I had with Linda had been the greatest possible fun: it would be untrue and ungrateful to Aunt Sadie to deny that; I had even quite enjoyed the long dark hours we spent in the Peeresses' gallery; but there had been a curious unreality about it all, it was not related, one felt, to life. Now I had my feet firmly planted on the ground. I was allowed to do what I liked, see whom I chose, at any hour, peacefully, naturally, and without breaking rules, and it was wonderful to bring my friends home and have them greeted in a friendly, if somewhat detached manner, by Davey, instead of smuggling them up the back stairs for fear of a raging scene in the hall.

During this happy time I became happily engaged to Alfred Wincham, then a young don at, now Warden of, St. Peter's College, Oxford. With this kindly scholarly man I have been perfectly happy ever since, finding in our home at Oxford that refuge from the storms and puzzles of life which I had always wanted. I say no more about him here: this is Linda's story, not mine.

We saw a great deal of Linda just then; she would come and chat for hours on end. She did not seem to be unhappy, though I felt sure she was already waking from her Titania-trance, but was obviously lonely, as her husband was at his work all day and at the House in the evening. Lord Merlin was abroad, and she had, as yet, no other very intimate friends; she missed the comings and goings, the cheerful bustle and hours of pointless chatter which had made up the family life at Alconleigh. I reminded her how much, when she was there, she had longed to escape, and she agreed, rather doubtfully, that it was wonderful to be on one's own. She was much pleased by my engagement, and liked Alfred.

'He has such a serious, clever look,' she said. 'What pretty little black babies you'll have, both of you so dark.'

He only quite liked her; he suspected that she was a tough nut, and rather, I must own, to my relief, she never exercised over him the spell in which she had entranced Davey and Lord Merlin.

One day, as we were busy with wedding invitations, she came in and announced:

'I am in pig, what d'you think of that?'

'A most hideous expression, Linda dear,' said Aunt Emily, 'but I suppose we must congratulate you.'

'I suppose so,' said Linda. She sank into a chair with an enormous sigh. 'I feel awfully ill, I must say.'

'But think how much good it will do you in the long run,' said Davey, enviously, 'such a wonderful clear-out.'

'I see just what you mean,' said Linda. 'Oh, we've got such a ghastly evening ahead of us. Some important Americans. It seems Tony wants to do a deal or something, and these Americans will only do the deal if they take a fancy to me. Now can you explain that? I know I shall be sick all over them, and my father-in-law will be so cross. Oh, the horror of important people—you are lucky not to know any.'

Linda's child, a girl, was born in May. She was ill for a long time before, and very ill indeed at her confinement. The doctors told her that she must never have another child, as it would almost certainly kill her if she did. This was a blow to the Kroesigs, as bankers, it seems, like kings, require many sons, but Linda did not appear to mind at all. She took no interest whatever in the baby she had got. I went to see her as soon as I was allowed to. She lay in a bower of blossom and pink roses, and looked like a corpse. I was expecting a baby myself, and naturally took a great interest in Linda's.

'What are you going to call her—where is she, anyway?'

'In Sister's room—it shrieks. Moira, I believe.'

'Not Moira, darling, you can't. I never heard such an awful name.'

'Tony likes it, he had a sister called Moira who died, and what d'you think I found out (not from him, but from their old nanny)? She died because Marjorie whacked her on the head with a hammer when she was four months old. Do you call that interesting? And then they say we are an uncontrolled family—why even Fa has never actually murdered anybody, or do you count that beater?'

'All the same, I don't see how you can saddle the poor little thing with a name like Moira, it's too unkind.'

'Not really, if you think. It'll have to grow up a Moira if the Kroesigs are to like it (people always grow up to their names I've noticed) and they might as well like it because frankly, I don't.'

'Linda, how can you be so naughty, and, anyway, you can't possibly tell whether you like her or not, yet.'

'Oh, yes I can. I can always tell if I like people from the start, and I don't like Moira, that's all. She's a fearful Counter-Hon, wait till you see her.'

At this point the Sister came in, and Linda introduced us.

'Oh, you are the cousin I hear so much about,' she said. 'You'll want to see the baby.'

She went away and presently returned carrying a Moses basket full of wails.

'Poor thing,' said Linda indifferently. 'It's really kinder not to look.'

'Don't pay any attention to her,' said the Sister. 'She pretends to be a wicked woman, but it's all put on.'

I did look, and, deep down among the frills and lace, there was the usual horrid sight of a howling orange in a fine black wig.

'Isn't she sweet,' said the Sister. 'Look at her little hands.'

I shuddered slightly, and said:

'Well, I know it's dreadful of me, but I don't much like them as small as that; I'm sure she'll be divine in a year or two.'

The wails now entered on a crescendo, and the whole room was filled with hideous noise.

'Poor soul,' said Linda. 'I think it must have caught sight of itself in a glass. Do take it away, Sister.'

Davey now came into the room. He was meeting me there to drive me down to Shenley for the night. The Sister came back and shooed us both off, saying that Linda had had enough. Outside her room, which was in the largest and most expensive nursing home in London, I paused, looking for the lift.

'This way,' said Davey, and then, with a slightly self-conscious giggle: '*Nourri dans le sérail, j'en connais les détours.* Oh, how are you, Sister Thesiger? How very nice to see you.'

'Captain Warbeck—I must tell Matron you are here.'

And it was nearly an hour before I could drag Davey out of this home from home. I hope I am not giving the impression that Davey's whole life was centred round his health. He was fully occupied with his work, writing, and editing a literary review, but his health was his hobby, and, as such, more in evidence during his spare time, the time when I saw most of him. How he enjoyed it ! He seemed to regard his body with the affectionate preoccupation of a farmer towards a pig—not a good doer, the small one of the litter, which must somehow be made to be a credit to the farm. He weighed it, sunned it, aired it, exercised it, and gave it special diets, new kinds of patent food and medicine, but all in vain. It never put on so much as a single ounce of weight, it never became a credit to the farm, but, somehow it lived, enjoying good things, enjoying its life, though falling victim to the ills that flesh is heir to, and other, imaginary ills as well, through which it was nursed with unfailing care, with concentrated attention, by the good farmer and his wife.

Aunt Emily said at once, when I told her about Linda and poor Moira :

'She's too young. I don't believe very young mothers ever get wrapped up in their babies. It's when women are older that they so adore their children, and maybe it's better for the children to have young unadoring mothers and to lead more detached lives.'

'But Linda seems to loathe her.'

'That's so like Linda,' said Davey. 'She has to do things by extremes.'

'But she seemed so gloomy. You must say that's not very like her.'

'She's been terribly ill,' said Aunt Emily. 'Sadie was in despair. Twice they thought she would die.'

'Don't talk of it,' said Davey. 'I can't imagine the world without Linda.'

CHAPTER XI

LIVING in Oxford, engrossed with my husband and young family, I saw less of Linda during the next few years than at any time in her life. This, however, did not affect the intimacy of our relationship, which remained absolute, and, when we did meet, it was still as though we were seeing each other every day. I stayed with her in London from time to time, and she with me in Oxford, and we corresponded regularly. I may as well say here that the one thing she never discussed with me was the deterioration of her marriage; in any case it would not have been necessary, the whole thing being as plain as relations between married people ever can be. Tony was, quite obviously, not good enough as a lover to make up, even at first, for his shortcomings in other respects, the boredom of his company and the mediocrity of his character. Linda was out of love with him by the time the child was born, and, thereafter, could not care a rap for the one or the other. The young man she had fallen in love with, handsome, gay, intellectual and domineering, melted away upon closer acquaintance, and proved to have been a chimera, never to have existed outside her imagination. Linda did not commit the usual fault of blaming Tony for what was entirely her own mistake, she merely turned from him in absolute indifference. This was made easier by the fact that she saw so little of him.

Lord Merlin now launched a tremendous Kroesig-tease. The Kroesigs were always complaining that Linda never went out, would not entertain, unless absolutely forced to, and did not care for society. They told their friends that she was a country girl, entirely sporting, that if you went into her drawing-room she would be found training a retriever with dead rabbits hidden behind the sofa cushions. They pretended that she was an amiable, half-witted, beautiful rustic, incapable of helping poor Tony, who was obliged to battle his way through life alone. There was a grain of truth in all this, the fact being that the Kroesig circle of acquaintances was too ineffably boring; poor Linda, having been unable to make any headway at all in it, had given up the struggle, and retired to the more congenial company of retrievers and dormice.

Lord Merlin, in London for the first time since Linda's marriage, at once introduced her into his world, the world towards which she had always looked, that of smart bohemianism; and here she found her feet, was entirely happy, and had an immediate and great success. She became very gay and went everywhere. There is no more popular unit in London society than a young, beautiful, but perfectly respectable woman who can be asked to dinner without her husband, and Linda was soon well on the way to having her head turned. Photographers and gossip writers dogged her footsteps, and indeed one could not escape the impression, until half an hour of her company put one right again, that she was becoming a bit of a bore. Her house was full of people from morning till night, chatting. Linda, who loved to chat, found many congenial spirits in the carefree, pleasure-seeking London of those days, when unemployment was rife as much among the upper as the lower classes. Young men, pensioned off by their relations, who would sometimes suggest in a perfunctory manner that it might be a good thing if they found some work, but without seriously helping them to do so (and, anyhow, what work was there for such as they?) clustered round Linda like bees round honey, buzz, buzz, buzz, chat, chat, chat. In her bedroom, on her bed, sitting on the stairs outside while she had a bath, in the kitchen while she ordered the food, shopping, walking round the park, cinema, theatre, opera, ballet, dinner, supper, night clubs, parties, dances, all day, all night—endless, endless, chat.

'But what do you suppose they talk about?' Aunt Sadie, disapproving, used to wonder. What, indeed?

Tony went early to his bank, hurrying out of the house with an air of infinite importance, an attaché case in one hand and a sheaf of newspapers under his arm. His departure heralded the swarm of chatterers, almost as if they had been waiting round the street corner to see him leave, and thereafter the house was filled with them. They were very nice, very good-looking, and great fun—their manners were perfect. I never was able, during my short visits, to distinguish them much one from another, but I saw their attraction, the unfailing attraction of vitality and high spirits. By no stretch of the imagination, however, could they have been called 'important', and the Kroesigs were beside themselves at this turn of affairs.

Tony did not seem to mind; he had long given up Linda as hopeless from the point of view of his career, and was rather pleased and flattered by the publicity which now launched her as a beauty. 'The beautiful wife of a clever young M.P.' Besides, he found that they were invited to large parties and balls, to which it suited him very well to go, coming late after the House, and where there were often to be found not only Linda's unimportant friends, with whom she would amuse herself, but also colleagues of his own, and by no means unimportant ones, whom he could buttonhole and bore at the bar. It would have been useless, however, to explain this to the old Kroesigs, who had a deeply rooted mistrust of smart society, of dancing, and of any kind of fun, all of which led, in their opinion, to extravagance, without compensating material advantages. Fortunately for Linda, Tony at this time was not on good terms with his father, owing to a conflict of policies in the bank; they did not go to Hyde Park Gardens as much as when they were first married, and visits to Planes, the Kroesig house in Surrey, were, for the time being, off. When they did meet, however, the old Kroesigs made it clear to Linda that she was not proving a satisfactory daughter-in-law. Even Tony's divergence of views was put down to her, and Lady Kroesig told her friends, with a sad shake of the head, that Linda did not bring out the best in him.

Linda now proceeded to fritter away years of her youth, with nothing whatever to show for them. If she had had an intellectual upbringing the place of all this pointless chatter, jokes and parties might have been taken by a serious interest in the arts, or by reading; if she had been happy in her marriage that side of her nature which craved for company could have found its fulfilment by the nursery fender; things being as they were, however, all was frippery and silliness.

Alfred and I once had an argument with Davey about her, during which we said all this. Davey accused us of being prigs, though at heart he must have known that we were right.

'But Linda gives one so much pleasure,' he kept saying, 'she is like a bunch of flowers. You don't want people like that to bury themselves in serious reading; what would be the good?'

However, even he was forced to admit that her behaviour to poor little Moira was not what it should be. (The child was fat, fair, placid, dull and backward, and Linda still did not like her; the Kroesigs, on the other hand, adored her, and she spent more and more time, with her nanny, at Planes. They loved having her there, but that did not stop them from ceaseless criticism of Linda's behaviour. They now told everybody that she was a silly society butterfly, hard-hearted neglecter of her child.)

Alfred said, almost angrily:

'It's so odd that she doesn't even have love affairs. I don't see what she gets out of her life, it must be dreadfully empty.'

Alfred likes people to be filed neatly away under some heading that he can understand; careerist, social climber, virtuous wife and mother, or adulteress.

Linda's social life was completely aimless; she simply collected around her an assortment of cosy people who had the leisure to chat all day; whether they were millionaires or paupers, princes or refugee Rumanians, was a matter of complete indifference to her. In spite of the fact that, except for me and her sisters, nearly all her friends were men, she had such a reputation for virtue that she was currently suspected of being in love with her husband.

'Linda believes in love,' said Davey, 'she is passionately romantic. At the moment I am sure she is, subconsciously, waiting for an irresistible temptation. Casual affairs would not interest her in the least. One must hope that when it comes it will not prove to be another Bottom.'

'I suppose she is really rather like my mother,' I said, 'and all of hers have been Bottoms.'

'Poor Bolter!' said Davey; 'but she's happy now, isn't she, with her white hunter?'

Tony soon became, as was to be expected, a perfect mountain of pomposity, more like his father every day. He was full of large, clear-sighted ideas for bettering the condition of the capitalist classes, and made no bones of his hatred and distrust of the workers.

'I hate the lower classes,' he said one day, when Linda and I were having tea with him on the terrace of the House of Commons. 'Ravening beasts, trying to get my money. Let them try, that's all.'

'Oh, shut up, Tony,' said Linda, bringing a dormouse out of her pocket, and feeding it with crumbs. 'I love them, anyway I was brought up with them. The trouble with you is you don't know the lower classes and you don't belong to the upper classes, you're just a rich foreigner who happens to live here. Nobody ought to be in Parliament—who hasn't lived in the country, anyhow part of their life—why, my old Fa knows more what he's talking about, when he does talk in the House, than you do.'

'I have lived in the country,' said Tony. 'Put that dormouse away, people are looking.'

He never got cross, he was far too pompous.

'Surrey,' said Linda, with infinite contempt.

'Anyhow, last time your Fa made a speech, about the Peeresses in their own right, his only argument for keeping them out of the House was that, if once they got in, they might use the Peers' lavatory.'

'Isn't he a love?' said Linda. 'It's what they all thought, you know, but he was the only one who dared to say it.'

'That's the worst of the House of Lords,' said Tony. 'These back-woodsmen come along just when they think they will, and bring the whole place into disrepute with a few dotty remarks, which get an enormous amount of publicity and give people the impression that we are governed by a lot of lunatics. These old peers ought to realize that it's their duty to their class to stay at home and keep quiet. The amount of excellent, solid, necessary work done in the House of Lords is quite unknown to the man in the street.'

Sir Leicester was expecting soon to become a peer, so this was a subject close to Tony's heart. His general attitude to what he called the man in the street was that he ought constantly to be covered by machine-guns: this having become impossible, owing to the weakness, in the past, of the great Whig families, he must be doped into submission with the fiction that huge reforms, to be engineered by the Conservative party, were always just round the next corner. Like this he could be kept quiet indefinitely, as long as there was no war. War brings people together and opens their eyes, it must be avoided at all costs, and especially war with Germany, where the Kroesigs had financial interests and many relations. (They were originally a Junkers family, and snobbed their Prussian connections as much as the latter looked down on them for being in trade.)

Both Sir Leicester and his son were great admirers of Herr Hitler; Sir Leicester had been to see him during a visit to Germany, and had been taken for a drive in a Mercedes-Benz by Dr. Schacht.

Linda took no interest in politics, but she was instinctively and unreasonably English. She knew that one Englishman was worth a hundred foreigners, whereas Tony thought that one capitalist was worth a hundred workers. Their outlook upon this, as upon most subjects, differed fundamentally.

CHAPTER XII

By a curious irony of fate it was at her father-in-law's house in Surrey that Linda met Christian Talbot. The little Moira, aged six, now lived permanently at Planes: it seemed a good arrangement as it saved Linda, who disliked housekeeping, the trouble of running two establishments, while Moira was given the benefit of country air and food. Linda and Tony were supposed to spend a couple of nights there every week, and Tony generally did so. Linda, in fact, went down for Sunday about once a month.

Planes was a horrible house. It was an overgrown cottage, that is to say, the rooms were large, with all the disadvantages of a cottage, low ceilings, small windows with diamond panes, uneven floorboards, and a great deal of naked knotted wood. It was furnished neither in good nor in bad taste, but simply with no attempt at taste at all, and was not even very comfortable. The garden which lay around it would be a lady water-colourist's heaven, herbaceous borders, rockeries and water-gardens were carried to a perfection of vulgarity, and flaunted a riot of huge and hideous flowers, each individual bloom appearing twice as large, three times as brilliant as it ought to have been and if possible of a different colour from that which nature intended. It would be hard to say whether it was more frightful, more like glorious Technicolour, in spring, in summer, or in autumn. Only in the depth of winter, covered by the kindly snow, did it melt into the landscape and become tolerable.

One April Saturday morning, in 1937, Linda, with whom I had been staying in London, took me down there for the night, as she sometimes did. I think she liked to have a buffer between herself and the Kroesigs, perhaps especially between herself and Moira. The old Kroesigs were by way of being very fond of me, and Sir Leicester sometimes took me for walks and hinted how much he wished that it had been me, so serious, so well educated, such a good wife and mother, whom Tony had married.

We motored down past acres of blossom.

'The great difference,' said Linda, 'between Surrey and proper, real country, is that in Surrey, when you see blossom, you know there will be no fruit. Think of the Vale of Evesham, and then look at all this pointless pink stuff—it gives you quite a different feeling. The garden at Planes will be a riot of sterility, just you wait.'

It was. You could hardly see any beautiful, pale, bright, yellow-green of spring, every tree appeared to be entirely covered with a waving mass of pink or mauve tissue-paper. The daffodils were so thick on the ground that they too obscured the green, they were new varieties of a terrifying size, either dead white or dark yellow, thick and fleshy; they did not look at all like the fragile friends of one's childhood. The whole effect was of a scene for musical comedy, and it exactly suited Sir Leicester, who, in the country, gave a surprisingly adequate performance of the old English squire. Picturesque. Delightful.

He was pottering in the garden as we drove up, in an old pair of corduroy trousers, so much designed as an old pair that it seemed improbable that they had ever been new, an old tweed coat on the same lines, secateurs in his hand, a depressed Corgi at his heels, and a mellow smile on his face.

'Here we are,' he said heartily. (One could almost see, as in the strip advertisements, a bubble coming out of his head thinks—'You are a most unsatisfactory daughter-in-law, but nobody can say it's our fault, we always have a welcome and a kind smile for you.') 'Car going well, I hope? Tony and Moira have gone out riding, I thought you might have passed them. Isn't the garden looking grand just now, I can hardly bear to go to London and leave all this beauty with no one to see it. Come for a stroll before lunch—Foster will see to your gear—just ring the front-door bell, Fanny, he may not have heard the car.'

He led us off into Madam Butterfly-land.

'I must warn you,' he said, 'that we have got rather a rough diamond coming to lunch. I don't know if you've ever met old Talbot who lives in the village, the old professor? Well, his son, Christian. He's by way of being rather a Communist, a clever chap gone all wrong, and a journalist on some daily rag. Tony can't bear him, never could as a child, and he's very cross with me for asking him today, but I always think it's as well to see something of these Left-wing fellows. If people like us are nice to them they can be tamed wonderfully.'

He said this in the tone of one who might have saved the life of a Communist in the war, and, by this act, turned him, through gratitude, into a true blue Tory. But in the first world war Sir Leicester had considered that, with his superior brain, he would have been wasted as cannon fodder, and had fixed himself in an office in Cairo. He neither saved nor took any lives, nor did he risk his own, but built up many valuable business contacts, became a major and got an O.B.E., thus making the best of all worlds.

So Christian came to luncheon, and behaved with the utmost intransigence. He was an extraordinarily handsome young man, tall and fair, in a completely different way from that of Tony, thin and very English-looking. His clothes were outrageous—he wore a really old pair of grey flannel trousers, full of little round moth-holes in the most embarrassing places, no coat, and a flannel shirt, one of the sleeves of which had a tattered tear from wrist to elbow.

'Has your father been writing anything lately?' Lady Kroesig asked, as they sat down to luncheon.

'I suppose so,' said Christian, 'as it's his profession. I can't say I've asked him, but one assumes he has, just as one assumes that Tony has been banking something lately.'

He then planted his elbow, bare through the rent, on to the table between himself and Lady Kroesig and swivelling right round to Linda, who was on his other side, he told her, at length and in immense detail, of a production of *Hamlet* he had seen lately in Moscow. The cultured Kroesigs listened attentively, throwing off occasional comments calculated to show that they knew *Hamlet* well—'I don't think that quite fits in with my idea of Ophelia,' or 'But Polonius was a very old man,' to all of which Christian turned an utterly deaf ear, gobbling his food with one hand, his elbow on the table, his eyes on Linda.

After luncheon he said to Linda:

'Come back and have tea with my father, you'd like him,' and they went off together, leaving the Kroesigs to behave for the rest of the afternoon like a lot of hens who have seen a fox.

Sir Leicester took me to his water-garden, which was full of enormous pink forget-me-nots, and dark-brown irises, and said:

'It is really rather too bad of Linda, little Moira has been so much looking forward to showing her the ponies. That child idolizes her mother.'

She didn't, actually, in the least. She was fond of Tony and quite indifferent to Linda, calm and stolid and not given to idolatry, but it was part of the Kroesigs' creed that children should idolize their mothers.

'Do you know Pixie Townsend?' he asked me suddenly.

'No,' I said, which was true, nor did I then know anything about her. 'Who is she?'

'She's a very delightful person.' He changed the subject.

Linda returned just in time to dress for dinner, looking extremely beautiful. She made me come and chat while she had her bath—Tony was reading to Moira upstairs in the night nursery. Linda was perfectly enchanted with her outing. Christian's father, she said, lived in the smallest house imaginable, an absolute contrast to what Christian called the Kroesighof, because, although absolutely tiny, it had nothing whatever of a cottage about it—it was in the grand manner, and full of books. Every available wall space was covered with books, they lay stacked on tables and chairs and in heaps on the floor. Mr. Talbot was the exact opposite of Sir Leicester, there was nothing picturesque about him, or anything to indicate that he was a learned man, he was brisk and matter-of-fact, and had made some very funny jokes about Davey, whom he knew well.

'He's perfect heaven,' Linda kept saying, her eyes shining. What she really meant, as I could see too clearly, was that Christian was perfect heaven. She was dazzled by him. It seemed that he had talked without cease, and his talk consisted of variations upon a single theme—the betterment of the world through political change. Linda, since her marriage, had heard no end of political shop talked by Tony and his friends, but this related politics entirely to personalities and jobs. As the persons all seemed to her infinitely old and dull, and as it was quite immaterial to her whether they got jobs or not, Linda had classed politics as a boring subject, and used to go off into a dream when they were discussed. But Christian's politics did not bore her. As they walked back from his father's house that evening he had taken her for a tour of the world. He showed her Fascism in Italy, Nazism in Germany, civil war in Spain, inadequate Socialism in France, tyranny in Africa, starvation in Asia, reaction in America and Right-wing blight in England. Only the U.S.S.R., Norway and Mexico came in for a modicum of praise.

Linda was a plum ripe for shaking. The tree was now shaken, and down she came. Intelligent and energetic, but with no outlet for her energies, unhappy in her marriage, uninterested in her child, and inwardly oppressed with a sense of futility, she was in the mood either to take up some cause, or to embark upon a love affair. That a cause should now be presented by an attractive young man made both it and him irresistible.

CHAPTER XIII

THE poor Alconleighs were now presented with crises in the lives of three of their children almost simultaneously. Linda ran away from Tony, Jassy ran away from home, and Matt ran away from Eton. The Alconleighs were obliged to face the fact, as parents must sooner or later, that their children had broken loose from control and had taken charge of their own lives. Distracted, disapproving, worried to death, there was nothing they could do; they had become mere spectators of a spectacle which did not please them in the least. This was the year when the parents of our contemporaries would console themselves, if things did not go quite as they hoped for their own children, by saying: 'Never mind, just think of the poor Alconleighs!'

Linda threw discretion, and what worldly wisdom she may have picked up during her years in London society, to the winds; she became an out-and-out Communist, bored and embarrassed everybody to death by preaching her new-found doctrine, not only at the dinner-table, but also from a soap-box in Hyde Park, and other equally squalid rostra, and finally, to the infinite relief of the Kroesig family, she went off to live with Christian. Tony started proceedings for divorce. This was a great blow to my aunt and uncle. It is true that they had never liked Tony, but they were infinitely old-fashioned in their ideas; marriage, to their way of thinking, was marriage, and adultery was wrong. Aunt Sadie was, in particular, profoundly shocked by the light-hearted way in which Linda had abandoned the little Moira. I think it all reminded her too much of my mother, and that she envisaged Linda's future from now on as a series of uncontrollable bolts.

Linda came to see me in Oxford. She was on her way back to London after having broken the news at Alconleigh. I thought it was really very brave of her to do it in person, and indeed, the first thing she asked for (most unlike her) was a drink. She was quite unnerved.

'Goodness,' she said. 'I'd forgotten how terrifying Fa can be—even now, when he's got no power over one. It was just like after we lunched with Tony; in the business-room just the same, and he simply roared, and poor Mummy looked miserable, but she was pretty furious too, and you know how sarcastic she can be. Oh, well, that's over. Darling, it's heaven to see you again.'

I hadn't seen her since the Sunday at Planes when she met Christian, so I wanted to hear all about her life.

'Well,' she said, 'I'm living with Christian in his flat, but it's very small, I must say, but perhaps that is just as well, because I'm doing the housework, and I don't seem to be very good at it, but luckily he is.'

'He'll need to be,' I said.

Linda was notorious in the family for her unhandiness, she could never even tie her own stock, and on hunting days either Uncle Matthew or Josh always had to do it for her. I so well remember her standing in front of a looking-glass in the hall, with Uncle Matthew tying it from behind, both the very picture of concentration, Linda saying: 'Oh, now I see. Next time I know I shall be able to manage.' As she had never in her life done so much as make her own bed, I could not imagine that Christian's flat could be very tidy or comfortable if it was being run by her.

'You are horrid. But oh how dreadful it is, cooking, I mean. That oven—Christian puts things in and says: "Now you take it out in about half an hour". I don't dare tell him how terrified I am, and at the end of half an hour I summon up all my courage and open the oven, and there is that awful hot blast hitting one in the face. I don't wonder people sometimes put their heads in and leave them out of sheer misery. Oh, dear, and I wish you could have seen the Hoover running away with me, it suddenly took the bit between its teeth and made for the lift shaft. How I shrieked—Christian only just rescued me in time. I think housework is far more tiring and frightening than hunting is, no comparison, and yet after hunting we had eggs for tea and were made to rest for hours, but after housework people expect one to go on just as if nothing special had happened.' She sighed.

'Christian is very strong,' she said, 'and very brave. He doesn't like it when I shriek.'

She seemed tired I thought and rather worried, and I looked in vain for signs of great happiness or great love.

'So what about Tony—how has he taken it?'

'Oh, he's awfully pleased, actually, because he can now marry his mistress without having a scandal, or being divorced, or upsetting the Conservative Association.'

It was so like Linda never to have hinted, even to me, that Tony had a mistress.

'Who is she?' I said.

'Called Pixie Townsend. You know the sort, young face, with white hair dyed blue. She adores Moira, lives near Planes, and takes her out riding every day. She's a terrific Counter-Hon, but I'm only too thankful now that she exists, because I needn't feel in the least bit guilty—they'll all get on so much better without me.'

'Married?'

'Oh, yes, and divorced her husband years ago. She's frightfully good at all poor Tony's things, golf and business and Conservatism, just like I wasn't, and Sir Leicester thinks she's perfect. Goodness, they'll be happy.'

'Now I want to hear more about Christian, please.'

'Well, he's heaven. He's a frightfully serious man, you know, a Communist, and so am I now, and we are surrounded by comrades all day, and they are terrific Hons, and there's an anarchist. The comrades don't like anarchists, isn't it queer? I always thought they were the same thing, but Christian likes this one because he threw a bomb at the King of Spain; you must say it's romantic. He's called Ramon, and he sits about all day and broods over the miners at Oviedo because his brother is one.'

'Yes, but, darling, tell about Christian.'

'Oh, he's perfect heaven—you must come and stay—or perhaps that wouldn't be very comfortable—come and see us. You can't think what an extraordinary man he is, so detached from other human beings that he hardly notices whether they are there or not. He only cares for ideas.'

'I hope he cares for you.'

'Well, I think he does, but he is very strange and absent-minded. I must tell you, the evening before I ran away with him (I only moved down to Pimlico in a taxi, but running away sounds romantic) he dined with his brother, so naturally I thought they'd talk about me and discuss the whole thing, so I couldn't resist ringing him up at about midnight and saying: "Hullo, darling, did you have a nice evening, and what did you talk about?" and he said: "I can't remember—oh, guerrilla warfare, I think".'

'Is his brother a Communist too?'

'Oh, no, he's in the Foreign Office. Fearfully grand, looks like a deep-sea monster—you know.'

'Oh, that Talbot—yes, I see. I hadn't connected them. So now what are your plans?'

'Well, he says he's going to marry me when I'm divorced. I think it's rather silly, I rather agree with Mummy that once is enough, for marriage, but he says I'm the kind of person one marries if one's living with them, and the thing is it would be bliss not to be called Kroesig any more. Anyway, we'll see.'

'Then what's your life? I suppose you don't go to parties and things now, do you?'

'Darling, such killing parties, you can't think—he won't let us go to ordinary ones at all. Grandi had a dinner-dance last week, and he rang me up himself and asked me to bring Christian, which I thought was awfully nice of him actually—he always has been nice to me—but Christian got into quite a temper and said if I couldn't see any reason against going I'd better go, but nothing would induce him to. So in the end, of course, neither of us went, and I heard afterwards it was the greatest fun. And we mayn't go to the Ribs or to . . .' and she mentioned several families known as much for their hospitality as for their Right-wing convictions.

'The worst of being a Communist is that the parties you may go to are—well—awfully funny and touching, but not very gay, and they're always in such gloomy places. Next week, for instance, we've got three, some Czechs at the Sacco and Vanzetti Memorial Hall at Golders Green, Ethiopians at the Paddington Baths, and the Scotsboro' boys at some boring old rooms or other. You know.'

'The Scotsboro' boys,' I said. 'Are they really still going? They must be getting on.'

'Yes, and they've gone downhill socially,' said Linda, with a giggle. 'I remember a perfectly divine party Brian gave for them—it was the first party Merlin ever took me to so I remember it well, oh, dear, it was fun. But next Thursday won't be the least like that. (Darling, I am being disloyal, but it is such heaven to have a chat after all these months. The comrades are sweet, but they never chat, they make speeches all the time.) But I'm always saying to Christian how much I wish his buddies would either brighten up their parties a bit or else giving them, because I don't see the point of sad parties, do you? And Left-wing people are always sad because they mind dreadfully about their causes, and the causes are always going so badly. You see, I bet the Scotsboro' boys will be electrocuted in the end, if they don't die of old age first, that is. One does feel so much on their side, but it's no good, people like Sir Leicester always come out on top, so what can one do? However, the comrades don't seem to realize that, and, luckily for them, they don't know Sir Leicester, so they feel they must go on giving these sad parties.'

'What do you wear at them?' I asked, with some interest, thinking that Linda, in her expensive-looking clothes, must seem very much out of place at these baths and halls.

'You know, that was a great tease at first, it worried me dreadfully, but I've discovered that, so long as one wears wool or cotton, everything is all right. Silk and satin would be the blunder. But I only ever do wear wool and cotton, so I'm on a good wicket. No jewels, of course, but then I left them behind at Bryanston Square, it's the way I was brought up but I must say it gave me a pang. Christian doesn't know about jewellery—I told him, because I thought he'd be rather pleased I'd given them all up for him, but he only said: "Well, there's always the Burma Jewel Company." Oh, dear, he is such a funny man, you must meet him again soon. I must go, darling, it has so cheered me up to see you.'

I don't quite know why, but I felt somehow that Linda had been once more deceived in her emotions, that this explorer in the sandy waste had only seen another mirage. The lake was there, the trees were there, the thirsty camels had gone down to have their evening drink; alas, a few steps forward would reveal nothing but dust and desert as before.

A few minutes only after Linda had left me to go back to London, Christian and the comrades, I had another caller. This time it was Lord Merlin. I liked Lord Merlin very much, I admired him, I was predisposed in his favour, but I was by no means on such intimate terms with him as Linda was. To tell the real truth he frightened me. I felt that, in my company, boredom was for him only just round the corner, and that, anyhow, I was merely regarded as pertaining to Linda, not existing on my own except as a dull little don's wife. I was nothing but the confidante in white linen.

'This is a bad business,' he said abruptly, and without preamble, though I had not seen him for several years. 'I'm just back from Rome, and what do I find—Linda and Christian Talbot. It's an extraordinary thing that I can't ever leave England without Linda getting herself mixed up with some thoroughly undesirable character. This is a disaster—how far has it gone? Can nothing be done?'

I told him that he had just missed Linda, and said something about her marriage with Tony having been unhappy. Lord Merlin waved this remark aside—it was a disconcerting gesture and made me feel a fool.

'Naturally she never would have stayed with Tony—nobody expected that. The point is that she's out of the frying-pan into an empty grate. How long has it been going on?'

I said I thought it was partly the Communism that had attracted her.

'Linda has always felt the need of a cause.'

'Cause,' he said scornfully. 'My dear Fanny, I think you are mixing up cause with effect. No, Christian is an attractive fellow, and I quite see that he would provide a perfect reaction from Tony, but it is a disaster. If she is in love with him he will make her miserable, and, if not, it means she has embarked upon a career like your mother's, and that, for Linda, would be very bad indeed. I don't see a ray of comfort anywhere. No money either, of course, and she needs money, she ought to have it.'

He went to the window, and looked across the street at Christ Church gilded by the westerly sun.

'I've known Christian,' he said, 'from a child—his father is a great friend of mine. Christian is a man who goes through the world attached to nobody—people are nothing in his life. The women who have been in love with him have suffered bitterly because he has not even noticed that they are there. I expect he is hardly aware that Linda has moved in on him—his head is in the clouds and he is always chasing after some new idea.'

'This is rather what Linda has just been saying.'

'Oh, she's noticed it already? Well, she is not stupid, and, of course at first it adds to the attraction—when he comes out of the clouds he is irresistible, I quite see that. But how can they ever settle down? Christian has never had a home, or felt the need for one; he wouldn't know what to do with it—it would hamper him. He'll never sit and chat to Linda, or concentrate upon her in any way, and she is a woman who requires, above all things, a great deal of concentration. Really it is too provoking that I should have been away when this happened, I'm sure I could have stopped it. Now, of course, nobody can.'

He turned from the window and looked at me so angrily that I felt it had all been my fault—actually I think he was unaware of my presence.

'What are they living on?' he said.

'Very little. Linda has a small allowance from Uncle Matthew, I believe, and I suppose Christian makes something from his journalism. I hear the Kroesigs go about saying that there is one good thing, she is sure to starve.'

'Oh, they do, do they?' said Lord Merlin, taking out his notebook. 'Can I have Linda's address, please, I am on my way to London now.'

Alfred came in, as usual unaware of exterior events and buried in some pamphlet he was writing.

'You don't happen to know,' he said to Lord Merlin, 'what the daily consumption of milk is in the Vatican City?'

'No, of course not,' said Lord Merlin angrily. 'Ask Tony Kroesig, he'll be sure to. Well, good-bye, Fanny, I'll have to see what I can do.'

What he did was to present Linda with the freehold of a tiny house far down Cheyne Walk. It was the prettiest little dolls' house that ever was seen, on that great bend of the river where Whistler had lived. The rooms were full of reflections of water and full of south and west sunlight; it had a vine and a Trafalgar balcony. Linda adored it. The Bryanston Square house, with an easterly outlook, had been originally dark, cold, and pompous. When Linda had had it done up by some decorating friend, it had become white, cold, and tomblike. The only thing of beauty that she had possessed was a picture, a fat tomato-coloured bathing-woman, which had been given her by Lord Merlin to annoy the Kroesigs. It had annoyed them, very much. This picture looked wonderful in the Cheyne Walk house, you could hardly tell where the real water-reflections ended and the Renoir ones began. The pleasure which Linda derived from her new surroundings, the relief which she felt at having once and for all got rid of the Kroesigs, were, I think, laid by her at Christian's door, and seemed to come from him. Thus the discovery that real love and happiness had once more eluded her was delayed for quite a long time.

CHAPTER XIV

THE Alconleighs were shocked and horrified over the whole Linda affair, but they had their other children to think of, and were, just now, making plans for the coming out of Jassy, who was as pretty as a peach. She, they hoped, would make up to them for their disappointment with Linda. It was most unfair, but very typical of them, that Louisa, who had married entirely in accordance with their wishes and had been a faithful wife and most prolific mother, having now some five children, hardly seemed to count any more. They were really rather bored by her.

Jassy went with Aunt Sadie to a few London dances at the end of the season, just after Linda had left Tony. She was thought to be rather delicate, and Aunt Sadie had an idea that it would be better for her to come out properly in the less strenuous autumn season, and, accordingly, in October, took a little house in London into which she prepared to move with a few servants, leaving Uncle Matthew in the country, to kill various birds and animals. Jassy complained very much that the young men she had met so far were dull and hideous, but Aunt Sadie took no notice. She said that all girls thought this at first, until they fell in love.

A few days before they were to have moved to London Jassy ran away. She was to have spent a fortnight with Louisa in Scotland, had put Louisa off without telling Aunt Sadie, had cashed her savings, and, before anybody even knew that she was missing, had arrived in

America. Poor Aunt Sadie received, out of the blue, a cable saying:
'On way to Hollywood. Don't worry. Jassy.'

At first the Alconleighs were completely mystified. Jassy had never
shown the smallest interest in stage or cinema, they felt certain she had
no wish to become a film star, and yet, why Hollywood? Then it
occurred to them that Matt might know something, he and Jassy being
the two inseparables of the family, and Aunt Sadie got into the Daimler
and rolled over to Eton. Matt was able to explain everything. He told
Aunt Sadie that Jassy was in love with a film star called Gary Coon (or
Carey Goon, he could not remember which), and that she had written
to Hollywood to ask him if he were married, telling Matt that if he
proved not to be she was going straight out there to marry him herself.
Matt said all this, in his wobbling half grown-up, half little-boy voice,
as if it were the most ordinary situation imaginable.

'So I suppose,' he ended up, 'that she got a letter saying he's not
married and just went off. Lucky she had her running away money.
What about some tea, Mum?'

Aunt Sadie, deeply preoccupied as she was, knew the rules of behaviour and what was expected of her, and stayed with Matt while he
consumed sausages, lobsters, eggs, bacon, fried sole, banana mess and
a chocolate sundae.

As always in times of crisis, the Alconleighs now sent for Davey, and,
as always, Davey displayed a perfect competence to deal with the
situation. He found out in no time that Carey Goon was a second-rate
film actor whom Jassy must have seen when she was in London for the
last parties of the summer. He had been in a film then showing called
One Splendid Hour. Davey got hold of the film, and Lord Merlin put it on
in his private cinema for the benefit of the family. It was about pirates,
and Carey Goon was not even the hero, he was just a pirate and seemed
to have nothing in particular to recommend him; no good looks, talent,
or visible charm, though he did display a certain agility shinning up
and down ropes. He also killed a man with a weapon not unlike the
entrenching tool, and this, we felt, may have awakened some hereditary
emotion in Jassy's bosom. The film itself was one of those of which it is
very difficult for the ordinary English person, as opposed to the film fan,
to make head or tail, and every time Carey Goon appeared the scene
had to be played over again for Uncle Matthew, who had come determined that no detail should escape him. He absolutely identified the
actor with his part, and kept saying:

'What does the fella want to do that for? Bloody fool, he might know
there would be an ambush there. I can't hear a word the fella says—
put that bit on again, Merlin.'

At the end he said he didn't think much of the cove, he appeared to
have no discipline and had been most impertinent to his commanding
officer. 'Needs a haircut! and I shouldn't wonder if he drinks.'

Uncle Matthew said how-do-you-do and good-bye quite civilly to Lord Merlin. He really seemed to be mellowing with age and misfortune.

After great consultations it was decided that some member of the family, not Aunt Sadie or Uncle Matthew, would have to go to Hollywood and bring Jassy home. But who? Linda, of course, would have been the obvious person, had she not been under a cloud and, furthermore, engrossed with her own life. But it would be of no use to send one bolter to fetch back another bolter, so somebody else must be found. In the end, after some persuasion ('madly inconvenient just now that I have started this course of *piqûres*') Davey consented to go with Louisa— the good, the sensible Louisa.

By the time this had been decided, Jassy had arrived in Hollywood, had broadcast her matrimonial intentions to all and sundry, and the whole thing appeared in the newspapers, which devoted pages of space to it, and (it was a silly season with nothing else to occupy their readers) turned it into a sort of serial story. Alconleigh now entered upon a state of siege. Journalists braved Uncle Matthew's stock-whips, his bloodhounds, his terrifying blue flashes, and hung around the village, penetrating even into the house itself in their search for local colour. Their stories were a daily delight. Uncle Matthew was made into something between Heathcliff, Dracula, and the Earl of Dorincourt, Alconleigh a sort of Nightmare Abbey or House of Usher, and Aunt Sadie a character not unlike David Copperfield's mother. Such courage, ingenuity and toughness were displayed by these correspondents that it came as no surprise to any of us when, later on, they did so well in the war. 'War report by So-and-So——'

Uncle Matthew would then say:

'Isn't that the damned sewer I found hiding under my bed?'

He greatly enjoyed the whole affair. Here were opponents worthy of him, not jumpy housemaids, and lachrymose governesses with wounded feelings, but tough young men who did not care what methods they used so long as they could get inside his house and produce a story.

He also seemed greatly to enjoy reading about himself in the newspapers and we all began to suspect that Uncle Matthew had a hidden passion for publicity. Aunt Sadie, on the other hand, found the whole thing very distasteful indeed.

It was thought most vital to keep it from the press that Davey and Louisa were leaving on a voyage of rescue, as the sudden surprise of seeing them might prove an important element in influencing Jassy to return. Unfortunately, Davey could not embark on so long and so trying a journey without a medicine chest, specially designed. While this was being made they missed one boat, and, by the time it was ready, the sleuths were on their track—this unlucky medicine chest having played the same part that Marie Antoinette's *nécessaire* did in the escape to Varennes.

Several journalists accompanied them on the crossing, but did not reap much of a reward, as Louisa was prostrated with sea-sickness and Davey spent his whole time closeted with the ship's doctor, who asserted that his trouble was a cramped intestine, which could easily be cured by manipulation, rays, diet, exercises and injections, all of which, or resting after which, occupied every moment of his day.

On their arrival in New York, however, they were nearly torn to pieces, and we were able, in common with the whole of the two great English-speaking nations, to follow their every move. They even appeared on the newsreel, looking worried and hiding their faces behind books.

It proved to have been a useless trip. Two days after their arrival in Hollywood Jassy became Mrs. Carey Goon. Louisa telegraphed this news home, adding, 'Carey is a terrific Hon.'

There was one comfort, the marriage killed the story.

'He's a perfect dear,' said Davey, on his return. 'A little man like a nut. I'm sure Jassy will be madly happy with him.'

Aunt Sadie, however, was neither reassured nor consoled. It seemed hard luck to have reared a pretty love of a daughter in order for her to marry a little man like a nut, and live with him thousands of miles away. The house in London was cancelled, and the Alconleighs lapsed into such a state of gloom that the next blow, when it fell, was received with fatalism.

Matt, aged sixteen, ran away from Eton, also in a blaze of newspaper publicity, to the Spanish war. Aunt Sadie minded this very much, but I don't think Uncle Matthew did. The desire to fight seemed to him entirely natural, though, of course, he deplored the fact that Matt was fighting for foreigners. He did not take a particular line against the Spanish reds, they were brave boys and had had the good sense to bump off a lot of idolatrous monks, nuns and priests, a proceeding of which he approved, but it was surely a pity to fight in a second-class war when there would so soon be a first-class one available. It was decided that no steps should be taken to retrieve Matt.

Christmas that year was a very sad one at Alconleigh. The children seemed to be melting away like the ten little nigger boys. Bob and Louisa, neither of whom had given their parents one moment of disquiet in their lives, John Fort William, as dull as a man could be, Louisa's children, so good, so pretty but lacking in any sort of originality, could not make up for the absence of Linda, Matt and Jassy, while Robin and Victoria, full as they were of jokes and fun, were swamped by the general atmosphere, and kept themselves to themselves as much as possible in the Hons' cupboard.

Linda was married in the Caxton Hall as soon as her divorce was through. The wedding was as different from her first as the Left-wing parties were different from the other kind. It was not exactly sad, but dismal, uncheerful, and with no feeling of happiness. Few of Linda's friends, and none of her relations except Davey and me were there; Lord Merlin sent two Aubusson rugs and some orchids but did not turn up himself. The pre-Christian chatters had faded out of Linda's life, discouraged, loudly bewailing the great loss she was in theirs.

Christian arrived late, and hurried in, followed by several comrades.

'I must say he is wonderful-looking,' Davey hissed in my ear, 'but oh, bother it all !'

There was no wedding breakfast, and, after a few moments of aimless and rather embarrassed hanging about in the street outside the hall, Linda and Christian went off home. Feeling provincial, up in London for the day and determined to see a little life, I made Davey give me luncheon at the Ritz. This had a still further depressing effect on my spirits. My clothes, so nice and suitable for the George, so much admired by the other dons' wives ('My dear, where did you get that lovely tweed?'), were, I now realized, almost bizarre in their dowdiness; it was the floating panels of taffeta all over again. I thought of those dear little black children, three of them now, in their nursery at home, and of dear Alfred in his study, but just for the moment this thought was no consolation. I passionately longed to have a tiny fur hat, or a tiny ostrich hat, like the two ladies at the next table. I longed for a neat black dress, diamond clips and a dark mink coat, shoes like surgical boots, long crinkly black suède gloves, and smooth polished hair. When I tried to explain all this to Davey, he remarked absentmindedly :

'Oh, but it doesn't matter a bit for you, Fanny, and, after all, how can you have time for *les petits soins de la personne* with so many other, more important things to think of.'

I suppose he thought this would cheer me up.

Soon after her marriage the Alconleighs took Linda back into the fold. They did not count second weddings of divorced people, and Victoria had been severely reprimanded for saying that Linda was engaged to Christian.

'You can't be engaged when you're married.'

It was not the fact of the ceremony which had mollified them, in their eyes Linda would be living from now on in a state of adultery, but they felt the need of her too strongly to keep up a quarrel. The thin end of the wedge (luncheon with Aunt Sadie at Gunters) was inserted, and soon everything was all right again between them. Linda went quite often to Alconleigh, though she never took Christian there, feeling that it would benefit nobody were she to do so.

Linda and Christian lived in their house in Cheyne Walk, and, if Linda was not as happy as she had hoped to be, she exhibited, as usual, a wonderful shop-front. Christian was certainly very fond of her, and, in his way, he tried to be kind to her, but, as Lord Merlin had prophesied, he was much too detached to make any ordinary woman happy. He seemed, for weeks on end, hardly to be aware of her presence; at other times he would wander off and not reappear for days, too much engrossed in whatever he was doing to let her know where he was or when she might expect to see him again. He would eat and sleep where he happened to find himself—on a bench at St. Pancras' station, or just sitting on the doorstep of some empty house. Cheyne Walk was always full of comrades, not chatting to Linda, but making speeches to each other, restlessly rushing about, telephoning, typewriting, drinking, quite often sleeping in their clothes, but without their boots, on Linda's drawing-room sofa.

Money troubles accrued. Christian, though he never appeared to spend any money, had a disconcerting way of scattering it. He had few, but expensive amusements, one of his favourites being to ring up the Nazi leaders in Berlin, and other European politicians, and have long teasing talks with them, costing pounds a minute. 'They never can resist a call from London,' he would say, nor, unfortunately, could they. At last, greatly to Linda's relief, the telephone was cut off, as the bill could not be paid.

I must say that Alfred and I both liked Christian very much. We are intellectual pinks ourselves, enthusiastic agreers with the *New Statesman*, so that his views, while rather more advanced than ours, had the same foundation of civilized humanity, and he seemed to us a great improvement on Tony. All the same, he was a hopeless husband for Linda. Her craving was for love, personal and particular, centred upon herself; wider love, for the poor, the sad, and the unattractive, had no appeal for her, though she honestly tried to believe that it had. The more I saw of Linda at this time, the more certain I felt that another bolt could not be very far ahead.

Twice a week Linda worked in a Red bookshop. It was run by a huge, perfectly silent comrade, called Boris. Boris liked to get drunk from Thursday afternoon, which was closing day in that district, to Monday morning, so Linda said she would take it over on Friday and Saturday. An extraordinary transformation would then occur. The books and tracts which mouldered there month after month, getting damper and dustier until at last they had to be thrown away, were hurried into the background, and their place taken by Linda's own few but well-loved favourites. Thus for *Whither British Airways?* was substituted *Round the World in Forty Days*, *Karl Marx, the Formative Years* was replaced by *The Making of a Marchioness*, and *The Giant of the Kremlin* by *Diary of a Nobody*, while *A Challenge to Coal-Owners* made way for *King Solomon's Mines*.

Hardly would Linda have arrived in the morning on her days there, and taken down the shutters, than the slummy little street would fill with motor cars, headed by Lord Merlin's electric brougham. Lord Merlin did great propaganda for the shop, saying that Linda was the only person who had ever succeeded in finding him *Froggie's Little Brother* and *Le Père Goriot*. The chatters came back in force, delighted to find Linda so easily accessible again, and without Christian, but sometimes there were embarrassing moments when they came face to face with comrades. Then they would buy a book and beat a hasty retreat, all except Lord Merlin, who had never felt disconcerted in his life. He took a perfectly firm line with the comrades.

'How are you today?' he would say with great emphasis, and then glower furiously at them until they left the shop.

All this had an excellent effect upon the financial side of the business. Instead of showing, week by week, an enormous loss, to be refunded from one could guess where, it now became the only Red bookshop in England to make a profit. Boris was greatly praised by his employers, the shop received a medal, which was stuck upon the sign, and the comrades all said that Linda was a good girl and a credit to the Party.

The rest of her time was spent in keeping house for Christian and the comrades, an occupation which entailed trying to induce a series of maids to stay with them, and making sincere, but sadly futile, efforts to take their place when they had left, which they usually did at the end of the first week. The comrades were not very nice or very thoughtful to maids.

'You know, being a Conservative is much more restful,' Linda said to me once in a moment of confidence, when she was being unusually frank about her life, 'though one must remember that it is bad, not good. But it does take place within certain hours, and then finish, whereas Communism seems to eat up all one's life and energy. And the comrades are such Hons, but sometimes they make me awfully cross, just as Tony used to make one furious when he talked about the workers. I often feel rather the same when they talk about us—you see, just like Tony, they've got it all wrong. I'm all for them stringing up Sir Leicester, but if they started on Aunt Emily and Davey, or even on Fa, I don't think I could stand by and watch. I suppose one is neither fish, flesh, nor good red herring, that's the worst of it.'

'But there is a difference,' I said, 'between Sir Leicester and Uncle Matthew.'

'Well, that's what I'm always trying to explain, Sir Leicester grubs up his money in London, goodness knows how, but Fa gets it from his land, and he puts a great deal back into the land, not only money, but work. Look at all the things he does for no pay—all those boring meetings, County Council, J.P., and so on. And he's a good landlord, he takes trouble. You see, the comrades don't know the country—they didn't know you could get a lovely cottage with a huge garden for 2s. 6d.

a week until I told them, and then they hardly believed it. Christian knows, but he says the system is wrong, and I expect it is.'

'What exactly does Christian do?' I said.

'Oh, everything you can think of. Just at the moment he's writing a book on famine—goodness; it's sad—and there's a dear little Chinese comrade who comes and tells him what famine is like, you never saw such a fat man in your life.'

I laughed.

Linda said, hurriedly and guiltily:

'Well, I may seem to laugh at the comrades, but at least one does know they are doing good not harm, and not living on other people's slavery like Sir Leicester, and really you know I do simply love them, though I sometimes wish they were a little more fond of chatting, and not quite so sad and earnest and down on everybody.'

CHAPTER XV

EARLY in 1939, the population of Catalonia streamed over the Pyrenees into the Roussillon, a poor and little-known province of France, which now, in a few days, found itself inhabited by more Spaniards than Frenchmen. Just as the lemmings suddenly pour themselves in mass suicide off the coast of Norway, knowing neither whence they come nor whither bound, so great is the compulsion that hurls them into the Atlantic, thus half a million men, women and children suddenly took flight into the bitter mountain weather, without pausing for thought. It was the greatest movement of population, in the time it took, that had ever hitherto been seen. Over the mountains they found no promised land: the French government, vacillating in its policy, neither turned them back with machine-guns at the frontier, nor welcomed them as brothers-in-arms against Fascism. It drove them like a herd of beasts down to the cruel salty marshes of that coast, enclosed them, like a herd of beasts, behind barbed-wire fences, and forgot all about them.

Christian, who had always, I think, had a half-guilty feeling about not having fought in Spain, immediately rushed off to Perpignan to see what was happening, and what, if anything, could be done. He wrote an endless series of reports, memoranda, articles and private letters about the conditions he had found in the camps, and then settled down to work in an office financed by various English humanitarians with the object of improving the camps, putting refugee families in touch again, and getting as many as possible out of France. This office was run by a young man who had lived many years in Spain called Robert

Parker. As soon as it became clear that there would not be, as at first was expected, an outbreak of typhus, Christian sent for Linda to join him in Perpignan.

It so happened that Linda had never before been abroad in her life. Tony had found all his pleasures, hunting, shooting, and golf, in England, and had grudged the extra days out of his holiday which would have been spent in travelling; while it would never have occurred to the Alconleighs to visit the Continent for any other purpose than that of fighting. Uncle Matthew's four years in France and Italy between 1914 and 1918 had given him no great opinion of foreigners.

'Frogs,' he would say, 'are slightly better than Huns or Wops, but abroad is unutterably bloody and foreigners are fiends.'

The bloodiness of abroad, the fiendishness of foreigners, had, in fact, become such a tenet of the Radlett family creed that Linda set forth on her journey with no little trepidation. I went to see her off at Victoria, she was looking intensely English in her long blond mink coat, the *Tatler* under her arm, and Lord Merlin's morocco dressing-case, with a canvas cover, in her hand.

'I hope you have sent your jewels to the bank,' I said.

'Oh, darling, don't tease, you know how I haven't got any now. But my money,' she said with a self-conscious giggle, 'is sewn into my stays. Fa rang up and begged me to, and I must say it did seem quite an idea. Oh, why aren't you coming? I do feel so terrified—think of sleeping in the train, all alone.'

'Perhaps you won't be alone,' I said. 'Foreigners are greatly given, I believe, to rape.'

'Yes, that would be nice, so long as they didn't find my stays. Oh, we are off—good-bye, darling, do think of me,' she said, and, clenching her suède-covered fist, she shook it out of the window in a Communist salute.

I must explain that I know everything that now happened to Linda, although I did not see her for another year, because afterwards, as will be shown, we spent a long quiet time together, during which she told it all to me, over and over again. It was her way of re-living happiness.

Of course the journey was an enchantment to her. The porters in their blue overalls, the loud, high conversations, of which, although she thought she knew French quite well, she did not understand a single word, the steamy, garlic-smelling heat of the French train, the delicious food, to which she was summoned by a little hurried bell, it was all from another world, like a dream.

She looked out of the window and saw chateaux, lime avenues, ponds and villages exactly like those in the *Bibliothèque Rose*—she thought she must, at any moment, see Sophie in her white dress and unnaturally small black pumps cutting up goldfish, gorging herself on new bread and cream, or scratching the face of good, uncomplaining

Paul. Her very stilted, very English French, got her across Paris and into the train for Perpignan without a hitch. Paris. She looked out of the window at the lighted dusky streets, and thought that never could any town have been so hauntingly beautiful. A strange stray thought came into her head that, one day, she would come back here and be very happy, but she knew that it was not likely, Christian would never want to live in Paris. Happiness and Christian were still linked together in her mind at this time.

At Perpignan she found him in a whirl of business. Funds had been raised, a ship had been chartered, and plans were on foot for sending six thousand Spaniards out of the camps to Mexico. This entailed an enormous amount of staff work, as families (no Spaniard would think of moving without his entire family) had to be reunited from camps all over the place, assembled in a camp in Perpignan, and taken by train to the port of Cette, whence they finally embarked. The work was greatly complicated by the fact that Spanish husbands and wives do not share a surname. Christian explained all this to Linda almost before she was out of the train; he gave her an absent-minded peck on the forehead and rushed her to his office, hardly giving her time to deposit her luggage at an hotel on the way and scouting the idea that she might like a bath. He did not ask how she was or whether she had had a good journey—Christian always assumed that people were all right unless they told him to the contrary, when, except in the case of destitute, coloured, oppressed, leprous, or otherwise unattractive strangers, he would take absolutely no notice. He was really only interested in mass wretchedness, and never much cared for individual cases, however genuine their misery, while the idea that it is possible to have three square meals a day and a roof and yet be unhappy or unwell, seemed to him intolerable nonsense.

The office was a large shed with a yard round it. This yard was permanently full of refugees with mountains of luggage and quantities of children, dogs, donkeys, goats, and other appurtenances, who had just struggled over the mountains in their flight from Fascism, and were hoping that the English would be able to prevent them being put into camps. In certain cases they could be lent money, or given railway tickets enabling them to join relations in France and French Morocco, but the vast majority waited hours for an interview, only to be told that there was no hope for them. They would then, with great and heart-breaking politeness, apologize for having been a nuisance and withdraw. Spaniards have a highly developed sense of human dignity.

Linda was now introduced to Robert Parker and to Randolph Pine, a young writer who, having led a more or less playboy existence in the South of France, had gone to fight in Spain, and was now working in Perpignan from a certain feeling of responsibility towards those who had once been fellow soldiers. They seemed pleased that Linda had arrived, and were most friendly and welcoming, saying that it was nice to see a new face.

'You must give me some work to do,' said Linda.

'Yes, now what can we think of for you?' said Robert. 'There's masses of work, never fear, it's just a question of finding the right kind. Can you speak Spanish?'

'No.'

'Oh, well, you'll soon pick it up.'

'I'm quite sure I shan't,' said Linda doubtfully.

'What do you know about welfare work?'

'Oh, dear, how hopeless I seem to be. Nothing, I'm afraid.'

'Lavender will find her a job,' said Christian, who had settled down at his table and was flapping over a card index.

'Lavender?'

'A girl called Lavender Davis.'

'No! I know her quite well, she used to live near us in the country. In fact she was one of my bridesmaids.'

'That's it,' said Robert. 'She said she knew you, I'd forgotten. She's wonderful, she really works with the Quakers in the camps, but she helps us a great deal too. There's absolutely nothing she doesn't know about calories and babies' nappies, and expectant mummies, and so on, and she's the hardest worker I've ever come across.'

'I'll tell you,' said Randolph Pine, 'what you can do. There's a job simply waiting for you, and that is to arrange the accommodation on this ship that's going off next week.'

'Oh, yes, of course,' said Robert, 'the very thing. She can have this table and start at once.'

'Now look,' said Randolph. 'I'll show you. (What delicious scent you have, Après l'Ondée? I thought so.) Now here is a map of the ship— see—best cabins, not such good cabins, lousy cabins, and battened down under the hatches. And here is a list of the families who are going. All you have to do is to allocate each family its cabin—when you have decided which they are to have, you put the number of the cabin against the family—here—you see? And the number of the family on the cabin here, like that. Quite easy, but it takes time, and must be done so that when they arrive on the boat they will know exactly where to go with their things.'

'But how do I decide who gets the good ones and who is battened? Awfully tricky, isn't it?'

'Not really. The point is it's a strictly democratic ship run on republican principles, class doesn't enter into it. I should give decent cabins to families where there are small children or babies. Apart from that do it any way you like. Take a pin if you like. The only thing that matters is that it should be done, otherwise there'll be a wild scramble for the best places when they get on board.'

Linda looked at the list of families. It took the form of a card index, the head of each family having a card on which was written the number and names of his dependants.

'It doesn't give their ages,' said Linda. 'How am I to know if there are young babies?'

'That's a point,' said Robert. 'How is she to?'

'Quite easy,' said Christian. 'With Spaniards you can always tell. Before the war they were called either after saints or after episodes in the life of the Virgin—Anunciacion, Asuncion, Purificacion, Concepcion, Consvelo, etc. Since the Civil War they are all called Carlos after Charlie Marx, Federigo after Freddie Engels or Estalina (very popular until the Russians let them down with a wallop), or else nice slogans like Solidaredad-Obrera, Libertad, and so on. Then you know the children are under three. Couldn't be simpler, really.'

Lavender Davis now appeared. She was indeed the same Lavender, dowdy, healthy and plain, wearing an English country tweed and brogues. Her short brown hair curled over her head, and she had no make-up. She greeted Linda with enthusiasm, indeed, it had always been a fiction in the Davis family that Lavender and Linda were each other's greatest friends. Linda was delighted to see her, as one always is delighted to see a familiar face, abroad.

'Come on,' said Randolph, 'now we're all here let's go and have a drink at the Palmarium.'

For the next weeks, until her private life began to occupy Linda's attention, she lived in an atmosphere of alternate fascination and horror. She grew to love Perpignan, a strange little old town, so different from anything she had ever known, with its river and broad quays, its network of narrow streets, its huge wild-looking plane trees, and all around it the bleak vine-growing country of the Roussillon bursting into summery green under her very eyes. Spring came late and slowly, but when it came it was hand-in-hand with summer, and almost at once everything was baking and warm, and in the villages the people danced every night on concrete dancing floors under the plane trees. At week-ends the English, unable to eradicate such a national habit, shut up the office and made for Collioure on the coast, where they bathed and sunbathed and went for Pyrenean picnics.

But all this had nothing to do with the reason for their presence in these charming surroundings—the camps. Linda went to the camps nearly every day, and they filled her soul with despair. As she could not help very much in the office owing to her lack of Spanish, nor with the children, since she knew nothing about calories, she was employed as a driver, and was always on the road in a Ford van full of supplies, or of refugees, or just taking messages to and from the camps. Often she had to sit and wait for hours on end while a certain man was found and his case dealt with; she would quickly be surrounded by a perfect cor-course of men talking to her in their heavy guttural French. By this time the camps were quite decently organized; there were rows of orderly though depressing huts, and the men were getting regular meals, which, if not very appetizing, did at least keep body and soul together. But the sight of these thousands of human beings, young and healthy, herded behind wire away from their womenfolk, with nothing on earth to do day after dismal day, was a recurring torture to Linda. She began to think that Uncle Matthew had been right—that abroad, where such things could happen, was indeed unutterably bloody, and that foreigners, who could inflict them upon each other, must be fiends.

One day as she sat in her van, the centre, as usual, of a crowd of Spaniards, a voice said:

'Linda, what on earth are you doing here?'

And it was Matt.

He looked ten years older than when she had last seen him, grown up, in fact, and extremely handsome, his Radlett eyes infinitely blue in a dark-brown face.

'I've seen you several times,' he said, 'and I thought you had been sent to fetch me away so I made off, but then I found out you are married to that Christian fellow. Was he the one you ran away from Tony with?'

'Yes,' said Linda. 'I'd no idea, Matt. I thought you'd have been sure to go back to England.'

'Well, no,' said Matt. 'I'm an officer, you see—must stay with the boys.'

'Does Mummy know you're all right?'

'Yes, I told her—at least if Christian posted a letter I gave him.'

'I don't suppose so—he's never been known to post a letter in his life. He is funny, he might have told me.'

'He didn't know—I sent it under cover to a friend of mine to forward. Didn't want any of the English to find out I was here, or they would start trying to get me home. I know.'

'Christian wouldn't,' said Linda. 'He's all for people doing what they want to in life. You're very thin, Matt, is there anything you'd like?'

'Yes,' said Matt, 'some cigarettes and a couple of thrillers.'

After this Linda saw him most days. She told Christian, who merely grunted and said: 'He'll have to be got out before the world war begins. I'll see to that,' and she wrote and told her parents. The result was a parcel of clothes from Aunt Sadie, which Matt refused to accept, and a packing-case full of vitamin pills from Davey, which Linda did not even dare to show him. He was cheerful and full of jokes and high spirits, but then there is a difference, as Christian said, between staying in a place because you are obliged to, and staying there because you think it right. But in any case, with the Radlett family, cheerfulness was never far below the surface.

The only other cheerful prospect was the ship. It was only going to rescue from hell a few thousand of the refugees, a mere fraction of the total amount, but, at any rate, they would be rescued, and taken to a better world, with happy and useful future prospects.

When she was not driving the van Linda worked hard over the cabin arrangements, and finally got the whole thing fixed and finished in time for the embarkation.

All the English except Linda went to Cette for the great day, taking with them two M.P.s and a duchess, who had helped the enterprise in London and had come out to see the fruit of their work. Linda went over by bus to Argelès to see Matt.

'How odd the Spanish upper classes must be,' she said, 'they don't raise a finger to help their own people, but leave it all to strangers like us.'

'You don't know Fascists,' Matt said gloomily.

'I was thinking yesterday when I was taking the Duchess round Barcarès—yes, but why an English duchess, aren't there any Spanish ones, and, come to that, why is it nothing but English working in Perpignan? I knew several Spaniards in London, why don't they come and help a bit? They'd be awfully useful. I suppose they speak Spanish.'

'Fa was quite right about foreigners being fiends,' said Matt, 'upper-class ones are, at least. All these boys are terrific Hons, I must say.'

'Well, I can't see the English leaving each other in the lurch like this, even if they did belong to different parties. I think it's shameful.'

Christian and Robert came back from Cette in a cheerful mood. The arrangements had gone like clockwork, and a baby which had been born during the first half-hour on the ship was named Embarcacion. It was the kind of joke Christian very much enjoyed. Robert said to Linda:

'Did you work on any special plan when you were arranging the cabins, or how did you do it?'

'Why? Wasn't it all right?'

'Perfect. Everybody had a place, and made for it. But I just wondered what you went by when you allocated the good cabins, that's all.'

'Well, I simply,' said Linda, 'gave the best cabins to the people who had *Labrador* on their card, because I used to have one when I was little and he was such a terrific . . . so sweet, you know.'

'Ah,' said Robert gravely, 'all is now explained. *Labrador* in Spanish happens to mean labourer. So you see under your scheme (excellent by the way, most democratic; the farm hands all found themselves in luxury while the intellectuals were battened. That'll teach them not to be so clever. You did very well. Linda, we were all most grateful.'

'He was such a sweet Labrador,' said Linda dreamily. 'I wish you could have seen him. I do miss not having pets.'

'Can't think why you don't make an offer for the *sangsue*,' said Robert.

One of the features of Perpignan was a leech in a bottle in the window of a chemist's shop, with a typewritten notice saying: SI LA SANGSUE MONTE DANS LA BOUTEILLE IL FERA BEAU TEMPS. SI LA SANGSUE DESCEND— L'ORAGE.'

'It might be nice,' said Linda, 'but I can't somehow imagine her getting very fond of one—too busy fussing about the weather all day, up and down, up and down—no time for human relationships.'

CHAPTER XVI

LINDA never could remember afterwards whether she had really minded when she discovered that Christian was in love with Lavender Davis, and, if so, how much. She could not at all remember her emotions at that time. Certainly wounded pride must have played a part, though perhaps less so with Linda than it would have with many women, as she did not suffer from much inferiority feeling. She must have seen that the past two years, her running away from Tony, all now went for nothing—but was she stricken at the heart, was she still in love with Christian, did she suffer the ordinary pangs of jealousy? I think not.

All the same, it was not a flattering choice. Lavender had seemed, for years and years, stretching back into childhood, to epitomize everything that the Radletts considered most unromantic: a keen girl guide, hockey player, tree climber, head girl at her school, rider astride. She had never lived in a dream of love; the sentiment was, quite obviously, far removed from her thoughts, although Louisa and Linda, unable to imagine that anybody could exist without some tiny spark of it, used to invent romances for Lavender—the games mistress at her school or Dr. Simpson of Merlinford (of whom Louisa had made up one of her non-sense rhymes—'He's doctor and king's proctor too, and she's in love with him, but he's in love with you'). Since those days she had trained as a nurse and as a welfare worker, had taken a course of law and political economy, and, indeed, might have done it all, Linda saw only too well, with the express intention of fitting herself to be a mate for Christian. The result was that in their present surroundings, with her calm assured confidence in her own ability, she easily outshone poor Linda. There was no competition, it was a walk-over.

Linda did not discover their love in any vulgar way—surprising a kiss, or finding them in bed together. It was all far more subtle, more dangerous than that, being quite simply borne in upon her week after week that they found perfect happiness in each other, and that Christian depended entirely on Lavender for comfort and encouragement in his work. As this work now absorbed him heart and soul, as he thought of nothing else and never relaxed for a moment, dependence upon Lavender involved the absolute exclusion of Linda. She felt uncertain what to do. She could not have it out with Christian; there was nothing tangible to have out, and, in any case, such a proceeding would have been absolutely foreign to Linda's character. She dreaded scenes and rows more than anything else in the world, and she had no illusions about what Christian thought of her. She felt that he really rather despised her for having left Tony and her child so easily, and that, in his opinion, she took a silly, light-hearted and superficial view of life. He liked serious, educated women, especially those who had made a study of welfare, especially Lavender. She had no desire to hear all this said. On the other hand she began to think that it would be as well for her to get away from Perpignan herself before Christian and Lavender went off together, as it seemed to her most probable that they would, wandering off hand in hand to search for and relieve other forms of human misery. Already she felt embarrassed when she was with Robert and Randolph, who were obviously very sorry for her and were always making little manœuvres to prevent her noticing that Christian was spending every minute of the day with Lavender.

One afternoon, looking idly out of the window of her hotel bedroom, she saw them walking up the Quai Sadi Carnot together, completely absorbed, utterly contented in each other's company, radiating happiness. Linda was seized by an impulse and acted on it. She packed her things, wrote a hasty letter to Christian saying that she was leaving him for good, as she realized that their marriage had been a failure. She asked him to look after Matt. She then burnt her boats by adding a postscript (a fatal feminine practice), 'I think you had much better marry Lavender.' She bundled herself and her luggage into a taxi and took the night train for Paris.

The journey this time was horrible. She was, after all, very fond of Christian, and as soon as the train had left the station, she began to ask herself whether she had not in fact behaved stupidly and badly. He probably had a passing fancy for Lavender, based on common interests, which would fade away as soon as he got back to London. Possibly it was not even that, but simply that he was obliged, for his work, to be with Lavender all the time. His absentminded treatment of Linda was, after all, nothing new, it had begun almost as soon as he had got her under his roof. She began to feel that she had done wrong to write that letter.

She had her return ticket, but very little money indeed, just enough, she reckoned, for dinner on the train and some food the next day. Linda always had to translate French money into pounds, shillings and pence before she knew where she was with it. She seemed to have about 18s. 6d. with her, so there could be no question of a sleeper. She had never before sat up all night in a train, and the experience appalled her; it was like some dreadful feverish illness, when the painful hours drag by, each one longer than a week. Her thoughts brought her no comfort. She had torn up her life of the past two years, all that she had tried to put into her relationship with Christian, and thrown it away like so much waste-paper. If this was to be the outcome why had she ever left Tony, her real husband for better for worse, and her child? That was where her duty had lain, and well she knew it. She thought of my mother and shuddered. Could it be that she, Linda, was from now on doomed to a life that she utterly despised, that of a bolter?

And in London what would she find? A little empty, dusty house. Perhaps, she thought, Christian would pursue her, come and insist that she belonged to him. But in her heart she knew that he would not, and that she did not, and that this was the end. Christian believed too sincerely that people must be allowed to do as they wish in life, without interference. He was fond of Linda, she knew, but disappointed in her, she also knew; he would not himself have made the first move to separate, but would not much regret the fact that she had done so. Soon he would have some new scheme in his head, some new plan for suffering mortals, any mortals, anywhere, so long as there were enough of them and their misery was great. Then he would forget Linda, and possibly also Lavender, as if they had never been. Christian was not in passionate quest of love, he had other interests, other aims, and it mattered very little to him what woman happened to be in his life at a given moment. But in his nature, she knew, there was a certain ruthlessness. She felt that he would not forgive what she had done, or try to persuade her to go back on it, nor, indeed, was there any reason why he should do so.

It could not be said, thought Linda, as the train pursued its way through the blackness, that her life so far had been a marked success. She had found neither great love nor great happiness, and she had not inspired them in others. Parting with her would have been no death blow to either of her husbands; on the contrary, they would both have turned with relief to a much preferred mistress, who was more suited to them in every way. Whatever quality it is that can hold indefinitely the love and affection of a man she plainly did not possess, and now she was doomed to the lonely, hunted life of a beautiful but unattached woman. Where now was love that would last to the grave and far beyond? What had she done with her youth? Tears for her lost hopes and ideals, tears of self-pity in fact, began to pour down her cheeks. The three fat Frenchmen who shared the carriage with her were in a snoring sleep, she wept alone.

Sad and tired as Linda was, she could not but perceive the beauty of

Paris that summer morning as she drove across it to the Gare du Nord. Paris in the early morning has a cheerful, bustling aspect, a promise of delicious things to come, a positive smell of coffee and croissants, quite peculiar to itself.

The people welcome a new day as if they were certain of liking it, the shopkeepers pull up their blinds serene in the expectation of good trade, the workers go happily to their work, the people who have sat up all night in night-clubs go happily to their rest, the orchestra of motor-car horns, of clanking trams, of whistling policemen tunes up for the daily symphony, and everywhere is joy. This joy, this life, this beauty did but underline poor Linda's fatigue and sadness, she felt it but was not of it. She turned her thoughts to old familiar London, she longed above all for her own bed, feeling as does a wounded beast when it crawls home to its lair. She only wanted to sleep undisturbed in her own bedroom.

But when she presented her return ticket at the Gare du Nord she was told, furiously, loudly and unsympathetically, that it had expired.

'*Voyons, madame—le* 29 *Mai. C'est aujourd'hui le* 30, *n'est-ce pas? Donc——!*' Tremendous shruggings.

Linda was paralysed with horror. Her 18s. 6d. was by now down to 6s. 3d., hardly enough for a meal. She knew nobody in Paris, she had absolutely no idea what she ought to do, she was too tired and too hungry to think clearly. She stood like a statue of despair. Her porter, tired of waiting beside a statue of despair, deposited the luggage at its feet and went grumbling off. Linda sank on to her suitcase and began to cry; nothing so dreadful had ever happened to her before. She cried bitterly, she could not stop. People passed to and fro as if weeping ladies were the most ordinary phenomenon at the Gare du Nord. 'Fiends! fiends!' she sobbed. Why had she not listened to her father, why had she ever come to this bloody abroad? Who would help her? In London there was a society, she knew, which looked after ladies stranded at railway stations; here, more likely, there would be one for shipping them off to South America. At any moment now somebody, some genial-looking old woman might come up and give her an injection, after which she would disappear for ever.

She became aware that somebody was standing beside her, not an old lady, but a short, stocky, very dark Frenchman in a black Homburg hat. He was laughing. Linda took no notice, but went on crying. The more she cried the more he laughed. Her tears were tears of rage now, no longer of self-pity.

At last she said, in a voice which was meant to be angrily impressive, but which squeaked and shook through her handkerchief:

'*Allez-vous en.*'

For answer he took her hand and pulled her to her feet.

'*Bonjour, bonjour,*' he said.

'*Voulez-vous vous en aller?*' said Linda, rather more doubtfully; here at least was a human being who showed signs of taking some interest in her. Then she thought of South America.

'*Il faut expliquer que je ne suis pas,*' she said, '*une esclave blanche. Je suis la fille d'un très important lord anglais.*'

The Frenchman gave a great bellow of laughter.

'One does not,' he said in the nearly perfect English of somebody who has spoken it from a child, 'have to be a Sherlock Holmes to guess that.'

Linda was rather annoyed. An Englishwoman abroad may be proud of her nationality and her virtue without wishing them to jump so conclusively to the eye.

'French ladies,' he went on, 'covered with *les marques extérieurs de la richesse* never never sit crying on their suitcases at the Gare du Nord in the very early morning, while *esclaves blanches* always have protectors, and it is only too clear that you are unprotected just now.'

This sounded all right, and Linda was mollified.

'Now,' he said, 'I invite you to luncheon with me, but first you must have a bath and rest and a cold compress on your face.'

He picked up her luggage and walked to a taxi.

'Get in, please.'

Linda got in. She was far from certain that this was not the road to Buenos Aires, but something made her do as he said. Her powers of resistance were at an end, and she really saw no alternative.

'Hotel Montalembert,' he told the taxi man. 'Rue du Bac. *Je m'excuse, madame,* for not taking you to the Ritz, but I have a feeling for the Hotel Montalembert just now, that it will suit your mood this morning.'

Linda sat upright in her corner of the taxi, looking, she hoped, very prim. As she could not think of anything pertinent to say she remained silent. Her companion hummed a little tune, and seemed vastly amused. When they arrived at the hotel, he took a room for her, told the liftman to show her to it, told the *concierge* to send her up a *café complet*, kissed her hand, and said:

'*A tout à l'heure*—I will fetch you a little before one o'clock and we will go out to luncheon.'

Linda had her bath and breakfast and got into bed. When the telephone bell rang she was so sound asleep that it was a struggle to wake up.

'*Un monsieur qui demande madame.*'

'*Je descends tout de suite,*' said Linda, but it took her quite half an hour to get ready.

CHAPTER XVII

'Ah! You keep me waiting,' he said, kissing her hand, or at least making a gesture of raising her hand towards his lips and then dropping it rather suddenly. 'That is a very good sign.'

'Sign of what?' said Linda. He had a two-seater outside the hotel and she got into it. She was feeling more like herself again.

'Oh, of this and that,' he said, letting in the clutch, 'a good augury for our affair, that it will be happy and last long.'

Linda became intensely stiff, English and embarrassed, and said, self-consciously:

'We are not having an affair.'

'My name is Fabrice—may one ask yours?'

'Linda.'

'Linda. *Comme c'est joli*. With me, it usually last five years.'

He drove to a restaurant where they were shown, with some deference, to a table in a red plush corner. He ordered the luncheon and the wine in rapid French, the sort of French that Linda frankly could not follow, then, putting his hands on his knees, he turned to her and said:

'*Allons, racontez, madame.*'

'*Racontez* what?'

'Well, but of course, the story. Who was it that left you to cry on that suitcase?'

'He didn't. I left him. It was my second husband and I have left him for ever because he has fallen in love with another woman—a welfare worker, not that you'd know what that is, because I'm sure they don't exist in France. It just makes it worse, that's all.'

'What a very curious reason for leaving one's second husband. Surely with your experience of husbands you must have noticed that falling in love with other women is one of the things they do? However, it's an ill wind, and I don't complain. But why the suitcase? Why didn't you put yourself in the train and go back to Monsieur the important lord, your father?'

'That's what I was doing until they told me that my return ticket had expired. I only had 6s. 3d., and I don't know anybody in Paris, and I was awfully tired, so I cried.'

'The second husband—why not borrow some money from him? Or had you left a note on his pillow—women never can resist these little essays in literature, and they do make it rather embarrassing to go back, I know.'

'Well, anyhow he's in Perpignan, so I couldn't have.'

'Ah, you come from Perpignan. And what were you doing there, in the name of heaven?'

'In the name of heaven we were trying to stop you frogs from teasing the poor Epagnards,' said Linda with some spirit.

'E-spa-gnols! So we are teasing them, are we?'

'Not so badly now—terribly at the beginning.'

'What were we supposed to do with them? We never invited them to come, you know.'

'You drove them into camps in that cruel wind, and gave them no shelter for weeks. Hundreds died.'

'It is quite a job to provide shelter, at a moment's notice, for half a million people. We did what we could—we fed them—the fact is that most of them are still alive.'

'Still herded in camps.'

'My dear Linda, you could hardly expect us to turn them loose on the countryside with no money—what would be the result? Do use your common sense.'

'You should mobilize them to fight in the war against Fascism that's coming any day now.'

'Talk about what you know and you won't get so angry. We haven't enough equipment for our own soldiers in the war against Germany that's coming—not any day, but after the harvest, probably in August. Now go on telling me about your husbands. It's so very much more interesting.'

'Only two. My first was a Conservative, and my second is a Communist.'

'Just as I guessed, your first is rich, your second is poor. I could see you once had a rich husband, the dressing-case and the fur coat, though it is a hideous colour, and no doubt, as far as one could see, with it bundled over your arm, a hideous shape. Still, *vison* usually betokens a rich husband somewhere. Then this dreadful linen suit you are wearing has ready-made written all over it.'

'You are rude, it's a very pretty suit.'

'And last year's. Jackets are getting longer you will find. I'll get you some clothes—if you were well dressed you would be quite good-looking, though it's true your eyes are small. Blue, a good colour, but small.'

'In England,' said Linda, 'I am considered a beauty.'

'Well, you have points.'

So this silly conversation went on and on, but it was only froth on the surface. Linda was feeling, what she had never so far felt for any man, an overwhelming physical attraction. It made her quite giddy, it terrified her. She could see that Fabrice was perfectly certain of the outcome, so was she perfectly certain, and that was what frightened her. How could she, Linda, with the horror and contempt she had always felt for casual affairs, allow herself to be picked up by any stray foreigner and, having seen him only for an hour, long and long and long to be in bed with him? He was not even good-looking, he was exactly like dozens of other dark men in Homburgs that can be seen in the streets of any French town. But there was something about the way he looked at her which seemed to be depriving her of all balance. She was profoundly shocked, and, at the same time, intensely excited.

After luncheon they strolled out of the restaurant into brilliant sunshine.

'Come and see my flat,' said Fabrice.

'I would rather see Paris,' said Linda.

'Do you know Paris well?'

'I've never been here before in my life.'

Fabrice was really startled.

'Never been here before?' he could not believe it. 'What a pleasure for me, to show it all to you. There is so much to show, it will take weeks.'

'Unfortunately,' said Linda, 'I leave for England tomorrow.'

'Yes, of course. Then we must see it all this afternoon.'

They drove slowly round a few streets and squares, and then went for a stroll in the Bois. Linda could not believe that she had only just arrived there, that this was still the very day which she had seen unfolding itself, so full of promise, through her mist of morning tears.

'How fortunate you are to live in such a town,' she said to Fabrice. 'It would be impossible to be very unhappy here.'

'Not impossible,' he said. 'One's emotions are intensified in Paris— one can be more happy and also more unhappy here than in any other place. But it is always a positive source of joy to live here, and there is nobody so miserable as a Parisian in exile from his town. The rest of the world seems unbearably cold and bleak to us, hardly worth living in.' He spoke with great feeling.

After tea, which they had out of doors in the Bois, he drove slowly back into Paris. He stopped the car outside an old house in the Rue Bonaparte, and said, again:

'Come and see my flat.'

'No, no,' said Linda. 'The time has now come for me to point out that I am *une femme sérieuse*.'

Fabrice gave his great bellow of laughter.

'Oh,' he said, shaking helplessly, 'how funny you are. What a phrase, *femme sérieuse*, where did you find it? And if so serious, how do you explain the second husband?'

'Yes, I admit that I did wrong, very wrong indeed, and made a great mistake. But that is no reason for losing control, for sliding down the hill altogether, for being picked up by strange gentlemen at the Gare du Nord and then immediately going with them to see their flat. And please, if you will be so kind as to lend me some money, I want to catch the London train tomorrow morning.'

'Of course, by all means,' said Fabrice.

He thrust a roll of banknotes into her hand, and drove her to the Hotel Montalembert. He seemed quite unmoved by her speech, and announced he would come back at eight o'clock to take her out to dinner.

Linda's bedroom was full of roses, it reminded her of when Moira was born.

'Really,' she thought with a giggle, 'this is a very penny-novelettish seduction, how can I be taken in by it?'

But she was filled with a strange, wild, unfamiliar happiness, and knew that this was love. Twice in her life she had mistaken something else for it; it was like seeing somebody in the street who you think is a friend, you whistle and wave and run after him, and it is not only not the friend, but not even very like him. A few minutes later the real friend appears in view, and then you can't imagine how you ever mistook that other person for him. Linda was now looking upon the authentic face of love, and she knew it, but it frightened her. That it should come so casually, so much by a series of accidents, was frightening. She tried to remember how she had felt when she had first loved her two husbands. There must have been strong and impelling emotion; in both cases she had disrupted her own life, upset her parents and friends remorselessly, in order to marry them, but she could not recall it. Only she knew that never before, not even in dreams, and she was a great dreamer of love, had she felt anything remotely like this. She told herself, over and over again, that tomorrow she must go back to London, but she had no intention of going back, and she knew it.

Fabrice took her out to dinner and then to a night club, where they did not dance, but chatted endlessly. She told him about Uncle Matthew, Aunt Sadie and Louisa and Jassy and Matt, and he could not hear enough, and egged her on to excesses of exaggeration about her family and all their various idiosyncrasies.

'*Et* Jassy—*et* Matt—*alors, racontez.*'

And she recounted, for hours.

In the taxi on their way home she refused again to go back with him or to let him come into the hotel with her. He did not insist, he did not try to hold her hand, or touch her at all. He merely said:

'*C'est une résistance magnifique, je vous félicite de tout mon cœur, madame.*'

Outside the hotel she gave him her hand to say good night. He took it in both of his and really kissed it.

'*A demain,*' he said, and got back into the taxi.

'*Allô—allô.*'

'Hullo.'

'Good morning. Are you having your breakfast?'

'Yes.'

'I thought I heard a coffee-cup clattering. Is it good?'

'It's so delicious that I have to keep stopping, for fear of finishing it too quickly. Are you having yours?'

'Had it. I must tell you that I like very long conversations in the morning, and I shall expect you to *raconter des histoires*.'

'Like Schéhérazade?'

'Yes, just like. And you're not to get that note in your voice of "now I'm going to ring off", as English people always do.'

'What English people do you know?'

'I know some. I was at school in England, and at Oxford.'

'No! When?'

'1920.'

'When I was nine. Fancy, perhaps I saw you in the street—we used to do all our shopping in Oxford.'

'Elliston & Cavell?'

'Oh, yes, and Webbers.'

There was a silence.

'Go on,' he said.

'Go on, what?'

'I mean don't ring off. Go on telling.'

'I shan't ring off. As a matter of fact I adore chatting. It's my favourite thing, and I expect you will want to ring off ages before I do.'

They had a long and very silly conversation, and, at the end of it, Fabrice said:

'Now get up, and in an hour I will fetch you and we will go to Versailles.'

At Versailles, which was an enchantment to Linda, she was reminded of a story she had once read about two English ladies who had seen the ghost of Marie Antoinette sitting in her garden at the Little Trianon. Fabrice found this intensely boring, and said so.

'*Histoires*,' he said, 'are only of interest when they are true, or when you have made them up specially to amuse me. *Histoires de revenants*, made up by some dim old English virgins, are neither true nor interesting. *Donc plus d'histoires de revenants, madame, s'il vous plaît.*'

'All right,' said Linda crossly. 'I'm doing my best to please—you tell me a story.'

'Yes, I will—and this story is true. My grandmother was very beautiful and had many lovers all her life, even when she was quite old. A short time before she died she was in Venice with my mother, her daughter, and one day, floating up some canal in their gondola, they saw a little palazzo of pink marble, very exquisite. They stopped the gondola to look at it, and my mother said: "I don't believe anybody lives there, what about trying to see the inside?"

'So they rang the bell, and an old servant came and said that nobody had lived there for many, many years, and he would show it to them if they liked. So they went in and upstairs to the *salone*, which had three windows looking over the canal and was decorated with fifteenth-century plaster work, white on a pale blue background. It was a perfect room. My grandmother seemed strangely moved, and stood for a long time in silence. At last she said to my mother:

' "If, in the third drawer of that bureau there is a filigree box containing a small gold key on a black velvet ribbon, this house belongs to me."

'And my mother looked, and there was, and it did. One of my grandmother's lovers had given it to her years and years before, when she was quite young, and she had forgotten all about it.'

'Goodness,' said Linda, 'what fascinating lives you foreigners do lead.'

'And it belongs to me now.'

He put his hand up to Linda's forehead and stroked back a strand of hair which was loose:

'And I would take you there tomorrow if——'

'If what?'

'One must wait here now, you see, for the war.'

'Oh, I keep forgetting the war,' said Linda.

'Yes, let's forget it. *Comme vous êtes mal coiffée, ma chère.*'

'If you don't like my clothes and don't like my hair and think my eyes are so small, I don't know what you see in me.'

'*Quand-même j'avoue qu'il y a quelque-chose,*' said Fabrice.

Again they dined together.

Linda said: 'Haven't you any other engagements?'

'Yes, of course. I have cancelled them.'

'Who are your friends?'

'*Les gens du monde.* And yours?'

'When I was married to Tony, that is, my first husband, I used to go out in the *monde*, it was my life. In those days I loved it. But then Christian didn't approve of it, he stopped me going to parties and frightened away my friends, whom he considered frivolous and idiotic, and we saw nothing but serious people trying to put the world right. I used to laugh at them, and rather long for my other friends, but now I don't know. Since I was at Perpignan perhaps I have become more serious myself.'

'Everybody is getting more serious, that's the way things are going. But, whatever one may be in politics, right, left, Fascist, Communist, *les gens du monde* are the only possible ones for friends. You see, they have made a fine art of personal relationships and of all that pertains to them—manners, clothes, beautiful houses, good food, everything that makes life agreeable. It would be silly not to take advantage of that. Friendship is something to be built up carefully, by people with leisure, it is an art, nature does not enter into it. You should never despise social life—*de la haute société*—I mean, it can be a very satisfying one,

entirely artificial of course, but absorbing. Apart from the life of the
intellect and the contemplative religious life, which few people are
qualified to enjoy, what else is there to distinguish man from the animals
but his social life? And who understand it so well and who can make it
so smooth and so amusing as *les gens du monde*? But one cannot have it
at the same time as a love affair, one must be whole-hearted to enjoy it,
so I have cancelled all my engagements.'

'What a pity,' said Linda, 'because I'm going back to London tomorrow morning.'

'Ah yes, I had forgotten. What a pity.'

'Allô—allô.'

'Hullo.'

'Were you asleep?'

'Yes, of course. What's the time?'

'About two. Shall I come round and see you?'

'Do you mean now?'

'Yes.'

'I must say it would be very nice, but the only thing is, what would
the night porter think?'

'Ma chère, how English you are. *Eh bien, je vais vous le dire—il ne se fera
aucune illusion.'*

'No, I suppose not.'

'But I don't imagine he's under any illusion as it is. After all, I come
here for you three times every day—you've seen nobody else, and
French people are quite quick at noticing these things, you know.'

'Yes,—I see——'

'Alors, c'est entendu—à tout à l'heure.'

The next day Fabrice installed her in a flat, he said it was *plus commode.* He said, 'When I was young I liked to be very romantic and run
all kinds of risks. I used to hide in wardrobes, be brought into the house
in a trunk, disguise myself as a footman, and climb in at windows. How
I used to climb! I remember once, halfway up a creeper there was a
wasps' nest—oh the agony—I wore a Kestos *soutien-gorge* for a week
afterwards. But now I prefer to be comfortable, to follow a certain
routine, and have my own key.'

Indeed, Linda thought, nobody could be less romantic and more
practical than Fabrice, no nonsense about him. A little nonsense, she
thought, would have been rather nice.

It was a beautiful flat, large and sunny, and decorated in the most
expensive kind of modern taste. It faced south and west over the Bois de
Boulogne, and was on a level with the tree-tops. Tree-tops and sky
made up the view. The enormous windows worked like windows of a
motor-car, the whole of the glass disappearing into the wall. This was

a great joy to Linda, who loved the open air and loved to sunbathe for hours with no clothes on, until she was hot and brown and sleepy and happy. Belonging to the flat, belonging, it was evident, to Fabrice, was a charming elderly *femme de ménage* called Germaine. She was assisted by various other elderly women who came and went in a bewildering succession. She was obviously most efficient, she had all Linda's things out of her suitcase, ironed and folded away, in a moment, and then went off to the kitchen, where she began to prepare dinner. Linda could not help wondering how many other people Fabrice had kept in this flat; however, as she was unlikely to find out, and, indeed, had no wish to know, she put the thought from her. There was no trace of any former occupant, not so much as a scribbled telephone number, or the mark of a lipstick anywhere to be seen; the flat might have been done up yesterday.

In her bath, before dinner, Linda thought rather wistfully of Aunt Sadie. She, Linda, was now a kept woman and an adulteress, and Aunt Sadie, she knew, wouldn't like that. She hadn't liked it when Linda had committed adultery with Christian, but he, at least, was English, and Linda had been properly introduced to him and knew his surname. Also, Christian had all along intended to marry her. But how much less would Aunt Sadie like her daughter to pick up an unknown, nameless foreigner and go off to live with him in luxury. It was a long step from lunching in Oxford to this, though Uncle Matthew would, no doubt, have considered it a step down the same road if he knew her situation, and he would disown her for ever, throw her out into the snow, shoot Fabrice, or take any other violent action which might occur to him. Then something would happen to make him laugh, and all would be well again. Aunt Sadie was a different matter. She would not say very much, but she would brood over it and take it to heart, and wonder if there had not been something wrong about her method of bringing up Linda which had led to this; Linda most profoundly hoped that she would never find out.

In the middle of this reverie the telephone bell rang. Germaine answered it, tapped on the bathroom door, and said:

'*M. le duc sera légèrement en retard, madame.*'

'All right—thank you,' said Linda.

At dinner she said:

'Could one know your name?'

'Oh,' said Fabrice. 'Hadn't you discovered that? What an extraordinary lack of curiosity. My name is Sauveterre. In short, *madame*, I am happy to tell you that I am a very rich duke, a most agreeable thing to be, even in these days.'

'How lovely for you. And, while we are on the subject of your private life, are you married?'

'No.'

'Why not?'

'My fiancée died.'

'Oh, how sad—what was she like?'

'Very pretty.'

'Prettier than me?'

'Much prettier. Very correct.'

'More correct than me?'

'*Vous—vous êtes une folle, madame, aucune correction. Et elle était gentille— mais d'une gentillesse, la pauvre.*'

For the first time since she knew him, Fabrice had become infinitely sentimental, and Linda was suddenly shaken by the pangs of a terrible jealousy, so terrible that she felt quite faint. If she had not already recognized the fact, she would have known now, for certain and always, that this was to be the great love of her life.

'Five years,' she said, 'is quite a long time when it's all in front of you.'

But Fabrice was still thinking of the fiancée.

'She died much more than five years ago—fifteen years in the autumn. I always go and put late roses on her grave, those little tight roses with very dark green leaves that never open properly—they remind me of her. *Dieu, que c'est triste.*'

'And what was her name?' said Linda.

'Louise. *Enfant unique du dernier Rancé.* I often go and see her mother, who is still alive, a remarkable old woman. She was brought up in England at the court of the Empress Eugénie, and Rancé married her in spite of that, for love. You can imagine how strange everybody found it.'

A deep melancholy settled on them both. Linda saw too clearly that she could not hope to compete with a fiancée who was not only prettier and more correct than she was, but also dead. It seemed most unfair. Had she remained alive her prettiness would surely, after fifteen years of marriage, have faded away, her correctness have become a bore; dead, she was embalmed for ever in her youth, her beauty, and her *gentillesse.*

After dinner, however, Linda was restored to happiness. Being made love to by Fabrice was an intoxication, quite different from anything she had hitherto experienced.

('I was forced to the conclusion,' she said, when telling me about this time, 'that neither Tony nor Christian had an inkling of what we used to call the facts of life. But I suppose all Englishmen are hopeless as lovers.'

'Not all,' I said, 'the trouble with most of them is that their minds are not on it, and it happens to require a very great deal of application. Alfred,' I told her, 'is wonderful.'

'Oh, good,' she said, but she sounded unconvinced I thought.)

They sat until late looking out of the open window. It was a hot evening, and, when the sun had gone, a green light lingered behind the black bunches of the trees until complete darkness fell.

'Do you always laugh when you make love?' said Fabrice.

'I hadn't thought about it, but I suppose I do. I generally laugh when I'm happy and cry when I'm not. I am a simple character, you know. Do you find it odd?'

'Very disconcerting at first, I must say.'

'But why—don't most women laugh?'

'Indeed, they do not. More often they cry.'

'How extraordinary—don't they enjoy it?'

'It has nothing to do with enjoyment. If they are young they call on their mothers, if they are religious they call on the Virgin to forgive them. But I have never known one who laughed except you. *Mais qu'est ce que vous voulez, vous êtes une folle.*'

Linda was fascinated.

'What else do they do?'

'What they all do, except you, is to say: "*Comme vous devez me mépriser*".'

'But why should you despise them?'

'Oh, really, my dear, one does, that's all.'

'Well, I call that most unfair. First you seduce them, then you despise them, poor things. What a monster you are.'

'They like it. They like grovelling about and saying "*Qu'est ce que j'ai fait? Mon Dieu, hélas Fabrice, que pouvez-bien penser de moi? O, que j'ai honte.*" It's all part of the thing to them. But you, you seem unaware of your shame, you just roar with laughter. It is very strange. *Pas désagréable, il faut avouer.*'

'Then what about the fiancée,' said Linda, 'didn't you despise her?'

'*Mais non, voyons*, of course not. She was a virtuous woman.'

'Do you mean to say you never went to bed with her?'

'Never. Never would such a thing have crossed my mind in a thousand thousand years.'

'Goodness,' said Linda. 'In England we always do.'

'*Ma chère, c'est bien connu, le côté animal des anglais.* The English are a drunken and an incontinent race, it is well known.'

'They don't know it. They think it's foreigners who are all those things.'

'French women are the most virtuous in the world,' said Fabrice, in the tones of exaggerated pride with which Frenchmen always talk about their women.

'Oh, dear,' said Linda sadly. 'I was so virtuous once. I wonder what happened to me. I went wrong when I married my first husband, but how was I to know? I thought he was a god and that I should love him for ever. Then I went wrong again when I ran away with Christian, but I thought I loved him, and I did too, much much more than Tony, but he never really loved me, and very soon I bored him, I wasn't serious enough, I suppose. Anyhow, if I hadn't done these things, I shouldn't have ended up on a suitcase at the Gare du Nord and I would never have met you, so, really, I'm glad. And in my next life, wherever I happen to be born, I must remember to fly to the boulevards as soon as I'm of marriageable age, and find a husband there.'

'*Comme c'est gentil*,' said Fabrice, '*et, en effet*, French marriages are generally very very happy you know. My father and mother had a cloudless life together, they loved each other so much that they hardly went out in society at all. My mother still lives in a sort of afterglow of happiness from it. What a good woman she is!'

'I must tell you,' Linda went on, 'that my mother and one of my aunts, one of my sisters and my cousin, are virtuous women, so virtue is not unknown in my family. And anyway, Fabrice, what about your grandmother?'

'Yes,' said Fabrice, with a sigh. 'I admit that she was a great sinner. But she was also *très grande dame*, and she died fully redeemed by the rites of the Church.'

CHAPTER XVIII

THEIR life now began to acquire a routine. Fabrice dined with her every night in the flat—he never took her out to a restaurant again—and stayed with her until seven o'clock the following morning. '*J'ai horreur de coucher seul*,' he said. At seven he would get up, dress, and go home, in time to be in his bed at eight o'clock, when his breakfast was brought in. He would have his breakfast, read the newspapers, and, at nine, ring up Linda and talk nonsense for half an hour, as though he had not seen her for days.

'Go on,' he would say, if she showed any signs of flagging. '*Allons, des histoires!*'

During the day she hardly ever saw him. He always lunched with his mother, who had the first-floor flat in the house where he lived on the ground floor. Sometimes he took Linda sight-seeing in the afternoon, but generally he did not appear until about half-past seven, soon after which they dined.

Linda occupied her days buying clothes, which she paid for with great wads of banknotes given her by Fabrice.

'Might as well be hanged for a sheep as a lamb,' she thought. 'And as he despises me anyway it can't make very much difference.'

Fabrice was delighted. He took an intense interest in her clothes, looked them up and down, made her parade round her drawing-room in them, forced her to take them back to the shops for alterations which seemed to her quite unnecessary, but which proved in the end to have made all the difference. Linda had never before fully realized the superiority of French clothes to English. In London she had been considered exceptionally well dressed, when she was married to Tony; she now realized that never could she have had, by French standards, the smallest pretensions to *chic*. The things she had with her seemed to her so appallingly dowdy, so skimpy and miserable and without line, that she went to the Galeries Lafayette and bought herself a ready-made dress there before she dared to venture into the big houses. When she did finally emerge from them with a few clothes, Fabrice advised her to get a great many more. Her taste, he said, was not at all bad, for an Englishwoman, though he doubted whether she would really become *élégante* in the true sense of the word.

'Only by trial and error,' he said, 'can you find out your *genre*, can you see where you are going. *Continuez, donc, ma chère, allez-y. Jusqu'à présent, ça ne vas pas mal du tout.*'

The weather now became hot and sultry, holiday, seaside weather. But this was 1939, and men's thoughts were not of relaxation but of death, not of bathing-suits but of uniforms, not of dance music but of trumpets, while beaches for the next few years were to be battle and not pleasure grounds. Fabrice said every day how much he longed to take Linda to the Riviera, to Venice and to his beautiful château in the Dauphiné. But he was a reservist, and would be called up any day now. Linda did not mind staying in Paris at all. She could sunbathe in her flat as much as she wanted to. She felt no particular apprehensions about the coming war, she was essentially a person who lived in the present.

'I couldn't sunbathe naked like this anywhere else,' she said, 'and it's the only holiday thing I enjoy. I don't like swimming, or tennis, or dancing, or gambling, so you see I'm just as well off here sunbathing and shopping, two perfect occupations for the day, and you, my darling love, at night. I should think I'm the happiest woman in the world.'

One boiling hot afternoon in July she arrived home wearing a new and particularly ravishing straw hat. It was large and simple, with a wreath of flowers and two blue bows. Her right arm was full of roses and carnations, and in her left hand was a striped bandbox, containing another exquisite hat. She let herself in with her latchkey, and stumped, on the high cork soles of her sandals, to the drawing-room.

The green venetian blinds were down, and the room was full of warm shadows, two of which suddenly resolved themselves into a thin man and a not so thin man—Davey and Lord Merlin.

'Good heavens,' said Linda, and she flopped down on to a sofa, scattering the roses at her feet.

'Well,' said Davey, 'you do look pretty.'

Linda felt really frightened, like a child caught out in some misdeed, like a child whose new toy is going to be taken away. She looked from one to the other. Lord Merlin was wearing black spectacles.

'Are you in disguise?' said Linda.

'No, what do you mean? Oh, the spectacles—I have to wear them when I go abroad, I have such kind eyes you see, beggars and things cluster round and annoy me.'

He took them off and blinked.

'What have you come for?'

'You don't seem very pleased to see us,' said Davey. 'We came, actually, to see if you were all right. As it's only too obvious that you are, we may as well go away again.'

'How did you find out? Do Mummy and Fa know?' she added, faintly.

'No, absolutely nothing. They think you're still with Christian. We haven't come in the spirit of two Victorian uncles, my dear Linda, if that's what you're thinking. I happened to see a man I know who had been to Perpignan, and he mentioned that Christian was living with Lavender Davis——'

'Oh good,' said Linda.

'What? And that you had left six weeks ago. I went round to Cheyne Walk and there you obviously weren't, and then Mer and I got faintly worried to think of you wandering about the Continent, so ill suited (we thought, how wrong we were) to look after yourself, and at the same time madly curious to know your whereabouts and present circumstances, so we put in motion a little discreet detective work, which revealed your whereabouts—your circumstances are now as clear as daylight, and I, for one, feel most relieved.'

'You gave us a fright,' said Lord Merlin crossly. 'Another time, when you are putting on this Cléo de Mérode act, you might send a postcard. For one thing, it is a great pleasure to see you in the part, I wouldn't have missed it for worlds. I hadn't realized, Linda, that you were such a beautiful woman.'

Davey was laughing quietly to himself.

'Oh, goodness, how funny it all is—so wonderfully old-fashioned. The shopping! The parcels! The flowers! So tremendously Victorian. People have been delivering cardboard boxes every five minutes since we arrived. What an interest you are in one's life, Linda dear. Have you told him he must give you up and marry a pure young girl yet?'

Linda said disarmingly: 'Don't tease, Dave. I'm *so* happy you can't think.'

'Yes, you look happy I must say. Oh, this flat is such a joke.'

'I was just thinking,' said Lord Merlin, 'that, however much taste may change, it always follows a stereotyped plan. Frenchmen used to keep their mistresses in *appartements*, each exactly like the other, in which the dominant note, you might say, was lace and velvet. The walls, the bed, the dressing-table, the very bath itself was hung with lace, and everything else was velvet. Nowadays for lace you substitute glass, and everything else is satin. I bet you've got a glass bed, Linda?'

'Yes—but——'

'And a glass dressing-table, and bathroom, and I wouldn't be surprised if your bath were made of glass, with goldfish swimming about in the sides of it. Goldfish are a prevailing motif all down the ages.'

'You've looked,' said Linda sulkily. 'Very clever.'

'Oh, what heaven,' said Davey. 'So it's true! He hasn't looked, I swear, but you see it's not beyond the bounds of human ingenuity to guess.'

'But there are some things here,' said Lord Merlin, 'which do raise the level, all the same. A Gauguin, those two Matisses (chintzy, but accomplished) and this Savonnerie carpet. Your protector must be very rich.'

'He is,' said Linda.

'Then, Linda dear, could one ask for a cup of tea?'

She rang the bell, and soon Davey was falling upon *éclairs* and *mille feuilles* with all the abandon of a schoolboy.

'I shall pay for this,' he said, with a devil-may-care smile, 'but never mind, one's not in Paris every day.'

Lord Merlin wandered round with his tea-cup. He picked up a book which Fabrice had given Linda the day before, of romantic nineteenth-century poetry.

'Is this what you're reading now?' he said. ' "*Dieu, que le son du cor est triste au fond des bois.*" I had a friend, when I lived in Paris, who had a boa constrictor as a pet, and this boa constrictor got itself inside a French horn. My friend rang me up in a fearful state, saying: "*Dieu, que le son du boa est triste au fond du cor.*" I've never forgotten it.'

'What time does your lover generally arrrive?' said Davey, taking out his watch.

'Not till about seven. Do stay and see him, he's such a terrific Hon.'

'No, thank you, not for the world.'

'Who is he?' said Lord Merlin.

'He's called the Duke of Sauveterre.'

A look of great surprise, mingled with horrified amusement, passed between Davey and Lord Merlin.

'Fabrice de Sauveterre?'

'Yes. Do you know him?'

'Darling Linda, one always forgets, under that look of great sophistication, what a little provincial you really are. Of course we know him, and all about him, and, what's more, so does everyone except you.'

'Well, don't you think he's a terrific Hon?'

'Fabrice,' said Lord Merlin with emphasis, 'is undoubtedly one of the wickedest men in Europe, as far as women are concerned. But I must admit that he's an extremely agreeable companion.'

'Do you remember in Venice,' said Davey, 'one used to see him at work in that gondola, one after another, bowling them over like rabbits, poor dears?'

'Please remember,' said Linda, 'that you are eating his tea at this moment.'

'Yes, indeed, and so delicious. Another *éclair*, please, Linda. That summer,' he went on, 'when he made off with Ciano's girl friend, what a fuss there was, I never shall forget, and then, a week later, he *plaqué-*'d her in Cannes and went to Salzburg with Martha Birmingham, and poor old Claud shot at him four times, and always missed him.'

'Fabrice has a charmed life,' said Lord Merlin. 'I suppose he has been shot at more than anybody, and, as far as I know, he's never had a scratch.'

Linda was unmoved by these revelations, which had been forestalled by Fabrice himself. Anyhow, no woman really minds hearing of the past affairs of her lover, it is the future alone that has the power to terrify.

'Come on, Mer,' said Davey. 'Time the *petite femme* got herself into a *négligée*. Goodness, what a scene there'll be when he smells Mer's cigar, there'll be a *crime passionel*, I shouldn't wonder. Good-bye, Linda darling, we're off to dine with our intellectual friends, you know, will you be lunching with us at the Ritz to-morrow? About one, then. Good-bye—give our love to Fabrice.'

When Fabrice came in he sniffed about, and asked whose cigar. Linda explained.

'They say they know you?'

'*Mais bien sûr—Merlin, tellement gentil, et l'autre Warbeck, toujours si malade, le pauvre. Je les connaissais à Venise.* What did they think of all this?'

'Well, they roared at the flat.'

'Yes, I can imagine. It is quite unsuitable for you, this flat, but it's convenient, and with the war coming——'

'Oh, but I love it. I wouldn't like anything else half so much. Wasn't it clever of them, though, to find me?'

'Do you mean to say you never told anybody where you were?'

'I really didn't think of it—the days go by, you know—one simply doesn't remember these things.'

'And it was six weeks before they thought of looking for you? As a family you seem to me strangely *décousu*.'

Linda suddenly threw herself into his arms, and said, with great passion:

'Never, never let me go back to them.'

'My darling—but you love them. Mummy and Fa, Matt and Robin and Victoria and Fanny. What is all this?'

'I never want to leave you again as long as I live.'

'Aha! But you know you will probably have to, soon. The war is going to begin, you know.'

'Why can't I stay here? I could work—I could become a nurse—well, perhaps not a nurse, actually, but something.'

'If you promise to do what I tell you, you may stay here for a time. At the beginning we shall sit and look at the Germans across the Maginot Line, then I shall be a great deal in Paris, between Paris and the front, but mostly here. At that time I shall want you here. Then somebody, we or the Germans, but I am very much afraid the Germans, will pour across the line, and a war of movement will begin. I shall have notice of that *étape*, and what you must promise me is that the very minute I tell you to leave for London you will leave, even if you can see no reason for doing so. I should be hampered beyond words in my duties if you were still here. So will you solemnly promise, now?'

'All right,' said Linda. 'Solemnly. I don't believe anything so dreadful could happen to me, but I promise to do as you say. Now will you promise that you will come to London as soon as it's all over and find me again. Promise?'

'Yes,' said Fabrice. 'I will do that.'

Luncheon with Davey and Lord Merlin was a gloomy meal. Preoccupation reigned. The two men had stayed up late and merrily with their literary friends, and showed every sign of having done so. Davey was beginning to be aware of the cruel pangs of dyspepsia, Lord Merlin was suffering badly from an ordinary straightforward hangover, and, when he removed his spectacles, his eyes were seen to be not kind at all. But Linda was far the most wretched of the three, she was, in fact, perfectly distracted by having overheard two French ladies in the foyer talking about Fabrice. She had arrived, as, from old habits of punctuality drummed into her by Uncle Matthew she always did, rather early. Fabrice had never taken her to the Ritz, she thought it delightful, she knew she was looking quite as pretty, and nearly as well dressed, as anybody there, and settled herself happily to await the others. Suddenly she heard, with that pang which the heart receives when the loved one's name is mentioned by strangers:

'And have you seen Fabrice at all?'

'Well, I have, because I quite often see him at Mme de Sauveterre's, but he never goes out anywhere, as you know.'

'Then what about Jacqueline?'

'Still in England. He is utterly lost without her, poor Fabrice, he is like a dog looking for its master. He sits sadly at home, never goes to parties, never goes to the club, sees nobody. His mother is really worried about him.'

'Who would ever have expected Fabrice to be so faithful? How long is it?'

'Five years, I believe. A wonderfully happy *ménage.*'

'Surely Jacqueline will come back soon.'

'Not until the old aunt has died. It seems she changes her will incessantly, and Jacqueline feels she must be there all the time—after all, she has her husband and children to consider.'

'Rather hard on Fabrice?'

'*Qu-est-ce que vous voulez?* His mother says he rings her up every morning and talks for an hour——'

It was at this point that Davey and Lord Merlin, looking tired and cross, arrived, and took Linda off to luncheon with them. She was longing to stay and hear more of this torturing conversation, but, eschewing cocktails with a shudder, they hurried her off to the dining-room, where they were only fairly nice to her, and frankly disagreeable to each other.

She thought the meal would never come to an end, and, when at last it did, she threw herself into a taxi and drove to Fabrice's house. She must find out about Jacqueline, she must know his intentions. When Jacqueline returned would that be the moment for her, Linda, to leave as she had promised? War of movement indeed!

The servant said that M. le Duc had just gone out with Madame la Duchesse, but that he would be back in about an hour. Linda said she would wait, and he showed her into Fabrice's sitting-room. She took off her hat, and wandered restlessly about. She had been here several times before, with Fabrice, and it had seemed, after her brilliantly sunny flat, a little dismal. Now that she was alone in it she began to be aware of the extreme beauty of the room, a grave and solemn beauty which penetrated her. It was very high, rectangular in shape, with grey boiseries and cherry-coloured brocade curtains. It looked into a courtyard and never could get a ray of sunshine, that was not the plan. This was a civilized interior, it had nothing to do with out-of-doors. Every object in it was perfect. The furniture had the severe lines and excellent proportions of 1780, there was a portrait by Lancret of a lady with a parrot on her wrist, a bust of the same lady by Bouchardon, a carpet like the one in Linda's flat, but larger and grander, with a huge coat of arms in the middle. A high carved bookcase contained nothing but French classics bound in contemporary morocco, with the Sauveterre crest, and open on a map table lay a copy of Redouté's roses.

Linda began to feel much more calm, but, at the same time, very sad. She saw that this room indicated a side of Fabrice's character which she had hardly been allowed to apprehend, and which had its roots in old civilized French grandeur. It was the essential Fabrice, something in which she could never have a share—she would always be outside in her sunny modern flat, kept away from all this, kept rigidly away even if their liaison were to go on for ever. The origins of the Radlett family were lost in the mists of antiquity, but the origins of Fabrice's family were not lost at all, there they were, each generation clutching at the next. The English, she thought, throw off their ancestors. It is the great strength of our aristocracy, but Fabrice has his round his neck, and he will never get away from them.

She began to realize that here were her competitors, her enemies, and that Jacqueline was nothing in comparison. Here, and in the grave of Louise. To come here and make a scene about a rival mistress would be utterly meaningless, she would be one unreality complaining about another. Fabrice would be annoyed, as men always are annoyed on these occasions, and she would get no satisfaction. She could hear his voice, dry and sarcastic:

'Ah! *Vous me grondez, madame?*'

Better go, better ignore the whole affair. Her only hope was to keep things on their present footing, to keep the happiness which she was enjoying day by day, hour by hour, and not to think about the future at all. It held nothing for her, leave it alone. Besides, everybody's future was in jeopardy now the war was coming, this war which she always forgot about.

She was reminded of it, however, when, that evening, Fabrice appeared in uniform.

'Another month I should think,' he said. 'As soon as they have got the harvest in.'

'If it depended on the English,' said Linda, 'they would wait until after the Christmas shopping. Oh, Fabrice, it won't last very long, will it?'

'It will be very disagreeable while it does last,' said Fabrice. 'Did you come to my flat today?'

'Yes, after lunching with those two old cross-patches I suddenly felt I wanted to see you very much.'

'*Comme c'est gentil,*' he looked at her quizzically, as though something had occurred to him, 'but why didn't you wait?'

'Your ancestors frightened me off.'

'Oh, they did? But you have ancestors yourself I believe, *madame?*'

'Yes, but they don't hang about in the same way as yours do.'

'You should have waited,' said Fabrice, 'it is always a very great pleasure to see you, both for me and for my ancestors. It cheers us all up.'

Germaine now came into the room with huge armfuls of flowers and a note from Lord Merlin, saying:

'Here are some coals for Newcastle. We are tottering home by the ferry-boat. Do you think I shall get Davey back alive? I enclose something which might, one day, be useful.'

It was a note for 20,000 francs.

'I must say,' said Linda, 'considering what cruel eyes he has, he does think of everything.'

She felt sentimental after the occurrences of the day.

'Tell me, Fabrice,' she said, 'what did you think the first moment you ever saw me?'

'If you really want to know, I thought: "*Tiens, elle ressemble à la petite Bosquet*".'

'Who is that?'

'There are two Bosquet sisters, the elder, who is a beauty, and a little one who looks like you.'

'*Merci beaucoup*,' said Linda, '*J'aimerais autant ressembler à l'autre.*'

Fabrice laughed. '*Ensuite, je me suis dit, comme c'est amusant, le côté demodé de tout ça*——'

When the war, which had for so long been pending, did actually break out some six weeks later, Linda was strangely unmoved by the fact. She was enveloped in the present, in her own detached and future-less life, which, anyhow, seemed so precarious, so much from one hour to another: exterior events hardly impinged on her consciousness. When she thought about the war it seemed to her almost a relief that it had actually begun, in so far as a beginning is the first step towards an end. That it had only begun in name and not in fact did not occur to her. Of course, had Fabrice been taken away by it her attitude would have been very different, but his job, an intelligence one, kept him mostly in Paris, and, indeed, she now saw rather more of him than formerly, as he moved into her flat, shutting up his own and sending his mother to the country. He would appear and disappear at all sorts of odd moments of the night and day, and, as the sight of him was a constant joy to Linda, as she could imagine no greater happiness than she always felt when the empty space in front of her eyes became filled by his form, these sudden apparitions kept her in a state of happy suspense and their relationship at fever point.

Since Davey's visit Linda had been getting letters from her family. He had given Aunt Sadie her address and told her that Linda was doing war work in Paris, providing comforts for the French army, he said vaguely, and with some degree of truth. Aunt Sadie was pleased about this, she thought it very good of Linda to work so hard (all night sometimes, Davey said), and was glad to hear that she earned her keep. Voluntary work was often unsatisfactory and expensive. Uncle Matthew thought it a pity to work for foreigners, and deplored the fact that his children were so fond of crossing oceans, but he also was very much in favour of war work. He was himself utterly disgusted that the War Office were not able to offer him the opportunity of repeating his exploit with the entrenching tool, or, indeed, any job at all, and he went about like a bear with a sore head, full of unsatisfied desire to fight for his King and country.

I wrote to Linda and told her about Christian, who was back in London, had left the Communist party and had joined up. Lavender had also returned: she was now in the A.T.S.

Christian did not show the slightest curiosity about what had happened to Linda; he did not seem to want to divorce her or to marry Lavender, he had thrown himself heart and soul into army life and thought of nothing but the war.

Before leaving Perpignan he had extricated Matt, who, after a good deal of persuasion, had consented to leave his Spanish comrades in order to join the battle against Fascism on another front. He went into Uncle Matthew's old regiment, and was said to bore his brother officers in the mess very much by arguing that they were training the men all wrong, and that, during the battle of the Ebro, things had been done thus and thus. In the end, his colonel, who was rather brighter in the head than some of the others, hit upon the obvious reply, which was, 'Well anyway, your side lost!' This shut Matt up on tactics, but got him going on statistics—'30,000 Germans and Italians, 500 German planes,' and so forth—which was almost equally dull and boring.

Linda heard no more about Jacqueline, and the wretchedness into which she had been thrown by those few chance words overheard at the Ritz was gradually forgotten. She reminded herself that nobody ever really knew the state of a man's heart, not even, perhaps specially not, his mother, and that in love it is actions that count. Fabrice had no time now for two women, he spent every spare moment with her and that in itself reassured her. Besides, just as her marriages with Tony and Christian had been necessary in order to lead up to her meeting with Fabrice, so this affair had led up to his meeting with her: undoubtedly he must have been seeing Jacqueline off at the Gare du Nord when he found Linda crying on her suitcase. Putting herself in Jacqueline's shoes, she realized how much preferable it was to be in her own: in any case it was not Jacqueline who was her dangerous rival, but that dim, virtuous figure from the past, Louise. Whenever Fabrice showed signs of becoming a little less practical, a little more nonsensical and romantic, it was of his fiancée that he would speak, dwelling with a gent'-sadness upon her beauty, her noble birth, her vast estates and her religious mania. Linda once suggested that, had the fiancée lived to become a wife, she might not have been a very happy one.

'All that climbing,' she said, 'in at other people's bedroom windows, might it not have upset her?'

Fabrice looked intensely shocked and reproachful and said that there never would have been any climbing, that, where marriage was concerned, he had the very highest ideals, and that his whole life would have been devoted to making Louise happy. Linda felt herself rebuked, but was not entirely convinced.

All this time Linda watched the tree-tops from her window. They had changed, since she had been in the flat, from bright green against a bright blue sky, to dark green against a lavender sky, to yellow against a cerulean sky, until now they were black skeletons against a sky of moleskin, and it was Christmas Day. The windows could no longer be opened until they disappeared, but, whenever the sun did come out, it shone into her rooms, and the flat was always as warm as a toast. On this Christmas morning Fabrice arrived, quite unexpectedly, before she was up, his arms full of parcels, and soon the floor of her bedroom was covered with waves of tissue paper through which, like wrecks and monsters half submerged beneath a shallow sea, appeared fur coats, hats, real mimosa, artificial flowers, feathers, scent, gloves, stockings, underclothes and a bulldog puppy.

Linda had spent Lord Merlin's 20,000 francs on a tiny Renoir for Fabrice : six inches of seascape, a little patch of brilliant blue, which she thought would look just right in his room in the Rue Bonaparte. Fabrice was the most difficult person to buy presents for, he possessed a larger assortment of jewels, knick-knacks and rare objects of all kinds than anybody she had ever known. He was delighted with the Renoir, nothing, he said, could have pleased him more, and Linda felt that he really meant it.

'Oh, such a cold day,' he said. 'I've just been to church.'

'Fabrice, how can you go to church when there's me?'

'Well, why not.'

'You're a Roman Catholic, aren't you?'

'Of course I am. What do you suppose? Do you think I look like a Calvinist?'

'But then aren't you living in mortal sin? So what about when you confess?'

'*On ne précise pas*,' said Fabrice carelessly, 'and, in any case, these little sins of the body are quite unimportant.'

Linda would have liked to think that she was more in Fabrice's life than a little sin of the body, but she was used to coming up against these closed doors in her relationship with him, and had learnt to be philosophical about it and thankful for the happiness that she did receive.

'In England,' she said, 'people are always renouncing each other on account of being Roman Catholics. It's sometimes very sad for them. A lot of English books are about this, you know.'

'*Les Anglais sont des insensés, je l'ai toujours dit*. You almost sound as if you want to be given up. What has happened since Saturday? Not tired of your war work, I hope?'

'No, no, Fabrice. I just wondered, that's all.'

'But you look so sad, *ma chérie*, what is it?'

'I was thinking of Christmas Day at home, I always feel sentimental at Christmas.'

'If what I said might happen does happen and I have to send you back to England, shall you go home to your father?'

'Oh, no,' said Linda, 'anyway, it won't happen. All the English papers say we are killing Germany with our blockade.'

'*Le blocus*,' said Fabrice impatiently, '*quelle blague! Je vais vous dire, madame, ils ne se fichent pas mal de votre blocus*. So where would you go?'

'To my own house in Chelsea, and wait for you to come.'

'It might be months, or years.'

'I shall wait,' she said.

The skeleton tree-tops began to fill out, they acquired a pinkish tinge, which gradually changed to golden-green. The sky was often blue, and, on some days, Linda could once more open her windows and lie naked in the sun, whose rays by now had a certain strength. She always loved the spring, she loved the sudden changes of temperature, the dips backward into winter and forward into summer, and, this year, living in beautiful Paris, her perceptions heightened by great emotion, she was profoundly affected by it. There was now a curious feeling in the air, very different from and much more nervous than that which had been current before Christmas, and the town was full of rumours. Linda often thought of the expression '*fin de siècle*'. There was a certain analogy, she thought, between the state of mind which it denoted and that prevailing now, only now it was more like '*fin de vie*'. It was as though everybody around her, and she herself, were living out the last few days of their lives, but this curious feeling did not disturb her, she was possessed by a calm and happy fatalism. She occupied the hours of waiting between Fabrice's visits by lying in the sun, when there was any, and playing with her puppy. On Fabrice's advice she even began to order some new clothes for the summer. He seemed to regard the acquisition of clothes as one of the chief duties of woman, to be pursued through war and revolution, through sickness, and up to death. It was as one who might say, 'whatever happens the fields must be tilled, the cattle tended, life must go on'. He was so essentially urban that to him the slow roll of the seasons was marked by the spring *tailleurs*, the summer *imprimés*, the autumn *ensembles*, and the winter furs of his mistress.

On a beautiful windy blue and white day in April the blow fell. Fabrice, whom Linda had not seen for nearly a week, arrived from the front looking grave and worried, and told her that she must go back to England at once.

'I've got a place for you in the aeroplane,' he said, 'for this afternoon.

You must pack a small suitcase, and the rest of your things must go after you by train. Germaine will see to them. I have to go to the Ministère de la Guerre, I'll be back as soon as possible, and anyhow in time to take you to Le Bourget. Come on,' he added, 'just time for a little war work.' He was in his most practical and least romantic mood.

When he returned he looked more preoccupied than ever. Linda was waiting for him, her box was packed, she was wearing the blue suit in which he had first seen her, and had her old mink coat over her arm.

'*Tiens*,' said Fabrice, who always at once noticed what she had on, 'what is this? A fancy-dress party?'

'Fabrice, you must understand that I can't take away the things you have given me. I loved having them while I was here, and while they gave you pleasure seeing me in them, but, after all, I have some pride. *Je n'étais quand-même pas élevée dans un bordel.*'

'*Ma chère*, try not to be so middle-class, it doesn't suit you at all. There's no time for you to change—wait, though——' He went into her bedroom, and came out again with a long sable coat, one of his Christmas presents. He took her mink coat, rolled it up, threw it into the waste-paper basket, and put the other over her arm in its place.

'Germaine will send your things after you,' he said. 'Come now, we must go.'

Linda said good-bye to Germaine, picked up the bulldog puppy, and followed Fabrice into the lift, out into the street. She did not fully understand that she was leaving that happy life behind her for ever.

CHAPTER XIX

At first, back in Cheyne Walk, she still did not understand. The world was grey and cold certainly, the sun had gone behind a cloud, but only for a time: it would come out again, she would soon once more be enveloped in that heat and light which had left her in so warm a glow, there was still much blue in the sky, this little cloud would pass. Then, as sometimes happens, the cloud, which had seemed at first such a little one, grew and grew, until it became a thick grey blanket smothering the horizon. The bad news began, the terrible days, the unforgettable weeks. A great horror of steel was rolling over France, was rolling towards England, swallowing on its way the puny beings who tried to stop it, swallowing Fabrice, Germaine, the flat, and the past months of Linda's life, swallowing Alfred, Bob, Matt, and little Robin, coming to swallow us all. London people cried openly in the buses, in the streets, for the English army which was lost.

Then, suddenly one day, the English army turned up again. There was a feeling of such intense relief, it was as if the war were over and won. Alfred and Bob and Matt and little Robin all reappeared, and, as a lot of French soldiers also arrived, Linda had a wild hope that Fabrice might be with them. She sat all day by the telephone, and when it rang and was not Fabrice she was furious with the unlucky telephoner—I know, because it happened to me. She was so furious that I dropped the receiver and went straight round to Cheyne Walk.

I found her unpacking a huge trunk, which had just arrived from France. I had never seen her looking so beautiful. It made me gasp, and I remembered how Davey had said, when he got back from Paris, that at last Linda was fulfilling the promise of her childhood, and had become a beauty.

'How do you imagine this got here?' she said, between tears and laughter. 'What an extraordinary war. The Southern Railway people brought it just now and I signed for it, all as though nothing peculiar were happening—I don't understand a word of it. What are you doing in London, darling?'

She seemed unaware of the fact that half an hour ago she had spoken to me, and indeed bitten my head off, on the telephone.

'I'm with Alfred. He's got to get a lot of new equipment and see all sorts of people. I believe he's going abroad again very soon.'

'Awfully good of him,' said Linda, 'when he needn't have joined up at all, I imagine. What does he say about Dunkirk?'

'He says it was like something out of the *Boy's Own*—he seems to have had a most fascinating time.'

'They all did, the boys were here yesterday and you never heard anything like their stories. Of course they never quite realized how desperate it all was until they got to the coast. Oh, isn't it wonderful to have them back. If only—if only one knew what had happened to one's French buddies——' She looked at me under her eyelashes, and I thought she was going to tell me about her life, but, if so, she changed her mind and went on unpacking.

'I shall have to put these winter things back in their boxes really,' she said. 'I simply haven't any cupboards that will hold them all, but it's something to do, and I like to see them again.'

'You should shake them,' I said, 'and put them in the sun. They may be damp.'

'Darling, you are wonderful, you always know.'

'Where did you get that puppy?' I said enviously. I had wanted a bulldog for years, but Alfred never would let me have one because of the snoring.

'Brought him back with me. He's the nicest puppy I ever had, so anxious to oblige, you can't think.'

'What about quarantine, then?'

'Under my coat,' said Linda laconically. 'You should have heard him grunting and snuffling, it shook the whole place, I was terrified, but he was so good. He never budged. And talking of puppies, those ghastly Kroesigs are sending Moira to America, isn't it typical of them? I've made a great thing with Tony about seeing her before she goes, after all I am her mother.'

'That's what I can't ever understand about you, Linda.'

'What?'

'How you could have been so dreadful to Moira.'

'Dull,' said Linda. 'Uninteresting.'

'I know, but the point is that children are like puppies, and if you never see puppies, if you give them to the groom or the gamekeeper to bring up, look how dull and uninteresting they always are. Children are just the same—you must give them much more than their life if they are to be any good. Poor little Moira—all you gave her was that awful name.'

'Oh, Fanny, I do know. To tell you the truth I believe it was always in the back of my mind that, sooner or later, I should have to run away from Tony, and I didn't want to get too fond of Moira, or make her too fond of me. She might have become an anchor, and I simply didn't dare let myself be anchored to the Kroesigs.'

'Poor Linda.'

'Oh, don't pity me. I've had eleven months of perfect and unalloyed happiness, very few people can say that, in the course of long long lives, I imagine.'

I imagined so too. Alfred and I are happy, as happy as married people can be. We are in love, we are intellectually and physically suited in every possible way, we rejoice in each other's company, we have no money troubles and three delightful children. And yet, when I consider my life, day by day, hour by hour, it seems to be composed of a series of pin-pricks. Nannies, cooks, the endless drudgery of house-keeping, the nerve-racking noise and boring repetitive conversation of small children (boring in the sense that it bores into one's very brain), their absolute incapacity to amuse themselves, their sudden and terrifying illnesses, Alfred's not infrequent bouts of moodiness, his invariable complaints at meals about the pudding, the way he will always use my toothpaste and will always squeeze the tube in the middle. These are the components of marriage, the wholemeal bread of life, rough, ordinary, but sustaining; Linda had been feeding upon honey-dew, and that is an incomparable diet.

The old woman who had opened the door to me came in and said was that everything, because, if so, she would be going home.

'Everything,' said Linda. 'Mrs. Hunt,' she said to me, when she had gone. 'A terrific Hon—she comes daily.'

'Why don't you go to Alconleigh,' I said, 'or to Shenley? Aunt Emily and Davey would love to have you, and I'm going there with the children as soon as Alfred is off again.'

'I'd like to come for a visit some time, when I know a little more what is happening, but at the moment I must stop here. Give them my love though. I've got such masses to tell you, Fanny, what we really need is hours and hours in the Hons' cupboard.'

After a good deal of hesitation Tony Kroesig and his wife, Pixie, allowed Moira to go and see her mother before leaving England. She arrived at Cheyne Walk in Tony's car, still driven by a chauffeur in uniform not the King's. She was a plain, stodgy, shy little girl, with no echo of the Radletts about her; not to put too fine a point on it she was a real little Gretchen.

'What a sweet puppy,' she said, awkwardly, when Linda had kissed her. She was clearly very much embarrassed.

'What's his name?'

'Plon-plon.'

'Oh. Is that a French name?'

'Yes, it is. He's a French dog, you see.'

'Daddy says the French are terrible.'

'I expect he does.'

'He says they have let us down, and what can we expect if we have anything to do with such people.'

'Yes, he would.'

'Daddy thinks we ought to fight with the Germans and not against them.'

'M'm. But Daddy doesn't seem to be fighting very much with anybody, or against anybody, or at all, as far as I can see. Now, Moira, before you go I have got two things for you, one is a present and the other is a little talk. The talk is very dull, so we'll get that over first, shall we?'

'Yes,' said Moira, apathetically. She lugged the puppy on to the sofa beside her,

'I want you to know,' said Linda, 'and to remember, please, Moira (stop playing with the puppy a minute and listen carefully to what I am saying) that I don't at all approve of you running away like this, I think it most dreadfully wrong. When you have a country which has given you as much as England has given all of us, you ought to stick to it, and not go wandering off as soon as it looks like being in trouble.'

'But it's not my fault,' said Moira, her forehead puckering. 'I'm only a child and Pixie is taking me. I have to do what I'm told, don't I?'

'Yes, of course, I know that's true. But you'd much rather stay, wouldn't you?' said Linda hopefully.

'Oh no, I don't think so. There might be air-raids.'

At this Linda gave up. Children might or might not enjoy air-raids actually in progress, but a child who was not thrilled by the idea of them was incomprehensible to her, and she could not imagine having conceived such a being. Useless to waste any more time and breath on this unnatural little girl. She sighed and said:

'Now wait a moment and I'll get your present.'

She had in her pocket, in a velvet box, a coral hand holding a diamond arrow, which Fabrice had given her, but she could not bear to waste anything so pretty on this besotted little coward. She went to her bedroom and found a sports wrist-watch, one of her wedding presents when she had married Tony and which she had never worn, and gave this to Moira, who seemed quite pleased by it, and left the house as politely and unenthusiastically as she had arrived.

Linda rang me up at Shenley and told me about this interview.

'I'm in such a temper,' she said, 'I must talk to somebody. To think I ruined nine months of my life in order to have that. What do your children think about air-raids, Fanny?'

'I must say they simply long for them, and I am sorry to say they also long for the Germans to arrive. They spend the whole day making booby-traps for them in the orchard.'

'Well that's a relief anyhow—I thought perhaps it was the generation. Actually, of course, it's not Moira's fault, it's all that bloody Pixie —I can see the form only too clearly, can't you? Pixie is frightened to death and she has found out that going to America is like the children's concert, you can only make it if you have a child in tow. So she's using Moira—well, it does serve one right for doing wrong.' Linda was evidently very much put out. 'And I hear Tony is going too, some Parliamentary mission or something. All I can say is what a set.'

All through those terrible months of May, June and July, Linda waited for a sign from Fabrice, but no sign came. She did not doubt that he was still alive, it was not in Linda's nature to imagine that anyone might be dead. She knew that thousands of Frenchmen were in German hands, but felt certain that, had Fabrice been taken prisoner (a thing which she did not at all approve of, incidentally, taking the old-fashioned view that, unless in exceptional circumstances, it is a disgrace), he would undoubtedly manage to escape. She would hear from him before long, and, meanwhile, there was nothing to be done, she must simply wait. All the same, as the days went by with no news, and as all the news there was from France was bad, she did become exceedingly restless. She was really more concerned with his attitude than with his safety—his attitude towards events and his attitude towards her. She felt sure that he would never be associated with the armistice, she felt sure that he would want to communicate with her, but she had no proof, and, in moments of great loneliness and depression, she allowed herself to lose faith. She realized how little she really knew of Fabrice, he had seldom talked seriously to her, their relationship having been primarily physical while their conversation and chat had all been based on jokes.

They had laughed and made love and laughed again, and the months had slipped by with no time for anything but laughter and love. Enough to satisfy her, but what about him? Now that life had become so serious, and, for a Frenchman, so tragic, would he not have forgotten that meal of whipped cream as something so utterly unimportant that it might never have existed? She began to think, more and more, to tell herself over and over again, to force herself to realize, that it was probably all finished, that Fabrice might never be anything for her now but a memory.

At the same time the few people she saw never failed when talking, as everybody talked then, about France, to emphasize that the French 'one knew,' the families who were '*bien*', were all behaving very badly, convinced Pétainists. Fabrice was not one of them, she thought, she felt, but she wished she knew, she longed for evidence.

In fact, she alternated between hope and despair, but as the months went by without a word, a word that she was sure he could have sent if he had really wanted to, despair began to prevail.

Then, on a sunny Sunday morning in August, very early, her telephone bell rang. She woke up with a start, aware that it had been ringing already for several moments, and she knew with absolute certainty that this was Fabrice.

'Are you Flaxman 2815?'

'Yes.'

'I've got a call for you. You're through.'

'*Allô—allô?*'

'Fabrice?'

'*Oui.*'

'Oh! Fabrice—*on vous attend depuis si longtemps.*'

'*Comme c'est gentil. Alors, on peut venir tout de suite chez vous?*'

'Oh, wait—yes, you can come at once, but don't go for a minute, go on talking, I want to hear the sound of your voice.'

'No, no, I have a taxi outside, I shall be with you in five minutes. There's too much one can't do on the telephone, *ma chère, voyons——*' Click.

She lay back, and all was light and warmth. Life, she thought, is sometimes sad and often dull, but there are currants in the cake and here is one of them. The early morning sun shone past her window on to the river, her ceiling danced with water-reflections. The Sunday silence was broken by two swans swinging slowly upstream, and then by the chugging of a little barge, while she waited for that other sound, a sound more intimately connected with the urban love affair than any except the telephone bell, that of a stopping taxicab. Sun, silence, and happiness. Presently she heard it in the street, slowly, slower, it stopped, the flag went up with a ring, the door slammed, voices, clinking coins, footsteps. She rushed downstairs.

Hours later Linda made some coffee.

'So lucky,' she said, 'that it happens to be Sunday, and Mrs. Hunt isn't here. What would she have thought?'

'Just about the same as the night porter at the Hotel Montalembert, I expect,' said Fabrice.

'Why did you come, Fabrice? To join General de Gaulle?'

'No, that was not necessary, because I have joined him already. I was with him in Bordeaux. My work has to be in France, but we have ways of communicating when we want to. I shall go and see him, of course, he expects me at midday, but actual.y I came on a private mission.'

He looked at her for a long time.

'I came to tell you that I love you,' he said, at last.

Linda felt giddy.

'You never said that to me in Paris.'

'No.'

'You always seemed so practical.'

'Yes, I suppose so. I had said it so often and often before in my life, I had been so romantic with so many women, that when I felt this to be different I really could not bring out all those stale old phrases again, I couldn't utter them. I never said I loved you, I never tutoyé'd you, on purpose. Because from the first moment I knew that this was as real as all the others were false, it was like recognizing somebody—there, I can't explain.'

'But that is exactly how I felt too,' said Linda, 'don't try to explain, you needn't, I know.'

'Then, when you had gone, I felt I had to tell you, and it became an obsession with me to tell you. All those dreadful weeks were made more dreadful because I was being prevented from telling you.'

'How ever did you get here?'

'*On circule*,' said Fabrice vaguely. 'I must leave again tomorrow morning, very early, and I shan't come back until the war is over, but you'll wait for me, Linda, and nothing matters so much now that you know. I was tormented, I couldn't concentrate on anything, I was becoming useless in my work. In future I may have much to bear, but I shan't have to bear you going away without knowing what a great great love I have for you.'

'Oh, Fabrice, I feel—well, I suppose religious people sometimes feel like this.'

She put her head on his shoulder, and they sat for a long time in silence.

When he had paid his visit to Carlton Gardens they lunched at the

Ritz. It was full of people Linda knew, all very smart, very gay, and talking with the greatest flippancy about the imminent arrival of the Germans. Had it not been for the fact that all the young men there had fought bravely in Flanders, and would, no doubt, soon be fighting bravely again, and this time with more experience, on other fields of battle, the general tone might have been considered shocking. Even Fabrice looked grave, and said they did not seem to realize——

Davey and Lord Merlin appeared. Their eyebrows went up when they saw Fabrice.

'Poor Merlin has the wrong kind,' Davey said to Linda.

'The wrong kind of what?'

'Pill to take when the Germans come. He's just got the sort you give to dogs.'

Davey brought out a jewelled box containing two pills, one white and one black.

'You take the white one first and then the black one——he really must go to my doctor.'

'I think one should let the Germans do the killing,' said Linda. 'Make them add to their own crimes and use up a bullet. Why should one smooth their path in any way? Besides, I back myself to do in at least two before they get me.'

'Oh, you're so tough, Linda, but I'm afraid it wouldn't be a bullet for me, they would torture me, look at the things I've said about them in the *Gazette*.'

'No worse than you've said about all of us,' Lord Merlin remarked.

Davey was known to be a most savage reviewer, a perfect butcher, never sparing even his dearest friends. He wrote under several pseudonyms, which in no way disguised his unmistakable style, his cruellest essays appearing over the name Little Nell.

'Are you here for long, Sauveterre?'

'No, not for long.'

Linda and Fabrice went in to luncheon. They talked of this and that, mostly jokes. Fabrice told her scandalous stories about some of the other lunchers known to him of old, with a wealth of unlikely detail. He spoke only once about France, only to say that the struggle must be carried on, everything would be all right in the end. Linda thought how different it would have been with Tony or Christian. Tony would have held forth about his experiences and made boring arrangements for his own future, Christian would have launched a monologue on world conditions subsequent to the recent fall of France, its probable repercussions in Araby and far Cashmere, the inadequacy of Pétain to deal with such a wealth of displaced persons, the steps that he, Christian, would have taken had he found himself in his, the Marshal's, shoes. Both would have spoken to her exactly, in every respect, as if she had been some chap in their club. Fabrice talked to her, at her, and for only her, it was absolutely personal talk, scattered with jokes and allusions private to them both. She had a feeling that he would not allow himself to be serious, that if he did he would have to embark on tragedy, and that he wanted her to carry away a happy memory of his visit. But he also gave an impression of boundless optimism and faith, very cheering at that dark time.

Early the next morning, another beautiful, hot, sunny morning, Linda lay back on her pillows and watched Fabrice while he dressed, as she had so often watched him in Paris. He made a certain kind of face when he was pulling his tie into a knot, she had quite forgotten it in the months between, and it brought back their Paris life to her suddenly and vividly.

'Fabrice,' she said. 'Do you think we shall ever live together again?'

'But of course we shall, for years and years and years, until I am ninety. I have a very faithful nature.'

'You weren't very faithful to Jacqueline.'

'Aha—so you know about Jacqueline, do you? *La pauvre, elle était si gentille—gentille, élégante, mais assommante, mon Dieu! Enfin*, I was immensely faithful to her and it lasted five years, it always does with me (either five days or five years). But as I love you ten times more than the others that brings it to when I am ninety, and, by then, *j'en aurai tellement l'habitude——*'

'And how soon shall I see you again?'

'*On fera la navette.*' He went to the window. 'I thought I heard a car—oh yes, it is turning round. There, I must go. *Au revoir*, Linda.'

He kissed her hand politely, almost absentmindedly, it was as if he had already gone, and walked quickly from the room. Linda went to the open window and leaned out. He was getting into a large motor-car with two French soldiers on the box and a Free French flag waving from the bonnet. As it moved away he looked up.

'*Navette—navette——*' cried Linda with a brilliant smile. Then she got back into bed and cried very much. She felt utterly in despair at this second parting.

CHAPTER XX

THE air-raids on London now began. Early in September, just as I had moved there with my family, a bomb fell in the garden of Aunt Emily's little house in Kent. It was a small bomb compared with what one saw later, and none of us were hurt, but the house was more or less wrecked. Aunt Emily, Davey, my children, and I, then took refuge at Alconleigh, where Aunt Sadie welcomed us with open arms, begging us to make it our home for the war. Louisa had already arrived there with her children, John Fort William had gone back to his regiment and their Scotch home had been taken over by the Navy.

'The more the merrier,' said Aunt Sadie, 'I should like to fill the house, and, besides, it's better for rations. Nice, too, for your children to be brought up all together, just like old times. With the boys away and Victoria in the Wrens Matthew and I would be a very dreary old couple here all alone.'

The big rooms at Alconleigh were filled with the contents of some science museum and no evacuees had been billeted there, I think it was felt that nobody who had not been brought up to such rigours could stand the cold of that house.

Soon the party received a very unexpected addition. I was upstairs in the nursery bathroom doing some washing for Nanny, measuring out the soap-flakes with wartime parsimony and wishing that the water at Alconleigh were not so dreadfully hard, when Louisa burst in.

'You'll never guess,' she said, 'in a thousand thousand years who has arrived.'

'Hitler,' I said stupidly.

'Your mother, Auntie Bolter. She just walked up the drive and walked in.'

'Alone?'

'No, with a man.'

'The Major?'

'He doesn't look like a major. He's got a musical instrument with him and he's very dirty. Come on, Fanny, leave those to soak——'

And so it was. My mother sat in the hall drinking a whisky and soda and recounting in her birdlike voice with what incredible adventures she had escaped from the Riviera. The major with whom she had been living for some years, always having greatly preferred the Germans to the French, had remained behind to collaborate, and the man who now accompanied my mother was a ruffianly-looking Spaniard called Juan, whom she had picked up during her travels, and without whom, she said, she could never have got away from a ghastly prison camp in Spain. She spoke of him exactly as though he were not there at all, which produced rather a curious effect, and indeed seemed most embarrassing until we realized that Juan understood no word of any language except Spanish. He sat staring blankly into space, clutching a guitar and gulping down great draughts of whisky. Their relationship was only too obvious, Juan was undoubtedly (nobody doubted for a moment, not even Aunt Sadie), the Bolter's lover, but they were quite incapable of verbal exchange, my mother being no linguist.

Presently Uncle Matthew appeared, and the Bolter told her adventures all over again to him. He said he was delighted to see her, and hoped she would stay as long as she liked, he then turned his blue eyes upon Juan in a most terrifying and uncompromising stare. Aunt Sadie led him off to the business-room, whispering, and we heard him say:

'All right then, but only for a few days.'

One person who was off his head with joy at the sight of her was dear old Josh.

'We must get her ladyship up on to a horse,' he said, hissing with pleasure.

My mother had not been her ladyship since three husbands, (four if one were to include the Major), but Josh took no account of this, she would always be her ladyship to him. He found a horse, not worthy of her, in his eyes, but not an absolute dud either, and had her out cubhunting within a week of her arrival.

As for me it was the first time in my life that I had really found myself face to face with my mother. When a small child I had been obsessed by her and the few appearances she had made had absolutely dazzled me, though, as I have said, I never had any wish to emulate her career. Davey and Aunt Emily had been very clever in their approach to her, they, and especially Davey, had gradually and gently and without in any way hurting my feelings, turned her into a sort of joke. Since I was grown up I had seen her a few times, and had taken Alfred to visit her on our honeymoon, but the fact that, in spite of our intimate relationship, we had no past life in common put a great strain upon us and these meetings were not a success. At Alconleigh, in contact with her morning, noon and night, I studied her with the greatest curiosity, apart from anything else, she was, after all, the grandmother of my children. I couldn't help rather liking her. Though she was silliness personified there was something engaging about her frankness and high spirits and endless good nature. The children adored her, Louisa's as well as mine, and she soon became an extra unofficial nurserymaid, and was very useful to us in that capacity.

She was curiously dated in her manner, and seemed still to be living in the 1920's. It was as though, at the age of thirty-five, having refused to grow any older, she had pickled herself, both mentally and physically, ignoring the fact that the world was changing and that she was withering fast. She had a short canary-coloured shingle (windswept) and wore trousers with the air of one still flouting the conventions, ignorant that every suburban shopgirl was doing the same. Her conversation, her point of view, the very slang she used, all belonged to the late 'twenties, that period now deader than the dodo. She was intensely unpractical, foolish, and apparently fragile, and yet she must have been quite a tough little person really, to have walked over the Pyrenees, to have escaped from a Spanish camp, and to have arrived at Alconleigh looking as if she had stepped out of the chorus of *No, No, Nanette*.

Some confusion was caused in the household at first by the fact that none of us could remember whether she had, in the end, actually married the Major (a married man himself and father of six) or not, and, in consequence, nobody knew whether her name was now Mrs. Rawl or Mrs. Plugge. Rawl had been a white hunter, the only husband she had ever lost respectably through death, having shot him by accident in the head during a safari. The question of names was soon solved, however, by her ration book, which proclaimed her to be Mrs. Plugge.

'This Gewan,' said Uncle Matthew, when they had been at Alconleigh a week or so, 'what's going to be done about him?'

'Well, Matthew dulling,' she larded her phrases with the word darling, and that is how she pronounced it. 'Hoo-arn saved my life, you know, over and over again, and I can't very well tear him up and throw him away, now can I, my sweet?'

'I can't keep a lot of dagoes here, you know.' Uncle Matthew said this in the same voice with which he used to tell Linda sthat she couldn't have any more pets, or if she did they must be kept in the stables. 'You'll have to make some other arrangements for him, Bolter, I'm afraid.'

'Oh, dulling, keep him a little longer, please, just a few more days, Matthew dulling,' she sounded just like Linda, pleading for some smelly old dog, 'and then I promise I'll find some place for him and tiny me to go to. You can't think what a lousy time we had together, I must stick to him now, I really must.'

'Well, another week if you like, but it's not to be the thin end of the wedge, Bolter, and after that he must go. You can stay as long as you want to, of course, but I do draw the line at Gewan.'

Louisa said to me, her eyes as big as saucers: 'He rushes into her room before tea and lives with her.' Louisa always describes the act of love as living with. 'Before tea, Fanny, can you imagine it?'

'Sadie, dear,' said Davey, 'I am going to do an unpardonable thing. It is for the general good, for your own good too, but it is unpardonable. If you feel you can't forgive me when I've said my say, Emily and I will have to leave, that's all.'

'Davey,' said Aunt Sadie in astonishment, 'what can be coming?'

'The food, Sadie, it's the food. I know how difficult it is for you in wartime, but we are all, in turns, being poisoned. I was sick for hours last night, the day before Emily had diarrhœa, Fanny has that great spot on her nose, and I'm sure the children aren't putting on the weight they should. The fact is, dear, that if Mrs. Beecher were a Borgia she could hardly be more successful—all that sausage mince is poison, Sadie. I wouldn't complain if it were merely nasty, or insufficient, or too starchy, one expects that in the war, but actual poison does, I feel, call for comment. Look at the menus this week—— Monday, poison pie; Tuesday, poison burger steak; Wednesday, Cornish poison——'

Aunt Sadie looked intensely worried.

'Oh, dear, yes, she is an awful cook, I know, but Davey, what can one do? The meat ration only lasts about two meals, and there are fourteen meals in a week, you must remember. If she minces it up with a little meat—poison meat (I do so agree with you really)—it goes much further, you see.'

'But in the country surely one can supplement the ration with game and farm produce? Yes, I know the home farm is let, but surely you could keep a pig and some hens? And what about game? There always used to be such a lot here.'

'The trouble is Matthew thinks they'll be needing all their ammunition for the Germans, and he refuses to waste a single shot on hares or partridges. Then you see Mrs. Beecher (oh, what a dreadful woman she is, though of course, we are lucky to have her) is the kind of cook who is quite good at a cut off the joint and two veg., but she simply hasn't an idea of how to make up delicious foreign oddments out of little bits of nothing at all. But you are quite, absolutely right, Davey, it's not wholesome. I really will make an effort to see what can be done.'

'You always used to be such a wonderful housekeeper, Sadie dear, it used to do one so much good, coming here. I remember one Christmas I put on four and a half ounces. But now I am losing steadily, my wretched frame is hardly more than a skeleton and I fear that, if I were to catch anything, I might peter out altogether. I take every precaution against that, everything is drenched in T.C.P., I gargle at least six times a day, but I can't disguise from you that my resistance is very low, very.'

Aunt Sadie said: 'It's quite easy to be a wonderful housekeeper when there are a first-rate cook, two kitchenmaids, a scullerymaid, and when you can get all the food you want. I'm afraid I am dreadfully stupid at managing on rations, but I really will try and take a pull. I'm very glad indeed that you mentioned it, Davey, it was absolutely right of you, and of course, I don't mind at all.'

But no real improvement resulted. Mrs. Beecher said 'yes, yes' to all suggestions, and continued to send up Hamburger steaks, Cornish pasty and shepherd pie, which continued to be full of poison sausage. It was very nasty and very unwholesome, and, for once, we all felt that Davey had not gone a bit too far. Meals were no pleasure to anybody and a positive ordeal to Davey, who sat, a pinched expression on his face, refusing food and resorting more and more often to the vitamin pills with which his place at the table was surrounded—too many by far even for his collection of jewelled boxes—a little forest of bottles, Vitamin A, vitamin B, vitamins A and C, vitamins B_3 and D, one tablet equals two pounds of summer butter—ten times the strength of a gallon of cod-liver oil—for the blood—for the brain—for muscle—for energy—anti-this and protection against that—all but one bore a pretty legend.

'And what's in this, Davey?'

'Oh, that's what the panzer troops have before going into action.'

Davey gave a series of little sniffs. This usually denoted that his nose was about to bleed, pints of valuable red and white corpuscles so assiduously filled with vitamins would be wasted, his resistance still further lowered.

Aunt Emily and I looked up in some anxiety from the rissoles we were sadly pushing round our plates.

'Bolter,' he said severely, 'you've been at my Mary Chess again.'

'Oh, Davey dulling, such a tiny droppie.'

'A tiny drop doesn't stink out the whole room. I'm sure you have been pouring it into the bath with the stopper out. It is a shame. That bottle is my quota for a month, it is too bad of you, Bolter.'

'Dulling, I swear I'll get you some more—I've got to go to London next week, to have my wiggie washed, and I'll bring back a bottle, I swear.'

'And I very much hope you'll take Gewan with you and leave him there,' growled Uncle Matthew. 'Because I won't have him in this house much longer, you know. I've warned you, Bolter.'

Uncle Matthew was busy from morning to night with his Home Guard. He was happy and interested and in a particularly mellow mood, for it looked as if his favourite hobby, that of clocking Germans, might be available again at any moment. So he only noticed Juan from time to time, and, whereas in the old days he would have had him out of the house in the twinkling of an eye, Juan had now been an inmate of Alconleigh for nearly a month. However, it was beginning to be obvious that my uncle had no intention of putting up with his presence for ever and things were clearly coming to a head where Juan was concerned. As for the Spaniard himself, I never saw a man so wretched. He wandered about miserably, with nothing whatever to do all day, unable to talk to anybody, while at mealtimes the disgust on his face fully equalled that of Davey. He hadn't even the spirit to play his guitar.

'Davey, you must talk to him,' said Aunt Sadie.

My mother had gone to London to have her hair dyed, and a family council was gathered in her absence to decide upon the fate of Juan.

'We obviously can't turn him out to starve, as the Bolter says he saved her life, and, anyhow, one has human feelings.'

'Not towards Dagoes,' said Uncle Matthew, grinding his dentures.

'But what we can do is to get him a job, only first we must find out what his profession is. Now, Davey, you're good at languages, and you're so clever, I'm sure if you had a look at the Spanish dictionary in the library you could just manage to ask him what he used to do before the war. Do try, Davey.'

'Yes, darling, do,' said Aunt Emily. 'The poor fellow looks too miserable for words at present, I expect he'd love to have some work.'

Uncle Matthew snorted.

'Just give me the Spanish dictionary,' he muttered. 'I'll soon find the word for "get out".'

'I'll try,' said Davey, 'but I can guess what it will be I'm afraid. G for gigolo.'

'Or something equally useless, like M for matador or H for hidalgo,' said Louisa.

'Yes. Then what?'

'Then B for be off,' said Uncle Matthew, 'and the Bolter will have to support him, but not anywhere near me, I beg. It must be made perfectly clear to both of them that I can't stand the sight of the sewer lounging about here any longer.'

When Davey takes on a job he does it thoroughly. He shut himself up for several hours with the Spanish dictionary, and wrote down a great many words and phrases on a piece of paper. Then he beckoned Juan into Uncle Matthew's business room and shut the door.

They were only there a short time, and, when they emerged, both were wreathed in happy smiles.

'You've sacked him, I hope?' Uncle Matthew said, suspiciously.

'No, indeed, I've not sacked him,' said Davey, 'on the contrary, I've engaged him. My dear, you'll never guess, it's too absolutely glamorous for words, Juan is a cook, he was the cook, I gather, of some cardinal before the Civil War. You don't mind I hope, Sadie. I look upon this as an absolute lifeline—Spanish food, so delicious, so unconstipating, so digestible, so full of glorious garlic. Oh, the joy, no more poison-burger —how soon can we get rid of Mrs. Beecher?'

Davey's enthusiasm was fully justified, and Juan in the kitchen was the very greatest possible success. He was more than a first class cook, he had an extraordinary talent for organization, and soon, I suspect, became king of the local black market. There was no nonsense about foreign dishes made out of little bits of nothing at all; succulent birds, beasts, and crustaceans appeared at every meal, the vegetables ran with extravagant sauces, the puddings were obviously based upon real ice-cream.

'Juan is wonderful,' Aunt Sadie would remark in her vague manner, 'at making the rations go round. When I think of Mrs. Beecher—really, Davey, you were so clever.'

One day she said: 'I hope the food isn't too rich for you now, Davey?'

'Oh no,' said Davey. 'I never mind rich food, it's poor food that does one such an infinity of harm.'

Juan also pickled and bottled and preserved from morning till night, until the store cupboard, which he had found bare except for a few tins of soup, began to look like a pre-war grocer's shop. Davey called it Aladdin's Cave, or Aladdin for short, and spent a lot of his time there, gloating. Months of tasty vitamins stood there in neat rows, a barrier between him and that starvation which had seemed, under Mrs. Beecher's régime, only just round the corner.

Juan himself was now a very different fellow from the dirty and disgruntled refugee who had sat about so miserably. He was clean, he wore a white coat and hat, he seemed to have grown in stature, and he soon acquired a manner of great authority in his kitchen. Even Uncle Matthew acknowledged the change.

'If I were the Bolter,' he said, 'I should marry him.'

'Knowing the Bolter,' said Davey, 'I've no doubt at all that she will.'

Early in November I had to go to London for the day, on business for Alfred, who was now in the Middle East, and to see my doctor. I went by the eight o'clock train, and, having heard nothing of Linda for some weeks, I took a taxi and drove straight to Cheyne Walk. There had been a heavy raid the night before, and I passed through streets which glistened with broken glass. Many fires still smouldered, and fire engines, ambulances, and rescue men hurried to and fro, streets were blocked, and several times we had to drive quite a long way round. There seemed to be a great deal of excitement in the air. Little groups of people were gathered outside shops and houses, as if to compare notes; my taxi-driver talked incessantly to me over his shoulder. He had been up all night, he said, helping the rescue workers. He described what he had found.

'It was a spongy mass of red,' he said ghoulishly, 'covered with feathers.'

'Feathers?' I said horrified.

'Yes. A feather bed, you see. It was still breathing, so I takes it to the hospital, but they says that no good to us, take it to the mortuary. So I sews it in a sack and takes it to the mortuary.'

'Goodness,' I said.

'Oh, that's nothing to what I have seen.'

Linda's nice daily woman, Mrs. Hunt, opened the door to me at Cheyne Walk.

'She's very poorly, ma'am, can't you take her back to the country with you? It's not right for her to be here, in her condition. I hate to see her like this.'

Linda was in her bathroom, being sick. When she came out she said:

'Don't think it's the raid that's upset me. I like them. I'm in the family way, that's what it is.'

'Darling, I thought you weren't supposed to have another baby.'

'Oh, doctors! They don't know anything, they are such fearful idiots. Of course I can, and I'm simply longing for it, this baby won't be the least bit like Moira, you'll see.'

'I'm going to have one too.'

'No—how lovely—when?'

'About the end of May.'

'Oh, just the same as me.'

'And Louisa, in March.'

'Haven't we been busy? I do call that nice, they can all be Hons together.'

'Now, Linda, why don't you come back with me to Alconleigh? Whatever is the sense of stopping here in all this? It can't be good for you or the baby.'

'I like it,' said Linda. 'It's my home, and I like to be in it. And besides, somebody might turn up, just for a few hours you know, and want to see me, and he knows where to find me here.'

'You'll be killed,' I said, 'and then he won't know where to find you.'

'Darling Fanny, don't be so silly. There are several million people living in London, do you really imagine they are all killed every night? Nobody is killed in air raids, there is a great deal of noise and a great deal of mess, but people really don't seem to get killed much.'

'Don't—don't——' I said. 'Touch wood. Apart from being killed or not it doesn't suit you. You look awful, Linda.'

'Not so bad when I'm made up. I'm so fearfully sick, that's the trouble, but it's nothing to do with the raids, and that part will soon be over now and I shall be quite all right again.'

'Well, think about it,' I said, 'it's very nice at Alconleigh, wonderful food——'

'Yes, so I hear. Merlin came to see me, and his stories of caramelized carrots swimming in cream made my mouth water. He said he was preparing to throw morality to the winds and bribe this Juan to go to Merlinford, but he found out it would mean having the Bolter too and he couldn't quite face that.'

'I must go,' I said uncertainly. 'I don't like to leave you, darling, I do wish you'd come back with me.'

'Perhaps I will later on, we'll see.'

I went down to the kitchen and found Mrs. Hunt. I gave her some money in case of emergency, and the Alconleigh telephone number, and begged her to ring me up if she thought there was anything I could do.

'She won't budge,' I said. 'I've done all I can to make her, but it doesn't seem to be any good, she's as obstinate as a donkey.'

'I know, madam. She won't even leave the house for a breath of air, sits by that telephone day in day out playing cards with herself. It ain't hardly right she should sleep here all alone in my opinion, either, but you can't get her to listen to sense. Last night, ma'am, whew! it was terrible, walloping down all night, and those wretched guns never got a single one, whatever they may tell you in the papers. It's my opinion they must have got women on those guns, and, if so, no wonder. Women!'

A week later Mrs. Hunt rang me up at Alconleigh. Linda's house had received a direct hit and they were still digging for her.

Aunt Sadie had gone on an early bus to Cheltenham to do some shopping, Uncle Matthew was nowhere to be found, so Davey and I simply took his car, full of Home Guard petrol, and drove to London, hell for leather. The little house was an absolute ruin, but Linda and her bulldog were unhurt, they had just been got out and put to bed in the house of a neighbour. Linda was flushed and excited, and couldn't stop talking.

'You see,' she said. 'What did I tell you, Fanny, about air raids not killing people. Here we are, right as rain. My bed simply went through the floor, Plon-plon and I went on it, most comfortable.'

Presently a doctor arrived and gave her a sedative. He told us she would probably go to sleep and that when she woke up we could drive her down to Alconleigh. I telephoned to Aunt Sadie and told her to have a room ready.

The rest of the day was spent by Davey in salvaging what he could of Linda's things. Her house and furniture, her beautiful Renoir, and everything in her bedroom was completely wrecked, but he was able to rescue a few oddments from the splintered, twisted remains of her cupboards, and in the basement he found, untouched, the two trunks full of clothes which Fabrice had sent after her from Paris. He came out looking like a miller, covered with white dust from head to foot, and Mrs. Hunt took us round to her own little house and gave us some food.

'I suppose Linda may miscarry,' I said to Davey, 'and I'm sure it's to be hoped she will. It's most dangerous for her to have this child—my doctor is horrified.'

However, she did not, in fact she said that the experience had done her a great deal of good, and had quite stopped her from feeling sick. She demurred again at leaving London, but without much conviction. I pointed out that if anybody was looking for her and found the Cheyne Walk house a total wreck they would be certain at once to get into touch with Alconleigh. She saw that this was so, and agreed to come with us.

CHAPTER XXI

WINTER now set in with its usual severity on those Cotswold uplands. The air was sharp and bracing, like cold water; most agreeable if one only goes out for short brisk walks or rides, and if there is a warm house to go back to. But the central-heating apparatus at Alconleigh had never been really satisfactory and I suppose that by now the pipes, through old age, had become thoroughly furred up—in any case they were hardly more than tepid. On coming into the hall from the bitter outside air one did feel a momentary glow of warmth; this soon lessened, and gradually, as circulation died down, one's body became pervaded by a cruel numbness. The men on the estate, the old ones that is, who were not in the army, had no time to chop up logs for the fires; they were occupied from morning till night, under the leadership of Uncle Matthew, in drilling, constructing barricades and blockhouses, and otherwise preparing to make themselves a nuisance to the German army before ending up as cannon-fodder.

'I reckon,' Uncle Matthew would say proudly, 'that we shall be able to stop them for two hours—possibly three—before we are all killed. Not bad for such a little place.'

We made our children go out and collect wood, Davey became an assiduous and surprisingly efficient woodman (he had refused to join the Home Guard, he said he always fought better out of uniform), but somehow, they only produced enough to keep the nursery fire going, and the one in the brown sitting-room, if it was lit after tea, and, as the wood was pretty wet, this only really got warm just when it was time to tear oneself away and go up the freezing stairs to bed. After dinner the two armchairs on each side of the fire were always occupied by Davey and my mother. Davey pointed out that it would be more trouble for everybody in the end if he got one of his chills; the Bolter just dumped herself down. The rest of us sat in a semi-circle well beyond the limits of any real warmth, and looked longingly at the little flickering yellow flames, which often subsided into sulky smoke. Linda had an evening coat, a sort of robe from head to foot, of white fox lined with white ermine. She wrapped herself in this for dinner, and suffered less than we others did. In the daytime she either wore her sable coat and a pair of black velvet boots lined with sable to match, or lay on the sofa tucked up in an enormous mink bedspread lined with white velvet quilting.

'It used to make me so laugh when Fabrice said he was getting me all these things because they would be useful in the war, the war would be fearfully cold he always said, but I see now how right he was.'

Linda's possessions filled the other females in the house with a sort of furious admiration.

'It does seem rather unfair,' Louisa said to me one afternoon when we were pushing our two youngest children out in their prams together. We were both dressed in stiff Scotch tweeds, so different from supple flattering French ones, in woollen stockings, brogues, and jerseys, knitted by ourselves, of shades carefully chosen to 'go with' though not 'to match' our coats and skirts. 'Linda goes off and has this glorious time in Paris, and comes back covered with rich furs, while you and I—what do we get for sticking all our lives to the same dreary old husbands? Three-quarter length shorn lamb.'

'Alfred isn't a dreary old husband,' I said loyally. But of course I knew exactly what she meant.

Aunt Sadie thought Linda's clothes too pretty.

'What lovely taste, darling,' she would say when another ravishing garment was brought out. 'Did that come from Paris too? It's really wonderful what you can get there, on no money, if you're clever.'

At this my mother would give tremendous winks in the direction of anybody whose eye she might happen to catch, including Linda herself. Linda's face would then become absolutely stony. She could not bear my mother; she felt that, before she met Fabrice, she had been heading down the same road herself, and she was appalled to see what lay at the end of it. My mother started off by trying a 'let's face it, dear, we are nothing but two fallen women' method of approach to Linda, which was most unsuccessful. Linda became not only stiff and cold, but positively rude to the poor Bolter, who, unable to see what she could have done to offend, was at first very much hurt. Then she began to be on her dignity, and said it was great nonsense for Linda to go on like this; in fact, considering she was nothing but a high-class tart, it was most pretentious and hypocritical of her. I tried to explain Linda's intensely romantic attitude towards Fabrice and the months she had spent with him, but the Bolter's own feelings had been dulled by time, and she either could not or would not understand.

'It was Sauveterre she was living with, wasn't it?' my mother said to me, soon after Linda arrived at Alconleigh.

'How do you know?'

'Everybody knew on the Riviera. One always knew about Sauveterre somehow. And it was rather a thing, because he seemed to have settled down for life with that boring Lamballe woman; then she had to go to England on business and clever little Linda nabbed him. A very good cop for her, dulling, but I don't see why she has to be so high-hat about it. Sadie doesn't know, I quite realize that, and of course wild horses wouldn't make me tell her, I'm not that kind of a girl, but I do think, when we're all together, Linda might be a tiny bit more jolly.'

The Alconleighs still believed that Linda was the devoted wife of Christian, who was now in Cairo, and, of course, it had never occurred to them for a moment that the child might not be his. They had quite forgiven her for leaving Tony, though they thought themselves distinctly broad-minded for having done so. They would ask her from time to time what Christian was doing, not because they were interested, but so that Linda shouldn't feel out of it when Louisa and I talked about our husbands. She would then be obliged to invent bits of news out of imaginary letters from Christian.

'He doesn't like his Brigadier very much,' or,

'He says Cairo is great fun, but one can have enough of it.'

In point of fact Linda never got any letters at all. She had not seen her English friends now for so long, they were scattered in the war to the ends of the earth, and, though they might not have forgotten about Linda, she was no longer in their lives. But, of course, there was only one thing she wanted, a letter, a line even, from Fabrice. Just after Christmas it came. It was forwarded in a typewritten envelope from Carlton Gardens with General de Gaulle's stamp on it. Linda, when she saw it lying on the hall table, became perfectly white. She seized it and rushed up to her bedroom.

About an hour later she came to find me.

'Oh, darling,' she said, her eyes full of tears. 'I've been all this time and I can't read one word. Isn't it torture? Could you have a look?'

She gave me a sheet of the thinnest paper I ever saw, on which were scratched, apparently with a rusty pin, a series of perfectly incomprehensible hieroglyphics. I could not make out one single word either, it seemed to bear no relation to handwriting, the marks in no way resembled letters.

'What can I do?' said poor Linda. 'Oh, Fanny.'

'Let's ask Davey,' I said.

She hesitated a little over this, but feeling that it would be better, however intimate the message, to share it with Davey than not to have it at all, she finally agreed.

Davey said she was quite right to ask him.

'I am very good at French handwriting.'

'Only you wouldn't laugh at it?' Linda said, in a breathless voice like a child.

'No, Linda, I don't regard it as a laughing matter any longer,' Davey replied, looking with love and anxiety at her face, which had become very drawn of late. But when he had studied the paper for some time, he too was obliged to confess himself absolutely stumped by it.

'I've seen a lot of difficult French writings in my life,' he said, 'and this beats them all.'

In the end Linda had to give up. She went about with the piece of paper, like a talisman, in her pocket, but never knew what Fabrice had written to her on it. It was cruelly tantalizing. She wrote to him at Carlton Gardens, but this letter came back with a note regretting that it could not be forwarded.

'Never mind,' she said. 'One day the telephone bell will ring again and he'll be there.'

Louisa and I were busy from morning to night. We now had one Nanny (mine) between eight children. Fortunately they were not at home all the time. Louisa's two eldest were at a private school, and two of hers and two of mine went for lessons to a convent Lord Merlin had most providentially found for us at Merlinford. Louisa got a little petrol for this, and she or I or Davey drove them there in Aunt Sadie's car every day. It can be imagined what Uncle Matthew thought of this arrangement. He ground his teeth, flashed his eyes, and always referred to the poor good nuns as 'those damned parachutists'. He was absolutely convinced that whatever time they could spare from making machine-gun nests for other nuns, who would presently descend from the skies, like birds, to occupy the nests, was given to the seduction of the souls of his grandchildren and great-nieces.

'They get a prize you know for anybody they can catch—of course you can see they are men, you've only got to look at their boots.'

Every Sunday he watched the children like a lynx for genuflexions, making the sign of the Cross, and other Papist antics, or even for undue interest in the service, and when none of these symptoms was to be observed he was hardly reassured.

'These Romans are so damned artful.'

He thought it most subversive of Lord Merlin to harbour such an establishment on his property, but only really what one might expect of a man who brought Germans to one's hall and was known to admire foreign music. Uncle Matthew had most conveniently forgotten all about 'Una voce poco fa', and now played, from morning to night, a record called 'The Turkish Patrol', which started piano, became forte, and ended up pianissimo.

'You see,' he would say, 'they come out of a wood, and then you can hear them go back into the wood. Don't know why it's called Turkish, you can't imagine Turks playing a tune like that, and of course there aren't any woods in Turkey. It's just the name, that's all.'

I think it reminded him of his Home Guard, who were always going into woods and coming out of them again, poor dears, often covering themselves with branches as when Birnam Wood came to Dunsinane.

So we worked hard, mending and making and washing, doing any chores for Nanny rather than actually look after the children ourselves. I have seen too many children brought up without Nannies to think this at all desirable. In Oxford, the wives of progressive dons did it often as a matter of principle; they would gradually become morons themselves, while the children looked like slum children and behaved like barbarians.

As well as looking after the clothes of our existing families we also had to make for the babies we were expecting, though they did inherit a good deal from brothers and sisters. Linda, who naturally had no store of baby clothes, did nothing of all this. She arranged one of the slatted shelves in the Hons' cupboard as a sort of bunk, with pillows and quilts from spare bedrooms, and here, wrapped in her mink bedspread, she would lie all day with Plon-plon beside her, reading fairy stories. The Hons' cupboard, as of old, was the warmest, the one really warm place in the house. Whenever I could I brought my sewing and sat with her there, and then she would put down the blue or the green fairy book,

Andersen or Grimm, and tell me at length about Fabrice and her happy life with him in Paris. Louisa sometimes joined us there, and then Linda would break off and we would talk about John Fort William and the children. But Louisa was a restless busy creature, not much of a chatter, and, besides, she was irritated to see how Linda did absolutely nothing, day after day.

'Whatever is the baby going to wear, poor thing,' she would say crossly to me, 'and who is going to look after it, Fanny? It's quite plain already that you and I will have to, and really, you know, we've got enough to do as it is. And another thing, Linda lies there covered in sables or whatever they are, but she's got no money at all, she's a pauper—I don't believe she realizes that in the least. And what is Christian going to say when he hears about the baby, after all, legally his, he'll have to bring a suit to illegitimize it, and then there'll be such a scandal. None of these things seems to have occurred to Linda. She ought to be beside herself with worry, instead of which she is behaving like the wife of a millionaire in peacetime. I've no patience with her.'

All the same, Louisa was a good soul. In the end it was she who went to London and bought a layette for the baby. Linda sold Tony's engagement ring, at a horribly low price, to pay for it.

'Do you ever think about your husbands?' I asked her one day, after she had been talking for hours about Fabrice.

'Well, funnily enough, I do quite often think of Tony. Christian, you see, was such an interlude, he hardly counts in my life at all, because, for one thing, our marriage lasted a very short time, and then it was quite overshadowed by what came after. I don't know, I find these things hard to remember, but I think that my feelings for him were only really intense for a few weeks, just at the very beginning. He's a noble character, a man you can respect, I don't blame myself for marrying him, but he has no talent for love.

'But Tony was my husband for so long, more than a quarter of my life, if you come to think of it. He certainly made an impression. And I see now that the thing going wrong was hardly his fault, poor Tony, I don't believe it would have gone right with anybody (unless I had happened to meet Fabrice) because in those days I was so extremely nasty. The really important thing, if a marriage is to go well, without much love, is very very great niceness—*gentillesse*—and wonderful good manners. I was never *gentille* with Tony, and often I was hardly polite to him, and, very soon after our honeymoon, I became exceedingly disagreeable. I'm ashamed now to think what I was like. And poor old Tony was so good-natured, he never snapped back, he put up with it all for years and then just ambled off to Pixie. I can't blame him. It was my fault from beginning to end.'

'Well, he wasn't very nice really, darling, I shouldn't worry yourself about it too much, and look how he's behaving now.'

'Oh, he's the weakest character in the world, it's Pixie and his parents who made him do that. If he'd still been married to me he would have been a Guards officer by now, I bet you.'

One thing Linda never thought about, I'm quite sure, was the future. Some day the telephone bell would ring and it would be Fabrice, and that was as far as she got. Whether he would marry her, and what would happen about the child, were questions which not only did not preoccupy her, but which never seemed to enter her head. Her mind was entirely on the past.

'It's rather sad,' she said one day, 'to belong, as we do, to a lost generation. I'm sure in history the two wars will count as one war and that we shall be squashed out of it altogether, and people will forget that we ever existed. We might just as well never have lived at all, I do think it's a shame.'

'It may become a sort of literary curiosity,' Davey said. He sometimes crept, shivering, into the Hons' cupboard to get up a little circulation before he went back to his writing. 'People will be interested in it for all the wrong reasons, and collect Lalique dressing-table sets and sha-green boxes and cocktail cabinets lined with looking-glass and find them very amusing. Oh good,' he said, peering out of the window, 'that wonderful Juan is bringing in another pheasant.'

(Juan had an invaluable talent, he was expert with a catapult. He spent all his odd moments—how he had odd moments was a mystery, but he had—creeping about the woods or down by the river armed with this weapon. As he was an infallible shot, and moreover, held back by no sporting inhibitions, that a pheasant or a hare should be sitting or a swan the property of the King being immaterial to Juan, the results of these sallies were excellent from the point of view of larder and stock-pot. When Davey really wanted to relish his food to the full he would recite, half to himself, a sort of little grace, which began: 'Remember Mrs. Beecher's tinned tomato soup.'

The unfortunate Craven was, of course, tortured by these goings on, which he regarded as little better than poaching. But his nose, poor man, was kept well to the grindstone by Uncle Matthew, and, when he was not on sentry-go, or fastening the trunks of trees to bicycle-wheels across the lanes to make barricades against tanks, he was on parade. Uncle Matthew was a byword in the county for the smartness of his parades. Juan, as an alien, was luckily excluded from these activities, and was able to devote all his time to making us comfortable and happy, in which he very notably succeeded.)

'I don't want to be a literary curiosity,' said Linda. 'I should like to have been a living part of a really great generation. I think it's too dismal to have been born in 1911.'

'Never mind, Linda, you will be a wonderful old lady.'

'You will be a wonderful old gentleman, Davey,' said Linda.

'Oh, me? I fear I shall never make old bones,' replied Davey, in accents of the greatest satisfaction.

And, indeed, there was a quality of agelessness about him. Although he was quite twenty years older than we and only about five years younger than Aunt Emily, he had always seemed much nearer to our generation than to hers, nor had he altered in any respect since the day when he had stood by the hall fire looking unlike a captain and unlike a husband.

'Come on, dears, tea, and I happen to know that Juan has made a layer-cake, so let's go down before the Bolter gets it all.'

Davey carried on a great meal-time feud with the Bolter. Her table manners had always been casual, but certain of her habits, such as eating jam with a spoon which she put back into the jam-pot, and stubbing out her cigarette in the sugar-basin, drove poor Davey, who was very ration-conscious, to a frenzy of irritation, and he would speak sharply to her, like a governess to a maddening child.

He might have spared himself the trouble. The Bolter took absolutely no notice whatever, and went on spoiling food with insouciance.

'Dulling,' she would say, 'whatever does it matter, my perfectly divine Hoo-arn has got plenty more up his tiny sleeve, I promise you.'

At this time there was a particularly alarming invasion scare. The arrival of the Germans, with full paraphernalia of airborne troops dressed as priests, ballet dancers, or what you will, was expected from one day to the next. Some unkind person put it about that they would all be the doubles of Mrs. Davis, in W.V.S. uniform. She had such a knack of being in several places at once that it already seemed as if there were a dozen Mrs. Davises parachuting about the countryside. Uncle Matthew took the invasion very seriously indeed, and one day he gathered us all together, in the business room and told us in detail the part that we were expected to play.

'You women, with the children, must go to the cellar while the battle is on,' he said, 'there is an excellent tap, and I have provisioned you with bully-beef for a week. Yes, you may be there several days, I warn you.'

'Nanny won't like that,' Louisa began, but was quelled by a furious look.

'While we are on the subject of Nanny,' Uncle Matthew said, 'I warn you, there's to be no question of cluttering up the roads with your prams, mind, no evacuation under any circumstances at all. Now, there is one very important job to be done, and that I am entrusting to you, Davey. You won't mind it I know, old boy, if I say that you are a very poor shot—as you know, we are short of ammunition, and what there is must, under no circumstances, be wasted—every bullet must tell. So I don't intend to give you a gun, at first, anyhow. But I've got a fuse and a charge of dynamite (I will show you, in a moment), and I shall want you to blow up the store-cupboard for me.'

'Blow up Aladdin,' said Davey. He turned quite pale. 'Matthew, you must be mad.'

'I would let Gewan do it, but the fact is, though I rather like old Gewan now, I don't altogether trust the fella. Once a foreigner always a foreigner in my opinion. Now I must explain to you why I regard this as a most vital part of the operations. When Josh and Craven and I and all the rest of us have been killed there is only one way in which you civilians can help, and that is by becoming a charge on the German army. You must make it their business to feed you—never fear, they'll do so, they don't want typhus along their lines of communication—but you must see that it's as difficult as possible for them. Now that store cupboard would keep you going for weeks, I've just had a look at it; why, it would feed the entire village. All wrong. Make them bring in the food and muck up their transport, that's what we want, to be a perfect nuisance to them. It's all you'll be able to do, by then, just be a nuisance, so the store cupboard will have to go, and Davey must blow it up.'

Davey opened his mouth to make another observation, but Uncle Matthew was in a very frightening mood and he thought better of it.

'Very well, dear Matthew,' he said sadly, 'you must show me what to do.'

But as soon as Uncle Matthew's back was turned he gave utterance to loud complaints.

'No, really, it is too bad of Matthew to insist on blowing up Aladdin,' he said. 'It's all right for him, he'll be dead, but he really should consider us a little more.'

'But I thought you were going to take those black and white pills,' said Linda.

'Emily doesn't like the idea, and I had decided only to take them if I were arrested, but now I don't know. Matthew says the German army will have to feed us, but he must know as well as I do that if they feed us at all, which is extremely problematical, it will be on nothing but starch—it will be Mrs. Beecher again, only worse, and I can't digest starch especially in the winter months. It is such a shame. Horrid old Matthew, he's so thoughtless.'

'Well, but Davey,' said Linda, 'how about us? We're all in the same boat, but we don't grumble.'

'Nanny will,' said Louisa with a sniff, which plainly said, 'and I wish to associate myself with Nanny.'

'Nanny! She lives in a world of her own,' said Linda. 'But we're all supposed to know why we're fighting, and, speaking for myself, I think Fa is absolutely right. And if I think that, in my condition——'

'Oh, you'll be looked after,' said Davey bitterly, 'pregnant women always are. They'll send you vitamins and things from America, you'll see. But nobody will bother about me, and I am so delicate, it simply won't do for me to be fed by the German army, and I shall never be able to make them understand about my inside. I know Germans.'

'You always said nobody understood as much about your inside as Dr. Meyerstein.'

'Use your common sense, Linda. Are they likely to drop Dr. Meyerstein over Alconleigh? You know perfectly well he's been in a camp for years. No, I must make up my mind to a lingering death—not a very pleasant prospect, I must say.'

Linda took Uncle Matthew aside after that, and made him show her how to blow up Aladdin.

'Davey's spirit is not so frightfully willing,' she said, 'and his flesh is definitely weak.'

There was a certain coldness between Linda and Davey for a little while after this, each thought the other had been quite unreasonable. It did not last, however. They were much too fond of each other (in fact, I am sure that Davey really loved Linda most in the world) and, as Aunt Sadie said, 'Who knows, perhaps the necessity for these dreadful decisions will not arise.'

So the winter slowly passed. The spring came with extraordinary beauty, as always at Alconleigh, with a brilliance of colouring, a richness of life, that one had forgotten to expect during the cold grey winter months. All the animals were giving birth, there were young creatures everywhere, and we now waited with longing and impatience for our babies to be born. The days, the very hours, dragged slowly by, and Linda began to say 'better than that' when asked the time.

'What's the time, darling?'

'Guess.'

'Half-past twelve?'

'Better than that, a quarter to one.'

We three pregnant women had all become enormous, we dragged ourselves about the house like great figures of fertility, heaving tremendous sighs, and feeling the heat of the first warm days with exaggerated discomfort.

Useless to her now were Linda's beautiful Paris clothes, she was down to the level of Louisa and me in a cotton smock, maternity skirt and sandals. She abandoned the Hons' cupboard, and spent her days, when it was fine weather, sitting by the edge of the wood, while Plon-plon, who had become an enthusiastic, though unsuccessful, rabbiter, plunged panting to and fro in the green mists of the undergrowth.

'If anything happens to me, darling, you will look after Plon-plon,' she said. 'He has been such a comfort to me all this time.'

But she spoke idly, as one who knows, in fact, that she will live for ever, and she mentioned neither Fabrice nor the child, as surely she would have done had she been touched by any premonition.

Louisa's baby, Angus, was born at the beginning of April. It was her sixth child and third boy, and we envied her from the bottom of our hearts for having got it over.

On the 28th May both our babies were born—both boys. The doctors who said that Linda ought never to have another child were not such idiots after all. It killed her. She died, I think, completely happy, and without having suffered very much, but for us at Alconleigh, for her father and mother, brothers and sisters, for Davey and for Lord Merlin a light went out, a great deal of joy that never could be replaced.

At about the same time as Linda's death Fabrice was caught by the Gestapo and subsequently shot. He was a hero of the Resistance, and his name has become a legend in France.

I have adopted the little Fabrice, with the consent of Christian, his legal father. He has black eyes, the same shape as Linda's blue ones, and is a most beautiful and enchanting child. I love him quite as much as, and perhaps more than, I do my own.

The Bolter came to see me while I was still in the Oxford nursing home where my baby had been born and where Linda had died.

'Poor Linda,' she said, with feeling, 'poor little thing. But, Fanny, don't you think perhaps it's just as well? The lives of women like Linda and me are not so much fun when one begins to grow older.'

I didn't want to hurt my mother's feelings by protesting that Linda was not that sort of woman.

'But I think she would have been happy with Fabrice,' I said. 'He was the great love of her life, you know.'

'Oh, dulling,' said my mother sadly. 'One always thinks that. Every, every time.'

LOVE IN A COLD CLIMATE

TO
LORD BERNERS

Part One

CHAPTER I

I am obliged to begin this story with a brief account of the Hampton family, because it is necessary to emphasize the fact once and for all that the Hamptons were very grand as well as very rich. A glance at Burke or at Debrett would be quite enough to make this clear, but these large volumes are not always available, while the books on the subject by Lord Montdore's brother-in-law, Boy Dougdale, are all out of print. His great talent for snobbishness and small talent for literature have produced three detailed studies of his wife's forebears, but they can only be read now by asking a bookseller to get them at second hand. (The bookseller will put an advertisement in his trade paper *The Clique*, 'H. Dougdale, any by'. He will be snowed under with copies at about a shilling each, and will then proudly inform his customer that he has 'managed to find what you want', implying hours of careful search on barrows, dirt cheap, at 30s. the three.) *Georgiana Lady Montdore and Her Circle*, *The Magnificent Montdores* and *Old Chronicles of Hampton*, I have them beside me as I write, and see that the opening paragraph of the first is:

'Two ladies, one dark, one fair, both young and lovely, were driving briskly towards the little village of Kensington on a fine May morning. They were Georgiana, Countess of Montdore and her great friend Walburga, Duchess of Paddington, and they made a delightfully animated picture as they discussed the burning question of the hour—should one, or should one not, subscribe to a parting present for poor, dear Princess Lieven?'

This book is dedicated, by gracious permission, to Her Royal Highness the Grand Duchess Peter of Russia, and has eight full-page illustrations.

It must be said that when this terrible trilogy first came out it had quite a vogue with the lending library public.

'The family of Hampton is ancient in the West of England, indeed Fuller, in his "Worthies", mentions it as being of stupendous antiquity.'

Burke makes it out just a shade more ancient than does Debrett, but both plunge back into the mists of medieval times, from which they drag forth ancestors with P. G. Wodehouse names, Ugs and Berts and Threds, and Walter Scott fates. 'His Lordship was attainted—beheaded—convicted—proscribed—exiled—dragged from prison by a furious mob—slain at the Battle of Crécy—went down in the White

Ship—perished during the third crusade—killed in a duel.' There were very few natural deaths to record in the early misty days. Both Burke and Debrett linger with obvious enjoyment over so genuine an object as this family, unspoilt by the ambiguities of female line and deed poll. Nor could any of those horrid books which came out in the nineteenth century, devoted to research and aiming to denigrate the nobility, make the object seem less genuine. Tall, golden-haired barons, born in wedlock and all looking very much alike, succeeded each other at Hampton, on lands which had never been bought or sold, until, in 1770, the Lord Hampton of the day brought back, from a visit to Versailles, a French bride, a Mademoiselle de Montdore. Their son had brown eyes, a dark skin and presumably, for it is powdered in all the pictures of him, black hair. This blackness did not persist in the family; he married a golden-haired heiress from Derbyshire and the Hamptons reverted to their blue and gold looks, for which they are famous to this day. The son of the Frenchwoman was rather clever and very worldly; he dabbled in politics and wrote a book of aphorisms. A great and life-long friendship with the Regent procured him, among other favours, an earldom. His mother's family having all perished during the Terror in France, he took her name as his title. Enormously rich, he spent enormously; he had a taste for French objects of art and acquired, during the years which followed the Revolution, a splendid collection of such things, including many pieces from the royal establishments, and others which had been looted out of the Hôtel de Montdore in the Rue de Varenne. To make a suitable setting for this collection he then proceeded to pull down, at Hampton, the large plain house that Adam had built for his grandfather, and to drag over to England stone by stone (as modern American millionaires are supposed to do) a Gothic French château. This he assembled round a splendid tower of his own designing, covered the walls of the rooms with French panelling and silks, and set it in a formal landscape which he also designed and planted himself. It was all very grand and very mad, and in the between-wars period of which I write, very much out of fashion. 'I suppose it is beautiful,' people used to say, 'but frankly I don't admire it.'

This Lord Montdore also built Montdore House in Park Lane and a castle on a crag in Aberdeenshire. He was really much the most interesting and original character the family ever produced, but no member of it deviated from a tradition of authority. A solid, worthy, powerful Hampton can be found on every page of English history, his influence enormous in the West of England and his counsels not unheeded in London.

The tradition was carried on by the father of my friend Polly Hampton. If an Englishman could be descended from the gods it would be he, so much the very type of English nobleman that those who believed in aristocratic government would always begin by pointing to him as a justification of their argument. It was generally felt, indeed, that if there were more people like him the country would not be in its present mess, even Socialists conceding his excellence, which they could afford to do since there was only one of him and he was getting on. A scholar, a Christian, a gentleman, finest shot in the British Isles, best-looking Viceroy we ever sent to India, a popular landlord, a pillar of the Conservative party, a wonderful old man, in short, who nothing common ever did or mean. My cousin Linda and I, two irreverent little girls whose opinion makes no odds, used to think that he was a wonderful old fraud, and it seemed to us that in that house it was Lady Montdore who really counted. Now Lady Montdore was for ever doing common things and mean and she was intensely unpopular, quite as much disliked as her husband was loved, so that anything he might do that was considered not quite worthy of him, or which did not quite fit in with his reputation, was immediately laid at her door. 'Of course she made him do it.' On the other hand I have often wondered whether without her to bully him and push him forward and plot and intrigue for him and 'make him do it', whether in fact, without the help of those very attributes which caused her to be so much disliked, her thick skin and ambition and boundless driving energy, he would ever have done anything at all noteworthy in the world.

This is not a popular theory. I am told that by the time I really knew him, after they got back from India, he was already old and tired out and had given up the struggle, and that, when he was in his prime, he had not only controlled the destinies of men but also the vulgarities of his wife. I wonder. There was an ineffectiveness about Lord Montdore which had nothing to do with age; he was certainly beautiful to look at, but it was an empty beauty like that of a woman who has no sex appeal, he looked wonderful and old, but it seemed to me that, in spite of the fact that he still went regularly to the House of Lords, attended the Privy Council, sat on many committees, and often appeared in the Birthday Honours, he might just as well have been made of wonderful old cardboard.

Lady Montdore, however, was flesh and blood all right. She was born a Miss Perrotte, the handsome daughter of a country squire of small means and no particular note, so that her marriage to Lord Montdore was a far better one than she could reasonably have been expected to make. As time went on, when her worldly greed and snobbishness, her terrible relentless rudeness, had become proverbial, and formed the subject of many a legendary tale, people were inclined to suppose that her origins must have been low or transatlantic, but, in fact, she was perfectly well-born and had been decently brought up, what used to be called 'a lady'; so that there were no mitigating circumstances, and she ought to have known better.

No doubt her rampant vulgarity must have become more evident and less controlled with the years. In any case her husband never seemed aware of it, and the marriage was a success. Lady Montdore soon embarked him upon a public career, the fruits of which he was able to enjoy without much hard work since she made it her business to see that he was surrounded by a horde of efficient underlings, and though he pretended to despise the social life which gave meaning to her existence, he put up with it very gracefully, exercising a natural talent for agreeable conversation and accepting as his due the fact that people thought him wonderful.

'Isn't Lord Montdore wonderful? Sonia, of course, is past a joke, but he is so brilliant, such a dear, I do love him.'

People liked to pretend that it was solely on his account that they ever went to the house at all, but this was great nonsense because the lively quality, the fun of Lady Montdore's parties had nothing whatever to do with him, and, hateful as she may have been in many ways, she excelled as a hostess.

In short, they were happy together and singularly well suited. But for years they suffered one serious vexation in their married life; they had no children. Lord Montdore minded this because he naturally wanted an heir, as well as for more sentimental reasons. Lady Montdore minded passionately. Not only did she also want an heir, but she disliked any form of failure, could not bear to be thwarted, and was eager for an object on which she could concentrate such energy as was not absorbed by society and her husband's career. They had been married nearly twenty years, and quite given up all idea of having a child when Lady Montdore began to feel less well than usual. She took no notice, went on with her usual occupations and it was only two months before it was born that she realized she was going to have a baby. She was clever enough to avoid the ridicule which often attaches to such a situation by pretending to have kept the secret on purpose, so that instead of roaring with laughter, everybody said, 'Isn't Sonia absolutely phenomenal?'

I know all this because my uncle Davey Warbeck has told me. Having himself for many years suffered, or enjoyed, most of the distempers in the medical dictionary he is very well up in nursing-home gossip.

The fact that the child, when it was born, turned out to be a daughter, never seems to have troubled the Montdores at all. It is possible that, as Lady Montdore was under forty when Polly was born, they did not at first envisage her as an only child and that by the time they realized that they would never have another they loved her so much that the idea of her being in any way different, a different person, a boy, had become unthinkable. Naturally they would have liked to have a boy, but only if it could have been as well as, and not instead of, Polly. She was their treasure, the very hub of their universe.

Polly Hampton had beauty, and this beauty was her outstanding characteristic. She was one of those people you cannot think of except in regard to their looks, which in her case were unvarying, independent of clothes, of age, of circumstances, and even of health. When ill or tired she merely looked fragile, but never yellow, withered or diminished; she was born beautiful and never, at any time when I knew her, went off or became less beautiful, but on the contrary her looks always steadily improved. The beauty of Polly and the importance of her family are essential elements of this story. But, whereas the Hamptons can be studied in various books of reference, it is not much use turning to old *Tatlers* and seeing Polly as Lenare, as Dorothy Wilding saw her. The bones of course are there, hideous hats, old-fashioned poses cannot conceal them, the bones and the shape of her face are always perfection. But beauty is more, after all, than bones, for while bones belong to death and endure after decay, beauty is a living thing; it is, in fact, skin deep, blue shadows on a white skin, hair falling like golden feathers on a white smooth forehead, it is embodied in the movement, in the smile and above all in the regard of a beautiful woman. Polly's regard was a blue flash, the bluest and most sudden thing I ever saw, so curiously unrelated to the act of seeing that it was almost impossible to believe that those opaque blue stones observed, assimilated, or did anything except confer a benefit upon the object of their direction.

No wonder her parents loved her. Even Lady Montdore, who would have been a terrible mother to an ugly girl, or to an eccentric, wayward boy, had no difficulty in being perfect to a child who must, it seemed, do her great credit in the world and crown her ambitions; literally, perhaps, crown. Polly was certainly destined for an exceptional marriage—was Lady Montdore not envisaging something very grand indeed when she gave her the name Leopoldina? Had this not a royal, a vaguely Coburg flavour which might one day be most suitable? Was she dreaming of an abbey, an altar, an Archbishop, a voice saying 'I, Albert Edward Christian George Andrew Patrick David take thee, Leopoldina'? It was not an impossible dream. On the other hand nothing could be more purely English, wholesome and unpretentious than 'Polly'.

My cousin Linda Radlett and I used to be borrowed from a very early age, to play with Polly, for, as so often happens with the parents of only children, the Montdores were always much preoccupied with her possible loneliness. I know that my own adopted mother, Aunt Emily, had the same feeling about me and would do anything rather than keep me alone with her during the holidays. Hampton Park is not far from Linda's home, Alconleigh, and she and Polly, being more or less of an age, each seemed destined to become the other's greatest friend. For some reason, however, they never really took to each other much, while Lady Montdore disliked Linda, and as soon as she was able to converse at all pronounced her conversation 'unsuitable'. I can see Linda now, at luncheon in the big dining-room at Hampton (that dining-room in which I have, at various times in my life, been so terrified that its very smell, a bouquet left by a hundred years of rich food, rich wine, rich cigars and rich women, is still to me as the smell of blood is to an animal), I can hear her loud sing-song Radlett voice, 'Did you ever have worms, Polly? I did, you can't imagine how fidgety they are. Then, oh the heaven of it, Doctor Simpson came and wormed me. Well you know how Doc. Simp. has always been the love of my life—so you do see——'

This was too much for Lady Montdore and Linda was never asked to stay again. But I went for a week or so almost every holidays, packed off there on my way to or from Alconleigh as children are, without ever being asked if I enjoyed it or wanted to go. My father was related to Lord Montdore through his mother. I was a well-behaved child and I think Lady Montdore quite liked me, anyhow she must have considered me 'suitable', a word which figured prominently in her vocabulary, because at one moment there was a question of my going to live there during the term, to do lessons with Polly. When I was thirteen, how-ever, they went off to govern India, after which Hampton and its owners became a dim, though always alarming, memory to me.

CHAPTER II

By the time the Montdores and Polly returned from India I was grown-up and had already had a season in London. Linda's mother, my Aunt Sadie (Lady Alconleigh), had taken Linda and me out to-gether, that is to say we went to a series of débutante dances where the people we met were all as young and as shy as we were ourselves, and the whole thing smelt strongly of bread and butter; it was quite unlike the real world, and almost as little of a preparation for it as children's parties are. When the summer ended Linda became engaged to be married, and I went back to my home in Kent, to another aunt and uncle, Aunt Emily and Uncle Davey, who had relieved my own divorced parents of the boredom and the burden of bringing up a child.

I was finding it dull at home, as young girls do when, for the first time, they have neither lessons nor parties to occupy their minds, and then one day into this dullness fell an invitation to stay at Hampton in October. Aunt Emily came out to find me, I was sitting in the garden, with Lady Montdore's letter in her hand.

'Lady Montdore says it will be rather a grown-up affair, mostly "young married people", she says, but she particularly wants you as company for Polly. There will be two young men for you girls, of course. Oh what a pity it happens to be Davey's day for getting drunk. I long to tell him, he'll be so much interested.'

There was nothing for it, however, but to wait; Davey had quite passed out and his stertorous breathing could be heard all over the house. My uncle's lapses into insobriety had no vice about them, they were purely therapeutic. The fact is he was following a new regime for perfect health, much in vogue at that time, he assured us, on the Continent.

'The aim is to warm up your glands with a series of jolts. The worst thing in the world for the body is to settle down and lead a quiet little life of regular habits; if you do that it soon resigns itself to old age and death. Shock your glands, force them to react, startle them back into youth, keep them on tip-toe so that they never know what to expect next, and they have to keep young and healthy to deal with all the surprises.'

Accordingly he ate in turns like Gandhi and like Henry VIII, went for ten-mile walks or lay in bed all day, shivered in a cold bath or sweated in a hot one. Nothing in moderation. 'It is also very important to get drunk every now and then.' Davey, however, was too much of a one for regular habits to be irregular otherwise than regularly, so he always got drunk at the full moon. Having once been under the influence of Rudolph Steiner he was still very conscious of the waxing and waning of the moon, and had, I believe, a vague idea that the waxing and waning of the capacity of his stomach coincided with its periods.

Uncle Davey was my one contact with the world; not the world of bread-and-butter misses but the great wicked world itself. Both my aunts had renounced it at an early age so that for them its existence had no reality, while their sister, my mother, had long since disappeared from view into its maw. Davey, however, had a modified liking for it, and often made little bachelor excursions into it from which he would return with a bag of interesting anecdotes. I could hardly wait to have a chat with him about this new development in my life.

'Are you sure he's too drunk, Aunt Emily?'

'Quite sure, dear. We must leave it until tomorrow.'

Meanwhile, as she always answered letters by return of post, she wrote and accepted. But the next day, when Davey reappeared looking perfectly green and with an appalling headache ('Oh, but that's splendid don't you see, such a challenge to the metabolism. I've just spoken to Dr. England and he is most satisfied with my reaction') he was rather doubtful whether she had been right to do so.

'My darling Emily, the child will die of terror, that's all.' He was examining Lady Montdore's letter. I knew quite well that what he said was true, I had known it in my heart ever since Aunt Emily had read me the letter, but nevertheless I was determined to go; the idea had a glittering fascination for me.

'I'm not a child any longer, Davey,' I said.

'Grown-up people have died of terror at Hampton before now,' he replied. 'Two young men for Fanny and Polly indeed! Two old lovers of two of the old ladies there if I know anything about it. What a look, Emily! If you intend to launch this poor child in high society you must send her away armed with knowledge of the facts of life, you know. But I really don't understand what your policy is. First of all you take care that she should only meet the most utterly innocuous people, keep her nose firmly to Pont Street—quite a point of view, don't think I'm against it for a moment—but then all of a sudden you push her off the rocks into Hampton and expect that she will be able to swim.'

'Your metaphors, Davey—it's all those spirits,' Aunt Emily said, crossly for her.

'Never mind the spirits and let me tell poor Fanny the form. First of all, dear, I must explain that it's no good counting on these alleged young men to amuse you, because they won't have any time to spare for little girls, that's quite certain. On the other hand who is sure to be there is the Lecherous Lecturer, and as you are probably still just within his age group there's no saying what fun and games you may not have with him.'

'Oh, Davey,' I said, 'you are dreadful.'

The Lecherous Lecturer was Boy Dougdale. The Radlett children had given him this name after he had once lectured at Aunt Sadie's Women's Institute. The lecture, it seemed (I was not there at the time), had been very dull, but the things the lecturer did afterwards to Linda and Jassy were not dull at all.

'You know what secluded lives we lead,' Jassy had told me when next I was at Alconleigh. 'Naturally, it's not very difficult to arouse our interest. For example, do you remember that dear old man who came and lectured on the Toll Gates of England and Wales? It was rather tedious, but we liked it—he's coming again, Green Lanes this time. Well, the Lecherous Lecturer's lecture was Duchesses, and of course, one always prefers people to gates. But the fascinating thing was after the lecture he gave us a foretaste of sex, think what a thrill. He took Linda up on to the roof and did all sorts of blissful things to her; at least, she could easily see how they would be blissful with anybody except the Lecturer. And I got some great sexy pinches as he passed the nursery landing. Do admit, Fanny.'

Of course, my Aunt Sadie had no inkling of all this; she would have been perfectly horrified. Both she and Uncle Matthew always had very much disliked Mr. Dougdale, and, when speaking of the lecture, she said it was exactly what she would have expected, snobbish, dreary and out of place with a village audience, but she had such difficulty filling up the Women's Institute programme month after month, in that remote district, that when he had himself written and suggested coming she had thought 'Oh, well——!' No doubt she supposed that her children called him the Lecherous Lecturer for alliterative rather than factual reasons, and indeed with the Radletts you never could tell. Why, for instance, would Victoria bellow like a bull and half kill Jassy whenever Jassy said, in a certain tone of voice, pointing her finger with a certain look, 'Fancy'? I think they hardly knew why themselves.

When I got home I told Davey about the Lecturer, and he had roared with laughter, but said I was not to breathe a word to Aunt Emily or there would be an appalling row, and the one who would really suffer would be Lady Patricia Dougdale, Boy's wife.

'She has enough to put up with as it is,' he said, 'and besides, what would be the good? Those Radletts are clearly heading for one bad end after another, except that for them nothing ever will be the end. Poor dear Sadie just doesn't realize what she has hatched out, luckily for her.'

All this had happened a year or two before the time of which I am writing, and the name of Lecturer for Boy Dougdale had passed into the family language, so that none of us children ever called him anything else, and even the grown-ups had come to accept it, though Aunt Sadie, as a matter of form, made an occasional vague protest. It seemed to suit him perfectly.

'Don't listen to Davey,' Aunt Emily said, 'he's in a very naughty mood. Another time we'll wait for the waning moon to tell him these things, he's only really sensible when he's fasting I've noticed. Now we shall have to think about your clothes, Fanny. Sonia's parties are always so dreadfully smart. I suppose they'll be sure to change for tea? Perhaps if we dyed your Ascot dress a nice dark shade of red that would do? It's a good thing we've got nearly a month.'

Nearly a month was indeed a comforting thought. Although I was bent on going to this house party, the very idea of it made me shake in my shoes with fright, not so much as the result of Davey's teasing as because ancient memories of Hampton now began to revive in force, memories of my childhood visits there and of how little, really, I had enjoyed them. Downstairs had been so utterly terrifying. It might be supposed that nothing could frighten somebody accustomed, as I was, to a downstairs inhabited by my uncle Matthew Alconleigh. But that rumbustious ogre, that eater of little girls, was by no means confined to one part of his house. He raged and roared about the whole of it, and indeed, the safest place to be in as far as he was concerned was downstairs in Aunt Sadie's drawing-room, since she alone had any control over him. The terror at Hampton was of a different quality, icy and dispassionate, and it reigned downstairs. You were forced down into it after tea, frilled up, washed and curled, when quite little, or in a tidy frock when older, into the Long Gallery, where there would seem to be dozens of grown-ups, all usually playing bridge. The worst of bridge is that out of every four people playing it one is always at liberty to roam about and say kind words to little girls.

Still, on the whole, there was not much attention to spare from the cards, and we could sit on the long white fur of the polar bear in front of the fireplace, looking at a picture book propped against its head, or just chatting to each other until welcome bedtime. It quite often happened, however, that Lord Montdore, or Boy Dougdale if he was there, would give up playing in order to amuse us. Lord Montdore would read aloud from Hans Andersen or Lewis Carroll and there was something about the way he read that made me squirm with secret embarrassment; Polly used to lie with her head on the bear's head, not listening, I believe, to a single word. It was far worse when Boy Dougdale organized hide and seek or sardines, two games of which he was extremely fond, and which he played in what Linda and I considered a "stchoopid" way. The word stupid, pronounced like that, had a meaning of its own in our language when we (the Radletts and I) were little; it was not until after the Lecturer's lecture that we realized that Boy Dougdale had not been stupid so much as lecherous.

When bridge was in progress we would at least be spared the attention of Lady Montdore, who, even when dummy, had eyes for nothing but the cards, but if by chance there should not be a four staying in the house she would make us play racing demon, a game which has always given me an inferiority feeling because I do pant along so slowly.

'Hurry up, Fanny—we're all waiting for that seven, you know. Don't be so moony, dear.'

She always won by hundreds, never missing a trick. She never missed a detail of one's appearance, either, the shabby old pair of indoor shoes, the stockings that did not quite match each other, the tidy frock too short and too tight, grown out of in fact—it was all chalked up on the score.

That was downstairs. Upstairs was all right, perfectly safe, anyhow, from intrusion, the nursery being occupied by nurses, the schoolroom by governesses, and neither being subject to visits from the Montdores who, when they wished to see Polly, sent for her to go to them. But it was rather dull, not nearly as much fun as staying at Alconleigh. No Hons' cupboard, no talking bawdy, no sallies into the woods to hide the steel traps or to unstop an earth, no nests of baby bats being fed with fountain-pen fillers in secret from the grown-ups, who had absurd ideas about bats, that they were covered with vermin, or got into your hair. Polly was a withdrawn, formal little girl, who went through her day with the sense of ritual, the poise, the absolute submission to etiquette of a Spanish Infanta. You had to love her, she was so beautiful and so friendly, but it was impossible to feel very intimate with her.

She was the exact opposite of the Radletts who always 'told' everything. Polly 'told' nothing and if there were anything to tell it was all bottled up inside her. When Lord Montdore once read us the story of the Snow Queen (I could hardly listen, he put in so much expression) I remember thinking that it must be about Polly and that she surely had a glass splinter in her heart. What did she love? That was the great puzzle to me. My cousins and I poured out love on each other, on the grown-ups, on a variety of animals and above all on the characters (often historical or even fictional) with whom we were IN love. There was no reticence and we all knew everything there was to know about each other's feelings for every other creature, whether real or imaginary. Then there were the shrieks. Shrieks of laughter and happiness and high spirits which always resounded through Alconleigh, except on the rare occasions when there were floods. It was shrieks or floods in that house, usually shrieks. But Polly did not pour or shriek, and I never saw her in tears. She was always the same, always charming, sweet and docile, polite, interested in what one said, rather amused by one's jokes, but all without exuberance, without superlatives, and certainly without any confidences.

Nearly a month then to this visit about which my feelings were so uncertain. All of a sudden, not only not nearly a month but now, today, now this minute, and I found myself being whirled through the suburbs of Oxford in a large black Daimler. One mercy, I was alone, and there was a long drive, some twenty miles, in front of me. I knew the road well from my hunting days in that neighbourhood. Perhaps it would go on nearly for ever. Lady Montdore's writing-paper was headed Hampton Place, Oxford, station Twyfold. But Twyfold, with the change and hour's wait at Oxford which it involved, was only inflicted upon such people as were never likely to be in a position to get their own back on Lady Montdore, anybody for whom she had the slightest regard being met at Oxford. 'Always be civil to the girls, you never know who they may marry' is an aphorism which has saved many an English spinster from being treated like an Indian widow.

So I fidgeted in my corner, looking out at the deep intense blue dusk of autumn, profoundly wishing that I could be safe back at home or going to Alconleigh or indeed anywhere rather than to Hampton. Well-known landmarks kept looming up, it got darker and darker but I could just see the Merlinford road with its big signpost. Then in a moment, or so it seemed, we were turning in at lodge gates. Horrors! I had arrived.

CHAPTER III

A SCRUNCH of gravel; the motor car gently stopped, and exactly as it did so the front door opened, casting a panel of light at my feet. Once inside, the butler took charge of me, removed my nutria coat (a coming-out present from Davey) led me through the hall, under the great steep Gothic double staircase up which rushed a hundred steps, half-way to heaven, meeting at a marble group which represented the sorrows of Niobe, through the octagonal antechamber, through the green drawing-room and the red drawing-room into the Long Gallery where, without asking it, he pronounced my name very loud and clear and then abandoned me.

The Long Gallery was, as I always remember it being, full of people. On this occasion there were perhaps twenty or thirty; some sat round a tea table by the fire while others, with glasses instead of cups in their hands, stood watching a game of backgammon. This group was composed, no doubt, of the 'young married' people to whom Lady Montdore had referred in her letter. In my eyes, however, they seemed far from young, being about the age of my own mother. They were chattering like starlings in a tree, did not break off their chatter when I came in, and when Lady Montdore introduced me to them, merely stopped it for a moment, gave me a glance and went straight on with it again. When she pronounced my name, however, one of them said:

'Not by any chance the Bolter's daughter?'

Lady Montdore paused at this, rather annoyed, but I, quite used to hearing my mother referred to as the Bolter—indeed nobody, not even her own sisters, ever called her anything else—piped up 'Yes'.

It then seemed as though all the starlings rose in the air and settled on a different tree, and that tree was me.

'The Bolter's girl?'

'Don't be funny—how could the Bolter have a grown-up daughter?'

'Veronica—do come here a minute—do you know who this is? She's the Bolter's child, that's all——!'

'Come and have your tea, Fanny,' said Lady Montdore. She led me to the table and the starlings went on with their chatter about my mother in 'eggy-peggy', a language I happened to know quite well.

'Egg-is shegg-ee reggealleggy, pwegg-oor swegg-eet? I couldn't be more interested, considering that the very first person the Bolter ever bolted with was Chad, wasn't it, darling? Lucky me got him next, but only after she had bolted away from him again.'

'I still don't see how it can be true. The Bolter can't be more than thirty-six, I know she can't. Roly, you know the Bolter's age, we all used to go to Miss Vacani's together, you in your tiny kilt, poker and tongs on the floor for the sword dance. Can she be more than thirty-six?'

'That's right, bird-brain, just do the sum. She married at eighteen, eighteen plus eighteen equals thirty-six, correct? No?'

'Yes. Steady on though, what about the nine months?'

'Not nine, darling, nothing like nine, don't you remember how bogus it all was and how shamingly huge her bouquet had to be, poor sweet? It was the whole point.'

'Veronica's gone too far as usual—come on, let's finish the game.'

I had half an ear on this riveting conversation and half on what Lady Montdore was saying. Having given me a characteristic and well-remembered look, up and down, a look which told me what I knew already, that my tweed skirt bulged behind and why had I no gloves (why, indeed, left them in the motor no doubt, and how would I ever have the courage to ask for them?), she remarked in a most friendly way that I had changed more in five years than Polly had, but that Polly was now much taller than me. How was Aunt Emily? And Davey?

That was where her charm lay. She would suddenly be nice just when it seemed that she was about to go for you tooth and nail, it was the charm of a purring puma. She now sent one of the men off to look for Polly.

'Playing billiards with Boy, I think,' and poured me out a cup of tea.

'And here,' she said, to the company in general, 'is Montdore.'

She always called her husband Montdore to those she regarded as her equals, but to border-line cases such as the estate agent or Dr. Simpson he was Lord Montdore, if not His Lordship. I never heard her refer to him as 'my husband', it was all part of the attitude to life that made her so generally unbeloved, a determination to show people what she considered to be their proper place and keep them in it.

The chatter did not continue while Lord Montdore, radiating wonderful oldness, came into the room. It stopped dead, and those who were not already standing up, respectfully did so. He shook hands all round, a suitable word for each in turn.

'And this is my friend Fanny? Quite grown-up now, and do you remember that last time I saw you we were weeping together over the Little Match Girl?'

Perfectly untrue, I thought. Nothing about human beings ever had the power to move me as a child. Black Beauty now——!

He turned to the fire, holding his large, thin white hands to the blaze, while Lady Montdore poured out his tea. There was a long silence in the room. Presently he took a scone, buttered it, put it in his saucer, and turning to another old man said, 'I've been wanting to ask you——'

They sat down together, talking in low voices, and by degrees the starling chatter broke loose again.

I was beginning to see that there was no occasion to feel alarmed in this company, because, as far as my fellow guests were concerned, I was clearly endowed with protective colouring; their momentary initial interest in me having subsided I might just as well not have been there at all, and could keep happily to myself and observe their antics. The various house parties for people of my age that I had been to during the past year had really been much more unnerving, because there I knew that I was expected to play a part, to sing for my supper by being, if possible, amusing. But here, a child once more among all these old people, it was my place to be seen and not heard. Looking round the room I wondered vaguely which were the young men Lady Montdore had mentioned as being specially invited for Polly and me. They could not yet have arrived as certainly none of these were the least bit young, all well over thirty I should have said and probably all married, though it was impossible to guess which of the couples were husbands and wives, because they all spoke to each other as if they all were, in voices and with endearments which, in the case of my aunts, could only have meant that it was their own husbands they were addressing.

'Have the Sauveterres not arrived yet, Sonia?' said Lord Montdore coming up for another cup of tea.

There was a movement among the women. They turned their heads like dogs who think they hear somebody unwrapping a piece of chocolate.

'Sauveterres? Do you mean Fabrice? Don't tell me Fabrice is married? I couldn't be more amazed.'

'No, no, of course not. He's bringing his mother to stay, she's an old flame of Montdore's—I've never seen her, and Montdore hasn't for quite forty years. Of course, we've always known Fabrice, and he came to us in India. He's such fun, a delightful creature. He was very much taken up with the little Ranee of Rawalpur, in fact they do say her last baby——'

'Sonia——!' said Lord Montdore, quite sharply for him. She took absolutely no notice.

'Dreadful old man the Rajah, I only hope it was. Poor creatures, it's one baby after another, you can't help feeling sorry for them, like little birds you know. I used to go and visit the ones who were kept in purdah and of course they simply worshipped me, it was really touching.'

Lady Patricia Dougdale was announced. I had seen the Dougdales from time to time while the Montdores were abroad because they were neighbours at Alconleigh and although my Uncle Matthew by no means encouraged neighbours, it was beyond even his powers to suppress them altogether and prevent them from turning up at the meets, the local point-to-points, on Oxford platform for the 9.10 and Paddington for the 4.45, or at the Merlinford market. Besides, the Dougdales had brought house parties to Alconleigh for Aunt Sadie's dances when Louisa and Linda came out and had given Louisa, for a wedding present, an antique pin cushion, curiously heavy because full of lead. The romantic Louisa, making sure it was curiously heavy because full of gold, 'somebody's savings don't you see?' had ripped it open with her nail scissors, only to find the lead, with the result that none of her wedding presents could be shown for fear of hurting Lady Patricia's feelings.

Lady Patricia was a perfect example of beauty that is but skin deep. She had once had the same face as Polly, but the fair hair had now gone white and the white skin yellow, so that she looked like a classical statue that has been out in the weather, with a layer of snow on its head, the features smudged and smeared by damp. Aunt Sadie said that she and Boy had been considered the handsomest couple in London, but of course that must have been years ago, they were old now, fifty or something, and life would soon be over for them. Lady Patricia's life had been full of sadness and suffering, sadness in her marriage and suffering in her liver. (Of course, I am now quoting Davey.) She had been passionately in love with Boy, who was younger than she, for some years before he had married her, which it was supposed that he had done because he could not resist the relationship with his esteemed Hampton family. The great sorrow of his life was childlessness, since he had set his heart on a quiverful of little half-Hamptons, and people said that the disappointment had almost unhinged him for a while, but that his niece Polly was now beginning to take the place of a daughter, he was so extremely devoted to her.

'Where is Boy?' Lady Patricia said when she had greeted, in the usual English way of greeting, the people who were near the fire, sending a wave of her gloves or half a smile to the ones who were further off. She wore a felt hat, sensible tweeds, silk stockings and beautifully polished calf shoes.

'I do wish they'd come,' said Lady Montdore, 'I want him to help me with the table. He's playing billiards with Polly—I've sent word once, by Rory—oh, here they are.'

Polly kissed her aunt and kissed me. She looked round the room to see if anybody else had arrived to whom she had not yet said 'How do you do?' (she and her parents, as a result, no doubt, of the various official positions Lord Montdore had held, were rather formal in their manners) and then turned back again to me.

'Fanny,' she said, 'have you been here long? Nobody told me.'

She stood there, rather taller now than me, embodied once more, instead of a mere nebulous memory of my childhood, and all the complicated feelings that we have for the human beings who matter in our lives came rushing back to me. My feelings for the Lecturer came rushing back too, uncomplicated.

'Ha!' he was saying, 'here, at last, is my lady wife.' He gave me the creeps, with his curly black hair going grey now, and his perky, jaunty little figure. He was shorter than the Hampton women, about an inch shorter than Lady Patricia, and tried to make up for this by having very thick soles to his shoes. He always looked horribly pleased with himself, the corners of his mouth turned up when his face was in repose, and if he was at all put out they turned up even more in a profoundly irritating smile.

Polly's blue look was now upon me, I suppose she also was rediscovering a person only half remembered, quite the same person really, a curly little black girl, Aunt Sadie used to say, like a little pony which at any moment might toss its shaggy mane and gallop off. Half an hour ago I would gladly have galloped, but now I felt happily inclined to stay where I was.

As we went upstairs together Polly put her arm round my waist saying, with obvious sincerity, 'It's too lovely to see you again. The things I've got to ask you! When I was in India I used to think and think about you—do you remember how we both had black velvet dresses with red sashes for coming down after tea and how Linda had worms? It does seem another life, so long ago. What is Linda's fiancé like?'

'Very good-looking,' I said, 'very hearty. They don't care for him much at Alconleigh, any of them.'

'Oh, how sad. Still, if Linda does—fancy, though, Louisa married and Linda engaged already! Of course, before India we were all babies really, and now we are of marriageable age, it makes a difference doesn't it.'

She sighed deeply.

'I suppose you came out in India?' I said. Polly, I knew, was a little older than I was.

'Well, yes I did, I've been out two years, actually. It was all very dull, this coming-out seems a great great bore—do you enjoy it, Fanny?'

I had never thought about whether I enjoyed it or not, and found it difficult to answer her question. Girls had to come out, I knew. It is a stage in their existence just as the public school is for boys, which must be passed before life, real life, could begin. Dances are supposed to be delightful; they cost a lot of money and it is most good of the grown-ups to give them, most good, too, of Aunt Sadie to have taken me to so many. But at these dances, although I quite enjoyed going to them, I always had the uncomfortable feeling that I missed something, it was like going to a play in a foreign language. Each time I used to hope that I should see the point, but I never did, though the people round me were all so evidently seeing it. Linda, for instance, had seen it clearly but then she had been successfully pursuing love.

'What I do enjoy,' I said, truthfully, 'is the dressing up.'

'Oh, so do I! Do you think about dresses and hats all the time, even in church? I do too. Heavenly tweed, Fanny, I noticed it at once.'

'Only it's bagging,' I said.

'They always bag, except on very smart little thin women like Veronica. Are you pleased to be back in this room? It's the one you used to have, do you remember?'

Of course I remembered. It always had my name in full, 'The Honble Frances Logan', written in a careful copperplate on a card on the door, even when I was so small that I came with my nanny, and this had greatly impressed and pleased me as a child.

'Is this what you're going to wear tonight?'

Polly went up to the huge red four-poster where my dress was laid out.

'How lovely—green velvet and silver, I call that a dream, so soft and delicious, too.' She rubbed a fold of the skirt against her cheek. 'Mine's silver lamé, it smells like a bird cage when it gets hot but I do love it. Aren't you thankful evening skirts are long again? But I want to hear more about what coming-out is like in England.'

'Dances,' I said, 'girls' luncheon parties, tennis if you can, dinner parties to go to, plays, Ascot, being presented. Oh, I don't know, I expect you can just about imagine.'

'And all going on like the people downstairs?'

'Chattering all the time? Well, but the downstairs people are old, Polly. Coming-out is with people of one's own age, you see.'

'They don't think they're old a bit,' she said, laughing.

'Well——' I said, 'all the same, they are.'

'I don't see them as so old myself, but I expect that's because they seem young beside Mummy and Daddy. Just think of it, Fanny, your mother wasn't born when Mummy married, and Mrs. Warbeck was only just old enough to be her bridesmaid. Mummy was saying so before you came. No, but what I really want to know about coming-out here is what about love? Are they all always having love affairs the whole time? Is it their one and only topic of conversation?'

I was obliged to admit that this was the case.

'Oh, bother. I felt sure, really, you would say that—it was so in India, of course, but I thought perhaps in a cold climate——! Anyway, don't tell Mummy if she asks you, pretend that English débutantes don't bother about love. She is in a perfect fit because I never fall in love with people; she teases me about it all the time. But it isn't any good because if you don't, you don't. I should have thought, at my age, it's natural not to.'

I looked at her in surprise, it seemed to me highly unnatural, though I could well understand not wanting to talk about such things to the grown-ups, and specially not to Lady Montdore if she happened to be one's mother. But a new idea struck me.

'In India,' I said, 'could you have fallen in love?' Polly laughed.

'Fanny darling, what do you mean? Of course I could have, why not? I just didn't happen to, you see.'

'White people?'

'White or black,' she said, teasingly.

'Fall in love with blacks?' What would Uncle Matthew say?

'People do, like anything. You don't understand about Rajahs, I see, but some of them are awfully attractive. I had a friend there who nearly died of love for one. And I'll tell you something, Fanny. I honestly believe Mamma would rather I fell in love with an Indian than not at all. Of course, there would have been a fearful row, and I should have been sent straight home, but even so she would have thought it quite a good thing. What she minds so much is the not at all. I know she's only asked this Frenchman to stay because she thinks no woman can resist him. They could think of nothing else in Delhi—I wasn't there at the time, I was in the hills with Boy and Auntie Patsy, we did a heavenly, heavenly trip—I must tell you about it but not now.'

'But would your mother like you to marry a Frenchman?' I said. At this time love and marriage were inextricably knotted in my mind.

'Oh, not marry, good gracious no. She'd just like me to have a little weakness for him, to show that I'm capable of it—she wants to see if I'm like other women. Well, she'll see. There's the dressing-bell—I'll call for you when I'm ready, I don't live up here any more, I've got a new room over the porch. Heaps of time, Fanny, quite an hour.'

CHAPTER IV

MY bedroom was in the tower, where Polly's nurseries had been when she was small. Whereas all the other rooms at Hampton were classical in feeling the tower rooms were exaggeratedly Gothic, the Gothic of fairy-story illustrations; and in this one the bed, the cupboards and the fireplace had pinnacles, the wallpaper was a design of scrolls and the windows were casements. An extensive work of modernization had taken place all over the house while the family was in India, and looking round I saw that in one of the cupboards there was now a tiled bathroom.

In the old days I used to sally forth, sponge in hand, to the nursery bathroom, which was down a terrifying twisting staircase, and I could still remember how cold it used to be outside, in the passages, though there was always a blazing fire in my room. But now the central heating had been brought up to date and the temperature everywhere was that of a hot-house. The fire which flickered away beneath the spires and towers of the chimney-piece was merely there for show, and no longer to be lighted at 7 a.m., before one was awake, by a little maid scuffling about like a mouse. The age of luxury was ended and that of comfort had begun. Being conservative by nature I was glad to see that the decoration of the room had not been changed at all, though the lighting was very much improved, there was a new quilt on the bed, the mahogany dressing-table had acquired a muslin petticoat and a triple looking-glass and the whole room and bathroom were close-carpeted. Otherwise everything was exactly as I remembered it, including two large yellow pictures which could be seen from the bed, Caravaggio's 'The Gamesters' and 'A Courtesan' by Raphael.

As I dressed for dinner I passionately wished that Polly and I could have spent the evening together upstairs, supping off a tray, as we used to do, in the schoolroom. I was dreading this grown-up dinner ahead of me because I knew that, once I found myself in the dining-room seated between two of the old gentlemen downstairs, it would no longer be possible to remain a silent spectator, I should be obliged to try and think of things to say. It had been drummed into me all my life, especially by Davey, that silence at meal times is anti-social.

'So long as you chatter, Fanny, it's of no consequence what you say, better recite out of the ABC than sit like a deaf mute. Think of your poor hostess, it simply isn't fair on her.'

In the dining-room, between the man called Rory and the man called Roly, I found things even worse than I had expected. The protective colouring, which had worked so well in the drawing-room, was now going on and off like a deficient electric light. I was visible. One of my neighbours would begin a conversation with me, and seem quite interested in what I was telling him when, without any warning at all, I would become invisible and Rory and Roly were both shouting across the table at the lady called Veronica, while I was left in mid-air with some sad little remark. It then became too obvious that they had not heard a single word I had been saying but had all along been entranced by the infinitely more fascinating conversation of this Veronica lady. All right then, invisible, which really I much preferred, able to eat happily away in silence. But no, not at all, unaccountably visible again.

'Is Lord Alconleigh your uncle then? Isn't he quite barmy? Doesn't he hunt people with bloodhounds by full moon?'

I was still enough of a child to accept the grown-ups of my own family without a question, and to suppose that each in their own way was more or less perfect, and it gave me a shock to hear this stranger refer to my uncle as quite barmy.

'Oh, but we love it,' I began, 'you can't imagine what fun——' No good. Even as I spoke I became invisible.

'No, no, Veronica, the whole point was he bought the microscope to look at his own——'

'Well, I dare you to say the word at dinner, that's all,' said Veronica, 'even if you know how to pronounce it which I doubt, it's too shame-making, not a dinner thing at all——' And so they went on backwards and forwards.

'I couldn't think Veronica much funnier, could you?'

The two ends of the table were quieter. At one Lady Montdore was talking to the Duc de Sauveterre, who was politely listening to what she said but whose brilliant, good-humoured little black eyes were nevertheless slightly roving, and at the other Lord Montdore and the Lecturer were having a lovely time showing off their faultless French by talking in it across the old Duchesse de Sauveterre to each other. I was near enough to listen to what they were saying, which I did during my periods of invisibility, and though it may not have been as witty as the conversation round Veronica it had the merit of being, to me, more comprehensible. It was all on these lines:

Montdore : 'Alors le Duc du Maine était le fils de qui?'

Boy :   'Mais, dites donc mon vieux, de Louis XIV.'

Montdore : 'Bien entendu, mais sa mère?'

Boy :   'La Montespan.'

At this point the duchess, who had been munching away in silence and not apparently listening to them, said, in a loud and very dis-approving voice,

'*Madame* de Montespan.'

Boy :   'Oui—oui—oui, parfaitement, Madame la Duchesse.' (In an English aside to his brother-in-law, 'The Marquise de Montespan was an aristocrat you know, they never forget it.')

'Elle avait deux fils d'ailleurs, le Duc du Maine et le Comte de Toulouse et Louis XIV les avait tous deux légitimé. Et sa fille a épousé le Régent. Tout cela est exacte, n'est ce pas, Madame la Duchesse?'

But the old lady, for whose benefit this linguistic performance was presumably being staged, was totally uninterested in it. She was eating as hard as she could, only pausing in order to ask the footman for more bread. When directly appealed to she said 'I suppose so'.

'It's all in Saint-Simon,' said Boy, 'I've been reading him again and so must you, Montdore, simply fascinating.' Boy was versed in all the court memoirs that had ever been written, thus acquiring a reputation for great historical knowledge.

'You may not like Boy, but he does know a lot about history, there's nothing he can't tell you.' All depending on what you wanted to find out. The Empress Eugénie's flight from the Tuileries, yes, the Tolpuddle

Martyrs' martyrdom, no. The Lecturer's historical knowledge was a sublimation of snobbery.

Lady Montdore now turned to her other neighbour, and everybody else followed suit. I got Rory instead of Roly, which was no change as both by now were entirely absorbed in what was going on on the other side of the table, and the Lecturer was left to struggle alone with the duchess. I heard him say:

'Dans le temps j'étais très lié avec le Duc de Souppes, qu'est-ce qu'il est devenu, Madame la Duchesse?'

'How, you are a friend to that poor Souppes?' she said, 'he is such an annoying boy.'

Her accent was very strange, a mixture of French and Cockney.

'Il habite toujours ce ravissant hôtel dans la rue du Bac?'

'I suppose so.'

'Et la vieille duchesse est toujours en vie?'

But his neighbour was now quite given over to eating and he never got another word out of her. She read the menu over and over again. She craned to see what the next dish looked like, when plates were given round after the pudding she touched hers and I heard her say approvingly to herself,

'Encore une assiette chaude, très—très bien.'

She was loving her food.

I was loving mine, too, especially now that the protective colouring was in perfect order again, and indeed continued to work for the rest of the evening with hardly another breakdown.

I thought what a pity it was that Davey could not be here for one of his overeating days. He always complained that Aunt Emily never really provided him with enough different dishes on these occasions to give his metabolism a proper shock.

'I don't believe you understand the least bit what I need,' he would say, crossly for him. 'I've got to be giddy, exhausted from overeating if it's to do me any good—that feeling you have after a meal in a Paris restaurant is what we've got to aim at, when you're too full to do anything but lie on your bed like a cobra for hours and hours, too full even to sleep. Now there must be a great many different courses, to coax my appetite—second helpings don't count, I must have them anyway, a great many different courses of really rich food, Emily dear. Naturally, if you'd rather, I'll give up the cure, but it seems a pity, just when it's doing me so much good. If it's the house books you're thinking of you must remember there are my starvation days. You never seem to take them into account at all.'

But Aunt Emily said the starvation days made absolutely no difference to the house books and that he might call it starvation but anybody else would call it four square meals.

Some two dozen metabolisms round this table were getting a jolly good jolt I thought, as the meal went on and on. Soup, fish, pheasant, beefsteak, asparagus, pudding, savoury, fruit. Hampton food, Aunt Sadie used to call it and indeed it had a character of its own which can best be described by saying that it was like mountains of the very most delicious imaginable nursery food, plain and wholesome, made of first-class materials, each thing tasting strongly of itself. But, like everything else at Hampton, it was exaggerated. Just as Lady Montdore was a little bit too much like a countess, Lord Montdore too much like an elder statesman, the servants too perfect and too deferential, the beds too soft and the linen too fine, the motor cars too new and too shiny and everything too much in apple-pie order, so the very peaches there were too peach-like. I used to think when I was a child that all this excellence made Hampton seem unreal compared with the only other houses I knew, Alconleigh and Aunt Emily's little house. It was like a noble establishment in a book or a play, not like somebody's home, and in the same way the Montdores, and even Polly, never quite seemed to be real flesh-and-blood people.

By the time I was embarked on a too peach-like peach I had lost all sense of fear, if not of decorum, and was lolling about as I would not have dared to at the beginning of dinner, boldly looking to right and to left. It was not the wine, I had only had one glass of claret and all my other glasses were full (the butler having paid no attention to my shakes of the head) and untouched; it was the food, I was reeling drunk on food. I saw just what Davey meant about a cobra, everything was stretched to its capacity, and I really felt as if I had swallowed a goat. I knew that my face was scarlet, and looking round I saw that so were all the other faces, except Polly's.

Polly, between just such a pair as Rory and Roly, had not made the least effort to be agreeable to them, though they had taken a good deal more trouble with her than my neighbours had with me. Nor was she enjoying her food. She picked at it with a fork, leaving most of it on her plate, and seemed to be completely in the clouds, her blank stare shining, like the ray from a blue lamp, in the direction of Boy, but not as though she saw him really or was listening to his terribly adequate French. Lady Montdore gave her a dissatisfied look from time to time, but she noticed nothing. Her thoughts were evidently far away from her mother's dinner table, and after a while her neighbours gave up the struggle of getting yes and no out of her, and, in chorus with mine, began to shout back-chat at the lady called Veronica.

This Veronica was small and thin and sparkling. Her bright gold hair lay on her head like a cap, perfectly smooth with a few flat curls above her forehead. She had a high bony nose, rather protruding pale blue eyes, and not much chin. She looked decadent I thought, my drunkenness putting that clever grown-up word into my mind, no doubt, but all the same it was no good denying that she was very, very pretty and that her clothes, her jewels, her make-up and her whole appearance were the perfection of smartness. She was evidently considered to be a great wit, and as soon as the party began to warm up after a chilly start it revolved entirely round her. She bandied repartee with the various Rorys and Rolys, the other women of her own age merely giggling away at the jokes but taking no active part in them, as though they realized it would be useless to try and steal any of her limelight, while the even older people who surrounded the Montdores at the two ends of the table kept up a steady flow of grave talk, occasionally throwing an indulgent glance at 'Veronica'.

Now that I had become brave I asked one of my neighbours to tell me her name, but he was so much surprised at my not knowing it that he quite forgot to answer my question.

'Veronica?' he said, stupefied. 'But surely you know Veronica.'

It was as though I had never heard of Vesuvius. Afterwards I discovered that her name was Mrs. Chaddesley Corbett and it seemed strange to me that Lady Montdore, whom I had so often been told was a snob, should have only a Mrs., not even an Hon. Mrs., to stay, and treat her almost with deference. This shows how innocent, socially, I must have been in those days, since every schoolboy (every Etonian, that is) knew all about Mrs. Chaddesley Corbett. She was to the other smart women of her day as the star is to the chorus and had invented a type of looks as well as a way of talking, walking and behaving which was slavishly copied by the fashionable set in England for at least ten years. No doubt the reason why I had never heard her name before was that she was such miles, in smartness, above the callow young world of my acquaintance.

It was terribly late when at last Lady Montdore got up to leave the table. My aunts never allowed such long sitting in the dining-room because of the washing-up and keeping the servants from going to bed, but that sort of thing simply was not considered at Hampton, nor did Lady Montdore turn to her husband, as Aunt Sadie always did, with an imploring look and a 'not too long, darling?' as she went, leaving the men to their port, their brandy, their cigars and their traditional dirty stories, which could hardly be any dirtier, it seemed to me, than Veronica's conversation had become during the last half hour or so.

Back in the Long Gallery some of the women went upstairs to 'powder their noses'. Lady Montdore was scornful.

'I go in the morning,' she said, 'and that is that. I don't have to be let out like a dog at intervals, thank goodness—there's nothing so common, to my mind.'

If Lady Montdore had really hoped that Sauveterre would exercise his charm on Polly and fill her mind with thoughts of love, she was in for a disappointment. As soon as the men came out of the dining-room, where they had remained for quite an hour ('This English habit', I heard him say, 'is terrible') he was surrounded by Veronica and her chorus and never given a chance to speak to anybody else. They all seemed to be old friends of his, called him Fabrice and had a thousand questions to ask about mutual acquaintances in Paris, fashionable foreign ladies with such unfashionable English names as Norah, Cora, Jennie, Daisy, May and Nellie.

'Are all Frenchwomen called after English housemaids?' Lady Montdore said, rather crossly, as she resigned herself to a chat with the old duchess, the group round Sauveterre having clearly settled down for good. He seemed to be enjoying himself, consumed, one would say, by some secret joke, his twinkling eyes resting with amusement rather than desire, on each plucked and painted face in turn, while in turn, and with almost too obvious insincerity, they asked about their darling Nellies and Daisies. Meanwhile, the husbands of these various ladies, frankly relieved, as Englishmen always are, by a respite from feminine company, were gambling at the other end of the long room, playing, no doubt, for much higher stakes than they would have been allowed to by their wives and with a solid, heavy masculine concentration on the game itself, undisturbed by any of the distractions of sex. Lady Patricia went off to bed; Boy Dougdale began by inserting himself into the group round Sauveterre but finding that nobody there took the slightest notice of him, Sauveterre not even answering when he asked about the Duc de Souppes, beyond saying evasively, 'I see poor Nina de Souppes sometimes' he gave up, a hurt, smiling look on his face. He came and sat with Polly and me and showed us how to play backgammon, holding our hands as we shook the dice, rubbing our knees with his, generally behaving, I thought, in a stchoopid and lecherous way. Lord Montdore and one or two other very old men went off to play billiards; he was said to be the finest billiards player in the British Isles.

Meanwhile poor Lady Montdore was being subjected to a tremendous interrogation by the duchess, who had relapsed through a spirit of contradiction perhaps, into her native tongue. Lady Montdore's French was adequate, but by no means so horribly wonderful as that of her husband and brother-in-law, and she was soon in difficulties over questions of weights and measures; how many hectares in the park at Hampton, how many metres high was the tower, what would it cost, in francs, to take a house boat for Henley, how many kilometres were they from Sheffield? She was obliged to appeal the whole time to Boy, who never failed her of course, but the duchess was not really very much interested in the answers, she was too busy cooking up the next question. They poured out in a relentless torrent, giving Lady Montdore no opportunity whatever to escape to the bridge table as she was longing to do. What sort of electric-light machine was there at Hampton, what was the average weight of a Scotch stag, how long had Lord and Lady Montdore been married ('tiens!'), how was the bath water heated, how many hounds in a pack of fox hounds, where was the Royal Family now? Lady Montdore was undergoing the sensation, novel to her, of being a rabbit with a snake. At last she could bear it no more and broke up the party, taking the women off to bed very much earlier than was usual at Hampton.

CHAPTER V

As this was the first time I had ever stayed away in such a large, grand grown-up house party I was rather uncertain what would happen about breakfast, so before we said good night I asked Polly.

'Oh,' she said vaguely, 'nine-ish, you know,' and I took that to mean, as it meant at home, between five and fifteen minutes past nine. In the morning, I was woken up at eight by a housemaid who brought me tea with slices of paper-thin bread and butter, asked me 'Are these your gloves, miss, they were found in the car?' and then, after running me a bath, whisked away every other garment within sight, to add them no doubt to the collection she had already made of yesterday's tweed suit, jersey, shoes, stockings and underclothes. I foresaw that soon I should be appearing downstairs in my gloves and nothing else.

Aunt Emily never allowed me to take her maid on visits as she said it would spoil me in case later on I should marry a poor man and have to do without one; I was always left to the tender mercies of house-maids when I went away from home.

So by nine o'clock I was bathed and dressed and quite ready for some food. Curiously enough, the immense dinner of the night before, which ought to have lasted me a week, seemed to have made me hungrier than usual. I waited a few minutes after the stable clock struck nine, so as not to be the first, and then ventured downstairs, but was greatly disconcerted in the dining-room to find the table still in its green baize, the door into the pantry wide open and the men-servants, in striped waistcoats and shirt sleeves, engaged upon jobs which had nothing to do with an approaching meal, such as sorting out letters and folding up the morning papers. They looked at me, or so I imagined, with surprise and hostility, I found them even more frightening than my fellow guests, and was about to go back to my bedroom as quick as I could when a voice behind me said:

'But it's terrible, looking at this empty table.'

It was the Duc de Sauveterre. My protective colouring was off, it seemed, by morning light, in fact, he spoke as if we were old friends. I was very much surprised, more so when he shook my hand, and most of all when he said, 'I also long for my porridge, but we can't stay here, it's too sad, shall we go for a walk while it comes?'

The next thing I knew I was walking beside him, very fast, running almost to keep up, in one of the great lime avenues of the park. He talked all the time, as fast as he walked.

'Season of mists,' he said, 'and mellow fruitfulness. Am I not brilliant to know that? But this morning you can hardly see the mellow fruitfulness, for the mists.'

And indeed there was a thin fog all round us, out of which loomed great yellow trees. The grass was soaking wet, and my indoor shoes were already leaking.

'I do love,' he went on, 'getting up with the lark and going for a walk before breakfast.'

'Do you always?' I said.

Some people did, I knew.

'Never, never, never. But this morning I told my man to put a call through to Paris, thinking it would take quite an hour, but it came through at once, so now I am at a loose end with time on my hands. Do I not know wonderful English?'

This ringing-up of Paris seemed to me a most dashing extravagance. Aunt Sadie and Aunt Emily only made trunk calls in times of crisis, and even then they generally rang off in the middle of a sentence when the three-minute signal went; Davey, it is true, spoke to his doctor in London most days, but that was only from Kent, and in any case Davey's health could really be said to constitute a perpetual crisis. But Paris, abroad!

'Is somebody ill?' I ventured.

'Not exactly ill, but she bores herself poor thing. I quite understand it, Paris must be terrible without me, I don't know how she can bear it. I do pity her, really.'

'Who?' I said, curiosity overcoming my shyness, and indeed it would be difficult to feel shy for long with this extraordinary man.

'My fiancée,' he said, carelessly.

Alas! Something had told me this would be the reply; my heart sank and I said dimly:

'Oh! How exciting! You are engaged?'

He gave me a sidelong whimsical look.

'Oh, yes,' he said, 'engaged!'

'And are you going to be married soon?'

But why, I wondered had he come away alone, without her? If I had such a fascinating fiancé I would follow him everywhere, I knew, like a faithful spaniel.

'I don't imagine it will be very soon,' he said gaily. 'You know what it is with the Vatican, time is nothing to them, a thousand ages in their sight are as an evening gone. Do I not know a lot of English poetry?'

'If you call it poetry. It's a hymn, really. But what has your marriage got to do with the Vatican, isn't that in Rome?'

'It is. There is such a thing as the Church of Rome, my dear young lady, which I belong to, and this Church must annul the marriage of my affianced—do you say affianced?'

'You could. It's rather affected.'

'My inamorata, my Dulcinea (brilliant?) must annul her marriage before she is at liberty to marry me.'

'Goodness! Is she married already?'

'Yes, yes, of course. There are very few unmarried ladies going about, you know. It's not a state that lasts very long with pretty women.'

'My Aunt Emily doesn't approve of people getting engaged when they are married. My mother is always doing it and it makes Aunt Emily very cross.'

'You must tell your dear Aunt Emily that in many ways it is rather convenient. But all the same, she is quite right, I have been a fiancé too often and far too long and now it is time I was married.'

'Do you want to be?'

'I am not so sure. Going out to dinner every night with the same person, this must be terrible.'

'You might stay in?'

'To break the habit of a lifetime is rather terrible too. The fact is, I am so accustomed now to the engaged state that it's hard to imagine anything different.'

'But have you been engaged to other people before this one?'

'Many many times,' he admitted.

'So what happened to them all?'

'Various unmentionable fates.'

'For instance, what happened to the last one before this?'

'Let me see. Ah, yes—the last one before this did something I couldn't approve of, so I stopped loving her.'

'But can you stop loving people because they do things you don't approve of?'

'Yes, I can.'

'What a lucky talent,' I said, 'I'm sure I couldn't.'

We had come to the end of the avenue and before us lay a field of stubble. The sun's rays were now beginning to pour down and dissolve the blue mist, turning the trees, the stubble and a group of ricks into objects of gold. I thought how lucky I was to be enjoying such a beautiful moment with so exactly the right person and that this was something I should remember all my life. The duke interrupted these sentimental reflections, saying:

'Behold how brightly breaks the morning,
Though bleak our lot our hearts are warm.

Am I not a perfect mine of quotations? Tell me, who is Veronica's lover now?'

I was once more obliged to confess that I had never seen Veronica before, and knew nothing of her life. He seemed less astounded by this news than Roly had been, but looked at me reflectively, saying:

'You are very young. You have something of your mother. At first I thought not, but now I see there is something.'

'And who do you think Mrs. Chaddesley Corbett's lover is?' I said. I was more interested in her than in my mother at the moment, and besides all this talk about lovers intoxicated me. One knew, of course, that they existed, because of the Duke of Monmouth and so on, but so near, under the very same roof as oneself, that was indeed exciting.

'It doesn't make a pin of difference,' he said, 'who it is. She lives, as all those sort of women do, in one little tiny group or set, and sooner or later everybody in that set becomes the lover of everybody else, so that when they change their lovers it is more like a cabinet reshuffle than a new government. Always chosen out of the same old lot, you see.'

'Is it like that in France?' I said.

'With society people? Just the same all over the world, though in France I should say there is less reshuffling on the whole than in England, the ministers stay longer in their posts.'

'Why?'

'Why? Frenchwomen generally keep their lovers if they want to because they know that there is one infallible method of doing so.'

'No!' I said, 'Oh, do tell.'

I was more fascinated by this conversation every minute.

'It's very simple. You must give way to them in every respect.'

'Goodness!' I said, thinking hard.

'Now, you see, these English *femmes du monde*, these Veronicas and Sheilas and Brendas, and your mother too though nobody could say she stays in one little set, if she had done that she would not be so *déclassée*, they follow quite a different plan. They are proud and distant, out when the telephone bell rings, not free to dine unless you ask them a week before—in short, *elles cherchent à se faire valoir*, and it never never succeeds. Even Englishmen, who are used to it, don't like it after a bit. Of course, no Frenchman would put up with it for a day. So they go on reshuffling.'

'They're very nasty ladies, aren't they?' I said, having formed that opinion the night before.

'Not at all, poor things. They are *les femmes du monde, voilà tout*, I love them, so easy to get on with. Not nasty at all. And I love *la mère* Montdore, how amusing she is, with her snobbishness. I am very very much for snobs, they are always so charming to me. I stayed with them in India, you know. She was charming and Lord Montdore pretended to be.'

'Pretended?'

'That man is made up of pretence, like so many of these stiff old Englishmen. Of course, he is a great great enemy of my country—dedicated to the undoing of the French empire.'

'Why?' I said, 'I thought we were all friends now.'

'Friends! Like rabbits and snakes. I have no love for Lord Montdore but he is rather clever. Last night after dinner he asked me a hundred questions on partridge shooting in France. Why? You can be very sure he had some reason for doing so.'

'Don't you think Polly is very beautiful?' I said.

'Yes, but she also is rather a riddle to me,' he replied. 'Perhaps she is not having a properly organized sex life. Yes, no doubt it is that which makes her so dreamy. I must see what I can do for her—only there's not much time.' He looked at his watch.

I said primly that very few well brought up English girls of nineteen have a properly organized sex life. Mine was not organized at all, I knew, but I did not seem to be so specially dreamy.

'But what a beauty, even in that terrible dress. When she has had a little love she may become one of the beauties of our age. It's not certain, it never is with Englishwomen. She may cram a felt hat on her head and become a Lady Patricia Dougdale, everything depends on the lover. So this Boy Dougdale, what about him?'

'Stupid,' I said, meaning, really, 'stchoopid.'

'But you are impossible, my dear. Nasty ladies, stupid men—you really must try and like people more or you'll never get on in this world.'

'How d'you mean, get on?'

'Well, get all those things like husbands and fiancés, and get on with them. They are what really matter in a woman's life, you know.'

'And children?' I said.

He roared with laughter.

'Yes, yes, of course, children. Husbands first, then children, then fiancés, then more children—then you have to live near the Parc Monceau because of the nannies—it's a whole programme having children, I can tell you, especially if you happen to prefer the Left Bank, as I do.'

I did not understand one word of all this.

'Are you going to be a Bolter,' he said, 'like your mother?'

'No, no,' I said. 'A tremendous sticker.'

'Really? I'm not quite sure.'

Soon, too soon for my liking, we found ourselves back at the house.

'Porridge,' said the duke, again looking at his watch.

The front door opened upon a scene of great confusion, most of the house party, some in tweeds and some in dressing-gowns, were assembled in the hall, as were various outdoor and indoor servants, while a village policeman, who in the excitement of the moment had brought his bicycle in with him, was conferring with Lord Montdore. High above our heads, leaning over the balustrade in front of Niobe, Lady Montdore, in a mauve satin wrap, was shouting at her husband :

'Tell him we must have Scotland Yard down at once, Montdore. If he won't send for them I shall ring up the Home Secretary myself. Most fortunately, I have the number of his private line. In fact, I think I'd better go and do it now.'

'No, no, my dear, please not. An Inspector is on his way I tell you.'

'Yes, I daresay, but how do we know it's the very best Inspector? I think I'd better get on to my friend, I think he'd be hurt with me if I didn't, the dear thing. Always so anxious to do what he can.'

I was rather surprised to hear Lady Montdore speak so affectionately of a member of the Labour Government, this not being the attitude of other grown-ups, in my experience, but when I came to know her better I realized that power was a positive virtue in her eyes and that she automatically liked those who were invested with it.

My companion, with that look of concentration which comes over French faces when a meal is in the offing, did not wait to hear any of this. He made a bee-line for the dining-room, but although I was also very hungry indeed after my walk, curiosity got the better of me and I stayed to find out what it all meant. It seemed that there had been a burglary during the night and that nearly everybody in the house, except Lord and Lady Montdore, had been roundly robbed of jewels, loose cash, furs and anything portable of the kind that happened to be lying about. What made it particularly annoying for the victims was that they had all been woken up by somebody prowling in their rooms, but had all immediately concluded that it must be Sauveterre, pursuing his well-known hobby, so that the husbands had merely turned over with a grunt, saying, 'Sorry, old chap, it's only me, I should try next door,' while the wives had lain quite still in a happy trance of desire, murmuring such words of encouragement as they knew in French. Or so, at least, they were saying about each other, and when I passed the telephone box on my way upstairs to change my wet shoes I could hear Mrs. Chaddesley Corbett's bird-like twitters piping her version of the story to the outside world. Perhaps the cabinet changes were becoming a little bit of a bore after all and these ladies did rather long, at heart, for a new policy.

The general feeling was now very much against Sauveterre, whose fault the whole thing clearly was. It became positively inflamed when he was known to have had a good night's rest, to have got up at eight to telephone to his mistress in Paris and then to have gone for a walk with that little girl. ('Not the Bolter's child for nothing,' I heard somebody say bitterly.) The climax was reached when he was seen to be putting away a huge breakfast of porridge and cream, kedgeree, eggs, cold ham and slice upon slice of toast covered with Cooper's Oxford. Very un-French, not at all in keeping with his reputation, unsuitable behaviour too, in view of the well-known frailty of his fellow guests. Britannia felt herself slighted by this foreigner, away with him! And away he went, immediately after breakfast, driving hell-for-leather to Newhaven to catch the boat for Dieppe.

'Castle life,' explained his mother, who placidly stayed until quite late on Monday, 'always annoys Fabrice and makes him nervous, poor boy.'

CHAPTER VI

THE rest of the day was rather disorganized. The men finally went off shooting, very late, while the women stayed at home to be interviewed by various Inspectors on the subject of their lost possessions. Of course, the burglary made a wonderful topic of conversation, and indeed nobody spoke of anything else.

'I couldn't care less about the diamond brooch, after all, it's well insured and now I shall be able to have clips instead, which will be far and away smarter. Veronica's clips always make me miserable, every time I see her, and besides, that brooch used to remind me of my bogus old mother-in-law too much. But I couldn't think it more hateful of them to have taken my fur tippet. Burglars never seem to realize one might feel the cold. How would they like it if I took away their wife's shawl?'

'Yes, it is a shame. I'm in a terrible do about my bracelet of lucky charms—no value to anybody else—really—too too sick-making. Just when I had managed to get a bit of hangman's rope, Mrs. Thompson too, did I tell you? Roly will never win the National now, poor sweet.'

'With me it's Mummy's little locket she had as a child. I can't think why my ass of a maid had to go and put it in, she never does as a rule.'

The brassy ladies became quite human as they mourned their lost trinkets, and now that the men were out of the house they suddenly seemed very much nicer. I am speaking of the Veronica chorus, for Mrs. Chaddesley Corbett herself, in common with Lady Montdore and Lady Patricia, was always exactly the same whatever the company.

At teatime the village policeman reappeared with his bicycle, having wiped the eye of all the grand detectives who had come from London in their shiny cars. He produced a perfect jumble-sale heap of objects which had been discarded by the burglars under a haystack, and nearly all the little treasures were retrieved, with high cries of joy, by their owners. As the only things which now remained missing were jewels of considerable value, and as these were felt to be the business of the

Insurance Companies, the party continued in a much more cheerful atmosphere. I never heard any of the women mention the burglary again though their husbands droned on rather about underwriters and premiums. There was now, however, a distinctly noticeable current of anti-French feeling. The Norahs and Nellies would have had a pretty poor reception if any of them had turned up just then, and Boy, if it was possible for him to have enough of a duchess, must have been having enough of this one, since all but he fled from the machine-gun fire of questions, and he was obliged to spend the next two days practically alone with her.

I was hanging about as one does at house parties, waiting for the next meal; it was not yet quite time to dress for dinner on Sunday evening. One of the pleasures of staying at Hampton was that the huge Louis XV map table in the middle of the long gallery was always covered with every imaginable weekly newspaper neatly laid out in rows and rearranged two or three times a day by a footman, whose sole occupation this appeared to be.

I seldom saw the *Tatler* and *Sketch*, as my aunts would have thought it a perfectly unwarranted extravagance to subscribe to such papers, and I was greedily gulping down back numbers when Lady Montdore called to me from a sofa where, ever since tea, she had been deep in talk with Mrs. Chaddesley Corbett. I had been throwing an occasional glance in their direction, wondering what it could all be about and wishing I could be a fly on the wall to hear them, thinking also that it would hardly be possible for two women to look more different. Mrs. Chaddesley Corbett, her bony little silken legs crossed and uncovered to above the knee, perched rather than sat on the edge of the sofa. She wore a plain beige kasha dress which must certainly have been made in Paris and certainly designed for the Anglo-Saxon market, and smoked cigarette after cigarette with a great play of long thin white fingers, flashing with rings and painted nails. She did not keep still for one moment though she was talking with great earnestness and concentration.

Lady Montdore sat well back on the sofa, both her feet on the ground. She seemed planted there, immovable and solid, not actually fat, but solid through and through. Smartness, even if she had sought after it, would hardly be attainable by her in a world where it was personified by the other, and had become almost as much a question of build, of quick and nervous movement, as of actual clothes. Her hair was shingled, but it was grey and fluffy, by no means a smooth cap; her eyebrows grew at will, and when she remembered to use lipstick and powder they were any colour and slapped on anyhow, so that her face, compared with that of Mrs. Chaddesley Corbett, was as a hay-field is to a lawn, her whole head looking twice as large as the polished

little head beside her. All the same she was not disagreeable to look at.
There was a healthiness and liveliness about her face which lent it a
certain attraction. Of course, she seemed to me, then, very old. She
was, in fact, about fifty-eight.

'Come over here, Fanny.'

I was almost too much surprised to be alarmed by this summons and
hurried over, wondering what it could all be about.

'Sit there,' she said, pointing to a needle-work chair, 'and talk to us.
Are you in love?'

I felt myself becoming scarlet in the face. How could they have
guessed my secret? Of course I had been in love for two days now, ever
since my morning walk with the Duc de Sauveterre. Passionately, but
as indeed I realized hopelessly, in love. In fact, the very thing that Lady
Montdore had intended for Polly had befallen me.

'There you are, Sonia,' said Mrs. Chaddesley Corbett triumphantly,
tapping a cigarette with nervous violence against her jewelled case and
lighting it with a gold lighter, her pale blue eyes never meanwhile leaving my face. 'What did I tell you? Of course she is, poor sweet, just look
at that blush, it must be something quite new and horribly bogus. I
know, it's my dear old husband. Confess, now! I couldn't mind less,
actually.'

I did not like to say that I still, after a whole week-end, had no idea
at all which of the many husbands present hers might be, but stam-
mered out as quick as I could:

'Oh no no, not anybody's husband, I promise.' Only a fiancé, and
such a detached one at that.

They both laughed.

'All right,' said Mrs. Chaddesley Corbett, 'we're not going to worm.
What we really want to know, to settle a bet, is, have you always fancied
somebody ever since you can remember? Answer truthfully please.'

I was obliged to admit that this was the case. From a tiny child,
ever since I could remember, in fact, some delicious image had been
enshrined in my heart, last thought at night, first thought in the
morning. Fred Terry as Sir Percy Blakeney, Lord Byron, Rudolph
Valentino, Henry V, Gerald du Maurier, blissful Mrs. Ashton at my
school, Steerforth, Napoleon, the guard on the 4.45, image had
succeeded image. Latterly it had been that of a pale pompous young
man in the Foreign Office who had once, during my season in London,
asked me for a dance, had seemed to me the very flower of cosmopolitan
civilization, and had remained the pivot of existence until wiped from
my memory by Sauveterre. For that is what always happened to these
images. Time and hateful absence blurred them, faded them but never
quite obliterated them until some lovely new broom image came and
swept them away.

'There you are you see,' Mrs. Chaddesley Corbett turned triumphantly to Lady Montdore. 'From kiddie-car to hearse, darling, I couldn't know it better. After all, what would there be to think about when one's alone, otherwise?'

What indeed? This Veronica had hit the nail on the head. Lady Montdore did not look convinced. She, I felt sure, had never harboured romantic yearnings and had plenty to think about when she was alone, which, anyhow, was hardly ever.

'But who is there for her to be in love with, and if she is, surely I should know it?' she said.

I guessed that they were talking about Polly, and this was confirmed by Mrs. Chaddesley Corbett saying:

'No, darling, you wouldn't, you're her mother. When I remember poor Mummy and her ideas on the subject of my ginks——'

'Now Fanny, tell us what you think? Is Polly in love?'

'Well, she says she's not, but——'

'But you don't think it's possible not to be fancying someone? Nor do I.'

I wondered. Polly and I had had a long chat the night before, sprawling on my bed in our dressing-gowns, and I had felt almost certain then that she was keeping something back which she would half have liked to tell.

'I suppose it might depend on your nature?' I said, doubtfully.

'Anyhow,' said Lady Montdore, 'there's one thing only too certain. She takes no notice of the young men I provide for her and they take no notice of her. They worship *me*, of course, but what is the good of that?'

Mrs. Chaddesley Corbett caught my eye and I thought she gave me half a wink. Lady Montdore went on,

'Bored and boring. I can't say I'm looking forward to bringing her out in London very much if she goes on like this. She used to be such a sweet easy child, but her whole character seems to have changed now she is grown-up. I can't understand it.'

'Oh, she's bound to fall for some nice chap in London, darling,' said Mrs. Chaddesley Corbett. 'I wouldn't worry too much if I were you. Whoever she's in love with now, if she is in love, which Fanny and I know she must be, is probably a kind of dream and she only needs to see some flesh-and-blood people for her to forget about it. It so often happens, with girls.'

'Yes, my dear, that's all very well, but she was out for two years in India you know. There were some very attractive men there, polo and so on, not suitable of course, I was only too thankful she didn't fall in love with any of them, but she could have, it would not have been unnatural at all. Why, poor Delia's girl fell in love with a Rajah, you know.'

'I couldn't blame her less,' said Mrs. Chaddesley Corbett. 'Rajahs must be perfect heaven, all those diamonds.'

'Oh no, my dear—any English family has better stones than they do. I never saw anything to compare with mine when I was there. But this Rajah was rather attractive, I must say, though of course Polly didn't see it, she never does. O dear, O dear! Now if only we were French; they really do seem to arrrange things so very much better. To begin with, Polly would inherit all this instead of those stupid people in Nova Scotia, so unsuitable—can you imagine Colonials living here —and to go on with we should find a husband for her ourselves, after which he and she would live partly at his place, with his parents, and partly here with us. Think how sensible that is. The old French tart was telling me the whole system last night.'

Lady Montdore was famous for picking up words she did not quite understand and giving them a meaning of her own. She clearly took the word tart to mean old girl, trout, body. Mrs. Chaddesley Corbett was delighted, she gave a happy little squeak and rushed upstairs saying that she must go and dress for dinner. When I came up ten minutes later she was still telling the news through bathroom doors.

After this Lady Montdore set out to win my heart, and, of course, succeeded. It was not very difficult. I was young and frightened, she was old and grand and frightening, and it only required an occasional hint of mutual understanding, a smile, a movement of sympathy to make me think I really loved her. The fact is that she had charm, and since charm allied to riches and position is almost irresistible, it so happened that her many haters were usually people who had never met her or people she had purposely snubbed or ignored. Those whom she made efforts to please, while forced to admit that she was indefensible, were very much inclined to say, '. . . but all the same she has been very nice to me and I can't help liking her'. She herself, of course, never doubted for one moment that she was worshipped, and by every section of society.

Before I left Hampton on Monday morning Polly took me up to her mother's bedroom to say good-bye. Some of the guests had left the night before, the others were leaving now, all rolling away in their huge rich motor cars, and the house was like a big school breaking up for the holidays. The bedroom doors we passed were open revealing litters of tissue paper and unmade beds, servants struggling with suitcases and guests struggling into their coats. Everybody seemed to be in a struggling hurry all of a sudden.

Lady Montdore's room, I remembered it of old, was enormous, more like a ballroom than a bedroom, and was done up in the taste of her own young days when she was a bride; the walls were panelled in pink silk covered with white lace, the huge wickerwork bed on a dais had curtains of pink shot-silk. The furniture was white with fat pink satin upholstery outlined in ribbon roses. Silver flower vases stood on all the tables, and there were many photographs in silver frames, mostly of royal personages, with inscriptions cordial in inverse ratio to the actual importance of the personage, reigning monarchs having contented themselves with merely a Christian name, an R, and perhaps a date, while ex-Kings and Queens, Archduchesses and Grand Dukes had scattered Dearest and Darling Sonia and Loving all over their trains and uniform trousers.

In the middle of all this silver and satin and silk, Lady Montdore cut rather a comic figure drinking strong tea in bed among masses of lace pillows, her coarse grey hair frizzed out and wearing what appeared to be a man's striped flannel pyjama top under a feathered wrap. The striped pyjamas were not the only incongruous touch in the room. On her lacy dressing-table with its big, solid silver looking-glass and among her silver and enamel brushes, bottles and boxes, with their diamond cypher, were a black Mason Pearson hair brush and a pot of Pond's cold cream, while dumped down in the middle of the royalties were a rusty nail-file, a broken comb and a bit of cotton wool. While we were talking, Lady Montdore's maid came in and with much clicking of her tongue was about to remove all these objects when Lady Montdore told her to leave them as she had not finished.

Her quilt was covered with newspapers and opened letters and she held *The Times* neatly folded back at the Court Circular, probably the only part of it she ever looked at, since news, she used to say, can always be gleaned, and far more entertainingly too, from those who make it. I think she felt it comfortable, rather like reading prayers, to begin the day with Mabell, Countess of Airlie having succeeded the Lady Elizabeth Motion as lady-in-waiting to the Queen. It indicated that the globe was still revolving in accordance with the laws of nature.

'Good morning, Fanny dear,' she said, 'this will interest you, I suppose.'

She handed me *The Times* and I saw that Linda's engagement to Anthony Kroesig was announced at last.

'Poor Alconleighs,' she went on, in tones of deep satisfaction. 'No wonder they don't like it! What a silly girl, well, she always has been in my opinion. No place. Rich, of course, but banker's money, it comes and it goes and however much of it there may be it's not like marrying all this.'

'All this' was a favourite expression of Lady Montdore's. It did not mean all this beauty, this strange and fairy-like house set in the middle of four great avenues rushing up four artificial slopes, the ordered spaces of trees and grass and sky seen from its windows, or the joy given by the treasures it contained, for she was not gifted with an aesthetic sense and if she admired anything at all it was rather what might be described as stockbroker's picturesque. She had made herself a little garden in the park, copied from one she had seen at a Chelsea flower show, in which rambler roses, forget-me-nots, and cyprus trees were grouped round an Italian well-head, and here she would often retire to see the sunset. 'So beautiful it makes me want to cry.' She had all the sentimentality of her generation, and this sentimentality, growing like a green moss over her spirit, helped to conceal its texture of stone, if not from others at any rate from herself. She was convinced that she was a woman of profound sensibility.

'All this', on her lips, meant position allied to such solid assets as acres, coal mines, real estate, jewels, silver, pictures, incunabula, and other possessions of the sort. Lord Montdore owned an almost incredible number of such things, fortunately.

'Not that I ever expected poor little Linda to make a suitable marriage,' she went on. 'Sadie is a wonderful woman, of course, and I'm devoted to her, but I'm afraid she hasn't the very smallest idea how to bring up girls.'

Nevertheless, no sooner did Aunt Sadie's girls show their noses outside the schoolroom than they were snapped up and married, albeit unsuitably, and perhaps this fact was rankling a little with Lady Montdore, whose mind appeared to be so much on the subject.

The relations between Hampton and Alconleigh were as follows. Lady Montdore had an irritated fondness for Aunt Sadie, whom she half admired for an integrity which she could not but recognize and half blamed for an unworldliness which she considered out of place in somebody of her position; she could not endure Uncle Matthew and thought him mad. Uncle Matthew, for his part, revered Lord Montdore, who was perhaps the only person in the world whom he looked up to, and loathed Lady Montdore to such a degree that he used to say he longed to strangle her. Now that Lord Montdore was back from India Uncle Matthew continually saw him at the House of Lords and on the various county organizations which they both attended, and he would come home and quote his most banal remark as if it were the utterance of a prophet—'Montdore tells me——, Montdore says——'. And that was that, useless to question it; what Lord Montdore believed on any subject was final in the eyes of my uncle.

'Wonderful fella, Montdore. What I can't imagine is how we ever got on without him in this country all those years. Terribly wasted, among the blackamoors, when he's the kind of fella we need so badly here.'

He even broke his rule about never visiting other people's houses in favour of Hampton. 'If Montdore asks us I think we ought to go.'

'It's Sonia who asks us,' Aunt Sadie would correct him, mischievously.

'The old she-wolf. I shall never know what can have come over Montdore to make him marry her. I suppose he didn't realize at the time how utterly poisonously bloody she is.'

'Darling—darling——!'

'Utterly bloody. But if Montdore asks us I think we should go.'

As for Aunt Sadie, she was always so vague, so much in the clouds, that it was never easy to know what she really thought of people, but I believe that though she rather enjoyed the company of Lady Montdore in small doses, she did not share my uncle's feelings about Lord Montdore, for when she spoke of him there was always a note of disparagement in her voice.

'Something silly about his look,' she used to say, though never in front of Uncle Matthew, for it would have hurt his feelings dreadfully.

'So that's Louisa and poor Linda accounted for,' Lady Montdore went on. 'Now you must be the next one, Fanny.'

'Oh no,' I said. 'Nobody will ever marry me.' And indeed I could not imagine anybody wanting to, I seemed to myself so much less fascinating than the other girls I knew, and I despised my looks, hating my round pink cheeks and rough curly black hair which never could be made to frame my face in silken cords, however much I wetted and brushed it, but would insist on growing the wrong way, upwards, like heather.

'Nonsense. And don't you go marrying just anybody, for love,' she said. 'Remember that love cannot last, it never never does, but if you marry all this it's for your life. One day, don't forget, you'll be middle-aged and think what that must be like for a woman who can't have, say, a pair of diamond ear-rings. A woman of my age needs diamonds near her face, to give a sparkle. Then at meal times, sitting with all the unimportant people for ever and ever. And no motor. Not a very nice prospect, you know. Of course,' she added as an afterthought, 'I was lucky, I had love as well as all this, but it doesn't often happen, and when the moment comes for you to choose, just remember what I say. I suppose Fanny ought to go now and catch her train—and when you've seen her off, will you find Boy please and send him up here to me, Polly? I want to think over the dinner party for next week with him. Good-bye, then, Fanny—let's see a lot of you now we're back.'

On the way down we ran into Boy.

'Mummy wants to see you,' said Polly, gravely posing, her blue look upon him. He put his hand to her shoulder and massaged it with his thumb.

'Yes,' he said, 'about this dinner party, I suppose. Are you coming to it, old girl?'

'Oh, I expect so,' she said. 'I'm out now, you know.'

'I can't say I look forward to it very much. Your mother's ideas on *placement* get vaguer and vaguer. The table last night was totally mad, the *duchesse* is still in a temper about it! Sonia really shouldn't have people at all if she doesn't intend to treat them properly.'

A phrase I had often heard on the lips of my Aunt Emily, with reference to animals.

CHAPTER VII

BACK at home I was naturally unable to talk of anything but my visit. Davey was much amused and said he had never known me so chatty.

'But my dear child,' he said, 'weren't you petrified? Sauveterre and the Chaddesley Corbetts——! Far worse even than I had expected.'

'Well yes, at first I thought I'd die. But nobody took any notice of me really except Mrs. Chaddesley Corbett and Lady Montdore——'

'Oh! And what notice did they take, may I ask?'

'Well, Mrs. Chaddesley Corbett said Mummy bolted first of all with Mr. Chaddesley Corbett.'

'So she did,' said Davey, 'that boring old Chad, I'd quite forgotten. But you don't mean to say Veronica told you so? I wouldn't have thought it possible, even of her.'

'No, I heard her tell, in eggy-peggy.'

'I see. Well then, what about Sonia?'

'Oh, she was sweet to me.'

'She was, was she? This is indeed sinister news.'

'What is sinister news?' said Aunt Emily, coming in with her dogs. 'It's simply glorious out, I can't imagine why you two are stuffing in here on such a heavenly day.'

'We're gossiping about this party you so unwisely allowed Fanny to go to. And I was saying that if Sonia has really taken a fancy to our little one, which it seems she has, we must look out for trouble, that's all.'

'What trouble?' I said.

'Sonia's terribly fond of juggling with people's lives. I never shall forget when she made me go to her doctor. I can only say he very nearly killed me; it's not her fault if I'm here today. She's entirely unscrupulous, she gets a hold over people much too easily with her charm and her prestige and then forces her own values on them.'

'Not on Fanny,' Aunt Emily said, with confidence, 'look at that chin.'

'You always say look at Fanny's chin but I never can see any other signs of her being strong-minded. Those Radletts make her do whatever they like.'

'You'll see,' said Aunt Emily. 'Siegfried is quite all right again by the way, he's had a lovely walkies.'

'Oh, good,' said Davey. 'Olive oil's the thing.'

They both looked affectionately at the Pekingese, Siegfried.

But I wanted to get some more interesting gossip out of Davey about the Hamptons. I said coaxingly:

'Go on Dave, do go on telling about Lady Montdore. What was she like when she was young?'

'Exactly the same as she is now.'

I sighed. 'No, but I mean what did she look like?'

'I tell you, just the same,' said Davey. 'I've known her ever since I was a little tiny boy and she hasn't changed one scrap.'

'Oh, Davey——' I began. But I left it at that. It's no good, I thought, you always come up against this blank wall with old people, they always say about each other that they have never looked any different, and how can it be true? Anyway, if it is true, they must have been a horrid generation, all withered or blowsy, and grey at the age of eighteen, knobbly hands, bags under the chin, eyes set in a little map of wrinkles, I thought crossly, adding up all these things on the faces of Davey and Aunt Emily as they sat there, smugly thinking that they had always looked exactly the same. Quite useless to discuss questions of age with old people, they have such peculiar ideas on the subject. 'Not really old at all, only seventy', you hear them saying, or 'quite young, younger than me, not much more than forty'. At eighteen this seems great nonsense, though now, at the more advanced age which I have reached, I am beginning to understand what it all meant because Davey and Aunt Emily in their turn seem to me to look as they have looked ever since I knew them first, when I was a little child.

'Who else was there,' asked Davey, 'the Dougdales?'

'Oh, yes. Isn't the Lecturer stchoopid?'

Davey laughed. 'And lecherous?' he said.

'No, I must say not actually lecherous, not with me.'

'Well, of course, he couldn't be with Sonia there, he wouldn't dare. He's been her young man for years, you know.'

'Don't tell me!' I said, fascinated. That was the heaven of Davey, he knew everything about everybody, quite unlike my aunts, who, though they had no special objection to our knowing gossip, now that we were grown-up, had always forgotten it themselves, being totally uninterested in the doings of people outside their own family. 'Davey! How could she?'

'Well, Boy is very good-looking,' said Davey, 'I should say rather, how could he? But as a matter of fact, I think it's a love-affair of pure convenience, it suits them both perfectly. Boy knows the Gotha by heart and all that kind of thing, he's like a wonderful extra butler, and Sonia on her side gives him an interest in life. I quite see it.'

One comfort, I thought, such elderly folk couldn't do anything, but again I kept it to myself because I knew that nothing makes people crosser than being considered too old for love, and Davey and the Lecturer were exactly the same age, they had been at school together. Lady Montdore, of course, was even older.

'Let's hear about Polly,' said Aunt Emily, 'and then I really must insist on you going out of doors before tea. Is she a real beauty, just as we were always being told, by Sonia, that she would be?'

'Of course she is,' said Davey, 'doesn't Sonia always get her own way?'

'So beautiful you can't imagine,' I said. 'And so nice, the nicest person I ever met.'

'Fanny is such a hero-worshipper,' said Aunt Emily, amused.

'I expect it's true though, anyway, about the beauty,' said Davey, 'because, quite apart from Sonia always getting what she wants, Hamptons do have such marvellous looks, and, after all, the old girl herself is very handsome. In fact, I see that she would improve the strain by giving a little solidity—Montdore looks too much like a collie dog.'

'And who is this wonderful girl to marry?' said Aunt Emily. 'That will be the next problem for Sonia. I can't see who will ever be good enough for her?'

'Merely a question of strawberry leaves,' said Davey, 'as I imagine she's probably too big for the Prince of Wales, he likes such tiny little women. You know, I can't help thinking that now Montdore is getting older he must feel it dreadfully that he can't leave Hampton to her. I had a long talk about it the other day with Boy in the London Library. Of course, Polly will be very rich—enormously rich, because he can leave her everything else, but they all love Hampton so much, I think it's very sad for them.'

'Can he leave Polly the pictures at Montdore House? Surely they must be entailed on the heir?' said Aunt Emily.

'There are wonderful pictures at Hampton,' I butted in. 'A Raphael and a Caravaggio in my bedroom alone.'

They both laughed at me, hurting my feelings rather.

'Oh, my darling child, country-house bedroom pictures! But the ones in London are a world-famous collection, and I believe they can all go to Polly. The young man from Nova Scotia simply gets Hampton and everything in it, but that is an Aladdin's Cave you know, the furniture, the silver, the library—treasures beyond value. Boy was saying they really ought to get him over and show him something of civilization before he becomes too transatlantic.'

'I forget how old he is,' said Aunt Emily.

'I know,' I said, 'he's six years older than me, about twenty-four now. And he's called Cedric, like Lord Fauntleroy. Linda and I used to look him up when we were little to see if he would do for us.'

'You would, how typical,' said Aunt Emily. 'But I should have thought he might really do for Polly—settle everything.'

'It would be too much unlike life,' said Davey. 'Oh, bother, talking to Fanny has made me forget my three o'clock pill.'

'Take it now,' said Aunt Emily, 'and then go out please, both of you.'

From this time on I saw a great deal of Polly. I went to Alconleigh, as I did every year, for some hunting, and from there I often went

over to spend a night or two at Hampton. There were no more big
house parties, but a continual flow of people, and in fact the Montdores and Polly never seemed to have a meal by themselves. Boy
Dougdale came over nearly every day from his own house at Silkin,
which was only about ten miles away. He quite often went home to
dress for dinner and came back again to spend the evening, since Lady
Patricia it seemed was not at all well, and liked to go to bed early.

Boy never seemed to me quite like a real human being and I think
this is because he was always acting some part. Boy the Don Juan
alternated with Boy the Old Etonian, squire of Silkin, and Boy the
talented cosmopolitan. In none of these parts was he quite convincing.
Don Juan only made headway with very unsophisticated women,
except in the case of Lady Montdore and she, whatever their relationship may have been in the past, had come to treat him more as a lady
companion or private secretary than as a lover. The squire played
cricket in a slightly arch manner with village youths, and lectured
village women, but never seemed like a real squire, for all his efforts,
and the talented cosmopolitan gave himself away whenever he put
brush to canvas or pen to paper.

He and Lady Montdore were much occupied, when they were in
the country, with what they called 'their art', producing enormous
portraits, landscapes and still lifes by the dozen. In the summer they
worked out of doors, and in the winter they installed a large stove in a
north-facing bedroom and used it as a studio. They were such great
admirers of their own and each other's work that the opinion of the outside world meant but little to them. Their pictures were always framed
and hung about their two houses, the best ones in rooms and the others
in passages.

By the evening Lady Montdore was ready for some relaxation.

'I like to work hard all day,' she would say, 'and then have agreeable
company and perhaps a game of cards in the evening.'

There were always guests for dinner, an Oxford don or two with
whom Lord Montdore could show off about Livy, Plotinus and the
Claudian family, Lord Merlin, who was a great favourite of Lady
Montdore and who published her sayings far and wide, and the more
important county neighbours, strictly in turns. They seldom sat down
fewer than ten people; it was very different from Alconleigh.

I enjoyed these visits to Hampton. Lady Montdore terrified me less
and charmed me more, Lord Montdore remained perfectly agreeable
and colourless, Boy continued to give me the creeps and Polly became
my best-friend-next-to-Linda.

Presently Aunt Sadie suggested that I might like to bring Polly back
with me to Alconleigh, which I duly did. It was not a very good time
for a visit there since everybody's nerves were upset by Linda's engagement, but Polly did not seem to notice the atmosphere, and no doubt

her presence restrained Uncle Matthew from giving vent to the full violence of his feelings while she was there. Indeed, she said to me, as we drove back to Hampton together after the visit, that she envied the Radlett children their upbringing in such a quiet, affectionate household, a remark which could only have been made by somebody who had inhabited the best spare room, out of range of Uncle Matthew's early morning gramophone concerts, and who had never happened to see that violent man in one of his tempers. Even so, I thought it strange, coming from Polly, because if anybody had been surrounded by affection all her life it was she; I did not yet fully understand how difficult the relations were beginning to be between her and her mother.

CHAPTER VIII

POLLY and I were bridesmaids at Linda's wedding in February, and when it was over I motored down to Hampton with Polly and Lady Montdore to spend a few days there. I was grateful to Polly for suggesting this, as I remembered too well the horrible feeling of anti-climax there had been after Louisa's wedding, which would certainly be ten times multiplied after Linda's. Indeed, with Linda married, the first stage of my life no less than of hers was finished, and I felt myself to be left in a horrid vacuum, with childhood over but married life not yet beginning.

As soon as Linda and Anthony had gone away Lady Montdore sent for her motor car and we all three huddled on to the back seat. Polly and I were still in our bridesmaids' dresses (sweet-pea tints, in chiffon) but well wrapped up in fur coats and each with a Shetland rug wound round our legs, like children going to a dancing class. The chauffeur spread a great bearskin over all of us and put a foot warmer under our silver kid shoes. It was not really cold, but shivery, pouring and pouring with rain as it had been all day, getting dark now. The inside of the motor was like a dry little box, and as we splashed down the long wet shiny roads, with the rain beating against the windows, there was a specially delicious cosiness about being in this little box and knowing that so much light and warmth and solid comfort lay ahead.

'I love being so dry in here,' as Lady Montdore put it, 'and seeing all those poor people so wet.'

She had done the journey twice that day, having driven up from Hampton in the morning, whereas Polly had gone up the day before, with her father, for a last fitting of her bridesmaid's dress and in order to go to a dinner-dance.

First of all we talked about the wedding. Lady Montdore was

wonderful when it came to picking over an occasion of that sort, with her gimlet eye nothing escaped her, nor did any charitable inhibitions tone down her comments on what she had observed.

'How extraordinary Lady Kroesig looked, poor woman! I suppose somebody must have told her that the bridegroom's mother should have a bit of everything in her hat—for luck perhaps. Fur, feathers, flowers and a scrap of lace—it was all there and a diamond brooch on top to finish it off nicely. Rose diamonds—I had a good look. It's a funny thing that these people who are supposed to be so rich never seem to have a decent jewel to put on—I've often noticed it. And did you see what mingy little things they gave poor Linda? A cheque—yes, that's all very well but for how much, I wonder? Cultured pearls, at least I imagine so, or they would have been worth quite £10,000, and a hideous little bracelet. No tiara, no necklace, what will the poor child wear at Court? Linen, which we didn't see, all that modern silver and a horrible house in one of those squares by the Marble Arch. Hardly worth being called by that nasty German name, I should say. And Davey tells me there's no proper settlement—really, Matthew Alconleigh isn't fit to have children if that's all he can do for them. Still, I'm bound to say he looked very handsome coming up the aisle, and Linda looked her very best too, really lovely.'

I think she was feeling quite affectionately towards Linda for having removed herself betimes from competition, for although not a great beauty like Polly she was certainly far more popular with young men.

'Sadie, too, looked so nice, very young and handsome, and the little things so puddy.' She pronounced the word pretty like that.

'Did you see our dessert service, Fanny? Oh, did she, I'm glad. She could change it, as it came from Goodes, but perhaps she won't want to. I was quite amused, weren't you, to see the difference between our side of the church and the Kroesig side. Bankers don't seem to be much to look at—so extraordinarily unsuitable having to know them at all, poor things, let alone marry them. But those sort of people have got megalomania nowadays, one can't get away from them. Did you notice the Kroesig sister? Oh, yes, of course, she was walking with you, Fanny. They'll have a job to get her off!'

'She's training to be a vet,' I said.

'First sensible thing I've heard about any of them. No point in cluttering up the ballrooms with girls who look like that, it's simply not fair on anybody. Now Polly, I want to hear exactly what you did yesterday.'

'Oh—nothing very much.'

'Don't be so tiresome. You got to London at about twelve, I suppose?'

'Yes, we did,' said Polly, in a resigned voice. She would have to account for every minute of the day, she knew, quicker to tell of her own accord than to have it pumped out of her. She began to fidget with her bridesmaid's wreath of silver leaves. 'Wait a moment,' she said, 'I must take this off, it's giving me a headache.'

It was twisted into her hair with wire. She tugged and pulled at it until finally she got it off and flung it down on the floor.

'Ow,' she said, 'that did hurt! Well yes then, let me think. We arrived. Daddy went straight to his appointment and I had an early luncheon at home.'

'By yourself?'

'No, Boy was there. He'd looked in to return some books, and Bullitt said there was plenty of food so I made him stay.'

'Well then, go on. After luncheon?'

'Hair.'

'Washed and set?'

'Yes, naturally.'

'You'd never think it. We really must find you a better hairdresser. No use asking Fanny I'm afraid, her hair always looks like a mop.'

Lady Montdore was becoming cross, and, like a cross child, was seeking to hurt anybody within reach.

'It was quite all right until I had to put that wreath on it. Well then, tea with Daddy at the House, rest after tea, dinner you know about, and bed,' she finished in one breath. 'Is that all?'

She and her mother seemed to be thoroughly on each other's nerves, or perhaps it was having pulled her hair with the wreath that made her so snappy. She flashed a perfectly vicious look across me at Lady Montdore. It was suddenly illuminated by the headlights of a passing motor. Lady Montdore neither saw it nor, apparently, noticed the edge in her voice and went on:

'No, certainly not. You haven't told me about the party yet. Who sat next you at dinner?'

'Oh, Mummy, I can't remember their names.'

'You never seem to remember anybody's name, it is too stupid. How can I invite your friends to the house if I don't know who they are?'

'But they're not my friends, they were the most dreadful, dreadful bores you can possibly imagine. I couldn't think of one thing to say to them.'

Lady Montdore sighed deeply.

'Then after dinner you danced?'

'Yes. Danced, and sat out and ate disgusting ices.'

'I'm sure the ices were delicious. Sylvia Waterman always does things beautifully. I suppose there was champagne?'

'I hate champagne.'

'And who took you home?'

'Lady Somebody. It was out of her way because she lives in Chelsea.'

'How extraordinary,' said Lady Montdore, rather cheered up by the idea that some poor ladies have to live in Chelsea. 'Now who could she possibly have been?'

The Dougdales had also been at the wedding and were to dine at Hampton on their way home; they were there when we arrived, not having, like us, waited to see Linda go away. Polly went straight upstairs. She looked tired and sent a message by her maid to say that she would have her dinner in bed. The Dougdales, Lady Montdore and I dined, without changing, in the little morning-room where they always had meals if there were fewer than eight people. This room was perhaps the most perfect thing at Hampton. It had been brought bodily from France and was entirely panelled in wood carved in a fine, elaborate pattern, painted blue and white; three cupboards matched three french windows and were filled with eighteenth-century china. Over cupboards, windows and doorways were decorative paintings by Boucher, framed in the panelling.

The talk at dinner was of the ball which Lady Montdore intended to give for Polly at Montdore House.

'May Day, I think,' she said.

'That's good,' said Boy, 'it must either be the first or the last ball of the season, if people are to remember it.'

'Oh, not the last, on any account. I should have to invite all the girls whose dances Polly had been to, and nothing is so fatal to a ball as too many girls.'

'But if you don't ask them,' said Lady Patricia, 'will they ask her?'

'Oh, yes,' said Lady Montdore shortly, 'they'll be dying to have her. I can pay them back in other ways. But, anyhow, I don't propose to take her about in the débutante world very much (all those awful parties, S.W. something), I don't see the point of it. She would become quite worn out and meet a lot of unsuitable people. I'm planning to let her go to not more than two dances a week, carefully chosen. Quite enough for a girl who's not very strong. I thought later on, if you'll help me, Boy, we could make a list of women to give dinners for my ball. Of course, it must be perfectly understood that they are to ask the people I tell them to; can't have them paying off their own friends and relations on me.'

After dinner, we went back to the Long Gallery. Boy settled down to his petit-point while we three women sat with idle hands. He had a talent for needlework, had hemstitched some of the sheets for the Queen's doll's house and had covered many chairs at Silkin and at Hampton. He was now making a fire-screen for the Long Gallery which he had designed himself in a sprawling Jacobean pattern, the theme of it was supposed to be flowers from Lady Montdore's garden, but these flowers really looked more like horrid huge insects. Being young and deeply prejudiced it never occurred to me to admire his work. I merely thought how too dreadful it was to see a man sewing and how hideous he looked, his grizzled head bent over the canvas, into which he was deftly stitching various shades of khaki. He had the same sort of thick coarse hair as mine and I knew that the waves in it, the little careless curls (boyish) must have been carefully wetted and pinched in before dinner.

Lady Montdore had sent for paper and a pencil in order to write down the names of dinner hostesses. 'We'll put down all the possible ones and then weed,' she said. But she soon gave up this occupation in order to complain about Polly, and though I had already heard her on the subject when she had been talking with Mrs. Chaddesley Corbett, the tone of her voice was now much sharper and more aggrieved.

'One does everything for these girls,' she said, 'everything. You wouldn't believe it, perhaps, but I assure you I spend quite half my day making plans for Polly—appointments, clothes, parties and so on. I haven't a minute to see my own friends, I've hardly had a game of cards for months, I've quite given up my art—in the middle of that nude girl from Oxford, too—in fact, I devote myself entirely to the child. I keep the London house going simply for her convenience. I hate London in the winter, as you know, and Montdore would be quite happy in two rooms without a cook (all that cold food at the club), but I've got a huge staff there eating their heads off, entirely on her account. You'd think she'd be grateful, at least, wouldn't you? Not at all. Sulky and disagreeable, I can hardly get a word out of her.'

The Dougdales said nothing. He was sorting out wools with great concentration, and Lady Patricia lay back, her eyes closed, suffering, as she had suffered for so long, in silence. She was looking more than ever like some garden statue, her skin and her beige London dress exactly the same colour, while her poor face was lined with pain and sadness, the very expression of antique tragedy.

Lady Montdore went on with her piece, talking exactly as if I were not there.

'I take endless trouble so that she can go and stay in nice houses, but she never seems to enjoy herself a bit, she comes home full of complaints and the only ones she wants to go back to are Alconleigh and Emily Warbeck. Both pure waste of time! Alconleigh is a madhouse—of course, I love Sadie, everybody does, I think she's wonderful, poor dear, and it's not her fault if she has all those eccentric children— she must have done what she can—but they are their father over again. No more need be said. Then I like the child to be with Fanny and one has known Emily and Davey all one's life—Emily was our bridesmaid and Davey was an elf in the very first pageant I ever organized—but the fact remains, Polly never meets anybody there, and if she never meets people how can she marry them?'

'Is there so much hurry for her to marry?' said Lady Patricia.

'Well, you know, she'll be twenty in May, she can't go on like this for ever. If she doesn't marry what will she do, with no interests in life, no occupation. She doesn't care for art or riding or society. She hardly has a friend in the world—oh, can you tell me how Montdore and I came to have a child like that—when I think of myself at her age. I remember so well Mr. Asquith saying he had never met anybody with such a genius for improvisation——'

'Yes, you were wonderful,' said Lady Patricia, with a little smile. 'But after all, she may be slower at developing than you were, and, as you say, she's not twenty yet. Surely it's rather nice to have her at home for another year or two?'

'The fact is,' replied her sister-in-law, 'girls are not nice, it's a perfectly horrid age. When they are children, so sweet and puddy, you think how delightful it will be to have their company later on, but what company is Polly to Montdore or to me? She moons about, always half cross and half tired, and takes no interest in any mortal thing, and what she needs is a husband. Once she is married we shall be on excellent terms again, I've so often seen it happen. I was talking to Sadie the other day and she agreed, she says she has had a most difficult time lately with Linda—Louisa, of course, was never any trouble, she had a nicer character and then she married straight out of the schoolroom. One thing you can say about the Radletts, no delay in marrying them off, though they might not be the sort of marriages one would like for one's own child. A banker and a dilapidated Scotch peer—still, there it is, they are married. What can be the matter with Polly? So beautiful and no B.A. at all.'

'S.A.,' said Lady Patricia faintly, 'or B.O.'

'When we were young none of that existed, thank goodness. S.A. and B.O., perfect rubbish and bosh—one was a beauty or a *jolie-laide* and that was that. All the same, now they have been invented I suppose it is better if the girls have them, their partners seem to like it and Polly hasn't a vestige, you can see that. But how differently,' she said with a sigh, 'how differently life turns out from what we expect! Ever since she was born, you know, I've worried and fussed over that child, and thought of the awful things that might happen to her—that Montdore might die before she was settled and we should have no proper home, that her looks would go (too beautiful at fourteen I feared), or that she would have an accident and spend the rest of her days in a spinal chair —all sorts of things, I used to wake up in the night and imagine them, but the one thing that never even crossed my mind was that she might end up an old maid.'

There was a rising note of aggrieved hysteria in her voice.

'Come now, Sonia,' said Lady Patricia rather sharply, 'the poor girl is still in her teens. Do wait at least until she has had a London season

before you call her an old maid—she'll find somebody she likes there
soon enough you can be quite sure.'

'I only wish I could think it, but I have a strong feeling she won't, and
that what's more they won't like her,' said Lady Montdore, 'she has no
come-hither in her eye. Oh, it is really too bad. She leaves the light on
in her bathroom night after night too, I see it shining out——'

Lady Montdore was very mean about modern inventions such as
electric light.

CHAPTER IX

As her mother had predicted, summer came and went without any
change in Polly's circumstances. The London season duly opened with
a ball at Montdore House which cost £2000, or so Lady Montdore told
everybody, and was certainly very brilliant. Polly wore a white satin
dress with pink roses at the bosom and a pink lining to the sash (touches
of pink as the *Tatler* said), chosen in Paris for her by Mrs. Chaddesley
Corbett and brought over in the bag by some South American diplomat, a friend of Lady Montdore's, to save duty, a proceeding of which
Lord Montdore knew nothing and to which would have perfectly horrified
him had he known. Enhanced by this dress, and by a little make-up,
Polly's beauty was greatly remarked upon, especially by those of a
former generation, who were all saying that since Lady Helen Vincent,
since Lily Langtry, since the Wyndham sisters (according to taste),
nothing so perfect had been seen in London. Her own contemporaries,
however, were not so greatly excited by her. They admitted her beauty
but said that she was dull, too large. What they really admired were
the little skinny goggling copies of Mrs. **Chaddesley Corbett** which
abounded that season. The many dislikers of Lady Montdore said
that she kept Polly too much in the background, and this was hardly
fair because, although it is true to say that Lady Montdore automatically filled the foreground of any picture in which she figured, she
was only too anxious to push Polly in front of her, like a hostage, and
it was not her fault if she was for ever slipping back again.

On the occasion of this ball many of the royalties in Lady Montdore's
bedroom had stepped from their silver frames and come to life, dustier
and less glamorous, poor dears, when seen in all their dimensions; the
huge reception rooms at Montdore House were scattered with them,
and the words Sir or Ma'am could be heard on every hand. The
Ma'ams were really quite pathetic, you would almost say hungry-
looking, so old, in such sad and crumpled clothes, while there were
some blue-chinned Sirs of dreadfully foreign aspect. I particularly
remember one of them because I was told that he was wanted by the

police in France and not much wanted anywhere else, especially not, it seemed, in his native land where his cousin, the King, was daily expecting the crown to be blown off his head by a puff of east wind. This Prince smelt strongly, but not deliciously, of camelias, and had a *fond de teint* of brilliant sunburn.

'I only ask him for the sake of my dear old Princess Irene,' Lady Montdore would explain if people raised their eyebrows at seeing him in such a very respectable house. 'I never shall forget what an angel she was to Montdore and me when we were touring the Balkans (one doesn't forget these things). I know people do say he's a daisy, whatever that may be, but if you listen to what everybody says about everybody you'll end by never having anybody, and besides, half these rumours are put about by anarchists, I'm positive.'

Lady Montdore loved anybody royal. It was a genuine emotion, quite disinterested, since she loved them as much in exile as in power, and the act of curtsying was the consummation of this love. Her curtsies, owing to the solid quality of her frame, did not recall the graceful movement of wheat before the wind. She scrambled down like a camel, rising again backside foremost like a cow, a strange performance, painful it might be supposed to the performer, the expression on whose face, however, belied this thought. Her knees cracked like revolver shots but her smile was heavenly.

I was the only unmarried woman to be asked to dine at Montdore House before the dance. There was a dinner party of forty people with a very grand Sir and Ma'am indeed, on account of whom everybody was punctual to the minute, so that all the guests arrived simultaneously and the large crowd in Park Lane was rewarded by good long stares into the queuing motor cars. Mine was the only cab.

Upstairs a long wait ensued, without cocktails, and even the most brassy people, even Mrs. Chaddesley Corbett, began to twitter with nerves, as though they were being subjected to an intolerable strain; they stood about piping stupidities in their fashionable voices. At last the butler came up to Lord Montdore and murmured something, upon which he and Lady Montdore went down into the hall to receive their guests, while the rest of us, directed by Boy, formed ourselves into a semicircle. Very slowly Lady Montdore led this tremendous Sir and Ma'am round the semicircle, making presentations in the tone of voice, low, reverent but distinct, which my aunts used for responses in church. Then, arm through exalted arm, the four of them moved off, still in slow motion, through the double doors into the dining-room, leaving the rest of us to sort ourselves out and follow. It all went like clockwork.

Soon after dinner, which took a long time and was Hampton food at its climax, crest and top, people began to arrive for the ball. Lady Montdore in gold lamé, and many diamonds, including her famous pink diamond tiara, Lord Montdore, genial, noble, his long thin legs in silk stockings and knee breeches, the Garter round one of them, its ribbon across his shirt front and a dozen miniatures dangling on his chest, and Polly in her white dress and her beauty, stood shaking hands at the top of the stairs for quite an hour and a very pretty sight it was to see the people streaming past them. Lady Montdore, true to her word, had invited very few girls and even fewer mammas. The guests were therefore neither too young nor too old to decorate but were all in their glittering prime.

Nobody asked me to dance. Just as no girls had been invited to the ball so also were there very few young men except such as were firmly attached to the young married set, but I was quite happy looking on, and since there was not a soul I knew to see me, no shame attached to my situation. All the same I was delighted when the Alconleighs, with Louisa and Linda and their husbands, Aunt Emily and Davey, who had been dining together, appeared, as they always did at parties, nice and early. I became assimilated into their cheerful group and we took up a position, whence we could have a good view of the proceedings, in the picture gallery. This opened into the ballroom on one hand and the supper-room on the other, there was a great deal of coming and going and at the same time never any crowd so that we could see the dresses and jewels to their best advantage. Behind us hung a Correggio St. Sebastian, with the usual Buchmanite expression on his face.

'Awful tripe,' said Uncle Matthew, 'fella wouldn't be grinning, he'd be dead with all those arrows in him.'

On the opposite wall was the Montdore Botticelli which Uncle Matthew said he wouldn't give 7s. 6d. for, and when Davey showed him a Leonardo drawing he said his fingers only itched for an india-rubber.

'I saw a picture once,' he said, 'of shire horses in the snow. There was nothing else, just a bit of broken down fence and three horses. It was dangerous good—Army and Navy. If I'd been a rich man I'd have bought that—I mean you could see how cold those poor brutes must have felt. If all this rubbish is supposed to be valuable, that must be worth a fortune.'

Uncle Matthew, who absolutely never went out in the evening, let alone to balls, would not hear of refusing an invitation to Montdore House, though Aunt Sadie, who knew how it tormented him to be kept awake after dinner, and how his poor eyes would turn back to front with sleepiness, had said:

'Really, darling, as we are between daughters, two married, and two not yet out, there's no occasion whatever for us to go if you'd rather not. Sonia would understand perfectly—and be quite glad of our room, I daresay.'

But Uncle Matthew had gloomily replied, 'If Montdore asks us to his ball it is because he wants to see us there. I think we ought to go.'

Accordingly, with many groans, he had squeezed himself into the knee breeches of his youth, now so perilously tight that he hardly dared sit down, but stood like a stork beside Aunt Sadie's chair, and Aunt Sadie had got all her diamonds out of the bank and lent some to Linda and some to Aunt Emily and even so had quite a nice lot left for herself, and here they were chatting away happily enough with their relations and with various county figures who came and went, and even Uncle Matthew seemed quite amused by it all until a dreadful fate befell him, he was made to take the German Ambassadress to supper. It happened like this. Lord Montdore, at Uncle Matthew's very elbow, suddenly exclaimed in horror:

'Good heavens, the German Ambassadress is sitting there quite alone.'

'Serve her right,' said Uncle Matthew. It would have been more prudent to have held his tongue. Lord Montdore heard him speak, without taking in the meaning of his words, turned sharply round, saw who it was, seized him by the arm and said:

'My dear Matthew, just the very man—Baroness von Ravensbrück, may I present my neighbour, Lord Alconleigh? Supper is quite ready in the music room—you know the way, Matthew.'

It was a measure of Lord Montdore's influence over Uncle Matthew that my uncle did not then and there turn tail and bolt for home. No other living person could have persuaded him to stay and shake hands with a Hun, let alone take it on his arm and feed it. He went off, throwing a mournful backward glance at his wife.

Lady Patricia now came and sat by Aunt Sadie and they chatted, in rather a desultory way, about local affairs. Aunt Sadie, unlike her husband, really enjoyed going out so long as it was not too often, she did not have to stay up too late, and she was allowed to look on peacefully without feeling obliged to make any conversational effort. Strangers bored and fatigued her; she only liked the company of those people with whom she had day-to-day interests in common, such as country neighbours or members of her own family, and even with them she was generally rather absent-minded. But on this occasion it was Lady Patricia who seemed half in the clouds, saying yes and no to Aunt Sadie and what a monstrous thing it was to let the Skilton village idiot out again specially now it was known what a fast runner he was since he had won the asylum 100 yards.

'And he's always chasing people,' Aunt Sadie said indignantly.

But Lady Patricia's mind was not on the idiot. She was thinking, I am sure, of parties in those very rooms when she was young, and how much she had worshipped the Lecturer, and what agony it had been when he had danced and flirted, she knew, with other people, and how perhaps it was almost sadder for her that now she could care about nothing any more but the condition of her liver.

I knew from Davey ('Oh, the luck' as Linda used to say, 'that Dave is such an old gossip, poor simple us if it weren't for him!') that Lady Patricia had loved Boy for several years before he had finally proposed to her, and had indeed quite lost hope. And then how short-lived was her happiness, barely six months before she had found him in bed with a kitchen maid.

'Boy never went out for big stuff,' I once heard Mrs. Chaddesley Corbett say, 'he only ever liked bowling over the rabbits, and now, of course, he's a joke.'

It must be hateful, being married to a joke.

Presently she said to Aunt Sadie, 'When was the first ball you ever came to, here?'

'It must have been the year I came out, in 1906. I well remember the excitement of actually seeing King Edward in the flesh and hearing his loud foreign laugh.'

'Twenty-four years ago, fancy,' said Lady Patricia, 'just before Boy and I were married. Do you remember how, in the war, people used to say we should never see this sort of thing again, and yet look! Only look at the jewels.'

Presently, as Lady Montdore came into sight, she said:

'You know, Sonia really is phenomenal. I'm sure she's better-looking and better-dressed now than she has ever been in her life.'

One of those middle-aged remarks I used to find incomprehensible. It did not seem to me that Lady Montdore could be described either as good-looking or as well-dressed; she was old and that was that. On the other hand nobody could deny that on occasions of this sort she was impressive, almost literally covered with great big diamonds, tiara, necklace, ear-rings, a huge Palatine cross on her bosom, bracelets from wrist to elbow over her suède gloves, and brooches wherever there was possible room for them. Dressed up in these tremendous jewels, surrounded by the exterior signs of 'all this', her whole demeanour irradiated by the superiority she so deeply felt in herself, she was, like a bull-fighter in his own ring, an idol in its own ark, the reason for and the very centre of the spectacle.

Uncle Matthew, having made his escape from the Ambassadress with a deep bow expressive of deep disgust, now came back to the family party.

'Old cannibal,' he said, 'she kept asking for more fleisch. Can't have swallowed her dinner more than an hour ago—I pretended not to hear, wouldn't pander to the old ogress, after all, who won the war? And what for, I should like to know? Wonderful public-spirited of Montdore to put up with all this foreign trash in his house—I'm blowed if I would. I ask you to look at that sewer!' He glared in the direction of a blue-chinned Sir who was heading for the supper-room with Polly on his arm.

'Come now, Matthew,' said Davey, 'the Serbs were our allies you know.'

'Allies!' said Uncle Matthew, grinding his teeth. The word was as a red rag to a bull and naughty Davey knew this and was waving the rag for fun.

'So that's a Serb, is it? Well, just what one would expect, needs a shave. Hogs, one and all. Of course, Montdore only asks them for the sake of the country. I do admire that fella, he thinks of nothing but his duty—what an example to everybody!'

A gleam of amusement crossed Lady Patricia's sad face. She was not without a sense of humour and was one of the few people Uncle Matthew liked, though he could not bring himself to be polite to Boy, and gazed furiously into space every time he passed our little colony, which he did quite often, squiring royal old ladies to the supper-room. Of his many offences in the eyes of Uncle Matthew, the chief was that, having been A.D.C. to a general in the war, he was once discovered by my uncle sketching a château behind the lines. There must clearly be something wrong about a man who could waste his time sketching, or indeed, undertake the duties of an A.D.C. at all, when he might be slaughtering foreigners all day.

'Nothing but a blasted lady's maid,' Uncle Matthew would say whenever Boy's name was mentioned. 'I can't stick the sewer. Boy indeed! Dougdale! What does it all mean? There used to be some perfectly respectable people called Blood at Silkin in the Old Lord's time. Major and Mrs. Blood.'

The Old Lord was Lord Montdore's father. Jassy once said, opening enormous eyes, 'He *must* have been old,' upon which Aunt Sadie had remarked that people do not remain the same age all their lives, and he had no doubt been young in his time just as one day, though she might not expect it, Jassy herself would become old.

It was not very logical of Uncle Matthew so exaggeratedly to despise Boy's military record, and was just another example of how those he liked could do no wrong and those he disliked no right, because Lord Montdore, his great hero, had never in his life heard the cheerful sound of musketry or been near a battle; he would have been rather elderly to have taken the field in the Great War, it is true, but his early years had vainly offered many a jolly fight, chances to hack away at native flesh, not to speak of Dutch flesh in that Boer war which had provided Uncle Matthew with such radiant memories, having given him his first experience of bivouac and battle.

'Four days in a bullock waggon,' he used to tell us, 'a hole as big as your fist in my stomach, and maggoty! Happiest time of my life. The only thing was one got rather tired of the taste of mutton after a bit, no beef in that campaign, you know.'

But Lord Montdore was a law unto himself, and had even got away with the famous Montdore Letter to the *Morning Post* which suggested that the war had gone on long enough and might be brought to an end, several months before the cowardly capitulation of the Hun had made this boring adjournment necessary. Uncle Matthew found it difficult to condone such spoiling of sport but did so by saying that Lord Montdore must have had some good reason for writing it which nobody else knew anything about.

My thoughts were now concentrated upon the entrance to the ball-room door, where I had suddenly perceived the back of somebody's head. So he had come after all. The fact that I had never thought he would (such a serious character) had in no way mitigated my dis-appointment that he had not; now, here he was. I must explain that the image of Sauveterre, having reigned in my hopeless heart for several months, had recently been ousted and replaced by something more serious, with more reality and promise.

The back of a head, seen at a ball, can have a most agitating effect upon a young girl, so different from the backs of other heads that it might be surrounded by a halo. There is the question, will he turn round, will he see her, and if so will he merely give a polite good-evening or invite her to dance? Oh, how I wished I could have been whirling gaily round in the arms of some fascinator instead of sitting with my aunts and uncles, too obviously a wallflower. Not that it mattered. There were a few moments of horrible suspense before the head turned round, but when it did he saw me, came straight over, said good-evening more than politely, and danced me away. He thought he would never get here, it was a question of borrowed, but mislaid, knee-breeches. Then he danced with Aunt Emily, again with me, and with Louisa, having engaged me to have supper after that.

'Who is that brute?' said Uncle Matthew, grinding his teeth as my young man went off with Louisa, 'why does he keep coming over here?'

'He's called Alfred Wincham,' I said, 'shall I introduce him to you?'

'For pity's sake, Fanny!'

'What an old Pasha you are,' said Davey. And indeed, Uncle Matthew would clearly have preferred to keep all his female relations in a condition if not of virginity at any rate of exaggerated chastity, and could never bear them to be approached by strange men.

When not dancing I went back and sat with my relations. I felt calmer now, having had two dances and the promise of supper, and was quite happy to fill in the time by listening to my elders as they conversed.

Presently Aunt Sadie and Aunt Emily went off to have supper to-gether; they always liked to do this at parties. Davey moved up to sit next Lady Patricia and Uncle Matthew stood by Davey's chair, sleep-ing on his feet as horses can, patiently waiting to be led back to his stable. 'It's this new man Meyerstein,' Davey was saying. 'You simply must go to him, Patricia, he does it all by salt elimination. You skip in order to sweat out all the salt in your organism, and eat saltless meals, of course. Too disgusting. But it does break down the crystals.'

'Do you mean skip with a skipping-rope?'

'Yes, hundreds of times. You count. I can do three hundred at a go, as well as some fancy steps, now.'

'But isn't it horribly tiring?'

'Nothing tires Davey—fella's as strong as a bull,' said Uncle Matthew, opening one eye.

Davey cast a sad look at his brother-in-law and said that of course it was desperately tiring, but well worth it for the results.

Polly was dancing now with her uncle, Boy. She did not look radiant and happy as such a spoilt darling should at her coming-out ball, but tired and pinched about the mouth, nor was she chattering away like the other women.

'I shouldn't care for one of my girls to look like that,' Aunt Sadie said, 'you'd think she had something on her mind.'

And my new friend Mr. Wincham said, as we danced round before going to supper, 'Of course she's a beauty, I quite see that she is, but she doesn't attract me, with that sulky expression, I'm sure she's very dull.'

I began to deny that she was either sulky or dull when he said 'Fanny' to me, the first time he ever had, and followed this up with a lot of things which I wanted to listen to very carefully so that I could think them over later on, when I was alone.

Mrs. Chaddesley Corbett shouted at me, from the arms of the Prince of Wales, 'Hullo, my sweet! What news of the Bolter? Are you still in love?'

'What's all this?' said my partner. 'Who is that woman? Who is the Bolter? And is it true that you are in love?'

'Mrs. Chaddesley Corbett,' I said. I felt that the time was not yet ripe to begin explaining about the Bolter.

'And how about love?'

'Nothing,' I said, rather pink, 'just a joke.'

'Good. I should like you to be on the verge of love but not yet quite in it. That's a very nice state of mind, while it lasts.'

But of course, I had already dived over that verge and was swimming away in a blue sea of illusion towards, I supposed, the islands of the blest, but really towards domesticity, maternity and the usual lot of womankind.

A holy hush now fell upon the crowd as the Royals prepared to go home, the very grand Royals serene in the knowledge that they would find the traditional cold roast chicken by their beds, not the pathetic Ma'ams and sinister Sirs who were stuffing away in the supper-room as if they were far from sure they would ever see so much food again, nor the gay young Royals who were going to dance until morning with little neat women of the Chaddesley Corbett sort.

'How late they have stayed, what a triumph for Sonia,' I heard Boy saying to his wife.

The dancers divided like the Red Sea forming a lane of bowing and curtsying subjects, down which Lord and Lady Montdore conducted their guests.

'Sweet of you to say so, Ma'am. Yes, at the next Court. Oh, how kind of you.'

The Montdores came back into the picture gallery, beaming happily and saying, to nobody in particular:

'So simple, so easy, pleased with any little thing one can do for them, such wonderful manners, such a memory. Astounding how much they know about India, the Maharajah was amazed.'

They spoke as though these Princes are so remote from life as we know it that the smallest sign of humanity, the mere fact even that they communicated by means of speech, was worth noting and proclaiming.

The rest of the evening was spent by me in a happy trance, and I remember no more about the party as such. I know that I was taken back to the Goring Hotel, where we were all staying, at five o'clock on a fine May morning by Mr. Wincham, who had clearly shown me, by then, that he was not at all averse to my company.

CHAPTER X

So Polly was now 'out' in London society, and played her part during the rest of the season, as she had at the ball, with a good enough grace, the performance only lacking vitality and temperament to make it perfect. She did all the things her mother arranged for her, went to the parties, wore the clothes and made the friends that Lady Montdore thought suitable and never branched out on her own or gave any possible cause for complaint. She certainly did nothing to create an atmosphere of fun, but Lady Montdore was perhaps too much employed herself in that very direction to notice that Polly, though good and acquiescent, never for one moment entered into the spirit of the many entertainments they went to. Lady Montdore enjoyed it all prodigiously, appeared to be satisfied with Polly, and was delighted with the publicity that, as the most important and most beautiful débutante of the year, she was receiving. She was really too busy, in too much of a whirl of society while the season was going on, to wonder whether Polly was being a success or not; when it was over they went to Goodwood, Cowes, and Scotland, where no doubt among the mists and heather she had time to take stock of the situation. They vanished from my life for many weeks.

By the time I saw them again, in the autumn, their relationship was back to what it had been before and they were clearly very much on each other's nerves. I was now living in London myself, Aunt Emily having taken a little house in St. Leonard's Terrace for the winter. It was a happy time in my life, as presently I became engaged to Alfred Wincham, the same young man whose back view had so much disturbed me at the Montdore ball. During the weeks that preceded my engagement I saw a great deal of Polly. She would telephone in the morning.

'What are you up to, Fanny?'

'Aching,' I would reply, meaning aching with boredom, a malaise from which girls, before national service came to their rescue, were apt to suffer considerably.

'Oh, good. So can I bend you to my will? You can't think how dull, but if you are aching anyway? Well then, I've got to try on that blue velvet hat at Madame Rita, and go and fetch the gloves from Debenhams—they said they would have them today. Yes, but the worst is to come—I couldn't possibly bend you to have luncheon with my Aunt Edna at Hampton Court and afterwards to sit and chat while I have my hair done? No, forget I said anything so awful—anyway, we'll see. I'll be round for you in half an hour.'

I was quite pliable. I had nothing whatever to do and enjoyed bouncing round London in the big Daimler, while Polly went about the business which is demanded of a beauty. Although society, at present, had no attractions for her, she was very much interested in her own appearance and would never, I think, have given up bothering about it as Lady Patricia had.

So we went to Madame Rita, and I tried on all the hats in the shop while Polly had her fitting, and wondered why it was that hats never seemed to suit me, something to do with my heather-like hair perhaps, and then we drove down to Hampton Court where Polly's old great-aunt, the widow of a general, had an apartment. She sat all day dealing out cards to herself as she waited for eternity.

'And yet I don't believe she aches, you know,' said Polly.

'I've noticed,' I said, 'that married ladies and even widows never ache. There is something about marriage that seems to stop it for good, I wonder why?'

Polly did not answer. The very word marriage always shut her up like a clam, it was a thing that had to be remembered in her company.

The afternoon before my engagement was to be announced in *The Times*, Aunt Emily sent me round to Montdore House to tell the news. It is not at all my nature to be one of those who 'drop in', I like to be invited by people to their houses at a given time, so that when I arrive they are expecting me and have made their dispositions accordingly, but I saw Aunt Emily's point when she said that, after all Lady Montdore's kindness to me, and considering that Polly was such a very great friend, I could hardly allow them to become aware of my engagement by reading it casually, in the paper.

So round I went, trembling rather. Bullitt, the butler, always frightened me into a fit. He was like Frankenstein's monster and one had to follow his jerky footsteps as though through some huge museum before arriving at the little green room, the only room in the house which did not seem as if it had been cleared ready for a reception, in which they always sat. Today, however, the front door was opened by a footman of more human aspect, and, furthermore, he told me the good news that Her Ladyship had not yet come in but Lady Polly was there alone, so off we trudged and presently discovered her amid the usual five o'clock paraphernalia of silver kettle on flame, silver teapot, Crown Derby cups and plates and enough sugary food to stock a pastrycook's shop. She was sitting on the arm of a chair reading the *Tatler*.

'Heavenly *Tatler* day,' she said, 'it really does help with the aching. I'm in and Linda's in, but not you this week. Faithful of you to come, I was just wishing somebody nice would—now we can have our tea.'

I was uncertain how she would take my engagement, I had in fact never spoken to her of Alfred since I had begged her to get him asked to the ball, she always seemed so much against young men or any talk of love. But when I told her the news she was enthusiastic and only reproached me with having been so secretive.

'I remember you made me ask him to the ball,' she said. 'But then you never mentioned him again, once.'

'I didn't dare to talk about it,' I said, 'in case—well—it really was of too much importance.'

'Oh, I do understand that. I'm so glad you **were longing** for it before he asked you, I never believe in the other sort, the ones who have to make up their minds, you know. How lucky you are, oh, fancy being able to marry the person you love. You don't know your luck.' Her eyes were full of tears, I saw. 'Go on,' she said. 'Tell everything.'

I was rather surprised at this show of feeling, so unusual with Polly, but in my selfish state of great new happiness did not pause to consider what it might mean. Besides, I was, of course, longing to tell.

'He was terribly nice to me at your ball, I hadn't a bit expected that he would come to London for it because for one thing, knee-breeches. I knew how he wouldn't have any, and then he's so busy always and hates parties, so you can imagine when I saw him I was all excited. Then he asked me to dance, but he danced with old Louisa too and even Aunt Emily so I thought, oh, well, he doesn't know anybody else, it must be that. So then he took me to supper and said he liked my dress and he hoped I'd go and see him at Oxford, and then he said something which showed he'd remembered a conversation we had had before. You know how encouraging that always is. After that he asked me to Oxford, twice, once he had a luncheon party and once he was alone, but in the holidays he went to Greece. Oxford holidays are terribly long, you know. Not even a postcard, so I thought it was all off. Well, on Thursday I went to Oxford again and this time he proposed to me and look——' I said, showing a pretty old ring, a garnet set in diamonds.

'Don't say he had it on him like in *The Making of a Marchioness*,' said Polly.

'Just like, except that it's not a ruby.'

'Quite the size of a pigeon's egg though. You are lucky.'

Lady Montdore now appeared. She bustled in still wearing her outdoor clothes and seemed unusually mellow.

'Ah! The girls!' she said, 'talking balls, I suppose, as usual! Going to the Gravesends' tonight, Fanny? Give me some tea, I'm quite dead, such an afternoon with the Grand Duchess, I've just dropped her at Kensington Palace. You'd never believe that woman was nearly eighty, she could run us all off our feet you know, and such a dear, so human, one doesn't mind what one says to her. We went to Woollands to get some woollens—she does feel the cold. Misses the double windows so she tells me.'

It must have been rather sad for Lady Montdore (though with her talent for ignoring disagreeable subjects she probably never even realized the fact) that friendship with royal personages only ever began for her when their days of glory were finished. Tsarkoe-Selo, Schönbrunn, the Quirinal, Kotrocheny Palace, Miramar, Laecken and the island of Corfu had never known her, unless among an enormous crowd in the state apartments. If she went to a foreign capital with her husband she would, of course, be invited to official receptions, while foreign rulers who came to London would attend her big parties, but it was all very formal. Crowned heads may not have had the sense to keep their crowns but they were evidently not too stupid to realize that give Lady Montdore an inch and she would take an ell. As soon as they were exiled, however, they began to see her charm, and another kingdom gone always meant a few more royal habitués at Montdore House; when they were completely down-and-out and had got through whatever money they had managed to salt away, she was allowed to act as lady-in-waiting and go with them to Woollands.

Polly handed her a cup of tea and told her my news. The happy afterglow from her royal outing immediately faded, and she became intensely disagreeable.

'Engaged?' she said. 'Well, I suppose that's very nice. Alfred what did you say? Who is he? What is that name?'

'He's a don, at Oxford.'

'Oh, dear, how extraordinary. You don't want to go and live at Oxford, surely? I should think he had better go into politics and buy a place—I suppose he hasn't got one by the way? No, or he wouldn't be a don, not an English don at least, in Spain of course, it's quite different —dons are somebody there, I believe. Let's think—yes, why shouldn't your father give you a place as a wedding present? You're the only child he's ever likely to have. I'll write to him at once—where is he now?'

I said vaguely that I believed in Jamaica, but did not know his address.

'Really, what a family! I'll find out from the Colonial Office and write by bag, that will be safest. Then this Mr. Thing can settle down and write books. It always gives a man status if he writes a book, Fanny, I advise you to start him off on that immediately.'

'I'm afraid I haven't much influence with him,' I said, uneasily.

'Oh, well, develop it dear, quick. No use marrying a man you can't influence. Just look what I've done for Montdore, always seen that he takes an interest, made him accept things (jobs, I mean) and kept him up to the mark, never let him slide back. A wife must always be on the look-out, men are so lazy by nature, for example, Montdore is for ever trying to have a little nap in the afternoon, but I won't hear of it, once you begin that, I tell him, you are old, and people who are old find themselves losing interest, dropping out of things and then they might as well be dead. Montdore's only got me to thank if he's not in the same condition as most of his contemporaries, creeping about the Marlborough Club like dying flies and hardly able to drag themselves as far as the House of Lords. I make Montdore walk down there every day. Now, Fanny dear, the more I think of it, the more it seems to me quite ridiculous for you to go marrying a don, what does Emily say?'

'She's awfully pleased.'

'Emily and Sadie are hopeless. You must ask my advice about this sort of thing, I'm very glad indeed you came round, we must think how we can get you out of it. Could you ring him up now and say you've changed your mind, I believe it would be kindest in the long run to do it that way.'

'Oh, no, I can't.'

'Why not, dear? It isn't in the paper yet.'

'It will be tomorrow.'

'That's where I can be so helpful. I'll send for Geoffrey Dawson now and have it stopped.'

I was quite terrified. 'Please——' I said, 'oh, please not!'

Polly came to my rescue. 'But she wants to marry him, Mummy, she's in love, and look at her pretty ring!'

Lady Montdore looked, and was confirmed in her opposition. 'That's not a ruby,' she said, as if I had been pretending it was. 'And as for love I should have thought the example of your mother would have taught you something—where has love landed her? Some ghastly white hunter. Love indeed—whoever invented love ought to be shot.'

'Dons aren't a bit the same as white hunters,' said Polly. 'You know how fond Daddy is of them.'

'Oh, I daresay they're all right for dinner, if you like that sort of thing. Montdore does have them over sometimes, I know, but that's no reason why they should go marrying people. So unsuitable, megalomania, I call it. So many people have that, nowadays. No, Fanny, I'm very much distressed.'

'Oh, please don't be,' I said.

'However, if you say it's settled, I suppose there's no more I can do, except to try and help you make a success of it. Montdore can ask the Chief Whip if there's something for you to nurse, that will be best.'

It was on the tip of my tongue to say that what I hoped to be nursing before long would be sent by God and not the Chief Whip but I restrained myself, nor did I dare to tell her that Alfred was not a Tory.

The conversation now turned upon the subject of my trousseau, about which Lady Montdore was quite as bossy though less embarrassing. I was not feeling much interest in clothes at that time, all my thoughts being of how to decorate and furnish a charming little old house which Alfred had taken me to see after placing the pigeon's egg on my finger, and which, by a miracle of good luck, was to be let.

'The important thing, dear,' she said, 'is to have a really good fur coat, I mean a proper, dark one.' To Lady Montdore, fur meant mink; she could imagine no other kind except sable, but that would be specified. 'Not only will it make all the rest of your clothes look better than they are but you really needn't bother much about anything else as you need never take it off. Above all, don't go wasting money on underclothes, there is nothing stupider—I always borrow Montdore's myself. Now for evening a diamond brooch is a great help, so long as it has good big stones. Oh, dear, when I think of the diamonds your father gave that woman, it really is too bad. All the same, he can't have got through everything, he was enormously rich when he succeeded, I must write to him. Now, dear, we're going to be very practical. No time like the present.'

She rang for her secretary and said my father's address must be found out.

'You could ring up the Under Secretary for Colonies with my compliments, and will you make a note that I will write to Lord Logan tomorrow.'

She also told her to make a list of places where linen, underclothes and house furnishings could be obtained at wholesale prices.

'Bring it straight back here for Miss Logan when it is ready.'

When the secretary had gone Lady Montdore turned to Polly and spoke to her exactly as if I had gone too, and they were alone. It was a habit she had, and I always found it very embarrassing, as I never quite knew what she expected me to do, whether to interrupt her by saying good-bye, or simply to look out of the window and pretend that my thoughts were far away. On this occasion, however, I was clearly expected to wait for the list of addresses, so I had no choice.

'Now, Polly, have you thought of a young man yet, for me to ask down on the third?'

'Oh, how about John Coningsby?' said Polly, with an indifference which I could plainly see must be maddening to her mother. Lord Coningsby was her official young man, so to speak. She invited him to everything, and this had greatly pleased Lady Montdore to begin with since he was rich, handsome, agreeable and an 'eldest son', which meant in Lady Montdore's parlance the eldest son of a peer (never let Jones or Robinson major think of themselves for one moment as eldest sons). Too soon, however, she saw that he and Polly were excellent friends and would never be anything else, after which she regretfully lost all interest in him.

'Oh, I don't count John,' she said.

'How d'you mean you don't count him?'

'He's only a friend. Now, I was thinking in Woollands—I often do have good ideas in shops—how would it be to ask Joyce Fleetwood?'

Alas, the days when I, Albert Christian George Andrew Patrick David, was considered to be the only person worthy of taking thee, Leopoldina, must have become indeed remote if Joyce Fleetwood was to be put forward as a substitute. Perhaps it was in Lady Montdore's mind that, since Polly showed no inclination to marry an established, inherited position, the next best thing would be somebody who might achieve one by his own efforts. Joyce Fleetwood was a noisy, self-opinionated young Conservative M.P. who had mastered one or two of the drearier subjects of debate, agriculture, the Empire, and so on, and was always ready to hold forth upon them in the House. He had made up to Lady Montdore who thought him much cleverer than he really was; his parents were known to her, they had a place in Norfolk.

'Well, Polly?'

'Yes, why not?' said Polly. 'It's a shower-bath when he talks, but do let's, he's so utterly fascinating, isn't he?'

Lady Montdore now lost her temper and her voice got quite out of control. I sympathized with her really, it was too obvious that Polly was wilfully provoking her.

'It's perfectly stupid to go on like this.'

Polly did not reply. She bent her head sideways and pretended to be deeply absorbed in the headlines, upside-down, of the evening paper which lay on a chair by her mother. She might just as well have said out loud, 'All right, you horrible vulgar woman, go on, I don't care, you are nothing to me,' so plain was her meaning.

'Please listen when I speak to you, Polly.'

Polly continued to squint at the headlines.

'Polly, will you please pay attention to what I'm saying?'

'What were you saying? Something about Mr. Fleetwood?'

'Let Mr. Fleetwood be, for the present. I want to know what, exactly, you are planning to do with your life. Do you intend to live at home and go mooning on like this for ever?'

'What else can I do? You haven't exactly trained me for a career, have you?'

'Oh, yes, indeed I have. I've trained you for marriage which, in my opinion (I may be old-fashioned), is by far the best career open to any woman.'

'That's all very well, but how can I marry if nobody asks me?'

Of course, that was really the sore point with Lady Montdore, nobody asking her. A Polly gay and flirtatious, surrounded by eligible suitors, playing one off against the others, withdrawing, teasing, desired by married men, breaking up her friends' romances, Lady Montdore would have been perfectly happy to watch her playing that game for several years if need be, so long as it was quite obvious that she would finally choose some suitably important husband and settle down with him. What her mother minded so dreadfully was that this acknowledged beauty should appear to have no attraction whatever for the male sex. The eldest sons had a look, said, 'Isn't she lovely?' and went off with some chinless little creature from Cadogan Square. There had been three or four engagements of this sort lately which had upset Lady Montdore very much indeed.

'And why don't they ask you? It's only because you give them no encouragement. Can't you try to be a little jollier, nicer with them, no man cares to make love to a dummy, you know, it's too discouraging.'

'Thank you, but I don't want to be made love to.'

'Oh, dear, oh, dear! Then what is it you do want?'

'Leave me alone Mother, please.'

'To stay on here, with us, until you are old?'

'Daddy wouldn't mind, a bit.'

'Oh, yes he would, make no mistake about that. Not for a year or two perhaps, but in the end he would. Nobody wants their girl to be hanging about for ever, a sour old maid, and you'll be the sour kind, that's too obvious already, my dear, wizened-up and sour.'

I could hardly believe my ears; could this be Lady Montdore speaking, in such frank and dreadful terms, to Polly, her beautiful paragon, whom she used to love so much that she was even reconciled to her being a daughter and not an heir? It seemed to me terrible, I went cold in my very backbone. There was a long and deeply embarrassing silence, broken by Frankenstein's monster who jerked into the room and said that the King of Portugal was on the telephone. Lady Montdore stumped off and I seized the opportunity to escape.

'I hate her,' said Polly, kissing me good-bye. 'I hate her, and I wish she were dead. Oh, Fanny, the luck of not being brought up by your own mother—you've no idea what a horrible relationship it can be.'

'Poor Polly,' I said, very much upset. 'How sad. But when you were little it wasn't horrible?'

'Always, always horrible. I've always hated her from the bottom of my heart.'

I did not believe it.

'She isn't like this the whole time?' I said.

'More and more. Better make a dash for it, love, or you'll be caught again. I'll ring up very soon——'

CHAPTER XI

I was married at the beginning of the Christmas vacation, and when Alfred and I returned from our honeymoon we went to stay at Alconleigh while our little house in Oxford was being got ready. This was an obvious and convenient arrangement as Alfred could go into Oxford every day for his work, and I was at hand to supervise the decoration of the house, but, although Alconleigh had been a second home to me from my babyhood, it was not without misgivings that I accepted Aunt Sadie's invitation to take my husband there for a long visit, at the very outset of our married life. My Uncle Matthew's likes and dislikes were famous for their violence, for the predomination of the latter over the former, and for the fact that he never made the slightest attempt to conceal them from their object; I could see that he was already prejudiced against poor Alfred. It was an accepted fact in the family that he loathed me; furthermore he also hated new people, hated men who married his female relations, hated and despised those who did not practise blood sports. I felt there was but little hope for Alfred, especially as, culmination of horror, 'the fella reads books'.

True, all this had applied to Davey when he had first appeared upon the scene, engaged to Aunt Emily, but Uncle Matthew had taken an unreasoning fancy to Davey from the very beginning, and it was not to be hoped that such a miracle could repeat itself. My fears, however, were not entirely realized. I think Aunt Sadie had probably read the riot act before our arrival, meanwhile I had been doing my best with Alfred. I made him have his hair cropped like a guardsman, explained to him that if he must open a book he should do so only in the privacy of his bedroom, and specially urged great punctuality at meal times.

Uncle Matthew, as I told him, liked to get us all into the dining-room at least five minutes before the meal was ready. 'Come on,' he would say, 'we'll go and sit in.' And in the family would sit, clasping hot plates to their bosoms (Aunt Sadie had once done this, absent-mindedly, with a plate of artichoke soup), all eyes upon the pantry door.

I tried to explain these things to Alfred, who listened patiently though uncomprehendingly, I also tried to prepare him for the tremendous impact of my uncle's rages, so that I got the poor man, really quite unnecessarily, into a panic.

'Do let's go to the Mitre,' he kept saying.

'It may not be too bad,' I replied, doubtfully.

And it was not, in the end, too bad at all. The fact is that Uncle Matthew's tremendous and classical hatred for me, which had begun when I was an infant and which had cast a shadow of fear over all my childhood, had now become more legend than actuality. I was such an habitual member of his household, and he such a Conservative, that this hatred, in common with that which he used to nurture against Josh, the groom, and various other old intimates, had not only lost its force but I think had, with the passage of years, actually turned into love; such a lukewarm sentiment as ordinary avuncular affection being of course foreign to his experience. Be that as it may, he evidently had no wish to poison the beginning of my married life, and made quite touching efforts to bottle up whatever irritation he felt at Alfred's shortcomings, ·his unmanly incompetence with his motor car, vagueness over time and fatal disposition to spill marmalade at breakfast. The fact that Alfred left for Oxford at nine o'clock, only returning in time for dinner, and that we spent Saturday to Monday of every week in Kent with Aunt Emily, made our visit just endurable to Uncle Matthew, and incidentally to Alfred himself, who did not share my unquestioning adoration for all members of the Radlett family.

The Radlett boys had gone back to their schools, and my cousin Linda, whom I loved best in the world after Alfred, was now living in London, expecting a baby, but, though Alconleigh was never quite the same without her, Jassy and Victoria were at home (none of the Radlett girls went to school) so the house resounded as usual with jingles and jangles and idiotic shrieks. There was always some joke being run to death at Alconleigh and just now it was headlines from the *Daily Express* which the children had made into a chant and intoned to each other all day.

Jassy: '*Man's* long *agony in* a lift-*shaft.*'
Victoria: 'Slowly *crushed* to *death* in a *lift.*'

Aunt Sadie became very cross about this, said they were really too old to be so heartless, that it wasn't a bit funny, only dull and disgusting, and absolutely forbade them to sing it any more. After this they tapped it out to each other, on doors, under the dining-room table, clicking with their tongues or blinking with their eyelids, and all the time in fits of naughty giggles. I could see that Alfred thought them terribly silly, and he could hardly contain his indignation when he found out that they did no lessons of any sort.

'Thank heavens for your Aunt Emily,' he said. 'I really could not have married somebody quite illiterate.'

Of course, I too thanked heavens more than ever for dear Aunt Emily, but at the same time Jassy and Victoria made me laugh so much, and I loved them so much, that it was impossible for me to wish them very different from what they were. Hardly had I arrived in the house than I was lugged off to their secret meeting-place, the Hons' cupboard, to be asked what IT was like.

'Linda says it's not all it's cracked up to be,' said Jassy, 'and we don't wonder when we think of Tony.'

'But Louisa says, once you get used to it, it's utter utter utter blissikins,' said Victoria, 'and we do wonder, when we think of John.'

'What's wrong with poor Tony and John?'

'Dull and old. Come on then Fanny—tell.'

I said I agreed with Louisa, but refused to enter into details.

'It is unfair, nobody ever tells. Sadie doesn't even know, that's quite obvious, and Louisa is an old prig, but we did think we could count on Linda and you. Very well then, we shall go to our marriage beds in ignorance, like Victorian ladies, and in the morning we shall be found stark staring mad with horror and live sixty more years in an expensive bin, and then perhaps you'll wish you had been more helpful.'

'Weighted down with jewels and Valenciennes costing thousands,' said Victoria. 'The Lecturer was here last week and he was telling Sadie some very nice sexy stories about that kind of thing—of course, we weren't meant to hear but you can just guess what happened, Sadie didn't listen and we did.'

'I should ask the Lecturer for information,' I said. 'He'd tell.'

'He'd show. No thank you very much.'

Polly came over to see me. She was pale and thinner, had rings under her eyes and seemed quite shut up in herself, though this may have been in contrast with the exuberant Radletts. When she was with Jassy and Victoria she looked like a swan, swimming in the company of two funny little tumbling ducks. She was very fond of them. She had never got on very well with Linda, for some reason, but she loved everybody else at Alconleigh, especially Aunt Sadie, and was more at her ease with Uncle Matthew than anybody I ever knew, outside his own family circle. He, for his part, bestowed on her some of the deference he felt for Lord Montdore, called her Lady Polly, and smiled every time his eyes fell on her beautiful face.

'Now children,' said Aunt Sadie, 'leave Fanny and Polly to have a little chat, they don't want you all the time, you know.'

'It is unfair—I suppose Fanny's going to *tell* Polly now. Well, back to the medical dictionary and the Bible. I only wish these things didn't look quite so sordid in cold print. What we need is some clean-minded married woman, to explain, but where are we to find her?'

Polly and I had a very desultory little chat, however. I showed her photographs of Alfred and me in the South of France, where we had been so that he could meet my poor mother the Bolter, who was living there now with a nasty new husband. Polly said the Dougdales were off there next week as Lady Patricia was feeling the cold so dreadfully that winter. She told me also that there had been a huge Christmas party at Hampton and that Joyce Fleetwood was in disgrace with her mother for not paying his bridge debts.

'So that's one comfort. We've still got the Grand Duchess, poor old thing. Goodness she's dull—not that Mummy seems to think so. Veronica Chaddesley Corbett calls her and Mummy Ma'am and Super-Ma'am.'

I did not like to ask if Polly and her mother were getting on any better, and Polly volunteered nothing on that subject, but she looked, I thought, very miserable. Presently she said she must go.

'Come over soon and bring Alfred.'

But I dreaded the impact of Lady Montdore upon Alfred even more than that of Uncle Matthew, and said he was too busy but I would come alone sometime.

'I hear that she and Sonia are on very bad terms again,' Aunt Sadie said when Polly had driven off.

'The hell-hag,' said Uncle Matthew, 'drown her if I were Montdore.'

'Or he might cut her to pieces with nail scissors like that French duke the Lecherous Lecturer was telling you all about, Sadie, when you weren't listening and we were.'

'Don't call me Sadie, children, and don't call Mr. Dougdale the Lecherous Lecturer.'

'Oh, dear. Well, we always do behind your backs so you see it's bound to slip out sometimes.'

Davey arrived. He had come to stay for a week or so for treatment at the Radcliffe Infirmary. Aunt Emily was becoming more and more attached to all her animals and could seldom now be persuaded to leave them, for which, on this occasion, I was thankful, since our Sundays in Kent really were an indispensable refuge to Alfred and me.

'I met Polly in the drive,' Davey said, 'we stopped and had a word. I think she looks most dreadfully unwell.'

'Nonsense,' said Aunt Sadie, who believed in no illness except appendicitis. 'There's nothing wrong with Polly, she needs a husband, that's all.'

'Oh! How like a woman!' said Davey. 'Sex, my dear Sadie, is not a sovereign cure for everything, you know. I only wish it were.'

'I didn't mean sex at all,' said my aunt, very much put out by this interpretation. Indeed, she was what the children called 'against' sex, that is to say it never entered into her calculations. 'What I said, and what I meant, was she needs a husband. Girls of her age, living at home, are hardly ever happy and Polly is a specially bad case because she has nothing whatever to do, she doesn't care for hunting, or parties, or anything much that I can see, and she doesn't get on with her mother. It's true that Sonia teases and lectures her and sets about it all the wrong way, she's a tactless person, but she is perfectly right, you know. Polly needs a life of her own, babies, occupations and interests— an establishment, in fact—and for all that she must have a husband.'

'Or a lady of Llangollen,' said Victoria.

'Time you went to bed, miss, now off you go both of you.'

'Not me, it's not nearly my bedtime yet.'

'I said both of you, now begone.'

They dragged themselves out of the room as slowly as they dared and went upstairs, stamping out 'Man's long agony' on the bare boards of the nursery passage so that nobody in the whole house could fail to hear them.

'Those children read too much,' said Aunt Sadie. 'But I can't stop them. I honestly believe they'd rather read the label on a medicine bottle than nothing at all.'

'Oh, but I love reading the labels of medicine bottles,' said Davey, 'they're madly enjoyable, you know.'

CHAPTER XII

THE next morning when I came down to breakfast I found everybody, even the children, looking grave. It seemed that by some mysterious local tom-tom Aunt Sadie had learnt that Lady Patricia Dougdale had died in the night. She had suddenly collapsed, Lord Montdore was sent for, but by the time he could arrive she had become unconscious, and an hour later was dead.

'Oh, poor Patricia,' Aunt Sadie kept saying, very much upset, while Uncle Matthew, who cried easily, was mopping his eyes as he bent over the hot plate, taking a sausage, or in his parlance, a 'banger', with less than his usual enthusiasm.

'I saw her only last week,' he said, 'at the Clarendon Yard.'

'Yes,' said Aunt Sadie. 'I remember you told me. Poor Patricia, I always liked her so much, though of course, all that about being delicate was tiresome.'

'Well, now you can see for yourself that she was delicate,' said Davey triumphantly. 'She's dead. It killed her. Doesn't that show you? I do wish I could make you Radletts understand that there is no such thing as imaginary illness. Nobody who is quite well could possibly be bothered to do all the things that I, for instance, am obliged to, in order to keep my wretched frame on its feet.'

The children began to giggle at this, and even Aunt Sadie smiled because they all knew that so far from it being a bother to Davey it was his all-absorbing occupation, and one which he enjoyed beyond words.

'Oh, of course, I know you all think it's a great great joke, and no doubt Jassy and Victoria will scream with laughter when I finally do conk out, but it's not a joke to me, let me tell you, and a liver in that state can't have been much of a joke to poor Patricia, what's more.'

'Poor Patricia, and I fear she had a sad life with that boring old Lecturer.'

This was so like Aunt Sadie. Having protested for years against the name Lecturer for Boy Dougdale she was now using it herself, it always happened; very soon no doubt we should hear her chanting 'Man's long agony'.

'For some reason that I could never understand, she really loved him.'

'Until lately,' said Davey. 'I think for the past year or two it has been the other way round, and he had begun to depend on her, and then it was too late, she had stopped bothering about him.'

'Possibly. Anyway, there it is, all very sad. We must send a wreath, darling, at once. What a time of year—it will have to come from Oxford, I suppose—oh, the waste of money.'

'Send a wreath of frog spawn frog spawn frog spawn, lovely lovely frog spawn it is my favourite thing,' sang Jassy.

'If you go on being so silly, children,' said Aunt Sadie, who had caught a look of great disapproval on Alfred's face, 'I shall be obliged to send you to school, you know.'

'But can you afford to?' said Victoria, 'you'd have to buy us plimsolls and gym tunics, underclothes in a decent state and some good strong luggage. I've seen girls going off to school, they are covered with expensive things. Of course, we long for it, pashes for the prefects and rags in the dorm. School has a very sexy side you know, Sadie—why, the very word "mistress" Sadie, you know——'

But Aunt Sadie was not really listening; she was away in her cloud and merely said:

'Mm, very naughty and silly, and don't call me Sadie.'

Aunt Sadie and Davey went off to the funeral together. Uncle Matthew had his Bench that day, and particularly wanted to attend in order to make quite sure that a certain ruffian, who was to come up before it, should be committed to the Assizes, where, it was very much to be hoped, he would get several years and the cat. One or two of Uncle Matthew's fellow beaks had curious, modern ideas about justice and he was obliged to carry on a strenuous war against them, in which he was greatly assisted by a retired Admiral of the neighbour-hood.

So they had to go to the funeral without him, and came back in low spirits.

'It's the dropping off the perches,' said Aunt Sadie. 'I've always dreaded when that begins. Soon we shall all have gone—oh well, never mind.'

'Nonsense,' Davey said, briskly. 'Modern science will keep us alive, and young, too, for many a long day yet. Patricia's insides were a terrible mess—I had a word with Dr. Simpson while you were with Sonia and it's quite obviously a miracle she didn't die years ago. When the children have gone to bed I'll tell you.'

'No, thank you,' said Aunt Sadie, while the children implored him to go then and there with them to the Hons' cupboard and tell.

'It is unfair, Sadie doesn't want to hear the least bit, and we die to.'

'How old was Patricia?' said Aunt Sadie.

'Older than we are,' said Davey. 'I remember when they married she was supposed to be quite a bit older than Boy.'

'And he was looking a hundred in that bitter wind.'

'I thought he seemed awfully cut up, poor Boy.'

Aunt Sadie, during a little graveside chat with Lady Montdore, had gathered that the death had come as a shock and surprise to all of them, that, although they had known Lady Patricia to be far from well, they had no idea that she was in immediate danger; in fact, she had been greatly looking forward to her trip abroad the following week. Lady Montdore, who resented death, clearly thought it most inconsiderate of her sister-in-law to break up their little circle so suddenly, and Lord Montdore, devoted to his sister, was dreadfully shaken by the midnight drive with a death-bed at the end of it. But surprisingly enough, the one who had taken it hardest was Polly. It seemed that she had been violently sick on hearing the news, com-pletely prostrated for two days, and was still looking so unwell that her mother had refused to take her to the funeral.

'It seems rather funny,' said Aunt Sadie, 'in a way. I'd no idea she was so particularly devoted to Patricia, had you, Fanny?'

'Nervous shock,' said Davey. 'I don't suppose she's ever had a death so near to her before.'

'Oh, yes she has,' said Jassy. 'Ranger.'

'Dogs aren't exactly the same as human beings, my dear Jassy.'

But to the Radletts they were exactly the same, except that to them dogs on the whole had more reality than people.

'So tell about the grave,' said Victoria.

'Not very much to tell, really,' said Aunt Sadie. 'Just a grave, you know, lots of flowers and mud.'

'They'd lined it with heather,' said Davey, 'from Craigside. Poor Patricia, she did love Scotland.'

'And where was it?'

'In the graveyard, of course, at Silkin—between the Wellingtonia and the Blood Arms, if you see where I mean. In full view of Boy's bedroom window, incidentally.'

Jassy began to talk fast and earnestly:

'You will promise to bury me here, whatever happens, won't you, won't you, there's one exact place I want, I note it every time I go to church, it's next door to that old lady who was nearly a hundred.'

'That's not our part of the churchyard—miles away from grand-father.'

'No, but it's the bit I want. I once saw a dear little dead baby vole there. Please please please don't forget.'

'You'll have married some sewer and gone to live in the Antipodes,' said Uncle Matthew who had just come in. 'They let that young hog off, said there was no evidence. Evidence be damned, you'd only got to look at his face to see who did it, afternoon completely wasted, the Admiral and I are going to resign.'

'Then bring me back,' said Jassy, 'pickled. I'll pay, I swear I will. Please, Fa, you must.'

'Write it down,' said Uncle Matthew, producing a piece of paper and a fountain-pen, 'if these things don't get written down they are for-gotten. And I'd like a deposit of ten bob please.'

'You can take it out of my birthday present,' said Jassy, who was scribbling away with great concentration. 'I've made a map like in *Treasure Island*,' she said. 'See?'

'Yes, thank you, that's quite clear,' said Uncle Matthew. He went to the wall, took his master-key from his pocket, opened a safe, and put in the piece of paper. Every room at Alconleigh had one of these wall-safes, whose contents would have amazed and discomfited the burglar who managed to open them. Aunt Sadie's jewels, which had some very good stones, were never kept in them, but lay glittering about all over the house and garden, in any place where she might have taken them off and forgotten to put them on again, on the downstairs wash-basin, by the flower-bed she had been weeding, sent to the laundry pinning up a suspender. Her big party pieces were kept in the bank. Uncle Matthew himself possessed no jewels and despised all men who did. (Boy's signet ring and platinum and pearl evening watch chain were great causes for tooth-grinding.) His own watch was a large loudly ticking object in gun-metal, tested twice a day by Greenwich mean time on a chronometer in the business-room, and said to gain three seconds a week. This was attached to his key ring across his mole-skin waistcoat

by an ordinary leather bootlace, in which Aunt Sadie often tied knots
to remind herself of things.

The safes, nevertheless, were full of treasures, if not of valuables, for
Uncle Matthew's treasures were objects of esoteric worth, such as a
stone quarried on the estate and said to have imprisoned for two
thousand years a living toad; Linda's first shoe; the skeleton of a mouse
regurgitated by an owl; a tiny gun for shooting blue-bottles; the hair
of all his children made into a bracelet; a silhouette of Aunt Sadie done
at a fair; a carved nut; a ship in a bottle; altogether a strange mixture
of sentiment, natural history and little objects which from time to time
had taken his fancy.

'Come on, do let's see,' said Jassy and Victoria, making a dash at the
door in the wall. There was always great excitement when the safes
were opened, as they hardly ever were, and seeing inside was considered
a treat.

'Oh! The dear little bit of shrapnel, may I have it?'

'No, you may not. It was once in my groin for a whole week.'

'Talk about death,' said Davey. 'The greatest medical mystery of
our times must be the fact that dear Matthew is still with us.'

'It only shows,' said Aunt Sadie, 'that nothing really matters the
least bit so why make these fearful efforts to keep alive?'

'Oh, but it's the efforts that one enjoys so much,' said Davey, and
this time he was speaking the truth.

CHAPTER XIII

I THINK it was about a fortnight after Lady Patricia's funeral that
Uncle Matthew stood, after luncheon, outside his front door, watch in
hand, scowling fiercely, grinding his teeth and awaiting his greatest
treat of all the year, an afternoon's chubb fuddling. The Chubb Fuddler
was supposed to be there at half-past two.

'Twenty-three and a quarter minutes past,' Uncle Matthew was
saying furiously, 'in precisely six and three-quarter minutes the
damned fella will be late.'

If people did not keep their appointments with him well before the
specified time he always counted them as being late, he would begin to
fidget quite half an hour too soon, and wasted, in this way, as much time
as people do who have no regard for it, besides getting himself into a
thoroughly bad temper.

The famous trout stream that ran through the valley below Alconleigh was one of Uncle Matthew's most cherished possessions. He was
an excellent dry-fly fisherman, and was never happier, in and out of

the fishing-season, than when messing about the river in waders and inventing glorious improvements for it. It was the small boy's dream come true. He built dams, he dug lashers, he cut the weed and trimmed the banks, he shot the herons, he hunted the otters, and he restocked with young trout every year. But he had trouble with the coarse fish, especially the chubb, which not only gobble up the baby trout but also their food, and they were a great worry to him. Then, one day he came upon an advertisement in *Exchange and Mart*. 'Send for the Chubb Fuddler.'

The Radletts always said that their father had never learnt to read, but in fact he could read quite well, if really fascinated by his subject, and the proof is that he found the Chubb Fuddler like this all by himself. He sat down then and there and sent. It took him some time, breathing heavily over the writing-paper and making, as he always did, several copies of the letter before finally sealing and stamping it.

'The fella says here to enclose a stamped and addressed envelope but I don't think I shall pander to him, he can take it or leave it.'

He took it. He came, he walked along the river bank, and sowed upon its waters some magic seed, which soon bore magic fruit for up to the surface, flapping, swooning, fainting, choking, thoroughly and undoubtedly fuddled, came hundreds upon hundreds of chubb. The entire male population of the village, warned beforehand and armed with rakes and landing-nets, fell upon the fish, several wheelbarrows were filled and the contents taken off to be used as manure for cottage gardens or chubb pie, according to taste.

Henceforward chubb fuddling became an annual event at Alconleigh, the Fuddler appearing regularly with the snowdrops, and to watch him at his work was a pleasure which never palled. So here we all were, waiting for him, Uncle Matthew pacing up and down outside the front door, the rest of us just inside on account of the bitter cold but peering out of the window, while all the men on the estate were gathered in groups down at the river's edge. Nobody, not even Aunt Sadie, wanted to miss a moment of the fuddling except, it seemed, Davey, who had retired to his room saying:

'It isn't madly me, you know, and certainly not in this weather.'

A motor car was now heard approaching, the scrunch of wheels and a low, rich hoot, and Uncle Matthew, with a last look at his watch, was just putting it back in his pocket when down the drive came, not at all the Chubb Fuddler's little Standard, but the huge black Daimler from Hampton Park containing both Lord and Lady Montdore. This was indeed a sensation! Callers were unknown at Alconleigh, anybody rash enough to try that experiment would see no sign of Aunt Sadie or the children, who would all be flat on the floor out of sight, though Uncle Matthew, glaring most embarrassingly, would stand at a window in full view, while they were being told 'not at home'. The neighbours had long ago given it up as a bad job. Furthermore, the Montdores, who considered themselves King and Queen of the neighbourhood, never called, but expected people to go to them, so from every point of view it seemed most peculiar. I am quite sure that if anybody else had broken in upon the happy anticipation of an afternoon's chubb fuddling Uncle Matthew would have bellowed at them to 'get out of it', possibly even have hurled a stone at them. When he saw who it was, however, he had one moment of stunned surprise and then leapt forward to open the door of the motor, like a squire of olden times leaping to the stirrup of his liege lord.

The hell-hag, we could all see at once, even through the window, was in a dreadful state. Her face was blotchy and swollen as from hours of weeping, she seemed perfectly unaware of Uncle Matthew and did not throw him either a word or a look as she struggled out of the car, angrily kicking at the rug round her feet, she then tottered with the gait of a very old woman, legs all weak and crooked, towards the house. Aunt Sadie, who had dashed forward, put an arm round her waist and took her into the drawing-room, giving the door a great 'keep out, children' bang. At the same time Lord Montdore and Uncle Matthew disappeared together into my uncle's business-room; Jassy, Victoria and I were left to goggle at each other with eyes like saucers, struck dumb by this extraordinary incident. Before we had time to begin speculating on what it could all mean, the Fuddler drove up, punctual to the very minute.

'Damned fella,' Uncle Matthew said afterwards, 'if he hadn't been so late we should have started by the time they arrived.'

He parked his little tinpot of a motor in line with the Daimler and bustled, all happy smiles, up to the front door. At his first visit he had gone modestly up the back drive, but the success of his magic had so put Uncle Matthew on his side that he had told him, in future, to come to the front door, and always gave him a glass of port before starting work. He would no doubt have given him Imperial Tokay if he had had any.

Jassy opened the door before the Fuddler had time to ring and then we all hung about while he drank his port, saying 'Bitter, isn't it?' and not quite knowing what to be at.

'His Lordship's not ill, I hope?' he said, surprised no doubt not to have found my uncle champing up and down as usual, his choleric look clearing suddenly into one of hearty welcome as he hurried to slap the Fuddler's back and pour out his wine.

'No no, we think he'll be here in a moment. He's busy.'

'Not so like His Lordship to be late, is it?'

Presently a message came from Uncle Matthew that we were to go down to the river and begin. It seemed too cruel to have the treat without him, but the fuddling had, of course, to be concluded by daylight. So we shivered out of the house, into the temporary shelter of the Fuddler's Standard and out again into the full blast of a north wind which was cutting up the valley. While the Fuddler sprinkled his stuff on the water we crept back into his car for warmth and began to speculate on the reason for the extraordinary visit now in progress. We were simply dying of curiosity.

'I guess the Government has fallen,' said Jassy.

'Why should that make Lady Montdore cry?'

'Well, who would do all her little things for her?'

'There'd soon be another lot for her to fag—Conservatives this time perhaps. She really likes that better.'

'D'you think Polly is dead?'

'No no, they'd be mourning o'er her lovely corpse, not driving about in motor cars and seeing people.'

'Perhaps they've lost all their money and are coming to live with us,' said Victoria. This idea cast a regular gloom, seeming as it did rather a likely explanation. In those days, when people were so rich and their fortunes so infinitely secure, it was quite usual for them to think that they were on the verge of losing all their money, and the Radlett children had always lived under the shadow of the workhouse, because Uncle Matthew, though really very comfortably off with about £10,000 a year gross, had a financial crisis every two or three years and was quite certain in his own mind that he would end up on parish relief.

The Fuddler's work was done, his seed was sown and we got out of the motor with our landing-nets. This was a moment that never failed to thrill, the river banks were dotted with people all gazing excitedly into the water and very soon the poor fish began to squirm about the surface. I landed a couple of whales and then a smaller one, and just as I was shaking it out of the net a well-known voice behind me, quivering with passion, said:

'Put it back at once, you blasted idiot—can't you see it's a greyling, Fanny? O my God, women—incompetent—and isn't that my landing-net you've got there? I've been looking for it all over the place.'

I gave it up with some relief. Ten minutes at the water's edge was quite enough in that wind. Jassy was saying 'Look look, they've gone', and there was the Daimler crossing the bridge, Lord Montdore sitting very upright in the back seat, bowing a little from side to side, almost like royalty. They overtook a butcher's van and I saw him lean forward and give the driver a gracious salute for having got out of the way. Lady Montdore was hardly visible, bundled up in her corner. They had gone, all right.

'Come on, Fanny,' said my cousins, downing tools, 'home, don't you think? Too cold here,' they shouted at their father, but he was busy cramming a giant chubb in its death throes into his hare pocket, and took no notice.

'And now,' said Jassy, as we raced up the hill, 'for worming it all out of Sadie.'

It was not, in fact, necessary to do any worming, Aunt Sadie was bursting with her news. She was more human and natural with her younger children than she had ever been with the elder ones. Her attitude of awe-inspiring vagueness alternating with sudden fits of severity, which had combined with Uncle Matthew's rages to drive Louisa and Linda and the boys underground, so that their real lives were led in the Hons' cupboard, was very much modified with regard to Jassy and Victoria. She was still quite as vague, but never very severe, and far more companionable. She had always been inclined to treat her children as if they were all exactly the same age, and the younger ones were now benefiting from the fact that Louisa and Linda were married women who could be spoken to, and in front of, without reserve.

We found her and Davey in the hall, she was quite pink with interest, and as for Davey he was looking as much excited as if he had developed some fascinating new symptom.

'Come on,' said the children, question-marks all over their faces. 'Tell.'

'You'll never believe it,' said Aunt Sadie, addressing herself to me, 'Polly Hampton has informed her poor mother that she is going to marry Boy Dougdale. Her uncle, if you please! Did you ever hear such a thing? The wretched Patricia, not cold in her grave——'

'Well,' said Jassy, aside, 'cooling, in this weather——'

'Miserable old man!' Aunt Sadie spoke in tones of deep indignation and was clearly a hundred per cent. on Lady Montdore's side. 'You see, Davey, how right Matthew has been about him all these years?'

'Oh, poor Boy, he's not so bad,' Davey said, uncomfortably.

'I don't see how you can go on standing up for him after this, Davey.'

'But Sadie,' said Victoria. 'How can she marry him if he's her uncle?'

'Just exactly what I said. But it seems, with an uncle by marriage, that you can. Would you believe that anything so disgustingly dreadful could be allowed?'

'I say,' said Jassy. 'Come on, Dave.'

'Oh, no dear, thank you. Marry one of you demons? Not for any money!'

'What a law!' said Aunt Sadie, 'whenever was it passed? Why, it's the end of all family life, a thing like that.'

'Except it's the beginning for Polly.'

'Who told Lady Montdore?' Of course, I was fascinated. This key-piece of the jigsaw made everything quite clear, and now I could not imagine how I could ever have been so stupid as to have missed it.

'Polly told her,' said Aunt Sadie. 'It happened like this. They hadn't seen Boy since the funeral because he caught a bad cold at it and stayed indoors—Sonia got an awful cold there too and still has it, but he had spoken to Sonia every day on the telephone, as he always does. Well, yesterday they both felt a bit better and he went over to Hampton with the letters he'd had about poor Patricia from Infantas and things, and they had a good gloat over them, and then a long discussion about what to put on the tombstone. It seems they more or less settled on "She shall not grow old as we that are left grow old".'

'Stupid!' said Jassy. 'She had grown old already!'

'Old! A few years older than me,' said Davey.

'Well——!' said Jassy.

'That's enough, miss. Sonia says he seemed terribly low and un-happy, talking about Patricia and what she'd always been to him, and how empty the house seems without her—just what you'd expect after twenty-three years or something. Miserable old hypocrite! Well, he was supposed to stay for dinner, without dressing because of his cold. Sonia and Lord Montdore went upstairs to change, and when Sonia came down again she found Polly, still in her day clothes, sitting on that white rug in front of the fire. She said, "What are you doing, Polly, it's very late. Go up and dress. Where's Boy then?" Polly got up and stretched herself and said, "He's gone home and I've got something to tell you. Boy and I are going to be married!" At first, of course, Sonia didn't believe it, but Polly never jokes as you know, and she very soon saw she was in deadly earnest, and then she was so furious she went sort of mad—how well I can understand that—and rushed at Polly and boxed her ears, and Polly gave her a great shove into an arm-chair and went upstairs. I imagine that Sonia was perfectly hysterical by then; anyway, she rang for her maid who took her up and put her straight to bed. Meanwhile, Polly dressed, came down again and calmly spent the evening with her father without saying a single word about it all to him, merely telling him that Sonia had a headache and wouldn't dine. So this morning poor Sonia had to tell him, she said it was terrible, because he so adores Polly. Then she tried to ring up Boy but the wretched coward has gone away, or pretends to have, leaving no address. Did you ever hear such a story?'

I was speechless with interest. Davey said:

'Personally, and speaking as an uncle, the one I feel for over all this is the unhappy Boy.'

'Oh, no, Davey, nonsense. Just imagine the Montdores' feelings—while they were trying to argue her out of it this morning she told them she'd been in love with him since before they went to India, when she was a little girl of fourteen.'

'Yes, very likely, but how do we know he wanted her to be in love with him? If you ask me I don't suppose he had the very faintest idea of it.'

'Come now, Davey, little girls of fourteen don't fall in love without any encouragement.'

'Alas, they do,' said Jassy, 'look at me and Mr. Fosdyke. Not one word, not one kindly glance has he ever thrown me, and yet he is the light of my life.'

Mr. Fosdyke was the local M.F.H.

I asked if Lady Montdore had had an inkling of all this before, knowing really quite well that she had not, as everything always came straight out with her and neither Polly nor Boy would have had one moment's peace.

'Simply no idea at all, it was a complete bolt from the blue. Poor Sonia, we know she has her faults but I can't think she has deserved this. She said Boy had always been very kind about taking Polly off her hands when they were in London, to the Royal Academy and so on, and Sonia was pleased because the child never seemed to have anybody to amuse her. Polly wasn't a satisfactory girl to bring out, you know, I'm very fond of her myself, I always have been, but you could see that Sonia was having a difficult time in many ways. Oh, poor Sonia, I do feel—now children, will you please go up and wash your fishy hands before tea?'

'This is the very limit, you're obviously going to say things while we're away. What about Fanny's fishy hands, then?'

'Fanny's grown-up, she'll wash her hands when she feels like it. Off you go.'

When they were safely out of the room she said, in horror, to Davey and me:

'Just imagine, Sonia, who had completely lost control of herself (not that I blame her), sort of hinted to me that Boy had once been her own lover.'

'Darling Sadie, you are such an innocent,' Davey said, laughing. 'It's a famous famous love affair which everybody except you has known all about for years. I sometimes think your children are right and you don't know the facts of life.'

'Well, all I can say is, I'm thankful I don't How perfectly hateful. Do you think Patricia knew?'

'Of course she did and she was only too glad of it. Before his affair with Sonia began, Boy used to make Patricia chaperone all the dismal little débutantes that he fancied, and they would sob out broken hearts on her shoulder, and beg her to divorce him, very last thing he wanted, naturally. She had a lot of trouble with him, you know.'

'I remember a kitchen maid,' Aunt Sadie said.

'Oh yes, it was one thing after another before Sonia took him on, but she had some control over him and Patricia's life became much easier and more agreeable, until her liver got so bad.'

'All the same,' I said, 'we know he still went for little girls, because look at Linda.'

'Did he?' said Aunt Sadie, 'I have sometimes wondered—Ugh! What a man! How you can think there's anything to be said for him, Davey, and how can you pretend he hadn't the faintest idea Polly was in love with him? If he made up to Linda like that, of course he must have done the same with her.'

'Well, Linda's not in love with him, is she? He can't be expected to guess that because he strokes the hair of a little girl when she's fourteen she's going to insist on marrying him when she grows up. Bad luck on a chap I call it.'

'Davey, you're hopeless! And if I didn't know quite well that you're only teasing me I should be very cross with you.'

'Poor Sonia,' said Davey. 'I feel for her, her daughter and her lover at a go—well, it often happens but it can't ever be very agreeable.'

'I'm sure it's the daughter she minds,' said Aunt Sadie, 'she hardly mentioned Boy, she was moaning and groaning about Polly, so perfectly beautiful, being thrown away like that. I should be just the same, I couldn't bear it for any of mine—that old fellow, they've known all their lives, and it's worse for her, Polly being the only one '·

'And such a treasure, so much the apple of their eye. Well, the more I see of life the more profoundly thankful I am not to have any children.'

'Between two and six they are perfect,' said my aunt, rather sadly I thought, 'after that I must say they are a worry, the funny little things. Then another horror for Sonia is wondering what went on all those years between Polly and Boy. She says last night she couldn't sleep for thinking of times when Polly pretended to have been to the hairdresser and obviously hadn't—that sort of thing—she says it's driving her mad.'

'It needn't,' I said firmly. 'I'm quite sure nothing ever happened. From various things I can remember Polly saying to me, I'm quite sure her love for the Lecturer must always have seemed hopeless to her. Polly's very good, you know, and she was very fond of her aunt.'

'I daresay you're right, Fanny. Sonia herself said that when she came down and found Polly sitting on the floor she thought at once "the girl looks as if she had been making love", and said she'd never seen her look like that before, flushed, her eyes simply huge and a curl of tousled hair hanging over her forehead—she was absolutely struck by her appearance, and then Polly told her——'

I could so well imagine the scene, Polly sitting, it was a very characteristic attitude with her, on the rug, getting up slowly, stretching, and then carelessly and gracefully implanting the cruel banderillas, the first movement of a fight that could only end in death.

'What I guess,' I said, 'is that he stroked a bit when she was fourteen and she fell in love then without him having any idea of it. Polly always bottles things up, and I don't expect anything more happened between them until the other evening.'

'Simply too dreadful,' said Aunt Sadie.

'Anyhow, Boy can't have expected to get engaged there and then, or he wouldn't have had all that talk about the Infanta's letter and the gravestone, would he?' said Davey. 'I expect what Fanny says is true.'

'You've been telling things—it is unfair—Fanny's hands are still foully fishy.' The children were back, out of breath.

'I do wonder what Uncle Matthew and Lord Montdore talked about in the business-room,' I said. I could not imagine such a tale being unfolded between those two, somehow.

'They topicked,' said Aunt Sadie. 'I told Matthew afterwards, I've never seen anybody so angry. But I haven't told you yet what it was that Sonia really came about. She's sending Polly here for a week or two.'

'No!' we all cried in chorus.

'Oh, the utter fascination!' said Jassy. 'But why?'

'Polly wants to come, it was her idea, and Sonia can't endure the sight of her for the present, which I can well understand. I must say I hesitated at first, but I am very fond of that little girl, you know, I really love her, and if she stays at home her mother will have driven her into an elopement within a week. If she comes here we might be able to influence her against this horrible marriage—and I don't mean you, children. You'll please try and be tactful for once in your lives.'

'I will be,' said Jassy, earnestly, 'it's dear little Vict. you must speak to, there's no tack in her, and personally I think it was a great mistake ever to have told her at all—ow—help—help—Sadie, she's killing me——'

'I mean both of you,' said Aunt Sadie, calmly, taking no notice whatever of the dog-fight in progress, 'you can talk about the chubb at dinner, that ought to be a safe subject.'

'What?' they said, stopping the fight, 'she's not coming today?'

'Yes, she is. After tea.'

'Oh, what a thrill. Do you think the Lecturer will have himself carried into the house dressed up as a sack of wood?'

'They shan't meet under my roof,' Aunt Sadie said firmly. 'I promised Sonia that, but of course, I pointed out that I can't control what Polly does elsewhere, I can only leave that to her own sense of what is in good taste, while she is staying with me.'

CHAPTER XIV

POLLY soon made it clear that Aunt Sadie need have no misgivings about her behaviour while at Alconleigh. Her self-possession was complete, the only exterior indication that her life was at a crisis being an aura of happiness which transformed her whole aspect. Nothing she said or did was at all out of the usual or could have led anybody to suppose that she had recently been involved in scenes of such intensity, and it was obvious that she held no communication of any sort with Boy. She never went near the telephone, she did not sit all day scribbling letters, received very few, and none, so the children informed me, with a Silkin postmark; she hardly ever left the house and then only to get a breath of air with the rest of us, certainly not in order to go for long solitary walks which might end in lovers' meetings.

Jassy and Victoria, romantic like all the Radletts, found this incomprehensible and most disappointing. They had expected to be plunged into an atmosphere of light opera, and had supposed that the Lecturer would hang, sighing but hopeful, about the precincts, that Polly would hang, sighing but expectant, out of a moonlit window, to be united, and put on the first stage of their journey to Gretna Green, by the ingenuity and enterprise of their two young friends.

They lugged a mattress and stocks of food into the Hons' cupboard in case Boy wanted to hide there for a day or two. They had thought of everything, so they informed me, and were busy making a rope ladder. But Polly would not play.

'If you have any letters for the post, Polly, you know what I mean, a letter—we could easily run down to the village with it on our bikes.'

'Darling, you are kind, but they'll go just as quickly if I put them on the hall table, won't they?'

'Oh, of course, you can do that if you like, but everybody will read the envelope and I just thought—— Or any messages? There's a telephone in the village post-office, rather public, but you could talk in French.'

'I don't know French very well. Isn't there a telephone here?'

'Oh, it's a brute, extensions all over the place. Now there's a hollow tree in the park quite big enough for a man to hide in—quite dry and comfy—shall we show you?'

'You must, one day. Too cold to go out today, I think.'

'You know there's a frightfully nice little temple in a wood the other side of the river, would you like us to take you there?'

'Do you mean Faulkner's Folly, where they have the meets? But Jassy I know it quite well, I've often seen it. Very pretty.'

'What I really mean is the key is kept under a stone, and we could show you exactly where so that you could go inside.'

'There's nothing to see inside except cobwebs,' I said, 'it was never finished, you know.'

Jassy made a furious face at me. 'Tackless,' she muttered.

'Let's go there next summer, darlings,' said Polly, 'for a picnic. I can't enjoy anything out of doors in this weather, my eyes water too much.'

The children slouched away, discouraged.

Polly exploded with laughter. 'Aren't they too heavenly? But I don't really see the point of making all these great efforts to spend a few minutes with Boy in freezing cold temples, or to write to him about nothing at all when very soon I shall be with him for the whole rest of my life. Besides, I don't want to annoy Lady Alconleigh when she is being such an angel to have me here.'

Aunt Sadie herself, while applauding Polly's attitude, which relieved her of any need to worry, found it most unnatural.

'Isn't it strange,' she said, 'you can see by looking at her that she is very happy, but if it weren't for that nobody could guess that she was in love. My girls always get so moony, writing reams all day, jumping when the telephone bell rings and so on, but there's none of that with Polly. I was watching her last night when Matthew put *Che Gelida Manina* on the gramophone, she didn't look a bit sentimental. Do you remember what an awful time we had with Linda when Tony was in America—never out of floods?'

But Polly had been brought up in a harder school for the emotions than had the Radletts, with a mother determined to find out everything that was in her mind and to mould her very thoughts to her own wishes. One could only admire the complete success with which she had countered both of these aims. Clearly her character had a steely quality incomprehensible to my cousins, blown hither and thither as they were upon the winds of sentiment.

I managed to have a few long talks alone with Polly at this time, but it was not very easy. Jassy and Victoria hardly left us for a single minute, so frightened were they of missing something; furthermore, they were shameless eavesdroppers, while hair-brushing chats at bed-time were ruled out by the fact of my so recent marriage. Mercifully the children went riding every day, when an hour or so of peace could be counted on; there was no hunting just then because of foot-and-mouth disease.

Gradually the whole thing came out. Polly's reserve, it is true, never really broke down, but every now and then the landscape was illuminated and its character exposed to view by flashes of startling frankness. It all seemed to have been very much as we had thought. For instance, I said to her something about when Boy proposed and she replied, quite carelessly:

'Oh, Boy never proposed to me at all, I don't think he ever would have, being that kind of a person—I mean, so wonderfully unselfish and thinking that it matters for me, not being left things in wills and all that rubbish. Besides, he knows Mummy so well and he knew just what a hullabaloo she would make—he couldn't face it for me. No no, I always realized that I should have to do the proposing, and I did. It wasn't very difficult.'

So Davey was right, no doubt. The idea of such a marriage would never have entered the Lecturer's head if it had not been put there by Polly herself. After that it would clearly have been beyond flesh and blood to resist such a prize, greatest beauty and greatest heiress of her generation, potential mother of the children, the little half-Hamptons, he had always longed for. He could never have said no once it all lay at his feet waiting to be pocketed.

'After all, I've loved him ever since I can remember. Oh, Fanny— isn't being happy wonderful?'

I felt just the same myself and was able to agree with all my heart. But her happiness had a curiously staid quality, and her love seemed less like the usual enchanted rapture of the young girl, newly engaged, than a comfortable love of old establishment, love which does not need to assert itself by continually meeting, corresponding with and talking about its object, but which takes itself, as well as his response, for granted. The doubts and jealousies which can be so painful and make a hell almost of a budding love affair did not seem to have occurred to Polly, who took the simple view that she and Boy had hitherto been kept apart by one insuperable barrier, and that this barrier having been removed, the path to lifelong bliss lay at their feet.

'What can it matter if we have a few more weeks of horrid waiting when we are going to live together all the rest of our lives and be buried in the same grave?'

'Fancy being buried in the same grave with the Lecturer,' Jassy said, coming into my bedroom before luncheon.

'Jassy, I think it's too awful the way you listen at doors.'

'Don't tease, Fan, I intend to be a novelist (child novelist astounds the critics), and I'm studying human nature like mad.'

'I really ought to tell Aunt Sadie.'

'That's it. Join the revereds, now you are married, just like Louisa. No, but seriously Fanny, think of sharing a grave with that old Lecturer, isn't it disgusting? And anyway, what about Lady Patricia?'

'Well, she's nice and snug in one all to herself, lined with heather. She's quite all right.'

'I think it's shocking.'

Meanwhile, Aunt Sadie was doing what she could to influence Polly, but as she was much too shy to speak to her directly on such intimate subjects as sex and marriage she used an oblique method of letting fall an occasional reflection, hoping that Polly would apply it to her own particular case.

'Always remember, children, that marriage is a very intimate relationship, it's not just sitting and chatting to a person, there are other things, you know.'

Boy Dougdale, to her, was physically repulsive, as I think he generally was to those women who did not find him irresistible, and she thought that if Polly could be brought to a realization of the physical aspect of marriage she might be put off him for good.

As Jassy very truly observed, however, 'Isn't Sadie a scream, she simply doesn't realize that what put Polly on the Lecturer's side in the first place must have been all those dreadful things he did to her, like he once tried to with Linda and me, and that now what she really wants most in the world is to roll and roll and roll about with him in a double bed.'

'Yes, poor Sadie, she's not too hot on psychology,' said Victoria. 'Now I should say the only hope of curing Polly's uncle-fixation is to analyse her. Shall we see if she'd let us try?'

'Children, I absolutely forbid you to,' I said firmly, 'and if you do I promise I'll tell Aunt Sadie about the eavesdropping, so there.'

I knew what dreadful questions they would ask Polly and that as she was rather prim she would be shocked and angry. They were very much taken up at this time with the study and practice of psycho-analysis. They got hold of a book on the subject ('Elliston's library, would you believe it?') and several days of peace ensued while they read it out to each other in the Hons' cupboard, after which they proceeded to action.

'Come and be analysed,' was their parrot cry. 'Let us rid you of the poison that is clogging your mental processes, by telling you all about yourselves. Now, suppose we begin with Fa, he's the simplest proposition in the house.'

'What d'you mean, simple?'

'ABC to us. No no, not your hand you dear old thing, we've grown out of palmistry ages ago, this is science.'

'All right, let's hear it.'

'Well, so then you're a very straightforward case of frustration— wanted to be a gamekeeper, were obliged to be a lord—followed, as is usual, by the development of over-compensation so that now you're a psycho-neurotic of the obsessive and hysterical type engrafted on to a paranoid and schizoid personality.'

'Children, you are not to say these things about your father.'

'Scientific truths are nothing to object to, Sadie, and in our experience everybody enjoys learning about themselves. Would you care for us to test your intelligence level with an ink blot, Fa?'

'What's that?'

'We could do it to you all in turn and mark you if you like. It's quite easy, you show the subject an ordinary blot of ink on white paper, and, according to the picture it makes for each individual (you understand what I mean, does it look like a spider, or the Himalayas, everybody sees something different), a practised questioner can immediately assess his intelligence level.'

'Are you practised questioners?'

'Well, we've practised on each other and all the Joshes and Mrs. Aster. And we've noted the results in our scientific note-book, so come on.'

Uncle Matthew gazed at the blot for a while and then said that it looked to him very much like an ordinary ink blot, and reminded him of nothing so much as Stephens' Blue-Black.

'It's just as I had feared,' said Jassy, 'and shows a positively sub-human level—even Baby Josh did better than that. Oh, dear, sub-human, that's bad——'

Jassy had now overstepped the boundary in the perpetual game of Tom Tiddler's Ground that she played with her father. He roared at her in a sudden rage and sent her to bed. She went off chanting 'paranoid *and* schizoid, paranoid *and* schizoid' which had taken the place of 'Man's long agony'. She said to me afterwards, 'Of course, it's rather grave for all of us because, whether you believe in heredity or environment, either way we are boiled, shut up here with this old sub-human of a father.'

Davey now decided that it would be only kind to go over and see his old friend Lady Montdore, so he rang her up and was invited to luncheon. He stayed until after tea, and by good luck when he got back Polly was lying down in her bedroom, so he was able to tell all.

'She is in a rage,' he said, 'a rage. Simply frightening. She has taken what the French call a *coup de vieux*; she looks a hundred. I wouldn't care to be hated by anyone as much as she hates Boy. After all, you never know, there may be something in Christian Science; evil thoughts and so on, directed at us with great intensity, may affect the body. How she hates him. Just imagine, she has cut out the tapestry he made for that fire-screen, quite roughly, with a pair of scissors, and the screen is still there in front of the fire with an enormous hole in it. It gave me quite a shock.'

'Poor Sonia, how like her, somehow. And what does she feel about Polly?'

'She mourns her, and she's pretty cross with her, too, for being so underhand and keeping it a secret all these years. I said, "You really couldn't expect that she would tell you?" but she didn't agree. She asked me a lot of questions about Polly and her state of mind. I was obliged to say that her state of mind is not revealed to me, but that she is looking twice as pretty as before, if possible, so it can therefore be presumed that she is happy.'

'Yes, you can always tell by that, with girls,' said Aunt Sadie. 'If it weren't for that I wouldn't have thought she cared a bit, one way or the other. What a strange character she must have, after all.'

'Not so strange,' said Davey. 'Many women are rather enigmatic, and very few laugh when they are happy and cry when they are sad to the extent that your children do, my dear Sadie, nor do we all see everything in black and white. Life is over-simplified at Alconleigh, it's part of the charm and I'm not complaining, but you mustn't suppose that all human beings are exactly like Radletts, because it is not so.'

'You stayed very late.'

'Poor Sonia, she's lonely. She must be, dreadfully, if you come to think of it. We talked about nothing else, too, round and round the subject, every aspect of it. She asked me to go over and see Boy to find out if there's any hope of his giving up the idea and going abroad for a bit. She says Montdore's lawyer has written and told him that the day Polly marries him she will be completely cut out of her father's will and also Montdore will stop Patricia's allowance, which he was intending to give Boy for his life. Even so, she fears they will have enough to live on, but it might shake him, I suppose. I didn't promise to go, but I think perhaps I will, all the same.'

'Oh, but you must,' said Jassy. 'There's us to consider.'

'Children, do stop interrupting,' said Aunt Sadie. 'If you can't hold your tongues you will have to leave the room when we are having serious conversations—in fact,' she said, becoming strict all of a sudden, just as she used to be when Linda and I were little, 'I think you'd better go now. Go on, off with you.'

They went. As they reached the door Jassy said in a loud aside:

'This labile and indeterminate attitude to discipline may do permanent damage to our young psychology. I really think Sadie should be more careful.'

'Oh, no, Jassy,' Victoria said, 'after all, it's our complexes that make us so fascinating and unusual.'

When they had shut the door Davey said rather seriously:

'You know, Sadie, you do spoil them.'

'Oh, dear,' said Aunt Sadie, 'I'm afraid so. It comes of having so many children. One can force oneself to be strict for a few years, but after that it becomes too much of an effort. But Davey, do you honestly imagine it makes the smallest difference when they are grown-up?'

'Probably not to your children, demons one and all. But look how well we brought up Fanny.'

'Davey! You were never strict,' I said, 'not the least bit. You spoilt me quite completely.'

'Yes, now that's true,' said Aunt Sadie. 'Fanny was allowed to do all sorts of dreadful things—especially after she came out. Powder her nose, travel alone, go in cabs with young men—didn't she once go to a night-club? Fortunately for you, she seems to have been born good, though why she should have been, with such parents, is beyond me.'

Davey told Polly that he had seen her mother but she merely said: 'How was Daddy?'

'In London, House of Lords, something about India. Your mother doesn't look at all well, Polly.'

'Temper,' said Polly, and left the room.

Davey's next visit was to Silkin. 'Frankly, I can't resist it.' He bustled off in his little motor car on the chance of finding the Lecturer at home. He still refused to come to the telephone, giving out that he was away for a few weeks, but all other evidence pointed to the fact that he was living in his house, and indeed this now proved to be the case.

'Puzzled and lonely and gloomy, poor old boy, and he's still got an awful cold he can't get rid of. Sonia's evil thoughts, perhaps. He has aged, too. Says he has seen nobody since his engagement to Polly—of course, he has cut himself off at Silkin but he seems to think that the people he has run into, at the London Library and so on, have been avoiding him as if they already knew about it. I expect it's really because he's in mourning—or perhaps they don't want to catch his cold —anyway, he's fearfully sensitive on the subject. Then he didn't say so, but you can see how much he is missing Sonia—naturally, after seeing her every day all these years. Missing Patricia too, I expect.'

'Did you talk quite openly about Polly?' I asked.

'Oh, quite. He says the whole thing originated with her, wasn't his idea at all.'

'Yes, that's true. She told me that herself.'

'And if you ask me, it shocks him dreadfully. He can't resist it, of course, but it shocks him, and he fully expects to be a social outcast as the result. Now that would have been the card for Sonia to have played, if she had been clever enough to foresee it all. Too late once the words were spoken, of course, but if she could have warned Boy what was likely to happen and then rubbed in about how that would finish him for ever in the eyes of society, I think she might have stopped it. After all he's frightfully social, poor chap. He would hate to be ostracized. As a matter of fact, though I didn't say so to him, people will come round in no time once they are married.'

'But you don't really think they will marry?' said Aunt Sadie.

'My dear Sadie, after ten days in the same house with Polly, I don't doubt it for one single instant. What's more, Boy knows he's in for it all right whether he likes it or not—and of course he half likes it very much indeed. But he dreads the consequences, not that there'll be any.

People have no memory about that sort of thing, and after all, there's nothing to forget except bad taste.'

'Détournement de jeunesse?'

'It won't occur to the ordinary person that Boy could have made a pass at Polly when she was little, we would never have thought of it except for what he did to Linda. In a couple of years nobody outside the family will even remember what all the fuss was about.'

'I'm afraid you're right,' said my aunt. 'Look at the Bolter! Ghastly scandal after ghastly scandal, elopements, horse-whippings, puts herself up as a prize in a lottery, cannibal kings—I don't know what all—headlines in the papers, libel actions, and yet she only has to appear in London and her friends queue up to give parties for her. But don't encourage Boy by telling him. Did you suggest he might chuck it and go abroad?'

'Yes, I did, but it's no good. He misses Sonia, he is horrified in a way by the whole thing, hates the idea of his money being stopped, though he's not penniless himself, you know, he's got an awful cold and is down in the dumps, but at the same time you can see that the prospect dazzles him, and as long as Polly makes all the running, I bet you he'll play. Oh, dear, fancy taking on a new young wife at our age—how exhausting. Boy, too, who is cut out to be a widower, I do pity him.'

'Pity him indeed! All he had to do was to leave little girls alone.'

'You're so implacable, Sadie. It's a heavy price to pay for a bit of cuddling—I wish you could see the poor chap——!'

'Whatever does he do with himself all the time?'

'He's embroidering a counterpane,' said Davey, 'it's his wedding present for Polly. He calls it a bedspread.'

'Oh, really!' Aunt Sadie shuddered. 'He is the most dreadful man! Better not tell Matthew—in fact, I wouldn't tell him you've been over at all. He nearly has a fit every time he thinks of Boy now, and I don't blame him. Bedspread indeed!'

CHAPTER XV

SOON after this Polly announced to Aunt Sadie that she would like to go to London the following day, as she had an appointment there with Boy. We were sitting alone with Aunt Sadie in her little room. Although it was the first time that Polly had mentioned her uncle's name to anybody at Alconleigh, except me, she brought it out not only without a tremor of self-consciousness but as though she spoke of him all and every day. It was an admirable performance. There was a pause. Aunt Sadie was the one who blushed and found it difficult to control her voice, and when at last she replied it did not sound natural at all, but hard and anxious.

'Would you care to tell me what your plans are, Polly?'

'Please—to catch the 9.30 if it's convenient.'

'No, I don't mean your plans for tomorrow, but for your life.'

'You see, that's what I must talk about, with Boy. Last time I saw him we made no plans, we simply became engaged to be married.'

'And this marriage, Polly dear—your mind is made up?'

'Yes, quite. So I don't see any point in all this waiting. As we are going to be married whatever happens, what can it matter when? In fact, there is every reason why it should be very soon now. It's out of the question for me to go and live with my mother again and I can't foist myself on you indefinitely. You've been much too kind as it is.'

'Oh, my darling child, don't give that a thought. It never matters having people here so long as Matthew likes them. Look at Davey and Fanny, they're in no hurry to go, they know quite well we love having them.'

'Oh, yes, I know, but they are family.'

'So are you, almost, and quite as welcome as if you were. I have got to go to London in a few weeks, as you know, for Linda's baby, but that needn't make any difference to you, and you must stay on for as long as ever you like. There'll be Fanny, and when Fanny goes there are the children—they worship you, you are their heroine, it's wonderful for them having you here. So don't think about that again. Don't, for heaven's sake, rush into marriage because you think you have nowhere to live, because for one thing it's not the case at all, since you can live here, and anyhow, it could never be a sufficient reason for taking such a grave step.'

'I'm not rushing,' said Polly. 'It's the only marriage I could ever have made, and if it had continued to be impossible I should have lived and died a spinster.'

'Oh, no you wouldn't,' said Aunt Sadie, 'you've no idea how long life goes on and how many many changes it brings. Young people seem to imagine that it's over in a flash, that they do this thing, or that thing, and then die, but I can assure you they are quite wrong. I suppose it's no good saying this to you, Polly, as I can see your mind is made up, but since you have the whole of your life before you as a married woman why not make the most of being a girl? You'll never be one again. You're only twenty. Why be in such a hurry to change?'

'I hate being a girl, I've hated it ever since I grew up,' said Polly, 'and besides, do you really think a life-time is too long for perfect happiness? I don't.'

Aunt Sadie gave a profound sigh.

'I wonder why it is that all girls suppose the married state to be one of perfect happiness? Is it just clever old Dame Nature's way of hurrying them into the trap?'

'Dear Lady Alconleigh, don't be so cynical.'

'No no, you are quite right, I mustn't be. You've settled upon your future and nothing anybody can say will stop you, I'm sure, but I must tell you that I think you are making a terrible mistake. There, I won't say another word about it. I'll order the car for the 9.30, and will you be catching the 4.45 back or the 6.10?'

'Four forty-five please. I told Boy to meet me at the Ritz at one—I sent him a postcard yesterday.'

And by a miracle the said postcard had lain about all day on the hall table without either Jassy or Victoria spotting it. Hunting had begun again, and although they were only allowed out three times a fortnight the sheer physical exhaustion which it induced did a great deal towards keeping their high spirits within bounds. As for Uncle Matthew, who went out four days a week, he hardly opened an eye after tea-time, but nodded away standing up in his business-room, with the gramophone blaring his favourite tunes. Every few minutes he gave a great jump and rushed to change the needle and the disc.

That evening, before dinner, Boy rang up. We were all in the business-room listening to *Lakmé* on the gramophone, new records which had just arrived from the Army and Navy Stores. My uncle ground his teeth when the temple bells were interrupted by a more penetrating peal, and gnashed them with anger when he heard Boy's voice asking for Polly, but he handed her the receiver and pushed up a chair for her with the old-fashioned courtesy which he used towards those he liked. He never treated Polly as if she were a very young person and I believe he was really rather in awe of her.

Polly said 'Yes? Oh? Very well. Good-bye' and hung up the receiver. Even this ordeal had done nothing to shake her serenity.

She told us that Boy had changed the rendezvous, saying he thought it was pointless to go all the way to London, and suggesting the Mitre in Oxford as a more convenient meeting-place.

'So perhaps we could go in together, Fanny darling.'

I was going, anyhow, to visit my house.

'Ashamed of himself,' said Davey, when Polly had gone upstairs. 'Doesn't want to be seen. People are beginning to talk. You know how Sonia can never keep a secret, and once the Kensington Palace set gets hold of something it is all round London in a jiffy.'

'Oh, dear,' said Aunt Sadie, 'but if they are seen at the Mitre it will look far worse. I feel rather worried, I only promised Sonia they shouldn't meet here, but ought I to tell her? What do you think?'

'Shall I go over to Silkin and shoot the sewer?' said Uncle Matthew, half asleep.

'Oh, no, darling, please don't. What do you think, Davey?'

'Don't you worry about the old she-wolf—good Lord, who cares a brass button for her?'

If Uncle Matthew had not hated Boy so much he would have been quite as eager as his daughters were to aid and abet Polly in any enterprise that would fly in the face of Lady Montdore.

Davey said, 'I wouldn't give it a thought. It so happens that Polly has been perfectly open and above-board about the whole thing—but suppose she hadn't told you? She's always going into Oxford with Fanny, isn't she? I should turn the blind eye.'

So in the morning Polly and I motored to Oxford together, and I lunched, as I often did, with Alfred at the George. (If I never mention Alfred in this story it is because he is so totally uninterested in other human beings and their lives that I think he was hardly aware of what was going on. He certainly did not enter into it with fascination like the rest of us. I suppose that I and his children and perhaps an occasional clever pupil seem real to him, but otherwise he lives in a world of shadows and abstract thought.)

After luncheon I spent a freezing, exhausting and discouraging hour in my little house, which seemed hopelessly haunted by builders. I noted, with something like despair, that they had now made one of the rooms cosy, a regular home from home, with blazing fire, stewing tea and film-stars on the walls. As far as I could see they never left it at all to ply their trade, and indeed, I could hardly blame them for that, so terrible were the damp and cold in the rest of the house. After a detailed inspection with the foreman which merely revealed more exposed pipes and fewer floor-boards than last time I had been there, I went to the window of what was supposed to be my drawing-room to fortify myself with the view of Christ Church, so beautiful against the black clouds. One day, I thought (it was an act of faith), I would sit by that very window, open wide, and there would be green trees and a blue sky behind the college. I gazed on, through glass which was almost opaque with dirt and whitewash, forcing myself to imagine that summer scene, when, battling their way down the street, the east wind in their faces, Polly and the Lecturer appeared to view. It was not a happy picture, but that may have been the fault of the climate. No aimless dalliance hand in hand beneath warm skies for poor English lovers who, if circumstances drive them to making love out-of-doors, are obliged to choose between the sharp brisk walk and the stupefying stuffiness of the cinema. They stumped on out of my sight, hands in pockets, heads bowed, and plunged, one would have said, in gloom.

Before going home I paid a visit to Woolworth's, having been enjoined by Jassy to get her a goldfish bowl for her frog spawn. She had broken hers the day before and had only got the precious jelly to the spare-room bath just in time, she said, to save it. Alfred and I were obliged to use the nursery bathroom until Jassy got a new bowl. 'So you see how it's to your own advantage, Fanny, not to forget.'

Once inside Woolworth's I found other things that I needed, as one always does, and presently I ran into Polly and Boy. He was holding a mouse-trap, but I think it was shelter from the wind that they really sought.

'Home soon?' said Polly.

'Now, d'you think?' I was dead tired.

'Do let's.'

So we all three went to the Clarendon Yard, where our respective motor cars were waiting. The Lecturer still had a terrible cold, which made him most unappetizing, I thought, and he seemed very grumpy. When he took my hand to say good-bye he gave it no extra squeeze, nor did he stroke and tickle our legs when tucking us up in the rug, which he would certainly have done had he been in a normal state, and when we drove off he just walked gloomily away with no backward glance, jaunty wave or boyish shake of the curls. He was evidently at a low ebb.

Polly leaned forward, wound up the window between us and the chauffeur and said:

'Well, everything's settled, thank goodness. A month from today if I can get my parents' consent—I shall still be under age, you see. So the next thing is a tussle with Mummy. I'll go over to Hampton to-morrow if she's there and point out that I shall be of age in May, after which she won't be able to stop me, so hadn't she better swallow the pill and have done with it. They won't be wanting to have birthday celebrations for me now since in any case Daddy is cutting me off with a shilling.'

'Do you think he really will?'

'As if I cared! The only thing I mind about is Hampton and he can't leave me that even if he wants to. Then I shall say "Do you intend to put a good face on it and let me be married in the chapel (which Boy terribly wants for some reason, and I would rather like it, I must say), or must we sneak off and be done in London?" Poor Mummy. Now I'm out of her clutches I feel awfully sorry for her in a way. I think the sooner it's over the better for everybody.'

Boy, it was clear, was still leaving all the dirty work to Polly. Perhaps his cold was sapping his will power, or perhaps the mere thought of a new young wife at his age was exhausting him already.

So Polly rang up her mother and asked if she could lunch at Hampton the following day and have a talk. I thought it would have been more sensible to have had the talk without the additional strain imposed by a meal, but Polly seemed unable to envisage a country house call which did not centre round food. Perhaps she was right, since Lady Montdore was very greedy and therefore more agreeable during and after meals than at other times. In any case, this is what she suggested; she also told her mother to send a motor as she did not like to ask the Alconleighs for one two days running. Lady Montdore said very well, but that she must bring me. Lord Montdore was still in London and I suppose she felt she could not bear to see Polly alone. Anyhow, she was one of those people who always avoid a *tête-à-tête* if possible, even with their intimates. Polly said to me that she herself had just been going to ask if I could come too.

'I want a witness,' she added, 'if she says yes in front of you she won't be able to wriggle out of it again later.'

Poor Lady Montdore, like Boy, was looking very much down; not only old and ill (like Boy, she was still afflicted with Lady Patricia's funeral cold which seemed to have been a specially virulent germ), but positively dirty. The fact that she had never, at the best of times, been very well-groomed, had formerly been offset by her flourish and swagger, radiant health, enjoyment of life, and the inward assurance of superiority bestowed upon her by 'all this'. These supports had been cut away by her cold as well as by the simultaneous defection of Polly, which must have taken much of the significance out of 'all this', and of Boy, her constant companion, the last lover, surely, that she would ever have. Life, in fact, had become sad and meaningless.

We began luncheon in silence. Polly turned her food over with a fork, Lady Montdore refused the first dish, while I munched away rather self-consciously alone, enjoying the change of cooking. Aunt Sadie's food, at that time, was very plain. After a glass or two of wine, Lady Montdore cheered up a bit and began to chat. She told us that the dear Grand Duchess had sent her such a puddy postcard from Cap d'Antibes, where she was staying with other members of the Imperial family. She remarked that the Government really ought to make more effort to attract such important visitors to England.

'I was saying so only the other day to Ramsay,' she complained. 'And he quite agreed with me, but of course, one knows nothing will be done, it never is in this hopeless country. So annoying. All the Rajahs are at Suvretta House again—the King of Greece has gone to Nice—the King of Sweden has gone to Cannes and the young Italians are doing winter sports. Perfectly ridiculous not to get them all here.'

'Whatever for,' said Polly, 'when there's no snow?'

'Plenty in Scotland. Or teach them to hunt, they'd love it, they only want encouraging a little.'

'No sun,' I said.

'Never mind. Make it the fashion to do without sun and they'll all come here. They came for my ball and Queen Alexandra's funeral—they love a binge, poor dears. The Government really ought to pay one to give a ball every year, it would restore confidence and bring important people to London.'

'I can't see what good all these old royalties do when they are here,' said Polly.

'Oh, yes, they do, they attract Americans and so on,' said Lady Montdore, vaguely. 'Always good to have influential people around you know, good for a private family and also good for a country. I've always gone in for them myself and I can tell you it's a very great mistake not to. Look at poor dear Sadie, I've never heard of anybody important going to Alconleigh.'

'Well,' said Polly, 'and what harm has it done her?'

'Harm! You can see the harm all round. First of all the girls' husbands'—on this point Lady Montdore did not lean, suddenly remembering no doubt her own situation in respect of daughters' husbands, but continued, 'Poor Matthew has never got anything has he—I don't only mean jobs, but not even a V.C. in the war and goodness knows he was brave enough. He may not be quite cut out to be a Governor, I grant you that, especially not where there are black people, but don't tell me there's nothing he could have got, if Sadie had been a little cleverer about it. Something at Court, for instance. It would have calmed him down.'

The idea of Uncle Matthew at Court made me choke into my pancake, but Lady Montdore took no notice and went on:

'And now I'm afraid it will be the same story with the boys. I'm told they were sent to the very worst house at Eton because Sadie had nobody to advise her or help her at all when the time came for them to go there. One must be able to pull strings in life, everything depends on that in this world, I'm afraid, it's the only way to be successful. Luckily for me, I like important people best and I get on with them like a house on fire, but even if they bored me I should have thought it my duty to cultivate them, for Montdore's sake.'

When we had finished our meal we installed ourselves in the Long Gallery, the butler brought in a coffee tray which Lady Montdore told him to leave. She always had several cups of strong black coffee. As soon as he had gone she turned to Polly and said sharply, 'So what is it you want to say to me?'

I made a half-hearted attempt to go, but they both insisted on me staying. I knew they would.

'I want to be married in a month from now,' said Polly, 'and to do that I must have your consent as I'm not of age until May. It seems to me that as it is only a question of nine weeks, when I shall marry anyhow, you might as well agree and get it over, don't you think?'

'I must say that's very puddy—your poor aunt—when the breath has hardly left her body.'

'It doesn't make the slightest difference to Aunt Patricia whether she has been dead three months or three years so let's leave her out of it. The facts are what they are. I can't live at Alconleigh much longer,

I can't live here with you, hadn't I better start my new life as soon as possible?'

'Do you quite realize, Polly, that the day you marry Boy Dougdale your father is going to alter his will?'

'Yes, yes, yes,' said Polly impatiently, 'the times you've told me!'

'I've only told you once before.'

'I've had a letter about it, Boy has had a letter about it. We know.'

'I wonder whether you also know that Boy Dougdale is a very poor man? They lived, really, on Patricia's allowance, which, of course, in the ordinary way your father would have continued during Boy's lifetime. That will also stop if he marries you.'

'Yes. It was all in the letters.'

'And don't count on your father changing his mind because I've no intention of allowing him to.'

'I'm quite sure you haven't.'

'You think it doesn't matter being poor, but I wonder if you realize what it is like.'

'The one who doesn't realize,' said Polly, 'is you.'

'Not from experience I'm glad to say, but from observation I do. One's only got to look at the hopeless, dreary expression on the faces of poor people to see what it must be.'

'I don't agree at all, but anyhow, we shan't be poor like poor people. Boy has £800 a year, besides what he makes from his books.'

'The parson here and his wife have £800 a year,' said Lady Montdore. 'And look at their faces——!'

'They were born with those—I did better, thanks to you. In any case, Mummy, it's no good going on and on arguing about it, because everything is as much settled as if we were married already, so it's just pure waste of time.'

'Then why have you come? What do you want me to do?'

'First, I want to have the wedding next month, for which I need your consent, and then I also want to know what you and Daddy prefer about the actual marriage ceremony itself—shall we be married here in the chapel or shall I go off without you to London for it? We naturally don't want anybody to be there except Fanny and Lady Alconleigh, and you, if you'd care to come. I must say I would love to be given away by Daddy——'

Lady Montdore thought for a while, and finally said, 'I think it is quite intolerable of you to put us in this position and I shall have to talk it over with Montdore, but frankly, I think that if you intend to go through with this indecent marriage at all costs, it will make the least talk if we have it here, and before your birthday. Then I shan't have to explain why there are to be no coming-of-age celebrations, the tenants have begun asking about that already. So I think you may take it that you can have the marriage here, and next month, after which, you incestuous little trollop, I never want to set eyes on either you or your uncle again, as long as I live. And please don't expect a wedding present from me.'

Tears of self-pity were pouring down her cheeks. Perhaps she was thinking of the magnificent parure in its glass case against which, had things been otherwise, so many envious noses would have been pressed during the wedding reception at Montdore House. 'From the Bride's Parents.' Her dream of Polly's wedding, long and dearly cherished, had ended in a sad awakening indeed.

'Don't cry, Mummy, I'm so very very happy.'

'Well, I'm not,' said Lady Montdore, and rushed furiously from the room.

CHAPTER XVI

EXACTLY one month later, Davey, Aunt Sadie and I drove over to Hampton together for the wedding, our ears full of the lamentations of Jassy and Victoria who had not been invited.

'Polly is a horrible Counter-Hon and we hate her,' they said, 'after we made our fingers bleed over that rope ladder, not to speak of all the things we would have done for her, smuggling the Lecturer up to the Hons' cupboard, sharing our food with him—no risk we wouldn't have taken to give them a few brief moments of happiness together, only they were too cold-blooded to want it, and now she doesn't even ask us to the wedding. Do admit, Fanny.'

'I don't blame her for a single minute,' I said, 'a wedding is a very serious thing, naturally she doesn't want gusts of giggles the whole way through it.'

'And did we gust at yours?'

'I expect so, only it was a bigger church and more people, and I didn't hear you.'

Uncle Matthew on the other hand was asked, and said that nothing would induce him to accept.

'Wouldn't be able to keep my hands off the sewer,' he said. 'Boy!' he went on, scornfully, 'there's one thing, you'll hear his real name at last, just note it down for me please, I've always wanted to know what it is, to put in a drawer.'

It was a favourite superstition of Uncle Matthew's that if you wrote somebody's name on a piece of paper and put it in a drawer, that person would die within the year. The drawers at Alconleigh were full of little slips bearing the names of those whom my uncle wanted out of the way, private hates of his and various public figures such as Bernard Shaw, de Valera, Gandhi, Lloyd George and the Kaiser, while every single drawer in the whole house contained the name Labby, Linda's old dog. The spell hardly ever seemed to work, even Labby having lived far beyond the age usual in Labradors, but he went hopefully on, and if one of the characters did happen to be carried off in the course of nature he would look pleased but guilty for a day or two.

'I suppose we must all have heard his name when he married Patricia,' Aunt Sadie said, looking at Davey, 'but I can't remember it, can you? Though I have an idea it was one of those surnames, Stanley, or Norman. Such a thousand thousand years ago. Poor Patricia, what can she be thinking now?'

'Was she married in the chapel at Hampton too?' I said.

'No, in London, and I'm trying to remember where. Lord Montdore and Sonia were married in the Abbey, of course. I well remember that, because Emily was a bridesmaid and I was so furiously jealous, and my Nanny took me, but outside because Mamma thought we would see more like that than if we were stuck away behind a tomb. It was like a royal wedding, almost. Of course, I was out by the time Patricia married—St. Margaret's, Westminster, I think—yes, I'm nearly sure it was. I know we all thought she was awfully old for a white wedding, thirty or something terrible.'

'But she was beautiful,' said Davey.

'Very much like Polly, of course, but she never had that something extra, whatever it is, that makes Polly such a radiant beauty. I only wish I knew why these lovely women have both thrown themselves away on that old Lecturer—so unnatural.'

'Poor Boy,' said Davey, with a deeply sympathetic sigh.

Davey, who had been in Kent with Aunt Emily since finishing his cure, had come back to Alconleigh in order to be best man. He had accepted, so he said, for poor Patricia's sake, but really, I think, because he longed to go to the wedding; he also very much enjoyed the excuse it gave him to bustle about between Silkin and Hampton and see for himself all that was going on in those two stricken homes.

Polly had gone back to Hampton. She had taken no steps whatever towards getting a trousseau, and as the engagement and wedding were to be announced simultaneously in *The Times*, 'took place very quietly, owing to deep mourning, at Hampton Park' (all these little details arranged by Davey), she had no letters to write, no presents to unpack, and none of the business that usually precedes a wedding. Lord Montdore had insisted that she should have an interview with his lawyer, who came all the way from London to explain to her formally that everything hitherto set aside in her father's will, for her and her children, that is to say Montdore House, Craigside Castle and their contents, the property in Northumberland with its coal mines, the valuable and extensive house property in London, one or two docks and about two million pounds sterling would now all go to her father's only male heir, Cedric Hampton. In the ordinary course of events, he would merely have inherited Hampton itself and Lord Montdore's titles, but as the result of this new will, Cedric Hampton was destined to be one of the five or six richest men in England.

'And how is Lord Montdore taking it?' Aunt Sadie asked Davey when he brought back this news from Hampton, via a visit to Boy at Silkin.

'Quite impossible to say. Sonia is wretched, Polly is nervous, but Montdore is just as usual. You couldn't guess that anything out of the ordinary was happening to him.'

'I always knew he was an old stick. Had you realized he was so rich, Davey?'

'Oh, yes, one of the very richest.'

'Funny when you think how stingy Sonia is, in little ways. How long d'you imagine he'll keep it up, cutting off Polly, I mean?'

'As long as Sonia is alive. I bet you she won't forgive, and, as you know, he is entirely under her thumb.'

'Yes. So what does Boy say to living with a wife, on £800 a year?'

'Doesn't like it. He talks of letting Silkin and going to live somewhere cheap, abroad. I told him he'll have to write more books. He doesn't do so badly with them, you know, but he is very low, poor old fellow, very.'

'I expect it will do him good to get away,' I said.

'Well, yes,' said Davey expressively. 'But——'

'I do wonder what Cedric Hampton is like.'

'So do we all—Boy was talking about it just now. It seems they don't really know where he is even. The father was a bad lot and went to Nova Scotia, fell ill there and married his nurse, an elderly Canadian woman, who had this one child, but he (the father) is dead and nothing more is known except the bare fact that there is this boy. Montdore gives him some small allowance, paid into a Canadian bank every year. Don't you think it's very odd he hasn't taken more interest in him, considering he will have his name and is the only hope of this ancient family being carried on?'

'Probably he hated the father.'

'I don't believe he ever knew him. They are quite a different generation—second cousins once removed—something like that. No, I put it down to Sonia, I expect she couldn't bear the idea of Hampton going away from Polly and pretended to herself that this Cedric did not really exist—you know what a one she is for shutting her eyes to things she doesn't like. I should imagine she'll be obliged to face up to him now, Montdore is sure to want to see him under these new circumstances.'

'Sad, isn't it, the idea of some great lumping colonial at Hampton!'

'Simply tragic!' said Davey. 'Poor Montdores, I do feel for them.'

Somehow, the material side of the business had never been fully borne in upon me until Davey went into these facts and figures, but now I realized that 'all this' was indeed something tremendous to be so carelessly thrown into the lap of a total stranger.

When we arrived at Hampton, Aunt Sadie and I were shown straight into the chapel, where we sat alone. Davey went off to find Boy. The chapel was a Victorian building among the servants' quarters. It had been constructed by the 'old lord', and contained his marble effigy in Garter robes with that of Alice, his wife, some bright stained glass, a family pew designed like a box at the opera, all red plush with curtains, and a very handsome organ. Davey had engaged a first class organist from Oxford, who now regaled us with some Bach preludes. None of the interested parties seemed to have bothered to take a hand in any of the arrangements. Davey had chosen all the music and the gardener had evidently been left to himself with the flowers, which were quite overwhelming in their magnificence, the exaggerated hothouse flowers beloved of all gardeners, arranged with typical florist's taste. I began to feel dreadfully sad. The Bach and the flowers induced melancholy, besides, look at it as you would, this marriage was a depressing business.

Boy and Davey came up the aisle, and Boy shook hands with us. He had evidently got rid of his cold, at last, and was looking quite well; his hair, I noticed, had received the attention of a damp comb to induce little waves and a curl or two, and his figure, not bad at all, especially from behind, was set off by his wedding clothes. He wore a white carnation, and Davey a red one. But though he was in the costume of a bridegroom, he had not the spirit to add this new part to his repertory with any conviction and his whole attitude was more appropriate to a chief mourner. Davey even had to show him where to stand, by the altar steps. I never saw a man look so hopeless.

The clergyman took up his position, a very disapproving expression on his face. Presently a movement at our left indicated that Lady Montdore had come into the family pew, which had its own entrance. It was impossible to stare, but I could not resist a glance and saw that she looked as if she were going to be sick. Boy also glanced, after which his back view became eloquent of a desire to slink in beside her and have a good long gossip. It was the first time he had seen her since they had read the Infanta's letters together.

The organist from Oxford stopped playing Bach, which he had been doing with less and less interest during the last few minutes, and paused. Looking round, I saw that Lord Montdore was standing at the entrance to the chapel. He was impassive, well-preserved, a cardboard earl, and might have been about to lead his daughter up the aisle of Westminster Abbey to marry the King of England for all that could be read into his look.

'O Perfect Love, all Human Thought Transcending' rang out, sung by an invisible choir in the gallery. And then, up the aisle, one large white hand on her father's arm, dispelling the gloomy embarrassment which hung like a fog in the chapel, came Polly, calm, confident and noble, radiating happiness. Somehow, she had got herself a wedding dress (did I recognize a ball dress of last season? No matter) and was in a cloud of white tulle and lilies of the valley and joy. Most brides have difficulty with their expression as they go to the altar, looking affected, or soulful, or, worst of all, too eager, but Polly simply floated along on waves of bliss, creating one of the most beautiful moments I have ever experienced.

There was a dry, choking sound on our left, the door of the family pew was slammed, Lady Montdore had gone.

The clergyman began to intone the wedding service. 'Forasmuch,' and so on, 'Who giveth this woman to be married to this man?' Lord Montdore bowed, took Polly's bouquet from her and went into the nearest pew.

'Please say after me, "I, Harvey, take thee, Leopoldina".' A look from Aunt Sadie.

It was soon over. One more hymn, and I was left alone while they all went behind a screen to sign the register. Then the burst of Mendelssohn and Polly floated out again as she had come, only on the arm of a different well-preserved old man.

While Polly and Boy changed into their going-away things we waited in the Long Gallery to say good-bye and see them off. They were motoring to the Lord Warden at Dover for the night, and going abroad the following day. I half expected that Polly would send for me to go upstairs and chat, but she did not, so I stayed with the others. I think she was so happy that she hardly noticed if people were with her or she was alone; perhaps she really preferred the latter. Lady Montdore put in no further appearance, Lord Montdore talked to Davey, congratulating him upon an anthology he had recently published, called *In Sickness and in Health.* I heard him say that, to his mind, there was not quite enough Browning, but that apart from that it would all have been his own choice.

'But Browning was so healthy,' objected Davey. The stress throughout the book was upon sickness.

A footman handed round glasses of champagne. Aunt Sadie and I settled down, as one always did, somehow, at Hampton, to a prolonged scrutiny of *Tatler, Sketch* and *Bystander,* and Polly took so long that I even got on to *Country Life* before she appeared. Through my happy haze of baronets' wives, their children, their dogs, their tweeds and their homes, or just their huge faces, wave of hair on the forehead held by a diamond clip, I was conscious that the atmosphere in the Long

Gallery, like that in the chapel, was one of embarrassment and gloom. When Boy reappeared, I saw him give a puzzled glance at the fire-screen with its jagged hole and then, as he realized what had happened to it, he turned his back on the room, and stood gazing out of the window. Nobody spoke to him. Lord Montdore and Davey sipped champagne, having exhausted the topic of the anthology, in silence.

At last Polly came in wearing her last year's mink coat and a tiny brown hat. Though the cloud of tulle had gone the cloud of joy still enveloped her, she was perfectly unselfconscious, hugged her father, kissed us all, including Davey, took Boy by the arm and led him to the front door. We followed. The servants, looking sad, and the elder ones sniffing, were gathered in the hall, she said good-bye to them, had some rice thrown over her, rather half-heartedly, by the youngest housemaid, got into the big Daimler, followed, very half-heartedly, by Boy, and was driven away.

We said good-bye politely to Lord Montdore and followed suit. As we went up the drive I looked back. The footmen had already shut the front door, and it seemed to me that beautiful Hampton, between the pale spring green of its lawns and the pale spring blue of the sky, lay deserted, empty and sad. Youth had gone from it and henceforward it was to be the home of two lonely old people.

Part Two

CHAPTER I

MY real life as a married woman, that is to say life with my husband in our own house, now began. One day I went to Oxford and a miracle seemed to have taken place. There was paper on all the walls of my house, the very paper I had chosen, too, and looking even prettier than I had hoped it would, the smell of cheap cigarettes, cement, stewed tea and dry rot had gone, and in its place there was a heavenly smell of new paint and cleanliness, the floor boards were all smooth and solid, and the windows so clean that they seemed to be glassless. The day was perfect, spring had come and my home was ready; I felt too happy for words. To set the seal upon this happiness, the wife of a professor had called, her card and her husband's two cards had carefully been put by the workmen on a chimney piece: Professor and Mrs. Cozens, 209 Banbury Road. Now, at last, I was a proper grown-up married lady on whom people called. It was very thrilling.

I had at this time a romantic but very definite picture in my mind of what life was going to be like in Oxford. I imagined a sort of Little Gidding, a community of delightful, busy, cultivated people, bound together by shared intellectual tastes and by their single-minded exertions on behalf of the youth entrusted to their care. I supposed that the other wives of dons would be beautiful, quiet women, versed in all the womanly arts but that of coquetry, a little worn with the effort of making a perfection of their homes at the same time as rearing large families of clever children, and keeping up with things like Kafka, but never too tired or too busy for long, serious discussions on subjects of importance, whether intellectual or practical. I saw myself, in the day-time, running happily in and out of the houses of these charming creatures, old houses with some important piece of architecture framed in the windows as Christ Church was in mine, sharing every detail of their lives, while the evenings would be spent listening to grave and scholarly talk between our husbands. In short I saw them as a tribe of heavenly new relations, more mature, more intellectual Radletts. This happy intimacy seemed to be heralded by the cards of Professor and Mrs. Cozens. For one moment the fact that they lived in the Banbury Road struck a note of disillusionment, but then it occurred to me that of course the clever Cozenses must have found some little old house in that unpromising neighbourhood, some nobleman's folly, sole reminder of long-vanished pleasure grounds, and decided to put up with the Banbury Road for the sake of its doorways and cornices, the rococo detail of its ceilings and the excellent proportions of its rooms.

I never shall forget that happy, happy day. The house at last was mine, the workmen had gone, the Cozenses had come, the daffodils were out in the garden, and a blackbird was singing fit to burst its lungs. Alfred looked in and seemed to find my sudden rush of high spirits quite irrational. He had always known, he said, that the house would be ready sooner or later, and had not, like me, alternated between faith and black moods of scepticism. As for the Cozenses, in spite of the fact that I realized by now that one human being, in Alfred's eyes, was exactly the same as another, I did find his indifference with regard to them and their cards rather damping.

'It's so terrible,' I wailed, 'because I can't return the call, our cards haven't come yet. Oh, yes, they are promised for next week, but I long to go now, this very minute, don't you see?'

'Next week will do quite well,' Alfred said, shortly.

Soon an even more blissful day dawned; I woke up in my own bed in my own bedroom, done up in my own taste and arranged entirely to suit me. True, it was freezing cold and pouring with rain on this occasion, and, since I had as yet no servant, I was obliged to get up very early and cook Alfred's breakfast, but I did not mind. He was my own husband, and the cooking took place in my own kitchen; it all seemed like heaven to me.

And now, I thought, for the happy sisterhood on which I had pinned my hopes. But alas, as so often happens in life, this turned out rather differently from what I had expected; I found myself landed with two sisters indeed, but they were very far removed from the charming companions of my dream. One was Lady Montdore and the other was Norma Cozens. At this time I was not only young, barely twenty, but extremely simple. Hitherto all human relationships had been with members of my family or with other girls (schoolfellows and débutantes) of my own age, they had been perfectly easy and straightforward and I had no idea that anything more complicated could exist; even love, with me, had followed an exceptionally level path. I supposed, in my simplicity, that when people liked me I ought to like them back as much, and that whatever they expected of me, especially if they were older people, I was morally bound to perform. In the case of these two, I doubt if it ever occurred to me that they were eating up my time and energy in a perfectly shameless way. Before my children were born I had time on my hands and I was lonely. Oxford is a place where social life, contrary to what I had imagined, is designed exclusively for celibate men, all the good talk, good food and good wine being reserved for those gatherings where there are no women; the whole tradition is in its essence monastic, and as far as society goes wives are quite superfluous.

I should never have chosen Norma Cozens to be an intimate friend, but I suppose that her company must have seemed preferable to hours of my own, while Lady Montdore did at least bring a breath of air which, though it could not have been described as fresh, had its origins in the great world outside our cloister, a world where women do count for something more than bed-makers.

Mrs. Cozens's horizon also extended beyond Oxford, though in another direction. Her maiden name was Boreley, and the Boreley family was well known to me, since her grandfather's huge 1890 Elizabethan house was situated not far from Alconleigh and they were the new rich of the neighbourhood. This grandfather, now Lord Driersley, had made his money in foreign railroads, he had married into the landed gentry and produced a huge family, all the members of which, as they grew up and married, he settled on estates within easy motoring distance of Driersley Manor; they, in their turns, became notable breeders, so that the Boreley tentacles had spread by now over a great part of the West of England and there seemed to be absolutely no end of Boreley cousins, aunts, uncles, brothers and sisters and their respective in-laws. There was very little variety about them; they all had the same cross, white guinea-pig look, thought alike, and led the same sort of lives, sporting, country lives; they seldom went to London. They were respected by their neighbours for the conformity to the fashion of the day, for their morals, for their wealth and for their excellence at all kinds of sport. They did everything that they ought to do in the way of sitting on Benches and County Councils, walking hound puppies and running Girl Guides, one was an M.P., another an M.F.H. In short, they were pillars of rural England. Uncle Matthew, who encountered them on local business, loathed them all, and they were collectively in many drawers under the one name, Boreley, I never quite knew why. However, like Gandhi, Bernard Shaw and Labby the Labrador, they continued to flourish, and no terrible Boreley holocaust ever took place.

My first experience of Oxford society, as the wife of a junior don, was a dinner party given in my honour by the Cozenses. The Waynflete Professor of Pastoral Theology was the professor of Alfred's subject, and was, therefore, of importance in our lives and an influence upon Alfred's career. I understood this to be so without Alfred exactly putting it into words. In any case I was of course anxious that my first Oxford appearance should be a success, anxious to look nice, make a good impression, and be a credit to my husband. My mother had given me an evening dress from Mainbocher which seemed specially designed for such an occasion, it had a white pleated chiffon skirt, and black silk jersey top with a high neck and long sleeves, which was tucked into a wide, black, patent-leather belt. Wearing this with my only jewel, a diamond clip sent by my father, I thought I was not only nicely, but also suitably, dressed. My father, incidentally, had turned a deaf ear to Lady Montdore's suggestion that he should buy me a place, and had declared himself to be too utterly ruined even to increase my allowance on my marriage. He did, however, send a cheque and this pretty jewel.

The Cozenses' house was not a nobleman's folly. It was the very worst kind of Banbury-Road house, depressing, with laurels. The front door was opened by a slut. I had never seen a slut before but recognized the genus without difficulty as soon as I set eyes on this one. Inside the hall Alfred and I and the slut got rather mixed up with a large pram. However, we sorted ourselves out and put down our coats, and then she opened a door and shot us, without announcing our names, into the terrible Cozens' drawing-room. All this to the accompaniment of shrill barking from four Border terriers.

I saw at once that my dress would not do. Norma told me afterwards, when pointing out the many fearful gaffes which I was supposed to have made during the course of the evening, that as a bride I would have been expected to wear my wedding dress at our first dinner party. But, even apart from that blunder, a jersey top, however Parisian, was obviously unacceptable for evening wear in high Oxford society. The other women present were either in lace or marocain, décolleté to the waist behind, and with bare arms. Their dresses were in shades of biscuit, and so were they. It was a cold evening following upon a chilly day. The Cozenses' hearth was not laid for a fire, but had a piece of pleated paper in the grate. And yet these naked ladies did not seem to be cold; they were not blue and goosey as I should have been, nor did they shiver. I was soon to learn that in donnish circles the Oxford summer is considered to be horribly hot, and the Oxford winter nice and bracing, but that no account is taken of the between seasons or of the findings of the thermometer; cold is never felt. Apart from there being no fire, the room was terribly cheerless. The hard little sofa, the few and hard little armchairs were upholstered in a cretonne of so dim and dismal a pattern that it was hard to imagine anybody, even a Boreley, actually choosing it, to imagine them going into a shop, taking a seat, having cretonnes thrown over a screen one after another and suddenly saying, all excited, 'That's the very thing for me—stop!' The lights were unshaded and held in chromium-plated fittings, there was no carpet on the floor, just a few slippery rugs, the walls were of shiny cream paint, and there were no pictures, objects or flowers to relieve the bareness.

Mrs. Cozens, whose cross, creased Boreley face I recognized from my hunting days, greeted us heartily enough, and the Professor came forward with a shadow of Lord Montdore's manner, an unctuous geniality which may have originated with the Church, though his version of it was as that of a curate to Lord Montdore's cardinal. There were three other couples to whom I was introduced, all dons and their wives. I was perfectly fascinated to see these people among whom I was henceforward to live. They were ugly and not specially friendly, but no doubt, I supposed, very brilliant.

The food at dinner, served by the slut in a gaunt dining-room, was so terrible that I felt deeply sorry for Mrs. Cozens, thinking that something must have gone wrong. I have had so many such meals since then that I do not remember exactly what it was; I guess, however, that it began with tinned soup and ended with dry sardines on dry toast, and that we drank a few drops of white wine. I do remember that the conversation was far from brilliant, a fact which, at the time, I attributed to the horrible stuff we were trying to swallow, but which I now know was more likely to have been due to the presence of females; dons are quite used to bad food but become paralysed in mixed company. As soon as the last sardine tail had been got down, Mrs. Cozens rose to her feet, and we went into the drawing-room, leaving the men to enjoy the one good item of the whole menu, excellent vintage port. They only reappeared just before it was time to go home.

Over the coffee, sitting round the pleated paper in the fireplace, the other women talked of Lady Montdore and Polly's amazing marriage. It seemed that, while their husbands all knew Lord Montdore slightly, none of them knew Lady Montdore, not even Norma Cozens, though, as a member of an important county family, she had been inside

Hampton once or twice to various big functions. They all spoke, however, not only as if they knew her quite well, but as if she had done each of them personally some terrible wrong. Lady Montdore was not popular in the county, and the reason was that she turned up her nose at the local squires and their wives as well as at the local tradesmen and their wares, ruthlessly importing both her guests and her groceries from London.

It is always interesting, and usually irritating, to hear what people have to say about somebody whom they do not know but we do. On this occasion I positively squirmed with interest and irritation. Nobody asked for my opinion, so I sat in silence, listening. The dominant thought of the discussion was that Lady Montdore, wicked as hell, had been envious of Polly, her youth and her beauty, ever since she grew up, had snubbed her and squashed her and kept her out of sight as much as possible, and that, furthermore, as soon as Polly got an admirer Lady Montdore had somehow managed to send him about his business, finally driving her into the arms of her uncle as the only escape from an unhappy home.

'Now I happen to know for a fact that Polly' (they all called her Polly, though none of them knew her) 'was on the point of getting engaged to Joyce Fleetwood, only just the other day, too—he stayed at Hampton for Christmas and it was all going like a house on fire. His own sister told me. Well, Lady Montdore got rid of him in double quick time, you see.'

'Yes, and wasn't it just the same with John Coningsby? Polly was madly in love with him, and no doubt he'd have come up to scratch in the end, but when Lady Montdore twigged what was going on she had him out on his ear.'

'And in India too, it happened several times, Polly only had to fancy a young man for him to vanish mysteriously.' They spoke as if Lady Montdore were an enchantress in a fairy tale.

'She was jealous, you know, of her being supposed to be such a beauty (never could see it myself, don't admire that flat fish look).'

'You'd think she'd want to get her off all the quicker.'

'You can't tell how jealousy is going to take people.'

'But I've always heard that Dougdale was Lady Montdore's own lover.'

'Of course he was, and that's exactly why she never imagined there could be anything between him and Polly. Serve her jolly well right, she ought to have let the poor girl marry all those others when she wanted to.'

'What a sly little thing though, under the very noses of her mother and her aunt like that.'

'I don't expect there's much to choose between them. The one I'm sorry for is poor old Lord Montdore, he's such a wonderful old man and she's led him the most awful dance you know for years, ever since they married. Daddy says she utterly ruined his career, and if it hadn't been for her he could have been Prime Minister or anything.'

'Well, but he was Viceroy,' I said, putting in my oar at last. I felt thoroughly on Lady Montdore's side against these hideous people.

'Yes he was, and everybody knows she nearly lost us India—I believe the harm she did there was something terrible. Daddy has a great friend, an Indian judge, you should hear his stories! Her rudeness——!'

'Of course, lots of people say Polly isn't Lord Montdore's child at all. King Edward, I've heard.'

'It doesn't seem to make much difference now whose child she is, because he's cut her out of his will and some American gets it all.'

'Australian, I heard. Imagine an Australian at Hampton, sad when you come to think of it.'

'And the whole thing is that old woman's fault, the old tart. That's all she is when you come to think of it, needn't give herself such airs.'

I suddenly became very furious. I was well aware of Lady Montdore's faults, I knew that she was deplorable in many ways, but it seemed to me to be wrong of people who had never even met her and knew nothing at first hand, to speak of her like this. I had a feeling that they did so out of an obscure jealousy, and that she only had to take any of these women up and bestow a flicker of her charm upon them for them to become her grovelling toadies.

'I hear she made a ghastly scene at the wedding,' said the don's wife whose Daddy knew an Indian judge. 'Screamed and yelled and had hysterics.'

'She didn't,' I said.

'Why, how do you know?'

'Because I was there.'

They looked at me curiously and rather angrily, as though I ought to have spoken up sooner, and changed the subject to the eternal ones of children's illnesses and servants' misdeeds.

I hoped that at my next dinner party I should be meeting the noble, thoughtful, intellectual women of my Oxford dream, if, indeed, they existed.

After this Norma Cozens took a fancy to me for some reason, and used to drop into my house on her way to or from the huge walks she went for every day with the Border terriers. I think she was the crossest person I ever met, nothing was ever right for her, and her conversation, which consisted of lectures, advice and criticism, was punctuated with furious sighs, but she was not a bad old thing, good-natured at heart, and often did me little kindnesses. I came to like her in the end the best of all the dons' wives; she was at least natural and unpretentious and brought her children up in an ordinary way. Those I found impossible to get on with were the arty-crafty ones with modern ideas, and ghastly children who had never been thwarted or cleaned up by the hand of a nanny. Norma was a type with which I was more familiar, an ordinary country hunting woman, incongruous, perhaps, in academic circles, but with no nonsense and certainly no nastiness about her. Anyhow, there she was, self-constituted part of my new life, and accepted by me as such without question.

CHAPTER II

A MORE difficult and exacting relationship was the one which now developed between me and Lady Montdore. She haunted my house, coming at much odder and more inconvenient times than Norma (who was very conventional in such ways), and proceeded to turn me into a lady-in-waiting. It was quite easy; nobody has ever sapped my will-power as she did, and like Lord Montdore, but unlike Polly, I was quite completely under her thumb. Even Alfred lifted his eyes for a moment from pastoral theology and saw what was going on. He said he could not understand my attitude, and that it made him impatient.

'You don't really like her, you're always complaining about her, why not say you are out when she comes?'

Why not, indeed? The fact was that I had never got over the physical feeling of terror which Lady Montdore had inspired in me from childhood, and though with my reason I knew now what she was, and did not care for what I knew, though the idol was down from its pedestal, the bull-fighter back in his ready-made suit, and she was revealed as nothing more or less than a selfish old woman, still I remained in awe of her. When Alfred told me to pretend to be out when she came I knew that this would be impossible for me.

'Oh, no, darling, I don't think I could do that.'

He shrugged his shoulders and said no more. He never tried to influence me, and very rarely commented on, or even appeared to notice, my behaviour and the conduct of my life.

Lady Montdore's plan was to descend upon me without warning, either on her way to or from London, or on shopping expeditions to Oxford, when she would take me round with her to fetch and carry and check her list. She would engage all my attention for an hour or two, tiring me out, exactly as small children can, with the demands she made of concentration upon her, and then vanish again, leaving me dissatisfied with life. As she was down on her own luck, but would have considered it a weakness to admit it even to herself, she was obliged to bolster up 'all this', to make it seem a perfect compensation for what she had lost by denigrating the circumstances of other people. It was even a help to her, I suppose, because otherwise I cannot account for her beastliness, to run down my poor little house, so unpretentious, and my dull little life, and she did so with such conviction that, since I am easily discouraged, it often took days before everything seemed all right again.

Days, or a visit from some member of the Radlett family. The Radletts had the exactly opposite effect, and always made me feel wonderful, owing to a habit known in the family as 'exclaiming'.

'Fanny's shoes——! Where? Lilley and Skinner? I must dash. And the lovely new skirt! Not a new suit, let's see—not lined with silk—Fanny! You are lucky, it is unfair!'

'Oh, dear, why doesn't my hair curl like that? Oh, the bliss of Fanny altogether—her eyelashes! You are lucky, it is unfair!'

These exclamations, which I remember from my very earliest childhood, now also embraced my house and household arrangements.

'The wallpaper! Fanny! Your bed—it can't be true. Oh, look at the darling little bit of Belleek—where did you find it? No! Do let's go there. And a new cushion! Oh, it is unfair, you are lucky to be you.'

'I say, Fanny's food! Toast at every meal! Not Yorkshire pudding! Why can't we live with Fanny always—the heaven of it here! Why can't I be you?'

Fortunately for my peace of mind, Jassy and Victoria came to see me whenever there was a motor car going to Oxford, which was quite often, and the elder ones always looked in if they were on their way to Alconleigh.

As I got to know Lady Montdore more intimately I began to realize that her selfishness was monumental, she had no thoughts except in relation to herself, could discuss no subject without cleverly edging it round to something directly pertaining to her. The only thing she ever wanted to know about people was what impression did she make on them, and she would do anything to find this out, sometimes digging traps for the unwary, into which, in my innocence, I was very apt to tumble.

'I suppose your husband is a clever man, at least so Montdore tells me. Of course, it's a thousand pities he is so dreadfully poor—I hate to see you living in this horrid little hovel, so unsuitable—and not more important, but Montdore says he has the reputation of being clever.'

She had dropped in just as I was having my tea, which consisted of a few rather broken digestive biscuits with a kitchen pot on a tray and without a plate. I was so busy that afternoon, and Mrs. Heathery, my maid of all work, was so busy too, that I had dashed into the kitchen and taken the tray myself, like that. Unfortunately, it never seemed to be chocolate cake and silver teapot day when Lady Mont-

dore came, though, such were the vagaries of my housekeeping while
I was a raw beginner, that these days did quite often, though quite
unaccountably, occur.

'Is that your tea? All right dear, yes, just a cup, please. How weak
you have it—no no, this will do quite well. Yes, as I was saying, Montdore spoke of your husband today at luncheon, with the Bishop. They
had read something of his and seem to have been quite impressed, so
I suppose he really is clever after all.'

'Oh, he is the cleverest man I ever met,' I said, happily. I loved to
talk about Alfred, it was the next best thing to being with him.

'So of course, I suppose he thinks I'm a very stupid person.' She
looked with distaste at the bits of digestives, and then took one.

'Oh no, he doesn't,' I said, inventing, because Alfred had never
put forward any opinion on the subject one way or another.

'I'm sure he must, really. You don't mean to tell me he thinks I'm
clever?'

'Yes, very clever. He p'r'aps doesn't look upon you as an intellectual——'

Crash! I was in the trap.

'Oh, indeed! Not an intellectual!'

I could see at once that she was terribly offended, and thrashed
about unhappily in my trap trying to extricate myself, to no avail,
however, I was in it up to the neck.

'You see, he doesn't believe that women ever are intellectuals hardly
hardly ever, perhaps one in ten million—Virginia Woolf perhaps——'

'I suppose he thinks I never read. Many people think that, because
they see me leading this active life, wearing myself out for others. I
might prefer to sit in a chair all day and read some book, very likely I
would, but I shouldn't think it right, in my position, to do so—I can't
only be thinking of myself, you see. I never do read books in the day-
time, that's perfectly true, I simply haven't a moment, but your
husband doesn't know, and nor do you, what I do at night. I don't
sleep well, not well at all, and at night I read volumes.'

Old volumes of the *Tatler*, I guessed. She had them all bound up from
before the war, and very fascinating they were.

'You know, Fanny,' she went on, 'it's all very well for funny little
people like you to read books the whole time, you only have yourselves
to consider, whereas Montdore and I are public servants in a way, we
have something to live up to, tradition and so on, duties to perform you
know, it's a very different matter. A great deal is expected of us, I
think and hope not in vain. It's a hard life, make no mistake about
that, hard and tiring, but occasionally we have our reward—when
people get a chance to show how they worship us, for instance, when
we came back from India and the dear villagers pulled our motor car
up the drive. Really touching! Now all you intellectual people never

have moments like that. Well,' she rose to leave, 'one lives and learns. I know now that I am outside the pale, intellectually. Of course, my dear child, we must remember that all those women students probably give your husband a very funny notion of what the female sex is really like. I wonder if he realizes that it's only the ones who can't hope for anything better that come here. Perhaps he finds them very fascinating —one never sees him in his own home, I notice.' She was working herself up into a tremendous temper now. 'And if I might offer you a little advice, Fanny, it would be to read fewer books, dear, and make your house slightly more comfortable. That is what a man appreciates, in the long run.'

She cast a meaning look at the plateless digestives, and went away without saying good-bye.

I was really upset to have annoyed her so stupidly and tactlessly, and felt certain that she would never come and see me again; funnily enough, instead of being relieved by this thought, I minded.

I had no time to brood over it, however, for hardly was she out of the house than Jassy and Victoria bundled in.

'Not digestives! Vict.—look, digestives! Isn't Fanny wonderful, you can always count on something heavenly—weeks since I tasted digestives, my favourite food, too.'

Mrs. Heathery, who adored the children and had heard their shrieks as they came in, brought up some fresh tea and a Fuller's cake, which elicited more exclamations.

'Oh, Mrs. Heathery, you angel on earth, not Fuller's walnut? How can you afford it, Fanny—we haven't had it at home since Fa's last financial crisis—but things are better you know, we are back to Bromo again now and the good writing-paper. When the loo paper gets thicker and the writing-paper thinner it's always a bad sign, at home.'

'Fa had to come about some harness, so he brought us in to see you, only ten minutes though. The thing is we've got a funny story about Sadie for you, so are you listening? Well, Sadie was telling how some people, before their babies are born, gaze at Greuze so that the babies shall look like it, and she said "You never know about these things, because when I was a little girl in Suffolk a baby was born in the village with a bear's head, and what do you think? Exactly nine months before a dancing bear had been in that neighbourhood." So Vict. said "But I can quite understand that, I always think bears are simply terribly attractive", and Sadie gave the most tremendous jump I ever saw and said, "You awful child, that's not what I mean at all". So are you shrieking, Fanny?'

'We saw your new friend Mrs. Cozens just now and her blissful Borders. You are so lucky to have new friends, it is unfair, we never do, really you know, we are the Lady of Shalott with our pathetic lives we lead. Even Davey never comes now horrible Polly's marriage is over.

Oh, by the way, we had a postcard from horrible Polly, but it's no use her bombarding us with these postcards—we can never never forgive.'

'Where was it from?'

'Seville, that's in Spain.'

'Did she sound happy?'

'Do people ever sound unhappy on postcards, Fanny? Isn't it always lovely weather and everything wonderful, on postcards? This one was a picture of a glorious girl called La Macarena, and the funny thing is this La Macarena is the literal image of horrible Polly herself. Do you think Lady Montdore gazed a bit before H.P was born?'

'You musn't say horrible Polly to me when I love her so much.'

'Well, we'll have to see. We love her in a way, in spite of all, and in a few years, possibly, we might forgive, though I doubt if we can ever forget her deep, base treachery. Has she written to you?'

'Only postcards,' I said. 'One from Paris and one from St. Jean de Luz.'

Polly had never been much of a letter-writer.

'I wonder if it's as nice as she thought, being in bed with that old Lecturer.'

'Marriage isn't only bed,' I said, primly, 'there are other things.'

'You go and tell that to Sadie. There's Fa's horn, we must dash or he'll never bring us again if we keep him waiting, and we promised we would the very second he blew. Oh, dear, back to the fields of barley and of rye, you are so lucky to live in this sweet little house in a glamorous town. Good-bye, Mrs. Heathery—the cake!'

They were still cramming it into their mouths as they went downstairs.

'Come in and have some tea,' I said to Uncle Matthew, who was at the wheel of his new big Wolseley. When my uncle had a financial crisis he always bought a new motor car.

'No thank you, Fanny, very kind of you but there's a perfectly good cup of tea waiting for me at home, and you know I never go inside other people's houses if I can possibly avoid it. Good-bye.'

He put on his green hat called a bramble, which he always wore, and drove away.

My next caller was Norma Cozens, who came in for a glass of sherry, but her conversation was so dull that I have not the heart to record it. It was a compound of an abscess between the toes of the mother Border terrier, the things the laundry does to sheets, how it looked to her as if the slut had been at her store cupboard so she was planning to replace her by an Austrian at 2s. a week cheaper wages, and how lucky I was to have Mrs. Heathery, but I must look out because new brooms sweep clean and Mrs. Heathery was sure not to be nearly as nice as she seemed.

I was very much mistaken if I thought that Lady Montdore was now out of my life for good. In less than a week she was back again. The door of my house was always kept on the latch, like a country-house door, and she never bothered to ring but just stumped upstairs, on this occasion it was five minutes to one and I plainly saw that I would have to share the little bit of salmon I had ordered for myself, as a treat, with her.

'And where is your husband today?'

She showed her disapproval of my marriage by always referring to Alfred like this and never by his name. He was still Mr. Thing in her eyes.

'Lunching in college.'

'Ah, yes? Just as well, so he won't be obliged to endure my un-intellectual conversation.'

I was afraid it would all start over again, including the working herself up into a temper, but apparently she had decided to treat my unlucky remark as a great joke.

'I told Merlin,' she said, 'that in Oxford circles I am not thought an intellectual, and I only wish you could have seen his face!'

When Mrs. Heathery offered the fish to Lady Montdore she scooped up the whole thing. No tiresome inhibitions caused her to ask what I would eat, and in fact I had some potatoes and salad. She was good enough to say that the quality of the food in my house seemed to be improving.

'Oh, yes, I know what I wanted to ask you,' she said. 'Who is this Virginia Woolf you mentioned to me? Merlin was talking about her too, the other day at Maggie Greville's.'

'She's a writer,' I said, 'a novelist really.'

'Yes, I see. And as she's so intellectual, no doubt she writes about nothing but station-masters.'

'Well, no,' I said, 'she doesn't.'

'I must confess that I prefer books about society people, not being myself a highbrow.'

'She did write a fascinating book about a society person,' I said, 'called Mrs. Dalloway.'

'Perhaps I'll read it then. Oh, of course, I'd forgotten—I never read, according to you, don't know how. Never mind. In case I have a little time this week, Fanny, you might lend it to me, will you? Excellent cheese, don't tell me you get this in Oxford?'

She was in an unusually good temper that day. I believe the fall of the Spanish throne had cheered her up, she probably foresaw a perfect swarm of Infantas winging its way towards Montdore House, besides, she was greatly enjoying all the details from Madrid. She said that the Duke of Barbarossa (this may not be the name, but it sounded like it) had told her the inside story, in which case he must also have told it to the Daily Express, where I had read word for word what she now kindly passed on to me, and several days before. She remembered to ask for Mrs. Dalloway before leaving, and went off with the book in her hand, a first edition. I felt sure that I had seen the last of it, but she brought it back the following week, saying that she really must write a book herself as she knew she could do much better than that.

'Couldn't read it,' she said. 'I did try, but it is too boring. And I never got to that society person you told me of. Now have you read the Grand Duchess's *Memoirs*? I won't lend you mine, you must buy them for yourself, Fanny, and that will help the dear duchess with another guinea. They are wonderful. There is a great deal, nearly a whole chapter, about Montdore and me in India—she stayed with us at Viceroy's House you know. She has really captured the spirit of the place quite amazingly, she was only there a week but one couldn't have done it better oneself, she describes a garden party I gave, and visits to the Ranees in their harems, and she tells what a lot I was able to do for those poor women of India, and how they worshipped me. Personally, I find memoirs so very much more interesting than any novel because they are true. I may not be an intellectual, but I do like to read the truth about things. Now in a book like the Grand Duchess's you can see history in the very making, and if you love history as I do (but don't tell your husband I said so dear, he would never believe it), if you love history, you must be interested to know the inside story, and it's only people like the Grand Duchess who are in a position to tell us that. And this reminds me, Fanny dear, will you put a call through to Downing Street for me please, and get hold of the P.M. or his secretary —I will speak myself when he is on the line. I'm arranging a little dinner for the Grand Duchess, to give her book a good start, of course, I don't ask you dear, it wouldn't be intellectual enough, just a few politicians and writers, I thought. Here is the number, Fanny.'

I was trying at this time to economize in every direction, having overspent myself on doing up the house, and I had made a rule never to telephone, even to Aunt Emily or to Alconleigh, if a letter would do as well, so it was most unwillingly that I did as she asked. There was a long wait on the line before I got the Prime Minister himself, after which Lady Montdore spoke for ages, the pip-pip-pips going at least five times, I could hear them, every pip an agony to me. First of all she fixed a date for her dinner party, this took a long time, with many pauses while he consulted his secretary, and two pip-pip-pips. Then she asked if there were anything new from Madrid.

'Yes,' she said, 'badly advised, poor man [pip-pip-pip] I fear. I saw Freddy Barbarossa last night (they are being so brave about it, by the way, quite stoical. Yes, at Claridges) and he told me . . .' here a flood of *Daily Express* news and views. 'But Montdore and I are very much worried about our own special Infanta—yes, a close friend of ours—oh, Prime Minister, if you could hear anything I should be so more than grateful. Will you really? You know, there is a whole chapter on Madrid in the Grand Duchess's book, it makes it very topical, rather splendid for her. Yes, a near relation. She describes the view [pip-pip-pip] from the Royal Palace—yes, very bleak, I've been there, wonderful sunsets though. I know, poor woman. Oh, she hated them at first, she had special opera glasses with black spots for the cruel moments.

'Have you heard where they are going? Yes, Barbara Barbarossa told me that too, but I wonder they don't come here. You ought to try and persuade them. Yes, I see. Well, we'll talk about all that, meanwhile, dear Prime Minister, I won't keep you any longer [pip-pip-pip] but we'll see you on the 10th. So do I. I'll send your secretary a reminder, of course. Good-bye.'

She turned to me, beaming, and said, 'I have the most wonderful effect on that man, you know, it's quite touching how he dotes on me, I really think I could do anything with him, anything at all.'

She never spoke of Polly. At first I supposed that the reason why she liked to see so much of me was that I was associated in her mind with Polly, and that sooner or later she would unburden herself to me, or even try and use me as go-between in a reconciliation. I soon realized, however, that Polly and Boy were dead to her; she had no further use for them since Boy could never be her lover again and Polly could never now, it seemed, do her credit in the eyes of the world; she simply dismissed them from her thoughts. Her visits to me were partly the outcome of loneliness and partly due to the fact that I was a convenient half-way house between London and Hampton and that she could use me as restaurant, cloakroom and telephone booth when in Oxford.

She was horribly lonely, you could see that. She filled Hampton every week-end with important people, with smart people, even just with people, but, although so great is the English predilection for country life, she generally managed to get these visits extended from Friday to Tuesday, even so, she was left with two empty days in the middle of the week. She went less and less to London. She had always preferred Hampton, where she reigned alone, to London where she faced a certain degree of competition, and life there without Polly to entertain for and without Boy to help her plot the social game had evidently become meaningless and dull.

CHAPTER III

IT was no doubt the dullness of her life which now deflected her thoughts towards Cedric Hampton, Lord Montdore's heir. They still knew nothing about him beyond the mere fact of his existence, which had hitherto been regarded as extremely superfluous since but for him the whole of 'all this', including Hampton, would have gone to Polly, and, although the other things she had been going to inherit were worth more money, it was Hampton they all loved so much. I have never made out his exact relationship to Lord Montdore, but I know that when Linda and I used to 'look him up' to see if he was the right age for us to marry it always took ages to find him, breathing heavily over the peerage, pointing, and going back and back.

  . . . . . . having had issue,

 ● Henry, b. 1875, who m. Dora, dau. of Stanley Honks Esq. of Annapolis, Nova Scotia, and d. 1913 leaving issue,

 ● Cedric, heir pres., b. 1907.

Just the right age, but what of Nova Scotia? An atlas, hastily consulted, showed it to be horribly marine. 'A transatlantic Isle of Wight' as Linda put it. 'No thanks.' Sea breezes, in so far as they are good for the complexion, were regarded by us as a means and not an end, for at that time it was our idea to live in capital cities and go to the Opera alight with diamonds, 'Who is that lovely woman?' and Nova Scotia was clearly not a suitable venue for such doings. It never seemed to occur to us that Cedric could perhaps have been transplanted from his native heath to Paris, London or Rome. Colonial, we thought, ignorantly. It ruled him out. I believe Lady Montdore knew very little more about him than we did. She had never felt interest or curiosity towards those unsuitable people in Canada, they were one of the unpleasant things of life and she preferred to ignore them. Now, however, left alone with an 'all this' which would one day, and one day fairly soon by the look of Lord Montdore, be Cedric's, she thought and spoke of him continually, and presently had the idea that it would amuse her to see him.

Of course, no sooner had she conceived this idea than she wanted him to be there the very next minute, and was infuriated by the delays that ensued. For Cedric could not be found.

I was kept informed of every stage in the search for him, as Lady Montdore could now think of nothing else.

'That idiotic woman has changed her address,' she told me. 'Montdore's lawyer has had the most terrible time getting in touch with her at all. Now fancy moving, in Canada. You'd think one place there would be exactly the same as another, wouldn't you? Sheer waste of money, you'd think. Well, they've found her at last, and now it seems that Cedric isn't with her at all, but somewhere in Europe, very odd of him not to have called on us in that case, so now, of course, there'll be more delays. Oh, dear, people are too inconsiderate—it's nothing but self, self, self, nowadays, nothing——!'

In the end Cedric was traced to Paris ('Simply extraordinary,' she said. 'Whatever could a Canadian be doing in Paris? I don't quite like it.') and an invitation to Hampton was given and accepted.

'He comes next Tuesday, for a fortnight. I wrote out the dates very carefully indeed, I always do when it is a question of a country-house visit, then there is no awkwardness about the length of it, people know exactly when they are expected to leave. If we like him he can come again, now we know that he lives in Paris, such an easy journey. But what do you suppose he is doing there, dear, I hope he's not an artist. Well, if he is we shall simply have to get him out of it—he must learn to behave suitably, now. We are sending to Dover for him, so that he'll arrive just in time for dinner. Montdore and I have decided not to dress that evening, as most likely he has no evening clothes, and one doesn't wish to make him feel shy at the very beginning of his visit, poor boy.'

This seemed most unlike Lady Montdore, who usually loved making people feel shy; it was well known to be one of her favourite diversions. No doubt Cedric was to be her new toy, and until such time as, inevitably I felt, just as Norma felt about Mrs. Heathery, disillusionment set in, nothing was to be too good for him, and no line of conduct too much calculated to charm him.

I began to think a great deal about Cedric, it was such an interesting situation and I longed to know how he would take it, this young man from the West, suddenly confronted with aristocratic England in full decadence, the cardboard earl, with his nobility of look and manner, the huge luxurious houses, the terrifying servants, the atmosphere of bottomless wealth. I remembered how exaggerated it had all seemed to me as a child, and supposed that he would see it with very much the same eyes and find it equally overpowering.

I thought, however, he might feel at home with Lady Montdore, especially as she desired to please, there was something spontaneous and almost childlike about her which could accord with a transatlantic outlook. It was the only hope, otherwise, and if he were at all timid, I thought, he would find himself submerged. Words dimly associated with Canada kept on occurring to me, the word lumber, the word shack, staking a claim (Uncle Matthew had once staked a claim, I knew, in Ontario in his wild young poker-playing days, with Harry Oakes). How I wished I could be present at Hampton when this lumber-jack arrived to stake his claim to that shack. Hardly had I formed the wish than it was granted, Lady Montdore ringing up to ask if I would go over for the night, she thought it would make things easier to have another young person there when Cedric arrived.

This was a wonderful reward, as I duly remarked to Alfred, for having been a lady-in-waiting.

Alfred said, 'If you have been putting yourself out all this time with a reward in view, I don't mind at all. I objected because I thought you were drifting along in the wake of that old woman merely from a lazy good-nature and with no particular motive. That is what I found degrading. Of course, if you were working for a wage, it is quite a different matter, so long, of course,' he said, with a disapproving look, 'as the wage seems to you worth while.'

It did.

The Montdores sent a motor car to Oxford for me. When I arrived at Hampton I was taken straight upstairs to my room, where I had a bath and changed, according to instructions brought me by Lady Montdore's maid, into a day dress. I had not spent a night at Hampton since my marriage. Knowing that Alfred would not want to go, I had always refused Lady Montdore's invitations, but my bedroom there was still deeply familiar to me. I knew every inch of it by heart. Nothing in it ever changed, the very books between their mahogany book-ends were the same collection that I had known and read there now for twelve years, or more than half my life: novels by Robert Hitchens and W. J. Locke, *Napoleon, The Last Phase* by Lord Rosebery, *The House of Mirth* by Edith Wharton, Hare's *Two Noble Lives*, *Dracula*, and a book on dog management. In front of them on a mahogany tallboy was a Japanese bronze tea-kettle with embossed water-lilies. On the walls, besides the two country-house old masters despised of Davey, were a Morland print, 'The Higglers preparing for Market', a Richmond water-colour of the 'old lord' in a kilt and an oil painting of Toledo either by Boy or Lady Montdore. Their styles were indistinguishable. It was in their early manner, and had probably hung there for twenty years. This room had a womb-like quality in my mind, partly because it was so red and warm and velvety and enclosed, and partly because of the terror with which I always used to be assailed by the idea of leaving it and venturing downstairs. This evening as I dressed I thought how lovely it was to be grown-up, a married woman, and no longer frightened of people. Of Lord Merlin a little, of the Warden of Wadham perhaps, but these were not panicky, indiscriminate social terrors, they could rather be classed as wholesome awe inspired by gifted elders.

When I was ready I went down to the Long Gallery, where Lord and Lady Montdore were sitting in their usual chairs one each side of the chimney-piece, but not at all in their usual frame of mind. They were both, and especially Lady Montdore, in a twitter of nerves, and looked up quite startled when I came into the room, relaxing again when they saw that it was only me. I thought that from the point of view of a stranger, a backwoodsman from the American continent, they struck exactly the right note. Lord Montdore, in an informal green velvet smoking-jacket, was impressive with his white hair and carved unchanging face, while Lady Montdore's very dowdiness was an indication that she was too grand to bother about clothes, and this too would surely impress. She wore printed black-and-white crêpe-de-chine, her only jewels the enormous half-hoop rings which flashed from her strong old woman's fingers, and sat as she always did, her knees well apart, her feet in their large buckled shoes firmly planted on the ground, her hands folded in her lap.

'We lit this little fire,' she said, 'thinking that he may feel cold after the journey.' It was unusual for her to refer to any arrangement in her house, people being expected to like what they found there, or else to lump it. 'Do you think we shall hear the motor when it comes up the drive? We generally can if the wind is in the west.'

'I expect I shall,' I said, tactlessly. 'I hear everything.'

'Oh, we're not stone deaf ourselves. Show Fanny what you have got for Cedric, Montdore.'

He held out a little book in green morocco, Gray's Poems.

'If you look at the fly-leaf,' he said, 'you will see that it was given to my grandfather by the late Lord Palmerston the day that Cedric's grandfather was born. They evidently happened to be dining together. We think that it should please him.'

I did so hope it would. I suddenly felt very sorry for these two old people, and longed for Cedric's visit to be a success and cheer them up.

'Canadians,' he went on, 'should know all about the poet Gray, because General Wolfe, at the taking of Quebec——'

There were footsteps now in the drawing-room, so we had not heard the motor after all. Lord and Lady Montdore got up and stood together in front of the fireplace as the butler opened the door and announced 'Mr. Cedric Hampton'.

A glitter of blue and gold crossed the parquet, and a human dragon-fly was kneeling on the fur rug in front of the Montdores, one long white hand extended towards each. He was a tall, thin young man, supple as a girl, dressed in rather a bright blue suit; his hair was the gold of a brass bed-knob, and his insect appearance came from the fact that the upper part of the face was concealed by blue goggles set in gold rims quite an inch thick.

He was flashing a smile of unearthly perfection, relaxed and happy he knelt there bestowing this smile upon each Montdore in turn.

'Don't speak,' he said, 'just for a moment. Just let me go on looking at you—wonderful, wonderful people!'

I could see at once that Lady Montdore was very highly gratified. She beamed with pleasure. Lord Montdore gave her a hasty glance to see how she was taking it, and when he saw that beaming was the note, he beamed too.

'Welcome,' she said, 'to Hampton.'

'The beauty,' Cedric went on, floating jointlessly to his feet. 'I can only say that I am drunk with it. England, so much more beautiful than I had imagined (I have never had very good accounts of England, somehow), this house, so romantic, such a repository of treasures, and above all, you—the two most beautiful people I have ever seen!'

He spoke with rather a curious accent, neither French nor Canadian, but peculiar to himself, in which every syllable received rather more emphasis than is given by the ordinary Englishman. Also he spoke, as it were, through his smile, which would fade a little, then flash out again, but which never altogether left his face.

'Won't you take off your spectacles?' said Lady Montdore. 'I should like to see your eyes.'

'Later, dear Lady Montdore, later. When my dreadful, paralysing shyness (a disease with me) has quite worn off. They give me confidence, you see, when I am dreadfully nervous, just as a mask would. In a mask one can face anything—I should like my life to be a perpetual *bal masqué*, Lady Montdore, don't you agree? I long to know who the Man in the Iron Mask was, don't you, Lord Montdore? Do you remember when Louis XVIII first saw the Duchesse d'Angoulême after the Restoration? Before saying anything else you know—wasn't it all awful or anything, he asked if poor Louis XVI had ever told her who the Man in the Iron Mask was? I love Louis XVIII for that—so like *One*.'

Lady Montdore indicated me. 'This is our cousin—and a distant relation of yours, Cedric—Fanny Wincham.'

He took my hand and looked long into my face, saying, 'I am enchanted to meet you' as if he really was. He turned again to the Montdores, and said, 'I am so happy to be here'.

'My dear boy, we are so happy to have you. You should have come before—we had no idea—we thought you were always in Nova Scotia, you see.'

Cedric was gazing at the big French map table. 'Riesener,' he said, 'this is a very strange thing, Lady Montdore, and you will hardly believe it, but where I live in France we have its pair—is that not a coincidence. Only this morning, at Chèvres, I was leaning upon that very table.'

'What is Chèvres?'

'Chèvres—Fontaine, where I live, in the Seine et Oise.'

'But it must be quite a large house,' said Lady Montdore, 'if that table is in it?'

'A little larger, in every dimension, than the central block at Versailles, and with much more water. At Versailles there only remain seven hundred *bouches* (how is *bouche* in English? Jets?). At Chèvres we have one thousand five hundred, and they play all the time.'

Dinner was announced. As we moved towards the dining-room Cedric stopped to examine various objects, touched them lovingly, and murmured:

'Weisweiller—Boulle—Caffieri—Jacob. How is it you come to have these marvels, Lord Montdore, such important pieces?'

'My great-grandfather (your great-great-grandfather), who was himself half French, collected it all his life. Some of it he bought during the sales of royal furniture after the Revolution and some came to him through his mother's family, the Montdores.'

'And the boiseries!' said Cedric, 'first quality Louis XV. There is nothing to equal this at Chèvres, it's like jewellery when it is so fine.'

We were now in the little dining-room.

'He brought them over too, and built the house round them.' Lord Montdore was evidently much pleased by Cedric's enthusiasm, he loved French furniture himself but seldom found anybody in England to share his taste.

'Porcelain with Marie-Antoinette's cypher, delightful. At Chèvres we have the Meisson service she brought with her from Vienna. We have many relics of Marie-Antoinette, poor dear, at Chèvres.'

'Who lives there?' asked Lady Montdore.

'I do,' he replied carelessly, 'when I wish to be in the country. In Paris I have an apartment of all beauty, *One's* idea of heaven.' Cedric made great use of the word one, which he pronounced with peculiar emphasis. Lady Montdore had always been a one for one, but she said it quite differently, 'w'n'. 'The first floor of the Hotel Pomponne—you see that? Purest Louis XIV. Tiny, you know, but all one needs, that is to say a bedroom and a bed-ballroom. You must come and stay with me there, dear Lady Montdore, you will live in my bedroom, which has comfort, and I in the bed-ballroom. Promise me that you will come.'

'We shall have to see. Personally, I have never been very fond of France, the people are so frivolous, I greatly prefer the Germans.'

'Germans!' said Cedric earnestly, leaning across the table and gazing at her through his goggles. 'The frivolity of the Germans terrifies even *One*. I have a German friend in Paris and a more frivolous creature, Lady Montdore, does not exist. This frivolity has caused me many a heartache, I must tell you.'

'I hope you will make some suitable English friends now, Cedric.'

'Yes, yes, that is what I long for. But please can my chief English friend be you, dear dearest Lady Montdore?'

'I think you should call us Aunt Sonia and Uncle Montdore.'

'May I really? How charming you are to me, how happy I am to be here—you seem, Aunt Sonia, to shower happiness around you.'

'Yes, I do. I live for others, I suppose that's why. The sad thing is that people have not always appreciated it, they are so selfish themselves.'

'Oh, yes, aren't they selfish? I too have been victim to the selfishness of people all my life. This German friend I mentioned just now, his selfishness passes comprehension. How one does suffer!'

'It's a he, is it?' Lady Montdore seemed glad of this.

'A boy called Klugg. I hope to forget all about him while I am here. Now, Lady Montdore—dearest Aunt Sonia—after dinner I want you to do me a great great favour. Will you put on your jewels so that I can see you sparkling in them? I do so long for that.'

'Really, my dear boy, they are down in the strong-room. I don't think they've been cleaned for ages.'

'Oh, don't say no, don't shake your head! Ever since I set eyes on you I have been thinking of nothing else, you must look so truly glorious in them. Mrs. Wincham (you are Mrs. I hope, aren't you, yes yes, I can tell that you are not a spinster), when did you last see Aunt Sonia laden with jewels?'

'It was at the ball for——' I stopped awkwardly, jibbing at the name, which was never now mentioned, but Cedric saved me from embarrassment by exclaiming:

'A ball! Aunt Sonia, how I would love to see you at a ball, I can so well imagine you at all the great English functions, coronations, Lords, balls, Ascot, Henley. What is Henley? No matter—and I can see you, above all, in India, riding on your elephant like a goddess. How they must have worshipped you there.'

'Well, you know, they did,' said Lady Montdore, delighted, 'they really worshipped us, it was quite touching. And of course, we deserved it, we did a very great deal for them, I think I may say we put India on the map. Hardly any of one's friends in England had ever even heard of India before we went there, you know.'

'I'm sure. What a wonderful and fascinating life you lead, Aunt Sonia. Did you keep a journal when you were in the East? Oh! please say yes, I would so love to read it.'

This was a very lucky shot. They had indeed filled a huge folio, whose morocco label, surmounted by an earl's coronet, announced 'Pages from our Indian Diary. M. and S.M.'

'It's really a sort of scrap-book,' Lord Montdore said, 'accounts of our journeys up-country, photographs, sketches by Sonia and our brother-in—that is to say a brother-in-law we had then, letters of appreciation from rajahs——'

'And Indian poetry translated by Montdore—"Prayer of a Widow before Suttee", "Death of an old Mahout", and so on, touching, it makes you cry.'

'Oh, I must read it all, every word, I can hardly wait.'

Lady Montdore was radiant. How many and many a time had she led her guests to 'Pages from Our Indian Diary', like horses to water, and watched them straying off after one half-hearted sip. Never before, I guess, had anybody so eagerly demanded to read it.

'Now you must tell us about your life, my dear boy,' said Lady Montdore. 'When did you leave Canada? Your home is in Nova Scotia, is it not?'

'I lived there until I was eighteen.'

'Montdore and I have never been in Canada—the States, of course, we spent a month once in New York and Washington and we saw Niagara Falls, but then we were obliged to come home, I only wish we could have gone on, they were quite touchingly anxious to have us, but Montdore and I cannot always do as we should like, we have our duties. Of course, that was a long time ago, twenty-five years I should think, but I daresay Nova Scotia doesn't alter much?'

'I am very very happy to say that kindly Nature has allowed a great sea-fog of oblivion to rise between me and Nova Scotia so that I hardly remember one single thing about it.'

'What a strange boy you are,' she said indulgently, but she was very well suited by the fact of the sea-fog, since the last thing she wanted would have been long-winded reminiscences of Cedric's family life in Canada; it was all no doubt much better forgotten, and especially the fact that Cedric had a mother. 'So you came to Europe when you were eighteen?'

'Paris. Yes, I was sent to Paris by my guardian, a banker, to learn some horrid sort of job, I quite forget what, as I never had to go near it. It is not necessary to have jobs in Paris, one's friends are so very very kind.'

'Really, how funny. I always thought the French were so mean.'

'Certainly not to *One*. My needs are simple, admittedly, but such as they are they have all been satisfied over and over again.'

'What are your needs?'

'I need a very great deal of beauty round me, beautiful objects wherever I look and beautiful people who see the point of *One*. And speaking of beautiful people, Aunt Sonia, after dinner the jewels? Don't, don't, please say no!'

'Very well, then,' she said, 'but now, Cedric, won't you take off your glasses?'

'Perhaps I could. Yes, I really think the last vestige of my shyness has gone.'

He took them off, and the eyes which were now disclosed, blinking in the light, were the eyes of Polly, large, blue, and rather blank. They quite startled me, but I do not think the Montdores were specially struck by the resemblance, though Lady Montdore said:

'Anybody can tell that you are a Hampton, Cedric. Please never let's see those horrid spectacles again.'

'My goggles? Specially designed by Van Cleef for me?'

'I hate spectacles,' said Lady Montdore firmly.

Lady Montdore's maid was now sent for, given the key of the safe from Lord Montdore's key-ring and told to bring up all the jewel cases. When dinner was over and we got back to the Long Gallery, leaving Lord Montdore to his port, but accompanied by Cedric, who was evidently unaware of the English custom which keeps the men in the dining-room after dinner and who followed Lady Montdore like a dog, we found the map-table covered with blue velvet trays each of which contained a parure of large and beautiful jewels. Cedric gave a cry of happiness and got down to work at once.

'In the first place, dear Aunt Sonia,' he said, this dress won't do. Let me see—ah, yes'—he took a piece of red brocade off the piano and draped her in it very cleverly, pinning it in place on one shoulder with a huge diamond brooch. 'Have you some maquillage in this bag, dear? And a comb?'

Lady Montdore rummaged about and produced a cheap lipstick and a small green comb with a tooth out.

'Naughty, naughty you,' he said, carefully painting her face, 'it cakes! Never mind, that will do for now. Not pulling your hair, am I? We've got to show the bone structure, so beautiful on you. I think you'll have to find a new coiffeur, Aunt Sonia—we'll see about that— anyway, it must go up—up—like this. Do you realize what a difference that makes? Now, Mrs. Wincham, will you please put out the top lights for me, and bring the lamp from that bureau over here. Thank you.'

He placed the lamp on the floor at Lady Montdore's feet and began to hang her with diamonds, so that the brocade was covered with them to her waist, finally poising the crown of pink diamonds on the top of her head.

'Now,' he said. 'Look!' and he led her to a looking-glass on the wall. She was entranced by the effect, which was indeed very splendid.

'My turn,' he said.

Although Lady Montdore seemed to be almost solid with diamonds the cases on the table still held many huge jewels. He took off his coat, his collar and tie, pulled open his shirt and clasped a great necklace of diamonds and sapphires round his neck, wound up another piece of silk into a turban, stuck a diamond feather in it and put it on his head. He went on talking all the time.

'You really must pat your face more, Aunt Sonia.'

'Pat?'

'With nourishing creams. I'll show you. Such a wonderful face, but uncultivated, neglected and starved. We must feed it up, exercise it and look after it better from now on. You'll soon see what a lot can be done. Twice a week you must sleep in a mask.'

'A mask?'

'Yes, back to masks, but this time I mean the sort you paint on at night. It goes quite hard, so that you look like the Commandeur in *Don Juan*, and in the morning you can't smile, not a glimmer, so you mustn't telephone until you've removed it with the remover, because you know how if you telephone smilelessly you sound cross, and if it happened to be *One* at the other end, *One* couldn't bear that.'

'Oh, my dear boy, I don't know about this mask. What would Griffith say?'

'If Griffith is your maid she won't notice a thing, they never do. We shall notice, though, your great new beauty. Those cruel lines!'

They were absorbed in each other and themselves, and when Lord

Montdore came in from the dining-room they did not even notice. He sat for a while in his usual attitude, the fingers of both hands pressed together, looking into the fire, and very soon crept off to bed. In the months which had passed since Polly's marriage he had turned into an old man, he was smaller, his clothes hung sadly on him, his voice quavered and complained. Before he went he gave the little book of poems to Cedric, who took it with a charming show of appreciation and looked at it until Lord Montdore was out of sight, when he quickly turned back to the jewels.

I was pregnant at this time and began to feel sleepy very soon after dinner. I had a look at the picture papers and then followed Lord Montdore's example.

'Good night,' I said, making for the door. They hardly bothered to answer. They were now standing each in front of a looking-glass, a lamp at their feet, happily gazing at their own images.

'Do you think it is better like that?' one would say.

'Much better,' the other would reply, without looking.

From time to time they exchanged a jewel ('Give me the rubies, dear boy.' 'May I have the emeralds if you've finished with them?') and he was now wearing the pink tiara, jewels lay all around them, tumbled on to the chairs and tables, even on the floor.

'I have a confession to make to you, Cedric,' she said, as I was leaving the room. 'I really rather like amethysts.'

'Oh, but I love amethysts,' he replied, 'so long as they are nice large dark stones set in diamonds. They suit *One* so well.'

The next morning when I went to Lady Montdore's room to say good-bye I found Cedric, in a pale mauve silk dressing-gown, sitting on her bed. They were both rubbing cream into their faces out of a large pink pot, it smelt delicious, and certainly belonged to him.

'And after that,' he was saying, 'until the end of her life (she only died just the other day), she wore a thick black veil.'

'And what did he do?'

'He left cards on all Paris, on which he had written "*mille regrets*".'

CHAPTER IV

FROM the moment that the Montdores first set eyes on Cedric there was no more question of his having come to Hampton for a fortnight, he was obviously there for good and all. They both took him to their hearts and loved him, almost at once, better than they had loved Polly for years, ever since she was a small child; the tremendous vacuum created by her departure was happily filled again, and filled by somebody who was able to give more than Polly had ever given in the way of companionship. Cedric could talk intelligently to Lord Montdore about the objects of art at Hampton. He knew an enormous amount about such things, though in the ordinary sense of the word he was uneducated, ill-read, incapable of the simplest calculation, and curiously ignorant of many quite elementary subjects. He was one of those people who take in the world through eye and ear, his intellect was probably worth very little, but his love of beauty was genuine. The librarian at Hampton was astounded at his bibliographical knowledge. It seemed, for instance, that he could tell at a glance whom a book had been bound for and by whom, and he said that Cedric knew much more than he did himself about eighteenth-century French editions. Lord Montdore had seldom seen his own cherished belongings so intelligently appreciated, and it was a great pleasure to him to spend hours with Cedric going over them. He had doted on Polly; she had been the apple of his eye in theory, but in practice she had never been in any respect a companion to him.

As for Lady Montdore, she became transformed with happiness during the months that followed, transformed, too, in other ways, Cedric taking her appearance in hand with extraordinary results. Just as Boy (it was the hold he had over her) had filled her days with society and painting, Cedric filled them with the pursuit of her own beauty, and to such an egotist this was a more satisfactory hobby. Facial operations, slimming cures, exercises, massage, diet, make-up, new clothes, jewels reset, a blue rinse for her grey hair, pink bows and diamond daisies in the blue curls; it kept her very busy. I saw her less and less, but each time I did she looked more unnaturally modish. Her movements, formerly so ponderous, became smart, spry and bird-like, she never sat now with her two legs planted on the ground, but threw one over the other, legs which, daily massaged and steamed, gradually lost their flesh and became little more than bone. Her face was lifted, plucked and trimmed, and looked as tidy as Mrs. Chaddesley Corbett's, and she learnt to flash a smile brilliant as Cedric's own.

'I make her say "brush" before she comes into a room,' he told me. 'It's a thing I got out of an old book on deportment and it fixes at once this very gay smile on one's face. Somebody ought to tell Lord Alconleigh about it.'

Since she had never hitherto made the smallest effort to appear younger than she was, but had remained fundamentally Edwardian-looking, as though conscious of her own superiority to the little smart ephemeral types, the Chaddesley Corbetts and so on, Cedric's production of her was revolutionary. In my opinion it was not successful for she made the sacrifice of a grand and characteristic appearance without really gaining in prettiness, but no doubt the effort which it involved made her perfectly happy.

Cedric and I became great friends and he visited me constantly in Oxford, just as Lady Montdore used to before she became so busy, and I must say that I greatly preferred his company to hers. During the later stages of my pregnancy, and after the baby was born, he would come and sit with me for hours on end, and I felt completely at my ease with him; I could go on with my sewing, or mending, without bothering about what I looked like, exactly as if he were one of my Radlett cousins. He was kind and thoughtful and affectionate, like a charming woman friend; better, because our friendship was marred by no tinge of jealousy.

Later on, when I had got my figure back after the baby, I began to dress and make myself up with a view to gaining Cedric's approbation, but I soon found that, with the means at my disposal, it was not much use. He knew too much about women and their accessories to be impressed by anything I could manage. For instance, if with a great effort I changed into silk stockings when I expected him, he could see at once that they were Elliston, 5s. 11d., all I could afford, and it really seemed more sensible to stick to lisle. Indeed, he once said to me:

'You know, Fanny, it doesn't matter a bit that you're not able to dress up in expensive clothes, there'd be no point in it anyway. You are like the Royal Family, my darling. Whatever you wear you look exactly the same, just as they do.'

I was not very much pleased, but I knew that he was right. I could never look fashionable, even if I tried as hard as Lady Montdore, with my heather-hair and round salubrious face.

I remember that my mother, during one of her rare visits to England, brought me a little jacket in scarlet cloth from Schiaparelli. It seemed to me quite plain and uninteresting except for the label in its lining, and I longed to put this on the outside so that people would know where it came from. I was wearing it, instead of a cardigan, in my house when Cedric happened to call, and the first thing he said was:

'Aha! So now we dress at Schiaparelli, I see! Whatever next?'

'Cedric! How can you tell?'

'My dear, one can always tell. Things have a signature, if you use your eyes, and mine seem to be trained over a greater range of objects than yours, Schiaparelli—Reboux—Fabergé—Violet le Duc—I can tell at a glance, literally a glance. So your wicked mother the Bolter has been here since last I saw you?'

'Might I not have bought it for myself?'

'No no, my love, you are saving up to educate your twelve brilliant sons, how could you possibly afford twenty-five pounds for a little jacket?'

'Don't tell me!' I said. 'Twenty-five pounds for this?'

'Quite that, I should guess.'

'Simply silly. Why, I could have made it myself.'

'But could you? And if you had would I have come into the room and said Schiaparelli?'

'There's only a yard of stuff in it, worth a pound, if that,' I went on, horrified by the waste of money.

'And how many yards of canvas in a Fragonard? And how much do planks of wood cost, or the skin of a darling goat before they are turned into commodes and morocco? Art is more than yards, just as *One* is more than flesh and bones. By the way, I must warn you that Sonia will be here in a minute, in search of strong tea. I took the liberty of having a word with Mrs. Heathery, the love of whose life I am, on my way up, and I also brought some scones from the Cadena which I deposited with her.'

'What is Lady Montdore doing now?' I said, beginning to tidy up the room.

'Now, this very minute? She is at Parkers, buying a birthday present for me. It is to be a great surprise, but I went to Parkers and prepared the ground and I shall be greatly surprised if the great surprise is not *Ackerman's Repository.*'

'I thought you turned up your nose at English furniture?' I said.

'Less and less. Provincial but charming is now my attitude and *Ackerman's Repository* is such an amusing book, I saw a copy the other day when Sonia and I went over to Lord Merlin's, and I long to possess it. I expect it will be all right. Sonia loves to give me these large presents, impossible to carry about; she thinks they anchor me to Hampton. I don't blame her, her life there must have been too dull for words, without me.'

'But are you anchored?' I said. 'It always seems to me that the place where you really belong is Paris—I can't imagine you staying here for ever.'

'I can't imagine it either, but the fact is, my darling, that the news from Paris is not too good. I told you, didn't I, that I left my German friend Klugg to look after my apartment and keep it warm for me? Now what do I hear? The baron came last week with a *camion* and took all the furniture, every stick, leaving poor Klugg to sleep on bare boards. I daresay he doesn't notice, he is always quite drunk by bedtime, but for waking up it can't be very nice, and meanwhile I am mourning my commodes. Louis XV—a pair—such *marqueterie*, such bronzes, really important pieces, *objets de musée*—well, often have I told you about them. Gone! The baron, during one fatal afternoon, took everything. Bitter work!'

'What baron?' I asked.

I knew all about Klugg, how hideous and drunken and brutal and German and unlettered he was, so that Cedric never could explain why he put up with his vagaries for a single moment, but the baron was a new figure to me. Cedric was evasive however. He was better than anybody I have ever known at not answering questions if he did not want to.

'Just another friend. The first night I was in Paris I went to the Opera, and I don't mind telling you, my darling, that all eyes were upon me, in my box, the poor artistes might just as well not have been on the stage at all. Well, one of the eyes belonged to the baron.'

'Two of the eyes, you mean,' I said.

'No dear, one. He wears a patch to make himself look sinister and fascinating. Nobody knows how much I hate barons, I feel exactly like King John whenever I think of them.'

'But Cedric, I don't understand. How could he take your furniture away?'

'How could he? How, indeed? Alas, he has, and that is that. My Savonnerie, my Sèvres, my sanguines, all my treasures gone and I confess I am very low about it, because, although they cannot compare in quality with what I see every day round me at Hampton, one does so love one's own things which one has bought and chosen oneself. I must say the Boulle at Hampton is the best I have ever seen—even at Chèvres we had no Boulle like that. Sensational. Have you been over since we began to clean the bronzes? Oh, you must come. I have taught my friend Archie how to unscrew the bits, scrub them with ammonia, and pour boiling water on them from a kettle so that they dry at once with no moisture left to turn them green. He does it all all day, and when he has finished it glitters like the cave of Aladdin.'

This Archie was a nice, handsome boy, a lorry-driver, whom Cedric had found with his lorry broken down near the gates of Hampton.

'For your ear alone, my darling, it was a stroke of thunder when I saw him. What one does so love about love is the time before they find out what *One* is like.'

'And it's also very nice,' I said, disloyally, 'before *One* finds out what they are like.'

Archie had now left his lorry for ever, and gone to live at Hampton to do odd jobs. Lady Montdore was enthusiastic about him.

'So willing,' she would say, 'so clever of Cedric to think of having him. Cedric always does such original things.'

Cedric went on, 'But I suppose you would think it more hideous than ever, Fanny. I know that you like a room to sparkle with freshness, whereas I like it to glitter with richness. That is where we differ at present, but you'll change. Your taste is really good, and it is bound to mature one day.'

It was true that my taste at this time, like that of the other young people I knew who cared about their houses, favoured pickled or painted furniture with a great deal of white, and upholstery in pale cheerful colours. French furniture with its finely chiselled ormolu (what Cedric called bronzes), its severe lines and perfect proportions was far above my head in those days, while Louis XIV needlework, of which there was a great amount at Hampton, seemed dark and stuffy. I frankly preferred a cheerful chintz.

Cedric's word with Mrs. Heathery had excellent results, and even Lady Montdore showed no signs of despising the tea which arrived at the same time as she did. In any case, now that she was happy again, she was much more good-natured about the attempts of the humble, such as myself, to regale her.

Her appearance still gave me quite a jump, though by now I really should have been getting accustomed to her flashing smile, her supple movements, and the pale blue curls, a little sparse upon the head, not unattractively so, but like a baby's curls. Today she was hatless, and wore a tartan ribbon to keep her hair in place. She was dressed in a plain but beautifully made grey coat and skirt, and as she came into the room, which was full of sun, she took her coat off with a curious, swift, double-jointed movement, revealing a piqué blouse and a positively girlish waist-line. It was warm spring weather just then, and I knew that she and Cedric did a lot of sun-bathing in a summer-house specially designed by him, as a result of which her skin had gone rather a horrid yellow, and looked as if it had to be soaked in oil to prevent it from falling into a thousand tiny cracks. Her nails were varnished dark red, and this was an improvement, since formerly they had been furrowed and not always quite clean. The old-fashioned hoops of enormous diamonds set in gold which used so stiffly to encircle her stiff fingers were replaced by square-cut diamonds in clusters of cabochon emeralds and rubies, her diamond ear-rings too had been reset, in the shape of cockle shells, and more large diamonds sparkled in a fashionable pair of clips at her throat. The whole thing was stunning.

But although her aspect was so much changed her personality remained the same, and the flashing (brush) smile was followed by the well-known up-and-down look.

'Is that your baby making that horrid noise, Fanny?'

'Yes. He never cries as a rule but his teeth are upsetting him.'

'Poor thing,' said Cedric, 'couldn't he go to the dentist?'

'Well, I've got your birthday present, Cedric. It can't be a surprise though, because it's all over the floor of the motor. They seemed to think, at Parker's, that you would like it—a book called *Ackerman's Suppository* or something.'

'Not *Ackerman's Suppository*—not really!' said Cedric, clasping his hands under his chin in a very characteristic gesture. 'How kind you are to me—how could you have guessed? Where did you find it? But, dearest, it's bad about the surprise. Birthday presents really ought to be surprises. I can't get Sonia to enter into the true spirit of birthdays, Fanny, what can *One* do about it?'

I thought *One* had done pretty well. Lady Montdore was famous for never giving presents at all, either for birthdays or at Christmas, and had never even relaxed this rule in favour of the adored Polly, though Lord Montdore used to make up for that by giving her several. But she showered presents, and valuable presents too, on Cedric, snatching at the smallest excuse to do so, and I quite saw that with somebody so intensely appreciative this must be a great pleasure.

'But I have got a surprise for you, as well as the books, something I bought in London,' she said, looking at him fondly.

'No!' said Cedric. I had the feeling he knew all about that, too. 'I shan't have one moment's peace until I've wormed it out of you—how I wish you hadn't told me.'

'You've only got to wait until tomorrow.'

'Well, I warn you I shall wake you up for it at six. Now finish your tea, dear, and come, we ought to be getting back, I'm in a little bit of a fuss to see what Archie has been up to with all those bronzes. He's doing the Boulle today and I have had a horrid idea—suppose he has reassembled it into a lorry by mistake? What would dearest Uncle Montdore say if he suddenly came upon a huge Boulle lorry in the middle of the Long Gallery?'

No doubt, I thought, but that both Lord and Lady Montdore would happily have got into it and been taken for a ride by Cedric. He had completely mesmerized them, and nothing that he could do ever seemed otherwise to them than perfection.

CHAPTER V

CEDRIC'S advent at Hampton naturally created quite a stir in the world outside. London society was not at first given the chance to form an opinion on him, because this was the year following the Financial Crisis—in fact, Cedric and the Crisis had arrived at about the same time, and Lady Montdore, though herself unaffected by it, thought that as there was no entertaining in London it was hardly worth while to keep Montdore House open. She had it shrouded in dust-sheets except for two rooms where Lord Montdore could put up if he wanted to go to the House of Lords.

Lady Montdore and Cedric never stayed there, they sometimes went to London, but only for the day. She no longer invited large house parties to Hampton. She said people could talk about nothing but money any more and it was too boring, but I thought there was another reason, and that she really wanted to keep Cedric to herself.

The county, however, hummed and buzzed with Cedric, and little else was talked of. I need hardly say that Uncle Matthew, after one look, found that the word sewer had become obsolete and inadequate. Scowling, growling, flashing of eyes and grinding of teeth, to a degree hitherto reserved for Boy Dougdale, were intensified a hundredfold at the mere thought of Cedric, and accompanied by swelling veins and apoplectic noises. The drawers at Alconleigh were emptied of the yellowing slips of paper on which my uncle's hates had mouldered all these years, and each now contained a clean new slip with the name, carefully printed in black ink, Cedric Hampton. There was a terrible scene at Oxford platform one day. Cedric went to the bookstall to buy *Vogue*, having mislaid his own copy. Uncle Matthew, who was waiting there for a train, happened to notice that the seams of his coat were piped in a contrasting shade. This was too much for his self-control. He fell upon Cedric and began to shake him like a rat; just then, very fortunately, the train came in, whereupon my uncle, who suffered terribly from train fever, dropped Cedric and rushed to catch it. 'You'd never think,' as Cedric said afterwards, 'that buying *Vogue Magazine* could be so dangerous. It was well worth it though, lovely Spring modes.'

The children, however, were in love with Cedric and furious because I would not allow them to meet him in my house, but Aunt Sadie, who seldom took a strong line about anything, had solemnly begged me to keep them apart, and her word with me was law. Besides, from my pinnacle of sophistication as wife and mother, I also considered Cedric unsuitable company for the very young, and when I knew that he was coming to see me I took great care to shooh away any undergraduates who might happen to be sitting about in my drawing-room.

Uncle Matthew and his neighbours seldom agreed on any subject. He despised their opinions, and they in their turn found his violent likes and dislikes quite incomprehensible, taking their cue as a rule from the balanced Boreleys. Over Cedric, however, all were united. Though the Boreleys were not haters in the Uncle Matthew class, they had their own prejudices, things they 'could not stick', foreigners, for example, well-dressed women and the Labour Party. But the thing they could stick least in the world were 'aesthetes—you know—those awful effeminate creatures—pansies'. When, therefore, Lady Montdore, whom anyhow they could not stick much, installed the awful effeminate pansy Cedric at Hampton, and it became borne in upon them that he was henceforth to be their neighbour for ever, quite an important one at that, the future Lord Montdore, hatred really did burgeon in their souls. At the same time they took a morbid interest in every detail of the situation, and these details were supplied to them by Norma, who got her facts, I am ashamed to say, from me. It tickled me so much to make Norma gasp and stretch her eyes with horror that I kept back nothing that might tease her and infuriate the Boreleys.

I soon found out that the most annoying feature of the whole thing to them was the radiant happiness of Lady Montdore. They had all been delighted by Polly's marriage, and even those people who might have been expected whole-heartedly to take Lady Montdore's side over it, such as the parents of pretty young daughters, having said with smug satisfaction, 'Serve her right'. They hated her and were glad to see her downed. Now, it seemed, the few remaining days of this wicked woman, who never invited them to her parties, were being suitably darkened with a sorrow which would surely bring her grey hairs to the grave. The curtain rises for the last act, and the stalls are filled with Boreleys all agog to witness the agony, the dissolution, the muffled drum, the catafalque, the procession to the vault, the lowering to the tomb, the darkness. But what is this? On to the dazzling stage springs Lady Montdore, lithe as a young cat, her grey hairs now a curious shade of blue, with a partner, a terrible creature from Sodom, from Gomorrah, from Paris, and proceeds to dance with him a wild fandango of delight. No wonder they were cross.

On the other hand, I thought the whole thing simply splendid, since I like my fellow-beings to be happy and the new state of affairs at Hampton had so greatly increased the sum of human happiness. An old lady, a selfish old creature admittedly, who deserved nothing at the end but trouble and sickness (but which of us will deserve better?) is suddenly presented with one of life's bonuses, and is rejuvenated, occupied and amused; a charming boy with a great love of beauty and of luxury, a little venal perhaps (but which of us is not if we get the opportunity to be?), whose life had hitherto depended upon the whims of barons, suddenly and respectably acquires two doting parents and a vast heritage of wealth, another bonus; Archie the lorry driver, taken from long cold nights on the road, long oily hours under his lorry, and put to polish ormolu in a warm and scented room; Polly married to the love of her life; Boy married to the greatest beauty of the age, five bonuses, five happy people, and yet the Boreleys were disgusted. They must indeed be against the human race, I thought, so to hate happiness.

I said all this to Davey and he winced a little. 'I wish you needn't go on about Sonia being an old old woman on the brink of the grave,' he said, 'she is barely sixty, you know, only about ten years older than your Aunt Emily.'

'Davey, she's forty years older than I am, it must seem old to me. I bet people forty years older than you are seem old to you, now do admit.'

Davey admitted. He also agreed that it is nice to see people happy, but made the reservation that it is only very nice if you happen to like them, and that although he was, in a way, quite fond of Lady Montdore, he did not happen to like Cedric.

'You don't like Cedric?' I said, amazed. 'How couldn't you, Dave? I absolutely love him.'

He replied that, whereas to an English rosebud like myself Cedric must appear as a being from another, darkly glamorous world, he, Davey, in the course of his own wild cosmopolitan wanderings, before he had met and settled down with Aunt Emily, had known too many Cedrics.

'You are lucky,' I said. 'I couldn't know too many. And if you think I find him darkly glamorous, you've got hold of the wrong end of the stick, my dear Dave. He seems to me like a darling Nanny.'

'Darling Nanny! Polar bear—tiger—puma—something that can never be tamed. They always turn nasty in the end, just you wait Fanny, all this ormolu radiance will soon blacken, and the last state of Sonia will be worse than her first, I prophesy. I've seen this sort of thing too often.'

'I don't believe it. Cedric loves Lady Montdore.'

'Cedric,' said Davey, 'loves Cedric, and furthermore he comes from the jungle, and just as soon as it suits him he will tear her to pieces and slink back into the undergrowth—you mark my words.'

'Well,' I said, 'if so, the Boreleys will be pleased.'

Cedric himself now sauntered into the room and Davey prepared to leave. I think after all the horrid things he had just been saying he was afraid of seeming too cordial to him in front of me. It was very difficult not to be cordial to Cedric, he was so disarming.

'I shan't see you again, Fanny,' Davey said, 'until I get back from my cruise.'

'Oh, are you going for a cruise—how delicious—where?' said Cedric.

'In search of a little sun. I give a few lectures on Minoan things and go cheap.'

'I do wish Aunt Emily would go too,' I said, 'it would be so good for her.'

'She'll never move until after Siegfried's death,' said Davey. 'You know what she is.'

When he had gone I said to Cedric:

'What d'you think, he may be able to go and see Polly and Boy in Sicily—wouldn't it be interesting?'

Cedric, of course, was deeply fascinated by anything to do with Polly.

'The absent influence, so boring and so overdone in literature, but I see now that in real life it can eat you with curiosity.'

'When did you last hear from her, Fanny?' he said.

'Oh, months ago, and then it was only a postcard. I'm so delighted about Dave seeing them because he's always so good at telling. We really shall hear how they are getting on, from him.'

'Sonia has still never mentioned her to me,' said Cedric, 'never once.'

'That's because she never thinks of her, then.'

'I'm sure she doesn't. This Polly can't be much of a personality, to have left such a small dent where she used to live?'

'Personality——' I said. 'I don't know. The thing about Polly is her beauty.'

'Describe it.'

'Oh, Cedric, I've described it to you hundreds of times.' It rather amused me to do so, though, because I knew that it teased him.

'Well,' I said, 'as I've often told you before, she is so beautiful that it's difficult to pay much attention to what she is saying, or to make out what she's really like as a person, because all you want to do is just gaze and gaze.'

Cedric looked sulky, as he always did when I talked like this.

'More beautiful than *One*?' he said.

'Very much like you, Cedric.'

'So you say, but I don't find that you gaze and gaze at *One*, on the contrary, you listen intently, with your eye out of the window.'

'She is very much like you, but all the same,' I said firmly, 'she must be more beautiful because there is that thing about the gazing.'

This was perfectly true, and not only said to annoy poor Cedric and make him jealous. He was like Polly, and very good-looking, but not an irresistible magnet to the eye as she was.

'I know exactly why,' he said, 'it's my beard, all that horrible shaving. I shall send to New York this very day for some wax—you can't conceive the agony it is, but if it will make you gaze, Fanny, it will be worth it.'

'Don't bother to do that,' I said. 'It's not the shaving. You do look like Polly, but you are not as beautiful. Lady Patricia also looked like her, but it wasn't the same thing. It's something extra that Polly has, which I can't explain, I can only tell you that it is so.'

'What extra can she possibly have except beardlessness?'

'Lady Patricia was quite beardless.'

'You are horrid. Never mind, I shall try it, and you'll see. People used to gaze before my beard grew, like mad, even in Nova Scotia. You are so fortunate not to be a beauty, Fanny, you'll never know the agony of losing your looks.'

'Thank you,' I said.

'And as talking about pretty Polly makes us both so disagreeable let's get on to the subject of Boy.'

'Ah now, nobody could say that Boy was pretty. No gazing there. Boy is old and grizzled and hideous.'

'Now Fanny, that's not true, dear. Descriptions of people are only interesting if they happen to be true, you know. I've seen many photographs of Boy, Sonia's books are full of them, from Boy playing Diabolo, Boy in puttees for the war, to Boy with his bearer Boosee. After India I think she lost her Brownie, in the move perhaps, because

"Pages from Our Indian Diary" seems to be the last book, but that was only three years ago and Boy was still ravishing then, the kind of looks I adore, stocky and with deep attractive furrows all over his face—dependable.'

'Dependable!'

'Why do you hate him so much, Fanny?'

'Oh, I don't know, he gives me the creeps. He's such a snob, for one thing.'

'I like that,' said Cedric. 'I am one myself.'

'Such a snob that living people aren't enough for him, he has to get to know the dead, as well—the titled dead of course, I mean. He dives about in their Memoirs so that he can talk about his dear Duchesse de Dino, or "as Lady Bessborough so truly says". He can reel off pedigrees, he always knows just how everybody was related, royal families and things I mean. Then he writes books about all these people, and after that anybody would think they were his own personal property. Ugh!'

'Exactly as I had supposed,' said Cedric, 'a handsome, cultivated man, the sort of person I like the best. Gifted, too. His embroidery, really wonderful, and the dozens of *toiles* by him in the squash court are worthy of the Douanier himself, landscapes with gorillas. Original and bold.'

'Gorillas! Lord and Lady Montdore, and anybody else who would pose.'

'Well, it is original and bold to depict my aunt and uncle as gorillas, I wouldn't dare. I think Polly is a very lucky girl.'

'The Boreleys think you will end by marrying Polly, Cedric.' Norma had propounded this thrilling theory to me the day before. They thought that it would be a death blow to Lady Montdore, and longed for it to happen.

'Very silly of them, dear, I should have thought they only had to look at *One* to see how unlikely that is. What else do the Boreleys say about me?'

'Cedric, do come and meet Norma one day—I simply long to see you together.'

'I think not, dear, thank you.'

'But why? You're always asking what she says and she's always asking what you say, you'd much better ask each other and do without the middleman.'

'The thing is, I believe she would remind me of Nova Scotia, and when that happens my spirits go down, down, past *grande pluie* to *tempête*. The house-carpenter at Hampton reminds me, don't ask me why but he does, and I have to rudely look away every time I meet him. I believe that's why Paris suits me so well, there's not a shade of Nova Scotia there, and perhaps it's also why I put up with the Baron all those years. The Baron could have come from many a land of spices, but from Nova Scotia he could not have come. Whereas Boreleys abound there. But though I don't want to meet them I always like hearing about them, so do go on with what they think about *One*.'

'Well, so then Norma was full of you just now, when I met her out shopping, because it seems you travelled down from London with her brother Jock yesterday, and now he can literally think of nothing else.'

'Oh, how exciting. How did he know it was me?'

'Lots of ways. The goggles, the piping, your name on your luggage. There is nothing anonymous about you, Cedric.'

'Oh, good.'

'So according to Norma he was in a perfect panic, sat with one eye on you and the other on the communication cord, because he expected you to pounce at any minute.'

'Heavens! What does he look like?'

'You ought to know. It seems you were quite alone together after Reading.'

'Well, darling, I only remember a dreadful moustachioed murderer sitting in a corner. I remember him particularly, because I kept thinking, "Oh, the luck of being *One* and not somebody like that".'

'I expect that was Jock. Sandy and white.'

'That's it. Oh, so that's a Boreley, is it? And do you imagine people often make advances to him, in trains?'

'He says you gave him hypnotic stares through your glasses.'

'The thing is, he did have rather a pretty tweed on.'

'And then, apparently, you made him get your suitcase off the rack at Oxford, saying you are not allowed to lift things.'

'No, and nor I am. It was very heavy, not a sign of a porter as usual, I might have hurt myself. Anyway, it was all right because he terribly sweetly got it down for me.'

'Yes, and now he's simply furious that he did. He says you hypnotized him.'

'Oh, poor him, I do so know the feeling.'

'Whatever had you got in it, Cedric? He says it simply weighed a ton.'

'*Complets*,' Cedric said, 'and a few small things for my face. Very little, really. I have found a lovely new resting-cream I must tell you about, by the way.'

'And now they are all saying, "There you are—if he even fixed old Jock, no wonder he has got round the Montdores".'

'But why on earth should I want to get round the Montdores?'

'Wills and things. Living at Hampton.'

'My dear, come to that, Chèvres-Fontaine is twenty times more beautiful than Hampton.'

'But could you go back there now, Cedric?' I said.

Cedric gave me rather a nasty look and went on:

'But in any case I wish people would understand that there's never much point in hanging about for wills—it's just not worth it. I have a friend who used to spend months of every year with an old uncle in the Sarthe so as to stay in his will. It was torture to him, because he knew the person he loved was being unfaithful to him in Paris, and anyhow, the Sarthe is utterly lugubrious, you know. But all the same, he went pegging away at it. Then what occurs? The uncle dies, my poor friend inherits the house in the Sarthe, and now he feels obliged to live a living death there so as to make himself believe that there was some point after all in having wasted months of his youth in the Sarthe. You see my argument? It's a vicious circle, and there is nothing vicious about me. The thing is, I love Sonia, that's why I stay.'

I believed him, really. Cedric lived in the present. It would not be like him to bother about such things as wills; if ever there were a grass-hopper, a lily of the field, it was he.

When Davey got back from his cruise he rang me up and said he would come over to luncheon and tell me about Polly. I thought Cedric might as well come and hear it at first hand. Davey was always better with an audience even if he did not much like its component parts, so I rang up Hampton, and Cedric accepted to lunch with pleasure and then said could he possibly stay with me for a night or two?

'Sonia has gone for this orange cure—yes, total starvation except for orange juice, but don't mind too much for her, I know she'll cheat. Uncle Montdore is in London for the House and I feel sad, all alone here. I'd love to be with you and to do some serious Oxford sight-seeing, which there's never time for when I've got Sonia with me. That will be charming, Fanny, thank you, dear. One o'clock, then.'

Alfred was very busy just then and I was delighted to think I should have Cedric's company for a day or two. I cleared the decks by warning Aunt Sadie that he would be there, and telling my undergraduate friends that I should not be wanting them around for the present.

'Who is that spotty child?' Cedric had once said, when a boy who had been crouching by my fireplace got up and vanished at a look from me.

'I see him as the young Shelley,' I answered, sententiously, no doubt.

'And *I* see him as the young Woodley.'

Davey arrived first.

'Cedric is coming,' I said, 'so you mustn't begin without him.' I could see he was bursting with his news.

'Oh, Cedric, it is too bad, Fanny, I never come without finding that monster here, he seems to live in your house. What does Alfred think of him?'

'Doubt if he knows him by sight, to tell you the truth. Come and see the baby, Dave.'

'Sorry if I'm late, darlings,' Cedric said, floating in, 'one has to drive so slowly in England, because of the walking *Herrschaften*. Why are the English roads always so covered with these tweeded stumpers?'

'They are colonels,' I said, 'don't French colonels go for walks?'

'Much too ill. They have always lost a leg or two and been terribly gassed. I can see that French wars must have been far bloodier than English ones, though I do know a colonel, in Paris, who walks to the antique shops sometimes.'

'How do they take their exercise?' I asked.

'Quite another way, darling. You haven't started, about Boy, have you? Oh, how loyal. I was delayed by Sonia, too, on the telephone. She's in all her states—it seems they've had her up for stealing the nurses' breakfast—well, had her up in front of the principal, who spoke quite cruelly to her, and said that if she does it again, or gets one more bite of illicit food, she'll have her holiday. Just imagine, no dinner, one orange juice at midnight, and woken up by the smell of kippers. So naturally, the poor darling sneaked out and pinched one, and they caught her with it under her dressing-gown. I'm glad to say she'd eaten most of it before they got it away from her. The thing is she started off demoralized by finding your name in the visitors' book, Davey. Apparently she gave a scream and said, "But he's a living skeleton, whatever was he doing here?" and they said you had gone there to put on weight. What's the idea?'

'The idea,' said Davey, impatiently, 'is health. If you are too fat you lose and if you are too thin you gain. I should have thought a child could understand that. But Sonia won't stick it for a day, no self-discipline.'

'Just like *One*, poor darling,' said Cedric. 'But then, what are we to do to get rid of those kilos? Vichy, perhaps?'

'My dear, look at the kilos she's lost already,' I said, 'she's really so thin, ought she to get any thinner?'

'It's just that little extra round the hips,' said Cedric, 'a jersey and skirt is the test, and she doesn't look quite right in that yet—and there's a weeny roll round her ribs. Besides, they say the orange juice clears the skin. Oh, I do hope she sticks it for a few more days, for her own sake, you know. She says another patient told her of a place in the village where you can have Devonshire teas, but I begged her to be careful. After what happened this morning they're sure to be on the look-out and one more slip may be fatal, what d'you think, Davey?'

'Yes, they're madly strict,' said Davey. 'There'd be no point, otherwise.'

We sat down to our luncheon and begged Davey to begin his story.

'I may as well start by telling you that I don't think they are at all happy.'

Davey, I knew, was never a one for seeing things through rose-coloured spectacles, but he spoke so definitely and with so grave an emphasis that I felt I must believe him.

'Oh, Dave, don't say that. How dreadful.'

Cedric, who, since he did not know and love Polly, was rather indifferent as to whether she was happy or not, said:

'Now, Davey dear, you're going much too fast. New readers begin here. You left your boat——'

'I left my ship at Syracuse, having wired them from Athens that I would be arriving for one night, and they met me on the quay with a village taxi. They have no motor car of their own.'

'Every detail. They were dressed?'

'Polly wore a plain blue cotton frock and Boy was in shorts.'

'Wouldn't care to see Boy's knees,' I said.

'They're all right,' said Davey, standing up for Boy as usual.

'Well then, Polly? Beautiful?'

'Less beautiful' (Cedric looked delighted to hear this news) 'and peevish. Nothing right for her. Hates living abroad, can't learn the language, talks Hindustani to the servants, complains that they steal her stockings——'

'You're going much too fast, we're still in the taxi, you can't skip to stockings like this—how far from Syracuse?'

'About an hour's drive, and beautiful beyond words—the situation, I mean. The villa is on a south-easterly slope looking over olive trees, umbrella pines and vineyards to the sea—you know, the regular Mediterranean view that you can never get tired of. They've taken the house, furnished, from Italians and complain about it ceaselessly, it seems to be on their minds, in fact. I do see that it can't be very nice in winter, no heating except open fireplaces which smoke, bath-water never hot, none of the windows fit, and so on, you know. Italian houses are always made for the heat, and of course, it can be jolly cold in Sicily. The inside is hideous, all khaki and bog oak, depressing if you had to be indoors much. But at this time of year it's ideal, you live on a terrace, roofed in with vines and bougainvillea—I never saw such a perfect spot—huge tubs of geraniums everywhere—simply divine.'

'Oh, dear, as I seem to have taken their place in life, I do wish we could swop over sometimes,' said Cedric. 'I do so love Sicily.'

'I think they'd be all for it,' said Davey, 'they struck me as being very homesick. Well, we arrived in time for luncheon, and I struggled away with the food (Italian cooking, so oily).'

'What did you talk about?'

'Well, you know, really, it was one long wail from them about how difficult everything is, more expensive than they thought it would be and how the people—village people, I mean—don't really help but say yes yes the whole time and nothing gets done, and how they are supposed to have vegetables out of the garden in return for paying the gardener's wages but actually they have to buy everything and as they are sure he sells the vegetables in the village they suppose that it is their own that they buy back again; how when they first came there wasn't a kettle in the place and the blankets were as hard as boards and none of the electric light switches worked and no lamps by the beds—you know, the usual complaints of people who take furnished houses, I've heard them a hundred times. After luncheon it got very hot, which Polly doesn't like, and she went off to her room with everything drawn and I had a session with Boy on the terrace, and then I really saw how the land lay. Well, all I can say is I know it is wrong, not right, to arouse the sexual instincts of little girls so that they fall madly in love with you, but the fact is, poor old Boy is taking a fearful punishment. You see, he has literally nothing to do from morning to night, except water his geraniums, and you know how bad it is for them to have too much water; of course, they are all leaf as a result. I told him so. He has nobody to talk to, no club, no London Library, no neighbours, and of course, above all, no Sonia to keep him on the run. I don't expect he ever realized what a lot of his time used to be taken up by Sonia. Polly's no company for him, really, you can see that, and in many ways she seems dreadfully on his nerves. She's so insular, you know, nothing is right for her, she hates the place, hates the people, even hates the climate. Boy at least is very cosmopolitan, speaks beautiful Italian, prepared to be interested in the local folk-lore and things like that, but you can't be interested quite alone and Polly is so discouraging. Everything seems rot to her and she only longs for England.'

'Funny,' I said, 'that she should be quite so narrow-mindedly English when you think that she spent five years in India.'

'Oh, my dear child, the butler was grander and the weather was hotter but otherwise there wouldn't be much to choose between Hampton and Viceroy's House. If anything, Viceroy's House was the less cosmopolitan of the two, I should say, and certainly it was no preparation for Sicilian housekeeping. No, she simply loathes it, so there is the poor fellow, shut up month after month with a cross little girl he has known from a baby. Not much cop, you must admit.'

'I thought,' said Cedric, 'that he was so fond of dukes? Sicily is full of heavenly dukes, you know.'

'Fairly heavenly, and they're nearly always away. Anyhow, he doesn't count them the same as French or English dukes.'

'Well, that's nonsense, nobody could be grander than Pincio. But if he doesn't count them (I do see some of the others are a bit unreal) and if he's got to live abroad, I can't imagine why he doesn't choose Paris. Plenty of proper dukes there—fifty to be exact—Souppes told me so once, you know how they can only talk about each other, in that trade.'

'My dear Cedric, they are very poor—they can't afford to live in

England, let alone Paris. That's why they are still in Sicily, if it wasn't for that they'd come home now like a shot. Boy lost money in the crash last autumn, and he told me that if he hadn't got a very good let for Silkin they would really be almost penniless. Oh, dear, and when you think how rich Polly would have been——'

'No cruel looks at *One*,' said Cedric. 'Fair's fair, you know.'

'Anyway, it's a shocking business and only shows where dear old sex can land a person. I never saw anybody so pleased as Boy was when I appeared—like a dog let off a lead. Wanted to hear every single thing that's been going on—you could just see how lonely and bored he feels, poor chap.'

But I was thinking of Polly. If Boy was bored and lonely she was not likely to be very happy either. The success or failure of all human relationships lies in the atmosphere each person is aware of creating for the other, what atmosphere could a disillusioned Polly feel that she was creating for a bored and lonely Boy? Her charm, apart from her beauty, and husbands, we know, get accustomed to the beauty of their wives so that it ceases to strike them at the heart, her charm used to derive from the sphinx-like quality which came from her secret dream of Boy; in the early days of that dream coming true, at Alconleigh, happiness had made her irresistible. But I quite saw that with the riddle solved, and if the happiness were dissolved, Polly, without her own little daily round of Madame Rita, Debenhams and the hairdresser to occupy her, and too low in vitality to invent new interests for herself, might easily sink into sulky dumps. She was not at all likely to find consolation in Sicilian folk-lore, I knew, and probably not, not yet, anyhow, in Sicilian noblemen.

'Oh, dear,' I said. 'If Boy isn't happy I don't suppose Polly can be either. Oh, poor Polly.'

'Poor Polly—m'm—but at least it was her idea,' said Davey, 'my heart bleeds for poor Boy. Well, he can't say I didn't warn him, over and over again.'

'What about a baby?' I asked, 'any signs?'

'None that I could see, but after all, how long have they been married? Eighteen months? Sonia was eighteen years before she had Polly.'

'Oh, goodness!' I said. 'I shouldn't imagine the Lecturer, in eighteen years' time, will be able——'

I was stopped by a well-known hurt look on Davey's face.

'Perhaps that is what makes them sad,' I ended, rather lamely.

'Possibly. Anyhow, I can't say that I formed a happy impression.'

At this point Cedric was called to the telephone, and Davey said to me in a lowered voice:

'Entirely between you and me, Fanny, and this is not to go any further, I think Polly is having trouble with Boy.'

'Oh, dear,' I said, 'kitchen-maids?'

'No,' said Davey, 'not kitchen-maids.'

'Don't tell me!' I said, horrified.

Cedric came back and said that Lady Montdore had been caught red-handed having elevenses in the Devonshire tea-rooms and had been given the sack. She told him that the motor would call for him on its way, so that she would have a companion for the drive home.

'There now,' he said gloomily. 'I shan't have my little visit to you after all, and I had so been looking forward to it.'

It struck me that Cedric had arranged the orange cure less with a view to getting rid of kilos than to getting rid of Lady Montdore for a week or two. Life with her must have been wearing work, even to Cedric, with his unflagging spirits and abounding energy, and he may well have felt that he had earned a short rest after nearly a year of it.

CHAPTER VI

CEDRIC HAMPTON and Norma Cozens met at last, but though the meeting took place in my garden it was none of my arranging; a pure chance. I was sitting, one afternoon of Indian summer, on my lawn, where the baby was crawling about stark naked and so brown that he looked like a little Topsy, when Cedric's golden head appeared over the fence, accompanied by another head, that of a thin and ancient horse.

'I'm coming to explain,' he said, 'but I won't bring my friend, I'll attach him to your fence, darling. He's so sad and good, he won't do any harm, I promise.'

A moment later he joined me in the garden. I put the baby back in its pram and was turning to Cedric to ask what this was all about when Norma came up the lane which passes my garden on her afternoon trudge with her dogs. Now the Boreley family consider that they have a special mandate, bestowed from on high, to deal with everything that regards the horse. They feel it to be their duty no less than their right, and therefore the moment she saw Cedric's friend, sad and good, standing by my fence, Norma unhesitatingly came into the garden to see what she could do about it. I introduced Cedric to her.

'I don't want to interrupt you,' she said, her eye upon the famous piping of the seams, brown today, upon a green linen coat, vaguely Tyrolean in aspect, 'but there's a very old mare, Fanny, tied up to your fence. Do you know anything about it—whom does she belong to?'

'Don't, dear Mrs. Cozens, tell me that the first horse I have ever owned is a female!' said Cedric, with a glittering (brush) smile.

'The animal is a mare,' said Norma, 'and if she is yours I must tell you that you ought to be ashamed of yourself for keeping her in that dreadful condition.'

'Oh, but I only began keeping her ten minutes ago, and I hope that when you see her again, in a few months' time, you simply won't know her.'

'Do you mean to say that you bought that creature? She ought to go straight away to the kennels.'

'The kennels? But why—she's not a dog!'

'The knacker, the horse-butcher,' said Norma impatiently, 'she must be destroyed, put down immediately or I shall ring up the R.S.P.C.A.'

'Oh, please don't do that. I'm not being cruel to her, I'm being kind. That horrid man I bought her from, he was being beastly, he was taking her to the knacker. My plan was to save her from him, I couldn't bear to see the expression on her poor face.'

'Well, but what are you going to do with her, my dear boy?'

'I thought—set her free.'

'Set her free? She's not a bird, you know, you can't go setting horses free like that—not in England, anyway.'

'Yes I can. Not in Oxford perhaps, but where I live there is a *vieux parc, solitaire et glacé,* and it is my intention to set her free there, to have happy days away from knackers. Isn't knacker a hateful word, Mrs. Cozens?'

'The grazing at Hampton is let,' said Norma. It was the kind of detail the Boreleys could be counted on to tell you. Cedric, however, took no notice and went on:

'She was being driven down the street in a van with her head sticking out at the back, and I could see at once that she was longing for some nice person to get her out of this unpleasant situation, so I stopped the van and bought her. You could see how relieved she felt.'

'How much?'

'Well, I offered the man forty pounds, it was all I had on me, so he kindly let me have her for that.'

'Forty pounds!' cried Norma, aghast. 'Why, you could get a hunter for less than forty pounds.'

'But my dearest Mrs. Cozens, I don't want a hunter, it's the last thing, I'd be far too frightened. Besides, look at the time you have to get up—I heard them the other morning in the woods, half-past six. Well, you know, I'm afraid it's "up before seven *dead* before eleven" with *One*. No, I just wanted this special old clipper-clopper, she's not the horse to make claims on a chap, she won't want to be ridden all the time as a younger horse might, and there she'll be, if I feel like having a few words with her occasionally. But the great question now, which I came to tease practical Fanny with, is how to get her home?'

'And if you go buying up all the horses that are fit for the kennels, however do you imagine hounds are going to be fed?' said Norma, in great exasperation. She was related to several Masters of fox-hounds and her sister had a pack of beagles, so no doubt she was acquainted with all their problems.'

'I shan't buy up all the horses,' said Cedric, soothingly, 'only this one, which I took a liking for. Now, dear Mrs. Cozens, do stop being angry and just tell me how I can get her home, because I know you can help if you want to and I simply can't get over the luck of meeting you here at the very moment when I needed you so badly.'

Norma began to weaken, as people so very often did with Cedric. It was extraordinary how fast he could worm his way through a thick crust of prejudice, and, just as in the case of Lady Montdore, the people who hated him the most were generally those who had seen him from afar but never met him. But whereas Lady Montdore had 'all this' to help in her conquest of disapproval, Cedric relied upon his charm, his good looks and his deep inborn knowledge of human, and especially female, nature.

'Please,' he said, his eyes upon her, blinking a little.

I could see that he had done the trick; Norma was considering.

'Well,' she said at last, 'there are two ways of doing it. I can lend you a saddle and you can ride her over—I'm not sure she's up to it, but you could see——'

'No, Mrs. Cozens, no. I have some literary sense—Fauntleroy on his pony, gallant little figure, the wind in his golden curls, all right, and if my uncle had had the sense to get me over from Canada when I was younger we should have seen that very thing, I've no doubt. But the gloomy old don on Rosinante is quite another matter, and I can't face it.'

'Which gloomy old don?' asked Norma, with interest. 'But it makes no odds, she'd never get there. Twenty miles, now I come to think of it—and I expect she's as lame as a cat.'

She went to the fence and peered over.

'Those hocks——! You know, it honestly would be kinder—Oh, very well, very well. If nothing I can say will make you understand that the animal would be far happier dead, you'll have to get the horse-box. Shall I ring up Stubly now, on Fanny's telephone, and see if he can come round at once?'

'No! You wouldn't do that for me? Oh, dearest Mrs. Cozens, I can only say—angel! What a miracle that I met you!'

'Lie down,' she said, to the Borders, and went indoors.

'Sexually unsatisfied, poor her,' said Cedric, when she had gone.

'Really Cedric, what nonsense. She's got four children.'

'I can't help it. Look at all those wrinkles. She could try patting in muscle oil, of course, and I shall suggest it as soon as I get to know her a little better, but I'm afraid the trouble is more deep-seated. Of course,

I feel certain the Professor must be a secret queer—nobody but a queer would ever marry Norma, to begin with.'

'Why? She's not at all boyish?'

'No, dearest, it isn't that, but there is a certain type of Norma-ish lady which appeals to queers, don't ask me why, but so it is. Now supposing I arranged for her to come over every Tuesday and share a facial with Sonia, what do you think? The competition would be good for both of them, and it would cheer Sonia up to see a woman so much younger, so much more deeply haggard.'

'I wouldn't,' I said. 'Norma always says she can't stick Lady Montdore.'

'Does she know her? Of course, I doubt if anything short of a nice lift would fix Mrs. Cozens, but we could teach her "brush" and a little charm to help the Waynflete Prof. to do his work a bit better, or failing that, and I fear it's rather a desperate hope, some nice Woodley might come to the rescue. No, darling, not *One*,' he added, in response to a meaning look from me. 'The cuticles are too desperately anaphrodisiac.'

'I thought you never wanted to see her because she reminded you of Nova Scotia?'

'Yes, I thought she would, but she is too English. She fascinates me for that reason, you know how very very pro-English I am becoming. The cuticles are rather Nova Scotian but her soul is the soul of Oxfordshire and I shall cultivate her after this like mad.'

Some half an hour later, as Cedric went off, sitting by the driver of the horse box, Norma, panting a little from her efforts with the mare who had stubbornly refused at first to get into it, said:

'You know, that boy has some good in him after all. What a shame he couldn't have gone to a decent public school instead of being brought up in those shocking colonies.'

To my amazement, and great secret annoyance, Cedric and Norma now became extremely friendly, and he went to see her, when he was in Oxford, quite as often as he did me.

'Whatever do you talk about?' I said to him, crossly.

'Oh, we have cosy little chats about this and that. I love Englishwomen, they are so restful.'

'Well, I'm fairly fond of old Norma, but I simply can't imagine what you see in her, Cedric.'

'I suppose I see whatever you see,' he replied, carelessly.

After a bit, he persuaded her to give a dinner party, to which he promised to bring Lady Montdore. Lord Montdore never went out now, and was sinking happily into old age. His wife being provided with a companion for every hour of the day, he was not only allowed but positively encouraged to have a good long nap in the afternoon, and he generally either had his dinner in bed or shuffled off there immediately after dinner. The advent of Cedric must have proved an absolute blessing to him in more ways than one. People very soon got into the habit of asking Cedric with Lady Montdore instead of her husband, and it must be said that he was much better company; they were going out more now than when Cedric first arrived, the panic caused by the financial crisis was subsiding and people had begun to entertain again. Lady Montdore was much too fond of society to keep away from it for long, and Cedric, firmly established at Hampton, weighed down with many large expensive gifts, could surely now be shown to her friends without danger of losing him.

In spite of the fact that she was by way of being unable to stick Lady Montdore, Norma got into a perfect state over this dinner party, dropping in on me at all hours to discuss the menu and the fellow guests, and finally imploring me to come on the morning of the day to make a pudding for her. I said that I would do so on one condition, she must buy a quart of cream. She wriggled like an eel not to have to do this, but I was quite firm. Then she said would the top of the milk do? No, I said, it must be thick rich unadulterated cream. I said I would bring it with me and let her know how much I had paid for it, and she very reluctantly agreed. Although she was, I knew, very wealthy, she never spent a penny more than she could help on her house, her table or her clothes (except her riding-clothes, for she was always beautifully turned out in the hunting-field and I am sure her horses lived on an equine substitute for cream). So I went round, and, having provided myself with the suitable ingredients, I made her a crème Chantilly. As I got back to my own house the telephone bell was pealing away—Cedric.

'I thought I'd better warn you my darling that we are chucking poor Norma tonight.'

'Cedric, you simply can't, I never heard anything so awful, she has bought cream!'

He gave an unkind laugh and said:

'So much the better for those weedy tots I see creeping about the house.'

'But why should you chuck, are you ill?'

'Not the least bit ill thank you, love. The thing is that Merlin wants us to go over there for dinner, he has got fresh *foie gras*, and a fascinating Marquesa with eyelashes two inches long, he measured. Do you see how *One* can't resist it?'

'*One* must resist it,' I said, frantically. 'You simply cannot chuck poor Norma now, you'll never know the trouble she's taken. Besides, do think of us, you miserable boy, we can't chuck, only think of the dismal evening we shall have without you.'

'I know, poor you, won't it be lugubrious?'

'Cedric, all I can say is you are a sewer.'

'Yes, darling, *mea culpa*. But it's not so much that I want to chuck as that I absolutely know I shall. I don't even intend to, I fully intend not to, it is that something in my body will make me. When I've rung off from speaking to you, I know that my hand will creep back to the receiver again of its own accord, and I shall hear my voice, but quite against my will, mind you, asking for Norma's number, and then I shall be really horrified to hear it breaking this dreadful news to Norma. So much worse, now I know about the cream, too. But there it is. But what I rang you up to say is, don't forget you are on *One's* side—no disloyalty Fanny, please, I absolutely count, dear, on you not to egg Norma on to be furious. Because so long as you don't do that you'll find she won't mind a bit, not a bit. So, solidarity between working girls, and I'll promise to come over tomorrow and tell about the eyelashes.'

Oddly enough, Cedric was right and Norma was not in the least put out. His excuse, and he had told the truth, merely adding a touch of embroidery by saying that Lady Montdore had been at school with the Marquesa, was considered quite a reasonable one, since dinner with Lord Merlin was recognized at Oxford as being the very pinnacle of human happiness. Norma rang me up to say that her dinner party was postponed, in the voice of a society hostess who postpones dinner parties every day of the week. Then, lapsing into more normal Oxford parlance, she said:

'It's a bore about the cream, because they are coming on Wednesday now, and it will never keep in this weather. Can you come back and make another pudding on Wednesday morning, Fanny? All right, and I'll pay you for both lots together, if that suits you. Everybody is free and I think the flowers may last over, so see you then, Fanny.'

But on Wednesday, Cedric was in bed with a high temperature, and on Thursday he was rushed to London by ambulance and operated upon for peritonitis, lying between life and death for several days, and in the end it was quite two months before the dinner party could take place.

At last, however, the date was fixed again, another pudding was made, and, at Norma's suggestion, I invited my Uncle Davey to come and stay for it, to pair off with her beagling sister. Norma looked down on dons quite as much as Lady Montdore did, and as for undergraduates, although of course she must have known that such things existed, since they provided her husband and mine with a livelihood, she certainly never thought of them as human beings and possible diners-out.

It would never formerly have occurred to me that 'touching', a word often on Lady Montdore's lips (it was very much of her day), could come to have any relation to herself, but on the occasion of Norma's dinner, the first time I had seen Lady Montdore with Cedric since his illness, there was really something touching about her attitude towards him. It was touching to see this hitherto redoubtable and ponderous personage, thin, now, as a rake, in her little-girl dress of dark tulle over pink taffeta, with her little-girl head of pale blue curls, dark blue ribbons and a swarm of diamond bees, as she listened through her own conversation to whatever Cedric might be saying, as she squinted out of the corner of her eye to see if he was happy and amused, perhaps even just to be quite sure that he was actually there, in the flesh; touching to see with what reluctance she left the dining-room after dinner; touching to watch her as she sat with the rest of us in the drawing-room waiting for the men to return, silent, or speaking at random, her eyes fixed upon the door like a spaniel waiting for its master. Love with her had blossomed late and strangely, but there could be no doubt that it had now blossomed, and that this thorny old plant had very much altered in character to accord with the tender flowers and springtime verdure which now so unexpectedly adorned it. During the whole of the evening there was only one respect in which she behaved as she would have done in her pre-Cedric days. She piled wood and coal, without so much as a by your leave, on to the tiny fire, Norma's concession to the fact that winter had begun, so that by the end of the evening we sat in a mellow warmth such as I had never known in that room before.

The men, as they always do in Oxford, remained an inordinate length of time over their port, so long, in fact, that Lady Montdore, with growing impatience, suggested to Norma that they might be sent for. Norma, however, looked so absolutely appalled at the idea that Lady Montdore did not press it any further, but went on with her self-appointed task as stoker, one spaniel-eye on the door.

'The only way to make a good fire,' she said, 'is to put on enough coal. People have all kinds of theories about it, but it's really very simple. Perhaps we could ask for another scuttle, Mrs. Cozens? Very kind. Cedric mustn't get a chill, whatever happens.'

'Dreadful,' I said, 'him being so ill, wasn't it?'

'Don't speak of it. I thought I should die. Yes, well, as I was saying. It's exactly the same with coffee, you know, people have these percolators and things and get the Bolter to buy them special beans in Kenya, perfectly pointless. Coffee is good if it is made strong enough and nasty if it is not. What we had just now would have been quite all right if your cook had put in three times the amount, you know. What can they be talking about in the dining-room? It's not as if any of them were interested in politics.'

At last the door opened. Davey came in first, looking bored, and made straight for the fire. Cedric, the Professor and Alfred followed in a bunch, still pursuing a conversation which seemed to be interesting them deeply.

'Just a narrow edging of white——' I heard Cedric say, through the open door, as they came down the passage.

Later on I remembered to ask Alfred what could have led up to this remark, so typical of Cedric but so untypical of the conversation in that house, and he replied that they had been having a most fascinating talk on burial customs in the High Yemen.

'I fear,' he said, 'that you bring out the worst in Cedric Hampton, Fanny. He is really a most intelligent young man, interested in a large range of subjects, though I have no doubt at all that when he is with you he confines himself, as you do, to remarks in the nature of "and did you notice the expression on her face when she saw who was there?" because he knows that general subjects do not amuse you, only personalities. With those whose horizon is a little wider he can be very serious, let me tell you.'

The fact was that Cedric could bring out edgings of white to suit all tastes.

'Well, Fanny, how do you like it?' he asked me, giving a twitch to Lady Montdore's tulle skirt. 'We ordered it by telephone when we were at Craigside—don't you die for television—Mainbocher simply couldn't believe that Sonia had lost so much weight.'

Indeed, she was very thin.

'I sit in a steam barrel,' she said, looking fondly at Cedric, 'for an hour or two, and then that nice Mr. Wixman comes down twice a week when we are at Hampton and he beats and beats me and the morning is gone in a flash. Cedric sees the cook for me nowadays, I find I can't take very much interest in food, in my barrel.'

'But my dear Sonia,' said Davey, 'I hope you consult Dr. Simpson about all this? I am horrified to see you in such a state, really much too thin, nothing but skin and bones. You know, at our age, it's most dangerous to play about with one's weight, a terrible strain on the heart.'

It was generous of Davey to talk about 'our age', since Lady Montdore was certainly fourteen years older than he was.

'Dr. Simpson!' she said derisively. 'My dear Davey, he's terribly behind the times. Why, he never even told me how good it is to stand on one's head, and Cedric says in Paris and Berlin they've been doing it for ages now. I must say I feel younger every day since I learnt. The blood races through your glands you know, and they love it.'

'How d'you know they love it?' said Davey, with considerable irritation. He always scorned any régime for health except the one he happened to be following himself, regarding all others as dangerous superstitions imposed on gullible fools by unscrupulous quacks. 'We understand so very little about our glands,' he went on. 'Why should it be good for them? Did Dame Nature intend us to stand on our heads —do animals stand on their heads, Sonia?'

'The sloth,' said Cedric, 'and the bat hang upside down for hours on end—you can't deny that, Davey.'

'Yes, but do sloths and bats feel younger every day? I doubt it. Bats may, but I'm sure sloths don't.'

'Come on, Cedric,' said Lady Montdore, very much put out by Davey's remarks, 'we must be going home.'

Lady Montdore and Cedric now installed themselves at Montdore House for the winter and were seen no more by me. London society, having none of the prejudices against the abnormal which still exist among Boreleys and Uncle Matthews in country places, simply ate Cedric up, occasional echoes of his great success even reaching Oxford. It seemed that such an arbiter of taste, such an arranger of festivities, had not been known since the days of the beaux, and that he lived in a perfect welter of parties, dragging Lady Montdore along in his wake.

'Isn't she wonderful? You know, she's seventy—eighty—ninety——' her age went up by leaps and bounds. 'She's a darling, so young, so delicious, I do hope I shall be just like her when I'm a hundred.'

So Cedric had transformed her from a terrifying old idol of about sixty into a delicious young darling of about a hundred. Was anything beyond his powers?

I remember one icy day of late spring I ran into Mrs. Chaddesley Corbett, walking down the Turl with an undergraduate, perhaps her son, I thought, chinless, like her.

'Fanny!' she said. 'Oh, of course, darling, you live here, don't you? I'm always hearing about you from Cedric. He dotes on you, that's all.'

'Oh,' I said, pleased, 'and I'm so very fond of him.'

'Couldn't like him more, could you? So gay, so cosy, I think he's a perfect poppet. As for Sonia, it's a transformation, isn't it? Polly's marriage seems to have turned out to be a blessing in disguise for her. Do you ever hear from Polly now? What a thing to have done, poor sweet. But I'm mad about Cedric, that's all—everybody in London is —tiny Lord Fauntleroy. They're both dining with me this evening, I'll give them your love, shall I? See you very soon, darling, good-bye.'

I saw Mrs. Chaddesley Corbett perhaps once a year, she always called me darling and said she would see me very soon, and this always left me feeling quite unreasonably elated.

I got back to my house and found Jassy and Victoria sitting by the fire. Victoria was looking very green.

'I must do the talking,' Jassy said, 'Fa's new car makes poor Vict. sick and she can't open her mouth for fear of letting the sick out.'

'Go and let it out in the loo,' I said. Victoria shook her head vehemently.

'She hates being,' said Jassy, 'anything rather. We hope you're pleased to see us.'

I said that I was, very.

'And we hope you've noted how we never do come nowadays.'

'Yes, I have noted. I put it down to the hunting.'

'Stupid you are. How could one hunt, in this weather?'

'This weather only began yesterday, and I've heard of you from Norma, hunting away like anything up to now.'

'We don't think you quite realize how bitterly offended we feel over your behaviour to us the last year or two.'

'Now, now children, we've had this out a thousand times,' I said firmly.

'Yes, well, it's not very nice of you. After all, when you married we rather naturally expected that your home would open up all the delights of civilized society to us, and that sooner or later we should meet, in your salon, the brilliant wealthy titled men destined to become our husbands. "I loved her from the first moment I saw her, the leggy little girl with the beautiful sensitive face, who used to sprawl about Mrs. Wincham's drawing-room at Oxford." Well, then what happens? One of the richest *partis* in Western Europe becomes an *habitué de la maison* and are we thrown at his head by our cousin, naturally ambitious for our future, does she move heaven and earth to further this splendid match? Not even asked to meet him. Spoil sport.'

'Go on,' I said, wearily.

'No, well, we're only bringing it up'—Victoria here fled the room, Jassy took no notice—'in order to show our great magnanimity of soul. The fact is that we know a very interesting piece of news, and in spite of your counter-honnish behaviour we are going to tell it to you. But we want you to realize that it is pretty noble of us, when you take everything into account, his flashing eyes, his floating hair, only seen in the distance, it is such a shame, and I must wait for Vict. to come back or it would be too unfaithful, and can we have some tea, she's always starving after.'

'Does Mrs. Heathery know you're here?'

'Yes, she held Vict's head.'

'You don't mean to say she's been sick already?'

'It's always thrice—once in the car and twice when we get there.'

'Well, if Mrs. Heathery knows, tea will appear.'

It appeared simultaneously with Victoria.

'Fanny's loo! The bliss! It's got a carpet, Jassy, and it's boiling warm, one could stay there all day. Crumpets! Oh, Fanny!'

'What's this news you know?' I asked, pouring out milk for the children.

'I like tea now, please,' said Jassy, 'which shows how long since you saw us. I like tea and I almost like coffee. So the news is, Napoleon has left Elba and is on his way back.'

'Say it again.'

'Dense. Nobody would think that you were a hostess to the younger cosmopolitan intellectual set, noted for her brilliant repartee.'

'Do you mean Polly?' I said, light suddenly dawning.

'Very bright of you, dear. Josh was out exercising this morning and he stopped at the Blood Arms for a quick one, and that's what he heard. So we came dashing over to tell you, Fanny, in sickness and in health, so does one good turn not deserve another, Fanny?'

'Oh, do stop being such a bore,' I said, 'and go on telling. When?'

'Any day now. The tenants have gone and the house is being got ready, Lady Patricia's sheets and things, you know. She's going to have a baby.'

'Who is, Polly?'

'Well dear, who do you think? Not Lady Patricia. So that's what she's coming back for. So are you admitting that it was handsome of us to come over and tell you?'

'Very handsome,' I said.

'So will you invite us to luncheon one day soon?'

'Any day you like. I'll make chocolate profiterolles with real cream.'

'And what about closing our eyes with holy dread?'

'Cedric, if that's what you mean, is in London, but you can close them at Jock Boreley,' I said.

'Oh, Fanny, you brute. Can we go upstairs and see dear little David?'

CHAPTER VII

THE weather now became intensely cold, and much snow fell. The newspapers came out every day with horror stories of sheep buried in snowdrifts, of song-birds frozen to the branches on which they perched, of fruit trees hopelessly nipped in the bud, and the situation seemed dreadful to those who, like Mrs. Heathery, believe all they see in print without recourse to past experience. I tried to cheer her up by telling her, what, in fact, proved to be the case, that in a very short time the fields would be covered with sheep, the trees with birds and the barrows with fruit just as usual. But though the future did not disturb me I found the present most disagreeable, that winter should set in again so late in the spring, at a time when it would not be unreasonable to expect delicious weather, almost summer-like, warm enough to sit out of doors for an hour or two. The sky was overcast with a thick yellow blanket from which an endless pattern of black and white snowflakes came swirling down, and this went on day after day. One morning I sat by my window gazing idly at the pattern and thinking idle thoughts, wondering if it would ever be warm again, thinking how like a child's snowball Christ Church looked through a curtain of flakes, thinking too how cold it was going to be at Norma's that evening without Lady Montdore to stoke the fire, and how dull without Cedric and his narrow edging of white. Thank goodness, I thought, that I had sold my father's diamond brooch and installed central heating with the proceeds, then I began to remember what the house had been like two years before when the workmen were still in it, and how I had looked out through that very same pane of glass, filthy dirty then, and splashed with whitewash, and seen Polly struggling into the wind with her future husband. I half wanted and half did not want Polly in my life again, I was expecting another baby and felt tired, really, not up to much.

Then, suddenly, the whole tempo of the morning completely altered because here in my drawing-room, heavily pregnant, beautiful as ever, in a red coat and no hat, was Polly, and of course, all feelings of not wanting her melted away and were forgotten. In my drawing-room too was the Lecturer, looking old and worn.

When Polly and I had finished hugging and kissing and laughing and saying 'Lovely to see you' and 'Why did you never write?' she said:

'Can I bend you to my will?'

'Oh, yes, you can. I've got simply nothing to do, I was just looking at the snow.'

'Oh, the heaven of snow,' she said, 'and clouds, after all those blue skies. Now the thing is, Fanny, can I bend you until late this afternoon, because Boy has got an utter mass of things to do and I can't stand about much, as you see. But you must frankly tell me if I shall be in your way, because I can always go to Elliston's waiting-room—the blissful bliss of Elliston after those foreign shops, I nearly cried for happiness when we passed their windows just now—the bags! the cretonnes! the horror of abroad!'

'But that's wonderful,' I said, 'then you'll both lunch here?'

'Boy has to lunch with someone on business,' said Polly, quickly, 'you can go off then, darling, if you like, as Fanny says she can keep me, don't bother to wait any more. Then come back for me here when you've finished?'

Boy, who had been rubbing his hands together in front of the fire, went off rather glum, wrapping a scarf round his throat.

'And don't hurry a bit,' she called after him, opening the door again and shouting down the stairs. 'Now, darling Fanny, I want to do one final bend and make you lunch with me at Fullers—don't speak, you're going to say "Look at the weather", aren't you? but we'll ring up for a taxi. Fullers! You'll never know how much I used to long for Dover sole and walnut cake and just this sort of a day, in Sicily. Do you remember how we used to go there from Alconleigh when you were getting your house ready? I can't believe this is the same house, can you, or that we are the same people, come to that. Except I see you're the same darling Fanny, just as you were the same when I got back from India. Why is it that I, of all people, keep on having to go abroad? I do think it's too awful, don't you.'

'I only went just that once,' I said, 'it's very light, isn't it?'

'Yes, horrible glare. Just imagine if one had to live there for ever. You know we started off in Spain, and you'll never believe this but they are two hours late for every meal—two hours, Fanny—(can we lunch at half-past twelve today?), so of course, by then, you've stopped feeling hungry and only feel sick, then when the food comes it is all cooked in rancid oil, I can smell it now, it's on everybody's hair too, and to make it more appetizing there are pictures all round you of some dear old bull being tortured to death. They think of literally nothing all day but bulls and the Virgin. Spain was the worst of all, I thought. Of course, Boy doesn't mind abroad a bit, in fact he seems to like it, and he can talk all those terribly affected languages (darling, Italian! you'd die!), but I truly don't think I could have borne it much longer, I should have pined away with homesickness. Anyway, here I am.'

'What made you come back?' I said, really wondering how they could afford it, poor as Davey said they were. Silkin was not a big house, but it would require three or four servants.

'Well, you remember my Aunt Edna at Hampton Court? The good old girl died and left me all her money—not much, but we think we can just afford to live at Silkin. Then Boy is writing a book and he had to come back for that, London Library and Paddington.'

'Paddington?' I said, thinking of the station.

'Duke. Muniment room. Then there's this baby. Fancy, if one had to have a baby abroad, poor little thing, not a cow in the place. All the same, Boy doesn't much want to settle down here for good, I think he's still frightened of Mummy, you know—I am a bit, myself—not frightened, exactly, but bored at the idea of scenes. But there's really nothing more she can do to us is there?'

'I don't think you need worry about her a bit,' I said, 'your mother has altered completely in the last two years.'

I could not very well say my real thought, which was that Lady Montdore no longer cared a rap for Boy or for Polly, and that she would most likely be quite friendly to them now, it all depended upon Cedric's attitude, everything did nowadays, as far as she was concerned.

Presently, when we were settled at our table at Fullers, among the fumed oak and the daintiness ('Isn't everything clean and lovely—aren't the waitresses fair—you can't think how dark the waiters always are, abroad.') and had ordered our Dover soles, Polly said that now I must tell her all about Cedric.

'Do you remember,' she said, 'how you and Linda used to look him up to see if he would *do*?'

'Well, he wouldn't have *done*,' I said, 'that's one thing quite certain.'

'So I imagine,' said Polly.

'How much do you know about him?'

I suddenly felt rather guilty at knowing so much myself and hoped that Polly would not think I had gone over to the enemy's camp. It is so difficult for somebody who is as fond of sport as I am to resist running with the hare and hunting with the hounds whenever possible.

'Boy made friends, in Sicily, with an Italian called Pincio, he is writing about a former Pincio in his new book, and this wop knew Cedric in Paris, so he told us a lot about him. He says he is very pretty.'

'Yes, that's quite true.'

'How pretty, Fan, prettier than me?'

'No. One doesn't have to gaze and gaze at him like one does with you.'

'Oh, darling, you are so kind. Not any longer though, I fear.'

'Just exactly the same. But he is very much like you, didn't the duke say that?'

'Yes. He said we were Viola and Sebastian. I must say I die for him.'

'He dies for you, too. We must arrange it.'

'Yes, after the baby—not while I'm such a sight. You know how cissies hate pregnant ladies. Poor Pinchers would do anything to get out of seeing me, lately. Go on telling more about Cedric and Mummy.'

'I really think he loves your mother, you know. He is such a slave to her, never leaves her for a moment, always in high spirits—I don't believe anybody could put it on to that extent, it must be love.'

'I'm not surprised,' said Polly. 'I used to love her before she began about the marrying.'

'There!' I said.

'There what?'

'Well, you told me once that you'd hated her all your life, and I knew it wasn't true.'

'The fact is,' said Polly, 'when you hate somebody you can't imagine what it's like not hating them, it's just the same as with love. But of course, with Mummy, who is such excellent company, so lively, you do love her before you find out how wicked she can be. And I don't suppose she's in all that violent hurry to get Cedric off that she was with me.'

'No hurry,' I said.

Polly's blank blue look fell upon my face. 'You mean she's in love with him herself?'

'In love? I don't know. She loves him like anything, he makes such fun for her, you see, her life has become so amusing. Besides, she must know quite well that marriage isn't his thing exactly, poor Cedric.'

'Oh, no,' said Polly. 'Boy agrees with me that she knows nothing, nothing whatever about all that. He says she once made a fearful gaffe about Sodomites, mixing them up with Dolomites, it was all over

London. No, I guess she's in love. She's a great, great faller in love, you know, I used to think at one time that she rather fancied Boy, though he says not. Well, it's all very annoying because I suppose she doesn't miss me one little bit, and I miss her, often. And now tell me, how's my Dad?'

'Very old,' I said. 'Very old, and your mother so very young. You must be prepared for quite as much of a shock when you see her as when you see him.'

'No, really? How d'you mean, very young? Dyed hair?'

'Blue. But what one chiefly notices is that she has become thin and supple, quick little movements, flinging one leg over the other, suddenly sitting on the floor and so on. Quite like a young person.'

'Good gracious,' said Polly, 'and she used to be so very stiff and solid.'

'It's Mr. Wixman, Cedric's and her masseur. He pounds and pulls for an hour every morning, then she has another hour in a hay-box— full-time work, you know, what with the creaming and splashing and putting on a mask and taking it off again and having her nails done and her feet and then all the exercises, as well as having her teeth completely rearranged and the hairs zipped off her arms and legs—I truly don't think I could be bothered.'

'Operations on her face?'

'Oh, yes, but that was ages ago. All the bags and wrinkles gone, eyebrows plucked and so on. Her face is very tidy now.'

'Of course, it may seem odd here,' said Polly, 'but, you know, there are hundreds and hundreds of women like that abroad. I suppose she stands on her head and lies in the sun? Yes, they all do. She must be a sight, scene or no scene, I utterly can't wait for her, Fanny, when can we arrange it?'

'Not for the moment, they're in London now, fearfully busy with the Longhi Ball they are giving at Montdore House. Cedric came to see me the other day and could talk of nothing else—he says they won't be going to Hampton again until it's over.'

'What is a Longhi Ball?'

'You know, Venetian. Real water, with real gondolas floating on it, in the ballroom. "O sole mio" on a hundred guitars, all the footmen in masks and capes, no light except from candles in Venetian lanterns until the guests get to the ballroom, when a searchlight will be trained on Cedric and your mother, receiving from a gondola. Fairly different from your ball, Polly? Oh, yes, and I know, Cedric won't allow any Royalties to be asked at all, because he says they ruin everything, in London; he says they are quite different in Paris where they know their place.'

'Goodness!' said Polly, 'how times have changed. Not even old Super-Ma'am?'

'No, not even your mother's new Infanta. Cedric was adamant.'

'Fanny, it's your duty to go to it—you will, won't you?'

'Oh, darling, I can't. I feel so sleepy after dinner when I am pregnant, you know, I really couldn't drag myself. We shall hear about it all right, from Cedric.'

'And when does it take place?'

'Under a month from now, the sixteenth, I believe.'

'Why, that's the very day I'm expecting my baby, how convenient. Then when everything's all over we can meet, can't we? You will fix it, promise.'

'Oh, don't worry, we shan't be able to hold Cedric back. He's fearfully interested in you, you're Rebecca to him.'

Boy came back to my house just as we were finishing our tea, he looked perished with cold and very tired but Polly would not let him wait while some fresh tea was made. She allowed him to swallow a tepid cup and dragged him off.

'I suppose you've lost the key of the car, as usual,' she said unkindly on their way downstairs.

'No no, here it is, on my key-ring.'

'Miracle,' said Polly, 'well then, good-bye, my darling, I'll telephone and we'll do some more benders.'

When Alfred came in later on I said to him:

'I've seen Polly, just imagine, she spent the whole day here, and oh, Alfred! she's not a bit in love any more!'

'Do you never think of anything but who is or is not in love with whom?' he said, in tones of great exasperation.

Norma, I knew, would be just as uninterested, and I longed very much for Davey or Cedric to pick it all over with.

CHAPTER VIII

So Polly now settled into her aunt's house at Silkin. It had always been Lady Patricia's house more than Boy's, as she was the one who lived there all the time, while Boy flitted about between Hampton and London with occasional visits to the Continent, and it was arranged inside with a very feminine form of tastelessness, that is to say, no taste and no comfort either. It was a bit better than Norma's house, but not much, the house itself being genuinely old instead of Banbury Road old and standing in the real country instead of an Oxford suburb; it contained one or two good pieces of furniture, and where Norma would have had cretonnes the Dougdales had Boy's needlework. But there were many similarities, especially upstairs, where linoleum

covered the floors, and every bathroom, in spite of the childlessness of
the Dougdales, was a nursery bathroom, smelling strongly of not very
nice soap.

Polly did not attempt to alter anything. She just flopped into Lady
Patricia's bed, in Lady Patricia's bedroom whose windows looked out
on to Lady Patricia's grave. 'Beloved wife of Harvey Dougdale' said
the gravestone, which had been erected some weeks after poor Harvey
Dougdale had acquired a new beloved wife. 'She shall not grow old
as we that are left grow old.'

I think Polly cared very little about houses, which, for her, consisted
of Hampton and the rest, and that if she could no longer live at
Hampton she could not take much interest in any other house anywhere else. Whatever it was in life that Polly did care for, and time had
yet to disclose the mystery, it was certainly not her home. She was in
no sense what the French call a *femme d'intérieur* and her household
arrangements were casual to the verge of chaos. Nor, any longer, alas,
was it Boy. Complete disillusion had set in as far as he was concerned,
and she was behaving towards him with exactly the same off-hand
coldness that had formerly characterized her attitude towards her
mother, the only difference being that whereas she had always been a
little frightened of Lady Montdore it was Boy, in this case, who was a
little frightened of her.

Boy was busily occupied with his new book. It was to be called
Three Dukes, and the gentlemen it portrayed were considered by Boy to
be perfect prototypes of nineteenth-century aristocracy in their three
countries. The Dukes in question were Paddington, Souppes and
Pincio, all masters, it seemed, of the arts of anecdote, adultery and
gourmandise, members of the Paris Jockey Club, gamblers and
sportsmen. He had a photograph, the frontispiece for his book, of all
three together taken at a shoot at Landçut. They stood in front of an
acre of dead animals and, with their tummies, their beards, their deer-
stalker's hats and white gaiters, they looked like nothing so much as
three King Edwards all in a row. Polly told me that he had finished
Pincio while they were in Sicily, the present man having put the
necessary documents at his disposal, and was now engaged upon
Paddington with the assistance of the duke's librarian, motoring off to
Paddington Park every morning, notebook in hand. The idea was
that when that was finished he should go to France in pursuit of
Souppes. Nobody ever had the least objection to Boy 'doing' their
ancestors. He always made them charming and endowed them with
delightful vices, besides which it gave a guarantee, a hall-mark of
ancient lineage, since he never would take on anybody whose family
did not go back to well before the Conquest, in England, or who, if
foreign, could not produce at least one Byzantine Emperor, Pope or
pre-Louis XV Bourbon in their family tree.

The day of the Montdore House Ball came and went, but there was no sign of Polly's baby. Aunt Sadie always used to say that people unconsciously cheat over the dates when babies are expected in order to make the time of waiting seem shorter, but if that is so it certainly makes the last week or two seem endless. Polly depended very much on my company and would send a motor car most days to take me over to Silkin for an hour or two. The weather was heavenly at last, and we were able to go for little walks and even to sit in a sheltered corner of the garden, wrapped in rugs.

'Don't you love it,' Polly said, 'when it's suddenly warm like this after the winter, and all the goats and hens look so happy?'

She did not give me the impression that she was very much interested in the idea of having a baby, though she once said to me:

'Doesn't it seem funny to have talcum powder and things and boring old Sister waiting about, and all for somebody who doesn't exist?'

'Oh, I always think that,' I said, 'and yet the very moment they are there, they become such an integral part of your life that you can't imagine what it was like without them.'

'I suppose so. I wish they'd hurry up. So what about the ball—have you heard anything? You really ought to have gone, Fanny.'

'I couldn't have. The Warden of Wadham and Norma went—not together, I don't mean, but they are the only people I've seen so far. It seems to have been very splendid, Cedric changed his dress five times, he started with tights made of rose petals and a pink wig and ended as Doris Keane in Romance and a black wig, he had real diamonds on his mask. Your mother was a Venetian youth to show off her new legs, and they stood in a gondola giving away wonderful prizes to everybody—Norma got a silver snuff-box—and it went on till seven. Oh, how badly people do describe balls.'

'Never mind, there'll be the *Tatler.*'

'Yes, they said it was flash flash all night. Cedric is sure to have the photographs to show us.'

Presently Boy strolled up and said:

'Well, Fanny, what d'you hear of the ball?'

'Oh, we've just had the ball,' said Polly, 'can't begin all over again. What about your work?'

'I could bring it out here if you like.'

'You know I don't count your silly old embroidery as work.'

Boy's face took on a hurt expression and he went away.

'Polly, you are awful,' I said.

'Yes, but it's for his own good. He pretends he can't concentrate until after the baby now, so he wanders about getting on everybody's nerves when he ought to be getting on with Paddington. He must hurry, you know, if the book is to be out for Christmas, he's still got Souppes to do. Have you ever met Geoffrey Paddington, Fanny?'

'Well, I have,' I said, 'because Uncle Matthew once produced him for a house party at Alconleigh. Old.'

'Not the least bit old,' said Polly, 'and simply heavenly. You've no idea how nice he is. He came first to see Boy about the book and now he comes quite often, to chat. Terribly kind of him, don't you think? Mamma is his chief hate so I never saw him before I married—I remember she was always trying to get him over to Hampton and he never would come. Perhaps he'll be here one day when you are, I'd love you to meet him.'

I did meet him after that, several times, finding his shabby little Morris Cowley outside Silkin when I arrived. He was a poor man, since his ancestor, the great duke, left much glory but little cash, and his father, the old gentleman in spats, had lavished most of what there was on La Païva and ladies of the kind. I thought him friendly and very dull, and could see that he was falling in love with Polly.

'Don't you think he's terribly nice?' said Polly, 'and so kind of him to come when I look like this!'

'Your face is the same,' I said.

'I really quite long for him to see me looking ordinary—if I ever do. I'm losing hope in this baby being born at all.'

It was born, though, that very evening, took one look, according to the Radletts, at its father, and quickly died again.

Polly was rather ill and the Sister would not allow any visitors for about ten days after the baby was born, but as soon as she did I went over. I saw Boy for a moment in the hall, he looked even more gloomy than usual, poor Boy, I thought, left with a wife who now so clearly disliked him and not even a baby to make up for it.

Polly lay in a bower of blossom, and the Sister was very much in evidence. There should have been a purple-faced wailing monster in a Moses basket to complete the picture and I felt its absence as though it were that of a person well known to me.

'Oh, poor——' I began. But Polly had inherited a great deal of her mother's talent for excluding what was disagreeable, and I saw at once that any show of sympathy would be out of place and annoy her, so instead I exclaimed, Radlett-fashion, over two camellia trees in full bloom which stood one each side of her bed.

'Geof. Paddington sent them,' she said. 'Do admit that he's a perfect love, Fanny. You know, Sister was with his sister when she had her babies.'

But then whom had Sister not been with? She and Boy must have had some lovely chats, I thought, the first night or two when Polly was feverish and they had sat up together in his dressing-room. She kept on coming into the room while I was there, bringing a tray, taking away an empty jug, bringing some more flowers, any excuse to break in on our talk and deposit some nice little dollop of gossip. She had seen my condition at a glance, she had also realized that I was too small a fish for her net, but she was affability itself and said that she hoped I would come over every day now and sit with Lady Polly.

'Do you ever see Jeremy Chaddesley Corbett at Oxford?' she asked. 'He is one of my favourite babies.'

Presently she came in empty-handed and rather pink, almost, if such a thing were possible with her, rattled, and announced that Lady Montdore was downstairs. I felt that, whereas she would have bundled any of us into our coffins with perfect calm, the advent of Lady Montdore had affected even her nerves of iron. Polly, too, was thrown off her balance for a moment and said faintly:

'Oh! Is Mr.—I mean my—I really mean, is Boy there?'

'Yes, he's with her now. He sent word to say will you see her—if you don't want to, Lady Polly, I can say quite truthfully that you may not have another visitor today. You really ought not to, the first day, in any case.'

'I'll go,' I said, getting up.

'No, no, no, Fanny, you mustn't, darling. I'm not sure I will see her but I couldn't possibly be left alone with her, sit down again at once, please.'

There were voices in the garden outside.

'Do go to the window,' said Polly, 'is it them?'

'Yes, and Cedric is there too,' I said, 'and they're all three walking round the garden together.'

'No! But I must, I must see Cedric—Sister, do be a darling, go down and tell them to come up at once.'

'Now, Lady Polly, no. And please don't work yourself up, you must avoid any excitement. It's absolutely out of the question for you to see a stranger today—close relations was what Dr. Simpson said, and one at a time. I suppose your mother must be allowed up for a few minutes if you want her, but nobody else and certainly not a strange young man.'

'I'd better see Mummy,' Polly said, to me, 'or else this silly feud will go on for ever, besides, I really can't wait to see her hair and her legs. Oh, dear, though, the one I long for is Cedric.'

'She seems to be in a very friendly mood,' I said, still looking at them out of the window, 'laughing and chatting away. Very smart in navy blue with a sailor hat. Boy is being wonderful. I thought he might be knocked groggy by her appearance, but he's pretending not to notice, he's looking at Cedric all the time. They are getting on like mad.'

Most astute of him, I thought privately. If he hit it off with Cedric he would, very soon, be back in Lady Montdore's good graces, and then perhaps there could be a little modification of Lord Montdore's will.

'I die for the sailor hat, come on, let's get it over. All right then, Sister, ask her to come up—wait—give me a comb and a glass first, will you? Go on with the running commentary, Fanny.'

'Well, Cedric and Boy are chatting away like mad, I think Boy is admiring Cedric's suit, a sort of coarse blue tweed, very pretty, piped with scarlet. Lady Montdore is all smiles, having a good look round. You know the way she does.'

'I can just see it,' said Polly, combing her hair.

I did not quite like to say that Lady Montdore at this very moment was peering over the churchyard wall at her sister-in-law's grave. Boy and Cedric had left her there and were wandering off together towards the wrought-iron gates which led to the kitchen garden, laughing, talking and gesticulating.

'Go on,' said Polly, 'keep it up, Fanny.'

'There's Sister, she is floating up to your mother, who is simply beaming—they both are—I never saw such smiles, goodness, how Sister is enjoying it! Here they come. Your mother looks so happy, I feel quite sentimental, you can see how she must have been missing you, really, at the bottom of her heart, all this time.'

'Nonsense,' said Polly, but she looked rather pleased.

'Darling, I do so feel I shall be in the way. Let me escape now through Boy's dressing-room.'

'Oh, on no account whatever, Fanny. Fanny, you'll upset me if you do that—I absolutely insist on you staying here—I can't face her alone, beams or no beams.'

Perhaps it had occurred to her, as it now did to me, that Lady Montdore's beam would very likely fade at the sight of Polly in Lady Patricia's room, unchanged in almost every respect, in the very bed where Lady Patricia had breathed her last, and that her repugnance for what Polly had done would be given a new reality. Even I had found it rather unattractive until I had got used to the idea. But oversensibility had never been one of Lady Montdore's failings, and besides, the great flame of happiness that Cedric had lit in her heart had long since burnt up all emotions which did not directly relate to him. He was the only person in the world now who had any substance for her.

So the beam did not flicker, she positively radiated good humour as she kissed Polly first and then me. She looked round the room and said:

'You've moved the dressing-table, it's much better like that, more light. Lovely flowers, dear, these camellias—can I have one for Cedric's button-hole? Oh, from Paddington, are they? Poor Geoffrey, I fear he's a bit of a megalomaniac, I haven't been over there once since he succeeded. His father now was very different, a charming man, great friend of ours, King Edward was very fond of him, too, and of course, Loelia Paddington was perfectly lovely—people used to stand on chairs, you know. So the poor little baby died, I expect it was just as well, children are such an awful expense, nowadays.'

Sister, who came back into the room just in time to hear this remark, put her hand to her heart and nearly fainted. That was going to be something to tell her next patients about, never, in all her sisterhood, can she have heard its like from a mother to an only daughter. But Polly, gazing open-mouthed at her mother, taking in every detail of the new appearance, was quite unmoved, it was too typical of Lady Montdore's whole outlook on life for somebody who had been brought up by her to find it odd or upsetting. In any case, I doubt if she minded much about the baby herself, she seemed to me rather like a cow whose calf has been taken away from it at birth, unconscious of her loss.

'What a pity you couldn't have come to the ball, Fanny,' Lady Montdore went on. 'Just only for half an hour, to have a look. It was really beautiful. A lot of Cedric's friends came from Paris for it, in most striking dresses, and I am bound to say, though I have never liked the French, they were very civil indeed and so appreciative of anything one did for them. They all said there hadn't been such a party since the days of Robert de Montesquieu and I can believe it—it cost £4,000, you know, the water for the gondolas was so heavy, for one thing. Well, it shows these foreigners that England isn't done for, yet, excellent propaganda. I wore all my diamonds and I have given Cedric a revolving diamond star (goes by clockwork) and he wore it on his shoulder—most effective, I must say. We thoroughly enjoyed every minute and I wish you could read the letters I've had about it, really touching, people have had so little pleasure the last year or two and it makes them all the more grateful, of course. Next time we come over I'll bring the photographs, they give a wonderful idea of what it was like.'

'What was your dress, Mummy?'

'Longhi,' said Lady Montdore, evasively. 'Veronica Chaddesley Corbett was very good as a prostitute (they were called something different in those days) and Davey was there, Fanny, have you heard from him? He was the Black Death. Everybody made a real effort, you know—it's a terrible pity you girls couldn't have come.'

There was a pause. She looked round the room and said with a sigh :

'Poor Patricia—well, never mind, that's all over now. Boy was telling us about his book, such an excellent idea, *Three Dukes*, and Cedric is very much interested because young Souppes, the son of the Prince des Ressources, whom we used to see at Trouville, is a friend of his. Chèvres-Fontaine, which Cedric used to take every summer, belongs to his first cousin. Isn't it a curious coincidence? So of course, Cedric can tell Boy a great many things he never knew about them all, and they think later on they might go to Paris together to do some research, in fact, we might all go, wouldn't that be amusing?'

'Not me,' said Polly, 'no more abroad for me, ever.'

At this point Boy came into the room and I discreetly left it in spite of a furious look from the bed. I went into the garden to find Cedric.

He was sitting on the church-yard wall, the pale sunshine on his golden hair, which I perceived to be tightly curled, an aftermath of the ball, no doubt, and plucking away with intense concentration at the petals of a daisy.

'He loves me he loves me not he loves me he loves me not, don't interrupt my angel, he loves me he loves me not, oh, heaven heaven heaven! He loves me! I may as well tell you, my darling, that the second big thing in my life has begun.'

A most sinister ray of light suddenly fell upon the future.

'Oh, Cedric,' I said. 'Do be careful!'

I need not have felt any alarm, however, Cedric managed the whole thing quite beautifully. As soon as Polly had completely recovered her health and looks, he put Lady Montdore and Boy into the big Daimler and rolled away with them to France. The field was thus left to a Morris Cowley which, sure enough, could be seen day after day in the drive at Silkin. Before very long, Polly got into it and was taken to Paddington Park, where she remained.

Then the Daimler rolled back to Hampton.

'So here we all are, my darling, having our lovely cake and eating it too, *One's* great aim in life.'

'Yes, I know,' I said, 'the Boreleys think it's simply terrible.'

THE BLESSING

TO
EVELYN WAUGH

Part One

CHAPTER I

'THE foreign gentleman seems to be in a terrible hurry, dear.'

And indeed the house, though quite large, what used to be called a family house, in Queen Anne's Gate, was filled with sounds of impatience. Somebody was stamping about, moving furniture, throwing windows up and down, and clearing his throat exaggeratedly.

'Ahem! Ahem!'

'How long has he been here, Nanny?'

'Nearly an hour I should think. He played the piano, very fast and loud, for a while, which seemed to keep him quiet. He's only started this shindy since John went and told him you were in and would be down presently.'

'You go, darling, and tell him he must wait while I change out of these trousers,' said Grace, who was vigorously cleaning her neck with cotton wool. 'Oh, the dirt. What I need is a bath.'

The drawing-room door was now flung open.

'Do I see you or not?' The voice was certainly foreign.

'All right—very well. I'll come down now, this minute.'

She looked at Nanny, laughing, and said, 'He might go through the floor, like Rumpelstiltskin.'

But Nanny said, 'Put on a dress dear, you can't go down like that.'

'Shall I come upstairs?' said the voice.

'No, don't, here I am,' and Grace ran down, still in her A.R.P. trousers.

The Frenchman, tall, dark and elegant, in French Air Force uniform, was on the drawing-room landing, both hands on the banister rail. He seemed about to uproot the delicate woodwork. When he saw Grace he said 'Ah!' as though her appearance caused him gratified surprise, then, 'Is this a uniform? It's not bad. Did you receive my note?'

'Only now,' said Grace. 'I've been at the A.R.P. all day.'

They went into the drawing-room. 'Your writing is very difficult. I was still puzzling over it when I heard all that noise—it was like the French revolution. You must be a very impatient man.'

'No. But I don't like to be kept waiting, though this room has more compensations than most, I confess.'

'I wouldn't have kept you waiting if I'd known a little sooner—why didn't you . . .'

He was no longer listening, he had turned to the pictures on the walls. 'I do love this Olivier,' he said. 'You must give it to me.'

'Except that it belongs to Papa.'

'Ah, yes, I suppose it does. Sir Conrad. He is very well known in the Middle East—I needn't tell you, however. The Allingham Commission, ah! cunning Sir Conrad. He owes something to my country, after that.' He turned from the picture to Grace, looking at her rather as if she were a picture, and said, 'Natoire, or Rosalba. You could be by either. Well, we shall see, and time will show.'

'Papa loves France.'

'I'm sure he does. The Englishmen who love France are always the worst.'

'The worst?'

'Each man kills the thing he loves, you know. Never mind.'

'You've come from Cairo?' she said. 'I thought I read Cairo in your letter and something about Hughie? You saw him?'

'The fiancé I saw.'

'And you've come to give me news of him?'

'Good news—that is to say no news. Why is this picture labelled Drouais?'

'I suppose it is by Drouais,' said Grace with perfect indifference. Brought up among beautiful things she took but small account of them.

'Indeed? What makes you think so?'

'Are you an art dealer?'

'An art deal-ee.'

'But you said you had news. Naturally I supposed it was the reason for your visit, to tell this news.'

'Have you any milk chocolate?'

'No, I'm sure we haven't.'

'Never mind.'

'Would you like a cocktail—or a glass of sherry?'

'Sherry, with delight.'

'Did you enjoy Cairo? Hughie says it's great fun.'

'The museum is wonderful—but of course no pictures, while the millionaires, poor dears, have wonderful pictures, for which they've paid wonderful prices (from those ateliers where Renoirs and Van Goghs are painted on purpose for millionaires), but which hardly satisfy one's cravings. Even their Corots are not always by Trouillebert. You see exactly how it is. So this afternoon I went to the National Gallery—shut. That is war. Now you will understand what an oasis I have found in Sir Conrad's drawing-room, though I must have a word with him some time about this Drouais, so called.'

'I'm afraid you won't see many pictures in London now,' said Grace. 'Papa has sent all his best ones to the country, and most people have shut up their houses, you know.'

'Never mind. I love London, even without pictures, and English women I love.'

'Do you? Don't we seem terribly dowdy?'

'Of course. That's what makes you so amusing and mysterious. What can you possibly do, all day?'

'Do?'

'Yes. How do you fill those endless eons of time when Frenchwomen are having their hair washed, trying on hats, visiting the collections, discussing with the *lingère*—what is *lingère* in English?'

'Underclothes-maker.'

'Hours they spend with the underclothes-maker. What a funny word —are you sure? Anyhow, Frenchwomen always give one to understand that arranging themselves is full-time work. Now you English, like flowers in a basket, are not arranged, which is quite all right when the flowers are spring flowers.' He gave her another long, approving look. 'But how do you fill in the time? That is the great puzzle.'

'I'm afraid,' she said, laughing, 'that we fill it in (not now, of course, but before the war) buying clothes and hats and having our hair washed. Perhaps the results were not quite the same, but I assure you that great efforts were made.'

'Please don't tell me. Do leave me in the dark, it makes you so much more interesting. Do let me go on believing that the hours drift by in a dream, that those blind blue eyes which see nothing, not even your father's pictures, are turned inward upon some Anglo-Saxon fairyland of your own. Am I not right?'

He was quite right, though perhaps she hardly knew it herself. She thought it over and then said,

'Just before the war I used to have a terribly thrilling dream about escaping from the Germans.'

'One must always escape from Germans. They are so very dull.'

'But now my life is as flat as a pancake, and I can hardly bear it. I quite—almost—long for bombs.'

'I am sorry to have to say that when life is flat it is our own fault. To me it is never flat.'

'Are you never bored?'

'I am sometimes bored by people, but never by life.'

'Oh how lucky.'

'Perhaps I'll take you out dancing. But where? The night clubs here must be terrible.'

'It depends on who you go with.'

'I see. Like all night clubs everywhere. So, I pick you up at eight? I love the black-out. I am trained to be a night bomber—I have flown behind the German lines dropping delightful leaflets, so of course I can find my way by the stars. This gives me confidence, sometimes misplaced I am obliged to own. Then we'll dine at the Connaught Hotel, where I'm staying, and where they have a very good *plat sucré*. What is *plat sucré* in English?—don't tell me, I know, pudding.'

'How d'you know such wonderful English?'

'My mother was. Still it is rather wonderful, isn't it? I can recite the whole of the *Excursion*, but not now. So, eight o'clock, then.'

'I'll be quite ready,' said Grace.

The Frenchman ran downstairs and out of the house, and she saw him from the window running towards St. James's Park. Then she went up to her room, pulled a lot of clothes from various drawers and cupboards, laid them on her bed, and hovered about wondering what on earth she should wear. Nothing seemed somehow quite suitable.

Nanny came in. 'Good gracious! The room looks like a jumble sale.'

'Run me a bath, darling, I'm going out to dinner with that Frenchman.'

'Are you, dear? And what's his name?'

'Bother, I never asked him.'

'Oh well,' said Nanny, 'one French name is very much like another, I daresay.'

CHAPTER II

His name was Charles-Edouard de Valhubert. About a month later he said to Grace, 'Perhaps I will marry you.'

Grace, in love as never before, tried to keep her head and not to look as if about to faint with happiness.

'Will you?' she said. 'Why?'

'In ten days I go back to the Middle East. The war will begin soon, anything may happen, and I need a son.'

'How practical you are.'

'Yes. I am French. *Mais après le mariage,—mince de—nettoyage,—La belle-mère!—on s'assied dessus!*' he sang. He was for ever singing little snatches of songs like that. 'But you won't have a *belle-mère*, unfortunately, since she died, poor dear, many years ago.'

'I must remind you,' said Grace, 'that I am engaged to somebody else.'

'I must remind you that your behaviour lately has not been the behaviour of a faithful fiancée.'

'A little flirtation means nothing at all. I am engaged, and that's that.'

'Engaged. But not married and not in love.'

'Fond.'

'Indeed?'

'You really did see Hughie in Cairo?'

'I saw him plain. He said "Going to London are you? Do look up Grace." Not very clever of him. So I looked up. He is very dull.'

'Very handsome.'

'Yes. So perhaps on Wednesday?'

'Wednesday what?'

'The marriage? I will now go and call on your father—where can I find him?'

'At this time of day he'll be at the House.'

'How little did I ever think I should end up as the son-in-law of the Allingham Commission. How strange is one's fate. Then I'll come back and take you out to dinner.'

The next day Sir Conrad Allingham went to see Mrs. O'Donovan, a widow with whom he had had for many years a loving friendship. Sir Conrad preferred actually making love, a pastime to which he devoted a good deal of energy, with those whose profession it is, finding it embarrassing, never really able to let himself go, with women whom he met in other circumstances. But he liked the company of women to an extent rare among Englishmen, and often went to chat for an hour or so with Mrs. O'Donovan in her light sunny little house which looked over Chelsea Hospital. She was always at home, always glad to receive a visitor, and had a large following among the more intellectual of the right-wing politicians. Her regard for Sir Conrad was special; she spoke of him as 'my Conrad' and was out to other callers when he came to see her. It was said that he never took a step without asking her advice first.

He said, without preamble, 'Have you seen Charles-Edouard de Valhubert?'

'Priscilla's son?'

'Yes.'

'Is he in London?'

'He's been in London several weeks, courting Grace so it seems.'

'Conrad! How extraordinary! What's he like?'

'Really, you know, irresistible. Came to see me at the House yesterday—wants to marry her. I knew nothing—but nothing. I thought Grace was buried in that First Aid Post, and, of course, I've been busy myself. Rather too bad of her really—here I am presented with this *fait accompli*.'

'Well, but what about Hughie?'

'What indeed? Mind you, my sympathies with Hughie are limited—he ought to have married her before he went away.'

'Poor Hughie, he was longing to. He thought it wouldn't be fair.'

'What rubbish though. He leaves a position utterly undefended, he can't be surprised if it falls into—well, Allied hands. I never cared for him as you know, quite half-baked and tells no jokes. However, she didn't ask my advice when she became engaged to him, nor did she ask it before breaking the engagement (if, indeed, she has remembered to do so). Clearly it doesn't matter what I think. So much for Hughie. He has made his exit all right.'

'I can see that you're pleased, really.'

'Yes and no. Valhubert is quite a chap I will say, tall, attractive (very much like his father to look at, much better dressed). He is clearly great fun. But I don't like the idea of Grace marrying a frog, to tell the truth.'

'Conrad! With your love for the French?' Mrs. O'Donovan loved the French too. She had once spent several months in Paris as a child; it had touched her imagination in some way, and she had hankered to live there ever since. This love was one of the strongest links between her and Sir Conrad. They both belonged to the category of English person, not rare among the cultivated classes, and not the least respectable of their race, who can find almost literally nothing to criticize where the French are concerned.

'Only because of Grace's special character,' he said. 'Try and picture her mooning about in Paris society. She would be a lamb among wolves; it makes me shudder to think of it.'

'I'm not sure—after all she's a beauty, and that means a great deal more in France than it does here.'

'Yes, with the men. I'm thinking of the women. They'll make short work of our poor Grace, always in the clouds.'

'Perhaps her clouds will protect her.'

'In a way, but I'm afraid she's deeply romantic, and Valhubert has a roving eye if ever there was one. Don't I remember that Priscilla was very unhappy? There used to be rumours——'

Mrs. O'Donovan delved in her mind for everything she had known, long ago now and buried away, about Priscilla de Valhubert. Among other things she brought to the surface was the memory that when she had first heard of Priscilla's engagement she had felt exactly what she was feeling now, that it was really rather unfair. Mrs. O'Donovan was as much like a Frenchwoman as it is possible for any Anglo-Saxon to be. She spoke the language faultlessly. Her clothes, her scent, the food she ate, the wine she drank, all, in fact, that makes life agreeable, came from France. There was a bidet in her bathroom; she had her afternoon rest on a chaise-longue; she hardly read a word of anything but French; her house was a centre for visiting Frenchmen; the cheese appeared before the pudding at her table, and her dog, a poodle, was called Blum.

In London she was considered the great authority on everything French, to all intents and purposes a Frenchwoman, and she had therefore, quite naturally, come to have a proprietary feeling with regard to France. So it had seemed unfair then that Priscilla, just as it seemed unfair now that Grace, ordinary, rather dull English girls, should marry these fascinating men and sink back with no further effort to the enjoyment of all the delights of French civilization.

Mrs. O'Donovan had never wanted to marry any particular Frenchman, and had been exceedingly happy with her own husband, so that this feeling was nothing if not irrational. All the same, as jealousy does, it stung.

'Yes, very unhappy,' she said, 'partly because she never felt comfortable in Paris society (she never quite learnt French) but chiefly, as you say, owing to the terrible unfaithfulness of Charles-René, which really, I believe, killed her in the end.'

'Oh—killed her,' said Sir Conrad. 'I don't suppose she died of love all the same. French doctors, more likely. When did Charles-René die?'

'Years ago. Fifteen years I should think—very soon after Priscilla. Is old Madame de Valhubert still alive? And Madame Rocher?'

'No idea—never knew them.'

'Madame Rocher des Innouïs is, or was, Madame de Valhubert's sister. Madame de Valhubert herself was always a kind of saint, as far as I can remember, and Madame Rocher was not. I knew them when I was a child, they were friends of my mother.'

'Oh well,' said Sir Conrad testily, 'nobody tells me anything. Nothing was said about any relations. I just talked with the chap for half an hour, mostly about my Drouais, which, according to him, is by some pupil of Nattier. Terrible rot. I did ask him why he wanted to marry her. They won't have many interests in common, unless Grace makes an effort to educate herself at last.' Grace's dreamy illiteracy always exasperated her father.

'What did he say?'

'He said she is so beautiful and so good.'

'And so rich,' said Mrs. O'Donovan.

'It can't be that, my dear Meg. The Valhuberts have always been immensely rich.'

'Yes, but nobody, and especially no French person, ever minds having a bit more you know.'

'I don't somehow feel it's that. Wants a son before he gets killed, more likely. The marriage, if you please, is tomorrow.'

'Tomorrow?'

'Yes, well, what can I do? Grace is of age—twenty-three, time she did marry, in fact—and in love, radiant with love, I must say. Valhubert is more than old enough to know his own mind, twenty-eight it appears, and is off to the war. They have decided, without asking me, that they will marry tomorrow. It remains for me to make a settlement and look pleasant.'

In spite of all this peppery talk, Mrs. O'Donovan, who knew him so well, could see that 'her' Conrad was not really displeased at the turn of events. He always rather liked the unexpected, so long as it did not interfere with his personal comfort, and was infinitely tolerant towards any manifestation of love. He had taken a fancy to Valhubert, who, since he was off to the war, would not be removing Sir Conrad's house-keeper and companion for months, possibly years to come. He who was so fond of Paris would be glad to have a solid family foothold there when the war was over, while the incompatibility of the couple, as well as Grace's broken heart, were, after all, only matters for speculation.

'Where are they to be married?' she asked. 'Shall I come?'

'I hope so indeed, and to luncheon afterwards. Twelve o'clock at the Caxton Hall.'

Mrs. O'Donovan, who was, of course, a Roman Catholic, was shocked and startled. 'A civil marriage only? Conrad, is that wise? The Valhuberts are an intensely Catholic family you know.'

'I know. I did think it rather odd. But Grace is not a Catholic yet, though I suppose in time she will become one. Anyway,' he said, getting up to go, 'that's what they've arranged. Nobody asked my advice about any of it, naturally. When I think how I used to turn to my dear old father—never moved a step without his approval——'

'Are you sure?' she said laughing. 'I seem to remember a river party —something about the Derby—a journey to Vienna——'

'Yes, yes, I don't say I was never young. I am speaking about broad outlines of policy——'

Grace went out and bought a hat, and dressing for her wedding con-sisted in putting on this hat. As the occasion was so momentous she took a long time, trying it a little more to the right, to the left, to the back. While pretty in itself, a pretty little object, it was strangely un-becoming to her rather large, beautiful face. Nanny fussed about the room in a rustle of tissue paper.

'Like this, Nan?'

'Quite nice.'

'Darling, you're not looking. Or like this?'

'I don't see much difference.' Deep sigh.

'Darling! What a sigh!'

'Yes, well I can't say this is the sort of wedding I'd hoped for.'

'I know. It's a shame, but there you are. The war.'

'A foreigner.'

'But such a blissful one. Oh dear, oh dear, this hat. What is wrong with it d'you think?'

'Very nice indeed I expect, but then I always liked Mr. Hugh.'

'Hughie is bliss too, of course, but he went off.'

'He went to fight for King and Country, dear.'

'Well, Charles-Edouard is going to fight for President and Country. I don't see much difference except that he is marrying me first. Oh darling, this hat. It's not quite right, is it?'

'Never mind, dear, nobody's going to look at you.'

'On my wedding day?'

But when Charles-Edouard met them at the registry office he looked at her and said, 'This hat is terrible, perhaps you'd better take it off.'

Grace did so with some relief, shook out her pretty golden hair, and gave the hat to Nanny, who, since it was made of flowers, looked rather like a small, cross, elderly bridesmaid clasping a bouquet.

They went for their honeymoon to Sir Conrad's house, Bunbury Park in Wiltshire, and were very happy. When, during the lonely years which followed, Grace tried to recall those ten short days, the picture that always came to her mind was of Charles-Edouard moving furniture. The central block of the house having been requisitioned by soldiers, he and Grace occupied three rooms in one of the wings, and Charles-Edouard now set himself the task of filling these rooms with objects of art. He seemed not to feel the piercing cold of the unheated hall, with its dome and marble floor, where most of the furniture had been put away, but bustled about in semi-darkness, lifting dust sheets, scrambling under pyramids of tables and chairs, opening cupboards and peering into packing cases, like a squirrel in search of nuts. From time to time, with a satisfied grunt, he would pounce upon some object and scurry off with it. If he could not move it alone he made the soldiers help him. It took eight of them to lug the marble bust of an Austrian archduke up the stairs into Grace's bedroom. Nanny and the housekeeper clearly thought Charles-Edouard was out of his head, and exchanged very meaning looks and sniffs while the archduke was making his painful progress. One of Marie Antoinette's brothers, bewigged and be-medalled, the Fleece upon his elaborately folded stock, he now entirely dominated the room with his calm, stupid, German face.

'He looks dull,' said Grace.

'But so beautiful. You look too much at the subject—can't you see that it's a wonderful piece of sculpture?'

'Come for a walk, Charles-Edouard, the woods are heavenly today.'

It was early spring, very fine and dry. The big beeches, not yet in leaf, stood naked on their copper carpet, while the other trees had petti-coats of pale green. The birds were already tuning up an orchestra as if preparing to accompany those two stars of summer the cuckoo and the nightingale as soon as they should make their bow. It seemed a pity to spend such days creeping about under dust sheets.

'Nature I hate,' said Charles-Edouard, as he went on with his self-appointed task. So she walked in the sunny woods alone, until she dis-covered that if she could propose an eighteenth-century mausoleum, Siamese dairy, wishing well, hermit's grotto or cottage orné as the object for a walk, he would accompany her. He strode along at an enormous speed, often breaking into a run, seizing her hand and drag-ging her with him. '*Il neige des plumes de tourterelles*', he sang.

Her father's park abounded in follies, quite enough to last out their visit. What did they talk about all day? She never could remember. Charles-Edouard sang his little songs, made his little jokes, and told her a great deal about the objects he found under the dust sheets, so that names like Carlin, Cressent, Thomire, Reisener and Gouthière always thereafter reminded her of their honeymoon. Her room became transformed from a rather dull country house bedroom into a corner of the Wallace Collection. But he hardly talked about himself at all, or his family, or life in Paris, or what they would do after the war. A fortnight from their wedding day he left England and went back to Cairo.

Grace soon realized that she was expecting a child. When the air raids began Sir Conrad sent her to live at Bunbury, and here, in a bedroom full of works of art collected by his father, Sigismond de Valhubert opened his eyes upon the calm, stupid face of an Austrian archduke.

CHAPTER III

'He is a little black boy—oh, he is black. I never expected you to have a baby with such eyes, it doesn't seem natural or right.'

'I don't know,' said Grace. 'I think one gets tired of always gazing into these blue eyes. I like this better.'

'Such a funny sort of name, too,' Nanny went on, 'not like anything. If he'd been called after his father he could have been Charlie, or Eddy, but Sigi——! Well, I don't care to say it in the street, makes people look round.'

'But you're so seldom in streets, darling.'

'Salisbury. People stop and look at him as it is.'

'That's because he's such a love. Anyway, I think he's a blessing.'

And so of course did Nanny, though she would have thought him an even more blessed blessing had he resembled his mother more and his father less.

Grace stayed on at Bunbury. She had not meant to, she had meant to go back to London and the A.R.P. as soon as Sigi was weaned, but somehow, in the end, she stayed on. She fell into various country jobs, ran a smallholding, and looked after the baby as much as Nanny allowed. Sir Conrad went down to see her at week-ends, and sometimes she spent a few days with him in London. So the years of the war went by calmly and rather happily for Grace, who never much minded being alone. She had a placid, optimistic nature, and was never tortured by anxious thoughts about Charles-Edouard, or doubted that he would return safely in due course. Nor did she doubt that when, in due course, he had safely returned, their marriage would be one of Elysian happiness.

Her father and Mrs. O'Donovan selected many books for her to read, in preparation for a French life. They told her she ought to be studying the religious writings of the seventeenth, the drama and philosophy of the eighteenth, the prose and politics of the nineteenth centuries. They sent her, as well as quantities of classics and many novels and *mémoires*, Michelet in sixteen morocco volumes and Sainte-Beuve in sixteen paper ones; they sent her Bodley's *France* and Brogan's *Third Republic*, saying she would feel a fool if she did not understand the French electoral, judicial, and municipal systems. Grace did make spasmodic efforts to get on with all this homework, but she was too mentally lazy and untrained to do more than nibble at it. In the evenings she liked to turn on the wireless, think of Charles-Edouard, and stitch away at a carpet destined to be literally laid at his feet. It was squares of petit point, in a particularly crude Victorian design of roses and lilies of the valley and blue ribbons. Grace thought it too pretty for words.

She lived in a dream of Charles-Edouard, so that as the years went on he turned, in her mind, into somebody quite divorced from all reality and quite different from the original. And the years did go on. He came back for three hectic days in July 1940 which hardly counted, so little did Grace see of him, and after that seemed to go further and further away, Fort Lamy, Ceylon, and finally Indo-China. When the war ended he was not immediately demobilized, his return was announced again and again, only to be put off, so that it was more than seven years after their wedding when at last the telephone bell rang and Grace heard his voice, speaking from Heath Row. This time he was unannounced; she had thought him still in the East.

'Our Ambassador was on the 'plane with me, and he is sending me straight down in his motor,' he said. 'It seems I'll be with you in an hour or two.'

Grace felt that, whereas the seven years had gone in a flash, this hour or two would never never end. She went up to the nursery. Sigi was having his bath before bedtime.

'Don't let him go to sleep,' she said to Nanny. 'Guess what, darling—his father will be here presently.'

Nanny received this news with the air of one resigned to the inevitable fact that all things, especially good things, have their term. She gave a particularly fearful sniff and said, 'Well, I only hope he won't over-excite the poor little fellow. You know what it's like getting him off, evenings, as well as I do.'

'Oh Nanny, just for once, darling, it wouldn't matter if he stayed up all night.'

She left the nursery and wandered down the drive to the lodge, where she sat on one of the stone stumps that, loosely chained together, enclosed grassy mounds on either side of the gates. There was no traffic on the little road outside the park, and beyond it, bordered by clumps of wild rose bushes, the deep woods were full of song. It was high summer now, that week when cuckoo and nightingale give their best, their purest performances. The evening was warm, but she felt glad of a cardigan; she had begun to shiver like a nervous dog.

At last the motor drove up. Charles-Edouard sprang out of it and hugged her, and then she remembered exactly what he was like as a real person, and the other, dream Charles-Edouard, was chased into the back of her mind. Not quite chased away, she often thereafter remembered him with affection, but separated from reality.

They got back into the motor and drove up to the house.

'You are looking very beautiful,' he said, 'and very happy. I was afraid you might have become sad, all these years and years down here, away from me.'

'I longed terribly for you.'

'I know. You must have.'

'Don't tease, Charles-Edouard. But if we had to be separated I would rather have been here than anywhere. I love the country you know, and besides, I had plenty to do.'

'What did you do?'

'Oh, goats and things.'

'Goats must be very dull.'

'No, really not. Then of course there was Sigi. Are you excited for him?'

'Very very much excited.'

'Come then, let's go straight up to the nursery.'

But outside Grace's bedroom Charles-Edouard caught her hand and pointed sternly to the door. 'I must see if the archduke is still there,' he said, and they went in.

Grace said presently, 'If you had been killed in the war it would have finished me off.'

'Ah! Would you have died? That's very nice.'

'Yes, I couldn't have gone on living.'

'And would it have been a violent death by poison or a slow death by misery?'

'Which would you prefer?'

'Poison would be very flattering.'

'All right then, poison. Now come on, let's go to Sigi.'

In the day nursery, Nanny's face was a picture of disapproval. 'Funny thing,' she said, 'I thought I heard a car quite half an hour ago. Time he went off to sleep, poor mite.'

They went through into the night nursery. Sigi was standing on his bed. He had black, silky curls and clever little black eyes, and he was always laughing.

'Have you seen me before?' he said to his father.

'Never. But I can guess who you are.'

'Sigismond de Valhubert, a great boy of nearly seven. Are you my papa?'

'Let me present myself—Charles-Edouard de Valhubert.' They shook hands.

'What are you?'

'I am a colonel in the French Air Force, retired. And what are you going to be?'

'A superman,' said the child.

Charles-Edouard was much gratified by this reply. 'Always the same old story,' he said, '*l'Empereur, la gloire, hommage à la Grande Armée.* I shall have a lot to tell you about the Marshal of France, your ancestor. Do you know that at home we have a standard from the battlefield of Friedland?'

Sigi looked intensely puzzled, and Grace said, 'I'm afraid his superman isn't Napoleon, not yet at least, but Garth.'

'Goethe?'

'Oh dear—no. Garth. It's a strip—I can't explain, I'll have to show you some time. It's rather horrible really, but we don't seem able to do without it.'

'Garth, you know, in the *Daily*,' Sigismond said. His grandfather had forbidden him to call it the *Mirror* so he compromised with the *Daily*. 'When I'm big I'm going to have a space ship like Garth and go to the——'

'But what do you know, Sigismond? Can you count? Can you read, and can you name the forty Kings of France?'

'Forty?' said Grace. 'Are there really? Poor little boy.'

'Well eighteen are Louis and ten are Charles. It's not as bad as it sounds. I always forget the others myself.'

'Isn't he a darling?' said Grace, as they went downstairs.

'A darling. Rather dull, but a darling.'

'He's not dull a bit,' she said indignantly, 'though he may be a little young for his age. It comes from living all alone with me in the country, if he is.'

'So perhaps tomorrow I take you both home to France.'

'Tomorrow? Oh no, Charles-Edouard, not——'

'We can't stay here. I've seen all the leaning towers and pavilions and rotundas and islands and rococo bridges, I've moved the furniture and rehung the pictures. There's nothing whatever to do, and we have our new life to begin. So——?'

'Oh darling, but tomorrow. What about the packing?'

'Don't bother. We're going straight to Provence, you'll only want cotton dresses, and you must have all new when we get to Paris anyhow.'

'Yes, but Nanny. What will she say?'

'I don't know. The 'plane is at twelve, giving us time to catch the night train to Marseilles. We leave here at nine. I've arranged everything and ordered a motor to take us. I suppose you've got the passports as I told you to last year?'

'But Nanny——' wailed poor Grace.

Charles-Edouard began to sing a song about sardines. '*Marinées, argentées, leurs petits corps décapités. . . .*'

CHAPTER IV

CHARLES-EDOUARD, Grace, Sigismond and Nanny arrived at Marseilles in a torrid heat wave. Grace and the child were tired after the night in the train, but Charles-Edouard and Nanny were made of sterner stuff. His songs and jokes flowed like a running river, except when he was actually asleep, and so did Nanny's complaints. These were a recitative of nursery grievance in which certain motifs constantly recurred. 'No time to write to Daniel Neal—all those nice toys left behind—the beautiful rocking-horse Mrs. O'Donovan gave us—his scooter with rubber tyres and a bell—poor little mite, grown out of his winter coat, how shall we ever get another—what shall I do without my wireless?—the Bengers never came, you know, dear, from the Army and Navy—shall we get the *Mirror* there and my *Woman and Beauty*? Oh I say, I never took those books back to Boots, what will the girl think of me—that nice blouse I was having made in the village——' Then the chorus, much louder than the rest, 'Shame, really.'

They were met at the station by Charles-Edouard's valet Ange-Victor in a big, rather old-fashioned Bentley. Ange-Victor was crying with joy, and it seemed as if he and Charles-Edouard would never stop hugging each other. At last they stowed the luggage into the motor, Grace and Sigi crammed into the front seats beside Charles-Edouard, with valet and nurse behind, and he drove hell for leather up the narrow, twisting, crowded road which goes from Marseilles to Aix.

'I'm a night bomber, have no fear,' he shouted to Grace as she cringed in her corner clasping Sigi. The hot air rushed past them, early as it was the day was already a scorcher. Charles-Edouard was singing '*Malbrouck s'en va t-en guerre et ne reviendra pas*'.

'But I am back,' he said triumphantly. 'Never never did I expect to come back. Five fortune-tellers said I should be killed.'

And he turned right round, in the teeth of an enormous lorry, to ask Ange-Victor if Madame André, in the village, still told the cards.

'Shall I tell your fortune now?' said Grace. 'If you don't drive much more carefully there will soon be a widow, a widower, an orphan and two childless parents in this family.'

'Try and remember that I am a night bomber,' said Charles-Edouard. 'I have driven aeroplanes over the impenetrable jungle, how should I have an accident on my old road I've known from a baby? Here we turn,' he said, wrenching the motor, under the very bonnet of another lorry, across the road and down a lane to the left of it. 'And there,' he said a few minutes later, 'is Bellandargues.'

The Provençal landscape, like that of Tuscany, which it so much resembles, is marked by many little hills humping unexpectedly in the middle of vineyards. These often have a cluster of cottages round their lower slopes, overlooked by a castle, or the ruin of a castle, on the summit. Such was Bellandargues. The village lay at the foot of a hill, and above it, up in the blue sky, hung the castle, home, for many generations, of the Valhubert family.

As they drove into the village it presented a gay and festive appearance, all flags for the return of Charles-Edouard. A great streamer, with '*Vive la Libération, Hommage à M. le Maire*', was stretched across the street: the village band was playing, and a crowd was gathered in the market-place, waving and cheering. Charles-Edouard stopped the motor. M. Mignon, the chemist, made a long speech, recalling the sad times they had lived through since Charles-Edouard was last there, and saying with what deep emotion they had all heard him when he had spoken on the London radio in July 1940.

'Hm. Hm.' Charles-Edouard had a certain face which betrayed, to those who knew him well, inward laughter tinged with a guilty feeling. His eyes laughed but his mouth turned down at the corners. He made this face now, remembering so well the speech at the B.B.C.; how he had been exchanging looks as he delivered it with the next speaker, on the other side of a glass screen. She was a pretty little Dutch girl, and he had taken her out to tea, he remembered, before going back to Grace. M. Mignon made a fine and flowery peroration, Charles-Edouard spoke in reply, the village band then struck up again while he and Grace shook hundreds of hands. Great admiration was lavished upon Sigi, pronounced to be the image of his papa; he jumped up and down on the seat, laughing and clapping, until Nanny said he was thoroughly above himself and pinned him to her lap.

'Well,' said Grace, when at last they drove on, 'if you never thought you'd be son-in-law to the Allingham Commission, it certainly never occurred to me that I should marry a mayor.' She turned round and said, 'Wasn't that delightful, Nan?'

'Funny-looking lot, aren't they? Not too fond of washing, if you ask me. Fearful smell of drains, dear.'

The road up through the village got steeper and steeper, the side alleys were all flights of steps. Charles-Edouard changed down into bottom gear. They bounced through a gateway, climbed another slope, came out on to a big, flat terrace, bordered with orange trees in tubs, and drew up at the open front door of the castle. The village was now invisible; far below them, shimmering in the heat and punctuated with umbrella pines, lay acre upon acre of vivid green landscape.

As she got out of the motor Grace thought to herself how different all this was going to look in a few weeks, when it had become familiar. Houses are entirely different when you know them well, she thought, and on first acquaintance even more different from their real selves, more deceptive about their real character than human beings. As with human beings, you can have an impression, that is all. Her impression of Bellandargues was entirely favourable, one of hot, sleepy, beautiful magnitude. She longed to be on everyday terms with it, to know the rooms that lay behind the vast windows of the first floor, to know what happened round the corner of the terrace, and where the staircase led to, just visible in the interior darkness. It is a funny feeling to visit your home for the first time and have to be taken about step by step like a blind person.

An old butler ran out of the door, saying he had not expected them for another half-hour. There was more hugging and crying, and then Charles-Edouard gave him rapid instructions about Nanny being taken straight to her rooms and a maid sent to help her unpack.

'And Madame la Marquise?' he said.

The butler replied that Madame la Marquise must be in the drawing-room. He said again that they had arrived before they were expected.

'Come then,' Charles-Edouard said, taking Sigi by the hand. 'Come, Grace.'

'Go with the butler, Nan,' said Grace. 'I'll be up as soon as I can.'

'Yes, well, don't keep Sigi too long, dear. He's filthy after that train.'

Her words fell on air, Grace was pursuing husband and son into the shadows of the house and up the stairs. Somewhere a Chopin waltz was being played, but Grace did not consciously hear it, though she remembered it afterwards.

'Wait, wait, Charles-Edouard,' she cried. 'Who is this Marquise?'

'My grandmother.'

'Charles-Edouard, dearest, stop one minute, I didn't know you had a grandmother—oh, do stop and explain——'

'There's nothing to explain. In here.' He held open a door for her. Grace walked into a huge room, dark and panelled, with a painted ceiling. Furniture was dotted about in it; like shrubs in a desert the pieces seemed to grow where they stood, following no plan of arrangement, and dotted about among them were human figures. There was an old man painting at an easel, an old lady at a piano playing the Chopin waltz, while another old lady, in the embrasure of a window, was deep in conversation with an ancient priest. She looked quickly round as the door opened, and then ran towards Grace.

'So soon?' she cried, 'and nobody downstairs to meet you? It's that wretched stable clock, always slow.' She kissed Grace on both cheeks, and then again, saying, 'A beauty! What a beauty! Well done, Charles-Edouard,' she said, hugging him. 'This is wonderful happiness, my child.'

Now there was a perfect hubbub of greetings and introductions. 'Tante Régine—M. le Curé, how are you? Yes, yes, I quite realized that,' said Charles-Edouard when M. le Curé began to explain that he had not been down in the village because M. Mignon was in charge of the welcome there. 'Grace, this is M. de la Bourlie, and this is M. le Curé, Grace, who has been M. le Curé here—for how long?'

Madame de Valhubert said, 'M. le Curé arrived here, a young priest, the same summer that I arrived, a young bride. We shall have seen sixty grape harvests together this year.'

Tante Régine became rather fidgety while her sister was speaking, and said to Grace in an aside, 'But I am much younger, I was always the baby—fifteen—twenty years younger than Françoise.'

Their faces were the same, soft, white faces with black eyes, but while Madame de Valhubert's was framed in soft white hair and her clothes were very much like those of a nun, Madame Rocher, painted and powdered, had her red hair cut in the latest way and wore such a beautiful, simple, desirable cotton dress that Grace could look at nothing else in the room.

'Dear Tante Régine, I'm very much pleased to see you,' said Charles-Edouard. 'And Octave?'

Octave was her late husband's nephew, the present holder of his title, whom Madame Rocher had brought up and then, because he bored her, had pushed into the army. The old Marquis had left her every penny of the enormous fortune which came to him through his mother, so she was able to behave in a very high-handed manner with his relations.

'Oh poor Octave, no luck at all, as usual,' said Madame Rocher. 'He is still with his regiment, still only a captain. Of course, if it hadn't been for this wretched war he would be at least a colonel by now.'

'Hm. Hm.' said Charles-Edouard, bursting with inward laughter. 'And I, in spite of this wretched war, am a colonel, do you know that? Grandmother, did you know that I am a colonel?'

'Yes, yes, we know a great deal about you here. Little Béguin, who was invalided home after the Libération, was full of your exploits.'

'Indeed I did splendidly,' said Charles-Edouard laughing. 'I am a colonel and I have a son—where is this son, by the way?'

He dragged Sigi out from behind a curtain, where he was hiding in a most unusual state of shyness.

'Sigismond, come and kiss the hand of your ancestress. Now that you are a French boy we should like to see some manners, please.'

Sigi became quite scarlet with embarrassment, but the old lady, taking two boxes of sweets from a table, held them out to him and said, 'You can kiss my hand another time, darling, but now choose which you'll have, a chocolate or a marron glacé. A little bribery never spoils anything,' she said to Charles-Edouard as Sigi carefully made his choice. 'Well?'

'Well, I do love chocolate, certainly I do, but I suppose I ought to choose the one with the silver paper on account of the poor lepers.'

'What, my child?'

'You see Nanny—well you haven't met her yet—she keeps a silver-paper ball, and when it weighs a pound she sends it up and one poor leper can live on that—oh for years, probably. They hardly need anything at all Nanny says, quite contented with a handful of rice from time to time, but it's ages now since Nanny sent up, silver paper is so terribly rare in these days. She will be pleased.'

'But this child has saintly thoughts!' cried Madame de Valhubert. 'M. le Curé, did you understand? The little one is already planning for the lepers. It is wonderful, so young. How he does look like you, Charles-Edouard, the image of what you were at that age, though I don't remember that you had such gratifying preoccupations.'

'Yes, isn't he the very picture,' said Charles-Edouard, 'but I'm afraid he's not as brilliant as I was. Now if you will excuse us perhaps I'll show Grace the rest of the house before luncheon, and take St. François Xavier up to his nursery.'

Outside, on the staircase, Nanny was hovering with a face of leaden reproach. She pounced upon Sigi and hurried him off, muttering her recitative under her breath. She was very slightly in awe of Charles-Edouard, and would only let herself go, Grace knew, when alone with her. The words 'unbearably close, here' were just distinguishable, a look of terrifying malice flashed in the direction of Charles-Edouard, and she was gone. Grace absolutely dreaded the day when she would be obliged to have it out with him about Nanny. She had known, as a child, that her father and mother used to have it out at intervals, until her mother, by dying, had saddled Sir Conrad with Nanny for ever. She gave Charles-Edouard a nervous, laughing look, but he did not notice it; he put his arm round her waist, and they went slowly up the stairs.

Then she went back to what she had been wondering as they came out of the drawing-room. 'But why didn't you tell me about your grandmother—well, really, all these people?'

'I have one very firm rule in life,' he said, 'which is never to talk to people about other people they have never seen. It is very dull, since people are only interested when you know them, and furthermore it can

lead to misunderstandings. You and my grandmother, having no pre-
conceived ideas about each other——'

'You haven't got a wife hidden away in some other room, I hope?'

'No wife.'

'Oh good. But of course it's just like in *Rebecca*. By degrees I shall find
out all about your past.'

'Oh my past! It's such a long time ago now.'

'So tell me more, now I've seen them. Who is the old man?'

'M. de la Bourlie? He is my grandmother's lover.'

'Her lover?' Grace was very much startled. 'Isn't she rather old to
have a lover?'

'Has age to do with love?' Charles-Edouard looked so much surprised
that Grace said,

'Oh well—I only thought. Anyway, perhaps there's nothing in it.'

He roared with laughter, saying, 'How English you are. But M. de la
Bourlie has visited my grandmother every single day for forty-six years,
and in such a case you may be sure that there is always love.'

'He doesn't live here, too?'

'No. He has a beautiful house in Aix. He generally comes over in the
afternoon, but today, of course, he has come early, dying of curiosity to
see l'Anglaise. They all must be, we shall have the whole neighbourhood over. It will be very dull. Never mind.'

'Why don't they marry?' said Grace.

'Who? Oh my grandmother. Well, but poor Madame de la Bourlie.'

'Poor her anyway. In England, when there is a long love affair like
that people always end by marrying.'

'And in America if you hold a woman's hand you are expected to go
round next day with the divorce papers. The Anglo-Saxons are very
fond of marriage, it is very strange.'

'I've never seen a pale green wig before.'

'He's worn that wig ever since I was a little boy. He has been a
tremendous lady-killer in his time, wig and all.'

'And when I am old like your grandmother, will you love me still?'

'It depends.'

'How horrid. Depends on what?'

'It all depends, entirely, on you.'

'Charles-Edouard, was the reason you didn't tell me about your
grandmother because you thought I wouldn't like the idea of sharing
my house with another woman?'

Charles-Edouard looked immensely surprised. 'It never occurred to
me for a single minute,' he said. 'It's not your house, exactly, but a
family house, you know. But we shall hardly ever be here.'

'Oh! I thought it was my new home?'

'One of them. Our real home is in Paris, and there my grandmother,
though she lives in the house, has a separate establishment. You will

love her you know. For one thing French people (and you are French now) always love their relations, and then my grandmother is a saint.'

'Yes,' said Grace, 'I see that. I know I shall. It was so charming the way she gave those chocolates to Sigi when she saw he didn't want to kiss her hand. But how sad, Charles-Edouard, to have this lovely house and not to live in it?'

'Oh dearest Grace, for living the country is really impossible. It is too dull. I am obliged to come down here on business, but I could never never live here.'

'What business?'

'I must explain that, whereas in England the country is for pleasure and the town for business, here it is the exact opposite. We French have all our pleasure in Paris, where we have nothing to do except amuse ourselves, but we work really hard in the country. I have a lot of work when I am here, local business, since I am the mayor, and much family business, looking after my property.'

They had reached a wide landing, arranged like a room, with old-fashioned, chintz furniture. Two great windows from floor to ceiling were open upon an expanse of pale blue sky. Charles-Edouard led her through one of them on to a balcony, and, waving at the green acres far below, he said,

'There grows the wealth of the Valhubert family.'

'D'you mean that vegetable? But what is it? I was wondering.'

'Vegetable indeed! Have you never been in the country in France before? How strange. These are vineyards.'

'No!' said Grace. She had supposed all her life that vineyards were covered with pergolas, such as, in Surrey gardens, support Miss Dorothy Perkins, heavy with bunches of hot-house grapes, black for red wine, white for champagne. Naboth's vineyard, in the imagination of Grace, was Naboth's pergola, complete with crazy paving underfoot.

However she did not explain all this to Charles-Edouard, but merely said, 'I've never seen one before. I thought they would be different, somehow.'

Grace's bedroom was at the top of the house. It was a large, white-panelled room with many windows, from most of which, so high up was it, so hanging in the firmament, nothing was visible but sky. But on one side two French windows opened on to a tiny garden of box hedges and standard roses, which looked like a stage set forming part of the room itself.

'Very English,' said Charles-Edouard, 'you will feel at home here.'

It had been arranged by his mother with old-fashioned chintz and embroidered white muslin.

'The garden!' said Grace. 'I never saw anything so lovely.'

'Every floor of this house has a terrace. It is built on the side of a hill, you see. Here are your bathroom and dressing-room, and here are my rooms. So we are all alone together.'

'Literally in heaven,' said Grace, with a happy sigh.

'Now perhaps I'll take you to the nursery; we go down again and up this little staircase. Here we are.'

'Oh, what a lovely nursery—isn't it lovely, Nan, much the biggest we've ever had, and so light—and what a view!'

This was Grace's technique with Nanny. She would open an offensive of enthusiasm, hoping to overcome and silence the battery of complaints before Nanny could begin firing them off. It almost never worked, she could see it not working now, though for the moment she was shielded by the presence of Charles-Edouard. Nanny remained silent and went on with what she was at, grimly unpacking toys from a hamper.

'I'll come back,' said Charles-Edouard. 'I want a word with Ange-Victor.'

Grace's heart sank, but she rattled bravely on. 'You've got a garden, too, isn't it delightful? I love it being surrounded by those pretty red roofs against the sky, like Kate Greenaway. Look at the plants growing out of them, what are they, I wonder? Doesn't it all smell delicious? I long for you to see my bedroom; it is so pretty. Tell you what, darling, I'll get you a garden chair, then you'll be able to sit out here of an evening.'

Nanny looked over her shoulder to make sure that Charles-Edouard had gone, and then spoke. 'Horribly draughty I should think, with all those roofs. Smutty, too, I daresay. Aren't the stairs awful? I shan't be able to manage them many times a day, in this heat. Well, I've been trying to unpack, but there's nowhere to put anything, you know—shame, really—no nice shelves for our toys. No mantelpieces, either, for my photographs and the ornaments. Funny sort of rooms, aren't they? Not very homy. I'd like to show you the bathroom and lavatory, dear—nothing but a cupboard—no window at all, really most insanitary—it would never be allowed at home.'

'How fascinating,' said Grace, 'look, it's built in the thickness of the wall, this big bathroom.'

'Perhaps it may be. Then what is that guitar-shaped vase for, I wonder? Oh, well, it'll do to put the things to soak. Not very nice, is it? Leading out of our bedroom like that?'

'Never mind, in this lovely weather you can leave everything wide open—it's quite different from England.'

'Different!' a deep sniff, 'I should say it is.'

'Look at the swing! How amusing! That will quite make up to Sigi for leaving his rocking-horse behind.'

'Yes, well it's a funny place for a swing, in our bedroom.'

'It's all so huge, isn't it? And like being out of doors, with these great windows everywhere. Heavenly, really. Look, here's a cupboard, darling—the size of a room, too. Hadn't you noticed it? You can put everything here—and see, there's a light for it. That is nice.'

'Just smell inside, dear—horribly musty, I'm afraid. Then I was wanting to speak to you about these roofs—the little monkey will be up on them in no time. My goodness! I knew it! Come down this instant, Sigi, what did I tell you? You are not to climb on those roofs— what d'you think you're doing? It's most dangerous.'

'I'm Garth on the mountains of the moon.'

Charles-Edouard reappeared, saying, 'Oh, do be Napoleon crossing the Alps. This Garth is really too dull. The roofs are quite safe, Nanny, I lived on them when I was his age, mountaineering and exploring. I must get out my old *Journal des Voyages* for him, since I suppose he is rather young for Jules Verne?'

Nanny having retreated into the nursery, 'don't know how you can stand the glare', Charles-Edouard pulled at the neck of Grace's cotton dress and implanted a kiss on her shoulder.

'Ugh! You soppy things,' said Sigismond, 'I don't like all this daft kissing stuff.'

'You'll like it all right one day,' said Charles-Edouard. 'That big bell means luncheon time. Good appetite, Sigi.'

As they went back through the nursery a man-servant was laying the table on a thick, white linen tablecloth. 'Good appetite, Nanny,' said Charles-Edouard. Nanny did not reply. She was looking with stupefied disapproval at a bottle of wine which had just been put down in front of her.

CHAPTER V

VERY hungry, accustomed to English post-war food, Grace thought the meal which followed the most delicious she had ever eaten. The food, the wine, the heat and the babel of French talk, most of which was quite incomprehensible to her untuned ear, induced a half-drunk, entirely happy state of haziness. When, after nearly two hours, the party rose from the table, she was floating on air. Everybody wandered off in different directions, and Charles-Edouard announced that he was going to be shut up in the library for the afternoon with his tenants and the agent.

'Will you be happy?' he said, stroking Grace's hair and laughing at her for being, as he could see, so tipsy.

'Oh I'm sleepy and happy and hot and sleepy and drunk and happy and sleepy. It's too too blissful being so drunk and happy.'

'Then go to sleep, and when I've finished we'll do whatever you like. Motor down to the sea if you like, and bathe. I'm sleepy myself, but the *régisseur* has convened all these people to see me—they've been waiting too long already—I must go to them, so there it is. See you presently.'

'All right. I'll go and have a little word with Nanny and then a lovely hot sleep. Oh the weather! Oh the bliss of everything! Oh how happy I am!'

Charles-Edouard gave her a very loving look as he went off. He thought he was going to like her even more in France than in England, and was well satisfied to have come back accompanied by this happy beauty.

Alas for the hot, tipsy sleep! Nanny sobered and woke her up all right, her expression alone was a wave of icy water. Grace did not even bother to say 'Wasn't the luncheon delicious? Did you enjoy it?' She just stood and meekly waited for the wave to break over her head.

'Well, dear, we've had nothing to eat since you saw us, nothing whatever. Course upon course of nasty greasy stuff smelling of garlic—a month's ration of meat, yes, but quite raw you know—shame, really—I wasn't going to touch it, let alone give it to Sigi, poor little mite.'

'Nanny says the cheese was matured in manure,' Sigi chipped in, eyes like saucers.

'I wish you could have smelt it, dear, awful it was, and still covered with bits of straw. Makes you wonder, doesn't it? Well, we just had a bite of bread and butter and a few of Mrs. Crispin's nice rock cakes I happened to have with me. Not much of a dinner, was it? Funny-looking bread here, too, all crust and holes, I don't know how you'd make a nice bit of damp toast with that. Poor little hungry boy—never mind, it's all right now, darling, your mummy will go to the kitchen for us and ask for some cold ham or chicken—a bit of something plain—some tomatoes, without that nasty, oily, oniony dressing, and a nice floury potato, won't you, dear?'

These words were uttered in tones of command. An order had been issued, there was nothing of the request about them.

'Goodness, I've no idea what floury potato is in French,' said Grace, playing for time. 'Didn't you like the food, Sigi?'

'It's not a question of like it or not like it. The child will eat anything, as you know, but I'm not going to risk having him laid up with a liver attack. This heat wave is quite trying enough without that, thank you very much, not to mention typhoid fever, or worse, I only wish you could have smelt it, that's all I say.'

'I did smell it, we had it downstairs—delicious.'

'Well it may be all right for grown-up people, if that's the sort of thing they go in for,' said Nanny, with a tremendous sniff, 'but give it to the child I will not, and personally I'd rather go hungry.' This, however, she had no intention of doing. 'Now, dear,' she said briskly, 'just go and get us a bite of something plain, that's a good girl.'

'I'm so dreadfully sorry, Mummy, I've got pains in my tummy. Listen, it rumbles, just like Garth when he'd been floating for weeks on that iceberg.'

Sigi looked so pathetic that Grace said, 'Oh all right then. I don't know where the kitchen is, but I'll see what I can do. I think it's all great rubbish,' she added in a loud aside as she slammed the nursery door behind her.

She wandered off uncertainly, hardly able, in that big, complicated house built at so many different dates, on so many different levels, to find her way to the first-floor rooms. At last she did so, looked into the drawing-room, and was almost relieved that there was nobody there. Her mission seemed to her so absurd, and really so ill-mannered, that she quite longed for it to fail. She assumed that everybody except Charles-Edouard would be happily asleep by now, and only wished that she were too. Loud French voices came from the library, apart from them the house was plunged in silence. She stood for a moment by the library door but did not dare to open it, thinking how furious Sir Conrad would be at such an interruption. The dining-room was empty; no sign of any servant. She went through it, and found a stone-flagged passage, which she followed, on and on, up and down steps, until she came to a heavy oak door. Perhaps this led to the kitchen; she opened it timidly. A strangely dark and silent kitchen, if so, with cool but not fresh air smelling of incense. She stood peering into the gloom; it was quite some moments before she realized that this must be a chapel. Then, not two yards from her, she saw Madame de Valhubert, a lace shawl over her head, praying deeply. Grace shut the door and fled, in British embarrassment, back to the nursery.

'I can't find the kitchen, or one single person to ask,' she said, in a hopeless voice. Nanny gave Grace a look. 'Where's Papa then?'

'At a meeting. Well Nan you do know, we should never have dared disturb my papa at a meeting, should we? I don't see how I can. Are you sure you haven't any food with you, to make do just for now?'

'Nothing whatever.'

'No groats?'

'Groats isn't much of a dinner. The poor little chap's hungry after all that travelling. We didn't get much of a dinner yesterday if you remember, in that aeroplane, expecting every moment to be our last.'

Sigismond now began to grizzle. 'Mummy I do want my dinner, please, please, Mummy.'

'Oh all right then,' said Grace furiously. There was clearly nothing for it but to set forth again, to summon up all her courage, and put her head round the library door. Abashed by the sudden silence that fell and the looks of surprise and interest on eight or ten strange masculine faces, she said to Charles-Edouard, who was the furthest from her so that she had to say it across the whole room, 'I'm so sorry to interrupt, but could I possibly have a word with you?'

He came out at once, shut the door, put his arms round her, and said, 'You were quite right to come. It was very dull in there, and now we'll go to your room.'

'Oh no,' said Grace, 'It wasn't for that.'

'How d'you mean? it wasn't for that. What is "that", anyway?' he said, laughing.

'Oh don't laugh at me, it was terrible going in there. I was so terribly frightened, but I had to. It's about Nanny.'

'Yes, yes, I know. We must have a long talk about Nanny, but not now. First we go upstairs—what must be must be, and quickly too.'

'No, first we go to the kitchen and ask for a floury potato for Nanny, who is waxy, in a bait, I mean, because they've had no luncheon.'

Grace, by now, was really rather hysterical.

'Had no luncheon!' cried Charles-Edouard, 'this is too much. I must find my Grandmother.'

'Oh they had it all right, they just couldn't eat it.'

'What d'you mean, Grace? I'm sure they had the same as we did. You said yourself it was delicious.'

'Yes, of course it was, and I'm furious with Nanny for complaining, but the fact is Nannies never can bear new food you know, it's my own fault, I ought to have remembered that. Now dear, dearest Charles-Edouard, do come to the kitchen and help to find something she can eat.'

'Very well. And tomorrow we send her back to England.'

There. Grace's heart sank.

'But who would look after poor little Sigi?'

'M. le Curé must find him a tutor. This child is quite unlettered, I had a long talk with him in the train. He knows nothing, and can't even read.'

'But of course not, poor little boy. He isn't seven yet!'

'When I was five,' said Charles-Edouard, 'I had read all Dumas, père.'

'I've noticed everybody thinks they themselves could read when they were five.'

'Ask M. le Curé.'

'Anyway you must have been too sweet for words,' said Grace. 'I only wish I'd known you then.'

'I was exceedingly brilliant. Now here is the kitchen, and here, by great good luck, is M. André, the head chef. Will you please explain exactly what it is that you do want?'

While some of the household slept (though sharp attacks of insomnia characterized that afternoon) and Madame de Valhubert prayed, Madame Rocher des Innouïs and M. de la Bourlie took themselves off to a little garden, deeply shaded by an ilex tree, to have a nice chat about Grace. One summer long ago they had conducted a violent love affair under the very noses of Madame de Valhubert, Madame de la Bourlie, M. Rocher, and Prince Zjebrowski, the lover of Madame Rocher. It had really been a *tour de force* of its kind; they had succeeded in hoodwinking all the others, none of whom had ever had the slightest suspicion of it. After that they had remained on cosy, rather conspiratorial terms.

'We must begin by saying that she is beautiful—more beautiful, perhaps, than Priscilla.' Madame Rocher spread out the ten yards of her Dior skirt and settled herself comfortably with cushions. 'But not, as anyone can see, a society woman. Of good family, yes perhaps, but perfectly green in worldly matters. She told me, at luncheon, that she has hardly been out in society since the war, but spent all those years looking after goats. Of course the English are very eccentric, you don't know that, Sosthène, you have never crossed the Channel, but you can take it from me that they are all half mad, a country of enormous, fair, mad atheists. Why did she look after goats? We shall never know. But looking after goats can hardly be considered as a good preparation for life with Charles-Edouard, and I am bound to say I feel uneasy for her. They are not married religiously, by the way.'

'Oh! How do you know?'

'I asked her.'

'What an extraordinary question to ask.'

'After all, I am Charles-Edouard's aunt.'

'I meant what an extraordinary idea. It would never have occurred to me that they might not be.'

'It occurred to me. I know England, Sosthène. We went every year for the Horse Show, don't forget.'

'Shall you tell Françoise?'

'Of course not, on no account, and nor must you. It would upset her dreadfully.'

'Speaking frankly then, nothing matters very much.'

'I don't agree at all. It's true that they can easily be divorced, and that Charles-Edouard will be able to marry again without waiting for an annulment, but before that happens he will have made her totally miserable. Charles-Edouard is a good, warm-hearted boy, he won't be able to help making her miserable, but he will suffer too. Oh dear, what could have induced him to marry an Englishwoman—these English with their terrible jealousy—it will be the story of Priscilla all over again, you'll see.'

'But the English husbands then, how do they manage?'

'English husbands? They go to their clubs, their boat race, their Royal Academy—they don't care for making love a bit. So they are always perfectly faithful to their wives.'

'What about the Gaiety Girls?'

'I don't think they exist any more. You are behind the times, my poor Sosthène, it is the gaiety boys now, if anything. But they have no temperament. Now Charles-Edouard cannot—he really cannot—see a pretty woman without immediately wanting to sleep with her. What foolishness, then, to go and marry an Anglo-Saxon.'

'You talk as if Latins are never jealous.'

'It is quite different for a Frenchwoman, she has ways and means of defending herself. First of all she is on her own ground, and then she has all the interest, the satisfaction, of making life impossible for her rival. Instead of sad repining her thoughts are concentrated on plot and counterplot, the laying of traps and the springing of mines. Paris divides into two camps, she has to consider most carefully what forces she can put in the field, she must sum up the enemy strength, and prepare her stratagem. Whom can she enlist on her side? There is all society to be won over, the hostesses, the old men who go to tea parties, and the families of those concerned. Then there is the elegance, the manicurists, the *vendeuses*, the *modistes*, the *bottiers* and the *lingères*. A foothold among the tradesmen who serve her rival's kitchen may prove very useful; we must not, of course, forget the fortune-tellers, while a concierge can play a cardinal role. The day is not long enough for all the contrivances to be put on foot, for the consultations with her women friends, the telephoning, the messages, the sifting and deep consideration of all news and all fresh evidence. Finally, and not the least important, she has her own lover to comfort and advise her. Ah! Things are very different for a Frenchwoman. But these poor English roses just hang their lovely heads and droop and die. Did Priscilla ever defend herself for a single moment? Don't you remember how painful it was to us, for years, to see how terribly she suffered? And now I suppose we are condemned to live through it all over again with this Grace.'

M. de la Bourlie thought how much he would have liked to appropriate to himself one of these loving, faithful and defenceless goddesses. When Madame de la Bourlie finally succumbed to a liver attack, he thought, why should he not take a little trip to London? But then he remembered his age.

'So hard to believe that we are all over eighty now,' he said peevishly.

'Yes, it must be, but what has that to do with Charles-Edouard? Poor boy, he has certainly made an unwise marriage. All the same I rather like this Grace, I can't help it, she is so lovely, and there is something direct about her which I find charming. I also think her tougher, a tougher proposition than poor Priscilla was, more of a per-

sonality. There was never any hope for Priscilla, and I'm not quite so
sure about Grace. If I can help her I will. Should I try to prepare her
a little while she is here? Warn her about Albertine, for instance? What
do you advise?'

'I don't think it ever does much good, to warn,' said M. de la Bourlie,
thinking how furious he would be, in Charles-Edouard's place, if somebody were to warn his exquisite new wife about his intoxicating old
mistress.

'No good at all,' agreed Madame Rocher, 'you are quite right. And
then it's not as if it were only Albertine. I'd have to warn against every
pretty woman and every *jolie-laide* at every dinner and every luncheon
that they go to. I'd have to warn against Rastaquoueres and Ranees,
Israelites and Infantas, Danes and Duchesses, Greeks and Cherokee
Indians. I'd have to give her a white list and a black list, and now, I
suppose, since he has just come back from Indo-China, a yellow list as
well. No, it would really be too exhausting, the young people must work
it out for themselves—everybody has storms and troubles at their age
no doubt, and there is no point in getting mixed up in them. All the
same, I do wish so very much that Charles-Edouard could have
married a good, solid, level-headed little French woman of the world
instead of this beautiful goat-herd.'

The long summer days went by, slowly at first and then gathering
speed, as days do which are filled from dawn to dusk with idleness.
Grace spent most of the morning on the terrace outside her bedroom
sewing away at her carpet. Charles-Edouard liked to see her doing it;
her fair, bent head and flashing, white hands made such a pretty
picture, but he decided that the day the carpet was finished it would
have to be overtaken by some rather fearful accident, a pot of spilt
indelible ink, or a spreading burn. Charles-Edouard was not one to
cherish an object, especially so large and ugly an object as this was going
to be, for reasons of sentiment.

After luncheon there was the siesta, and then Charles-Edouard and
she would often drive down to the sea for a bathe. He had countless
friends and acquaintances on the coast to whose villas they could go
and from whose rocks they could swim, but Grace's complete lack of
suitable clothes protected her from a really social life, from dinner
parties and visits to the Riviera. For this she was thankful. She liked the
sleepy existence at Bellandargues, though Charles-Edouard complained
of its dullness. His crony there was Madame Rocher, who poured into
his ears an endless saga, her own version of all that had happened to all
his friends since he had last seen them in 1939. It sounded simply
terrific to Grace, whenever she overheard any of it. Madame Rocher
was bored herself, longing to be off to yachts and palazzos and villas at
which various impatient hosts and hostesses were said to be awaiting

her. But this year she had decided to obey her doctor, and to stay quietly at Bellandargues for at least a month. She kept herself amused by the overwhelming interest she took in all that happened in house, village, and neighbourhood. When Grace and Charles-Edouard went off on their bathing expeditions she was able to tell them a great deal about their hosts, and what they were likely to find in the way of a household.

'Is it today you go to the English Lesbians? The nephew of the old one is there, I believe—if he is her nephew. They've just bought a refrigerator, what extravagance!'

'The Italian ménage à trois? Have you explained to Grace that *she* only likes boys of sixteen and *they* get them for her? An excellent cook, I hear, this year.'

'Those two pederasts? Poor people, they are being horribly black-mailed by an ex-convict who lives in the village. But their rocks have never been nicer.'

And so on.

'Your aunt sees life through a veil of sex,' Grace said to Charles-Edouard when, for the third or fourth time, the company, represented to her by Madame Rocher as steeped in lurid vice, had turned out to be an ordinary, jolly house party.

'And who's to say she's wrong?'

'Well, I do think to call Mrs. Browne and Lady Adela the English Lesbians is going rather too far. Anybody can see they've never heard of such a thing, poor darlings.'

'Then it's time somebody told them. More fun for them, if they know.'

'Charles-Edouard! And that dear old Italian lady with her two nice friends and all their grandchildren. I can't believe it!'

'One must never entirely discount Tante Régine's information on these subjects.'

One day when they were going to see an intensely pompous French duke and his wife, Madame Rocher hissed through the window of the motor at Grace, 'Reds.'

'Dear Tante Régine, come now!' Even Charles-Edouard was laughing.

'That family have always been Orleanists, my dear boy, and you very well know it. Impossible to be more to the Left.'

As they drove back in the beautiful evening light Charles-Edouard said, 'Shall we go to Venice? You could buy some clothes in Cannes on our way.'

Grace's heart sank. 'I'm happy here—aren't you, Charles-Edouard?'

'The evenings here are so terrible,' he said. 'I can get through the day, but the evenings——!'

'I love them,' she said, 'they must have been exactly the same for hundreds of years.'

She dreaded leaving Bellandargues, she felt she could cope with life there. The world that awaited them outside its walls was so infinitely complicated, according to Madame Rocher.

'Very well,' said Charles-Edouard, 'if you like it so much we'll stay until we go to Paris. I like it all right except for after dinner.'

Certainly the evenings were not very gay. The party repaired for coffee and tisane to a small salon where they chatted or played bridge until bed-time. Hot night noises floated in through the open windows. 'Why do French ducks quack all night?' Grace had asked. 'Those are frogs, my dearest, our staple diet you know.' Sometimes Madame Rocher played Chopin. It really was rather dull. Then Charles-Edouard discovered that she knew how to tell fortunes by cards, after which there was no more Chopin and no more gossiping. Grace was left at the bridge table while Charles-Edouard bullied Madame Rocher in a corner.

'Come on, Tante Régine, to work, to work!'

'But I've told you all I can.'

'That was yesterday. Today some new and hitherto unknown factor may have changed the whole course of my existence. Come, come!'

Madame Rocher, completely good-natured, would take up the cards and go on to the end of her invention. 'No wonder those five fortune-tellers said you would be killed in the war—they simply had to, to get rid of you.'

'Once more, Tante Régine—do I cut in three this time?'

'That's it, flog the poor old horse till it drops.'

'I passed by Madame André's cottage this afternoon, and made her tell the cards. She is much more dramatic than you, Tante Régine— dark ladies and fair ladies—wicked ladies of all sorts abound chez Madame André.'

'Yes, but I am handicapped by the presence of your wife,' said Madame Rocher, laughing.

'Oh!' said Grace, from the bridge table, 'you mustn't be. I'm not a bit a jealous person. I don't know what it is to be jealous.'

Madame Rocher raised her eyebrows, Madame de Valhubert and M. de la Bourlie looked sadly at each other across the table, and M. le Curé said, 'I declare a little slam.'

'That's very naughty, M. le Curé,' said Grace, 'now we shall be two down.'

CHAPTER VI

'Iт's about this Mr. Labby, dear.'

Charles-Edouard, who always got things done at once when he had decided upon them, had produced a young abbé to give Sigismond his lessons, and of course M. l'Abbé and Nanny were, from the very first, at daggers drawn. That is to say, Nanny's dagger was drawn, but it hardly penetrated the thick, black, clerical robes of the priest, who seemed quite unaware of her existence. That was his weapon.

'Oh Nan! But he seems nice, don't you think? So gentle. And Sigi loves him.'

Indeed that was partly the trouble. Sigi was always running off to be with M. l'Abbé, adored his lessons, had asked for longer hours, and Nanny was jealous.

'That's as may be,' she said darkly, 'you never can tell with these foreign clergymen, but it's his little brain I'm thinking of. Their little brains are so easily taxed. I wish you could hear him scream of a night. He's nothing but a bundle of nerves, all on edge—awful dreams he has, poor little fellow. I was wondering if these lessons aren't too much for him.'

'No, darling, of course not. We all learnt to read, you know. I was reading *The Making of a Marchioness* when Mummy died, I remember it so well.'

It was a memory that she always found rather disturbing. The little girl, with her nose in the book, had felt that she ought to feel sad, and yet all she wanted was to get on with the story. Sir Conrad had come into the nursery, tears pouring down his cheeks, at the very moment when Emily Fox-Seaton was setting out for the fish, and Grace had been distinctly annoyed by the interruption. Later on in life she had pondered over this apparent heartlessness with some astonishment. Did little children, then, not feel sorrow, or was it that the book had provided her with a refuge from the tragic, and perhaps embarrassing, reality?

She did not remember feeling sorrow at the loss of her mother, though she had often been seized with a physical longing for the soft lap and scented bosom of that intensely luxurious woman.

'I was only six—do you admit, Nanny?'

'Practically seven, and girls are always more forward.'

'Besides, you know, he simply must learn French.'

Nanny sniffed. 'He's learning French quick enough from that Canary. Another thing I wanted to talk to you about, when he's with Canary and all those other little devils they go off together goodness knows where, and I wouldn't be surprised if they bathe in the pond.'

'I expect they do.' Grace had, indeed, often seen them at it, and very pretty they looked popping naked in and out of the green water of a Renaissance fountain on the edge of the village. 'But it doesn't matter. Sigi's papa says he always bathed there when he was a child. It's perfectly safe.'

'Oh perfectly safe until the poor little chap gets polio-myelitis and spends the rest of his life in a wheel chair. I wish to goodness he'd never taken up with that Canary, he's a perfect menace.'

Canari, the little yellow-headed son of Mignon the chemist, was Sigi's friend. 'M. l'Abbé is teaching me to pray. I prayed for a friend and I got Canari.'

Every afternoon, at the hottest time of the day, Sigi would race down to the vineyard to meet Canari and his band of maquisards. He was seen no more until Nanny rang the bell for Dick Barton, when he would race back up the hill. Nanny now had a powerful wireless installed, which turned the nursery into for ever England with 6 o'clock news, 9 o'clock news, Music While You Work, and Twenty Questions. The *Daily Mirror*, too, had begun to arrive, bringing Garth in person, and so had *Woman and Beauty*, since when the nursery front had been distinctly calmer.

'But we mustn't worry too much, Nanny darling. Sigi is a little boy, growing up fast now, he's bound to dash off, you know, that's what little boys are like. I think it's a lovely life for him here, I only wish we could stay for ever.'

'You love M. l'Abbé, don't you, Sigismond?' said Grace, next morning. He always sat on her bed while she had her breakfast, a great bowl of coffee with fresh white bread, served on old Marseilles china. It was in many ways her favourite moment of the day; she drank her coffee looking at the hot early morning sky through muslin curtains; everything in the room was pretty, and the little boy on the end of her bed, in a white cotton jersey and red linen trousers, the prettiest object of all.

'I love M. l'Abbé and I revere him, and I've got a new ambition now. I wish to be able to converse with him in Latin.'

'French first, darling.'

'No, Mummy, the Romans were civilized before the Gauls, M. l'Abbé says. He tells some smashing stories about these Romans, and I've a new idea for Nanny. Supposing we got her into an arena with a particularly fierce bear?'

'Oh, poor Nanny. Where will you find the bear?'

'One of our maquisards comes from the Pyrenees, and they've got three bears there, wild, to this day. I showed him a picture of Garth digging a cunning pit, covered with leaves and branches——'

'Not Garth still?' said Charles-Edouard, coming in with the morning's letters. 'Run along, Sigi,' he said, holding the door and shooing him with a newspaper.

'Why do you always say run along, Papa?' He dragged through the door, looking crestfallen.

'It's what my mother used to say to me. "Run along, Charles-Edouard." The whole of my childhood was spent running along. I did hate it, too. Off with you! That was another.' He shut the door, and gave Grace her letters.

'If you didn't like it,' she said, 'I can't think why you inflict it on the poor little boy. I don't think he sees enough of us, and he never sees us together.'

'That's not the point. The point is that we see quite enough of him,' said Charles-Edouard. 'There is nothing so dull as the conversation of small children.'

'It amuses me.'

'It does sometimes amuse women. They've got a childish side themselves, nature's way of enabling them to bear the prattle. And while we are on the subject, M. l'Abbé tells me that Nanny won't leave them alone at lesson time, she's always fussing in with some excuse or other. It's very annoying. Perhaps you'd speak to her about it?'

'I do know. I was afraid you'd be cross.'

'Well, speak.'

'Yes, I'll try. But you know what it is with Nanny, I'm dreadfully under her thumb. She thinks M. l'Abbé is taxing his little brain.'

'But his little brain has got to be taxed, it's there for that. Let Nanny wait till he's reading for his bachot if she wants to see him taxed—going on to twelve and one at night—poor little green face—rings under his eyes—attempted suicide—breakdowns——'

'Oh, Charles-Edouard, you are a brute,' said Grace, quite horrified. He laughed, and began kissing her arm and shoulder.

'All this loony kissing again,' Sigi appeared in the window, 'over the pathless Himalayas, that's where I've come.'

'Yes, I wondered how long it would be before you found the way,' said Charles-Edouard.

'Shall I tell you something? I've just seen the *Daily*, and Garth has renounced the love of women.'

'Oh he's like that, is he?'

'He's an Effendi now. What's an Effendi, Papa?'

'Talk about taxing his brain,' said Charles-Edouard.

'Well I know, but if it wasn't for Garth and Dick Barton he'd never go near the nursery, and poor Nanny would have a stroke looking for him on the roof and in the vineyards all day.'

'Now Sigismond, just go back over those trackless paths, will you?'

'In other words run along and off with you. All right, if I must.'

'M. l'Abbé talks about teaching him Latin.'

'Yes?' Charles-Edouard was opening his letters.

'Seems rather a waste of time?'

'Latin is a waste of time?' he said, putting a letter in his pocket and looking at Grace with surprise. 'Surely he must learn it before he goes to Eton?'

'Well it won't be the right pronunciation. Do we want Sigi to go to Eton?'

'Why not, for a bit? Then he can be top in English when he goes to St. Cyr.'

'But I don't think they can go to Eton for a bit. Oh dear, I thought the thing about being French was you had your blessing always at home.'

'Do we always want him at home?'

'I do. Anyway you have to be put down for Eton before your parents are married now—long before you are conceived, so I think this dream will come to nothing.'

Charles-Edouard, who was still reading his letters, said, 'Brighton College then, it's all the same.'

'Please can I come to the sea with you?'

'Not today darling. We're lunching with some grown-up people.'

'It is unfair. I want to take a photograph of a huge, frightening wave.'

'But today it will be flat calm. Next time there's a mistral we'll take you.'

'I'm so hot. I do so want to bathe.'

'Don't you bathe in the fountain, with Canari?'

'I'm brouillé with le chef.'

'Not brouillé with Canari?'

'Yes I am. It was convenu that the maquisards should come here and be chasseurs alpins on the roof one day and the next I should spend with them doing sabotage in the village. Well, they came here, and yesterday I went down to the village and he was under the lime tree with les braves, and he said "*va-t-en. On ne veut pas de toi*".'

'But why, Sigi?'

'I don't know. But I don't care, not a bit, I want to go to the sea and swim under water and spear an octopus.'

'When you are older.'

'When shall I be older?'

'All in due course. Run along now and find M. l'Abbé.'

'He is reading his bréviaire.'

'Well, Nanny then. Anyway, run along, darling.'

That night, at dinner, Madame de Valhubert said, 'Do you know our poor little maquisard spent the whole afternoon by himself in the salon? He looked the picture of woe. In the end Régine and I had to play cards with him for very pity.'

'It's that wretched Canari,' said Grace, 'he has sent him packing, and nobody knows why. Oh, I do hope they'll make it up soon, or the poor duck will have no more fun at all. I feel quite worried. Couldn't you go down and speak to M. Mignon, Charles-Edouard, and find out what it is?'

Charles-Edouard laughed, looked round the table at the others, who were all smiling, and said, 'Alas, my influence with Mignon is but limited I fear.'

'But why? He made that nice speech.'

'That was the solidarité de la libération. It just held long enough for him to make the speech. Now we are back among all the old feuds again. A very good sign that peace is really here.'

'M. le Curé, couldn't you do something?' said Grace.

At this there was a general laugh. M. le Curé lifted his hands, saying that Grace did not quite grasp the situation. M. Mignon, he said, was a Radical Socialist. If Grace had not spent the years of the war so idly, stitching dreams into an ugly carpet or leading goats to browse on black-berries, if she had taken the advice of her father and concentrated instead upon Messrs. Bodley and Brogan, whose works lay among a huge heap of unopened books behind the back stairs, these words would have meant something to her, and what was to follow would have been avoided. But as she looked completely blank Charles-Edouard began to explain.

'Not only is M. Mignon, *père*, a Radical Socialist of the deepest dye—Canari doesn't go to our school, I would have you observe, but to the Instituteur—but he is actually a Freemason.'

'Well, in that case it's a pity my father's not here to have a word with him. They could wear their aprons, and do whatever it is together.'

Charles-Edouard tried to kick Grace under the table, but she was too far for him to reach her. She went blandly on:

'Papa is one of the top Freemasons, at home, you know. Couldn't we tell M. Mignon that? It might help.'

Silence fell, so petrifyingly cold that she realized something was very wrong, but couldn't imagine what.

Madame de Valhubert's black eyes went with a question mark to Charles-Edouard. Madame Rocher and M. de la Bourlie exchanged glances of mournful significance; M. le Curé and M. l'Abbé gazed at their plates and Charles-Edouard looked extremely put out, as Grace had never seen him look before. At last he said, to his grandmother, 'Freemasons are quite different in England, you know.'

'Oh! Indeed?'

'The Grand Master, there, is a member of the Royal Family—is that not so, Grace?'

'I don't know,' said Grace. 'I don't really know much about them.'

'With the English anything is possible,' said Madame Rocher. 'What did I tell you, Sosthène?'

'Oh no, but all the same,' muttered the old man, 'this is too much.'

There was another long silence, at the end of which Madame de Valhubert rose from the table, and they all went into the little salon. The evening dragged much worse than usual, and the party dispersed for the night very early indeed.

'What have I done?' said Grace in her bedroom.

'It's not your fault,' said Charles-Edouard, crossly, for him, not knowing that it was entirely her fault for neglecting the information Sir Conrad had put at her disposal, 'but I must beg you never again to speak of Freemasons before French people. Take a lover—take two— turn Lesbian—steal valuable boxes off your friends' tables—anything, anything, but don't say that your father is a Freemason. It will need ten years of virtuous life before this is forgiven, and it will never be forgotten. La fille du francmaçon! Well, I'll see my grandmother in the morning and try to explain——' He was laughing again now, but Grace saw that he was really very much embarrassed by what she had done.

Madame de Valhubert having rushed to the chapel, Madame Rocher went down with M. de la Bourlie to his motor, and they stood for a moment on the terrace together.

'You see!' she said, 'daughter of Freemasons! What did I tell you? No wonder she was married by a mayor, all is now plain as daylight. Can they, I wonder, really be considered decent people in England? I must find out. Poor Charles-Edouard, I see his path beset by thorns. Terrible for the Valhuberts, especially as they have had this sort of trouble in the family once—well not freemasonry, of course, but that dreadful Marshal. All so carefully lived down ever since. No wonder Françoise is upset—she will be on her knees all night, I feel sure.'

M. de la Bourlie was greatly shocked at the whole affair. Even were he not over eighty, even were Madame de la Bourlie not still alive, a beautiful English wife now ceased to be any temptation to him. He had learnt his lesson.

Grace's blunder had one good result however. Sigi got back into the Canari set, from which he had been expelled, had he but known it, on grounds of clericalism. His adherence to M. l'Abbé had been doing him no good among the maquisards.

M. le Curé was unable to keep the extraordinary pronouncement of young Madame de Valhubert to himself; he told one or two gossips, and the news spread like wild-fire, causing the greatest possible sensation in the village. The Catholics, adherents of the M.R.P. and so on, were very much shocked, but the rest of the population was jubilant. The daughter of a Freemason was an unhoped-for addition to the

Valhubert family. Nanny, whose resistance to M. l'Abbé stiffened every day, came to be regarded as the very champion of anti-clericalism. The position of Charles-Edouard remained anomalous, a certain mystery seemed to surround his opinions, and nobody knew exactly where he stood. On one hand there was the Freemason wife, on the other it was he and nobody else who had summoned M. l'Abbé to teach his child. Since he was popular, jolly, and a good landlord, since his war record was above reproach, and they knew, from his own voice on the radio, that he had been one of the very first to join General de Gaulle, he tended to be claimed as one of themselves by all sections of the community while they awaited further evidence from which to draw further conclusions.

Charles-Edouard did manage to convince his grandmother that freemasonry in England was regarded by decent, and even royal, families as perfectly correct. It took some doing, but finally he succeeded.

'Very well then,' she said. 'I believe you, my child. But as we are on disagreeable topics, why this marriage by a mayor? Why not a priest?'

'Ah!' he said. 'You know?'

'Yes, I know.'

'The fact is I was not quite sure. I married this foreign woman after a very short courtship, I was off to the war, perhaps for years, she was engaged to somebody else when I first met her, and might have—I didn't think so, but there was no proof—an unstable character. And she was a heathen. The English, you know, are nearly all heathens, like freemasonry, it is a perfectly respectable thing to be, over there. Should she have got tired of waiting and gone off with somebody else, I didn't want to be debarred for ever, or at any rate for years, from a proper marriage. If she, or her father, had made the least objection to the civil marriage. if they had even mentioned it, I would have got a priest, but the subject was never raised. It was very odd. They regarded the whole thing as perfectly normal and natural. Sigismond has been baptized, by the way. I wrote and asked for that, and it was immediately done, just as if I had asked for him to be vaccinated.'

'And now?' said Madame de Valhubert.

'Grace is still a heathen, but you can see for yourself that she is a soul worth saving. In due course we shall convert her; it will be time enough then to be married in church.'

'Charles-Edouard, you have brought home a heathen concubine instead of a wife! You are living in mortal sin, my child.'

'Dearest grandmother, you know me well enough to know that I am generally living in mortal sin. We must trust, for my soul, to the mercy of God. As regards Grace, all will turn out for the best, you will see.'

Grace would have been intensely surprised if she could have overheard this conversation. They both spoke as if he had picked up the daughter of a cannibal king in darkest Africa, whereas she thought of herself as a perfectly ordinary Christian. Something of this occurred to Charles-Edouard.

'Please, grandmother, if you speak with Grace about this, don't say that she is only a concubine. She wouldn't like it. Trust me—I'm sure everything will be all right, meanwhile you can look upon us as fiancés.'

'Very well,' said the old lady. 'I won't say a word on any religious subject. It is your responsibility, Charles-Edouard, and you know as well as I do where your duty lies in this matter.'

'But,' she thought to herself, 'there are other things I must have out with her before they go back to Paris.'

'I suppose Charles-Edouard must seem very English to you, dear child,' she began, next time she found herself alone with Grace.

'English?' Grace was amused and surprised. For her Charles-Edouard was the forty kings of France rolled into one, the French race in person walking and breathing.

'Indeed at first sight he is very English. His clothes, his figure, that enormous breakfast of ham and eggs, his aptitude for business. But you know him very little, dearest, as yet. You have been married (if one can call it a marriage) for seven years and yet here you are, strangers, on a honeymoon, with a big child. It's a very odd situation, and not the least curious and wonderful part is that you are both so happy. But I repeat that so far you have only seen the English side of your husband. He is getting restless here (I know him so well) and very soon, probably at a day's notice, he will take you off to Paris. When you are there you will begin to see how truly French he is.'

'But he seems so French to me already. How can he seem even more so in Paris? In what way?'

'I am giving you a word of warning, just one. In Paris you and he will be back in his own world of little friends all brought up together. I advise you to be very very sensible. Behave as if you were a thousand years old, like me.'

'You think I shall be jealous. Tante Régine thinks so too, I can see. But I never am. It's not part of my nature. I'm not insensitive, it isn't that, I can mind things quite terribly, but jealous I am not.'

'Alas, my dear child, you are in love, and there is no love in this world without jealousy.'

'And I may not have known Charles-Edouard for long, but I do know him very well. He loves me.'

'Yes, yes, indeed he does. That is quite plain. And so do we all, dear child, and that is why I am talking to you like this, in spite of everything. I tell you too that if you are very sensible he will love you for ever, and in time everything will be regulated in your lives and you will be a truly happy couple, for ever.'

'That's what Charles-Edouard tells me. All right, I am very sensible, so he will love me for ever. Don't I look sensible?'

'Alas, I know these practical, English looks and how they are deceptive. So reassuringly calm on the surface, and underneath what a turmoil. And then the world reflected in distorting glasses. Latin women see things so clearly as they are; above all they understand men.'

'I never know quite what it means, to understand men.'

'Don't you, dear? It's very simple, it can be said in a few words. Put them first. A woman who puts her husband first seldom loses him.'

'Well I daresay,' said Grace with some indignation, 'that a woman who lets her husband do exactly as he likes, who shuts her eyes to every infidelity, and lets him walk over her, in fact, would never lose him.'

'Just so,' said Madame de Valhubert, placidly.

'And do you really advise that?'

'Oh I don't advise, the old must never advise. All I do say is remember that Charles-Edouard is a Frenchman—not an Englishman with a French veneer, but a deeply French Frenchman. If you want this to become a real marriage, a lifelong union (I don't speak of a sacrament), you must follow the rules of our civilization. A little life of your own, if you wish it, will never be held against you, so long as you always put your husband first.'

Grace was thoroughly shocked. 'I could have understood it if Tante Régine had spoken like that—would have expected it in fact, but your grandmother!' she said to Charles-Edouard.

'My grandmother is an extremely practical person,' he said, 'you can see it by the way she runs this house. You can always tell by that, with women.'

The next day Charles-Edouard made one of his sudden moves and whirled Grace off to Paris. Nanny and the little boy were left behind to follow in a week or two, escorted by the faithful Ange-Victor.

CHAPTER VII

THE Valhuberts' Paris house was of a later date than any part of Bellandargues, and had only been finished a month or two before the Revolution. It stood on the site of a Louis XIII house whose owner, planning to receive Marie Antoinette there, had pulled it down and built something more fashionable, to be worthy of her. The intended fête for the Queen never took place, and in the end it was Josephine, not Marie Antoinette, who was received as guest of honour in the round, white and gold music room. This was an episode in their family history very much glossed over by future Valhuberts, and most of all by

Charles-Edouard's grandmother. The truth was that the eldest son of Marie Antoinette's admirer, a soldier born and bred, had not been able to resist the opportunity of serving under the most brilliant of all commanders. He had joined the revolutionary army, had risen to the rank of General before he was thirty, and was killed at the battle of Friedland shortly after receiving his Marshal's bâton.

'Most fortunately,' Charles-Edouard said when recounting all this to Grace, 'or he would certainly have ended up as a Duke with some outlandish title. I prefer to be what I am.'

'Perhaps he would have refused.'

'Perhaps. But I've yet to hear of anybody refusing a dukedom.'

The family, after his death, had once more embraced a cautious Royalism, and a veil was drawn over this unfashionable patriotic outburst. Old Madame de Valhubert always pretended that she knew nothing of it, and, if anybody mentioned the Marshal, would say that he must have been some very distant relation of her husband's. All his relics, his portrait in uniform by Gros, the eagle which it had cost him his life to recapture, his medals, his sword, and his bâton were hidden away at Bellandargues in a little outhouse, locally known as le pavillon de la gloire, and even Charles-Edouard would not have dared bring them back into the salon during the lifetime of his grandmother.

'It will be the same with me,' he said. 'Sigi's great-granddaughter-in-law will hide away my Croix de Lorraine, my médaille de la résistance, and the badge of my squadron, and say that I was some distant relation of her husband's. They are terrible, French families.'

The house, long, three-storied, lay between courtyard and garden. Old Madame de Valhubert, when in Paris, occupied one of the lodges in the courtyard. 'She moved in there during the war, after the Germans had looted the main block, and now she likes it so much that she has stayed on.' The other lodge housed the servants. The ground floor of the house itself consisted of five enormous drawing-rooms leading out of each other, the middle one being the famous round music room, masterpiece of the brothers Rousseau. Over this, the same shape and almost as elaborately decorated, was Grace's bedroom. These rooms were on the garden side, facing the south and with a wide view of trees.

'What an enormous garden, for a town,' said Grace.

'It used to be three times as long, but some of it was taken, alas, in the time of Haussman to make the horrible rue de Babel, well named. However, we can't complain, many houses in this neighbourhood suffered more—many wonderful houses either lost their gardens altogether, or were even pulled down. Paris was only saved from complete ruination by the fall of Napoleon III. Bismarck really saved us, funnily enough!'

As Charles-Edouard had quite openly joined the Free French under his own name, everything he possessed was confiscated during the war and would have been taken off to Germany had it not been for the initiative of Louis, his old butler, who had piled pictures and furniture in the cellar, built a wall to hide them, and, to make the wall convincing, put a wash basin with brass taps against it.

'We had so little time,' he said, when explaining all this to Grace and Charles-Edouard, 'that we had to connect the taps with an ordinary bucket of water hung up on the other side of the wall. Oh how we prayed the Germans wouldn't run them very long. All was well, however. They came, they tested the taps for a minute, just as we hoped they would, and went away again. Oh what a relief!'

'And they never requisitioned the house?'

'They didn't like this side of the river—too many dark, old, twisting streets; they felt more comfortable up by the Etoile in big, modern buildings. They just carted off everything they could see, and never came back again. Fortunately, as I've been here so long I knew which were the best pieces (we didn't dare hide everything). Later on we installed ventilation in the cellar, and the things were miraculously well preserved through those long, terrible winters. In all this we were helped by M. Saqué the builder—M. le Marquis will perhaps go and thank him.'

'Very probably I will,' said Charles-Edouard, more touched than he cared to admit by this recital. He loved his furniture and objects, and specially loved his pictures. He showed them to Grace before he even allowed her to go upstairs. It was a charming collection of minor masters with one or two high spots, an important Fragonard, a pair of Hubert Roberts, and so on. He was always adding to it, and had bought more than half the pictures himself.

The weeks which followed, spent by Grace alone with her husband in the empty town during unfashionable September, were the happiest she had ever known. Charles-Edouard, rediscovering, after seven long years, the stones of Paris, for which he had an almost unhealthy love, walked with her all day in the streets, and sometimes, when there was a moon, after dinner as well. Grace was a good walker, even for an Englishwoman, but he was indefatigable, and sometimes, as when they went to Versailles for the day, she had to cry for mercy. He was wonderful company. He knew the long, intricate histories of all the palaces of the Faubourg St. Germain and exactly where to find each one, hidden behind huge walls and carriage doorways.

'You could ring the bell there and have a peep,' he would say, 'nobody knows you as yet—but I shall remain here, out of sight.'

So Grace would ring, put her head round the wicket, apologize to the concierge, and be rewarded by a transparency of stone and glass and ironwork, placed, like her own house, between courtyard and trees. When the ground floor was the width of one room these trees would be visible through the two sets of windows.

'Well, did you like it?'

'Oh wonderful—I can't get over it. Charles-Edouard!'

'Please do not demonstrate in front of these policemen. Please remember that I am a well-known figure in this neighbourhood. Did you notice the sphinxes in the courtyard?'

Grace never noticed any details of that sort; her eye was quite untrained, and she was content to take in a general impression of beauty, to which she was very receptive. Unlike her husband, however, she really preferred natural beauty to things made by man.

'I am loving it, oh I am loving it. I didn't know Paris was like this. When I was at school here it was different—rue de la Pompe and Avenue Victor Hugo (the hours we spent in the Grand Magazin Jones!) in those days. And even so I was always happy here, but now——! I suppose it's got something to do with you as well, my happiness.'

'Something!' said Charles-Edouard. 'Everything.'

'How lucky I am! I could never have loved anybody else half as much.'

'I know.'

'Still, I wish you wouldn't say "I know" like that. You might say that you're lucky too.'

'I'm awfully nice,' he answered, 'never could you have found anybody as nice as I am. Admit that you amuse yourself when you are with me. Now look—the Fountain of Bouchardon, so beautiful. But how foolish to put those horrible modern flats just there.'

'You ought to have a Georgian Society,' said Grace. 'Do you think you're really the whole reason for my happiness?'

'Almost certainly.'

'Oh dear, I hope not, so dangerous when it all depends on one person. Perhaps the Blessing has a bit to do with it too.' But she knew that if so it was a very minor bit, much as she loved the pretty little boy.

'Look, the gateway of the Hotel de Bérulle, is it not a masterpiece of restraint and clever contrivance? See how a coach would be able to turn out of this narrow street, and drive in.'

'Oh, yes, how fascinating!'

'Please do not demonstrate——'

But he was really delighted at the way she was taking to everything French. He saw that, in spite of her bad education, she showed signs of a natural taste which could easily be developed. As for Charles-Edouard, art was a religion to him. If he had a few moments to spare he would run into the Louvre as his grandmother would run into church for a short prayer. The museums were awakening one after another from their war-time trance, and Charles-Edouard, intimate with all the curators, spent hours with them discussing and praising the many improvements.

Grace said, 'How strange it is that you, who really take in everything through the eyes, should hate the country so much.'

'Nature I hate. It is so dull in the country, that must be why. But Art I love.'

'And pretty ladies you love?' she said, as he turned to peer at a vision in black and white flashing by in a little Rolls Royce. September was nearing its close and the pretty ladies had begun to trickle back into the town, filling Grace with apprehension.

'Women I love,' he said with his guilty, interior laugh. 'But also I am a great family man, and that will be your hold over me.'

But how to have a hold, she thought, unless one's own feet are firmly planted on the ground? And how can they be so planted in a strange country, surrounded by strangers at the very beginning of a strange new life?

In due course Nanny and Sigi arrived on the night train from Marseilles, and that afternoon Grace took them across the river to the Tuileries gardens. Nanny was in a wonderfully mellow mood, delighted to have got away from the heat of Provence, from Canari, and, temporarily, at any rate, from M. l'Abbé. (He was coming to Paris after Christmas, when the lessons would be resumed.) Delighted, too, to be in a town again, where a child is so much easier to control than in the country. She entirely approved of the fact that the door to the street could only be opened by the concierge, and that the garden was surrounded by walls high as the ramparts of a city. No means of escape here for little boys. She was not even entirely displeased with the nursery accommodation; arranged for Charles-Edouard by his English mother it was like an old-fashioned nursery in some big London house, and had none of the strange bleakness of the rooms at Bellandargues.

Her smiles, however, always on the wintry side, soon vanished when she was confronted with the goat carts, the donkeys, the Guignol, and the happy crowd of scooting, skating children in the Tuileries gardens. Sigi had, of course, no sooner seen the goat carts than he was in one.

'We shall never get the little monkey away from these animals—is there nowhere else for us to go, dear, more like Hyde Park? I'm not going to stand the whole winter in this draughty-looking square waiting for him to ride round hour after hour.'

'Oh no, darling, you mustn't. We must ration him. But don't you think this is a charming place for children, more fun really than Hyde Park?'

Grace had been so much looking forward to bringing Sigi here and watching him enjoy all the treats that she had overlooked the certain disapproval of Nanny.

'Grace! I'm surprised to hear you say such a thing! Think of the Peter Pan monument, and the Dell! Goodness knows what he'll pick up from all these children. Anyway there's to be no question of him going inside that filthy-looking theatre, or whatever it is. I hope that's quite understood, dear.'

'Of course, Nan, just as you say.'

Nanny took Grace's arm and said in a low voice, 'Isn't that Mrs. Dexter over there?'

'Grace!'

'Carolyn!'

'I was just going to ring up your house and see if you were back. We've come to live here, isn't it lovely? I spoke to your papa on the telephone on our way through London and he gave me your number, but we've been so busy flat-hunting. Yes, now we've found a lovely one —only miles from you I'm afraid—up by the Parc Monceau. Is this Sigi? Seven, I suppose—he looks more. Poor little Foss will be rather young for him, but Nanny will be pleased to see you, Nanny, it will make all the difference. Which day can you come to tea? Then we must get together, Grace, and meet each other's husbands! Isn't it exciting?'

Carolyn Broadman was a lifelong friend of Grace. Their fathers had been friends and they had been at the same school. Carolyn was a little older and much cleverer, she was the head girl at school, revered by the others, many of whom had been passionately in love with her. She was tall, with curly, auburn hair and particularly piercing bright blue eyes. This colouring constituted her claim to beauty; her features were not very good, though her figure was excellent. She moved with more than the hint of a swagger, and Sir Conrad always called her Don Juan. She had certainly been one at school, coldly gathering up the poor little hearts laid at her feet and throwing them over her shoulder. Grace had not seen her since the war, but knew that she had married an enormously rich, important American whom she had met in Italy. As was to be expected she had become a female General in the war—were there such things as female Marshals she would, no doubt, have been one.

'Come back to tea now,' said Grace, 'and meet Charles-Edouard.'

'Darling I can't. I'm just off to our Embassy where they've got a cocktail party for some Senators—I must pick up Hector at his office and then go home and change for it. I promised I'd go early and help.'

So they chatted for a few minutes more and then parted with many plans for meeting again soon.

'Nice to see a clean English skin,' said Nanny, as they wandered back across the Pont de Solferino.

Charles-Edouard was in the hall, evidently on his way out.

'Well,' he said, 'what are the news?'

'I took Sigi and Nan—run along up darling, it's tea-time—to the Tuileries Gardens and who d'you think we met? An old friend of mine called Carolyn Dexter. Wasn't it funny?'

'Beautiful?'

'I don't know if you'd think so. Beautiful colouring.'

'That means red hair I suppose. Not my type.'

'And a wonderful figure, and she's terribly clever. She's married to a very important American called Hector Dexter.'

'So, go on. What did she tell you?'

'Well, they live up by the Parc Monceau. We must all meet someday soon.'

'Go on. What else?'

'Nothing else.'

'Ha! So you stood together in the Tuileries gazing into each other's eyes without a word?'

'You do tease me. We chattered like magpies.'

'But what about?'

'She was just off to a cocktail party at the American Embassy.'

'This is all very dull.'

'Don't be such a bully, Charles-Edouard.'

'You must tell me stories about what happens during your day, to amuse me. Do go on.'

'They have a little boy, but younger than Sigi, and Nanny is longing to go and meet their English nanny——'

Charles-Edouard's attention was wandering. '*Quand un Vicomte rencontre un autre Vicomte,*' he sang. '*Qu'est-ce qu'ils se racontent? Des histoires de Vicomtes.*' He picked up his hat.

'Are you going out?'

'Yes.'

'Back to tea?'

'No.'

Grace had her tea in the nursery, that day and subsequently. Charles-Edouard was never in at tea-time because he now resumed an afternoon habit of many years' standing, he visited Albertine Marel-Desboulles. She was one of the little friends, all brought up together, about whom Madame de Valhubert had wanted to warn Grace, and quite the most dangerous of them. She and Charles-Edouard had had the same nurse as children (passed on to Charles-Edouard's mother by Albertine's, since Albertine was older). When he was eighteen and she a young married woman they had had a short but enthusiastic love affair; this had simmered down to a sentimental friendship in which love, physical love at any rate, still played a part. Charles-Edouard found her more entertaining than anybody; she was certainly quite the reverse of dull, always having something to recount. Not plain slices of life served up on a thick white plate, but wonderful confections embellished with the aromatic and exotic fruits of her own sugary imagination, presented in just such a way as to tempt the appetite of such sophisticated admirers as he. She had endless tales to spin around their mutual friends, could discuss art and objects of art with his own collector's enthusiasm as well as with imaginative knowledge, and, what specially appealed to Charles-Edouard, would talk by the hour, also with imaginative knowledge and with collector's enthusiasm, about himself. She was an accomplished fortune-teller. Like a child who knows where the sweets are kept, Charles-Edouard always went straight to the japanese lacquer commode, in the right-hand corner of whose top drawer lay packs of cards.

'How many years since I have done this?' she said, shuffling and dealing, her long, spidery fingers bright with diamonds.

'You said I would be killed in the war, I remember,' said Charles-Edouard.

'I said I couldn't quite see in what circumstances you would be coming back. Suppose I had told you it would be complete with an English wife and a son, that would indeed have been a coup for me. Unfortunately I didn't foresee anything so improbable. Please cut the cards. However, I see her now, clear as daylight, surrounded by old maids, not another man in her orbit. She must be very faithful. Nice for you to have this faithful wife. Good. Cut the cards. Yes. Now here we have a surprise, not that it surprises me very much. Not English, and not your wife, but a sparkling beauty, a brilliant. There is an enormous amount of interesting incident round you and your relationship with this brilliant. Cut the cards. This is for you. Yes, here you are and with all your talents, your charm, your wit, your good nature, watching yourself as you live your life, and fascinated by the spectacle.'

'Ah!' said Charles-Edouard, 'this is very nice. How I love being rubbed the right way.'

'Cut three times. I am bound to tell you that there will be a few little tiresomenesses, to do with the brilliant. You won't be careful enough, or you'll be unlucky—there'll be a torrent of tears, but they won't be your tears, so never mind. Cut the cards. Nothing different—you again, between the brilliant and the wife. I can't tell any more today.'

She leaned her head on her hand and looked at him with blue, lollipop eyes, which seemed out of place among her pointed Gothic features. Everything about her was long and thin, except for these round, blue eyes; she was an exceedingly odd-looking woman.

'So! How do you find marriage?'

'Rather dull,' said Charles-Edouard, 'but I rather like it, and I love my wife. She is original, she amuses me.'

'And lovely?' said Madame Marel.

'She will be, when she is arranged. No doubt you will see her at the Fertés on the 10th.'

'Yes indeed. We shall all be there, all agog. You haven't changed much, Charles-Edouard, except that you are better looking than ever.'

'Ah!' said Charles-Edouard. He got up and locked the door.

'No need to do that,' she said smiling. 'Pierre would never let anybody else in when he knows you are here.'

Presently Charles-Edouard, lying relaxed among the cushions of an enormous sofa, said, 'So tell me, since all these years what have you become?'

'Oh it's a long story—or rather a long book of short stories.'

'Yes, I expect it is. And now——?'

'Nothing very much. I have an Englishman who is madly in love with me—I don't believe I've ever been loved so violently, with such really suicidal mania, as by this Englishman.'

'Ah, these English, they are terrible.'

'You may laugh, but it is no joke at all. The evidences of his love simply pour into the house—I don't know what the concierge can think, it is full-time work carrying them across the courtyard. Flowers, telegrams, letters, parcels, all the day.'

'Does he live here?'

'Better than that, in London. But he flies over to see me at least once a week, and then the tears, the scenes, the jealousy, the temperament. It is wearing me out, and I ought really to get rid of him.'

'Why don't you?'

'Because of the bourgeois thrift I learnt from my dear husband. Never throw anything away, it might come in useful. Besides, I do love to be loved.'

'And what is his name?'

'It's not an interesting name—Palgrave, Hughie Palgrave.'

'It is interesting to me, however,' said Charles-Edouard, 'since Hughie Palgrave was once engaged to my wife.'

CHAPTER VIII

As soon as she had some presentable clothes Charles-Edouard began taking Grace to see his relations. 'Very dull,' he said, 'but what must be, must be.' So at 6.30 every day they would put themselves into a little lift which shook and wavered up to the drawing-room of some old aunt or cousin of the family. These lifts, these drawing-rooms and these old ladies differed very little from each other. The rooms were huge, cold and magnificent, with splendid pieces of furniture arranged to their worst advantage and mixed up with a curious assortment of objects which had been collected during the course of long married lives. The old ladies were also arranged to their worst advantage, and covered with a curious assortment of jewellery. Prominent upon a black cardigan they generally wore the rosette of the Legion of Honour.

'We might be going in for a literary prize,' said Charles-Edouard, as for the fifth time they tottered up in the fifth little lift.

'Why might we?'

'This is how you win a literary prize in France. First you write a book —that is of no importance, however. Then you go and see my aunts, treat them with enormous deference, and laugh loudly at the jokes my uncles make over the porto.'

'I don't understand.'

'No wonder. All the literary prizes here are given by my aunts.'

'And won by other aunts?'

'Not usually. Their works, of an unreadable erudition, are crowned by the Academy. That is different, though my aunts have great power there also, and have managed to insert my uncles under the cupola all right.'

'Does Tante Régine give prizes?'

'Heavens no! She is in quite a different world. You will find her (she's coming back next week, by the way) at all the parties, the dress collections, the private views, the first nights. It's another product altogether. The Novembre de la Fertés, my grandmother's and Tante Régine's family, have never gone in for intellect—nor have the Rocher des Innouïs. All these clever old girls are Valhubert relations—their cradles were rocked by Alphonse Daudet and the Abbé Liszt. Ah! Ma tante! Bonjour mon oncle. So, this is Grace.'

'Grace! Sit here where we can see you, dear child, and tell us—so cut off from England for so long—all about Mr. Charles Morgan.'

The rest of the company consisted, as usual, of earnest, dowdy young women, following in the footsteps of their elders, of old men so courtly in manner that they seemed dedicated to eternal courtship, and one or two bright, overgrown boys. They put Grace on a high-backed needle-work chair facing the window, sat round her in a semi-circle, and plied her with weak port wine, biscuits, and questions. They passed from Mr. Charles Morgan, about whom she knew lamentably little, to Miss Mazo de la Roche, about whom she knew less. They gave her to understand that one of the most serious deprivations caused by the war had been that of Les Whiteoaks, Les Jalna. Then they fired questions at her from all sides, wanting to know about English novelists, dramatists, lesser country houses, boy scouts, gardens, music, essayists, and the government of Britain, until she felt like an ambulating Britain in Pictures. Their knowledge of England was quite astonishing, very much like the knowledge some astronomer might have of the moon after regarding it for many a long night through a telescope.

Grace felt that they were trying to place her. Not, as Tante Régine was always trying, to place her in English society, to find out whom she knew and if her family was really, in spite of the freemason father, quite respectable, but in another way. Some of them had read Sir Conrad's

Life of Fouquet. They pronounced it honourable, and assumed, from the fact of its existence, that Grace must have been brought up in intellectual circles. They wanted to place her views and inclinations, her turn of mind. They wanted to know if she was Oxford or Cambridge, whether she preferred *The Times* or the *Daily Telegraph*, what she felt about Shakespeare and Bacon. Their questions were not at all hard to answer, but she felt that by her answers to these, possibly deceptively, simple questions, she was being for ever judged.

She found it a great strain, and had said so to Charles-Edouard after the last tea-party.

'But that is what French people are like,' he had replied, shrugging his shoulders. 'In France you are always in a witness box. You'll get used to it. But you must sharpen your wits a little, my dearest, if you want a favourable verdict.'

The old uncles did not play much part in all this. They were still, after a lifetime of marriage, lost in admiration at the brilliance of their wives, quite wrapped up in whatever these wonderful women were doing. So when they met each other out of doors, which happened continually, as they all lived in the same neighbourhood and all had Scotties to exercise, they would shout across the street, 'Good morning, and how is Benjamin Constant going on' (or whoever it was that the other's wife was known to be studying just then). 'Splendidly, splendidly. And the old stones of Provins?'

With Grace they were charming, making her feel that she was a pretty woman and that therefore nothing she said would ever be held against her. However she was shrewd enough to see that it was the aunts who counted. These aunts were a great surprise to Grace. She had hitherto supposed that, with the exception of a few very religious people like Madame de Valhubert, all Frenchwomen, of all ages, were entirely frivolous and given over to the art of pleasing. From which it will be deduced that the works of Mauriac and Balzac, like those of Brogan and Bodley, lay mouldering, their pages uncut, in the great heap behind the kitchen stairs at Bunbury.

'Are you happy?' Charles-Edouard said, as they walked home. It was some days, he had noticed, since Grace had said how happy she was, of her own accord.

'I am perfectly happy,' she said, 'but I can't feel at home yet.'

'You felt at home at Bellandargues, why not here?'

'Bellandargues was the country.' She found it hard to explain to Charles-Edouard how different was life in Paris from anything she had ever known, so complicated and artificial that her only refuge of reality was the nursery. The other rooms in her house, with their admirable decoration and gold-encrusted furniture, so rich that to enter one of them was like opening a jewellery box, belonged to the Valhuberts past, present, and future, but she could not feel as yet that they belonged to her. The smiling servants maintained the life of the house undirected by her; the comings and goings in the courtyard, the cheerful bustle of a large establishment, would all go on exactly the same if she were not there. In short she played not the smallest part in this place, which was, nevertheless, her home.

Charles-Edouard had quite fallen back into his pre-war existence. He spent the morning telephoning to friends whose very names she did not know; in the afternoon he ran from one antiquary to another; he was out a great deal, and always out at tea-time.

Every fortnight or so he went for the inside of a day to Bellandargues to perform his mayoral duties, and very occasionally he stayed there the night. 'I do hate to sleep out of Paris,' he used to say, and did so as seldom as he possibly could.

Grace herself was quite busy, an unaccustomed busyness, since it was all concerned with clothes. Madame Rocher's vendeuse had taken charge of her, and kept her nose to the grindstone, making her get more and more dresses for more and more occasions; big occasions, a ball, Friday night at Maxims, the opera, the important dinner party; little occasions, the theatre, dinner at home alone, or with one or two friends, luncheons at home, luncheon in a restaurant; and odd occasions, luncheon or dinner in the country (nothing so lugubrious as a week-end party was envisaged), and the voyage.

'Could I not travel in my morning suit?'

'It is always better to travel with brown accessories.'

'I am perfectly happy,' she repeated, 'only not quite at my ease yet. Perhaps a little homesick.'

But more than ever passionately in love with Charles-Edouard.

The first big occasion to which Grace went in Paris was a dinner given for her by the Duchesse de la Ferté. At this dinner Grace's pre-conceived ideas about the French, already shaken by the porto parties, were blown sky high. She knew, or thought she knew, that French-women were hideously ugly, but with an ugliness redeemed by great vivacity and perfect taste in dress. Perfect taste she took to mean quiet, unassuming taste—'better be under- than over-dressed' her English mentors such as Carolyn's mother used to say. Then she imagined that all Frenchmen were small and black, at best resembling Charles Boyer, her own husband's graceful elegance being easily accounted for, in her view, by his English blood.

So all in all she was unprepared for the scene that met her eyes on entering the Fertés's big salon. The door opened upon a kaleidoscope of glitter. The women, nearly all beauties, were in huge crinolines, from which rose naked shoulders and almost naked bosoms, sparkling with jewels. They moved on warm waves of scent, their faces were gaily painted with no attempt at simulating nature, their hair looked cleaner and glossier than any hair she had ever seen. Almost more of a surprise to Grace were the men, tall, handsome, and beautifully dressed. The majority of both men and women were fair with blue eyes, in fact they had the kind of looks which are considered in England to be English looks at their best. Grace saw that these looks in the women were greatly enhanced by over-dressing, always so much more becoming, whatever Carolyn's mother might say, than the reverse. That the atmosphere was of untrammelled sex did not surprise her, except in so far as that sex, outside a bedroom, could be so untrammelled.

Madame de la Ferté took Grace by the arm and led her round, introducing her to everybody. She was so much fascinated by what she saw that the terrible up and down examination accorded to a newcomer to the herd went on without her even being aware of it, and it was a long time before she realized how under-dressed, under-painted and under-scented she must seem. The jewels however, which Charles-Edouard had forced her to put on against her own inclination, were second to nobody's. Her face, too, though lacking the sparkle of the French faces, had no rival in that room for beauty of line and structure.

The party waited some time for the arrival of a young Bourbon and of a certain not so young woman who, to underline the fact that she was now his mistress, liked to arrive late in queenly fashion. The affair was being discussed by the group round Grace, the rapid quality of whose talk, so precise, so funny, so accomplished, so frighteningly well-informed, positively paralysed her. Her own brain seemed to struggle along in the rear. Charles-Edouard, swimming in his native waters, was happy and animated as she had never seen him.

A moment before the arrival of the Prince, his mistress came in on her husband's arm. She curtsied lower than anybody, murmuring, 'Monseigneur!'

'They left the luncheon together, they must have been in bed the whole afternoon.'

'I don't think so. She had a fitting at Dior.'

When the late arrivals had shaken hands with the company they all went in to dinner. Grace sat beside her host, the brother of Madame de Valhubert and Madame Rocher. He seemed a thousand years old, very frail, and wore a shawl over his shoulders. Opposite her was Charles-Edouard, between his hostess and a majestic old woman who had swept in to dinner holding in one hand the train of her dress and in the other a large ebony ear-trumpet. During the hush which fell while people were finding their places and settling down she said to Charles-Edouard, in the penetrating voice of a deaf person, but with a very confidential look as if she thought she was whispering:

'Are you still in love with Albertine?'

Charles-Edouard, not at all put out, took the trumpet and shouted into it, 'No. I'm married now and I have a son of seven.'

'So I heard. But what has that to do with it?'

Grace tried to look as if she had heard nothing. She was wondering desperately what she could talk about to M. de la Ferté when, greatly to her relief, he turned to her and said that he had just read *Les Hauts de Hurlevent* by a talented young English writer.

'I wondered if you knew her,' he said. 'Mademoiselle Emilie Brontë.'

This was indeed a lifeline. 'I really know her sister Charlotte better.'

'Ah! She has a sister?'

'Several. They all write books.'

'But no brothers?'

'One brother, but he's a bad lot. Nobody ever mentions him.'

'This Mademoiselle Brontë tells of country-house life in England. It must be very strange—well of course one knows it is. They do such curious things, I find. I should like to read other books by her talented family.'

'I wonder whether they've been translated.'

'No matter. My concierge's son knows English, he can translate them for me.'

M. de Tournon, on Grace's other side, was handsome, blond, and young, and when the time came for them to talk he opened the conversation in English, saying 'You are new to Paris life, so I am going to explain some very important things to you, which you may not have understood, about society here.'

'I wish you would,' she said gratefully.

'Footnotes, as it were, to the book you are reading.'

'Just what I require.'

'We will begin, I think, with precedence, since precedence precedes everything else. Now in England (and here I break off to explain that I know England extremely well; let me give you my credentials, Mary Marylebone and Molly Waterloo are two of my most intimate friends). Now what I am going to explain first is this. Please do not imagine that social life is easy here, as it is in England. It is a very very different matter. I will explain why. In England, as we know, everybody has a number, so when you give a dinner it is perfectly easy to place your guests—you look up the numbers, seat them accordingly, and they just dump down without any argument. Placement, such a terrible worry to us in France, never bothers you at all.'

'Are you sure,' said Grace, 'about these numbers? I've never heard of them. Placement doesn't bother us because nobody minds where they sit, at home.'

'People always mind. I mean the numbers in the beginning of the peerage. I subscribe to your peerage, such a beautiful book, and then I know where I am with English visitors. I only wish we had such a thing here, but we have not, and as a result the complications of precedence are terrible. There is the old French nobility and that of the Holy

Roman Empire (Lorraine, Savoy, and so on). These are complicated enough in themselves, but then we have the titles created by Napoleon, at the Restoration, by the July monarchy and Napoleon III. There are the Bourbon bastards and the Bonaparte bastards. I think you have no special place for your big bastards in England?'

'I don't think there are any.'

He looked at her with pity and reeled off some well-known English family names. Grace saw that she was doing badly in this witness box.

'Mrs. Jordan alone had about eighteen children,' he said. 'After all, royal blood is not nothing. But to come back to France. Suppose you have asked three dukes to dinner, which do you put first? You ring up the protocol—good, but the dukes meanwhile ring you up, each putting forward his claim. Then, my dear, you will positively long to be back in England, where you can have any number of dukes and members of the Academy at the same time. Where do you place Academicians, in England?'

'R.A.s?' said Grace. 'I don't know any.'

'Indeed! Now here, when you get to the dining-room, those of your guests who think themselves badly placed, if they don't leave at once, will turn their plates in protest and refuse the first course (though if it looks very delicious they may take it when it is handed round again).'

'Goodness!' said Grace, 'so what is the solution?'

'Do not ask more than one duke at a time.'

'But supposing they are friends?'

'Never will they be friends to that extent. But it shows how you are fortunate over there, you could ask all twenty-six—am I not right in saying there are twenty-six?'

'I haven't the faintest idea,' said Grace.

'I think so. You could ask all twenty-six to the same dinner without making a single enemy. Unimaginable. To go on with our lesson. Whereas in England the host and hostess sit at the ends of the table, here they face each other across the middle, the ends being reserved for low people, those who have married for love and so on. Two years of love, we say here, are no compensation for a lifetime at the end of the table.'

'Might not the end be more amusing?'

'No. It is not amusing to be with one's near relations and the people other people have married for love. Because near relations of the house go to the end, you and Charles-Edouard would be there tonight, except that this dinner is being given in your honour. Juliette, as you see, is there; as you also see, she is far from liking it.'

The young woman he indicated was the prettiest of them all, and the most dressed-up. She wore white tulle with swags of blue taffeta which matched her eyes, her skin looked as if a light were shining through it, and her hair fell on her shoulders in fat, chestnut curls. She was very lively and very young, hardly more than a child.

'Who is she?'

'Juliette Novembre de la Ferté, daughter-in-law of the house. The other end is her husband, watching with his jealous eye, poor Jean, and much good will it do him. She is the great success of the year.'

'How old is she?'

'Eighteen?—nineteen? Very soon she will have to begin her family, poor dear. Jean will have to take her to the country if he wants the necessary number, and wants them to be his.'

'Necessary number?'

'Yes, hasn't Charles-Edouard explained? We all have to have six nowadays if we are to prevent everything—but everything—being taken away in taxation. So most of us took advantage of the war years and just devoted ourselves to procreation. My wife and I have four (we prayed for twins—in vain, alas). Very soon we shall have to make up our minds again. Oh, how we were bored, I never shall forget it. We had our house full of Germans, how they were middle-class and dreary.'

Grace, who regarded Germans as frightening rather than dreary, was very much surprised and more so when he went on:

'There was one not so bad, a Graf, who sang little lieder after dinner, a charming baritone. But we had moments of grave disquietude, you know, caused by the maquisards. They were well-intentioned, but so tactless—at one moment we thought they would kill our baritone, and then, only think, there might have been a battle!'

'In wars,' said Grace, 'you rather expect battles.'

'Not in one's own château, my dear! How we were relieved when the Germans went away—just packed up one day and went—and we saw two nice young Guards officers of good family, Etonians, coming up the drive. Because please don't think I was on the side of the Germans. Why, when I saw them swarming over the hill (we lived in the unoccupied zone), I put out my hand and took down my gun. There and then I made a vow never to shoot again until they were out of France.'

'You mean, never to shoot birds again?'

'And rabbits and pigs, yes. You may not think much of this vow, but I live for shooting, it is my greatest joy.'

'Then why didn't you join the maquis and shoot the Germans?'

'Oh no, my dear, one couldn't do that.'

'Why not?'

'For many reasons. My brother-in-law joined a maquis, dreadful people, he soon had to give that up. They weren't possible, I assure you.'

'Well they may not have been possible, but they were on our side, and I love them for it.'

'Oh! my dear, we were all on your side, so you must love us all in that case.'

After dinner Charles-Edouard made a bee-line for Juliette Novembre. Grace heard him say, 'If you were Juliette de Champeaubert how is it I don't remember you? Jeanne Marie is one of my very greatest friends.'

'Oh I've only just been invented,' she said gaily, 'but before I was invented I used to hang out of the window, waiting to see you get into that pretty black motor you had in those days. My governess used to pull me back by my hair.'

'No! But that's awfully nice,' said Charles-Edouard. 'Come—I want to see my uncle's Subleyras again.'

They went off together into another room. Somebody said, 'It was quite indicated that those two would take to each other—she might be made for Charles-Edouard.'

M. de Tournon brought his wife over to Grace. He wanted her to see for herself this uncouth girl Charles-Edouard had so oddly married, in order to be able to talk about her when they got home. Madame de Tournon was Italian, more really beautiful and more elegant than Juliette Novembre but with much less sparkle.

'I am a cousin of yours now,' she said. 'Let's all sit here. So tell me what you have been doing in Paris since you arrived—there haven't been any dinners so far, have there? We only got back ourselves last night—we came back for this.'

'Really I've done very little. I've bought some clothes.'

'Is that Dior? Yes, I could see. But are they making these high necks now?'

'I had it altered—it seemed too naked.'

'Oh no, my dear,' said Madame de Tournon, 'you've got beautiful breasts, so why hide them up like that? It spoils the line. What else?'

'I've met Charles-Edouard's aunts.'

Madame de Tournon made a little face of sympathy. 'Any cocktail parties?'

'There have been one or two, but I never go to them, I hate them. Charles-Edouard goes. I don't terribly like lunching out either,' she went on. 'If I had my way I'd never go out before dinner-time.'

The Tournons looked at each other in growing amazement as she spoke.

'But listen,' cried Madame de Tournon, 'nobody can dine out more than eight times in a week. But if one lunches every day and goes to, say, three cocktails, as well as dining out, one can go to forty houses in a week. We often have, haven't we, Eugène?'

'Sometimes more, in the summer. I wish you could see us in July, fit for a nursing home by the time we get to the seaside.'

'Where do you go to the seaside as a rule?' asked Grace, thinking of them on the sands of some French Eastbourne with their four tots.

'Always Venice. Say what you like, it's the only place in August.'

'But is it fun for the children?'

They stared at her. 'We don't take the children to Venice—poor little things, what on earth would they do there? Besides, the children don't need a change, they don't have an exhausting season in Paris, they lead a perfectly healthy outdoor life in the Seine et Marne.'

Charles-Edouard and Juliette only reappeared when a general move was being made to go home. In the hall, as they were putting on their coats, Juliette flourished a hand for Charles-Edouard to kiss, saying, 'Good-bye for the present then, wickedness, I will consider your proposition.' She and her husband then got into the lift which took them to their own apartments.

'What proposition?' said Grace, in the motor.

'No proposition.'

'Oh dear! Need we dine out very often?'

'What d'you mean?'

'Let's dine together, alone, in future.'

'It would be very dull,' said Charles-Edouard.

'Such a terrible man I sat next to.'

'Eugène? He's a friendly old thing.'

'You can't think what he's like when he talks about the war.'

'I know. I saw him at a picture dealer's the other day and we had it all. But you mustn't be too hard on old Eugène—he joined up quite correctly in '39 and fought quite bravely in '40. His father was killed quite correctly in 1917. These Eugènes are not so rotten, it is the State of Denmark.'

The Tournons, meanwhile, were discussing Grace.

'My dear, the lowest peasant of the Danube knows more than she—just fancy, she had never heard of the English order of precedence, didn't know how many dukes there are in England, and didn't seem to think any of it mattered.'

'And did you hear what she said about taking the children to Venice? She must be backward, I'm afraid.'

'Allingham. What is this name? I must write at once to Molly Waterloo and ask her if they are people one can know. Poor Charles-Edouard—I pity him really.'

'Everything will be all right. Madame Rocher told my mother they are not married religiously.'

Madame Rocher had gone to Venice the week after Grace and Charles-Edouard left Bellandargues, and there she had managed to do quite a lot of harm to Grace, not wilfully at all, not intending mischief, but because she was utterly incapable of holding her tongue on any subject of general interest. Interest was very much centred, at the moment, on Charles-Edouard and his marriage.

Everybody thought it a pity that he, with his name and his fortune, should have married an English Protestant. When it transpired that she was the daughter of a Freemason, the general disapproval knew no bounds, a Bolshevist would have been as gladly received. Those who were informed on political subjects pointed to the dire results, for France, of the Allingham Commission, and it was freely hinted that Grace was very likely in the pay of the Intelligence Service.

Rather soon, however, the pendulum swung back in her favour. Older, cosmopolitan Frenchmen, writers, diplomats, and the like, who did not only live for society and yet had great influence with the Tournons of the world, had known the charming, cultivated, francophile Sir Conrad, and had read his books. They said he was by no means to the Left in politics, a rigid Conservative, in fact. Silly old Régine must have got the Freemason story all wrong, so like her, for it could not possibly be true. As to the Allingham Commission, the prime mover in that was a terrible villain called Sparks, paid by Arabs, in whose hands poor Sir Conrad had been as putty, and furthermore the results of the Commission, while annoying to the French government of the day, had not in the long run done any harm to France. It was absurd to say that the Allinghams were not the sort of people you could know; even Eugène de Tournon was quite impressed when he saw in his peerage who Grace's mother had been.

The highbrow aunts, who, dowdy as they seemed, counted for a good deal in society, weighed in on her side, saying that, though not an intellectual, she was very nice and well brought up. Her beauty, too, was in her favour. At last the nine days' wonder came to an end, and Grace was accepted. She was a new girl, she must watch her step, but the general feeling was that she would do.

She and Charles-Edouard now dined out nearly every day, and after all these dinners Charles-Edouard would sit with Juliette Novembre, as far removed from the rest of the company as possible, until it was time to go home.

CHAPTER IX

CAROLYN DEXTER and Grace saw a good deal of each other, sitting on nursery fenders, and at first this was a comfort to Grace because of her need to feel at home somewhere. She felt at home with Carolyn. But as time went on Carolyn often irritated her dreadfully. Since marriage with the important Mr. Dexter the swagger and self-assurance which had made her so fascinating to the other girls at her school had deteriorated into bossiness. She was for ever telling Grace what she ought to do and whom she and Charles-Edouard ought to see, and was also for ever enlarging upon the faults of the French. She had a particular grievance against the world of Parisians which was led by such young couples as the Tournons and the Novembre de la Fertés, not, oddly enough, on the grounds of their really frightening frivolity, but because they so seldom invited herself and her husband to their houses. In view of the importance of Mr. Dexter and the fact that she was the niece of a former British Ambassador to Paris, she had expected immediately to be asked everywhere, but, except for big, official parties, the Dexters moved almost entirely in an Anglo-American world. Mr. Dexter did not mind this at all. When he said, as he continually did, that he despised the French, he meant it. He had no wish to meet any, except those he was obliged to work with. But Carolyn was not quite so honest. If the French annoyed her it was very largely by ignoring her presence in their town.

Carolyn thought that Grace ought to give a dinner party for her, and said so in her extremely outspoken way. Grace replied, with perfect truth, that, for the moment, she and Charles-Edouard were taken up with his many relations. Carolyn did not accept this as easily as some people would have, and often returned to the charge.

'I hear you dined last night with the Polastrons. Are they relations of your husband?' she said, before even saying hullo to Grace, who had come to tea.

'Yes, I think so.'

'How are they related?'

'Perhaps they're not. But anyway, great old friends.'

'Great old friends, but not related. I thought you were only seeing relations at present?'

'Well, but Carolyn—I leave it all to Charles-Edouard, you know.'

She felt instinctively that Charles-Edouard would find the Dexters very dull.

'Let's have a cocktail,' said Carolyn. 'I'm exhausted. I've had an awful afternoon struggling with the garage people to do something about my car. Promised for yesterday—you know the sort of thing. Really I'm fed up with these wretched French.'

'I thought you loved France. You always used to.'

'I love France, but I can't say I love the French, nowadays. They are quite different, you know, since the war. Everybody says the same.'

Grace somehow felt sure that they were not quite different at all. She really did love them. She loved the servants in her house for their friendly efficiency, their faithfulness to Charles-Edouard; she loved the highbrow aunts, now that she was getting to know them, for being so clever and so serious, and she loved the gay young diners for being so pretty and so light-hearted. She even loved their snobbishness, it seemed to her such a tremendous joke, so particularly funny, somehow, nowadays. She was beginning to love the critical spirit of all and sundry. It kept people up to the mark, no doubt, and had filled her with the desire to improve her mind and sharpen her wits. She longed to make a better appearance in the box, and be a credit to Charles-Edouard. And she loved the people in the streets for smiling at her and noticing her new clothes.

'I don't say I hate them,' said Carolyn, 'but they irritate me, and I see their faults.'

'What faults?'

'Oh, you're sold to the French, Grace, it's hardly worth talking to you about them. Faults! They hit you in the eye if you're not blind. Never punctual—don't get things done—not reliable (you should hear Hector)—dirty—— The dirt! Look at the central heating here—just gusts of hot dust, impossible to keep anything clean. Then the butchers' shops—after living in America you feel ill to see them—flies all over the meat——'

'I like that,' said Grace. 'Meat can't be too meaty, for my taste.'

'Ugh! Anyhow, you can't like the rudeness——'

'Nobody's ever rude to me. They smile when they see me, even strangers in the street.'

'Trying to pick you up. And what about those dreadful policemen!'

'I always think they look like young saints, in their capes.'

'Saints! I must tell that to Hector, he'll roar.'

'I've never had anything but niceness from them—over Nanny's identity card and so on.'

'I expect your husband gives them enormous bribes.'

'Of course he doesn't.'

'I suppose even you will admit the French would do anything for money.'

'Perhaps they may—it's never crossed my path, but you may be right. Perhaps they are more frank and open about it than other people.'

'Frank and open is the word. They always frankly and openly marry for money, to begin with.'

'Charles-Edouard didn't.'

'Are you—— Oh well there may be exceptions, and I suppose he wouldn't need to. But at the time when our grandfathers were marrying actresses for love their contemporaries here were all marrying Jewesses for money. I was thinking of dozens of examples last night in bed.'

'I think they were quite right. Just look at it from the point of view of their grandchildren. Honestly now, which would you prefer as a grandmother—a clever old Jewess, who has brought brains and money and Caffieri commodes into the family, or some ass of an actress?'

'I can't understand you, Grace, you used to seem so very English at home.'

'Yes, well now,' said Grace, rather sadly, 'I'm nothing at all. But I would love to have been born a Frenchwoman, and I can't say more, can I?'

'Oh, you'll change your tune, I bet. By the way, I've been meaning to tell you—we quite often see Hughie.'

'Hughie! Does he live here too?'

'He was here with a military mission, now he's back in England, but he keeps coming over. Hector sees him at the Travellers and brings him in for a drink, most weeks. He's terribly in love with a French-woman here, a Madame Marel-Desboulles. Hector thinks it's a disaster for him, he has heard all about this Madame Marel and says she's no good.'

'Marel—Marel-Desboulles. Don't I know her?' Grace said vaguely.

The names and faces of the French people she met had not yet clicked into place, they floated round her mind separately, many names and many faces, all wonderfully romantic and new but not adding up into real people. So the name Marel-Desboulles had a familiar ring but no face, while the brilliant woman who played conversational ping-pong with Charles-Edouard, across a dinner-table, sometimes across a whole roomful of people all delighted by the speed and accuracy of the game, volley, volley, high lob with a spin, volley, cut, smash, had not yet acquired a surname. Grace only knew her as Albertine.

'He wants to marry her.'

Carolyn looked at Grace to see if she minded, but she hardly even seemed interested.

'And will he?'

'I don't think so. He says she is very Catholic and talks all the time of going into a convent—poor Hughie says he'll kill himself if she does. But Hector says nobody at the Travellers thinks there's much danger of that. What happened about your engagement to Hughie, Grace? I never really knew.'

'Oh, just that we were engaged, and he went to the war and I married Charles-Edouard instead. I'm afraid I didn't behave very well.'

'Pity, in a way.'

'I can't agree.'

'I meant nothing against your husband. I hear he is charming. I only meant pity to marry a Frenchman.'

Grace longed to retaliate with 'well then, what about marrying an American' but she knew that, while it is considered nowadays per-fectly all right to throw any amount of aspersions on poor old France and England, one tiny word reflecting anything but exaggerated love for rich new America is thought to be in the worst of taste. She was also, by nature, more careful of people's feelings than Carolyn. So she said, mildly, that she could not imagine any other sort of husband.

The two nannies clung to each other like drowning men. and Sigi was now taken every day for air and exercise to the Parc Monceau instead of the Tuileries Gardens. He was very cross about this, and complained bitterly to his mother.

'Pascal and I are so fond of each other. I never knew such an obliging goat, and now I never see him. It's a shame, Mummy.'

'Why don't you meet Nanny Dexter in the Tuileries sometimes for a change?' Grace said to her Nan.

'Oh no thank you, dear. We don't like those Tuileries. It's the draughtiest place in Paris. I only wish you would feel the stiff neck I caught there the other day, waiting for the little monkey to finish his ride. I don't think all those smelly animals are very nice, if you ask me, and the children there are a funny lot too. Some of them are black, dear, and one was distinctly Chinese. The Parc Monceau is a much better place for little boys.'

'Oh well, Nan, it's just as you like, of course, but when I went there I thought it fearfully depressing, such thousands of children, like a children's market or something, and all those castor-oil plants. Hideous.'

'Still you do see a little grass there,' said Nanny, 'and decent railings.'

'I hate the silly little baby Parc Monceau,' piped up Sigi, 'and I loathe dear little Foster Dexter aged four. Under the spreading chestnut tree, I loathe Foss and Foss loathes me.'

'Very stupid and naughty, Sigismond. Foster's a dear little chap—so easy too. Nanny Dexter has never had one minute's trouble with him since he was born, and they've been all over the place—oh they have travelled! I must say Mrs. Dexter's a marvellous mummy.'

'In what way?' Grace asked, with interest. She tried her best to be a marvellous mummy too, but her efforts never received much acknowledgment.

'Well, she has tea in the nursery every day.'

'But, Nanny, so do I—nearly every day.'

'And gives little Foss his bath often as not, and, what's more, every Saturday and Sunday Mr. Dexter gives him his bath. He is a nice daddy, Mr. Dexter.'

Unfortunately Grace was stumped by this. Nobody could say that Charles-Edouard was that sort of nice daddy; he never went near the nursery. He liked the idea of Sigi, and was delighted when people said the child was his living image, but a few minutes of his company at a time were more than sufficient. He was such a restless man that a few minutes of almost anybody's company at a time was more than sufficient.

Grace said to Charles-Edouard,
'You know my friend Carolyn?'
'The beautiful Lesbian?'

'No, no, Carolyn Dexter.'

'You said she was a Lesbian at school.'

'I said we were all in love with her, that's quite different. Besides, people are all sorts of things at school—Carolyn used to be a Communist then—we used to point her out to visitors as the school Communist—and look at her now! Marshall Plan up to the eyes. Anyway, can we dine there on Thursday?—I'm to let her know.'

'You keep our engagements, it's for you to say.'

'We are quite free, but I wanted to know if you'd like it.'

'Who will be there?'

'Well, it sounded like this, but I may have got it wrong. The Jorgmanns of *Life*, the Schmutzes of *Time*, the Jungfleisches, who are liaison between *Life* and *Time*, the Oberammergaus who have replaced the Pottses on the Un-American Activities Committee, European branch, the Rutters, who are liaison between the French Chamber of Commerce, the Radio-Diffusion Française and the *Chicago Herald Tribune*, and an important French couple the Tournons. Are the Tournons important really?'

'Of course they are, in their way, but it won't be those Tournons. It will be what we call les faux Tournons—he is chef de cabinet to Salleté, very dull, but she is rather nice.'

'Carolyn says these are all people you ought to meet.'

'Why ought I to meet them?'

'Now darling, do be serious for once. It's all that Aid and so on. They might like you, and it's so terribly important for them to like French people because of the Aid. Carolyn's always saying so, and she's very clever, as I've told you. She says what happens is that the important Americans who come here meet all the wrong sort of French. Then they go back to the middle of America and tell the people there, who hate foreigners anyway, that the French are undependable, and so nasty it would be better to cut the Aid and concentrate on Italy, where they are undependable too but so nice, and specially on Germany, where they are dependable and so wonderful, and leave the nasty French to rot. All because they meet the wrong sort. And all this is very discouraging to Hector Dexter, who is dying to help and aid the French more and more.'

'Well of course Hector Dexter would lose his job if they cut the Aid, that's very plain.'

'There you are, being French and cynical, just like Carolyn always says. And as if it would matter to Mr. Dexter whether he lost his job or not. He's far too important.'

Indeed the word important seemed, at that time, to have been coined only for Mr. Dexter, and his name never occurred either in print or in conversation without it. It seemed that he was one of the most, if not the most, important of living men.

'My dear child, do you really think, when a great country like America has settled on a certain policy with regard to another great country like France, it can be deflected from it by the Jungfleisches meeting the wrong sort of French person?'

'Carolyn says it can.'

'And what makes you think I'm the right sort of French person for them to meet?'

'Well look at what you did in the war.'

'But the Americans hate the people who were on their side in the war. It's one thing they can never forgive. I'm surprised you haven't noticed that. Never mind,' he said, seeing her face fall. 'We'll go, and I'll do my best to be nice, I promise you.'

CHAPTER X

THE Dexters invited their guests at eight, but only sat down to dinner at nine. The intervening hour was spent drinking cocktails while Hector Dexter talked about the present state of France.

'I have known France all my life. I came here as a kid; I came during my vacations from college; I came on my honeymoon with my first wife, the first Mrs. Dexter, and I was here during World War II. So I am in some sort qualified to make my diagnosis, and I have made my diagnosis, and my diagnosis is as follows, but first I would like to tell you all a little story which I think will help me to illustrate the point I am going to try if I can to make.

'Well it was just before the Ardennes counter-offensive; we were up in this little village near the frontier of Belgium, or no, maybe it was near the frontier of Luxembourg—it makes no odds really and doesn't affect my story. Now there was this boulanger in the village, and I think now I will if I may describe the state of the village. Well it had been bombed by the U.S. air force, precision bombed, if you see what I mean; it had then been bombed by the Luftwaffe quite regardless I am sorry to say (sorry because I am one who hopes very soon to see the Germans playing a very very important part in the family of nations), bombed, then, quite regardless of civilian property and military objectives. It had then been shelled by U.S. infantry and taken and occupied; it had then been shelled and retaken and reoccupied by the Reichswehr, and I am sorry to say that when it was reoccupied by the Reichswehr certain atrocities took place which I for one would rather forget. It had then been shelled and retaken and occupied by the U.S. infantry. And the rain was falling down day and night. I daresay you can picture the state of this village at the time of which I am telling you. But it so happened that the habitation of this boulanger was still intact.

It had been damaged of course, the windows were blown in and so on, but the walls were standing, a bit of roof was left and the big oven had suffered no impairment. So I went and asked him if he would care to have some U.S. army flour so that he could bake bread for those civilians who were left in the village. But this little old boulanger simply said what the hell, though he said it in French of course, what the hell, the Boches will be back again this evening and I don't see much point baking bread for the Boches to eat tonight.

'Now this little story is symbolical of what I see around me and of what we Americans in France are trying to fight against. There is a malaise in this country, a spirit of discontent, of nausea, of defatigation, of successlessness around us, here in this very city of Paris which I for one find profoundly discouraging.

'Now my son Heck junior is here temporarily with us, my son by the first Mrs. Dexter, an independent, earning, American male of some twenty-two summers. He trained to be a psychiatrist. In my view, everybody nowadays, whatever profession they intend eventually to embrace, ought to have this training. Now he has a column.'

Charles-Edouard, gazing all this time at Mrs. Jungfleisch, who happened to be very pretty, and wondering if there were another room he could sit in after dinner with her (but he knew really that the flat was not likely to have a suite of drawing-rooms), was startled out of his reverie by the word column.

'Doric?' he asked with interest, 'or Corinthian?'

But Mr. Dexter, in the full flood of locution, took no notice.

'And my son walks in the streets of this town—he is not here with us tonight because he prefers to eat alone using his eyes and his ears in some small, but representative bistro—and he claims that he can sense, by observing the faces of the ordinary citizens, and by various small actions they perform in the course of their daily round, he claims to observe this malaise in every observable walk of life, and I am sorry to say, sorry because I am very deeply sincere in my wish and desire to help the French people, that what my son senses as he goes about this city is entirely reflected in this column.'

And so on. Grace thought it exceedingly clever of Mr. Dexter to keep up such a flow, but she could see it was not quite doing for Charles-Edouard. If only he were more serious, she thought sadly, he could be just as wonderful, or more so, but he never seemed to care a bit about the things that really matter in the world. Even during the war he had done nothing, when she was with him anyhow, but make love, sing little snatches of songs, roar with laughter, and search for objects of art on which to feast his eyes. And yet he must have a serious side to his nature since he had been impelled to leave all these things he cared for and to fight long years in the East. She knew that he could have been demobilized much sooner if he had wished but that he had refused to leave his squadron until they all came home. She longed for him to get up and make a speech even cleverer than Mr. Dexter's, in defence of his country, but he only sat laughing inside himself and looking at pretty Mrs. Jungfleisch.

At last they went into dinner. Grace, who was by now accustomed to an easy flow of French chat from her dinner partners, was completely paralysed when Mr. Rutter opened the conversation by turning to her and saying, 'Tell me about yourself.' She was looking, as she always did, to see if Charles-Edouard was happy; it distressed her that he had been put as far as possible from pretty Mrs. Jungfleisch. He too clearly did not admire Carolyn, who was talking to him about Nanny, a subject that did not bring out the best in him.

'Myself?' she said, and fell dumb.

However Hector Dexter now tapped his plate for silence.

'I'm going to call on each person here,' he said, 'to say a few words on a subject with which we are all deeply preoccupied. I mean, of course, the A-bomb. I think Charlie Jungfleisch can speak for the ordinary citizen of our great United States of America, as he is just back from there. Aspinall Jorgmann will tell us what they are saying behind the Iron Curtain (Asp has just done this comprehensive six-day tour and we all want to know his impressions), Wilbur Rutter can speak of it as it will, or may, affect world prosperity, M. Tournon represents the French government at this little gathering, and M. de Valhubert——'

'Perhaps I will listen without joining in,' said Charles-Edouard, much to Grace's disappointment, 'as an amateur of pâte tendre, you will understand, I find the whole subject really too painful. My policy with regard to atom bombs is that of the ostrich.'

'Just as you like,' said Mr. Dexter. 'Then I call on Charlie. There is one thing we here in Europe are very very anxious to know, Charlie, and that is what, if any, air-raid precautions are being taken in New York?'

'Well, Heck, quite some precautions are being taken. In the first place the authorities have issued a very comprehensive little pamphlet entitled "The Bomb and You" designed to bring the bomb into every home and invest it with a certain degree of cosiness. This should calm and reassure the population in case of attack. There are plenty of guidance reunions, fork lunches, and so on where the subject is treated frankly, to familiarize it, as it were, and rob it of all unpleasantness. At these gatherings the speakers stress that the observation of certain rules of atomic hygiene ought to be a matter of everyday routine. Keep a white sheet handy, for example, since white offers the best protection against gamma rays. Then the folks are told what to do after the explosion. The importance of rest can hardly be overestimated; the protein contents of the diet should be increased—no harm in a glass of milk as soon as the bomb has gone off. If you feel a little queer, dissatisfied with your symptoms, send at once for the doctor. You follow me, it is elementary, of course, but these things cannot be too much emphasized. If the folks know just what they ought to do in the case of atomic explosion, such explosion is robbed of half, or one-third, its terrors.'

'Thank you, Charlie,' said Mr. Dexter. 'I for one feel a lot easier in my mind. There is nothing so dangerous as a policy of laisser-aller, and I am very glad that the great American public, if I may say so, M. de Valhubert, without offending your feelings, is not hiding its head in the sand, but is looking the Bomb squarely in the eye. Very glad indeed. And now I shall call on Asp for a few words. Tell us what they are thinking in the Russian-occupied countries, Asp.'

'Well, I have just had six very very interesting days in Poland, Czecho-Slovakia, Roumania, Bulgaria, the East or Russian-occupied part of Germany, and the East or Russian-occupied part of Austria, and I'm here to tell you that these countries, if not actually preparing for war, which I think they are, are undeniably being run on a war-time basis.'

'And did you talk with the ordinary citizens of these countries, Asp?'

'Why, no, Heck. For reasons of which I suppose you are all cognizant I did not, but I saw the key men and key women of our embassies and missions in these countries, and I gleaned enough material for three, or two, very very long and interesting articles which I hope you will all be reading for yourselves——'

And so it went on. Fortunately some more very important people came in after dinner, so Grace and Charles-Edouard were able to slip away without looking too rude. Charles-Edouard never managed to have a word with Mrs. Jungfleisch, who had settled down to a cosy chat with Mr. Jorgmann about conferences, vetos, and what Joe Alsop had told her when she saw him in Washington. Pretty Mrs. Jungfleisch, like Mr. Dexter, was deeply concerned about the present state of the world, and had no time for frivolous Frenchmen who preferred pâte tendre to atom bombs.

Charles-Edouard was particularly nice to Grace about this dinner, and insisted on asking the Dexters back the following week. The two couples dined alone together, rather quickly, and went to *Lorenzaccio*. If Charles-Edouard had suffered from boredom at the Dexter dinner, he had more than his revenge on Hector, who really could hardly sit still at *Lorenzaccio*, and said, quite rudely, in the entr'acte, that whoever would take this play to Broadway was heading for a very very serious financial loss indeed.

'But my dearest,' said Albertine, 'dinner with the wife's best friend and the best friend's husband is a classic. I could have warned you about that, as much a part of married life as babies, nannies, and in-laws. Of course a jolly bachelor like yourself had never envisaged such developments.'

'I wish I understood Americans,' said Charles-Edouard. 'They are very strange. So good, and yet so dull.'

'What makes you think they are so good?'

'You can see it, shining in their eyes.'

'That's not goodness, that's contact lenses—a kind of spectacle they wear next the eyeball. I had an American lover after the liberation and I used to tap his eye with my nail file. He was a very curious man. Imagine, his huge, healthy-looking body hardly functioned at all by itself. He couldn't walk a yard; I took him to Versailles, and half-way across the Galerie des Glaces he lay on the floor and cried for his mother. He couldn't do you know what without lavages, he could only digest yaghourt and raw carrots, he couldn't sleep without a sleeping draught or wake up without benzedrine, and he had to have a good strong blood transfusion every morning before he could face the day. It was like having another automaton in the house.'

'You had him in the house?'

Albertine, who hated too much intimacy, had never done this with any of her lovers.

'For the central heating, dearest,' she said apologetically. 'It was that very cold winter. Americans have no circulation of their own—even their motors are artificially heated in winter and cooled in summer. I never shall forget how hot he kept this room—my little thermometer sprang in one day from "rivières glacées" to "vers à soie", and even then he complained. Finally it reached Sénégale, all the marquetry on my Oeben began to spring, and I was obliged to divorce him. We were married, by the way.'

'Married?' Charles-Edouard was quite astounded.

'Yes, he could do nothing in bed without marriage lines. I tried everything. I even got an excellent aphrodisiac from the doctor. Useless. We had to go to the Consulate together, and after that he was splendid. The result is I've got an American passport, which never does any harm.'

'And what has become of him now?'

'Oh he's got the cutest little wife and the two loveliest kids, and he sends me boxes of cleansing tissues every Christmas.'

CHAPTER XI

MADAME DE VALHUBERT died suddenly the very day she was to have left Bellandargues for Paris. She made the journey all the same, and was buried in the family grave at the Père Lachaise. Charles-Edouard was very sad, cast down as Grace had never seen him. He said they must go into mourning in the old-fashioned, strict way which has been greatly relaxed in France since the war; it was a tribute, he said, that he owed to his grandmother. So Grace was no longer subjected to an enormous dinner party, reception or ball nearly every day, and this was a great comfort to her. Not a truly social person, these parties, as soon as they had ceased to frighten, had begun to bore her, and she envisaged almost with horror the endless succession there would be of them to the end of her life. She was very much happier now that, for the moment, they were ruled out. She did not have much more of her husband's company than usual; he continued to spend whole days at the sale-rooms in the Hôtel Drouot and with the antique dealers, and was still always out at tea-time. They never spent an evening at home together quietly; the moment he had swallowed his dinner he would drag Grace to a film, a play, or a concert.

Charles-Edouard's long absences from his house had never surprised her or struck her as needing an explanation. She had been brought up in the shadow of Parliament, Brooks's, White's and Pratts'; her own father was practically never at home, and she supposed that all men were engaged, for hours every day, on some masculine business, inexplicable, at any rate never explained, but quite innocent and normal.

But although she saw rather little of him it seemed to her that Charles-Edouard was cosier, more at home with her now, than when they had first arrived in France. It had never even occurred to her that she was, perhaps, more in love than he was. In her eyes all the evidence pointed to a great deal of love on his side. He was very nice to her, he made love continually, and she had not enough experience to look for any of the other signs that indicate the condition of a man's heart. Now that they were no longer going out she never saw Juliette, and assumed that Charles-Edouard never did either. This was certainly a relief, though the affair had annoyed rather than worried her. It seemed to her that it was too open to matter, she had taken it half as a joke, and teased him about it.

So Grace regarded herself as a perfectly happy woman whose marriage was entirely satisfactory, with one very small reservation.

'You know, Charles-Edouard,' she said to him, 'I can't help thinking it's a pity you never set eyes on our Blessing. I often wonder whether I see enough of him, but you are an absolute stranger to the poor little boy. Sigi,' she called, hearing him outside on the stairs, 'come in here. Who is this gentleman?'

'Papa!'

'Yes, quite right, but how did you guess?'

He looked his mother up and down. 'I say, Mummy, you are getting Frenchified.'

'Don't you think we all are, now we live in France?'

'Nanny isn't, and Nanny Dexter isn't, and Mrs. Dexter isn't.'

'Well, perhaps not. Are you just going out?'

'Oh yes, boring old Parc Monceau as usual.'

'Does he go to the Parc Monceau?' said Charles-Edouard. 'This is very foolish. Why not the Tuileries, or the Luxembourg, or the beautiful garden of the Musée Rodin? I should hate it if my childhood memories were of the Parc Monceau.'

'His little friend goes there.'

'My little friend indeed! Nanny's little friend. I loathe him. Anyway, I like grown-up people.'

'Ha!' said Charles-Edouard. 'How I agree with you, so do I. Will you chuck the Parc Monceau today and come for a walk with me instead?'

'With delight. And Mummy too?'

Grace thought it would be much better if they went off alone, without her, and said, 'I can't, darling, I've got to try on a hat. Go with Papa and I'll be here for tea when you get back.'

'Always hats! Wouldn't be much good in a tight fix with interior tribes, you and your old hats.' He was not displeased, however. His experience of walking with two grown-up people was that they chatted away together up there in the air while you were left to look for francs in the gutter.

'I think you underestimate the value of hats,' said Charles-Edouard. 'They can have a very civilizing influence on interior tribes. Look at Mummy——'

'Oh shut up, Charles-Edouard.'

'Cut the necking,' said Sigi.

'Where does the child learn this sort of language?'

'It's what I tell you. If he was more with us——'

'Where shall we go, Papa?'

> '*Promenons-nous dans les bois*
> *Pendant que le loup n'y est pas.*'

'No, not dans les bois. A street walk.'

'The most beautiful walk in the world then. Across the Beaux Arts bridge, through the Cour Carrée, under the Arc du Carousel (averting the eye from Gambetta) and across the Place de la Concorde. How would that be?'

'Then we could have a word with Pascal on the way?'

'Who is Pascal?'

'My goat.'

'Ah no. No words with goats.'

They set off hand in hand, Charles-Edouard dragging the child along at a furious speed. At the Arc du Carousel Charles-Edouard began reciting '*A la voix du vainqueur d'Austerlitz*—when you know that by heart,' he said, 'I'll give you a prize.'

'What sort of prize?'

'I don't know. A good sort.'

'How can I learn it?'

'It's written up there on the arch. At your age I used to read it every day. Oh how I loved the Emperor, at your age.'

'How can I read it when we never come here?'

'You must come. You must refuse the Parc Monceau and come.'

'But, Papa——'

'No excuses. Nothing so dull.'

Sigi waved at Pascal with his free hand, but was dragged on.

'You are too old for goats. I'll show you some horses. There, the flying horses of Coysevox, are they not wonderful?'

'Look, look, Papa! Mrs. Dexter in her lovely new Buick.'

'Come on, she's not my type. What is a Buick?'

'Papa! It's a motor, of course.'

'Ha! You know Buick and you've never heard of Coysevox. What a world to be young in. Now here are the chevaux de Marly—are they not beautiful?'

'Can I get up there and ride on one of them?'

'Ride on the chevaux de Marly? Certainly not, what an idea.'

They hurried on to Charles-Edouard's destination, the shop of an art dealer who had written to him about a pair of vases. Here Sigi was put to sit, kicking his heels, on one of those stools which, at Versailles, were kept exclusively for dukes. 'So now,' said the dealer, 'you are duc et pair de France.'

Charles-Edouard began an exhaustive examination of everything in the shop: the vases, a tray of jewelled boxes, an inkstand which had belonged to Catherine the Great, a pair of cherubs said to be by Pigalle, and so on. He always asked the price of everything, like a child in a toy shop, and roared with derisive laughter when he was told. He was the flail of the dealers, his technique being to arrive with the words, loudly enunciated before the other customers, 'Why don't you burn all this rubbish and get some decent stock?' But they respected his knowledge and his love of beautiful things.

Sigi gazed out of the plate-glass window. It was very dull being duc et pair de France for so long. In a window across the road there was a great heap of mattresses, as in the story of the Princess and the pea. The sight of these mattresses, combined with the endless æons of inactivity so terrible to a child, filled him with a great longing to jump up and down on them.

Presently Madame Marel came into the shop. Charles-Edouard, who had forgotten that he had half arranged to meet her there, was a little bit put out at being found with Sigi. He knew that all would be reported to Grace.

'How are you, my dear Albertine? Here are the vases—not bad, what do you say? But the price is the funniest thing I ever heard. M. Dupont does love to make me laugh. Now what of this bronze? I am thinking of it most seriously. I do love Louis XIV bronze, so delightfully solid, so proof against housemaids. Once you fall into Louis XV you are immediately in the domain of restored terre cuite and broken china, of things which must go behind glass in any case. I love them too, far too much, but there is something comfortable about this old satyr. As soon as M. Dupont has mentioned its real price I shall buy it—at present he is in the realms of romance. Such an imaginative man, such an artist in figures, M. Dupont. So—this is Sigismond.'

Sigi, rather unwillingly, but forced to it by a severe look from his father, kissed her hand.

'This is Sigi? Now all is explained—he is well worth it. Have you been here long? Very long? Poor little boy, not very amusing for you, sitting on that tabouret and thinking of what, I wonder? What were you thinking of, Sigismond?'

'The mattresses over there. I would like to jump and jump and jump and roll and roll and roll on them.'

'Already?' she said. 'How like your father. I'll tell you what, darling, shall we go over there and jump while he goes on breaking poor M. Dupont's heart? Shall we? Come on.'

'No, Albertine, certainly not. I am a well-known figure in Paris, please try and remember. It is quite out of the question.'

'He wants to so badly.'

'But this child has the most peculiar ambitions. On the way here he wanted to chat to a goat and to ride on the chevaux de Marly.'

'What a lovely idea, and how well I can understand it. Why don't we arrange it for him?'

'Try not to be foolish, Albertine. Flirt with the child if you can't help it, but keep within reason.'

'Your father has this pompous side to his nature, you know. When one comes up against that there's nothing to be done. Will you come to tea with me one day, if I collect some little friends?'

'He loathes little friends.'

'So much the better, he can come alone. There are lots of things in my house to amuse you—things that you wind up which do tricks. A dancing bear, a drinking monkey, a singing dog. Will you come?'

'Oh yes please,' said Sigi. He took greatly to this lady who was so nice to him and who smelt so delicious.

'Today?'

'Not today,' said Charles-Edouard rather hastily, 'I'm taking him home now, he has been out long enough. Say good-bye, Sigismond.'

Madame Marel said, in French, which she presumed the child would not understand, 'Then come straight on to me—tea will be ready and I've got many things to tell you.'

'Did you enjoy your walk with Daddy?' Grace asked as they sat down to tea. The two nannies had at last found an English grocer, so their tables were laden now with (for export only) such delicacies as Huntley and Palmer's biscuits, good black Indian tea, Tiptree's strawberry jam, Gentleman's Relish, and rich fruit cake.

At luncheon, chutney, Colman's mustard, and horse-radish sauce made it possible to swallow the nasty foreign-looking meat swimming in fat, and hardly a day went by without a sago pudding or castle cakes with Bird's custard.

Grace never went to the nursery without feeling rather like the maiden in the fairy story whose husband allowed her to have one room in the castle lined with nettles to make her feel at home again.

'I enjoyed it very much indeed. We saw Pascal in the distance, but he didn't see me.'

'You didn't have a drive?'

'Papa was in such a hurry. Then we saw Mrs. Dexter in her Buick but she's not his type, then we saw the chevaux de Marly but he was in too much of a hurry to let me ride on them, then we saw a huge heap of mattresses and I wanted to jump and jump up and down on them, but Papa wouldn't let me even though the lady we met said he ought to because it would be very amusing, and she said it was just like Papa, wanting to jump and roll on the mattresses.'

'You met a lady?'

'Yes, she smelt heavenly and Papa has gone to tea with her. I think she is his type.'

'A pretty lady?'

'Very Frenchified.'

'So on the whole you had a good time?'

'Smashing,' said Sigi with conviction, his hour of restless boredom on the tabouret quite forgotten.

When Charles-Edouard got back he found Grace in the little library next door to her bedroom where she generally sat when she was alone. She was tucked up on a chaise-longue looking pretty and comfortable and a little fragile, since she was expecting a child.

'Who was it you met on your walk? She's made a great hit with Sigi, he said she smelt too delicious.'

'Yes. I wish I knew what scent she uses, but it has always been a state secret. Albertine Marel-Desboulles.'

'Marel. Oh! Isn't that the woman Hughie's in love with?'

'Exactly. She tells me she has fourteen English suitors, it's very amusing.'

'Not very amusing for poor Hughie. He's terrified that she'll go into a convent, according to Carolyn. Do you think it's likely?'

Charles-Edouard roared with laughter. 'Convent indeed! Never, in a long life, have I heard anything so funny.'

'Where does she live?'

'Just round the corner in the rue de l'Université, in that house you always look at with the two balconies.'

'Oh, the lovely house. Does she live there?'

'As you would know if you ever listened to what I say. She has extraordinary furniture, and the most famous collection of old toys in the world. Her husband's family made all the toys for the French court from the time of Henri II to the Revolution.'

'Does she live with her husband?'

'He is dead. He was vastly rich and he died.'

'And she's an old friend of yours?'

'Since always. We had the same nurse.'

'Take me to see her one day?'

'Perhaps—I'm not sure. Albertine is not very fond of women.'

Three or four days later Grace was driving home at tea-time when she saw Charles-Edouard leaning against the great double doors of Madame Marel's house. He had evidently just rung the bell. A small side door flew open and he disappeared through it. For the first time since her marriage Grace felt a jealous, heart-sinking pang. By the time he came in, some two hours later, she was so nervous that she thought it better to speak.

'But Charles-Edouard,' she said, 'you went to tea with Madame Marel again today?'

Charles-Edouard always acted on the principle, with women, of telling the truth and then explaining it away so that it sounded highly innocent.

'Yes,' he said carelessly. 'It's an old habit of all my life. I go there every day, at tea-time.'

'Then you are in love with her?'

'Because I go to tea?' He raised his hand and shook his head reassuringly, but with his inward, guilty laugh.

Grace was not reassured. 'Because you go there every day. That's why you never come and have tea with us, in the nursery.'

'Only partly why.'

'When you told me about M. de la Bourlie visiting your grandmother every day you said in such a case there is always love. I remember so well, they were your very words, Charles-Edouard.'

'Now listen, my dearest Grace. As life goes on each person develops many different relationships with many different people, and each of these relationships is unique in quality. My relationship with you is perfect, is it not?'

'I thought so,' she answered sadly.

'If you think so it is so. Is it spoilt if I have another relationship, much less intense, much less important, but also perfect in its way, with Albertine Marel? Be frank now. You didn't mind me being alone for hours with my grandmother; you wouldn't mind if I went to a club, or spent hours with some old school friend, a man. You are not sad because the hours are not spent with you, you realize we can't be together every minute of the day; you mind because Albertine is a still desirable woman. And yet we are old school friends—nursery friends, in fact, and we share a great interest and hobby, that of collecting. I will tell you something very seriously, Grace. If you don't empty your mind and heart of sexual jealousy, if you let yourself give way to that, you will never be happy with me. Because I really cannot help liking the company of women. Do you understand what I have said?'

'It sounds all right,' said Grace.

'Try and remember it then.'

'Yes, I'll try.'

'Are you happy again?'

'Yes. But, oh dear, how nice it would be if you had tea here with us every day.'

'In the nursery? With Nanny? Are you mad?'

CHAPTER XII

On Madame de Valhubert's birthday, in February, Charles-Edouard, Grace and Sigismond went to the Père Lachaise with a bunch of spring flowers for her. It was beautiful weather, a respite between two particularly sharp spells of winter. The sun shone, the birds sang, and the blue gnomes who keep order in the streets of the dead were all beaming cheerfully. Even the floating widows looked as if they did not much object to being left alone a few more years above the ground.

'Have a good look at everything, Sigi,' said Charles-Edouard, 'you will be longer here than anywhere on earth.'

'Oh the funny little houses,' said the child, running from one to another and looking in, 'can I come and live in one?'

'All in good time. So, we'll pay some visits as we go.'

They climbed the long, steep hill, Charles-Edouard pulling Grace up by the hand.

'Many friends. Here are the Navarreins. The first ball I ever went to was in their house. M. de Navarrein was a link with the past, one of those things I never can remember. Let me see, his father was kissed by somebody whose great-great-grandfather had been held in the arms of le grand Condé. You know, it all depends on everyone concerned having children when they are ninety, really rather disgusting. There's the beautiful tomb of the Grandlieus—Madame de Grandlieu was my godmother, and she gave me the praying hands by Watteau which are over my bed.'

'Oh look,' said Grace, 'poor little Laetitia Hogg—younger than Sigi. What was she doing in Paris, and why did she die, I wonder?'

'One of those questions which are posed in graveyards. James and Mary Hogg must have loved her, since they bought her this tomb in perpetuity. Ha! the Politovskis, I'd not noticed them here before.' He went up to read the inscription, and began to laugh loudly. 'Oh no! This is too much! I've never heard such a thing! They've given themselves an S.A.R.! It's perfect, I can't wait to tell Tante Régine, what rubbish really. "Il conquit Naples et resta pur." Maybe he did, though not very likely, but even that doesn't entitle him to be a Royal Highness. Langeais and his wife, so charming. Sauveterre (poor Fabrice, give me one flower for him, how he would have laughed to see me here with wife and child). We've already passed enough friends to collect a large dinner party, a large amusing dinner party. Hélas, where are they all now, I wonder?'

'Having large, amusing dinner parties somewhere else,' said Grace, suddenly seeing herself as doomed to eternal dinner parties, 'wishing you were there and wondering what I'm like.'

'Yes, indeed. L'Anglaise! Intelligence Service! Fille de francmaçon,' said Charles-Edouard with his inward laugh. 'Here we are, this is the Avenue of the Marshals of France, our future home. Sigismond will spend some melancholic moments here, I hope, before it is his turn. Is it not beautiful up on this cliff, are we not lucky to be so well placed? Mind you, it is not the smart set, but at least we are not among presidents of the Republic, actors, duellists, and English pederasts. We have this pretty view and we have la gloire. Not bad, is it?'

'I feel sad,' said Grace, 'it reminds me of your dear grandmother's funeral.'

'I was very sad. Tired, and very sad. But there is only one thing I clearly remember of that whole day, the look of terrible triumph on the face of Madame de la Bourlie.'

'Oh surely not, at her age?'

'Age cannot blunt the hatred of a lifetime.'

They put their flowers at the base of a stone pyramid. It was a fine Empire tomb with bas reliefs of battles and battle trophies.

'Poor Grandmère, she can't be very much pleased with the neighbours—Masséna, Lefebvre, Moscowa, Davout—not at all for her, I'm afraid. Come here Sigismond, can you read this?'

'Famille Valhubert,' he spelt it out.

'This is your little house.'

'Can't I have one with a lace table-cloth and a door?'

'No. You will lie here with Grandmère and all of us.'

'Yes, but supposing I am killed in a stratospheric battle with Martians?'

'That I should applaud. You may or may not become a Marshal of

France, but you should always die in battle if you can, or you may live
to be shot by your fellow-countrymen, like poor Ney over there, who
was not fortunate enough to be killed by the enemy like Essling and
Valhubert. I hope you are paying attention to what I am telling you,
Sigismond. And now who would you like to see? I can offer you
painters, writers, musicians, cooks (Brillat-Savarin, the French Mrs.
Beeton, is here), and all the great bourgeois of Paris. The nineteenth-
century Russians, rastaquouères of their day, with huge, extravagant
tombs, Rumanian princes in miniature Saint Sophias, domed and
frescoed. Auguste Comte, the founder of positivism, might interest Sigi?
But you look very tired, my dearest, and I think we had better walk
gently back to the motor.'

The following day Grace had a miscarriage. They said she had perhaps walked too fast up the hill. It was not serious, quite early in her
pregnancy, but it pulled her down, depressed her spirits, and she was a
long time in bed. This was not a bad place just then. Late snow had
fallen, it lay in the garden, white and brown, under a low, dark sky.

But her room gave a sunny impression, yellow with spring flowers.
The mimosa was changed three times a day so that it should be always
fluffy. People were very kind; Ange-Victor said that Madame Auriol
herself would not have had more inquiries, flowers and books poured
into the house, and so, when she was well enough to receive them, did
visitors. Among those who came, and found Grace by chance alone,
was Albertine Marel-Desboulles.

'I never see you,' she said, smiling with all her great charm at Grace.
'Before Madame de Valhubert died I used to have the pleasure of that
lovely face to look at over the dinner-table—those huge, boring dinners
in the autumn. Now, though we live so near, you have vanished again.
But I have met the entirely delightful Sigismond.'

'I know. He told me. He thought you were heavenly.'

'When I heard you were ill I decided to call on you. Charles-Edouard
and I are the oldest friends in the world—foster-brother and sister in a
way, since we had the same nanny—well, to cut short all these explanations, here I am. How pretty you have made this room. I know it of
old because here we used to put our coats when Madame de Valhubert
gave her famous music parties.'

'I didn't know Madame de Valhubert was musical.'

'Oh well, music was not the only object of the parties, but the house
has this music room and Régine Rocher had a Polish lover who played
Chopin, so it all fitted in rather conveniently. As I was saying, then,
we used to come up here with our coats—it was a hundred years ago—
and in those days there was an Empire dressing-table with a marble
top, very ugly, I can see it now, and on this slab of horrid grey marble
there were hair-pins and safety-pins and papier à poudre for our shiny

noses. I must explain that this was thought very old-fashioned and a great joke even then. I am old, but not so old that I have ever not owned a powder puff. It was freezing up here, agony to take off our coats, so we only stayed a moment, I don't suppose anybody ever used the papier à poudre. Then we would go to the music room, where the Polish lover was fiercely thumping away with passionate glances at Régine, and Charles-Edouard couldn't be stopped from talking. He would sit next the prettiest woman, which sometimes happened to be me, and talk at the top of his voice, while Régine got more and more furious. But dear Madame de Valhubert, who literally never knew one note from another, not that it would have made much difference if she had, was quite delighted to see him enjoying himself so much.

'So I've known this room a long time, but it's never been as pretty as now. I can see that you are one of those women with a talent for living in a house, which is quite different from the talent for arranging houses, and far more precious.'

Of course Grace was completely won over. Presently the door opened again and the pretty head of Juliette Novembre, in a sable hat with violets, peeped round it.

'I've brought a camellia—can I come in, or are you talking secrets?' she said, like a child.

'Oh please, please come in.'

'Just look at her, la jolie,' said Albertine, 'what a seasonable hat.'

'I love my little bit of rabbit. How are you?' she said to Grace. 'Isn't it horrid? I had one last year.'

Albertine said, 'I'm longing to hear about the ball, Juliette.'

'Yes, but why didn't you come? We were all wondering.'

'I was discouraged. My new dress wasn't ready, and I do hate autumn clothes in the spring. So after dinner I went home. But as soon as I had sent the motor away I longed very much for the ball. I couldn't go to bed, I sat in my dressing-room until three consumed by this longing to be at the ball. Isn't it absurd, really! But to me a ball is still a miracle of pleasure. I see it with the eyes of a Tolstoy and not at all those of a Marcel Proust, and really, I promise you, it is terrible for me to miss one, even at my age. So now, torture me, tell us exactly what it was like.'

'Divine, a bal classique—no fancies, no embroideries. The prettiest women, in their prettiest clothes, a very good band, sucking pig for supper, wonderful champagne, in that house where everybody always looks their best. I loved it; I stayed to the end, which was after six. But nothing dramatic, Albertine, no fight, no elopement, nothing to tell really, hours and hours of smiling politeness.'

'I knew it, what I love the most. You have twisted a knife in my heart,' cried Albertine. 'Perhaps I ought to have gone, even in an old dress. But there—a ball to me is such a magical occasion that I cannot enjoy it wearing just anything. For days I have been seeing myself at that ball wearing my new dress, and when I found it couldn't be ready in time (nobody's fault, influenza in the workrooms), I didn't want to spoil the mental picture by going in another dress. Don't you understand?'

'Oh yes,' said Juliette. 'I'm just the same. I can't think of any occasion—a tea party even—without seeing an exact picture of how I shall look at it, down to shoes and stockings. I often wonder how social life—or life at all—can be much pleasure to people who don't care about dress. I'd hardly get myself out of bed in the morning if I hadn't something pretty and rather new to put on, and never get myself to a party. Now take all one's old relations, they love going out, but why? How can they enjoy it, really?'

'Oh their enjoyment comes from thinking of all the money they have saved by not dressing. They look at Régine Rocher and they add up what her clothes must have cost (you'll find they know, too, to a penny) and they feel as if somebody had given them a present of the amount.'

'Poor you, all that mourning,' Juliette said to Grace.

Like Albertine, she was out to please. They chatted away and Grace enjoyed herself. It was the enjoyment of frivolous, cosy, feminine company, of which she was very much starved. Carolyn, her only woman friend in Paris, could neither be described as frivolous nor cosy. She had many virtues, Grace knew that she was loyal and would be a rock in times of trouble, but she was not much fun, too restless and discontented. These two, rattling on with their nonsense, seemed to her perfectly fascinating, and she quite forgave Charles-Edouard for liking to be with them, it seemed so natural that he should.

Presently she sent for Sigi, who arrived hand in hand with his papa. Juliette became extremely animated, almost fidgety, making up to both father and son. Grace thought 'it's rather charming now, she's still only like a little girl, but at forty she will be terrible'. Albertine went to the chair on which she had put her things, produced a long, beautifully made wooden box, and gave it to Sigi.

'A present for you, darling. Open it.'

'What is it?' he said, pink and excited.

'It's called a kaleidoscope. Take it out. It was made for the poor little Dauphin,' she said to Grace.

'Oh you shouldn't! How good of you.'

Charles-Edouard took it from Sigi. 'You shut one eye, like Nelson, and see the stars. So.'

'Is it a telescope?'

'Better, you make your own stars as you go along. Venus—can you see? Shake it. Mars. Shake it. Jupiter as himself. Shake it. Jupiter as a swan.'

'Charles-Edouard, you'll muddle him.'

'Now here's another star you can see with the naked eye,' he said, pointing to Juliette. 'Doesn't she twinkle? She'll tell us all the gossip of the heavens. So, Juliette, tell.'

'Nothing to tell. I lead the life of a good little girl who does her lessons.'

'Ah yes? What lessons?'

'In the morning, I sing, coloratura, "Hark, hark the lark"; in the afternoon I paint a snowy landscape; and when it is night I go to the Louvre and see the statues lit up.' She looked at Charles-Edouard with huge, innocent, blue eyes.

'Hm, hm,' he said, clearly rather annoyed. Grace felt again that horrid pang or twinge of jealous uneasiness that she had had on seeing Charles-Edouard outside Albertine's house in the rue de l'Université. Only that morning he had promised to take her, when she was well again, to see the statues lit up, saying how beautiful was the Winged Victory, white in the black shadows and then black against a white wall. She could not help noticing his present embarrassment, and was quite sure that he must have been to see the statues with Juliette. Her feeling of not being able to blame him for liking to be with this pretty wriggler, this flapper of eyelids and purser of lips, suddenly gave way to a feeling that she blamed him very much, and indeed could hardly bear it.

Meanwhile Sigi was entranced with the kaleidoscope.

'Please,' he said, 'can I take it to bed when I go?'

'But this child is his father over again,' cried Albertine. 'The moment he sees something pretty he wants to take it to bed with him.'

Two large tears rolled down Grace's cheeks. She felt, all of a sudden, most exceedingly tired.

Sir Conrad now came over to visit Grace, though he refused to stay with her, preferring the freedom of an hotel. When in Paris he liked to submit himself to the rather strenuous attentions of a certain Hungarian countess, an old friend of before the war; after visiting her establishment he needed a restful morning, and did not feel up to much family life before luncheon-time.

Charles-Edouard introduced him to Madame Rocher, and this was a stroke of genius, they could have been made for each other. She came out of mourning and gave a large dinner party for him, at which he charmed everybody. The rumours about the Allinghams not being people to know were now for ever scotched. He and Madame Rocher embarked upon a shameless flirtation, and were soon on such intimate terms that she even taxed him with being a Freemason. Sir Conrad, who was of course perfectly aware of the implications of this in France, roared with laughter, did not make any definite statement but let it be understood that his daughter had, of course, been joking, and a very good joke too. Madame Rocher, who was no fool, began to see that Charles-Edouard must have been quite right in what he had said about English Freemasons. Henceforward she addressed Sir Conrad as Vénérable, referred to him as le Grand Maître, and all was merry as a marriage bell.

He liked Charles-Edouard more than ever. It would have surprised and gratified Grace to know that they had long, interesting discussions on political subjects when they were alone together, during which Charles-Edouard showed himself quite as serious, if not quite as long-winded, as Hector Dexter. One evening Charles-Edouard, though protesting that he himself only cared for society women, took his father-in-law round the brothels. These, having lately been driven underground by the ill-considered action of a woman Deputy, had become rather difficult for a foreigner to find.

Sir Conrad, who had never had many topics on which he could converse with his daughter, now found fewer even than when she was living with him.

'Are you happy?' he asked her, before leaving.

'Very happy.'

'Take care of yourself, darling. You don't look well.'

'I was quite ill. I shall be all right in a week or two.'

'Nanny hasn't changed much.'

'Oh dear no.'

'Well, sooner Charles-Edouard than me is all I can say. Must you keep her? Couldn't you get a governess soon, or a tutor or something?'

'Papa! Nanny!—I couldn't possibly do without her.'

'No, no, I suppose not. And as she seems to have the secret of eternal youth (sold her soul to the devil, no doubt) I suppose Sigi's children won't be able to do without her either. If we were savages she would undoubtedly be the chieftainess of the tribe.'

Back in London, Sir Conrad went straight off to see Mrs. O'Donovan and recount his visit.

'It's such a pity you didn't come,' he said, 'next time you really must. Grace would love to put you up, she asked me to tell you.'

'I don't believe I shall ever go back to Paris,' she said. 'I've known it too well and loved it too much, I couldn't bear to find all my friends old and poor and down at heels.'

'If it's only that,' he said with a short laugh, 'I've never seen them so prosperous, all living in their own huge houses, thousands of servants, guzzle, guzzle, guzzle, swig, swig, swig, just like old days.'

'Are they really so rich? But why?' she said querulously, as if they ought not to be.

'I suppose I don't have to enter into the economic reasons with you. You know as well as I do why it is.'

'In any case you can't deny they are all ten years older.'

'But the point is you'd think they were twenty years younger. They've all had Bogomoletz. That is something we must look into, you know. You get the liver of a newly killed young man (killed on the roads, of course, not on purpose) pumped into your liver, and the result is quite amazing.'

'My dear Conrad——'

'Or if you jib at that you can press unborn chickens on to your face before going out.'

'Thank you very much if by you, you mean me. *I* get one Polish egg a week on my ration.'

'Remarkable what your cook manages to do with that one Polish egg, I must say. Hens must lay enormous eggs in Poland, or are they ostriches? But to go back to our friends, none of them looks a day more than forty. I can't think why you're not pleased, you're supposed to love the French so much.'

'I think it's frightfully annoying, after all they've been through. Now I want to hear a great deal about other things. What is the exact situation at present?'

'Situation?'

Sir Conrad had come back in a very uppish mood, she thought, like a child after a treat.

'The political situation, of course. What does Blondin say, for instance?'

'My dear Meg, I didn't see Blondin, or any of them. I was entirely given over to pleasure and fun. But you know what the silly old fool says as well as I do, since I am well aware that, like me, you see all the French papers.'

Mrs. O'Donovan sighed. She did wish her English political friends could be a little more serious about the terrible state of the world. Sir Conrad, she thought, might well take a leaf out of the book of that important, well-informed Mr. Hector Dexter whom she had met the day before at a dinner party, and who had told her some interesting, if rather lowering, facts about present-day French mentality.

Sir Conrad was not unconscious of these critical thoughts, he knew Mrs. O'Donovan too well for that, but he was still a little drunk with all the pleasure and fun he had been having, so he went carelessly on.

'I want you to help me give a big, amusing dinner for Madame Rocher des Innouïs next month if she comes, as I hope she will, to stay at the French Embassy.'

'Régine Rocher,' said Mrs. O'Donovan faintly, 'don't tell me she's got the liver of a newly run-over young man.'

'I should think she's got everything she can lay her hands on. Anyhow she's remarkably pretty for what Charles-Edouard says is her age. He says she spends £8000 a year on clothes, and the result, I'm obliged to tell you, is top-hole.'

'Simply ridiculous, I should imagine.'

Mrs. O'Donovan, who was generally the driest of blankets, was proving such a wet one on this occasion that Sir Conrad took himself off to the House. Here he had a sensational success with all his traveller's tales about Bogomoletz and embryo chickens, not to mention detailed descriptions, unfit for the ears of a lady, of the goings-on chez Countess Arraczi.

CHAPTER XIII

'Our visit to London,' said Hector Dexter, 'was an integral success. I went to learn about the present or peace-time conditions there and to sense the present or peace-time mood of you Britishers, and I think that I fully achieved both these aims.'

The Dexters and Hughie Palgrave were dining with Grace. Charles-Edouard had told her earlier in the week that he was obliged to dine alone with Madame de la Ferté to talk family business.

'My uncle is so old now, he really makes no sense at all, and Jean is no use to her either. Nobody knows whether he is a case of arrested development or premature senile decay; she is having him injected for both, and the only result so far has been a poisoned arm. Why don't you ask some friends here to keep you company?'

Grace jumped at the idea of having the Dexters without Charles-Edouard. Although he never said they bored him, and indeed professed to admire Carolyn, whom he always referred to as 'la belle Lesbienne', she could somehow never bring herself to suggest inviting them again when he was there. As for Hughie, there would clearly be an awkwardness if he were to meet Charles-Edouard. She herself saw him quite often at the Dexters, and once a certain embarrassment between them was over they had become good friends again. They had never been much more than that, never passionate lovers.

'It's not the first time you've seen London, is it?' Grace said.

'No, Grace, it is not. I was in London during World War II and I will not pause now to say what I felt then about the effort which every class of you Britishers was putting forward at that time because what I felt then is expressed in my well-known and best-selling book *Global Vortex*. This time I found a very different atmosphere, much more relaxed and therefore much more difficult to sense, harder to describe.'

'Whom did you see?'

'We saw a very representative cross-section of your British life. We were in London and had a good time there, many very pleasant lunch parties and dinner parties and cocktail parties being given for us. We spent some nights with Carolyn's relatives in the North and had a good time there and some nights with some other relatives of Carolyn's near Oxford and had a good time there too.'

'So now what was your general impression, Heck?'

Hughie revered Hector, who seemed to him quite the cleverest man he had ever met. His own ambition was to go into politics as soon as he could get a seat to contest, and he liked picking Hector's brains on international subjects, or rather, allowing Hector's brains to flow over him in a glowing lava of thought.

'I must be honest with you, Hughie, my impression is not quite satisfactory.'

'Oh dear, that's bad. In what way?'

'An impression, I am sorry to say, of a great deal of misplaced levity.'

'Levity? I never see much levity at home; nothing much to levitate about, I shouldn't have said.'

'I must explain a little further. My government expects, and gets, reports from me on the political equilibrium, stability, and soundness of the various countries I visit. At first sight this stability, equilibrium, and soundness seem very great in Britain. At first sight. But there is a worm, a canker in this seemingly sound and perfect fruit which I for one find profoundly disquieting. I refer to the frivolous attitude you Britishers have adopted, just as it has been adopted here (the difference being that nobody expects the French to be serious whereas we do most certainly expect it of you Britishers), the frivolous attitude towards—we are all grown-up and I guess I can speak without embarrassing anybody— sexual perversion.'

'Have we adopted a frivolous attitude?' said Hughie. 'The poor old dears are always being run in, you know.'

'I think I will put it this way. I think it cannot be generally understood and realized in Britain, as we understand and realize it in the States, that morally and politically these people are lepers. They are sickly, morbose, healthless, chlorotic, unbraced, flagging, peccant, vitiated and contaminated, and when I use the word contaminated I use it very specifically in the political sense. But I think you British have absolutely no conception of the danger in your midst, of the harm these perverts can do to the state of which they are citizens. You seem to regard them as a subject for joking rather than as the object of a deep-seated, far-reaching purge.'

'But they're not in politics, Heck—hardly any, at least.'

'Not openly, no. That's their cunning. They work behind the scenes.'

'If you can call it work.'

'For the cause of Communism. The point I am trying to make is that they are dangerous because politically contaminated, a political contamination that can, in every traceable case, be traced to Moscow.'

'I say, hold on, Heck,' said Hughie. 'All the old queens I know are terrific old Tories.'

'I am bound to contradict you, Hughie, or rather I am bound to put forward my argument, and you are going to see that it is a powerful argument, to persuade you of the exact opposite of what you have just said and to persuade you that what you have just said is the exact opposite of the truth as known to my government. We Americans, you may know, have certain very very sure and reliable, I would even say infallible, sources of information. We have our Un-American Activities Committee sections, we have our F.B.I. agents, we have countless very very brilliant newspaper men and business men all over the world (men like Charlie Jungfleisch and Asp Jorgmann); we have also other sources which I am not at liberty to disclose to you, even off the record. And our sources of information inform us that nine out of every ten, and some say ninety-nine out of every hundred, of these morally sick persons are not only in the very closest sympathy but in actual contact with Moscow. And I for one entirely believe these sources.'

Hughie was unconvinced. 'But my dear Heck, in Russia you go to Siberia for that. I've got a friend of mine who's awfully worried about it in case they come——'

'Maybe you do, maybe you don't. There are some very curious anomalies, things you would hardly credit, Hughie, but of which our agents are cognizant, going on in that great amorphous blob of a country today. But I am not concerned with the pervert in Russia, my concern is with the pervert in Western Europe because my professional concern at the moment is with Western Europe, more especially in its moral and ethical aspect.'

'Then what about the pervert in America?' said Hughie.

'And I am very very glad to say that this very unpleasant problem does not exist in the States. We have no pederasts.'

'How funny,' said Grace, 'all the Americans here are.'

She was thinking of various gay, light-hearted fellows whom she met with Charles-Edouard and his friends. Mr. Dexter was displeased with this remark and did not reply, but Hughie said,

'Perhaps they have a bad time at home and all come here, like before the war one used to think all Germans were Jews. But honestly you know, Heck, what you've just said makes no sense, and the more one thinks of it the less sense it makes.'

'I will make one more attempt to explain my meaning to you, Hughie, and then we must go. If a man is morally sick, Hughie, he is morally sick, if he is sick in one sense he will be sick in another, and if he is sexually sick he will be politically sick as well.'

'But, poor old things, they're not sick,' said Hughie, 'they just happen to like boys better than girls. You can't blame them for that, it's awfully inconvenient, and they'd give anything to be different if they could. But I don't see that it's any reason for calling them Bolshevists. I probably know more about them than you do, having been at Eton and

Oxford, and if there's one thing they're not it's Bolshevists. Anything for a quiet life is their motto. I'm afraid, old man, you've got the wrong end of the stick there, and if this is what your infallible sources are telling you, I should advise a comb-out of the sources.'

The Dexters now got up to leave. The Jungfleisches, they explained, were giving a party for important people, and they had promised to be there early.

'Poor old Heck,' said Hughie when they had gone. 'He does see things in black and white. Funny, really, for such a clever man. I can't help remembering how all over the Russians he used to be, in Italy. He bit my head off the other day for reminding him, but it's true.'

'Like Carolyn,' Grace said, laughing, 'she used to be our school Communist. I know it was she, though now she pretends I've been mixing her up with another girl. She gets furious when I tease her about it.'

Hughie said, 'Let's go and have a glass of wine somewhere before bed-time, shall we?'

Grace felt tired, as she often did now, but it seemed rather a shame to send him away so early, and she consented.

'Just for an hour then,' she said.

They went to a White Russian night club, a stuffy, dark enclosed room filled with music from the Steppes. Cossacks, in boots and white blouses, have keened here night after night for thirty years over a life that has gone for ever. The hours of darkness seem too short for them to express the whole burden of their desolation, so that any reveller who will sit up and listen to the wails and whimpers of their violins until late into the next day becomes their brother and their best beloved. Whereas in other night places the band may be anxious to catch the last metro and go home, these Russians would rather anything than that a lack of customers should drive them out to the first metro. The little room has come to represent Holy Russia to them, and when they leave it in the morning exile begins again. It is really a place designed for lovers or for drunkards, people who like to sit all night engulfed in sound rather than for those who want an hour of sober chat.

Hughie had come to unburden himself about Albertine, and he had to talk very loud so as to be heard over the scream of the violins. From time to time the noise suddenly dropped to a dramatic hush, intended to represent the lull in a storm, and then Hughie's powerful English voice would ring out into the silence so that he was embarrassed, and Grace wanted to giggle. As soon as he had lowered it a gusty crescendo would swallow up his next sentence. It was a very fidgety way of confiding.

'Of course she'll never want to marry me, I know. I don't allow myself to think of it. She is far above me, far too clever and wonderful. She knows everything, not only all French literature but English and German too—she has even read Mrs. Henry Wood, for instance. I wish you could hear her reciting—by the hour, it's extraordinary. When I

think of all the years I've wasted—but I never guessed there was somebody like that just round the corner or I would have tried to educate
myself a bit. You can't be surprised she rather looks down on me, as it is.
So now I'm trying terribly hard to make up for lost time, just in case
one day she might think of marrying me. Not very likely, I know, but in
life things do sometimes happen. For instance she might be ruined and
need a home, or have a fearful accident and be quite disfigured, or
lose a leg——'

The words 'lose a leg', falling into one of the pools of sudden silence,
echoed round the room so that Grace could not help laughing.

'Lose a leg?' she said.

Hughie laughed himself, saying, 'Oh well, of course it sounds ridiculous; it's one of those things which I sometimes think of. After all Sarah
Bernhardt did, it can happen, and then she'd need somebody to push
her about. The worst of it is such hundreds of people do want to marry
her, she'd be unlikely to choose me. There's another terrible worry. She
talks of going into a convent. I wake up in the night and think about it.
Supposing one day I were to call at her house only to be told "Madame
Marel-Desboulles is no more. Pray for Sœur Angélique"?'

Grace laughed again, and said, 'You've been reading Henry James—
so do I, in the hopes of understanding them all better. But I don't think
Albertine is another Madame de Cintré, and nor do I think she'll ever
marry again. I guess you'll be able to go on like this for years, if it's any
consolation to you.'

'It's very much better than nothing, of course. So, as I say, I read a
lot to try to educate myself, but I must have let my mind go badly and
it's an awful strain. Have you ever tried the *Mémoires* of Saint-Simon?
Heavy weather, I can tell you. Then I try and see as many clever people
as I can. That's why I go such a lot to the Dexters.'

'D'you think them so very clever?'

'Carolyn is brilliant of course, she takes me sight-seeing and we go to
lectures. As for old Heck, well, if he is a bit muddle-headed about some
things, he's got the gift of the gab, hasn't he? I wish I could talk like
that, on and on.'

'I always think he talks as if he doesn't quite know English.'

'Really, Grace, what an idea. All those words—I'm English, but I
don't know what half of them mean. Albertine would like me much
better if I could put on an act like Hector, I'm sure she would. But when
I'm with her I seem to get so tongue-tied.'

At this moment a large party of people got up to go. The violinists
came forward, still playing, to try and persuade them to stay. They
surrounded them, playing with all their souls. But the people, though
smiling, were firm, and made a passage through the deeply bowing, still
playing Cossacks. When they had gone, and the violinists had returned
to the band, Grace suddenly perceived, in a very dark corner, hitherto

obscured by these other people, the figures of Charles-Edouard and Juliette. Their backs were turned, but she could see their faces in a look-ing-glass. They were evidently enjoying themselves enormously, heads close together, laughing and chattering sixteen to the dozen. Grace was particularly struck, stricken to the heart indeed, by Charles-Edouard's look, a happy, tender, and amused expression, which, she thought, she herself used to evoke at Bellandargues but which she had not seen of late.

She felt weak, as if she were bleeding to death. 'I'm so sorry,' she said, 'but I think I might faint. Could we go home please, Hughie?'

'Goodness,' he said, 'you are white, Grace.' He hurried her to the motor, full of self-reproach. 'I should never have suggested this, you're not strong enough yet.'

'Don't worry, it's nothing, I promise, I feel better already. I'm just a little tired, that's all. Don't come in,' she said, when they arrived at her house. 'My maid always waits for me—she's so old-fashioned; I'm so lucky. Good night, Hughie.'

When Charles-Edouard got back, not very late, she was in bed, cry-ing dreadfully.

'Why do you weep?' he said, with great solicitude.

'Because you're in love.'

'I am in love?'

'With Juliette.'

'Why do you say this?'

'I was at the Russian place. I saw you.'

Charles-Edouard looked very much taken aback. 'But you never go to night places.'

'I know. I hate them, but Hughie wanted to——'

'Ha! You've been out with Hughie?'

'I told you we were all going to dine here, me and Hughie and the Dexters. Well the Dexters went on to a party after dinner so Hughie and I—— Oh, Charles-Edouard, you're in love with her?'

He raised his hand, shook his head, and replied, 'Not at all.'

'Then why were you looking so happy?'

'Would I look happy if I were in love with Juliette? It would be very inconvenient, after all she is my cousin's wife. No, I look happy because I am happy—happy in my life and with you, and then I do love to go out with a pretty woman.'

'Why did you pretend you were going to dine with Tante Edmonde?'

'But my dear Grace, it was no pretence at all. I did dine there. It so happens that Juliette also was dining with her mother-in-law. Jean has gone to Picardy; she was alone in her flat so she dined downstairs. When I had finished talking with my aunt I took her out for half an hour before bedtime. I didn't want to come back here and find your dinner still going on.'

'Oh!' This sounded so reasonable. 'Oh dear, I'm sorry to make a scene and I do apologize.'

'For what? The rights of passion have been proclaimed once and for all in the French Revolution.'

'The worst part of the whole thing,' said Grace, tears beginning to well into her eyes again, 'is that what I minded so terribly was your look of happiness. I am supposed to love you and yet I mind you looking happy. When you were sad, when your grandmother died, I was sorry, of course, but I could easily bear it—now I find that what I can't bear is for you to look happy. What can it mean, it doesn't make sense.'

'That, I'm afraid,' said Charles-Edouard, 'is love.'

'But what can I do? I can't live with somebody whom I would rather see sad than happy. Perhaps I'd better go back to England?'

'No. Do stay.'

Grace laughed. 'You say that as if you were asking me for a weekend.'

'Do stay, for good.'

'I can't bear to make scenes, I'm ashamed of myself, it is dreadful.'

'You won't have to very often.'

'I shall begin to imagine all sorts of things whenever you go out.'

'That would be the greatest pity—imaginative women are terrible. Now let's calmly consider what did happen this evening. What did you actually see? Juliette and me, sitting quite properly at a table in a perfectly proper establishment. I was not looking unhappy, but then I have no reason to, I'm not a White Russian violinist. So! That is what you saw. Then your imagination got to work, and what did you imagine? That I had told you a lie, sneaked off to dine in a loving intimacy with Juliette and then taken her to a night club. Knowing me as you do, you might have thought it more probable that, if I were in love with Juliette, I would go straight to bed with her, but no! We choose the night club where we can be seen by all and sundry, and where in fact you see us, staying perhaps an hour, not more. I take her home, but only to the door. My aunt's concierge, like ours, has to get out of bed to let people in, so there could be no question of me going upstairs with Jean's wife; the whole of Paris would know it tomorrow if I did. I say good night in the street and come back here—it is still not one o'clock. I don't think any of this indicates the existence of a great and guilty passion for Juliette. You must be more reasonable, dearest. Shall I give you a piece of advice, quite as useful in love as in warfare? Save your ammunition, and only shoot when you see the whites of their eyes. Now in this particular case I would have you observe that I spent exactly the same sort of evening as you did. We both dined with a few rather dull people, and then went out with the least dull of them for an hour or so before bed.'

'Hughie isn't as pretty as Juliette.'

'Hughie is very handsome, and you know it. But I haven't come near to seeing the whites of his eyes yet. I shan't shoot this time, and nor must you.'

Grace was completely reassured. She went happily to sleep.

CHAPTER XIV

A few days later Grace lunched with Carolyn, and the talk was all of a certain guide who took personally conducted tours into the private houses of Paris. Carolyn said that she had followed one of these tours every day that week.

'I've been into such wonderful houses, which I would never have seen otherwise,' she said. 'He gets permission to visit anything that is "classé", and of course that means anything worth seeing. His lectures, too, are good and informative. Yesterday we went to Mansard's own house in the Marais.'

She described it to Grace. Carolyn was at her best on the subject of old Paris and really knew a great deal about it. She liked the monuments of the town better than its denizens who still threw her into a fever of irritation.

'Now I asked you not to be late,' she said, 'because this afternoon M. de la Tour is taking us to see a very famous private house, one of the hardest to get into, the Hôtel de Hauteserre in the rue de Varenne. I simply must go, and you'd better come too, Grace,. It's a chance we shan't have again for ages, and I believe the boiseries are unique.'

Grace had nothing much to do and was, like Hughie, for ever trying to scrape up a little culture. Besides, she thought, it might be something for Charles-Edouard with his perpetual 'What are the news?' She never had enough to tell him about her day. 'So, what did la belle Lesbienne recount? Or did you sit, as usual, gazing at each other in silence?' As her talk with Carolyn was never anything that could possibly interest him, being all about nannies, the Parc Monceau, and mutual friends at home, and as Grace had no talent for cooking up such plain food with either the spice of malice or the sauce of funniness, she was always obliged to leave it that they had gazed in silence. 'Very strange, this dumbness.'

After luncheon Carolyn drove her across the river to the rue de Varenne. Her exasperation with the French always reached boiling-point when she was driving a motor. As they went she told Grace about a dishonest mechanic who had put back her spare wheel unmended (she was never happier than when some little thing of this sort occurred, another stick with which to beat them), and punctuated her story with, 'Look at that! Did you ever see such driving? I shan't give way; I'm in my rights and he knows it. Disgusting. Oh get on. What a place to park. What people, really!'

It was one of those Paris afternoons when, by some trick of the light, the buildings look as if they are made of opaque, blue glass. Grace wondered how much Carolyn really did love the stones of Paris. She seemed not to notice, as they went by, the blue glass façade of the Invalides surmounted by its dome powdered with gold, but only the bad driving in the Esplanade.

Now when they arrived at their destination Grace saw that it was none other than the Ferté house. She had never known that its old name was Hôtel de Hauteserre, to her it had always been 83 rue de Varenne or the house of Tante Edmonde. She laughed, and said to Carolyn, 'But I know this house by heart—it belongs to Charles-Edouard's old great-uncle; we lunch or dine here every week of our lives. I don't think there's much point in me going in.'

'Nonsense,' said Carolyn, 'you'd better come along as you're here. M. de la Tour will tell you all about it, and very likely show you lots of things you hadn't ever suspected.'

Grace thought again that it would be something funny to tell Charles-Edouard, and that the idea of her sight-seeing in that house would be sure to amuse him. So she paid 100 francs at the door and went in with Carolyn. There was quite a crowd of people, and the guide was just beginning his lecture.

'This house,' he said, 'was built in 1713 by Boffrand for the famous— I should perhaps say notorious—Marquise de Hauteserre, who created a record by keeping the Régent as her lover for eighteen weeks. He was by no means her only lover, and they were, in fact, numberless. I am glad to be able to announce that when we have seen the state rooms, which are of an extraordinary beauty, we are to be allowed the great privilege, hardly ever accorded to tourists, of seeing Madame de Hauteserre's own bedroom. Madame la Duchesse has given me the key; she knows that we are all serious students of French art and not mere gaping sightseers.'

'Have you seen it?' whispered Carolyn to Grace.

'No.'

'There—what did I tell you?'

'This bedroom,' the guide continued, 'has an erotic ceiling, a thing rare in France though not uncommon in Italy, by Le Moine; a Régence bed of wonderful quality, and boiseries by Robert de Cotte. When I tell you that all this is quite unrestored, you will easily realize that what you are about to see is unique, of its sort, in Paris.'

They went upstairs into the reception rooms of the first floor which Grace knew so well, gold and white, blue and white, gold and blue with painted ceilings. The lecturer went at length into the history of every detail; they were nearly an hour examining these three rooms, and Grace began to feel tired. At last, in the Salon de Jupiter, where the Fertés usually sat after dinner, the lecturer went to a little door in the wall, which Grace had never noticed there. Taking a large key from his pocket he unlocked this door, saying, 'And now for the famous bedroom of Madame de Hauteserre.'

Grace happened to be standing beside him, and together they looked in. It was a tiny room decorated with a gold and white trellis; an alcove contained a bed, and on the bed, in a considerable state of disarray, were Juliette and Charles-Edouard.

The guide quickly slammed and relocked the door. He turned to the crowd, saying, 'Excuse me, I had quite forgotten, but of course the boiseries and the ceiling have gone to the Beaux Arts for repair.'

Nobody but Grace and the guide had seen into the room; greatly to her relief the tourists accepted his statement without dispute, if rather crossly. They had certainly had their money's worth in this beautiful house, although they had been looking forward to the erotic ceiling as a final titbit. Carolyn, still gazing at a panel in the Jupiter room, said, 'Oh, never mind, we've really seen enough for one day. Shall I give you a lift home, Grace?'

Grace got into the motor, talked away quite naturally, thanked Carolyn for the afternoon, and went into her house as if nothing had happened. She lay on the day bed in her library, saying to herself, 'This is the end.' But, as with some physical blow, she had not yet begun to feel any pain.

Presently Charles-Edouard came in.

'I looked for you in the nursery,' he said.

'Aren't you having tea with Madame Marel?'

'Not today, I never do on Wednesday, it's her day for receiving. Where do we dine? Oh yes, of course, I remember, Tante Régine. That's sure to be great fun. So, what are the news? Don't tell me, I can guess. You lunched, in an impenetrable silence, with la Dexter. Such a curious friendship, I find.'

'And after luncheon we went sight-seeing.'

'Indeed? Where?'

'The Hôtel de Hauteserre.'

Charles-Edouard looked at her, startled, and then said, quite angrily for him, 'Really, Grace, you are too extravagant. What could have induced you to pay 100 francs to see the house of your uncle, which you know perfectly well already? No—this is not sensible, and I'm very cross with you. Why, 100 francs was a dowry when my grandmother was young.'

'You pay for the lecturer. He shows all sorts of unexpected things.'

'I will take you over it one day. I know much more about it than any lecturer.'

'You would never show me what he did, this afternoon.'

'Ha!' said Charles-Edouard. He went to the window and looked out of it.

'This is very annoying,' he said presently.

'I thought so too. I've seen the whites of their eyes, Charles-Edouard.'

'Imbecile of a lecturer. He should know better than to come bursting into bedrooms like that.'

'Yes. Being French you'd think he would.'

'Perhaps I'll give up Juliette.'

'You needn't bother. I'm going back to England.'

'Do stay,' said Charles-Edouard.

'For the week-end?'

'No. For ever.'

'It's no good, Charles-Edouard. I'm too English; your behaviour makes me too miserable, and I can't bear it any more.'

'But my dear, that's nothing to do with being English. All women are the same; indeed if you were Spanish I daresay you would have killed me by now, or Juliette, or both. No, we've been particularly unlucky. This unspeakable lecturer, paid 100 francs to open bedroom doors in the middle of the afternoon! What could have induced Tante Edmonde to let him, she is out of her mind. I know what it is of course, she hopes to get off taxes by allowing the public into her house, but what a short-sighted action! Half that crowd must have been Treasury spies, nosing about to see how many signed pieces she owns, and the rest of course were burglars making lists of all the objects in the glass cases. I blame her terribly. Then I'm bound to say it was a little bit your own fault, wasting 100 francs and a whole afternoon in a house where you dine at least once a week. Bad luck, and bad management.'

'In fact everybody's fault but yours.'

'No, no, I blame myself most, for being so careless.'

'Oh dear! How cynical you are.'

'Not at all. I see things in the light of reality.'

'Yes. Well I also must try to be a realist. After this I could never again be happy with you because I should never again have an easy moment when you were out of my sight, never. You are wonderful at explaining things away until one happens to have seen with one's own eyes, but from now on the explanations won't be any good. So I shall go back to Papa.'

'And when do you leave?'

'Tomorrow. I shall take Sigi.'

'Yes, you must. And Nanny, too, perhaps?'

'And Nanny, too. And please excuse me to Tante Régine. I've got a headache, and there's a great deal of packing to be done.'

'Nanny, we're going home to England tomorrow.'

'What, all of us?'

'You and me and Sigismond.'

'Mm.' The tone was one of disapproval. 'Tomorrow, dear? And what about the packing?'

'The train isn't till 12.30 and there's Marie to help you. You must manage somehow, darling, please.'

'But how long are we going for?'

'For good. Now don't look sad, it will be London, not Bunbury. So think—Hyde Park every day, Daniel Neal, steam puddings, Irish stew——'

'Irish stew indeed. My sister says you never see a nice neck, these days. And Sigi's Papa?'

'He's not coming.'

'Mm.'

'Do be pleased, darling. I thought at least somebody would be.'

'Well dear, I've always said little boys ought to have a mummy and a daddy.'

'That can't be helped. And think of the hundreds who don't.'

'I'm wondering how I'm ever to get all his toys packed up in the time. Funny thing, one never gets any notice of these journeys.'

'Send Marie out to buy an extra hamper if there's no room.'

Next day there had to be a special motor to take Sigi's luggage; he had exactly twice as many items as his mother.

'Anybody would suppose that he was a famous cocotte,' said Charles-Edouard, who went to the station exactly as if he were seeing them off for a little change. Sigi skipped about on the platform, getting in everybody's way and saying, 'Can I ride on the engine, please, Papa?'

'Certainly not. And I hope you'll have learnt to read before I see you again.'

'Will you give me a prize if I can?'

'Perhaps. If you can read everything, and not only the little bit out of the *Journal des Voyages* you already know by heart.'

'What sort of prize?'

'A good sort.'

'Can I ride on the chevaux de Marly for my prize?'

'You can only ride on the chevaux de Marly when you know *A la voix du vainqueur d'Austerlitz* by heart.'

'How can I learn it, in England?'

'I can't imagine. Anyhow you can learn to read. Shall I tell you what will become of you if you can't read when you are grown up?'

'All grown-up people can read,' said the child, conclusively.

'Good-bye, Grace,' said Charles-Edouard. 'Do come back soon.'

'For a week-end?'

'No. For good.'

He kissed her hand and left them. He was quite surprised at how much he minded their departure.

CHAPTER XV

'What's all this about?' said Sir Conrad when Sigi, Nanny, and their baggage had been deposited in the nursery and he had Grace to himself.. 'I'm delighted to see you, it goes without saying, but why such short notice? Is it not rather hysterical?'

'Yes, well, you may call it so. I've left Charles-Edouard.'

'You've left your husband?'

'Yes.'

Sir Conrad was not surprised, since this sudden run for home could hardly, he knew, mean anything else.

'And are you going to tell me why?'

He did not doubt what the reason would be, broadly speaking, but was curious as to the details.

Grace told him at some length about her life in Paris.

'I could bear it when he went to tea every day with Madame Marel, though I didn't like it; I could even bear his terribly open flirtation at every party we went to, with Juliette Novembre, but what happened yesterday afternoon at the Hôtel de Hauteserre is more than I can endure or forgive.'

'What did happen?'

But when she told him Sir Conrad annoyed her very much indeed by bursting into a hearty laugh.

'I say, what bad luck! Now don't look so cross and prim, darling, I quite see it was horrible for you, and I'm very sorry, but I can't help thinking of Charles-Edouard too. You must admit it was bad luck on him, poor chap.'

'Perhaps it was. But lives can't be built entirely on luck.'

'No good saying that, as they always are. Luck, my darling, makes the world we live in. After all, it was by luck you met Charles-Edouard in the first place (bad luck for Hughie); by luck that he came back from the war safe and sound; by luck that you had that clever little Sigi— by luck, indeed, that you got your mother's large blue eyes and lovely legs and not my small green eyes and bow legs. Luck is a thing you can never discount. It may be unfair, it generally is, but you can't discount it. And if Charles-Edouard is having, as he seems to be, a run of bad luck you ought to be there, sympathizing with the poor chap. It doesn't seem right to go off and leave him all alone. I hoped I'd brought you up better than that.'

'You're talking as if he had lost all his money at the races.'

'Oh well, not quite so bad, thank goodness.'

'And as if you're on his side.'

'We must try and see his side of the question, I suppose.'

'I don't think you need, you're my father.'

'Now listen, my darling child. I love you, as you know, and only desire your happiness. This is your home, available for you whenever you need it. You can always come here, and even bring Nanny if you must, so please don't think I want to send you away. Quite the contrary, I like to have you here, it's a great pleasure. But it's my plain duty, as your father, to try to make you see things as they are, and, above all, to try and make you see Charles-Edouard as he is. I'm very fond of Charles-Edouard, and I presume that you are too, as you married him.

'Now he is a man who likes women in the French way of liking them, that is he likes everything about them, including hours of their company and going to bed with them. I suppose you would admit that this is part of his charm for you. But you hardly ever find a man, or anyhow a young man, with his liking for women who can be faithful to one woman. It's most exceedingly rare.'

'Yes, Papa, all this may be true about Charles-Edouard. But with me it's a question of how much I can stand, and I can't stand a life of constant suspicion and jealousy. Juliette, Albertine, the women he looks at in the street, the way he flirts with everybody, everybody, even Tante Régine, the way he kisses their hands, the way he answers the telephone when they ring up—oh no, it's too much for me, I can't.'

'My dear child, I always thought you had a healthy outlook on life, but this is positively morbid. You really must pull yourself together or I foresee great unhappiness for you in the future.'

'I shan't be unhappy a bit if I can marry an ordinary, faithful, English husband.'

Grace had been sustained during her journey by the mental picture of an idealized anglicized Charles-Edouard, whom she was to meet and marry in an incredibly short space of time. This vision had come to her when the light airiness of Northern France, with its young wheat, pink roads and large, white, rolling clouds, had been exchanged for the little, dark, enclosed Kentish landscape, safe and reassuring—home, in fact. She had looked out of the window at the iron grey sky pressing upon wasteful agriculture, coppices untouched by hand of woodman, tangles of blackberry and gorse, all so familiar to her eyes, and she was comforted by the thought that she could be an English countrywoman once more, gardening, going for walks, playing bridge with neighbours, a faithful English Charles-Edouard, tweeded and hearty, by her side. She would be quite happy, she thought, living in an oast-house, or a cottage with a twist of smoke on the edge of Mousehold Heath, or a little red villa with glass veranda in the Isle of Wight—anything, anywhere, so long as it was safe in England and she safely married to this tower of strength and reliability, this English Charles-Edouard.

'I'm afraid an ordinary faithful English husband will seem very plain pudding after the extraordinarily fascinating French one you are throwing away so carelessly,' said her father. 'People like Charles-Edouard don't grow on every tree, you know. The fact is women must choose in life what sort of a man it is that they do want—whether what is called a good husband, faithful to his wife but seldom seeing her, going off to the club and so on for his relaxation, or one that really loves women, loves his wife, probably, best and longest, but who also and inevitably feels the need for other relationships with other women.'

'Is that the sort of husband you were, Papa?'

'Yes, I'm afraid so. And as I never had a quarter the bad luck of poor Charles-Edouard, and as your mother was either entirely unsuspicious or else very very clever, it was a perfect success, and we were happy. But I didn't care to risk it again after her death, so here I am unmarried.'

'Don't you feel lonely sometimes?'

'Often. That's why I can't help being pleased to see you and the little boy back again, though I suppose if I had any moral sense whatever I'd send you off with a flea in your ear. May I ask what you are planning next?'

'Really, Papa, I hadn't thought.'

'You should try to think before you act, my dear child. Do you want a divorce?'

'Don't let's talk about it now, I'm so tired. Divorce sounds so horrible.'

'Yes, well, leaving your husband is rather horrible.'

'But I suppose it will come to that.'

Sigi now put in an appearance, saying 'Grandfather——'

'Yes, Sigi?'

'You know adultery——?'

Sir Conrad raised an eyebrow and Grace quickly intervened, saying, 'Really Nanny is too naughty, she will teach him these dreadful words out of the Bible. Adultery is for when you're older, darling.'

'Oh I see. A sort of pas devant thing?'

'Yes, that's just it. So Nanny must be pleased to be back in her own old nursery again?'

'Not a bit. Fluff under the carpet—she doesn't know what the girls are coming to these days. One thing she will say for Paris, the housemaids there did know their work. And she's just rung up her sister—offal is a thing you never see in London now. So Nanny's in a terrible dump. Grandfather——'

'Now what?'

'Are there cartridges again, and can I learn to shoot?'

'We'll have to talk to Black about that, when we go to Bunbury.'

'Oh good. Can you have a word with Nanny before dinner, Mum?'

Grace, who had been expecting this summons, sighed deeply and went upstairs.

Part Two

CHAPTER I

THE days of 'run along, Sigismond' were now in the past; nobody ever said it to him again. Grace, lonely and wretched, concentrated herself on the little boy, he was with her from first thing in the morning to his bedtime. He would arrive with her breakfast tray, open her letters, answer her telephone, and play with the things on her dressing-table. From time to time, in a desultory manner, she gave him reading lessons.

'You simply must be able to read books by the time you see Papa again,' she said.

'And when shall I see him again?'

'I expect it will be after the summer holidays.'

'Shall I go and stay with him?'

'I expect so.'

'In Paris, or Bellandargues?'

'Paris. He's not going to Bellandargues this year.'

'And you too?'

'We'll see when the time comes.'

'I say, Mummy, are you divorced?'

'Certainly not, darling. What do you know about divorce?'

'Well I've told you about Georgie in the Park? His mummy and daddy are divorced and he says it's an awfully good idea—you have a much better time all round, he says, when they are.'

'Goodness, darling——!'

'Actually his mummy and daddy have both married again, so he's got two of each now, and he says the new ones are smashing, really better than the original ones. You ought to see the things they give him, they're so lovely and rich. So shall you be marrying again, Mummy?'

'You seem to forget that I'm married already, to Papa.'

'Nanny told her sister she thought perhaps Mr. Palgrave. She always thought it would have been better, in the first place.'

'Don't fidget with that necklace, Sigi, you'll wear out the string.'

'Do you know what Mr. Palgrave gave me last time I saw him?'

'No, what?'

'Eleven bob.'

'What a funny sum.'

'Yes, well, Nanny always takes 10 per cent for her old lepers. I told him that and he very nicely made it up. I need a lot of money.'

'Why do you?'

'Because I'm saving up for a space ship when it's invented. Mum, when can I have a bike?'

'When we go to the country perhaps.'

'And why don't you marry Mr. Palgrave?'

'Because not.'

'Nanny says it's nicer for little boys to have a mummy and a daddy, but I expect it's best of all when they have two mummies and two daddies.'

'Shall we get on with the reading?'

They went for the summer holidays to Bunbury. At first Grace thought she would find it unbearable to be in a place so impregnated now with memories of Charles-Edouard, where they had spent their honeymoon, where she had lived all those years dreaming of him, and where he had come to find her after the war. But her father wanted to go there, it would be good for Sigismond, and it was, after all, her home, the home of her ancestors; it would belong to her when Sir Conrad died. Memories of Charles-Edouard were not the only ones connected with it. And, in any case, her thoughts were of him all day, wherever she was.

'One thing I must ask you,' she said to Sir Conrad. 'Will you give orders for the Archduke to be taken out of my room?'

'Certainly I will,' he replied. 'The proper place for that Archduke is the hall—I never could understand what he was doing upstairs. And while we are on the subject, I should very much like to see my Boucher back in the drawing-room, if you don't mind.'

In the end Grace's room became less like a corner of the Wallace Collection and more like an ordinary country-house bedroom. It was really more convenient.

Nanny, in so far as she was ever pleased by anything, was pleased to be back at Bunbury. Just as Grace had spent the war years dreaming of Charles-Edouard, so Nanny had spent them dreaming of Hyde Park and what fun it would be, now she had a boy once more, taking him there. But when at last, on their return from Paris, she had achieved this objective, the dream, as dreams so often do, had turned to ashes. The Park, she found, had lost its old character. Not only had the railings disappeared, the beautiful fleur-de-lis railings which used to surround it, the stout stumps of Rotten Row, the elegant Regency railings of the flower beds, and the railings on which children loved to walk a tight-rope at the edges of the paths, but so, to a very great extent, had the nannies. Increasing numbers of little boys, it seemed, while they had a multiplicity of mummies and daddies, had no nannies at all. They were no longer wheeled about in prams, morning and afternoon, as a matter of course, but when they needed fresh air they were hung out of windows in meat safes. As soon as they could toddle they toddled off to nursery schools, where they were taught to sing little songs, given a great deal of milk to drink, and kept strictly out of the way of their harassed parents. So Park society was not what it had been. There was no wide range of choice, as in the past, and the few nannies who were left clung together, a sad little bunch, like the survivors in an autumnal poultry yard, most of whose fellows had already gone to the pot. Nanny had few friends among them and pronounced them to be, on the whole, a very inferior type of person. But at Bunbury she had congenial gossips, the old housekeeper, the groom's wife, Mrs. Atkin the butler's wife, and Mrs. Black, to whom she was able to boast and brag about her year in France until they stretched their eyes. Anybody who knew how terribly she had complained during the whole of her sojourn there, or who could have heard her comments to Nanny Dexter on every aspect of French civilization, would have been amazed by the attitude she now assumed over the clanking cups of tea with her cronies.

'Say what you choose, France is a wonderful country—oh it is wonderful. Take the shops, dear, they groan with food, just like pre-war. I only wish you could see the meat, great carcasses for anybody to buy—the offal brimming over on to the pavement—animals like elephants. They could have suet every day if they knew how to make a nice suet pudding. But there is one drawback, nobody there can cook. They've got all the materials in the world but they cannot serve up a decent meal —funny, isn't it? It's the one thing I'm glad to be back for, you never saw such unsuitable food for a child—well I ended with a spirit lamp in the nursery, cooking for ourselves. There now—I wish you could have seen our nursery, a huge great room looking out over the garden, with a real English fireplace. Then I wish you could have seen the château, it is different from Bunbury—oh it is. Abroad, and no mistake. Like a castle in a book, at the top of a mountain, you quite expect to see knights in armour coming up on their horses. And warm! Well, imagine the worst heat wave you ever knew in your life, the summer of 1911 for instance, and double that. No, I didn't mind a bit, it simply didn't affect me, though the poor mite got rather peaky. You don't know what heat can be, in this country.'

Sir Conrad gave Sigi a little gun, and with it a great talking to on the handling of guns in general and the manners of a sportsman in particular.

'And just remember this,' he said in conclusion, 'never never let your gun pointed be at anyone. That it may unloaded be matters not a rap to me! And Black is going to keep it for you in the gun-room; he'll teach you to clean it and so on, and you may only use it when you are with him.'

So Sigi never left Black's side all the long summer days, trotting happily about the woods and pooping off at magpies and other vermin.

'There's something I do regret,' he remarked to his mother. 'I would like to show my gun to Canari. It's small, but you could kill a man with it if you got the vital spot. Now Canari isn't a silly little baby molly-coddle, like dear little Foster Dexter, or dear little Georgie in the Park. Canari is a maquisard, a brave, a dragon, and he would never sack me out of his bande again if I had this gun. They're terribly short of equipment in Canari's maquis, it's a shame.'

Grace could hardly bear to think of lovely Bellandargues shut up and empty all the summer and that, for the first time in living memory, the big salon would no longer be the scene of a conversation piece like that which was discovered when Charles-Edouard had first held open the door for her to walk in, and repeated thereafter every day of her visit; Madame Rocher at the piano, M. de la Bourlie at his canvas, and Madame de Valhubert deep in earnest talk with M. le Curé.

She had an uneasy feeling of guilt, exactly as if it were all her own fault and not that of Charles-Edouard.

Also she longed very much for the heat and light of Provence. They had come home to a typical English summer. Rain poured all day on to the high trees out of the low clouds, clouds which lifted and parted towards nightfall so that a pallid ray of north-western sunshine illumined the soaking landscape, a pallid ray of hope for the morrow.

'It's lovely now—we must go out. Don't you think the weather may have turned at last?'

The next morning those who, suffering in their bodies, or, like poor Grace, in their hearts, and who therefore slept little at a time, would awake with the birds to such a glorious glitter of sunshine from cloudless sky upon wet leaves that summer, it would seem, must be there at last. This happened nearly every morning to Grace, who would presently doze off again, rather happier. But long before breakfast the rain would be blowing in fine white sheets across her window, the promise of early morning quite forgotten. She would go down, later on, to the drawing-room, glad to find a little fire.

Charles-Edouard, she knew, had gone to Venice this year. He had taken a palazzo on the Grand Canal and was entertaining many Paris friends, among others Madame Rocher, the Novembre de la Fertés, and Albertine Marel-Desboulles. This had been a great blow to poor Hughie. He had cherished a hope all the summer that Albertine might have gone with him for a motor tour in Sweden. But as soon as the Venetian party offered itself, with Charles-Edouard and all her friends, the motor tour became, for various good reasons, impossible. Furthermore she discouraged Hughie from following her to Venice, saying vaguely that she would be taken up with the film festival. So he often came now to spend a day or two at Bunbury. He was trying to stand for Parliament, but had had no luck so far with the Selection Committees, partly of course, he said, because he was so stupid, and partly because he had no wife. He longed more than ever to be married to Albertine, even though he felt sure that in that case it would be her they would want as candidate and not him. He could just imagine the kind of speech she would make, bringing her point of view, inspired, sensible, and well expressed, to bear on all the problems under discussion.

'I, the soul of the French bourgeoisie, my solid legs planted on the solid earth, I Albertine Labé, descended from generations of timber merchants, who have always given good measure for good money, I have the gift of seeing things clearly and truthfully as they are. I cannot pretend. I feel the truth, I feel it here in my heart and here in my bowels as well as knowing it here in my brain. It is a power, this seeing and feeling and knowing truth, and it has been bred in me by my ancestors the merchants.

'And I tell you, I, Albertine Labé, bourgeoise, that it is this power of truthfulness and of knowing truth which is needed if we are to rebuild your England, rebuild my France, and rebuild our Europe.'

Just the stuff for the Selection Committees, he thought. There was another line of talk which ran, 'I who loathe the bourgeoisie, I who would rather burn charcoal in the woods than buy or sell anything whatever it might be, I who would rather freeze to death out of doors in the cruel winter of my native Lorraine than sit over a warm fire in a back shop, I, Albertine Labé de Lespay, aristocrat, child of knight and warrior, whose ancestors never touched money or even carried it on their persons because they thought it the dirtiest of dirt, I tell you that I know the truth, I know it here and here and here, and it is this truth, this virtue, this hatred of gold that is needed if we are to rebuild etc. etc'.

The second statement, actually, had more foundation in fact, since Albertine did not possess one drop of bourgeois blood, and her ancestors, a line of powerful princes, had only been timber merchants to the extent of owning vast forests in Lorraine. But the trend of the modern world had not escaped her notice, and the timber merchants were ever increasingly brought into play. Hughie was much too much dazzled by her to notice any discrepancy; both these statements had, at different times, bowled him over, as he assumed that they would bowl over the Selection Committees. He was unable to imagine anybody, even an English Conservative, standing up against the charm and brilliance of this extraordinary woman. With her by his side, to inspire and teach him, it seemed that no goal in the world would be unobtainable.

'Of course I'm glad to think of her in Venice,' he said, not gladly though, to Grace, as they sat over the little drawing-room fire, summer rain fiercely beating on the windows. 'She loves Italy so much, she needs the beauty. Then there is the important work she does there, with the films.'

'What work? She's frightfully rich, she doesn't need to work.'

'She doesn't need to, she does it for her country, for France. She is a moving power in the French film industry with her taste and knowledge and influence. No film is ever made there without first being submitted to her, you know. She has an infallible instinct. Yes, I love to think of her in Venice, but I do wish she would write to me. She won't, of course. "What is writing?" she said once. "Just a scratch of metal upon paper." Well, look at it that way and what is it?'

Grace, whose heart was also in Venice, and who would also have welcomed a scratch of metal upon paper, or even upon a postcard, sympathized with Hughie, but did not quite enjoy his interminable eulogies of Albertine, who seemed to her one of the many causes of her own wretchedness. She wondered if he was aware that Charles-Edouard went to tea with her every day, but was too polite and tactful to mention it.

'Don't you think young people nowadays manage their lives much worse than we used to?' Sir Conrad said to Mrs. O'Donovan, who had come down for a little country air. 'Surely you and I would have been more competent than either of those two in the same circumstances, and less gloomy? I'm tired of all the despondency in this house; it's getting me down. Why on earth don't they pack up and go off to Venice and have it out finally with these frogs?'

'Just imagine having anything out finally with Madame Marel,' she replied. 'As for Grace, you mustn't be too hard on her. I think she has received a terrible shock, and is still suffering from it. To see a thing like that with your own eyes can have really grave results, psychologically.'

'Oh nonsense, Meg. She ought to have another baby, that's all.'

'Having a baby is not a sovereign cure for everything, although all men, I know, think it is.'

'Anyhow she's in a thoroughly tiresome state of mind. I can't find out what it is she does want—divorce or what. She says one thing one day and another the next, and it's time something was settled, in my view.'

'What does he think, do you know?'

'Yes, I do. I've had a long letter from him. As I've often told you, I never understood why he wanted to marry her in the first place, but whatever the reason may have been it still seems to hold good, and he wants her back again.'

'Have you told her?'

'It wouldn't be any use me telling her in her present mood; he must come and tell her himself. But meanwhile she goes on havering and wavering about shall she or shan't she divorce until I'm tired of discussing it with her. She's grown up, and she must decide for herself which it is to be.'

'It really doesn't make a pin of difference,' said Mrs. O'Donovan. 'They weren't married in church, and therefore neither Charles-Edouard nor anybody else in Paris counts them as being properly married at all.'

'I suppose it would only make a difference if one of them wanted to marry again. The whole thing is thoroughly tiresome and annoying.

Well, after the holidays I'll run over to Paris and have a word with Charles-Edouard, that will be best. I'll tell him he must come and fetch her back if he wants her—I don't believe she'd ever resist him in flesh and blood. She'd much better stick to him, this fidgeting about with husbands is no good for women, it doesn't suit them. Hullo, Sigi, I didn't know you were there——'

'It's too wet to go out and too early for Dick Barton, and Mummy and Mr. Palgrave are talking about Madame Marel, as usual. If you go to Paris I wish you'd take me.'

'Why?'

'Because I want to learn the words of *A la voix du vainqueur d'Austerlitz*, and nobody knows them here.'

'Oh I do,' said Mrs. O'Donovan. 'I used to read them every morning of my life when I was a little girl with a hoop in the Tuileries Gardens. I'll teach them to you if you come along to my bedroom before dinner.'

CHAPTER II

THAT night Sigi was woken up by a tinkle of breaking glass under his open window. He nipped out of bed and looked down. The pantry window was underneath his and he saw a bit of broken glass shining on the gravel beside it; there seemed to be a light on in the pantry. Nanny was snoring away undisturbed in the next room, so it must be very late he knew; well after midnight. He crept out of his room and down the back stairs, feeling his way by the banisters. Sure enough there was a light shining under the pantry door. He put his eye to the keyhole and saw a man examining the door of the silver cupboard, big and heavy like that of a safe. Now Sigi, owing to a great friendship formed in early babyhood with Atkin the butler, knew all the little ways of this silver cupboard. He opened the pantry door and walked in. The burglar, a small, fair young man, turned quickly round and pointed a revolver at him.

'I don't care for these manners,' said Sigi, in a very governessy voice. 'Surely you know that never never should your gun pointed be at anyone. That it may unloaded be matters not a rap to me.'

'It's not only unloaded,' said the burglar, 'but it's not a gun at all. It's a dummy. You get into a terrible mess, in my trade, if you go carrying guns about.'

'Are you a burglar?'

'Yes, I try to be.'

'I think it's very careless of you not to wear gloves. What about the finger prints?'

'I know. I simply cannot work in gloves—never could—can't drive a car in them either. I'm not very good at my work as it is—look at this wretched door, I don't know how you'd open it.'

'Why do you do it then?'

'The hours suit me—can't get up in the morning, and everything you earn, such as it is, is tax free, with no overheads. There's a good deal to be said for it. I expect I shall improve.'

'How about prison?'

'Haven't had any yet. I'm so fearfully amateurish that nobody ever thinks I can be serious, and when I get caught they simply think it must be a joke.'

'Where I live it's not a joke at all, burgling. They come with machine-guns and wearing masks and they generally kill off the whole family and the concierge before they begin.'

'That must make it much easier.'

'Yes. Sometimes they only sausage them.'

'They what?'

'Tie them up like sausages, brr round and round, and gag them and put them in a cupboard, where they are found next day more dead than alive.'

'Where do you live then?'

'Paris. I'm a French boy.'

'You talk pretty good English for a French boy.'

'Yes, and I talk pretty good French for an English boy. Would you like me to open the silver cupboard for you?'

'Why? Do you know how to?'

'Of course I do. Mr. Atkin showed me. You blow on it, see? Like that.' The door swung slowly open. 'I always feel on the side of burglars because of Garth. So you go on and I'll keep cave.'

The burglar looked at him uncertainly. 'I suppose I'd better make sure,' he said, half to himself, and before Sigi realized what was happening he found himself gagged and trussed up.

'There you see. English burglars sausage people too sometimes,' said the young man, putting Sigi gently on the floor. 'I'm sorry, old fellow, it won't be for long, but really to leave you keeping cave would be carrying amateurishness too far.'

Sigi was perfectly outraged. 'All right then,' he said to himself.

The burglar went into the cupboard and began to examine its contents. Sigi waited a moment, then he rolled under the pantry table and kicked a certain catch he knew of. The cupboard door clanged to, and the burglar was trapped. Then Sigi began to roll and wriggle through the green baize swing-door into the dining-room, through the dining-room door, which luckily was open, into the hall, where he lay kicking the big gong until Sir Conrad appeared at the top of the stairs.

'Good gracious,' he said, when he saw Sigi rolling and wriggling like a little eel. 'My dear child,' he said, untying him, 'whatever have you been up to?'

'Ugh! That tasted awful. Grandfather, grandfather, I've got a burglar, in the silver cupboard.'

'What do you mean?'

'Yes, I promise. I did it with Mr. Atkin's patent catch—he's in there now. Come and see.'

'I say! Good boy!'

'And he's got a dummy gun.'

'Never mind. He won't dare use that. Go and get Atkin for me, will you?'

'Mr. Atkin—Mr. Atkin—Grandfather wants you—I've got a burglar in the silver cupboard! Mummy, Mummy, I've caught a burglar! Nanny, Nanny, I've got a burglar. I did it all by myself.'

Nanny, hurrying into her dressing-gown, said, 'Tut-tut, all this excitement in the middle of the night is very bad for little boys. You're coming straight back to bed, my child.'

But Sigi was off again in a flash, down to the pantry, where Sir Conrad was sitting on the edge of the table talking to the burglar and surrounded by quite a little crowd. Hughie now put in an appearance.

'Hullo, Hughie,' said the burglar.

'Oh! Hullo, Ozzie. It's you, is it?'

'That your nipper?'

'No. I wish he were.'

'Wouldn't mind having him for a partner. The child's an expert.'

'I was your partner till you sausaged me,' Sigi said furiously.

'The milk train,' said Sir Conrad, looking at the pantry clock, 'leaves at 6.15. Perhaps you'd better be off, it's more than an hour's walk. Or would you suggest that I should send you in the motor?'

'I wouldn't hear of it,' said the burglar. 'Good-bye,' he said, rather in the manner of one who, leaving a party first, says a general good-bye in order not to break it up. He climbed out through the open window and was gone.

'Grandfather! He was my burglar—I caught him, and now you've let him go. It is unfair.'

'Yes, well you couldn't keep him as a pet, you know.'

'I wanted to see the coppers put the bracelets on and drag him off in a Black Maria.'

'Sigismond, will you come back to bed this instant, please?'

'You were a very good, clever boy,' said Sir Conrad, 'and tomorrow I'll get you a bike with three speeds.'

'I don't want any old bike at all.'

'There you are, these high jinks always end in tears. Now come along, and look sharp about it.'

'Really, Papa,' said Grace, when a dejected Sigi had padded off with

Nanny. 'I'm not sure you ought to have turned him loose on the community like that, you know.'

'Oh my dear child, he hadn't done any harm. On the contrary, he spoke very nicely of my article on Turenne in the *Cornhill*, before you came down.'

CHAPTER III

THE long, cold, light summer came to an end. As soon as autumn began, warm, mellow, and golden, the Bunbury household removed itself to Queen Anne's Gate.

It was now agreed between Charles-Edouard and Grace, through the medium of Sir Conrad, that they had better be divorced. Sir Conrad told Grace that the situation must be regularized one way or the other.

'You must choose,' he said, 'between going back to France and living with your husband—far the best solution, in my view—or divorcing the poor chap. It's too unsatisfactory to spend the rest of your lives married and yet not married, impossible, really. Besides, I want to make certain financial arrangements for you. I know you never think about money, you've never had to, so far, but you might as well know that I can't live on my income any more. I'm eating up my capital like everybody else, and before it's all gone I propose to make some over to you and some to Sigismond, in the hopes that you'll be able to keep Bunbury when I am dead. Now I must have a word with Charles-Edouard about all this. We had better arrange the divorce at the same time.'

'Oh—oh——!'

'Darling Grace, you know what I think about it, don't you? But if you really can't live with him you'll have to make up your mind to it, I'm afraid. It has to be one thing or the other.'

'Papa, I couldn't just go back like that, it's not so easy. For one thing he hasn't asked me to.'

'He didn't ask you to go away. He assumes that you will go back when you feel like it. He wants you to, I know.'

'It was he who made it impossible for me to stay. If he really wants me he must come over and ask me, beg me, in fact, show that he is serious, and promise——'

'Promise what?' Sir Conrad gave her a very unsympathetic look. How could Charles-Edouard promise what she would want him to? He thought his daughter was being utterly unreasonable.

Grace burst into tears and left the room.

Sir Conrad went to Paris. Charles-Edouard was most friendly, and they had long talks on many subjects of interest to them both, including the future of Sigi.

'One can't tell, of course, what things will be like by the time he inherits,' said Sir Conrad, 'but it seems to become increasingly difficult for anybody to live in two countries. I wonder if he'll ever be able to keep Bellandargues and Bunbury. Oh dear, the ideal thing would have been if Grace had had this other child and I could have settled Bunbury on him, or her. Now I suppose I must wait and see if she marries again, or what happens. I would so much like to have it all tied up before I get too old. I'm quite against leaving these decisions to a woman, specially Grace, who is so unpractical.'

'That wretched miscarriage was at the beginning of all our troubles,' said Charles-Edouard. 'She was set on having that child; disappointment I think more than the actual illness pulled her down and made her nervous. Really so unlucky. Pregnant women, after all, don't have this tiresome mania for sight-seeing.'

'She is in a very nervous state indeed now,' said her father.

'Shall I go to London and see what I can do?'

'You can try, it would be the only way, and I suppose you'll succeed if she consents to see you. But I'm not at all sure, in her present mood, that she will. It's as if the whole thing had been too much for her, though presumably, in time, she'll become more reasonable.'

'Very well, I'll try. I'll say I've come to fetch the boy for a visit, then it will be quite natural to have a word with her between two trains. It won't be like a formal interview, which might put her off. I think I ought to be able to persuade her of how very very much I long for her, as it's quite true.'

'I'm sure she longs for you. What an idiotic situation, really.'

'But in case this all goes wrong, and since you are here, perhaps we'd better begin to arrange about a divorce. It means nothing whatever to me, as I've certainly no intention of marrying again, but if we are to live apart I'd rather be divorced, I'm tired of people asking where my wife is. So perhaps we'll visit my lawyer. I've had to make a change, such a nuisance, but the old one of all my life was a terrible collaborator and you don't realize what that means. Two hours of self-justification before one can get down to any business. There's no bore like a collabo in all the wide world. So, this afternoon then?

'By the way, Tante Régine is coming to luncheon. When I told her you were here she screamed like a peacock and rushed off to buy a new hat.'

The hat was very pretty, and Madame Rocher was in a cheerful bustle between, she said, the autumn collections, which were simply perfect this season (for some forty-five seasons now they had appeared simply perfect in her eyes) and the 'Bal des Innouïs'. This was a famous charity ball which she organized every other year in aid, not to put too fine a point on it, of her late husband's relations. The Rocher des Innouïs were an enormous tribe, as fabulously poor as she was fabulously rich, and she had devised this way of assisting them at a minimum cost to herself. With the proceeds of the ball she had built, and now maintained, the Hospice des Innouïs, which, situated on a salubrious slope of the Pyrenees, not only provided a delightful setting for the old age of the Rocher relations, but also kept them far away from the Hôtel des Innouïs. 'If I must entertain them,' she would say, 'I'd much rather do so at the Hospice than at home.' So strong are family ties in France that, had they lived within reach of Paris, Madame Rocher would have received visits from all at least once a week; as it was she descended upon them every summer laden with boxes of chocolates, kissed them tremendously several times on each cheek, and vanished away again in a cloud of dust and goodwill.

The ball was always great fun, an intensely elegant occasion, and Madame Rocher would cut the photographs of it out of *Match* and papers of that sort and send them to be pinned up on the walls of the Hospice. She often said how much she wished her dear cousins could have been there to see for themselves what they were missing.

'We have been in despair,' she said to Charles-Edouard and Sir Conrad, 'to know what to have as our motif this year. We've already had birds, flowers, masks, wigs, moustaches, sunshades, kings and queens. Now that darling, clever Albertine has got an entirely new idea; everybody is to suggest their own bête noir; not to be her, you understand, but to wear something that suggests her. It is very subtle—nobody but Albertine could have conceived it.'

'What a pretty idea,' said Charles-Edouard. 'Who is your bête noir, Tante Régine?'

'That I keep as a secret weapon. I said to M. Dior this morning, "If my dress is not delivered tomorrow, Dior, it will be you". Most efficacious. And the lovely Grace—will she be back in time for it?'

All Paris was eaten with curiosity as to the situation between Charles-Edouard and Grace. He had given out that she was paying a long visit to her father, and had never dropped the smallest hint, even to his most intimate friends, even to Albertine, that there was any sort of a breach. She was always said to be expected back in a week or two. So rumours were rife, some saying that she had eloped, and others that she had a disfiguring illness, but the great majority headed by the Tournons maintained that she must have gone into a home for persons of retarded intellect. 'A bit late,' they said, 'but modern science can do wonders. And,' they said, 'it will need to.'

Charles-Edouard was getting tired of this 'coming back soon', which made him look a fool, and he knew that Sir Conrad's visit would already have set tongues wagging. 'The lovely Grace,' he now told Madame Rocher, 'wishes to divorce.'

'Very English, and all in the best Freemason tradition,' she said. 'So now you will have her tied to your apron strings once more, mon cher Vénérable.'

Having made this excellent joke she could hardly wait to get home to her telephone and scatter the news that Charles-Edouard was a marriageable unit once more. She was going to have great fun. The little girls of all her friends and relations would have to be lined up and looked over, an occupation she would very much enjoy. Like horses, their pedigrees would have to be carefully considered; certain strains were better avoided altogether, Bourlie blood, for instance, had never been known to do a family much good, while certain others always seemed fatal in combination. A substantial dowry, while not absolutely necessary, never spoilt anything. She imagined the excitement of the various mammas, and thought how amusing it was going to be to see the discomfiture of those who had recently married their daughters to less eligible husbands. In short Madame Rocher foresaw some very agreeable hours ahead of her.

'Good-bye, cher Vénérable, all my best wishes to the Grand Orient,' she cried, waving a pink glove from the window of her motor.

'Well, Papa?'

'Well darling. Charles-Edouard was most reasonable, as I knew he would be. I like him more every time I see him.'

Grace thought her father looked old and sad, and she had a pang of conscience. This was all her fault.

'You look tired, Papa.'

'Yes, I am. The fact is we had a bit of a night out, last night.'

'I see.' Really it was too bad, at this moment of crisis in her life, that her father should regard the man she was going to divorce merely as a dog to go hunting with.

'Naturally you never spoke about me, at all!'

'Oh indeed we did. We spent hours with the lawyer, we arranged all about the divorce, the money and Sigi, every detail.'

Grace realized that she must have been entertaining, subconsciously, a hope which these words laid low, though what hope, exactly, she did not feel quite sure.

'Sigi? What about him?'

'You are each to have him six months of the year, to be divided up as seems most convenient, until he is ten, when he will live with his father during the terms and with you during the holidays.'

'He's to go to school in France?'

'He's a French boy, my dear. I've got a letter for you from Charles-Edouard.'

She took it with, once more, a feeling, a flicker of hope. It was the first time she had seen Charles-Edouard's writing on an envelope since

she left him. It was very formal, ending up 'affectueusement et respec-
tueusement', and was merely to ask whether the little boy could now go
to Paris for a while. She handed it to Sir Conrad, who said, 'Yes. If you
consent, Charles-Edouard will come over himself next week to fetch
him.'

'Oh, of course I do. Only I won't see Charles-Edouard, Papa.'

'That's entirely for you to say, my love.'

'No, no, no—it wouldn't do at all.'

But she knew that if Charles-Edouard really wanted her back he
would insist on seeing her, and that if he did so his cause was won.
Everything would be different once they had seen each other. Life
without him, here in London, had become so grey and meaningless
that she was beginning to feel she would put up with almost anything,
even the constant jealousy and suspicion she so much dreaded, to be
with him once more in Paris. Surely, she thought, he would not bother
to come himself for Sigi unless he wanted to see her, and if he wanted to
see her it could only be for one reason.

The days went by. Charles-Edouard was definitely expected, Nanny's
opposition to another move had been overcome, and Grace's will to
resist was evaporating. She kept up a façade of resistance, she did not
pack her things, or prepare to leave in any practical way, but the
citadel was ready to surrender.

He came over in the ferry, and was to return, an hour or so later, by
Golden Arrow. When he arrived at Queen Anne's Gate, Grace (it was
the last remaining gesture of independence) was still in bed. She never
got up early, and, in case by some horrible chance Charles-Edouard did
not ask her to go with them after all, she did not want to look as if
prepared there and then to step into the train. In fact she calculated that she could easily be ready in time; her maid could bring
the luggage later. She had had her bath, and was very carefully
made up.

Sir Conrad's motor had gone to the station to meet Charles-Edouard.
She heard it arrive; she heard his voice, and heard the front door slam.
'There's Papa,' she said to Sigismond. 'You run downstairs and ask him
if he'd like a cup of coffee in here before you go. Hurry——!'

Sigi was off in a flash. 'Papa—Papa—are we going on the boat? Is
there a storm? Can I stay on deck all the time?'

'Very likely you can. Where's your mummy? I want to see her.'

But Sigismond did not favour this idea at all. He wanted to travel, as
he had been told he would, alone with his papa, attention concentrated
on him. If Papa went upstairs, if he saw Mummy, that daft kissing stuff
would begin, 'Run along, Sigi,' and who knows? Grown-up people are
so unaccountable, Mummy might quite well decide to come back to
Paris with them, and it would be 'Go to Nanny, darling' all day and
every day as of old. Life had become considerably more fun with

Mummy and without Papa; it would be considerably more fun to go back to Paris with Papa but without Mummy.

'Mummy's in bed and asleep,' he said.

'Asleep—so late—are you sure?'

'Quite quite sure. She went out dancing last night—she expected to be out till any hour, and strict orders are she is not to be called.'

'And your grandfather?'

But Sir Conrad was away, shooting in the North.

Charles-Edouard considered what he should do.

Nanny appeared on the stairs, the footman was sent to fetch a taxi, Sigi's luggage being far too much for one motor, and the footman and Nanny went off to Victoria to register the heavy things.

'Now listen, Sigi,' said Charles-Edouard when they had gone, 'you run up to your mummy's room, say I'm here (wake her up if she's asleep) and ask if I can see her for a moment.'

'All right.' Sigi ran up, but not to his mother's room. He waited on the landing for a minute and then skipped downstairs again, curling up bits of his hair with one hand, as he always did when telling lies though nobody had ever noticed the fact, and saying, 'No good. The door's locked and she's written up "don't disturb". I tell you, she wants to sleep till luncheon.'

'Come on then,' said Charles-Edouard, taking Sigi by the hand, 'we'll walk to the station. I need a little air.' He felt furious with Grace, deeply hurt and deeply disappointed.

The front door slammed again and Grace was left alone in the house. Sigi had not even said good-bye to her.

'Well,' said Charles-Edouard, settled in the train with a large English breakfast before him and Sigi opposite. 'Come on now, what are the news? What have you been doing in England?'

'Oh Papa, I've had the whizz of a time. I caught a burglar all by myself—I cunningly trapped him in the silver cupboard—and I've saved up nearly £5 out of tips and Grandfather is investing it at 2½ per cent compound interest, and I've got a gun and I shot an ill thrush, it was kinder really, and I've got a bike wot fair mops it up.'

'You've got a what which does what?'

'Un vélo qui marche à toute vitesse,' he kindly explained.

'Good gracious! And I have to compete with all this?'

'Yes, you have. But it's quite easy—I only want to ride on the Chevaux de Marly.'

'Is that all? Which one?'

'I don't mind.'

'Ah! But do you know the words?'

The little boy shut his mouth tight and laughed at his father with shining black eyes.

'Sigismond. Do you?'

'I shall say the words when I am on the horse, and not before.'

'Then I fear,' said Charles-Edouard, 'that these words will remain for ever unspoken.'

In the Customs shed at Dover there was quite an excitement. The woman next to them was asked to hand over a coat she was carrying on her arm. From its pockets the Customs officer drew several pound notes. He then began to search her luggage, and produced pound notes from everything he touched, like a conjurer; from books and sponge bag and hot-water-bottle cover and bags and pockets and shoes, everything capable of containing a pound note seemed to do so. The poor lady, white and sad, was then led away. Sigismond looked on, perfectly fascinated.

'She won't catch the boat,' said Charles-Edouard with the smugness of one who, having an English father-in-law, was under no necessity to conduct any illicit currency operations.

'Won't she really, Papa? Why?'

'She's a silly fool, breaking a silly law in a very silly way.'

'So will she go to prison?'

'No, not for pound notes. Gold would have been more serious. I expect she'll miss the boat, that's about all,' said Charles-Edouard. 'Come come, up that gangway with you.'

CHAPTER IV

As soon as Madame Marel was back in the rue de l'Université from her summer holiday, which had included a long visit to Vienna after Charles-Edouard's Venetian party had broken up, Hughie rushed over to Paris. He only stayed there two days, returning to London in a thoughtful frame of mind, the very day that Sigi left with his father.

Grace rather wondered what could have happened, but he said nothing and she was not a woman to ask for confidences. As she now felt lonely without her little boy, and as Hughie seemed to be at a loose end, they began to see a great deal of each other. Nearly every week he drove her down to his country house for a few days.

This house, Yeotown Manor, in Hertfordshire, was like a large, rambling cottage. Part of it was really old, a little old manor, but most of the low, dark, inconvenient rooms, the huge beams, the oak doors with wooden bolts and latches, the linenfold panelling and inglenooks, while quite genuine of their sort, had a certain false air owing to the fact that they had been added to the structure by Hughie's mother out of old cottages which she had bought and carved up to serve her purpose. It had no beauty but a certain cosy charm, to which Grace was susceptible at that time since it was so completely English, so much the antithesis of anything she had known in France. Nothing in it reminded her of either of her French homes, or of Charles-Edouard. She was dreadfully saddened now by such memories, and only longed to put them from her.

Hughie always had a few people at week-ends, and perpetual games of bridge went on day and night. Thump thump thump went the radiogram, thumping its way through great heaps of jazz records from breakfast to bedtime, while Hughie and his guests sat by electric light at green baize tables, drink at their elbows, ash-trays filling all round them, shuffling, dealing, playing, and scoring.

At this time Grace was happier there than anywhere. She had always liked gambling, and now she flew to it as to a drug. Also she missed Charles-Edouard less acutely when she was with Hughie, whose masculine presence calmed her nerves. He had become very much more attentive to her of late; indeed, had she not known about Albertine, she would have supposed that he was courting her again. Onlookers, Mrs. O'Donovan for instance, and Carolyn Dexter, assumed that it would only be a matter of months before they married.

Time passed, and a morning came when Grace woke up at Yeotown feeling, if not quite happy, at least without a stifling blanket of unhappiness. This blanket had hitherto weighed upon her like something physical, so that there had been days when she had hardly been able to rise from under it and get out of bed. But on this particular morning it seemed to have gone. Through latticed windows the sun shone on a bank of beeches and on the few golden leaves which still clung to their branches. The sky was very blue, her room was warm, her bed intensely comfortable. When she rang the bell Hughie's housekeeper herself came in with the breakfast tray, followed by a housemaid with all the Sunday papers. The servants there were very fond of Grace and spoilt her as much as they could, hoping that she would marry Hughie. The breakfast was a delight, as it always was in that house, pretty to look at, piping hot, and carefully presented. Grace thought, not for the first time, that it would be difficult for somebody who led such an intensely comfortable life as she did to be quite submerged in unhappiness. There were too many daily pleasures, of which breakfast in bed was by no means the least. Perhaps too, she thought, this English life, so much more suitable for her than a French one, would in the end bring her more happiness. Here she was within her depth, she could do the things which were expected of her, and was not always having to try to learn and understand and do new things. It would have taken her years, she knew, to be able to tell at a glance whether an object was Louis XV or Louis Philippe, First or Third Empire; years before she could bring out suitable quotations from Racine or Apollinaire, write phrases in the manner of Gide and Proust, or even make, in good French, the kind of joke, naïve and yet penetrating, that is expected from an English person. Accomplishments of this sort seemed to be a necessity in France, the small change of daily intercourse. It had all been, quite frankly, a most terrible effort. The English, on the other hand, take people as they are, they don't expect that the last ounce of energy will be expended on them in the natural order of things, and are, indeed, pleased and flattered at the slightest attempt to entertain them.

She often had these moments of thinking that what had happened was really all for the best, but they never lasted very long. Today the reaction came as soon as she went downstairs. Thump thump thump went the radiogram, gobbling its waxen meal. Hughie was already shuffling the cards, the Dexters, who made up the party, already had glasses in their hands, and tedium loomed. The only hope was to get quickly to the game, but even that magic did not always work.

Hector Dexter had just made a tour of the Industrial North, and was telling, with his usual wealth of word and detail but with an unusual note of humanity, of life as it is lived in the factories. In these terrible, dark, Victorian buildings, he said, where daylight is never seen, the people sit at the same table going through the same motions hour after hour, day after day, with music while you work in the background. As Grace dealt the cards it occurred to her that week-ends at Yeotown were not unlike that. You sat by electric light at the same table hour after hour, going through the same motions, with music while you work thump thump thumping in the background, life passed by, the things of the mind neglected, the beautiful weather out of doors unfelt, unseen. 'One club, two no trumps. Three spades. Four spades. Game and rubber. I make that one a rubber of 16—pass me the washing book, old boy.'

'Luncheon is served,' said the butler.

A break, while you go to the canteen. Her life in Paris may have been difficult and exacting, she may have been a flustered witness ever in the box, ever trying not to give the game away to a ruthless cross-examining counsel, but it may also have been a more satisfactory existence than this. At least she had felt alive, she had been made to use whatever mind she possessed, and there had seemed to be point and purpose to each day. It had never merely been a question of getting through such hours as remain before the grave finally closes.

During luncheon Hector Dexter went on talking about his tour. 'I'm afraid I must be perfectly frank,' he said, 'and tell you that in my opinion this little island of yours is just like some little old grandfather clock that is running down, and if you ask me why is it running down I must reply because the machinery is worn out, deteriorated, degenerated and decayed, while the men who work this machinery are demoralized vitiated and corrupt, and if you ask me why this should be so I will give you my viewpoint on the history of Britain during the past fifty years.' His viewpoint on this subject was then exposed, in great detail. Hughie listened to him with rapturous interest, wondering how anybody could achieve so much knowledge and such a flow of words— oh would that he could pour out its like before the Selection Committees. He had another in front of him that week. Grace felt more than ever as if she were a factory hand, in the kind of factory where people come and chat to the workers on subjects of general interest. 'We are lucky enough to have here today the important Mr. Hector Dexter, who is going to talk to us about some of our problems, their roots in the past, and how they may be solved in the future.'

By the time they were drinking their coffee he had more or less finished with the roots, which were very dull and into which the word 'vision ' came a great deal, and was warming up to the remedy.

'Now you will ask me if I can see a remedy for this state of things, a state of things, mind, which I do not only observe and take cognizance of in your country but which I have observed and taken cognizance of in all the European countries, that is to say all those countries in Europe west of the so-called Iron Curtain, to which I am sent by my government in order to form my views in order to acquaint my government of those views which I have formed. Now what you need in this little old island, and what is needed in all the countries of Europe west of the so-called Iron Curtain, and even more I imagine, though I do not speak with personal experience, in all the countries of Europe east of the so-called Iron Curtain as well as in the backward lands of the Far East and the backward lands of Africa, is some greater precognition of and practice of (but practice cannot come without knowledge) our American way of living. I should like to see a bottle of Coca Cola on every table in England, on every table in France, on every——'

'But isn't it terribly nasty?' said Grace.

'No, ma'am, it most certainly is not. It tastes good. But that, if I may say so, is entirely beside the point which I am trying, if I can, to make. When I say a bottle of Coca Cola I mean it metaphorically speaking, I mean it as an outward and visible sign of something inward and spiritual, I mean it as if each Coca Cola bottle contained a djinn, and as if that djinn was our great American civilization ready to spring out of each bottle and cover the whole global universe with its great wide wings. That is what I mean.'

'Goodness!' said Hughie.

'I say,' said Grace, who was getting rather fidgety, 'oughtn't we to have another rubber before tea?'

Grace did all she could to avoid being left alone with Carolyn, but to no avail. Carolyn came into her bedroom while she was dressing for dinner and was quite extraordinarily tactless; she seemed not to have any consideration whatever for her friend's feelings.

'Well,' she began. 'So what happened, exactly? Didn't I tell you, it's not possible for an English girl to settle down with a French husband and be happy. What finally drove you away?'

'Nothing, Carolyn. I'm not finally driven away. I haven't been very well since my miscarriage, so I've been quietly at home with Papa.'

'Oh bunkum! I know you're going to divorce, Madame Rocher has told everyone so. I don't blame you, Grace, on the contrary, you're quite right. But now there's the problem of Sigi. You really must try and get him away from his father. I think it's my duty to tell you that Charles-Edouard is ruining that child. They're never apart, according to Nanny; he takes him to visit all his mistresses, has him down to dinner, keeps him up far too late and gives him wine. Nanny is quite in despair. You ought to see a lawyer and try and get a court injunction to stop it, you know.'

'But Sigi is a French boy. It's only right for him to be brought up at least half in France; Charles-Edouard won't do anything that's bad for him.'

'My dear Grace! I think it's your positive duty to get him away and bring him up yourself. Don't you lie down under it, show a little backbone.'

'I don't want to bring him up entirely myself. A boy needs his father.'

'Yes well, I'm coming to that. What we all hope is that you'll do as you ought to have done in the first place, marry Hughie. You're made for each other. Then he'll be a father to the boy, who couldn't have a better one. Hughie is through with the frogs for ever, he told Heck, no more sand in his eyes. He'll arrange for Sigi to go to Eton, and make a man of him.'

'Charles-Edouard used to be rather in favour of Eton—more than I was in fact.'

'Rather in favour! What a way to talk about Eton.' Carolyn's family, the Boreleys, were passionate Etonians.

'You're sending Foss there?' said Grace, hoping to change the subject. She couldn't bear discussing Sigi and Charles-Edouard, who were so much in her heart at the moment, with Carolyn. She had been half pleased and half tormented to hear from Nanny of Charles-Edouard's odd new passion for the child.

'It's a little different for us,' said Carolyn. 'Foss is an American boy and Heck thinks an Eton accent would do him a lot of harm when the time comes for him to get a job.'

'I wouldn't lie down under that,' said Grace. 'Show a little backbone, Carolyn.'

'Simply absurd, Grace. You don't seem to realize the unique position of the Union of States to which Hector and I belong. You can't compare them with any other country, because in a very few years they will be the absolute rulers of the world.'

'Oh. So we're going to be ruled by Foss, are we?'

'Yes, in a way. It's a privilege for a young man to be brought up there, as Foster will be. But France is finished and done for, and that's the difference.'

'It may be finished and done for, but it's far the most agreeable country to live in.'

'Well I notice you didn't stay there very long,' aid Carolyn, triumphantly having the last word.

There was a tinkle of cowbells, meaning that dinner was ready, and they went downstairs.

Early on Monday morning the Dexters drove away in their huge, sick-coloured motor from which issued puffs of heat and high strains of coloratura. They were to visit some more factories on their way to London.

Hughie said he would motor Grace up in time for dinner. He took her for a long walk and asked her to marry him.

'But what about Albertine?' she said, in great surprise. 'I don't think I want another husband who goes to tea at the rue de l'Université every day. Charles-Edouard always did, you know; how I hated it.'

'You needn't worry about that. I shall never see her again as long as I live.'

'Why? Has something happened?'

'Yes. When I went over to Paris in October she played me a thoroughly low and dirty trick which I shall never forgive. But it did have one good result, it showed me quite clearly that you and I ought never to have got mixed up with all these foreigners; we ought to have married in the first place. The sooner we do so now, forget all about these people and settle down to an ordinary English life, the better.'

'I often think that,' said Grace. 'What was it, Hughie?'

'I haven't told you before because it involves your husband, Grace, but now I hear you are divorcing anyhow, so I can. Well. I hadn't seen her since the summer, as you know; she was away for ages, first Venice and then Vienna. I spoke to her on the telephone as soon as I arrived. She was terrifically loving. I was to go round at six, take her to a varnishing, and then dine with her.

'I was there on the stroke of six, as you can imagine, and Pierre showed me into the little salon there is under her dressing-room, saying she was changing and would be down at once. I could hear her upstairs, getting ready as I supposed, walking to and fro. I imagined her at her dressing-table, going over to the cupboard, trying on one hat, changing it, perhaps changing her dress again. I'd so often seen it—she takes hours to get ready, and then she changes everything again, and so on. I was feeling most awfully romantic, so I got a bit of paper and wrote a little poem about her in her dressing-room and hearing the tap tap of her heels overhead. Fearful rot, of course, but I began longing to show it to her, and finally I thought "why not, I'll go upstairs and find her".

'I went into the dressing-room, but it was Maria, her Italian maid, who was walking up and down. I didn't think much of this, I thought Albertine must be in her bedroom and I went through, and sure enough there she was—in bed with your husband. Never had such a shock in my life. She must have told Maria to walk to and fro to keep me quiet downstairs. You see? Not very nice, was it? But I think that kills two birds with one stone; it kills Albertine for me and it ought to kill Valhubert for you.'

Grace tried not to laugh. The story did not upset her at all. Could she possibly, she thought, be coming round to the point of view of her father and Charles-Edouard on these matters?

'Very French,' she said.

'Yes, and I wish you could have heard her trying to explain it away on the telephone afterwards—very French too. "Come now, Hughie, Charles-Edouard is my foster-brother, we had the same nurse and drank the same milk, how could there be anything between him and me? We were having a little rest after luncheon." 'Course I just rang off.'

'Poor Hughie!'

'Funny thing is I honestly didn't mind, in fact it was really, after the first shock, a great relief. You see, I'm too English, just as you are, Grace, to cope with people like that. It's unsuitable, we shouldn't attempt it. And it showed me something else, too, that it's you I love, Grace. What I felt for Albertine was simply infatuation.'

'I always wish I knew the difference between infatuation and love,' said Grace.

'You are infatuated with your husband, but it can't last, it's not built on anything solid and very soon you'll begin to love me again. You like this place, don't you, and our life here, it suits you, and you like being with me. Then if I take up politics you'll like that; you're used to it, with your father, and you'll be a great help to me. You loved me all right before you met Valhubert, and I'm sure you will again, and you'll like having some real English children with blue eyes and things, more natural for you. Besides, we've both had the same experience now, it makes us understand each other as an outside person never would. So, when the divorce is over, Grace——?'

'Let's wait a bit,' said Grace. 'No hurry, is there? I'm pleased and touched to have been asked, but I can't say, yet. It all depends, very much, on Sigismond.'

'He'll be all for it, you'll see,' said Hughie with confidence. 'I'll think of every sort of amusing thing for him to do when he gets back.'

CHAPTER V

It did not take Sigi very long to notice that life in Paris alone with Charles-Edouard was a very different matter from family life there with a mummy you only saw at tea-time and a daddy you hardly ever saw at all. It was much more fun. He was with his father morning, noon, and night, and all the things they did together were delightful. They went to the antique shops and museums; Sigi learnt about marquetry and china and pictures and bronzes and was given a small cabinet to house an ivory collection of his own. They went to the Jockey Club, and though Sigi was left sitting, like a dog, in the hall, he didn't mind that because he collected small, but regular, sums in tips from various members who thought he looked bored and wanted to see him smile.

'Shall I belong to the Jockey Club when I'm grown up?'

'If I remember to do for you what my father did for me,' said Charles-Edouard, 'and get you in before you've made too many enemies among husbands. Husbands can be most terrible blackballers. But it's very dull.'

'Then why do we come so often?'

'I don't know.'

On the rare occasions when Charles-Edouard was at home in the evening Sigi dined downstairs with him, and this was the greatest treat of all. He was given a glass of wine, like his father, and made to guess the vintage. When he got it right Charles-Edouard gave him 100 francs.

'In England,' said Sigi, 'little boys don't have dinner.'

'No dinner?'

'Supper. And sometimes only high tea.'

'What is this, high tea?'

'Yes well, it's tea, you know, with cocoa and scones, and eggs if you've got hens and bacon if you've killed a pig, and marmalade and Bovril and kippers, and you have it late for tea, about six.'

'How terrible this must be!'

'Oh no—high tea is absolutely smashing. Until you come to supper-time, and then I must say you do rather long for supper.'

Nanny sat talking with the Dexter Nanny, who had come round for her evening off. They had been obliged to put Sigi to bed in the middle of their nice chat, which they both considered an outrageous bore. He now lay in the next room, on the verge of sleep but not quite off, and a certain amount of what they were saying penetrated his consciousness. It was all mixed up with noise from the B.B.C., which ran on in that nursery whatever the programme. Young, polite, rather breathy English voices were playing some sort of paper game; their owners hardly seemed to belong to the same race as the two Nannies, so dim their personalities, so indefinite their statements.

'The Marquee never used to look at him when Mummy was with us.

Funny, isn't it? It's as much as I can do now to get him up here for the time it takes to change his shoes—thoroughly spoilt he's getting—out of hand. More tea, dear?'

'Thanks, dear. But it's always like that with separated couples, in my opinion. I've seen it over and over. Because, you know, each one is trying to give the child a better time than the other. ' At these words Sigi woke right up and began listening with all his ears. 'Nothing can be worse for the children.'

'I know. Shame, really. Well I told Mummy—I don't care for these youths on the wireless much, do you?'

'Not at all. There seems to be nothing else nowadays, youth this and youth that. Nobody thought of it when I was young.'

'Yes well, as we were saying. If you ask me I rather expect they'll come together again, and I'm sure it's to be hoped they will. I know Mummy was awfully upset about something, but I don't suppose he's worse than most men, except for being foreign of course, and I think it's their plain duty to make it up for the sake of the poor little mite. That's what I shall tell Mummy when I see her again, and I shall warn her plainly that if he goes on like this, getting his own way with both of them as he does now, he'll become utterly spoilt and impossible. No use saying anything to the Marquee, he's always in such a tearing hurry, though I must say I'd like to give him a piece of my mind about these dinners—the poor little chap comes to bed half drunk if you ask me.'

It was while listening to this conversation that Sigismond first made up his mind, consciously, that his father and mother must never be allowed to come together again if there was anything he could do to prevent it.

Charles-Edouard always took Sigi with him now when he went, at five o'clock, to see Albertine. She gave them an enormous tea, after which Sigi would play with her collection of old toys and automata. The most fascinating, the one of which he never tired, was a toy guillotine. It really worked, and really chopped off the victim's head, to the accompaniment of sinister drums and the horrified gestures of the other dolls on the scaffold. Besides this there were many varieties of musical box, there were dancing bears, smoking monkeys, singing birds, and so on, and while Albertine told the cards Sigi was turned loose among them, with tremendous injunctions from Charles-Edouard to be very very careful as they were very very precious.

'Why are they more precious than other toys?'

'Because they are old.'

'Are old things always precious?'

'Yes.'

'In that case Nanny must be very precious.'

'Always this young man between you and the blonde lady you think about so much.'

'Could it be Hughie?' Charles-Edouard was very much puzzled. He knew that Grace was seeing a good deal of Hughie now, but had never given the matter a serious thought. 'Did he ever come back again, by the way, Albertine? What happened?'

'He was furious. I've never known a man so angry. I rang him up twice and explained everything, but each time he rang off without even saying good-bye. These English——!'

'How did you explain it?' said Charles-Edouard, very much amused.

'I told him the truth.'

'No wonder he rang off in a rage.'

'My dearest, you know as well as I do that there is never only one truth and always many truths. I told him that you, Charles-Edouard de Valhubert, and I, Albertine Labé de Lespay, had drunk the same milk when we were little, young babies.'

'What milk?'

'Come now, Charles-Edouard, we had the same nurse!'

'Old Nanny Perkins didn't have one drop of milk when I first knew her, and wasn't that amount younger when she was with you?'

'We had the same nurse, therefore, to all intents and purposes, we drank the same milk. We are foster-brother and sister—how could he think of us as anything else? The Anglo-Saxon mind reduces everything to sex, I've often noticed it. Cut three times. Very odd indeed—here is the young man again, keeping you apart. Surely surely she cannot love Hughie?'

'Oh yes she does,' Sigi piped up from his corner. 'He is the love of her life.'

'This is very strange,' said Charles-Edouard, genuinely surprised that anybody in a position to be in love with him could fancy Hughie.

Albertine was not displeased. 'Come here, Sigi, and tell us how you know.'

'When Mr. Palgrave is coming to see her, she looks like this,' he said, and did a lifelike imitation of his mother as she had looked after the front door had slammed that morning when Charles-Edouard came to fetch him away. He opened enormous eyes and smiled as if something heavenly were about to happen. 'She thinks the world of Mr. Palgrave, and so do I. He gives me pounds and pounds.' He was twisting his hair into curls as he spoke.

'Go on with the cards,' said Charles-Edouard, very much put out.

'Cut then. But why did you not have an explanation with her when you were in England?' she said in Italian, so that Sigi would not understand.

'She was in her room and refused to see me.'

'Unlike you not to gallop up the stairs.'

'In what way unlike me? I would have you observe, Albertine, that I have never forced my way into a woman's bedroom in my life.'

'Take four cards. What a curious thing—intrigues and misunder-standings, just like a Palais Royal farce, with this real old-fashioned villain plotting away in the background. Fancy Hughie being so wicked, it makes him more interesting, all of a sudden. I must send him a Christmas card. What do you want for Christmas, Sigi?'

'I want to ride on the cheval de Marly.'

'This child has an obsession.'

'And what else?'

'Nothing else.'

'Be very careful, Sigismond. Consider it well. Do you really want to wake up with an empty stocking, to find a tree loaded with no presents, to spend the whole day unpacking no parcels?'

'Well, what will you give me?'

'You must say what you want first. It's always like that. Then we have to consider whether we can afford it.'

Sigismond became very thoughtful and hardly spoke another word the rest of the evening.

'M.P.'s daughter divorces French Marquis,' Sigi, chanting this loudly, came into his father's bathroom. Charles-Edouard was shaving at the time.

'What do you know about this—who told you?'

'I heard Nanny clicking her tongue at the *Daily*, so I went and looked over her shoulder and saw it. I can read quite well now you see, how about a prize?'

'You couldn't read a word of *Monte Cristo* last night.'

'I can only read if it's in English and printed, and I want to. At first the marriage was a happy one—who are the other women, Papa? I know, Madame Marel and Madame Novembre.'

'Be quiet, Sigi. These are things you must not say.'

'Pas devant?'

'Pas du tout. If you do you'll be punished.'

'What sort of punishment?'

'A bad sort. And you'll never never be allowed to ride on the chevaux de Marly.'

'O.K. And if I don't speak, when can I ride?'

'I don't know.'

'So now you can't be married to Mummy again, can you?'

'Yes I can. Tomorrow, if she likes.'

'Oh!' His mouth went down at the corners.

'Why, Sigi? Don't you want us to be?'

'It wouldn't be the slightest good wanting, I'm afraid. My mummy is quite wrapped up in Hughie now.' His hand went to his hair and began twisting it.

'Mr. Palgrave.'

'He lets me call him Hughie.'

'How very unsuitable. But is she?' said Charles-Edouard. 'Is she really, Sigi? He is very dull.'

'That's nothing. Look how dull is Mr. Dexter, and yet Mrs. Dexter is quite wrapped up in him, the Nannies always say so.'

'What is all this wrapping up, Sigi?'

'Emballé. Like you are with Madame Novembre.'

'Hm. Hm. Get ready to go out and I'll take you to see Pascal.'

'Well if I can't ride on you know what, I suppose that dreary old Pascal will have to do.'

Now that Charles-Edouard's divorce was in the papers, great efforts were made, in many directions, to marry him, and nobody tried harder than his two mistresses.

Albertine, shuffling the cards, said, 'I have been noticing a very different trend in your fate. It seems to become more definite, more inescapable, every time I take up the pack. You have turned a corner, as one sometimes does in life, and a new landscape lies at your feet. For some days the cards have left the atmosphere of Palais Royal and have pointed to a grave decision—two grave decisions in fact—which lead to extraordinary happiness, to a journey and to advancement. Anybody who knew the rudiments of fortune-telling would see these bare facts, they repeat and repeat themselves; it now remains to interpret them, and that, of course, is more difficult. Cut the cards. There now. It looks very much like service to your country in some foreign land.'

'Indo-China?' Charles-Edouard looked puzzled. 'I'm rather old, now, it's only the regular army they want. Still, I suppose there would be something for me, though I can't say I'm absolutely longing to go back.'

'Oh I don't mean that, not military service. All the same, have you never thought that now your marriage is over it might be a good thing to go away for a while? To change your ideas?'

'But, Albertine, I never go away from Paris, you know that very well. I go to Bellandargues when I must, but otherwise I can't be got as far as St. Cloud even. What are you thinking of?'

'Let me tell you, calmly and clearly, what I see. Cut the cards. I will lay out the whole pack. Now. I see you in a foreign land, a civilized one, among white people, and I see you negotiating, treating, making terms and driving bargains, for France.

'There is a word for somebody who does all those things—ambassador. Why should you not, in fact, become an ambassador?'

'Me? Albertine, you must be mad!'

'So mad, my love? After all, you have been in the foreign service—there are still broken hearts in Copenhagen I believe.'

'Oh that Copenhagen—dinner at 6.30—never shall I forget it. But if you remember, I resigned because I can't bear to be away from Paris.

I was away seven years during and after the war, and that is enough for my lifetime, thank you very much.'

'I don't believe it. I believe you would like to serve your country once more, to put this time at her disposal, as well as your great courage, your charm and eloquence and gift for languages. You have extraordinary gifts, Charles-Edouard.'

'Well, but who is going to make me an ambassador all of a sudden?' he said, rather more favourably.

'I could help you there. I am on very good terms with the Foreign Minister, and, even more important, with Madame Salleté. I am practically certain it would be arranged. And that brings us back to the cards. You understand that you would need to be married for such an assignment; an unmarried ambassador (and especially if that ambassador were you, dear Charles-Edouard) is in a position to be gravely compromised. It wouldn't do at all. Salleté wouldn't consider it for a single moment. Now the cards, ever since they have taken on this new direction, as you might call it, have been pointing to re-marriage. An older wife, not only nearer your own age but older, mentally, than our poor dear Grace. A Frenchwoman, of course, who would be able to play her part; a widow, whom you could marry in church. Above all,' she said, lowering her voice, 'somebody who would be able to help you with the education of our beloved little Sigismond.'

Charles-Edouard saw just what she meant. 'Ah yes,' he said, 'but the fact is that I am obliged to remain in Paris precisely on Sigi's account. Presently he must go to the Condorcet as I did, while living here with me.'

'You don't feel that a cosmopolitan education is more precious for a boy of today?'

'Sigi will be bilingual whatever happens. I think he ought to go to school in France. And besides, I don't, I really don't, think I could accept any favour from Salleté.'

Albertine was much too clever to press her point. 'Think it over,' she said, calmly, 'and now, cut three times.'

Charles-Edouard did think it over, and soon began to feel that marriage with Albertine was perhaps not such a bad idea. He got on very well with her, old friend of all his life; she never failed to amuse him, they talked the same language, understood the fine shades of each other's character and behaviour; they knew the same people and had identical tastes. Albertine owned several pictures that Charles-Edouard had always coveted; he would give a great deal to see her big Claude Lorraine on his own walls, not to mention her Louis XIV commode in solid silver. No need for a quick decision, his divorce was not yet absolute, but some time, he thought, he might find out how Sigismond felt about it.

Juliette's approach was more direct. She rolled lazily over in

Madame de Hauteserre's bed (the door now bolted as well as locked), her eyes, which always became as big as saucers after making love, upon the erotic ceiling, and said, 'So I hear you have your divorce at last. What now, Charles-Edouard?'

'I'm tired. Perhaps I'll sleep for a few minutes.'

'No. Don't sleep. I want to talk. What are your plans?'

'No plans.'

'Charles-Edouard! But you must marry again.'

'No more marriage.'

'But my dearest, you'll be lonely.'

'I'm never lonely. It's people who can't amuse themselves who feel lonely, another word for bored. I am never bored, either.'

'Shall I tell you what I think?'

'No. Tell me a story, to amuse me.'

'Presently. I think you and I ought to go and see M. le Maire together.'

'And what about poor Jean?'

'I'm perfectly sick of poor Jean. He's the dullest boy in Paris.'

'I thought you wanted to be a duchess?'

'I will renounce it for your sake. I will be divorced and give up being a duchess, Charles-Edouard, and all for you.'

'How would you get an annulment?'

'There may be grounds for that.'

'It would take years and years.'

'But I thought we might be married by M. le Maire, as you were with Grace.'

'Yes, and a terrible mistake too. I will never be married again, except in church. No,' he said sleepily, 'of all the women in the world you are the one I would soonest marry, but, alas, it cannot be.'

'Why not?'

'Because of Sigismond. From now on my life must be dedicated to him.'

'But the poor child needs a mother. And little sisters, Charles-Edouard, darling, pretty little girls, surely you'd like that?'

'Well now, perhaps I would,' said Charles-Edouard. He turned over, laid his head between Juliette's breasts and went to sleep.

As it became increasingly obvious that the key to Charles-Edouard's heart was held by his little boy both Albertine and Juliette now proceeded to pay their court to Sigismond. Juliette employed exactly the same technique of seduction and cajolery as with his father; Albertine's approach, while she never neglected the uses of sex, was rather more subtle.

Juliette gave the little boy treat after treat. She took him to all the various circuses, to musical plays, to the cinema, and even to see the clothes at Christian Dior. Greatest treat of all, and a tremendous secret, she would drive him out of Paris in her pretty little open motor, and when they came to the straight, empty, poplar-bordered roads which lead to the east she would change places with him and let him take over the controls.

'Look, look, Madame Novembre, cent à l'heure,' he would cry in ecstasy as the speedometer went up and up. She bore it unflinchingly, though sometimes very much frightened.

After one of these clandestine outings they were drinking hot chocolate with blobs of cream in her pretty, warm little boudoir at the rue de Varenne. The mixture of camaraderie and sex in Juliette's approach to Sigi made her almost irresistible and the little boy was fascinated by her, though rather sleepy now from the cold afternoon air. Presently she said, 'We do have a good time together, eh, Sigismond?'

'Oh we do!'

'You'd like it to go on for ever, wouldn't you?'

'Yes please, I would.'

'For ever and ever. It easily could, you know. I could become your maman and live in the same house—would you like that?'

'Mm,' he said, his nose in the chocolate.

'Then you could drive my motor every day, not only sometimes, like now. We'd do all sorts of other lovely things, specially in the summer.'

'Could we have a speed-boat on the river?'

'Yes, that would be great fun.'

'And a glider perhaps.'

'Surely.'

'And I very much long for a piebald rat.'

'Well——' she said with a slight shudder, 'why not?'

'And what else?'

'Let's see what would be nice. Perhaps—little brothers and sisters?'

Sigi took his nose out of the chocolate and gave her a very sharp and wide-awake look. He finished the cup, put it down on the table and said, 'I think it's time to go home.'

Juliette realized at once that she had made a blunder, though she did not know quite how fatal it was going to be to her ambitions, and nor could she know that her words would be underlined that very evening by the two Nannies.

'That Madame November,' Sigi overheard, from his bed, 'is a perfect menace. She gets hold of the child, and the things they do—thoroughly unsuitable—dress shows, and awful sorts of films, and he says (not that I quite believe it, mind you, but you never know) that she lets him drive her car. Anyway she fills his little head with rubbish and spoils him, oh she does spoil him. If you ask my opinion it's the Marquee she's after and that's the way she's setting about it, and quite likely it would be all for the best if she got him. Because then little Master Grown-up would be back in the nursery for good, sure as eggs is eggs, no more high jinks, and the young person occupied with her own children likely as not.

'That child's getting ruined between the lot of them, and I don't mind who knows it. I can't do a thing with him any more.'

'Yes well,' said Nanny Dexter, 'none of it's any surprise to me.'

'Papa,' said Sigi next morning.

'Hullo! You're early today.'

'Yes, I've got something very important I want to talk about.'

'Well?'

'You know how you're wrapped up in Madame Novembre?'

'So you always tell me.'

'Were you thinking of marrying her?'

'Why, Sigismond?'

'Because she's not at all the type of person I would like to have as my maman—not at all.'

'Nothing,' said Charles-Edouard, 'could be further from my thoughts.'

But this was not perfectly true. The idea of marriage with Juliette had been occupying his mind of late, chiefly because, as he said to one of his men friends, it was so dreadfully tiresome always going to bed in the afternoon. However if Sigi felt like that about it the question would arise no more.

CHAPTER VI

ALBERTINE played upon the little boy's social sense, already very much developed.

'I have three invitations for you, darling, two parties and luncheon at the Ritz.'

'You know, Madame Marel, I'm very tired of parties. Always that silly old conjurer, he's getting on my nerves with his doves and rabbits. Can't I go to a ball?'

'You want to go to a ball now, do you? But for several reasons that is impossible. Firstly, how would you dress? Secondly, you are too small for dancing with grown-up people, and thirdly, as it is not the custom for boys of your age to go to balls you'd find that you would not enjoy yourself at it. You must wait for balls until you are older.'

Sigi's mouth went down at the corners and he looked very glum. He was not accustomed, now, to being refused things.

'What can we do?' Albertine said to Charles-Edouard when he had gone home. 'The poor little boy looked so sad. I must think this over.'

She thought it over, and presently had an idea of genius. She would give a ball for Sigi, a fancy-dress ball, 'Famous parents with their

famous children,' which would be the most sensational of the season.
Her first intention was that parents with their children only would be
allowed, no famous child admitted without a famous parent, and, far
more testing, no famous parent without his or her own famous child.
But this rule led to such shrieks down the telephone from Albertine's
many bachelor friends that she was finally obliged to relax it in favour
of uncles and aunts. Further she would not budge; nobody, she said,
would be allowed in without either their own child or their own
nephew or niece.

Never before had children been at such a premium. A great deal of
sharing out took place in families. 'If I have Stanislas and you take
Oriane that still leaves little Christophe to go with Jean'; fleets of aeroplanes were chartered to bring over nephews and nieces for the many
bachelors from Chile, Bolivia, and the Argentine who live in France,
while legal adoptions were hurried through at a rate never previously
known in the department of the Seine. The Tournons, and others who,
like them, had had several children in order to avoid taxation, now
sent to the country for them, and these little strangers suddenly found
themselves the very be-all and end-all of their parents' existence.

As was to be expected, the Tournons were positively dramatic in their
approach to the ball; indeed one night, shortly before it was to take
place, Madame de Tournon woke up screaming from a nightmare in
which her nursery had caught fire before her very eyes and all her now
priceless brood had perished in the flames. M. de Tournon calmed her
with difficulty, promising to go out as soon as the shops opened and buy
the latest form of fire-escape. Even so this dream, which had been a particularly vivid one, recurred to her at intervals for several days. She was
dreadfully shaken by it, and never felt quite comfortable again until the
ball had begun. Of course the great question was how should they go to
it. What famous couple, fair husband dark wife, with three boys and
one girl, was famous enough for the Tournon family? They racked
their brains, they refused all their invitations in order to stay quietly at
home, thinking. At last Eugène de Tournon said that they would never
have any truly original idea in the hurly-burly of a town, and that the
absolute peace and quiet of the country were essential to any such act of
creation. So away they went. They had not seen the country, except
through the windows of some fast-moving vehicle, for several years, and
they came back to Paris saying that people ought to go there more, it
really was rather pretty. Their friends were relieved to hear that the
journey had been a success, the great inspiration having come to them
as they walked down a forest glade—Henri II, Catherine de Medicis,
the three little kings and la Reine Margot. Almost every other family of
four children had had the same idea. Indeed there was very little
originality in the choice of characters; parents with only sons were
Napoleon, Eugénie, and the Prince Imperial; mothers with only

daughters Madame de Sévigné and Madame de Grignan; uncles with only nephews (of which there seemed to be dozens) Jerome or Lucien with l'Aiglon; families of a boy and a girl Louis XVI, Marie Antoinette and their children, and so on. Charles-Edouard decided upon Talleyrand and Delacroix, chiefly because Sigismond looked so charming in the black velvet coat and big, floppy bow tie of the artist. Albertine, in a wonderfully elaborate dress made of fig leaves, was Eve the Mother of All.

Madame Rocher des Innouïs alone was allowed to break the hard and fast rule about blood relations, but then she was a law unto herself, nobody in Paris, not even Albertine, would think of giving a party without her. She sent for two little orphans from the Hospice des Innouïs. 'After all,' she said, 'I am Tante Régine to everybody at the Hospice.' Two ugly little boys arrived, one very fat and one very thin. After some thought she dressed them in deer-stalkers, white spats and beards as Edward VII and the Tsar of Russia, going herself as the Queen of Denmark, 'Mother-in-law of Europe'. When they arrived Albertine murmured rather feebly, 'I said aunts, not mothers-in-law,' but of course she let them pass.

She was not so lenient, however, to Madame Novembre. Juliette had no possible excuse for being asked, except a niece, the daughter of her only sister who had married a Czech and gone to live in South Africa. This wretched spoilsport refused to deliver up her child, even on the receipt of several long, explanatory telegrams from Juliette. It must be said that the probability of such a refusal had been taken into the fullest consideration by Albertine when making her plans.

Juliette now became perfectly frantic, and told her husband there was nothing for it, they must adopt a child. But at this the worm turned. Jean Novembre may not have been very bright in the head, but he was impregnated with a deep respect for his own family tree. Never, he said, would he bestow the great name of Novembre de la Ferté, not to speak of the proportion of his income which, by the laws of adoption, he would be obliged to settle, on some little gutter-snipe, simply in order to allow Juliette to go to a ball. He said it was unreasonable of her to expect such a thing; he also pointed out that she was the one who had consistently refused to have children of their own, which he wanted very much.

'Everybody's doing it,' said Juliette.

'The rastaquouères and Israelites may be, and who cares? Paris can easily support the presence of a few more Montezumas and Montelevis, it makes no difference to anybody. But Novembre de la Ferté is quite another matter. It's entirely your own fault, Juliette. You have always mocked at Isabella de Tournon for having all those children—I tell you she's a clever woman, and now you see who has come best out of the affair.'

Finally Juliette was reduced to borrowing her concierge's child, a loathly specimen whom she hoped to pass off as the South African niece. Albertine was not deceived for a moment by this manœuvre, and Madame Vigée Lebrun and her daughter entered the house only to make an ignominious exit. 'Take that hideous child away this instant, Juliette. I know perfectly well who it is—I see it picking its nose every time I come into your courtyard. Off with you both and no argument. A rule is a rule : I refuse to make any exceptions.'

Very fortunately, three (really) famous (real) musicians, all excellent mimics, happened to be arriving at this moment. For weeks afterwards they re-enacted the scene, in high falsetto, at every Paris gathering. It became longer and more dramatic every time they did it, and was finally set to music and immortalized in the ballet 'Novembre Approche'.

A pair of young mothers now became the centre of interest. They had risen from their lying-in much sooner than the doctors would otherwise have allowed. (French doctors are always very good about recognizing the importance of social events, and certainly in this case had the patients been forbidden the ball they might easily have fretted themselves to death.) One came as the Duchesse de Berri with l'Enfant du Miracle, and the other as Madame de Montespan and the Duc du Maine. The two husbands, the ghost of the Duc de Berri, a dagger sticking out of his evening dress, and Louis XIV, were rather embarrassed really by the horrible screams of their so very young heirs, and hurried to the bar together. The noise was indeed terrific, and Albertine said crossly that had she been consulted she would, in this case, have permitted and even encouraged the substitution of dolls. The infants were then dumped down to cry themselves to sleep among the coats on her bed, whence they were presently collected by their mothers' monthly nurses. Nobody thereafter could feel quite sure that the noble families of Bregendir and Belestat were not hopelessly and for ever interchanged. As their initials and coronets were, unfortunately, the same, and their baby linen came from the same shop, it was impossible to identify the children for certain. The mothers were sent for, but the pleasures of society rediscovered having greatly befogged their maternal instincts, they were obliged to admit that they had no idea which was which. With a tremendous amount of guilty giggling they spun a coin for the prettier of the two babies and left it at that.

The famous parents and their famous children were now lined up for the entrée. Each group, heralded by a roll of drums, entered the ballroom by a small stage. Here they posed a few moments for the photographers, after which they joined the crowd on the ballroom floor. Very soon the famous parents dumped their famous offspring at the buffet and left them there while they went off to dance, flirt, gamble or gossip with other famous parents. The children happily stuffed away with cream and cake and champagne, all of which very soon combined with the lateness of the hour to produce a drowsy numbness. Every available sofa, chair, and settee now bore its load of sleeping babies; they lay on the floor round the edges of the rooms, under the buffet, and behind the window curtains. The grown-ups, all set for a jolly evening, waltzed carelessly among their bodies.

Presently two incongruous, iron-clad figures appeared, clicking their tongues, the Dexter and Valhubert nannies in search of their charges. They peered about, turning over an occasional body, and looking like nothing so much as two tragic mothers after some massacre of innocents. Sigi was found in the arms of the Reine Margot; Foss had crept into a corner and been terribly sick. Of course Carolyn knew that she ought never to have allowed him to come, she felt most extremely guilty about it; but the fact was that this ball had had the effect, in Paris, of a bull-fight in some small Spanish town—that is to say, disapprove of it as you might, the atmosphere it produced was such that it was really impossible to resist going to it. Bearing away the little bodies, their faces glowing with a just indignation, the two English nannies vanished into the night.

Charles-Edouard spent most of his evening with Madame de Tournon, whom he had always rather fancied but whom he had never so far courted because she was Juliette's greatest friend. He detested scenes and drama in his private life, and would go to almost any lengths, within reason, to avoid them.

Madame Rocher set her cap at Hector Dexter. She was organizing a gala at the Opera in June, to provide the Hospice des Innouïs with some new bath-chairs and other little comforts for the aged.

The Dexters were just the people to rope in for this gala, a big box, she thought, and possibly a row of stalls as well. Having been told that one certain way to the heart of every American was through his mother, she said,

'Your mother was a Whale, I believe, Mr. Dexter?'

'Why, yes, indeed, Madame des Innouïs, that is so.'

'My late husband, who knew America, was entertained there by the Whales; he has often and often told me that their house was an exact copy, but ten times the size, of—let me see—was it Courances or Château d'O?—one of those houses entirely surrounded by water anyhow.'

'This is another branch of the Whale family, Madame Innouïs. There are hundreds of Whales in the States since this family is a very very large and extensive one and I have a perfect multiplicity of aunts and uncles and cousins and other more distant relatives, spread over the whole extent of the U.S.A. and all originating as Whales.'

'How delightful.' Madame Rocher's attention was wandering. She longed to join the group round Janvier, Cocquelin and Daudet, the musicians, who were doing their imitation of Juliette's gate-crashing, Janvier leading in Daudet, Cocquelin as the outraged Albertine—not the polished affair it afterwards became but none the less funny for that —to the accompaniment of happy shrieks from their audience. First things first, however. She turned again to Mr. Dexter, saying, 'And have you any children yourself?'

'I am glad to be able to tell you yes, Mrs. Innouïs. I have a son and a daughter by my first wife, the first Mrs. Dexter, and a son by my second wife, and a son, who is here this evening costumed as George Washington, by my third wife, who is also here, costumed as George Washington's mother, I myself being costumed, as you can see, as George Washington's father. My eldest son, Heck junior, is not perhaps quite brilliant, but he is a very very well-integrated, human person. My daughter, Aylmer, is married, and happily married I am glad to say, to a young technician in a very prominent and important electrical concern. My son by my second wife is now at Yale, having a good time. In the States, Madame Innouïs, we believe in all young folk being happy, and we do all we humanly can to further their happiness.

'Now here in Europe a very different point of view seems to prevail. Here so many of the entertainments and parties seem to be given by old people for other old people. Now I am over forty, Madame Innouïs, but many and many's the time, in French houses, when I have been the youngest person present, and I've never yet, at any parties, seen really young folks, college boys and girls or teen-agers. How do your French teen-agers amuse themselves, Madame Innouïs?'

'They are young, surely that is enough,' she said indignantly. 'Surely they don't need to amuse themselves as well.'

'But in the States, Madame Innouïs, we think it our duty to make sure that precisely while they are young they are having the best years of their lives. Now in what way do the young folks here spend these best years of their lives, Madame Innouïs?'

'I believe they are entirely nourished on porto,' said Madame Rocher enigmatically. She decided that she must get away from Mr. Dexter come what might, and even if it had to be at the expense of that big box and two rows of stalls. She made a sign of command to Eugène de Tournon, who sprang forward, gave her his arm, and took her to supper.

'Many people don't realize at all,' she said, 'what I go through in order to support those dear good creatures at the Hospice. Champagne please, at once. He called me Madame Innouïs.'

'But everybody knows, Tante Régine, that you are a saint, an absolute, literal saint.'

'Yes indeed, Tante Régine,' said Charles-Edouard, at whose table they sat down, 'we shall find you on the ceiling one of these days, I've always thought that.'

'And where is our adorable little Sigi?' she asked, as a very tipsy Grand Dauphin tottered past the table, followed by Mademoiselle de Blois who, with that high whine peculiar to French children, was demanding another glass of champagne. The innocents were beginning to come to life again.

'That old dragon of a Nanny came and took him away. So stupid. As if one night out would do him any harm.'

'Poor little things.' Madame Rocher surveyed them through her lorgnette. 'I'm glad it's not me growing up now. What a world for them! Atom bombs, and no brothels. What will their parents do about that—after all you can't very well ask your own friends, can you? I suppose they'll all end up as pederasts.'

'Far the best thing to be, if you can fancy it,' said Charles-Edouard. 'Just imagine—no jealous husbands, what, Eugène? None of the terrible worries that make our lives so distracting. No pregnancies, no abortions, no divorce—I envy them.'

'Blackmail?'

'Blackmail indeed! They've only got to write a journal clearly stating what they are. You can't blackmail a man by threatening to tell the world what he has told the world already.

'Now supposing I were to write a journal making it quite plain how much I have loved women—to begin with nobody would buy it, and to go on with it would have a terrible effect on the husbands and I should be in worse odour than ever before. It's really most unfair.'

Charles-Edouard got up to shake hands with Mr. and Mrs. Dexter, saying, since they were clearly going to anyhow, 'Do come and sit here. We are talking about brothels, pederasts, and blackmail.'

'You don't surprise me at all,' said Carolyn.

The Dexters, having now lived two years in Paris, had become quite accepted as part of French society, and were asked everywhere. But Carolyn still could not get to like, or be in the least amused by, the French.

'I am very very happy to be able to tell you,' said Mr. Dexter, settling into his chair, 'that when our ancestors left little old Europe and shook its dust off their feet in order to found our great United States of America, those three things are three of the things they left behind them here on your continent.'

'Well then, perhaps you can tell us,' said Madame Rocher, 'how, in a country where there are no brothels, do the young men ever learn?'

'I am very very happy to be able to tell you, Madame Innouïs, that the young American male is brimming over with strong and lustful, but clean desire. He is not worn out, old, and complicated before his time, no ma'am, he does not need any education sentimental, it all comes to him naturally, as it ought to come, like some great force of nature. He dates up young, he marries young, he raises his first family young, and by the time he is ready to re-marry he is still young. And I am now going to give you a little apercoo of our American outlook on sex and marriage.

'We, in the States, are entirely opposed to physical relations between the sexes outside the cadre of married life. Now in the States it is usual for the male to marry at least four, or three times. He marries first straight from college in order to canalize his sexual desires, he marries a second time with more material ends in view—maybe the sister or the daughter of his employer—and much later on, when he has reached the full stature of his maturity, he finds his life's mate and marries her. Finally it may be, though it does not always happen, that when he has raised his last family with his life's mate and when she has ceased to feel an entire concentrated interest in him, but is sublimating her sexual instincts into other channels such as card games and literature, he may satisfy a longing, sometimes more paternal than sexual, for some younger element in his home, by marrying the friend of one of his children, or, as has occurred in certain cases known to me personally, of one of his grandchildren.

'In the States we just worship youth, Madame Innouïs, it seems to us that human beings were put on this earth to be young; youth seems to us the most desirable of all human attributes.'

'In that case I very much advise you to go in for Bogomoletz. The wonders it has done for me! Why my hair, which was quite red, has positively begun to go black at the roots.'

'My faith, Madame Innouïs, is pinned to this diet I follow. Perhaps you would care to hear of it. Well it was entirely invented by a very very good friend of mine and its basis is germ of wheat oil, milk fortified with powdered milk and molasses, and meat fortified with yaghourt. Now in my case this diet, very carefully followed over a period of months, has succeeded in strengthening, beyond belief, the tissues of certain very very important organs——'

'The usual conversation of the over-forties, I see,' said Albertine joining them. 'Let me just warn you all not to brush your faces. Little Lambesé was told to brush his face, to induce circulation or some rubbish, and he is still in his room, poor boy, marked as if he had encountered a savage beast.'

'After all, the face is not a suède shoe,' said Madame de Tournon. 'Is that why he's not here? He told me he was coming as a famous aunt.'

'Yes, and he wouldn't have been the only one.'

'I think it's very hard luck, and I'm sorry,' said Madame Rocher. 'Now supposing I make more money than I expect to at the Gala des Innouïs I will try and give Lambesé a Bogo; if anybody deserves one it is he.'

'I thought the lift had been such a great success, and if so why did he brush?'

'He thought nothing of it,' said Madame Marel. 'If you want that extra radiance, he was told, brush—brush. He did have some particular reason for wanting it—he brushed—and there he was looking like Paul in *Les Malheurs de Sophie*.'

It was past six when the ball ended. The famous parents gathered up their famous children, wilting and dishevelled, as accessories to fancy dress always are by the time a party is over, and carried them away. The last to leave was Henri II, with the three little Valois kings and la Reine Margot, but without Catherine de Medicis.

'Where is my wife?' he said, to everybody he saw.

'And where,' said Albertine, more in sorrow than surprise, 'is Charles-Edouard?'

CHAPTER VII

THE next day, after luncheon, Charles-Edouard and Sigi set out to walk to the Jockey Club, both feeling the need for a little fresh air after their various excesses of the previous night. They crossed the Place de la Concorde as only Frenchmen can, that is to say they sauntered through the traffic, chatting away, looking neither to right nor to left and assuming that the vehicles whizzing by would miss them, even if only by inches. (A miss is as good as a mile might be taken as their motto by French pedestrians.) The skirts of their coats were sometimes blown up by passing motors, but they were in fact, missed, and reached the other side in safety.

'So what did the Reine Margot tell you?'

'She isn't really the Reine Margot, she's Jeanne-Marie de Tournon.'

'And what did she tell you?'

'Nothing at all—it's easy.'

Sigi was sometimes quite as obstinate as his mother when it came to 'What are the news'.

'Ha!' said Charles-Edouard. 'So you lay together on that sofa, hour after hour, gazing into each other's eyes and saying nothing at all. How very strange!'

'She lives in the country all the year round. She is dull. I was dull when you first knew me and I lived always in the country.'

'Are you not dull now?'

'I am not. I can read and write and do difficult sums and I'm excellent company. I know all about the Emperor and I can say the words of —oh Papa, Papa, do look——'

Some workmen were engaged upon Coustou's horses. The right-hand one was being cleaned and the other, with the arm of its groom over its back, still had a long ladder poised against the stone mane.

'Papa! Can I?'

Charles-Edouard looked round. There was nobody very near them, and no policeman nearer than the Concorde bridge.

'Do you know the words?'

'Yes. You'll hear, when I'm up there.'

'On your honour, Sigi?'

'Honneur,' he cried, taking off his coat, 'à la Grande Armée!'

He nipped up the ladder, and, clambering with the agility of a monkey on to the horse's back, began to chant: '*A la voix du vainqueur d'Austerlitz l'empire d'Allemagne tombe. La confédération du Rhin commence. Les royaumes de Wurtembourg et de Bavière sont créés. Venise se réunit à la couronne de fer, et l'Italie toute entière se range sous les lois de son libérateur. Honneur à la Grande Armée.*'

The motors in the Champs Elysées and Place de la Concorde began to draw into the side and stop while their occupants got out to have a better view of the charming sight.

'It must be for the cinema,' they said to each other. 'C'est trop joli.'

And indeed the little boy, with his blue trousers, yellow jersey, and mop of bright black hair on the white horse, outlined against a dappled sky, made a fascinating picture. Charles-Edouard laughed out loud as he looked. Then, as several whistling policemen arrived on the spot, he decided to allow Sigismond to deal alone with the situation as it developed. He hailed a taxi and went home. It was quite another half-hour before Sigi dashed into the house with a very great deal to tell.

Photographers, it seemed, had appeared; a man with a megaphone had told him to stay where he was. The crowd, led by Sigi, had begun to sing his favourite song '*Les voyez vous, les hussars, les dragons, la garde*'. The firemen had arrived in a shrieking red car, had swarmed up more ladders to the horse, had carried him down and borne him home in triumph, shooting across red lights in the boulevard.

'So these words have not remained unsaid after all, Papa, you see?'

'If his mummy had been here,' came floating into the night nursery, 'none of this would ever have happened. That Madame Marel would never have given that wicked ball (poor little mites, I can't get them out of my head lying about in great heaps all over the shop), and the Marquee would never have taken him for a walk—once in a blue moon was how often we saw the Marquee when Mummy was here. Allowing him to ride up on that horse indeed; it's a mercy he didn't fall off and crack his little skull.'

Next morning Charles-Edouard drank the several cups of black coffee and ate the several slices of ham which constituted his so-called English breakfast, with Sigi, on the floor beside him, busily cutting photographs of himself out of half a dozen newspapers brought in by Ange-Victor.

'Now guess what I'm going to do,' said Charles-Edouard. 'Ring up Mummy and tell her all about it and see if she'd like to have you over there for a bit.'

'Oh good,' said Sigi. 'Can I go tomorrow?' He was longing to see his mother, boast to her about what Nanny called the high jinks of the last two days, and see what she could do, now, to amuse him.

'Yes, unless you think she'd like to come over and pay us a visit instead? What do you say, Sigismond? We can always try to persuade her, can't we?'

If Charles-Edouard had seen the look Sigi gave him he might have interpreted it correctly, but he had already taken up the telephone (he seldom sat out of reach of this instrument) and was dialling the foreign exchange number.

'I want a personal call to London,' he said, giving Grace's name and number. He then went off to have his bath. 'Sit by the telephone, Sigismond, and call me at once if it rings.'

Sigi perched on his father's bed, reflecting.

As soon as the water began to run loudly in the bathroom next door he lifted the receiver and cancelled the call to London. When the water stopped running Charles-Edouard heard 'That you, Mummy? We're coming back tomorrow. Yes, Nanny and me, on the Arrow. Yes. Unless you'd like to pay us a visit here, Papa says? Oh! Mum!' a tragic, reproachful note in the voice. 'Won't you even speak to him? Here he is, out of his bath—oh! She's cut off,' he said, handing the receiver to Charles-Edouard, who, indeed, only heard a dialling tone. He slammed it down furiously and went back to his bath, saying 'Go and tell Nanny to pack, will you?'

Sigi went slowly off, twisting his hair until it was a mass of tangles.

In London Grace cried over her coffee. 'Paris wants you' to her had meant that in a minute or two she might hear the voice of Charles-Edouard. But when her telephone bell rang again and she answered it with beating heart it was only to hear: 'Sorry you have been troubled. Paris has now cancelled the call.'

CHAPTER VIII

GRACE now had two suitors, Hughie Palgrave, and a new friend, Ed Spain. Ed Spain was a leading London intellectual, known to his contemporaries as the Captain or the Old Salt, which names he had first received at Eton, on account, no doubt, of some long-forgotten joke.

He had a sort of seafaring aspect, accentuated later in life by a neat beard; his build was that of a sailor, short and slight, and his keen blue eyes looked as if they had been concentrated for many years on a vanishing horizon. In fact he was a charming, lazy character who had had from his schooldays but one idea, to make a great deal of money with little or no effort, so that he could lead the life for which nature had suited him, that of a rich dilettante. When he left Oxford somebody had told him that one sure road to a quick fortune was the theatre. With his small capital he had bought an old suburban playhouse called, suitably enough, the Royal George, and had then sat back awaiting the success which was to make him rich. It never came. The Captain had too much intellectual honesty to pander to his audiences by putting on plays which might have amused them but which did not come up to his own idea of perfection. He gained prestige, he was said to have written a new chapter in theatrical history, but certainly never made his coveted fortune.

However he soon attracted to himself a band of faithful followers, clever young women all more or less connected with the stage and all more or less in love with the Captain, and these followers, by their energy and devotion, kept the Royal George afloat. He called them My Crew, and left the management of his theatre more and more in their hands as the years went on, a perfect arrangement for such a lazy man. The Crew were relentlessly highbrow, much more so, really, than the Captain, whose own tastes, within the limits of what was first-class of its kind, were catholic and jolly. The Crew only liked plays written by sad young foreigners with the sort of titles (*This Way to the Womb*, *Iscariot Interperson*) which never seem to attract family parties out for a cheerful evening. Unfortunately these are the mainstay of the theatre world. The Crew, however, cared nothing for so contemptible a public. Their criterion of a play was that it should be worthy of the Captain, and when they found such a work they did not rest until they had translated, adapted, and produced it at the Royal George.

They took charge, too, of the financial side of the venture, which they ran rather successfully on a system of intellectual blackmail. Nobody in a certain set in London at that time, no clever Oxford or Cambridge undergraduate, would dare to claim that he was abreast of contemporary thought unless he paid his annual subscription, entitling him to two stalls a month, to the Royal George. These subscriptions, payable through Heywood Hill's bookshop, ensured a good, regular income for the theatre, but would not necessarily have brought in an audience but for the Captain's own exertions. Nobody minded forking out a few pounds a year to feel that they were in the swim, but the agony of sitting through most of the plays was hardly endurable. However if the theatre was quite empty for too many performances the Crew was apt to get very cross; it was the Captain's job to see that this did not happen. He let it be understood that those who wished to keep in his good graces must put in an occasional appearance at the Royal George.

As he was one of the most amusing people in London, as his presence was a talisman that ensured the success of any party (so long as he was well fed and given what he considered his due in the way of superior French wines, otherwise he had been known to sulk outrageously) this exacting tribute was paid from time to time by his friends and acquaintances. There was no special virtue, however, in going to a first night, since the house was always full on these occasions. First nights at the Royal George were very interesting affairs, and the Captain himself allocated all the seats for them. M. de Tournon's anguish over the placing of dukes at his dinner-table found its London counterpart in the Captain's anguish over the placing, on these first nights, of the grand young men of literature and the arts. His own, or Royal box, only held four. Neither he nor the Crew were ever likely to forget the first night of *Factory* 46 when Jiři Mucha, Nanos Valaoritis, Umbro Apollonio, Chun Chan Yeh, and Odysseus Sikelberg had all graciously announced their intention of being present. The situation was saved by Sikelberg getting mumps, but only at the very last minute.

Grace and her father went with Mr. O'Donovan, who was what she called 'abonnée', to the first night of *Sir Theseus*. Naturally they were not in the Royal box, full, on this occasion, of darkies, but they were well placed, in the second row of the stalls. The Captain, who often saw Sir Conrad at White's, came and sat with them for part of the time, a signal honour. *Sir Theseus* was, in fact, *Phèdre*, written with a new slant, under the inspiration of modern psychological knowledge, by a young Indian. Phaedra was the oldest member of the Crew and really rather a terror, only kept on by the Captain because she was such an excellent cook. She was got up to look, as Sir Conrad said, like a gracious American hostess, with crimped blue hair and a housecoat. When she bore down upon Hyppolitus, whose disgust at her approach, as he cowered against the backcloth, had nothing to do with histrionic art, Sir Conrad said in his loud, politician's voice, 'She's got young Woodley on the ropes this time.' The Captain loved to laugh, as he did at this, though really he half-hated the sort of joke which implied that art might not be sacred. He half-loved and half-hated, too, the sort of person represented by Sir Conrad. If the Captain had known in which direction he wanted to set his compass, life would have been that much easier for him. However on this occasion, attracted by the beauty and elegance of Grace, he invited her father to bring her and Mrs. O'Donovan back to his house for supper after the play.

The Captain lived in a large, rambling, early nineteenth-century house, built to be an hotel or lodging-house, on the river, hard by the Royal George. This he shared with such members of the Crew who were able and willing to do housework. They lived in attics and cellars which no servant would have considered for a single moment, but which the clever Captain had invested with romance. 'Les toits de Paris' he would murmur, craning through a leaky skylight and squinting at les toits de Hammersmith, while the cellars, damp and dripping, were supposed to be the foundations of a famous convent, 'the English Port Royal'. He reserved for himself big, sunny rooms on the first floor furnished in the later manner (much later, some said) of Jacob. Here an excellent supper, withdrawn from oven and hay-box by Phaedra with the assistance of Oenone, was served to quite a large party, consisting mostly of critics and fellow highbrows, such as the editors of *Depth* and *Neoterism*. The Indian author of *Sir Theseus* lay on the floor reading a book and never spoke to anybody.

'What really wonderful champagne,' said Sir Conrad.

'I'm so glad you like it.' The Captain was pouring out two sorts of wine, a Krug 1928 for some and an Ayala for others. This had nothing to do with meanness; he really could not bear to see the bright, delicious drops disappear into a throat that would as soon receive any other form of intoxicant. There were many such throats among them on this occasion.

Presently those members of the Crew who had been engaged upon the more mechanical jobs at the theatre began to arrive. They looked very much alike, and might have been a large family of sisters; their faces were partially hidden behind curtains of dusty, blonde hair, features more or less obscured from view, and they were all dressed alike in duffle coats and short trousers, with bare feet, blue and rather large, loosely connected to unnaturally thin ankles. Their demeanour was that of an extreme sulkiness, and indeed they looked as if they might be on the verge of mutiny. But this appearance was quite misleading, the Captain had them well in hand; they hopped to it at the merest glance from him, emptying ash-trays and bringing more bottles off the ice. The Royal George, if not always a happy ship, was an intensely disciplined one. Like the Indian, however, the Crew added but little to the gaiety of the party. They sat in silent groups combing the dusty veils over their faces and thinking clever thoughts about *The Book of the It*, *The Sheldonian Synthesis*, *The Literature of Extreme Situations*, and other neglected masterpieces.

The Captain was very much struck by Grace with her French name and Paris clothes, a year old, but all the easier for that on an English eye. He knew about the General de Valhubert killed at Friedland because this General had been a great friend, indeed one of the few known friends, of General Chaderlos de Laclos. He took Grace to his library and showed her what he said was his greatest treasure, General de Valhubert's own copy of *Les Liaisons Dangereuses*. It was bound in red morocco with the Valhubert coat of arms, a stag and a rose tree, and the General had written a sort of journal, or series of notes, during one of his campaigns, all over the margins. It was a collector's piece of rare interest. That coat of arms, so familiar to Grace, who during her short and happy life in France had seen it every day on china, silver, carpets, books and linen, gave her a dreadful pang

'How strange. It must have been stolen from Bellandargues,' she said, looking sadly at the book.

'Thrown away, more likely. No respectable French family would have cared to have *Les Liaisons Dangereuses* lying about their house, in the nineteenth century.'

'Oh yes, that's it, of course. And then my husband always said they were really ashamed of the Marshal, though in another way pleased to have a Marshal of France in the family. All very complicated.'

'French people are complicated. Did you like the play?' he asked.

'Yes, though I like the real *Phèdre* better.' It was Charles-Edouard's favourite play, she remembered.

'The real *Phèdre* is wonderful poetry, but, as my friend Baggarat has shown us this evening, it is psychologically quite unsound. Racine's *Phèdre* has two psychological weaknesses—the first is that we can never believe in Hyppolite's love for Aracie, and the second we cannot understand why he should recoil in such horror from this fascinating woman who loves him.'

'Except that she was as old as the hills.'

'How do you know? My guess is that she was half-way between the ages of Thésée and Hyppolite, and still very attractive. But if Hyppolite was homosexual, everything is explained—he adores Hara-See the dancing boy, he loathes the idea of making love to a woman. I think my friend Baggarat has done a very fine piece of work, valuable for the future of the theatre.'

Grace was impressed. She liked the Captain very much, she liked his jolly, careless, piratical look, she thought his house most original and charming, and she was quite prepared to like the Crew. But the Crew despised her and made no effort to conceal the fact. They could not be the clever girls they were without seeing life a little bit through Marx-coloured spectacles, and to them Grace was the very personification of the rich bourgeoisie. They despised the rich bourgeoisie. Her presence in the house made them uneasy; superstitious, it was as though Jonah had come aboard the Royal George.

They sat in a sulky, silent group, combed their hair over their faces and watched the Captain through it. To their distress they saw that he was putting himself out to be as agreeable to Grace as if she had been Panayotis Canellopoulos in person. Why? What could he see in this spineless creature, who, unable to get on with her husband, had run back to her father like a spoilt child? When the various members of the

Crew had been unable to get on with their husbands they had struck proudly out on their own, taken rooms near the Deux Magots, hitch-hiked to Lithuania, or stowed away to the Caribbean. She was the sort of woman, with no self-respect, whom they positively execrated. They combed and watched, but if they harboured mutinous thoughts, they still hopped to it at a look from the Captain. In those days it seemed unthinkable that actual rebellion should ever break out on that ship while that Captain was at the helm.

The Captain soon fell in love with Grace, if that can be called love which has nothing physical in its composition. He was not attracted to her physically, she was too clean, too tidy, and too reserved for him; impossible to conceive of cuddling, or rumpling Grace. Her stiff Paris dresses, lined with buckram and padded petticoats, in themselves precluded such cosy goings on. He could not even imagine her sitting on his lap. But in every other way he loved her; he loved her elegance, her sad, romantic look, and the serious attention which she bestowed upon everything he said. Above all he loved his own mental picture of what life with her would be like if they were to marry. He imagined a small eighteenth-century villa not too far from London, where great luxury would prevail. Large, delicious, regular meals would arrive with no effort to himself, none of the expense of spirit which it cost him to keep Phaedra up to the mark; he would have a gentleman's library, a first-class cellar, intellectual friends would come and stay, he would be able to chuck the Royal George and write a masterpiece. Later, when Sir Conrad was dead, they would live at beautiful Bunbury. Sex would not play much part in all this. The French husband, it was to be hoped, would have satisfied her in that respect for ever, and after all people could live together very happily without it. He knew many cases. They would just have to sublimate their sexual desires, it was really quite easy.

Grace, too, had made a mental picture of what marriage with the Captain would be like, as women always do when they become aware that a man's thoughts have turned in that direction. Her picture was not so very different from his. As with his, sex was left out. They would live together like brother and sister, she thought, a long, quiet, cultivated life. She saw them as the Wordsworths, in a larger, warmer house, nearer to London and without Coleridge; as Charles and Mary Lamb without the madness; as Mr. and Mrs. Carlyle without the liver attacks. Visits to Paris came into this picture, since she could not imagine life always away from France, and revenge of some sort on Charles-Edouard for making her so very unhappy. She began to see a great deal of the Captain, whose intentions became increasingly clear.

Sir Conrad was not enthusiastic about either of his possible sons-in-law as such. Hughie was a nice, good creature, of course, but so boring, with his political pretensions. Sir Conrad thought that politics should be transacted, lightly, by clever men, and not ponderously by stupid ones. The Captain, whose company he very much enjoyed, seemed to him altogether too bohemian for marriage.

'Don't you think,' he said to Mrs. O'Donovan, 'that there may still be a chance of her marrying Charles-Edouard again? They both adore the boy, surely it's only reasonable to think that they ought to make some sacrifices on his account. After all, so little is wanted—a little discretion from Charles-Edouard and a little toleration from Grace. Mind you, it all depends on Grace. I happen to know that Charles-Edouard would take her back tomorrow, he still wants her.'

'It all depends,' said Mrs. O'Donovan rather severely, 'on Grace taking a more Christian view of the duties of a wife. I have been able to forgive her behaviour up to now on account of the shock she must have received, but she has got over that. She is certainly planning to marry again, and is making up her mind whether it shall be Hughie or the Captain. This ceremony, if you can call it that, in a registry office naturally meant nothing to her and marriage as a sacrament is quite outside her experience.'

'Yes, well, you're a Papist, Meg, so that's how you look at it. I think it all comes from a sort of silly pride. Anyhow it's most exceedingly tiresome. That wretched Carolyn with her mania for sight-seeing. I never could stand her, even as a child. The sort of woman who always manages to put her foot in it. Well she managed that time to some tune, it's enough to make you cry. Just when everything was going like a marriage bell. Grace was so happy with Charles-Edouard, and furthermore so happy, which is rare for an Englishwoman, living in Paris. She loved it.'

'Is that rare?' she said with a sigh. 'I know I should love it.'

'Most English people hate living in France. I always think it's got a great deal to do with French silver. They don't realize it's another alloy, they think that dark look means that it hasn't been properly cleaned, and that makes them hate the French. You know what the English are about silver, it's a fetish with them. I've so often noticed it. In the other war the silver at Bombon used to put up the backs of all our generals; they never could talk about anything else after a meal there with old Foch.'

'I like that rich, dark silver,' said Mrs. O'Donovan.

But then she liked everything French, indiscriminately and unreasonably, and her life in England, though it was all she had ever known, seemed to her a perpetual exile, so insistent was the beckoning from over the Channel.

CHAPTER IX

GRACE, called to the telephone in the middle of a rubber of bridge at Yeotown, came back and said to Hughie, 'Most mysterious—Sigi and Nanny have arrived in London. I think I must go back.'

'Don't do that. I'll send the motor for them. They'll be here by dinner-time.'

Dinner had begun when the little boy burst into the room and threw himself into his mother's arms, saying, 'D'you know what, Mum—I rode on a cheval de Marly.'

'No!'

'Yes I did—look!' He fished some very tattered newspaper cuttings out of one pocket, but somehow forgot to fish a letter from Charles-Edouard out of another. Charles-Edouard had written coldly but clearly stating that, in his view, it was their absolute duty to their child to re-marry as soon as possible. He had done so without much hope of moving Grace, but he wanted her to know quite definitely, to read in black and white, his views on the subject, and to make it clear that their continued estrangement was her own responsibility.

'My darling Sigi—however did you get up there? But first say how d'you do please to Mr. and Mrs. Fawcett and Hughie, and thank Hughie very very much for sending his motor. No—you don't kiss people's hands in England.'

'Please always kiss mine,' said Mrs. Fawcett. 'I love it, Sigismond.'

'Don't muddle him, Virginia, he must learn the difference.'

'Well, Mummy, I got up a ladder the workmen had left. Papa allowed me to and then he went home and left me there, and I rode for ages, it was so lovely up in the sky, and there was an enormous crowd to see me and I recited to them. Well first I said the words, that was for Papa, then we had "Waterloo, morne plaine", then we all sang "Les voyez-vous", and then the pompiers came and we had the "Marseillaise", all the verses, then they carried me down and took me home.'

'I never heard such a thing,' said Grace, with a look at Hughie which clearly said, 'Now what? We can never compete with this.' 'Ask Hughie if you may dine here with us as a great great treat.'

'Wouldn't be any treat at all in Paris, I always dine with Papa and have a glass of Bordeaux and 100 francs if I can tell the vintage.'

'You can have a glass of Bordeaux here,' said Hughie, 'only we call it claret, and half a crown if you can tell the vintage.'

He poured it out.

'Quite an honourable wine,' said Sigi, 'but not grand cru. I can only tell when it's grand cru.'

This remark having gone down, he saw, rather badly, Sigismond settled to a hearty meal.

Presently Hughie said to him, 'What do you do all day in Paris, Sigi?'

'In Paris,' said Sigi, 'I have two great friends. One is Madame Novembre de la Ferté, who gives me treats, allows me to drive her motor, and so on, and the other is Madame Marel, who gives me my lessons. They both give me very very expensive presents.'

'But doesn't M. l'Abbé give you your lessons any more?'

'He did for a while, but he's gone away. So now I have lessons with Madame Marel. I like it far better. I know masses of poetry by heart and we go to the jardin des plantes.' Sigi was curling up bits of his hair with one hand. 'And what d'you think we saw the turtles doing? Yes, but it wasn't her fault, they only do it once every three years—bad luck really. You ought to have heard them bellowing.'

'Well,' said Hughie, 'that doesn't amount to much. You've ridden a stone horse and driven a car—which you'll do every day of your life when you're grown up—and learnt poetry and heard turtles bellowing.'

'They weren't only bellowing,' said Sigi. 'Expensive presents, too—and a ball.'

He spoke very crossly. He was tired after the journey, more than half-asleep, and felt that he had not done himself justice or made it sufficiently clear that nobody in Paris could think of anything from morning till night but how best to keep him amused. However he was re-assured by Hughie's next words.

'What about learning to ride a real horse so that you can go hunting next winter?'

'O.K. Can I begin tomorrow?'

'No. Tomorrow is Sunday. You can begin on Monday.'

Grace left Sigi in the dining-room and went up to see Nanny.

'High time we did get back, in my opinion. Such goings on, dear. The Marquee does spoil him—oh he does, lets him do anything he says. That Madam November too and that Madam Marel—they fill his head with the most unsuitable ideas between them. Did he tell you about the ball?'

'He did say something. He's half-asleep, I think.'

'You'll hear it all, no doubt. I never saw such an exhibition in my life, those poor little mites, in ridiculous clothes for children (though I must say Sigi looked sweet) kept up I believe, some of them, till six in the morning. Nanny Dexter and I—the servants didn't want to let us in, but we weren't having any of that—we went and fetched our two away quite early on. Sigi was sound asleep, but poor little Foss, oh he was sick. I wish you could have seen the stuff he kept on bringing up. She hasn't got his little tummy right yet. The usual rush over the packing, of course, and nobody to meet us at Victoria, dear.'

'But, Nanny, nobody knew you were coming.'

'There now. The Marquee said he'd rung up and everything was arranged—oh well, French you know!'

Sigismond was very sleepy indeed, but not too sleepy to burn his father's letter to his mother in the empty nursery grate, with a match he had brought upstairs with him on purpose, while Nanny was running his bath.

The fact that Hughie now began to pay court to Sigismond just as, in Paris, Albertine and Juliette had paid court, and with the same end in view, that of becoming his step-parent, was clear as daylight to the little boy. Like his mother he had been quite doubtful whether the high level of amusement to which he had lately become accustomed could be maintained in England. Greatly to his surprise he found that it was positively surpassed. It so happened that Sigi had a natural aptitude for all forms of sport, and therefore very much enjoyed practising them. Hughie, an excellent athlete, gave up hours a day to coaching him; he played tennis, squash, and cricket with him, and taught him to ride. So of course Sigi loved being at Yeotown and very much approved of Hughie, whose stock, in consequence, soared with Grace. Visits to Yeotown became more and more frequent and prolonged, and very soon Sigi was quite ready to consider Hughie as an auxiliary papa. He realized that his mother could never have put on such a good show by herself.

Hughie said to Grace, 'This child must go to Eton—I'm sure they'd make a cricketer of him. Seems waste of excellent material for him to go to some French school where they do nothing but lessons.'

'But he was never put down for it,' said Grace.

'I can fix that, I'm sure. A word with Woodford. The boy is exceptional, you see.'

'Oh dear, I wonder whether Charles-Edouard would allow it. He did once seem to think of it, I remember.'

'It's my opinion that child can do anything he likes with his father. If he wants to go he'll go, it all depends on that.'

Hughie was one of those to whom Eton is bathed retrospectively in a light that never was on land or sea. He talked much of it to Sigi, who began to imagine himself as Captain and Keeper of this and that, and inclined very favourably to the idea. At last Hughie suggested that the three of them might go down for the day, take out his own nephew, Miles Boreley, and let Sigismond have a look round.

'We'll go down next Thursday, I'll ring up Miles's tutor now and arrange it. Once the child has seen it for himself the thing's a foregone conclusion—there'll be no holding him—he'll be as good as there.'

Miles Boreley was a sad little boy. He stood waiting for them at the Burning Bush, top hat crammed on to large, red ears, mouth slightly open, large, red hands hanging down. Though very plain, he had a disquieting look of his handsome uncle Hughie. They left the motor and walked with him towards Windsor. He said he had engaged a table for luncheon at a restaurant there.

It was one of those summer days when the cold of the Thames valley eats into the very bone, though the boys who slouched about the street with no apparent aim in view, looking like refugees in a foreign town, did not seem to notice it. Sigi's bright little eyes, which missed nothing, darted from one to another. He was amazed by their archaic blacks, clothes and general air of ill-being. Hughie, bathed in the light that never was, glanced at him from time to time, wondering if the magic had already begun to work. Had he known his Sigi better he would have been quite well aware that it had not. The corners of the mouth were drooping in a very tell-tale way.

They were shown their table in the restaurant and were settling themselves round it when Miles, looking with disfavour at the seat of his chair, asked if he could have a cushion. The waitress quite understood, and went off to get him one.

'Been in trouble, old boy?' said Hughie.

'Only been beaten by the library.'

'Bad luck. What for?'

'Changing the times sheet, as usual.'

'Oh I say, you shouldn't do that, you know.'

'You're telling me.'

'Beaten?' said Sigi. His blood ran cold.

'Yes, of course. Aren't you ever beaten?'

'Certainly not. I'm a French boy—I wouldn't allow such a thing.'

'What a sissy!'

'But do you like being beaten?'

'Not specially. But I shall like it all right when it's my turn to beat the others.'

Hughie said, 'When I got into the library I used to lay about me like Captain Bligh. I had a lot of leeway to make up—we'd had an awful time at m'tutor's from a brute called Kroesig. But I got my own back. How's the food this half, Miles?'

'Well you literally can't see it, there's so little. We buy everything at the sock shop now. M'tutor is married,' he explained for the benefit of Grace and Sigi, 'and Mrs. Woodford has got three children and a fur coat, all paid for by the housebooks, of course, and is saving up for more.'

'More children or more fur coats?'

'More of everything. She's literally the meanest miser you ever saw.'

'Yes, married tutors can be the devil,' said Hughie. 'Mine was a bachelor and I'm bound to say he never starved us, but m'dame used to steal our money.'

'Steal it!' said Grace. 'What a shame.'

'Well that's what we used to say. Rather like Miles and the fur coats, you know. These Eton rumours shouldn't be taken too seriously, they would none of them stand up to scientific investigation.'

Sigi looked relieved. 'What about the beating?' he said. 'Is that a rumour too?'

'Just take a look at my behind,' said Miles. 'I'll show you after. That will stand up to any amount of scientific investigation, as you'll see.'

A family party now came in. A woman, looking incredibly old to be the mother of children in their teens, was followed by two little girls and a stocky boy with a square of pink elastoplast on the back of his neck. They hurried through the restaurant and went upstairs.

Miles's mouth opened wider; he turned quite pink.

'Badger-Skeffington,' he said.

'No!' said Hughie, craning round to look. But they had disappeared.

'Badger-Skeffington!' said Grace, laughing hysterically. She was thinking that, wonderful as it seemed, some man must have gone to bed with that old lady only a few years before, since the youngest little girl was not more than twelve.

'What are you laughing at?' said Hughie.

'Such a funny name.'

'It may seem funny to you, but I can tell you, you haven't heard it for the last time. That boy is an extraordinary athlete; it's years since they've had such a boy there. Tell them, Miles.'

'Keeper of the Field, Keeper of Boxing, Captain of the XI. They'll be having a black-market lunch up there,' he said enviously. 'Badger-Skeffington's mother is a most famous black-marketeer.'

'Are you sure? She doesn't look a bit like that.'

'Didn't you notice how they were all weighed down with baskets and things? Tons of beefsteak. I expect, pots of cream, pounds of butter. That's why they go upstairs, so that nobody shall see what they are unpacking. They bribe the police with huge sums, it's well known.'

'Miles! I expect they have a farm.'

'So likely, in Ennismore Gardens. That's why Badger-Skeffington always wins everything—Daddy says he's literally full of food, like a French racehorse. They're nouveaux riches, you know.'

'Now hold on, Miles, that is not true. I often see Bobby Badger at my club, he's frightfully poor, it was a fearful effort to send the boy here at all, I believe.'

'Yes, I know, Uncle Hughie, the point is they are nouveaux riches and frightfully poor as well. There are lots like that here. Their fathers and mothers give up literally everything to send them.'

'Oh dear, how poor everybody seems to be, in England,' said Grace. 'It's too terrible when even the nouveaux riches are poor.'

'Yes, and while we are on the subject I would like to know exactly why it is they are all so stinking rich in France,' said Hughie stuffily. He was rich himself, but his capital seemed to be melting away at an alarming rate. 'It seems quite sinister to me.'

'Quite easy really. The French have always looked after their estates. They have foresters in their forests, not just gamekeepers, and their vineyards are a gold mine. In England, when I was a child anyhow, landed estates simply drained away the money—I remember quite well how my father and uncles used to talk as if it was a most tremendous luxury, owning land. There was never any idea of making it pay.'

'Hm,' said Hughie. Were he clever, like Albertine, had he the gift of the gab, like Heck, he would have been able, he thought bitterly, to prove to Grace the undoubted fact that the French are rich because they are wicked, while the English are poor because they are good. As he was neither clever nor gabby he was obliged to leave the last word with her. It was most annoying.

Some friends of Grace's now came in, accompanied by two charming little boys. They said 'hullo', looked with interest at Sigi, and went through to another room. 'See you later perhaps.'

'They look rather nice,' said Grace to Miles. 'Do you know them?'

'Who, Stocker?'

'Yes.'

'Yes, he's in my house.'

'Is he nice?' she persevered.

'He's just a boy.'

'Yes, I see. And the other?'

'The other one is a tug. We must only hope Badger-Skeffington doesn't see him. Badger-Skeffington is the scourge of the tugs.'

'What is a tug?' said Sigi.

'Somebody a bit brighter in the head than the rest,' said Grace, to tease Hughie. He was suddenly very much on her nerves. They had been too much lately at Yeotown, she thought, and decided they must have a few days in London, though no doubt Sigi would complain dreadfully at being dragged away from his riding and all the games.

After luncheon they went with Miles to his house, and there they followed him through a rabbit warren of passages and up and down little dark staircases. A deathly silence reigned.

'How empty it all seems,' said Grace. 'Where's everybody?'

'Having boys' dinner.'

'Very late.'

'Yes, well, it doesn't make much difference. Late or early there's literally nothing to eat.'

Miles's room, when they finally got to it, was extraordinarily bare and bleak. The walls were beige, the window curtains orange, and a black curtain hung from ceiling to floor in one corner. Over the empty fireplace there was a valedictory poem, illuminated and framed, on the closing of the Derby racecourse.

> There'll be no more racing at Derby
> It rings indeed like a knell, etc. etc.

It was terribly cold, colder than winter. Grace sat on the only chair, huddling into her fur coat, and the others stood round her as if she were a stove.

'Is this your bedroom?' Sigi said, taking in every detail.

'Yes, of course.'

'Is there a bed?' If he had been told that Miles slept on a heap of rags on the floor, like the concierges in Poland, he would not have been at all surprised.

'Here, of course,' said Miles scornfully. He lifted the black curtain to disclose an iron instrument against the wall. 'You pull it down at night, and the boys' maid makes it. And now, Uncle Hughie, if you'll excuse me, I must go off and do my time. Will you wait here or what?'

'I'm so terribly cold,' Grace said imploringly to Hughie. 'Couldn't we go home?'

'Well, rather bad luck on Miles when we've come to take him out. His time won't last more than three-quarters of an hour, you know.'

'Give him two pounds, he won't mind a bit,' she whispered.

'Oh I say, Uncle Hughie, thanks very much. Are you going, then?' he said, in tones of undisguised relief. 'Good-bye. Will you excuse me? —I shall be late.' He clattered away down the passage.

'Really, Grace—two pounds! I usually give him ten bob.'

'I'll go shares,' she said, 'put it on the bridge book. Worth it to me, I was dying of cold simply.'

The visit to Eton finished off Hughie's chances of marrying Grace for ever. Sigismond had seen a red light, and immediately took action.

'Mummy!'

'Hullo—you're early this morning!'

'Well yes, I've got something rather important to say. You know Hughie?'

'Yes.'

'Were you thinking of marrying him?'

'Why, darling?'

'The Nannies always say you will.'

'Would you like me to?'

'That's just the point. I would not.'

'Oh—Sigi——!'

'No use pretending, I would not.'

'Very well, darling. I promise I'll never marry anybody you don't

like. And now just go and tell Nanny to pack, will you? We're going up
to London after luncheon.'

Sigi gave his mother a nice hug and trotted off. He was not at all dissatisfied to find himself later in the day on the road back to London.
The riding and the games had been great fun, but if they were to lead to
the prison house, whose shades he had now seen for himself, they
simply were not worth it.

CHAPTER X

ALL this time the Captain had been going on with his pursuit of Grace,
and of course he too had seen that, if there were a way to her heart, that
heart so curiously absent, it would be through Sigismond.

'Bring him to *Sir Theseus* on Thursday afternoon,' he said.

'My dear Captain—is *Phèdre* very suitable for little boys?'

'Exquise Marquise, what about the Matinée Classique at the Français—is it not full of little boys seeing *Phèdre*?'

'All right then,' she said. It was a comfort to her to be with somebody
who knew about the Matinée Classique and other features of French
life. Hughie, in spite of all his efforts to educate himself in the Albertine
days, had never really got much further than the Ritz bar, and now his
love for everything French had turned to unreasonable hatred. Whenever Grace spoke to him of France he would say horrid little things
which annoyed her. Like many large, bluff and apparently good-
natured men, Hughie had a malevolent side to his character, and knew
exactly how to stick a pin where it hurt. He was always exceedingly
catty about the Captain, who spoke, however, rather charmingly of him.

'Why does he hate her so much?' asked Sigi, as Hyppolitus recoiled
in homosexual horror before the advancing Phaedra.

'Because she's his stepmother.'

'Oh. If Papa married Madame Marel would she be my stepmother
and would I hate her?'

'Sh—darling, don't talk so loud, it's rude to the actors.'

She couldn't very well have said it was disturbing to the audience. A
beautiful, hot day, one of the very few that summer, had not been helpful in filling the Matinée Classique with little scholars of modern
psychological drama, and the theatre was empty. Three or four members of the Crew sat about, balefully watching Grace through their
hair; the Captain, who always said he preferred to see his plays from
the back of the gallery, an excellent alibi, was having a guilty sun-bath
on the roof of his house.

'Mum?' Sigi was wriggling about, bored.

'Yes?'

'Where's Hyppolitus's own mummy?'

'I'm not sure, I think she's dead, we must ask the Captain.'

'Mummy? Sir Theseus what?'

'You must ask the Captain that too.'

'Well—what's happened to Hyppolitus now?'

'Darling, try and pay attention. Didn't you hear Theramenus saying how he had fallen off his bicycle and been run over by a lorry?'

'Coo! Phaedra is upset and no mistake.'

'Don't say coo. I'm always telling you.'

'Mummy, why has Sir Theseus adopted Hara-See?'

'I suppose he feels rather lonely, now everybody seems to be dead.'

'Will he have to make over some of his money to Hara-See?'

'I don't know. Here's the Captain, you must ask him.'

The Captain took them backstage and showed them the machinery, switchboard, and so on, all of which interested Sigi a great deal more than the play. After this he was allowed the run of the Royal George, to the displeasure of the younger members of the Crew, who had seen through their hair exactly how the land lay. Phaedra, however, took a great fancy to Sigi and spoilt him.

The Captain's courtship, meanwhile, was not making much real progress. He was hampered in it by Grace's failure to attract him sexually, by a shyness and feeling of discomfort in her presence that he never seemed to get over. While it may be possible to do without sex in married life, he began to realize that it is very difficult actually to propose to a beautiful young woman without ever having had any physical contact with her. A little rumpling and cuddling bridges many an awkward gulf. In fact it now seemed to him as if the impossibility of cuddling Grace was endangering his whole heavenly scheme. He blamed her bitterly for it. Why should she be so stiff and remote? Why not unbend, make things easier for him? It was very hard. He had thought so much, during many a wakeful night, of all that marriage with her would bring. The laurels of Madame Victoire, the griffins and castles of Madame de Pompadour, the dolphins and the fleur-de-lis; Château Yquem, Chambolle-Musigny, Mouton Rothschild. He could feel, he could see, he could taste them. Sometimes he thought that he would break down and cry like a child if all this and much more were to elude his grasp, simply because of his inability to grasp the waist of Grace.

Nothing was going well for the Captain at this time. Subscriptions to the Royal George were falling off at a disquieting rate, various creditors were pressing their claims, *Sir Theseus* could obviously not be made to run much longer, and, worst of all, the Crew was in a chronic bad temper. Only old Phaedra was nice to him now, but her varicose veins had got worse and the doctor said she must give up the kitchen while she was playing this long and arduous role. So he was at the mercy of the others for his comforts, and they gave expression to their feelings through the medium of housework. Smash and burn were the order of the day. His home life had never been so wretched.

It now became imperative to find another play with which to replace *Sir Theseus*. The Crew pushed their hair out of their eyes and read quantities of manuscripts, many of them in the original Catalan, Finnish, or Bantu, and wrote résumés of them for the Captain to see. He had told them, and indeed in their hearts they knew it, that this time they must put on something which would sell a few seats. 'For once,' he said, 'try and find a play with a plot. I believe that would help. Something, for once, that the critics could understand.'

One bright spot in the Captain's life just then was how well he was getting on with Sigismond. The little boy hung about the theatre, thoroughly stage-struck and told his mother, who of course repeated it, that he revered the Captain second only to M. l'Abbé.

The Captain, on his side, was entranced. Knowing as he did no children of that age, Sigi appeared to him a perfect miracle of grace and intelligence. He kept begging to be given a part in a play, and the Captain thought that, if something suitable could be found, it would be from every point of view a good idea. The child had received a great deal of publicity for having ridden the cheval de Marly, he was very pretty, possibly very talented, and the whole thing would bring the Captain into continual contact with Grace. Sitting with her in his box on the first night, both feeling rather emotional, it might suddenly become possible for him to take her hand, to press her knee, even to implant a kiss on a naked shoulder when nobody was looking.

Now it so happened that a certain member of the Crew had been teasing the Captain for quite a long time to put on a play she had translated from some Bratislavian dialect, and of which the protagonist was a little boy of ten. The Captain had read her translation, which, he thought, probably failed to convey the fiery poetry and political subtleties of the original. In English it seemed rather dreary. But now this play was being very much discussed on the Continent. It was put on in Paris, where it had a mixed reception, and was said to have run clandestinely for several months in Lvov. The Captain, with Sigi in mind, decided to have another look at it.

It was called *The Younker*. An old Communist, whose days had been spent wringing a livelihood from the bitter marsh land round his home, lay on his bed, ageing. He lay alone because, so ungovernable was his temper, no human dared approach him. His dog, a famous mangler, lay snarling by the empty hearth. His only son had married a foreign Fascist woman; for this he had turned him out. The son had gone to the foreign Fascist woman's land and there had died. The old man kept his savings in gold in a pot under his bed, and it came upon him that he would like to give this pot, before he died and before the Party got it, to his son's son, and that he would like to see this child before his old eyes failed. The younker arrived. He was a manly little fellow, not at all awed by his grandfather's ungovernable rages, or by his grand-father's dog, the mangler. Indeed he went everywhere with his little hand resting on its head. He brought love into that house, and presently he brought his mother, the Fascist woman, and she made the bed, which had never been made before. And by degrees this child, this innocent, loving little creature, bridged even the great political gap between his mother and his grandfather. They joined a middle-of-the-road party and all ended in happiness.

The Captain began to see possibilities in this play if it could be altered and adapted according to an idea he had, and put on with Sigi in the name part. The great difficulty would be to get round the Crew; if only he could achieve that he foresaw a box-office success at last.

He called a conference on the stage after the Saturday matinée. The Crew sat about in high-necked sweaters, shorts, and bare, blue feet, their heads bowed and their faces entirely obscured by the curtain of hair. Though he did not know it, they were in a dangerous mood. They had hardly set eyes on the Captain of late, either at home or in his theatre; he had been, they knew, to many parties, in rich, bourgeois houses, with Grace. Rumour even had it that he had been seen in Sir Conrad's box at the Ascot races. None of this had done him much good with his Crew.

The Captain began by saying that it was quite essential for the Royal George to have a monetary success. If it did not, he pointed out, they would no longer be able to satisfy their serious public with plays that they alone were brave enough to produce. They would, in fact, be obliged to shut their doors and put out their lights and close, leaving a very serious gap in the intellectual life of London. The Crew knew that all this was so. They sat quite still listening. The Captain went on to praise Fiona very highly for her translation of *The Younker*. He said he had been re-reading it, that it was very good, that he thought it would do. He then branched off into a disquisition on the psychology of audiences through the ages.

'The two greatest dramatists of the modern world,' he said, 'are Shakespeare and Racine.'

There was no sign of life from the figures round him; faceless and dumb, bowed immovably over their bare, blue feet, they waited for him to go on. The Captain knew that had he said Sartre and Lorca there would have been some response, a tremor, perhaps, parting the silky blonde curtains, or a nodding of the veiled heads. No such tremor, no such nodding, occurred. He began to feel nervous, to wonder whether he was going to fail in what he was attempting. But he had never failed, as yet, to master his Crew, and he thought all would be well.

'Now Shakespeare and Racine,' he went on, nervously for him, 'understood the psychology of the playgoer, and they both knew that there are two things that audiences cannot resist. The first (and if we are to take a lesson from these great men, as I think we should, this will give scope to Ulra when designing her set) is the appeal of the past. The second, I am afraid, discloses a weakness in human nature, a weakness which exists as strongly today as it did in the seventeenth century. Not to put too fine a point on it, audiences like a lord. Shakespeare knew what he was about, that can't be denied. You'll hardly find a single commoner in Shakespeare's plays, and when they do occur he doesn't even trouble to invent names for them. 1st gravedigger, 2nd soldier, and so on. You'd think he might have written some very penetrating studies of the burghers of Stratford, he must have had plenty of copy. Not a bit. Kings and lords, queens and ladies make up his dramatis personae. Webster the same. And who's to say they're wrong? "I am Duchess of Malfi still" makes us cry. "I am Mrs. Robinson still" wouldn't be at all the same thing.'

The Crew did not raise a titter at this joke, and the Captain had an uneasy feeling it had probably been made before. He hoped he was not losing his grip, and hurried on.

'As for Racine, his heroes and heroines are usually Imperial.

'Now I say that what was good enough for the Globe and the Théâtre Royal is good enough for the Royal George. Supposing, Fiona dear, that you were to rewrite The Younker, to set it in an English country house in the nineties, to change the violent old Communist into a violent old Earl? Write the part of the boy for our adorable little Sigismond—he should prove a tremendous attraction. If you do all this, as only you can, Fiona, if Ulra makes a really amusing set for it—a Victorian castle, Ulra, in the Gothic style, lace collar, velvet suit for the Younker—I think I can prophesy certain success. I think we could count on six months with the house packed. After that we shall be able to go on with what we are trying to do in this theatre, don't be afraid that I've lost sight of that. I won't keep you now,' he looked at his watch, 'I have to go to London, but I will be home for dinner.' They always dined after the evening performance in the Captain's house. 'We can talk it over then——'

Not a movement, the curtained figures sat as in a trance. He did not quite like it, but was not seriously alarmed; he had weathered too many a storm in that ship with that Crew, those hearts of oak.

When the Captain arrived home rather late for dinner the house was in darkness, and empty as the Marie Céleste. There were signs of recent human activity, a meal had evidently just been eaten and not cleared away, but nobody was there.

The Captain supposed that his Crew must have gone on shore. They sometimes did so of an evening and always, on these occasions, left some delectable titbit sizzling in the oven for him. But the kitchen was in darkness, the oven cold and bare. He peered into the bedroom usually occupied by Ulra to see if a sulking figure were not perhaps lolling on the bed. If so it must be stirred up, made to minister to his needs. Not only was there no sulking figure, but nylon hairbrush and broken comb had vanished from the dressing-table, crumpled underclothes no longer brimmed from half-open drawers, duffle coats and ragged ball dresses no longer bulged behind the corner curtain, there were no old shoes lying about on the deal floor and no old hats on the deal shelf. Ulra had clearly gone, and taken all her belongings. Down in the Port Royal, up beneath the Toits de Paris, the same state of affairs existed in every bedroom. The Captain's heart sank within him. This was desertion. Mutiny he could have dealt with, his dreaded cat o' nine tails, sarcasm, had but to be seen by the Crew for them to come to heel, but desertion was far more serious. They had almost certainly, he knew, gone off in a body to join the staff of Neoterism.

The Captain passed a sleepless night, during which he decided that there was only one course left for him to take. He must go and see Grace and persuade her to marry him. Not a bad thing, perhaps, to do it on an impulse, though he would have preferred to lead up to it with the triumphant success on the boards of Sigismond. He must try and whirl her to a registry office before either she or he had any more chance of thinking it over. Thinking it over was no good now, the time had come for action. Breakfastless, feeling rather sea-sick, the Captain set out for Queen Anne's Gate.

Now it so happened that on this particular day Grace had woken up sadder and more hopeless than at any time since leaving Paris. Her divorce had just become absolute, and she had finished her carpet. She had made a sort of bet with herself that before these two things happened there would have been a sign from Charles-Edouard; none had come. The weather, which always affected her spirits, remained terrible, as it had been so far the whole summer. Day after day it was a question of putting on winter clothes and crowning them, for no other reason than that the month was June, with a straw hat, through which the cold wind whistled horribly. She was putting on one of these hats to go out to a dull luncheon when her maid came in and said that the Captain was downstairs. This news cheered her up.

'Give him a glass of vodka—I'm just coming.'

The Captain was already pouring vodka down his throat in great gulps like a Russian and feeling much more confident that all would yet be well. The door opened, and, instead of Grace, Sigismond appeared.

'Good morning, Old Salt,' he said, too cockily for a child of his age the Captain thought, irritated. He must get rid of him, he had got to see Grace alone while the action of the vodka on his doubly empty stomach (no dinner, no breakfast) was having its excellent effect.

'And when do I go into rehearsal, Cap?'

This was too much for the Captain's nerves. He took Sigi by the shoulder, propelled him to the door, gave him a sharp push and said,

'It's your Mummy I want to see, not you. Run along to Nanny, there's a good boy.'

Sigi gave him a very baleful glance. Aware that he had done himself no good, the Captain felt about in his pocket. He had a shilling and a fiver, and if one seemed too little the other seemed immeasurably too much. He fished out the shilling, which Sigi pocketed without a word, going furiously upstairs. Nobody had ever insulted him with so small a coin in his life before.

Grace appeared. She looked very pretty and was pleased to see the Captain, quite approachable, he thought. He took the plunge.

'I've come on an impulse, to ask you to marry me, Grace.'

'Good heavens, Captain!'

'I suppose you think I ought to lead up to it, pave the way, break it like bad news. I don't. We're both grown-up people, and I think if I want to marry you the easiest thing is to say so straight out.'

'Yes, I expect you're quite right.'

'And please don't think it over. I hate the sort of people who are for ever thinking things over, horrid, calculating thoughts. Say yes now—and I'll go off and get a licence.'

Grace was seriously tempted to do so. She was feeling furious with Charles-Edouard, with his attitude of 'come back whenever you like but don't expect me to bother about you, or make it any easier for you', and with his manner of conveying it to her, indirectly, through Sir Conrad. Why did he never telephone, write, or make any direct approach? It was intolerable. She felt it would punish him if she were to marry the Captain, brilliant, sparkling, friend of Paris intellectuals, much more than if she were to marry someone like Hughie. Hughie could only be a stopgap, the Captain might well be a great new love.

'I don't want to think it over,' she said, 'but I shall have to consult Sigismond.'

The Captain was very much taken aback. 'Consult Sigi?'

'Oh Captain, if Sigi didn't like it I could never do it, you know. I've given him my word never to marry without asking him first.'

'It's mad. Little boys of that age change their ideas every few minutes—he might say yes one day and no the next, it would mean nothing at all. According to whether—well for instance according to whether one had last tipped him with a shilling or five pounds. Sigi is very fond of me, you must have noticed that for yourself. I shan't turn out to be a Mr. Murdstone, I can assure you—I am good-natured and I love children. I tell you this, so it must be true. What people say about themselves is always true. When they say "Don't fall in love with me, I shall make you very unhappy" you must believe them, just as you must

believe me when I tell you that both you and Sigi will have happy lives
once you are married to me. Quiet, uneventful, but happy.'

'Oh I do, Captain, I do believe it. I've known it really for a long
time.'

As Grace said this she looked positively cuddlable, and the Captain
was about to press her to his bosom when she saw the time, gave a
tremendous jump, said she was half an hour late for luncheon already
and fled—shouting from the staircase 'Come back at tea-time.'

'Tell me something, Sigi. You love the Captain, darling, don't you?'

'Shall I tell you what I think of the Captain?'

'Yes, that's what I'm asking you.'

'I think he's a bloody bastard, so there.'

'Sigismond—go to bed this instant. Nanny—Nanny——' Grace was
running furiously upstairs, 'Please put Sigismond to bed without any
supper and without Dick Barton. I won't have it, Sigi, you're not to
speak of grown-up people like that, do you understand? Oh no, it's too
much,' and she burst into tears. She had quite made up her mind that
she was going to marry the Captain and now this consolation was to be
denied her.

Sigi, rather puzzled and very cross, received pains and penalties, but
he had hit his target first. That night the Captain left London, alone,
for France. The Royal George had gone down, without her crew complete. Her new owner, having repainted, furbished up, and rechristened
her, more in the spirit of the age, The Broadway, opened triumphantly
that autumn with a dramatization of *Little Lord Fauntleroy*.

CHAPTER XI

MADAME ROCHER DES INNOUÏS, as old ladies sometimes do, now
got an idea into her head, and decided that she would not rest until she
had seen it carried out. The idea was that Grace and Charles-Edouard
must be brought together again, must be married properly this time,
that Grace must be converted, that they must have more children, and
do their duty by the one they had already. The present situation had
become impossible. Charles-Edouard quite clearly had no intentions of
marrying any of the nice, suitable girls vetted and presented by his aunt,
and was now in trouble with half the husbands of Paris. Grace, according to information received by Madame Rocher through the French
Embassy in London, was contemplating remarriage with some very
unsuitable sailor, and the child was being outrageously spoilt on both
sides of the Channel. Bad enough that a Valhubert should be written

about and photographed in *Samedi Soir*, it now seemed that his mother contemplated putting him on the London stage, while Sir Conrad, whom Madame Rocher loved but whom she did not trust a yard, was no doubt initiating him into the terrible rites of Freemasonry. Charles-Edouard's heir was on the way to becoming a publicity-monger, an actor, and a Nihilist; what must poor Françoise be thinking?

Madame Rocher took action. She arrived in London to stay with the French Ambassador, sent for Grace, and weighed in at once with what she had to say.

'Grace, my child, it is your duty to return to Paris and marry Charles-Edouard. Picture this unfortunate man, lonely, unhappy, reduced to pursuing the wives of all his friends, forced to go to bed at the most inconvenient times, and always with the risk of his motive being misunderstood. He may find himself trapped into some perfectly incongruous marriage before we know where we are. Then think of your little boy, brought up like this between the two of you, no continuity in his education. Nothing can be worse for a child than these six months of hysterical spoiling from each of you in turn. You are very reasonable, Grace dear, surely you must understand where it is that your duty lies.

'I know the English are fond of duty, it is their great speciality. We all admire you so much for having no black market, but what is the good of no black market if you will not do your duty by your own family, Grace? Have you thought of that?'

Grace, sick to death of living alone, longing night and day for Charles-Edouard, was unable to conceal from Madame Rocher's experienced eye the happiness these words gave her, and that in her case duty and inclination were the same.

'But Charles-Edouard never asks me to go back,' she said. 'I'm always hearing from my father that he wants me, but I've never had a direct communication from him. It makes it rather difficult.'

Madame Rocher gave a sigh of relief. The day, she saw, was won.

'It is perhaps not so very strange,' she said. 'Charles-Edouard has never been left before by a woman. He fully understands the technique of leaving, one might say he has brought it to a fine art, but being left is a new experience. No doubt it puzzles him, he is not quite sure how to deal with it. Could you not take the first step?'

'Oh Tante Régine! Yes, perhaps. But then what about Juliette and Albertine?'

'Back to them again? You are behind the times, my dearest. Juliette is quite finished. But let's try and be sensible about it. Charles-Edouard was sleeping with you, I suppose?'

Grace became rather pink, but she nodded.

'Well then, that's all right. Why not look upon these others as his hobby? Like hunting or racing, a pursuit that takes him from you of an afternoon sometimes, amuses him, and does you no harm?

'There's another thing I wanted to tell you. Of course one never can say for certain, and people vary in this respect, but very often at Charles-Edouard's age a man does begin, all the same, to settle down with his own wife. If you go back to him it would not surprise me in the least to see a very different Charles-Edouard five or ten years from now.

'Tea with Albertine, yes I expect so, she is one whom people never quite get out of their systems, I'm afraid, and Charles-Edouard had her in his long before he ever met you. But the Juliettes of this world have their little day, it is soon over, and sometimes they are not replaced. I think Charles-Edouard is a particularly hopeful case because of the great love he has of his home. Consider the hours and the energy he expends on it, rearranging his furniture and pictures, adding to his collections, pondering over almost insignificant details of the lighting, and so on. Think how much he hates to leave it, even for a short holiday at Bellandargues or in Venice. He goes away, complaining dreadfully, for a month while the servants have their holiday and is back before the dust sheets are off.

'All this can be very much on your side if you can manage to make him feel that you are part of his home, its goddess, in fact. I had a cousin, a terrible Don Juan, whose wife retrieved him, really, with her knitting. She sat through everything with this eternal ball of wool and click of needles—how we used to mock at her for it. But it was not stupid. In the end it became a symbol to him I think, a symbol of home life, and he so turned to her again that when they were old he seemed never to have cared for anybody else. Could you not try to see this whole problem rather differently, Grace? More like a Frenchwoman and less like a film star?'

Grace felt that she could, and knew that she longed to, since this different vision was clearly essential if she were to go home to Charles-Edouard.

'Yes, Tante Régine,' she said. 'I will try, I promise you. But Charles-Edouard must come and fetch me.'

'Oh—that! I shall have a word with him, and I can promise he'll be here next week. So all is settled then—good. And now, when do I see my dear Vénérable?'

'Ah well, the Vénérable dies for you. He rang up the Embassy to find out your plans—it seems they are taking you to the Ballet tonight, so he hopes that you will dine with us tomorrow. He's out shopping this very moment, trying to find something fit to offer you.'

'Wearing his apron, no doubt. But please tell him not to trouble. I love your English cuts, sirloins and saddles—you see how I remember, and I haven't been here since 1914. I love them just as they are. That excellent roast meat, those steak and kidney puddings, what could be more delicious? At eight o'clock then tomorrow?' She kissed Grace most affectionately on both cheeks.

Grace went home, a warm feeling at her heart. Everything was going to be all right now, she knew.

The dinner party for Madame Rocher consisted of an M.P., Clarkely by name, member of the Anglo-French Parliamentary Committee, Sir Henry and Lady Clarissa Teazle, owner of one of the big Sunday papers and his wife, noted francophiles, and, of course, Mrs. O'Donovan. Madame Rocher arrived in full Paris fig. Her breasts were contained (but only just, it seemed that they might spring out at any moment, and then how to coax them back again?) in pale blue glass bubbles embroidered on yellow silk; her pale blue skirt, carved, as it were, out of hundreds of layers of tulle, was rather short, and when she sat down it could be seen that she wore yellow silk breeches also embroidered at the knee with bubbles. Mrs. O'Donovan and Lady Clarissa could not take their eyes off bosom and knees, and exchanged many significant glances.

'What a joy,' Madame Rocher cried effusively, 'to see dear Meg. Why do you never come to Paris now? I know more than one who still dies of love for you there. Nobody,' she said to the company at large, 'certainly no foreigner, has ever had so much success in Paris as Madame Audonnevent.'

All the English guests had been chosen because they spoke excellent French, but they did not get much opportunity to air this accomplishment, since Madame Rocher was determined to practise her English, and, furthermore, never drew breath the whole evening.

Her theme was the delight, the ravishment, the ecstasies into which she had been thrown by her two days in London.

'This morning,' she said, 'I got up at eight, and imagine! I was ready for the opening at nine.'

'The opening?'

'Of the shops. Oh those shops! I have already bought all my hats for the Grande Semaine.'

'No! Where?' said Mrs. O'Donovan, hoping for the name of a talented little French modiste, kept perhaps in some secret mews by the ladies of the French Embassy.

'My dear, can you ask? D. H. Heavens, of course—in the basement. I never saw such beauties—the straw! the workmanship! the chic! I have got Christmas presents for all my friends—how they will be thrilled—of your famous English scent, the Yardley—so delicious, so well presented, such chic bottles. Then all my cotillon favours for the bal des Innouïs at the Woolworth—oh the joy just to wander in the Woolworth. The very names of the shops are a poem—the Scotch House—I bought a hundred mètres of tartan to cover all my furniture, many country bérets, and a lovely fur bag, in the Scotch House, while as for the Army and the Fleet! The elegance! I shall come over once a month now for the elegance alone.

'At Oopers I ordered a new Rolls Royce, of cane-work—you see the chic of that. From time to time, when I get a little tired, for all this shopping does tire me rather, I go to the Cadena Café and order a café crème and sit very happily watching your English beauties. They are a refreshment to the eye. I notice how sensible they are, they scorn the demi-toilette, and quite right too, there is nothing worse. They come out with no make-up, hardly having combed their hair even, to do their shopping. Then, of course, they go home and arrange themselves properly. Now I admire that. All or nothing, how I agree.

'So I had no time for luncheon as you can imagine, but who cares when you can have a bun and a cup of tea? The afternoon I spent in fittings!'

'Fittings?' Mrs. O'Donovan and Lady Clarissa were stunned by this recital.

'Junior Miss, my dear. All my little dresses for the plage. Don't ask me what Dior will say when he hears of Junior Miss. I'd rather not think. No thank you, no wine—when I am in England I drink nothing but whisky.'

Mr. Clarkely, more interested in French politics than English elegance, began asking a few questions about the Third Force, saying that he had made friends, through his Committee, with many of the Ministers, but Madame Rocher merely cried,

'Don't talk to me of these dreadful people—they think of nothing, day and night, but their stomachs and their mistresses.'

'Really?' said Mr. Clarkely. 'Are you sure?' It had not been his impression at all.

'On what do you suppose they squander their salaries—those huge augmentations for which they are always and for ever voting?' (Madame Rocher would have complained very much if she had found herself compelled to dress on the amount annually earned by a French Minister.) 'Stomachs, dear sir, and mistresses. The vast sums that dreadful Dexter gives them for tanks and aeroplanes, what d'you suppose happens to them? My nephew, a commandant, tells me there are no tanks and no aeroplanes and hardly even a popgun. Why? Because, my dear sir, these sums are spent on the stomachs and the mistresses of your friends.'

Mr. Clarkely was very much surprised. 'Surely not so and so,' he said, mentioning a certain prominent Minister noted for his dyspeptic austerity of life and devotion to work.

'All—all! Don't mention their names or I shall have an attack! All, I tell you, all! They take the best houses to live in, they have fleets of motors, they spend the day eating and drinking, and all night the relays of mistresses are shown up the escalier de service. It has ever been so, but let me tell you that the scandals of Wilson and Panama, of the death of Felix Faure even, are nothing, but nothing, to what goes on today. Give us back our King, my dear sir, and then speak to me of politics,' she said, rather as if her King were kept a prisoner in the Tower of London. 'More whisky, Vénérable, I pray.'

Mrs. O'Donovan whispered to Mr. Clarkely, 'It's no use asking that sort of Frenchwoman about politics—ask me. I know a great deal more than she does.'

But Mr. Clarkely went to tea once a week at St. Leonard's Terrace and had been told what Mrs. O'Donovan knew already. He had hoped for something more directly from the horse's mouth.

'Is she really so royalist?' he turned to Grace. Madame Rocher was telling Sir Conrad her summer plans and begging him to go with her to Deauville, Venice, and Monte Carlo.

'Like all the Faubourg,' said Grace, 'she has a photograph of the King on her piano, but I don't think she'd raise a finger to get him back. My husband says the French hate all forms of authority quite equally.'

After dinner Madame Rocher took Sir Conrad aside, saying, 'And tell me, mon cher Vénérable, how goes the Grand Orient? You know,' she said, breathing a scented whisper (not Yardley's) into his ear, 'that I have designs on one of your adherents?'

'I am most glad to hear it,' he replied, delightfully drowning in the great billows of sex that emanated from her in spite of her seventy-odd years. 'Come in here a minute and we will discuss ways and means together.'

CHAPTER XII

MADAME ROCHER'S journey turned out not to have been really necessary. The night of Sir Conrad's dinner party Sigismond was very sick and feverish; in the morning the doctor came, and said he must have his appendix out at once. He was taken by ambulance to a nursing home to be prepared for the operation, deeply interested in the whole affair.

'Shall I die? And go to the Père Lachaise? And see l'Empereur, like in Le Rêve? Well, I forgive Nanny for everything. Can I see the knife? I shall have a scar now, like Canari! oh good! When are you going to do it?'

'Not until tomorrow morning,' said the nurse, 'and don't get so excited.'

'Better give him something to keep him quiet,' said the doctor, after which Sigi became intensely drowsy. Grace sat with him until evening when Nanny came, prepared to spend the night in the nursing home. As there seemed no point in them both being there and as Nanny insisted on staying, Grace went back to Queen Anne's Gate. Charles-Edouard was getting out of a cab just as she arrived.

It seemed quite natural to see him, she felt no embarrassment or constraint, and nor, quite obviously, did he.

'Ravi de vous voir, ma chère Grace,' he said, kissing her hand in his rapid way.

She opened the door with her key and they went into the house together.

'So how is he? And when is the operation? I was out when your father telephoned or I could have been here sooner.'

'It doesn't matter,' she said, 'he's been asleep more or less all day and the operation isn't till the morning. There's no danger, and no need to worry.' She sat down rather suddenly, feeling giddy.

'You look tired.'

'Yes. I was up most of the night, and I've been at the nursing home ever since without much to eat. I shall feel better after dinner.'

The butler came into the hall. He looked uncertainly at Charles-Edouard's bag, left it where it was and said, 'Sir Conrad won't be back from the House until late.'

'Perhaps we could have dinner at once then, please.'

Charles-Edouard was delightful at dinner; he told her all the Paris gossip.

'I'm so very pleased to see you,' he said from time to time, and towards the end of the meal, 'You don't know how much I've missed you.'

'Oh, Charles-Edouard, I've been ill from missing you.'

'I thought I would open Bellandargues this summer. Sigi can get over his operation there. Won't you come?'

'For a week-end?'

'For good. Let's go upstairs.'

They went up. When they got to the drawing-room Grace opened the door, but Charles-Edouard took her hand and pointed further up.

'Charles-Edouard, we can't. We're not married.'

'We never have been married,' he said.

They went together into her bedroom.

'But I think we had better be,' he said, later on, 'and properly this time. For the sake of the child.'

Grace repeated happily and sleepily 'For the sake of the child.' Then she woke up a little more and said, 'But why, Charles-Edouard, did you never make a sign? A whole year and no sign?'

'No sign? When you refused to see me although I'd come all the way from Paris—when you told Sigi nothing would induce you to speak to me on the telephone—when you never answered the long letter I gave him for you. No sign? What more could I have done?'

So then it all came out. All poor Sigi's major acts of iniquity and minor acts of trouble-making were revealed before the horrified gaze of his parents.

'We seem to have given birth to a Borgia,' said Charles-Edouard at last.

'Rubbish!' Grace said indignantly, 'he's a dear, affectionate little boy. The whole thing was entirely our own fault for leaving him too much alone when we were happy and depending too much on him when we were lonely. We've been thoroughly selfish and awful with the poor darling from the very beginning, I see it all now. He only did it because he loves us and wants to be with us. When we were together we left him out and made him jealous, so of course he thought the best plan would be to keep us apart.'

'It's terrible all this jealousy. First you and then the child. What am I going to do about it?'

'You must try to be nicer, Charles-Edouard.'

'I must anyhow try to be more careful.'

'One thing, he did stop us marrying anybody else.'

'Were we seriously considering such a step?'

'I was, twice.'

'How extraordinary. Confess you would never have amused yourself so much as you do with me.'

'Amusement is not the only aim of marriage,' said Grace primly.

'Are you quite sure?'

They decided never to let Sigi realize that they knew all, but to keep a firm look-out for any underhand dealings in the future.

When Sir Conrad got back, very late, he found Charles-Edouard's suitcase still in the hall, the drawing-room empty and dark. He nodded to himself, and went happily to bed.

Next morning Sigismond, still very much interested, was lifted on to a trolley, 'Like the pudding tray at the Ritz,' he said, and was wheeled away. The last thing he knew was the surgeon's enormous eye gazing into his.

The very next minute, or half a lifetime later, he opened his eyes again. He was back in his bed. He saw the nurse and smiled at her. Then he saw his father and mother. They were holding hands. His mother leant over him. 'How d'you feel, darling?' Suddenly the full significance of all this became hideously apparent. He shut his eyes again with a shudder.

'He's not quite round,' said the nurse, 'he hasn't seen you yet.'

'Oh yes I have,' said Sigi, 'and I'm going to be sick.'

As soon as Sigismond was well enough to travel they all left for Paris on the Golden Arrow, complete with Nanny, the usual mountain of luggage, and Grace's carpet, a huge roll done up with straps.

'It will do for your bedroom at Bellandargues,' said Charles-Edouard.

'I meant it for your bedroom in Paris.'

But Charles-Edouard raised his hand, shook his head, and said, very kindly but firmly, 'No.'

Madame Rocher, who was already back in Paris and delighted by this turn of events, rang up Charles-Edouard the day before their journey. 'I've got Fr. Lanvin,' she said, 'he'll marry you on Thursday morning at eleven, and then Grace must be converted by him. He's far the best and quickest, he did the Princesse de Louville in no time.'

But Albertine, whom Charles-Edouard rang up to make quite sure that all Paris should know the facts of the case, begged him to go to her priest. 'Fr. Lanvin is quite all right, I'm sure, but I think you need somebody of a different calibre. Fr. Strogonoff is so gentle and understanding, and then he specializes in foreign converts——'

'Yes, I'm sure, Albertine, but you see my aunt has made the appointment now, I think we'd better keep it. We can always change, if Grace doesn't like him.' Grace thought it was just the way people go on about their dentists.

'What?' said Charles-Edouard, still on the telephone. 'No! Are you sure?'

He was listening with all his ears. Grace could hear Albertine's voice, quack, quack, quack, down the receiver, but could not hear what she was saying. Charles-Edouard seemed entranced by whatever it was.

'Oh how interesting. Go on. Yes. What a sensation! Don't you know any more? Don't cut off—wait while I tell Grace. The Dexters,' he said to Grace, 'have flown to Russia. They've been Communist spies from the very beginning, and they've gone. It will be in the papers tomorrow. Salleté has just told Albertine the whole story. Well then, Albertine dearest, good-bye, and we'll count on you Thursday at eleven. Saint Louis des Invalides. Nobody at all except Tante Régine and my father-in-law. Good-bye.'

'So——!' said Grace, all agog.

'Well, it seems the Americans have been rather suspicious of your friend Heck for quite a long time. At last they had enough evidence to arrest him—he must have got wind of it and he flew to Prague the day before yesterday. The latest information is that he has turned up in Moscow.'

'And Carolyn?'

'With Carolyn and little Foss.'

'Rather a comfort,' said Grace, 'to think that little Foss won't be ruling the world after all.'

'Rather a comfort,' said Charles-Edouard, 'to think that we shall never have to listen to Hector's views on anything again.'

'Poor Carolyn, will she like living in Russia? One thing, the Russians can't get on her nerves more than the French used to. So I was quite right, you see, she was a Communist at school. No wonder she got so cross when I reminded her.'

'And it seems that his real name is Dextrovitch.'

'He told me his mother was a Whale.'

'She was. His father, Dextrovitch, became an American just before he was born. They say they have evidence now that Hector has been a Bolshevist all his life, his father brought him up to be one. It's a most interesting story really. The father saw his two brothers shot by the Tsarist police, he escaped to America, married this rich Whale, and had Hector.'

'Can you beat it?' said Grace. 'Where's Papa—do let's go and tell him.'

Of course the journey to Paris was greatly enlivened for Grace, Charles-Edouard and Nanny by the Dexter story, which now filled all the newspapers. Hector Dexter, it seemed, was worth at least ten atom bombs to the Russians. He had held jobs of the highest responsibility for years, had always been *persona grata* at the White House, where he knew his way about better than anybody except the President himself, had never been denied access to any information anywhere, and was one of the most brilliant of living men. Great stress was laid upon how deeply he was beloved by his countless friends (good old Heck) in London, Paris, and New York. Many of these refused to believe that he had gone to Russia of his own accord, but were quite certain that the whole family must have been kidnapped, putting forward as evidence that Carolyn had left her fur coat behind. 'I suppose they've never heard of Russian sables,' Charles-Edouard said when Grace read this out to him.

Asp Jorgmann and Charlie Jungfleisch were interviewed in Paris. 'Whatever Heck may have done,' they said, 'he remains a very very good friend of ours.'

But the French Ambassador to London, who was on the train and with whom Charles-Edouard went to sit for a while, told him that his American colleagues regarded it as worth quite a lot of atom bombs to be relieved of good old Heck's company for ever. 'He's supposed to have gone straight off for a conference with Beria. Well, I feel awfully sorry for Beria.'

'Perhaps he won't mind as much as we do; we're always told the Russians have no sense of time,' said Charles-Edouard.

'It does seem strange, dear, such a good daddy. And fancy Mrs. Dexter, too. What will Nanny Dexter say?'

'You must ring her up the very minute we arrive and see if she's still there.'

Sigi sat by his mother in a fit of deep sulks, his mouth down at the corners, his clever little black eyes roving to and fro like those of an animal cornered at last. When the train was nearly at Dover the clever little black eyes suddenly had their attention fixed. The Bunbury burglar was walking up the Pullman on his way, no doubt, to the Trianon bar. Charles-Edouard was asleep in his corner, and Grace half-asleep in hers.

'Where are you going, Sigi?' she said, as he slipped out of his seat.

'Just to stretch my poor scar.'

'Well don't be long, we're nearly at Dover. You'll be able to lie down on the boat,' she said, 'poor darling.'

He sidled off, and found his burglar alone in the bar, drinking whisky.

'Good Lord,' said the burglar. 'It's you! Where are you off to?'

'Paris. I'm a French boy, like I told you. And I'm going home with my father and mother, but leaving my appendix in London.'

'Oh dear. They ought to have given it you in a bottle.'

'Are you coming to Paris too?'

'I hope so. If nothing awkward happens on the way.'

Sigi got very close to him and said confidentially, 'Have you got anything you'd rather I carried through the Customs for you? My papa travels to and fro the whole time, they all know him, he never has anything opened.'

The burglar looked at him and said, 'Whose side are you on now?'

Sigi began twisting up his curls. 'On your side, like I was last time, if you remember, until you sausaged me. But although it was very treacherous, what you did, I do feel I owe you a good turn to make up for shutting you in the cupboard.'

'Mm,' said the burglar doubtfully. They were passing through Dover Town station, sea and cliffs were in sight, seagulls mewed, and passengers began to fuss.

'White horses,' said Sigi. 'Poor Nanny.'

At last the burglar said, 'All right. If you like to give me a hand with this.' He passed him a small leather writing-case.

'Coo!' said Sigi. 'Heavy, isn't it?'

'Heavy because full of gold.'

'Can I see?'

'No. We're arriving. Be a good boy, bring it to me on the boat, cabin 11, can you remember? Then I'll give you a bit for a keepsake.'

'Oh here he is. You shouldn't wander off like that, darling, we were quite worried.' The train stopped with a bump.

'What's that satchel, dear?' Nanny asked as they went towards the Customs shed.

'I'm looking after it for Papa——'

'That makes eighteen pieces then—I'd only counted seventeen. Where is that porter going?'

Charles-Edouard told Grace and Nanny to go on board. 'I'll see to the luggage.' He gave Grace their tickets. 'And it's cabin No. 7.'

'Eighteen pieces of luggage, sir.'

'Thank you, Nanny. Run along, Sigi.'

'No, no,' said Sigi, 'this is the part I enjoy.'

Charles-Edouard laughed and said to Grace, 'We saw some idiot taken away last time, for smuggling, I suppose he hopes for the best again.'

'I do. Very much indeed.'

A huge heap of luggage, mostly, of course, belonging to Sigi, was piled on to the counter in the Customs shed. Charles-Edouard stood by, with his back to the counter, talking to a friend who was in the Ambassador's party. They were both roaring with laughter still about the Dexters.

Sigi put his little writing-case on top of the other things and said, confidentially, to the Customs man, 'If I were you, officer, I would take a look inside that.'

'These all your things, sir?' The officer leant forward and spoke rather loudly to Charles-Edouard, who replied, half-looking round, 'Yes, yes, all mine,' and went on talking with his friend. The officer, who knew Charles-Edouard by sight, began chalking the cases as he passed them.

Sigi, getting very fidgety, said, 'You mustn't mark that one without opening it first.'

The officer laughed. 'What are you up to? Smuggling?'

'Not me, my papa. Oh do look—do look inside.'

The officer good-naturedly snapped open the case, which seemed at first sight to contain coffee in half-pound bags. Still laughing, he took one out. Then his face changed. He tore open the bag and gave a loud whistle. Charles-Edouard was saying to his friend 'See you in a few minutes then.' The friend went on out of the shed and Charles-Edouard turned to the Customs officer who said, 'Excuse me, sir, is this your case?'

'I think so. If it's with the others,' he said, rather puzzled at the sudden gravity of the man's expression.

'Then I'm afraid I must ask you to follow me.'

'Follow you. Why?'

'This way, sir, please.'

'Yes, but why?'

'Your case is full of gold coins,' said the officer, showing him.

'Nom de nom,' said Charles-Edouard, very much taken aback. 'But wait a moment, that's not my case. I've never seen it before.'

'You've just said it was yours, sir.'

'Sigi—does this case belong to you?'

'Oh no, Papa, you gave it to me to hold, don't you remember?' Sigi was wildly twisting up his hair.

Two Englishwomen said to each other, 'Shame, making the child smuggle for him.'

Charles-Edouard gave Sigi a very searching look and said, 'Sigismond, what is all this? Now will you please go on board this minute, go to cabin 1, find M. l'Ambassadeur and ask him to come here.'

Sigi ran off and Charles-Edouard followed the Customs man into a back office.

When Sigi got on to the ship he made no effort to find cabin 1 or the Ambassador. Since he had time to get rid of, and did not want to run into his burglar, he made his way to the ladies' room, where, as he knew he would, he found Nanny lying down with her skirt off and occupying the entire attention of the stewardess, who stood over her with a bottle of sea-sick tablets. 'Not as bad as all that,' the stewardess was saying, 'bumpier this side. You go right off to sleep, dear, that'll be the best.'

'And what about the little monkey?'

'I'll be all right,' said Sigi. 'I'm just waiting for the boat to start and then I'll go and find Mummy. I've got some very interesting news for Mummy, but only when we've started.'

'Won't be long now,' said the stewardess, looking at her watch.

Meanwhile the Ambassador's servant had arrived in his cabin, saying, 'M. le Marquis de Valhubert is in trouble with the Customs and it doesn't look as if they will allow him to travel.'

The Ambassador did not hesitate. He had a word with the ship's captain and immediately went on shore again, accompanied by an officer who took him straight to the room where Charles-Edouard was talking with several Customs men.

'What is all this about?' said the Ambassador, in English.

Charles-Edouard said furiously, 'My child, who seems to be a member of the criminal classes, has planted a case full of gold coins on me. Don't ask me how he got them. I'm in a very awkward position indeed.'

The Ambassador said to the senior official, 'It's absolutely out of the question that M. de Valhubert should be smuggling gold. You need not consider it even as a possibility. There must be a mistake.'

'Yes, sir, we feel sure there is. But we must find out where all this gold comes from. Where is the little boy?'

'He went off to find you,' Charles-Edouard said to the Ambassador.

'I haven't seen him. My valet told me you'd been delayed, that's why I came.'

'It was most good of you, mon cher, I'm exceedingly grateful.'

'I could do no less.'

Another official now put his head round the door.

'Mr. Porter, please, one moment.'

Mr. Porter went out, and was back again almost at once.

'I think we've got to the bottom of it,' he said. 'A man has just been arrested on board. If I might have your name and address, sir, you've time to catch the boat, I'm very glad to say.'

Charles-Edouard gave him his card and hurried on board with the Ambassador.

Sigi's timing had gone a little bit wrong, and he had arrived in his mother's cabin rather before he meant to. Charles-Edouard, from outside, heard a well-known voice piping, 'He has always been wrapped up in Madame Novembre—it doesn't surprise me in the least. They're made for each other, and now they've gone off together—oh yes, Mummy, I saw them, I tell you, in her Cadillac.'

Charles-Edouard burst open the door, saying, in a voice which neither Sigi nor Grace had ever heard, and which turned Sigi to stone with terror, 'Sigismond'. This was followed by a tremendous box on the ears. The three of them stood looking at each other for a moment. Then Charles-Edouard, mastering his temper, said, 'What you need, my child, is a family of little brothers and sisters, and we must try to see that you get them. And now, please, run along and find Nanny.'

DON'T TELL ALFRED

CHAPTER I

ON the day which was to be such a turning-point in my life, I went to London by the 9.7. I had planned to do a little shopping; somebody had told me of Chinese robes in the sales, perfect for dinner at home since they would cover up everything. I was also going to see my naughty boy, Basil, a perennial worry to me; Aunt Sadie begged me to look in on Uncle Matthew and there was something I had long wanted to put to him. I had appointments to lunch with the one and to have tea with the other. It was a Saturday because that was Basil's half-holiday—he was cramming for the Foreign Office. We were to meet at a restaurant, then go back to his lodgings, what used to be called 'rooms' and is now called a 'service flat'. My idea was to do a little, surely much needed, tidying up there, as well as to collect some dirty clothes, and bring them back with me to have them washed or cleaned. I took a large canvas hold-all to contain them and the Chinese robe, if I bought it.

But, oh dear, I don't think I've ever looked such a fool as I did in that Chinese robe, with my brown walking shoes, enormous, beneath the hem, hair untidy from dragging off a hat, leather bag clasped to bosom because it had £28 in it and I knew that people snatched bags at sales. The assistant earnestly said think of the difference if I were carefully coiffée and maquillée and parfumée and manicurée and pedicurée, wearing Chinese sandals (next department, 35/6) and lying on a couch in a soft light. It was no good, however—my imagination could not get to work on all these hypotheses; I felt both hot and bothered; I tore the robe from me and fled from the displeasure of the saleswoman.

I had made my plan with Basil some days before, on the telephone. Like all the children he is quite incapable of either reading or writing a letter. I was rather more worried about him than usual; last time he had come to Oxford his clothes had been distinctly on the Teddy side while his hair combed (or rather pulled) over his forehead and worn in a bob at the back gave him a curiously horrid look. This, no doubt, is now the fashion and not in itself a cause for alarm. But when he was alone with me he had spoken about his future, saying that the prospect of the Foreign Service bored him and that he thought he could put his talent for languages to better account in some other career. The sinister words 'get rich quick' were uttered. I was anxious to see him again and ask a few questions. It was a blow, therefore, though not a great surprise, when he failed to turn up at the restaurant. I lunched there alone and then went off to find his service flat. The address he had given me, in Islington, turned out to be a pretty old house, come down in the world (soon no doubt to come down altogether). There were five or six bells at the front door with cards attached; one bell had no card but somebody had scribbled Baz on the wall beside it. I pressed it, without much hope. Nobody came. I went on pressing at intervals.

A sharp lad in Teddy costume was lounging in the street, eyeing me. Presently he came up and said, 'If it's old Baz you're after, he's gone to Spain.'

Rain, rain, go to Spain. 'And when will he be back again?'

'When he comes for the next batch. Old Baz is a travel agent now, didn't you know? Joined up with his Grandad—some people are lucky in their relations. Baz herds them out to the Costa Brava, goes into hiding while they live it up there and brings back the bodies a week later. Or that's the general idea—he's only just started the work.'

Travel agent—Grandad—what did the child mean? Was not this a line of talk intended to keep me here until a man who was walking up the street should be out of sight? There was nobody else about, this dread Teddy, armed, no doubt, with blades, was clearly after my bag and the £28. I gave him a nervous, idiotic smile. 'Thank you very much,' I said, 'that's just what I thought. Goodbye and thank you.'

The Euston Road was near and very soon I was in a good old No. 19 sagely ambling towards Sloane Street. This sort of thing always happened when I tried to see Basil. Oh well, one must put oneself in his shoes. Why should he want to spend his Saturday afternoon with a middle-aged mother? What a bore for a young man, on his own for the first time, to have to watch this elderly woman messing about in his room and taking away his suits. All the same, it was not like him to throw one over quite so callously; what could have happened? How could I find out? Meanwhile here I was in London on a Saturday afternoon with nothing to do until tea-time. We were passing the National Gallery, but I felt too dispirited to go in. I decided to walk off my bad temper in the Park.

Though I have lived in London for longish periods at various times in my life, I have never been a Londoner, so that its associations to me are more literary and historic than personal. Every time I visit it I am saddened by seeing changes for the worse: the growing inelegance; the loss of character; the disappearance of landmarks and their replacement by flat and faceless glass houses. When I got off my bus at Hyde Park Corner, I looked sadly at the huge hotel where Montdore House used to be, in Park Lane. When first built it had been hailed as a triumph of modern architecture, but although it had only stood there for three years it had already become shabby, the colour of old teeth, and in an odd way out of date. I stumped off towards Kensington Gardens. Somebody had told me that Knightsbridge Barracks were soon to go, so I said goodbye to them. I had never looked at them very carefully—I now saw that they were solid and well built in a pretty mixture of brick and stone. No masterpiece, but certainly far better than the glorified garage that would replace them. Wendy's Wishing Well is horribly altered, I noted, and what has happened to the trees in the Broad Walk? However, Kensington Palace is still there, though probably not for long, and eccentric old men are still sailing boats on the Round Pond, which has not, as yet, been dried and levelled and turned into a car park.

Presently, drops of rain began to fall. It was half past three. Uncle Matthew never minds one being early; I decided to make for his mews at once. If he were in he would be pleased to see me, if not I could wait for him in a little sheltered place where the dust-bins are kept.

Uncle Matthew had handed over Alconleigh to his only surviving son, Bob Radlett, keeping a small Regency house on the estate for himself. Aunt Sadie was delighted by this exchange; she liked being nearer the village; the new house got sunshine all day and it amused her to do it up. Indeed, newly painted from top to toe and containing what little good furniture there had been at Alconleigh, it had become a much more desirable residence than the other. But hardly had they moved into it than my uncle fell out with Bob: the eternal story of the old king and the young king. Bob had his own ideas about shooting and estate management; Uncle Matthew disagreed violently with every innovation. His son-in-law, Fort William, his brother-in-law, Davey Warbeck, and such neighbours as were on speaking terms with Uncle Matthew had all warned him that this would happen; they had been invited to mind their own business. Now that they had been proved right he refused to admit the real cause of his chagrin and persuaded himself that Bob's wife, Jennifer, was to blame. He pronounced his intense dislike for her; her vicinity, he said, was not to be endured. Poor Jennifer was quite inoffensive, she only wished to please and this was so obvious that even Uncle Matthew, when asked to explain the reason for his hatred, found himself at a loss. 'Meaningless piece of flesh,' he would mutter. Undeniable; Jennifer was one of those women whose meaning, if they have one, is only apparent to husband and children, but she certainly did not deserve such a torrent of hatred.

Of course Uncle Matthew could not remain in a place where he risked setting eyes on this loathed daughter-in-law. He took a flat in London, always known as The Mews, and seemed strangely contented in a town which he had hitherto regarded as a plague spot. Aunt Sadie remained peacefully in her nice new house, able to see a few friends and entertain her grandchildren without any fear of explosions. Uncle Matthew, who had been fond of his own children when they were young, took a very poor view of their progeny, while my aunt really liked them better, felt more at her ease with them, than she ever had with their parents.

At first domestic troubles raged in The Mews. There was no bed-room for a servant; daily women were found but Uncle Matthew pronounced them to be harlots; daily men smelt of drink and were impertinent. Luck favoured him in the end and he arrived at a perfect solution. One day, driving in a taxi to the House of Lords, he spied a pound note on the floor. On getting out, he handed it and his fare, plus, no doubt, an enormous tip (he was a great over-tipper), to the cabby who remarked that this was a nuisance because now he would be obliged to take it round to the Yard.

'Don't you do any such thing!' said Uncle Matthew, rather oddly, perhaps, for a legislator. 'Nobody will claim it. Keep it for yourself, my dear fellow.' The cabby thanked him warmly, both for the tip and the advice, and they parted on a chuckling note, like a pair of conspirators.

The next day, by chance, Uncle Matthew, having rung up his local shelter (or, as it is probably now called, Drivers' Rest and Culture Hall) for a cab to take him down to the House, got the same man. He told my uncle that, though he had quite seen the good sense of his advice, he had nevertheless taken the pound to Scotland Yard.

'Damned fool,' said Uncle Matthew. He asked him his name and what time he started his day. The name was Payne and he was on the streets at about half past eight. Uncle Matthew told him that, in future, he was to put his flag down when he left his garage and drive straight to The Mews.

'I like to get to Victoria Street every morning in time for the Stores to open so that would suit us both.' The Stores (Army and Navy) had ever been a magnet to my uncle; Aunt Sadie used to say she wished she could have a penny for each pound he had spent there. He knew most of the employees by name and used to take his constitutional in the magic precincts, ending up with a view from the bridge, whence he would note the direction of the wind. No sky was visible from The Mews.

Presently Payne and my uncle came to a very suitable arrangement. Payne would drop him at the Stores, return to The Mews and put in a couple of hours doing housework there. He would then go back for Uncle Matthew and drive him either to his club or home, in which case he would fetch him some hot luncheon from the Rest and Culture Hall, where according to my uncle, the cabbies do themselves exceed-ingly well. (I often feel pleased to remember this when waiting in a bitter wind for one of them to finish his nuts and wine.) For the rest of the day Payne was allowed to ply his trade on condition that between every fare he should ring up The Mews to see if anything were wanted. Uncle Matthew paid him, then and there, whatever was on the clock and a tip. He said this saved accounts and made everything easier. The system worked like a charm. Uncle Matthew was the envy of his peers, few of whom were so well looked after as he.

As I was walking along Kensington Gore a cab drew up beside me, Payne at the wheel. Taking no notice of his fare, who looked surprised and not delighted, he leant over to me and said, confidentially, 'His Lordship's out. If you're going to The Mews now I'd best give you the key. I'm to pick him up at St. George's Hospital after taking this gentleman to Paddington.' The fare now pulled down the window and said furiously, 'Look here, driver, I've got a train to catch, you know.'

'Very good, Sir,' said Payne. He handed me the key and drove away.

By the time I arrived it was raining hard and I was glad not to be obliged to sit on the dust-bin. Although we were already in July the day was turning chilly; Uncle Matthew had a little fire in his sitting-room. I went up to it, rubbing my hands. The room was small, dark and ugly, the old business room at Alconleigh in miniature. It had the same smell of wood fire and Virginia cigarettes and was filled, as the business room had always been, with hideous gadgets, most of which my uncle had invented himself years ago and which, it was supposed of each in turn, would make him rich beyond belief. There were the Alconsegar Ash Tray, the Alconstoke Fire Lighters, the Alconclef Record Rack and the Home Beautifier, a fly trap made of fretwork in the form of a Swiss chalet. They vividly evoked my childhood and the long evenings at Alconleigh with Uncle Matthew playing his favourite records. I thought with a sigh what an easy time parents and guardians had had in those days—no Teddy-boys, no Beards, no Chelsea set, no heiresses, or at least not such wildly public ones; good little children we seem to have been, in retrospect.

Tea was already laid out, silver hot-dishes containing scones and girdle cakes and a pot of Tiptree jam. You could count on a good tea, at The Mews. I looked round for something to read, picked up the *Daily Post* and fell upon Amyas Mockbar's Paris Page. Provincials like myself are kept in touch with fashionable and intellectual Europe in its last stronghold of civilized leisure by this Mr. Mockbar who, four times a week, recounts the inside story of Parisian lives, loves and scandals. It makes perfect reading for the housewife who is able to enjoy the chronicle without having to rub shoulders with the human horrors depicted therein; she lays down the paper more contented than ever with her lot. Today, however, the page was rather dull, consisting of speculations on the appointment of a new English Ambassador to Paris. Sir Louis Leone, it seemed, was due to retire after a mission of unusual length. Mockbar had always presented him as a diplomatic disaster, too brilliant, too social and much too pro-French. His beautiful wife was supposed to have made too many friends in Paris; reading between the lines, one gathered that Mockbar had not been among them. Now that the Leones were leaving, however, he was seized with an inexplicable tenderness for them. Perhaps he was saving his ammunition for the new Sir Somebody whom he confidently tipped as Sir Louis' successor.

I heard the taxi crawling into The Mews. It stopped, the door slammed, the meter rang, my uncle rattled some half-crowns out of his pocket, Payne thanked him and drove off. I went to meet Uncle Matthew as he came slowly up the stairs.

'How are you, my dear child?'

It was comfortable to be my dear child again; I was so accustomed to seeing myself as a mother—poor, neglected mother today, left to have her luncheon all alone. I looked at myself in a glass while Uncle Matthew went to the little kitchen to put on a kettle, saying 'Payne got everything ready, there's only the tea to make.' No doubt there was something in my appearance which made 'my dear child' not too ridiculous, even at the age of forty-five. I took off my hat and combed my hair which was as springy as ever, turned up all over my head and was neither faded nor grey. My face was not much lined; my eyes looked bright and rather young. I weighed the same as when I was eighteen. There was an unfashionable aspect about me which came from having lived most of my life in Oxford, as much out of the world as if it had been Tibet, but no doubt some such drastic treatment as a love affair (perish the thought) or change of environment could still transform my appearance; the material was there.

'Very civil of you to come, Fanny.'

I saw Uncle Matthew but seldom these days and never really got accustomed to finding him old, that is to say, no longer in the agreeable, seemingly endless autumn of life but plunged in its midwinter. I had known him so vigorous and violent, so rampageous and full of super-charged energy that it went to my heart to see him now, stiff and slow in his movements; wearing spectacles; decidedly deaf. Until we are middle-aged ourselves, old age is outside our experience. When very young, of course, everybody grown up seems old while the really old people with whom we come into contact, never having been different during the few years—short to them, endlessly long to us—of our acquaintance, seem more like another species than members of our own race in a different condition. But the day comes when those we have known in the prime of life approach its end; then we under-stand what old age really is. Uncle Matthew was only in his seventies but he was not well preserved. He had gone through life with one lung, the other having been shot away in the Boer War. In 1914, on the reserve of officers, he had arrived in France with the first hundred thousand and spent two years in the trenches before being invalided home. After that he had hunted, shot and played lawn tennis as though he had been perfectly fit. I can often remember, as a child, seeing him fight to get his breath—it must have been a strain on the heart. He had known sorrow too, which always ages people. He had suffered the deaths of three of his children and those his three favourites. Having lost a child myself I know that nothing more terrible can befall a human being; mine, having died as a baby, left no gap comparable with the disappearance of Linda and the two boys he was so proud of.

When he came back with the tea, looking like some old shepherd of the hills who had invited one to his chimney-corner, I said, 'Whom were you visiting at St. George's?'

'Why, Davey! I thought you couldn't have known he was there or you would have come.' Davey Warbeck was my uncle, widower of Aunt Emily who had snatched me from my own, unmaternal, mother and brought me up.

'Indeed I would have. Whatever is he in for now?' There was no terror in my voice as I asked; Davey's health was his hobby and he spent much of his life in nursing homes and hospitals.

'Nothing serious. It seems they have got a few human spare parts, frozen, don't you know, from America. Davey came up from the country to give them the once over. He says it was hard to know what to choose, they were all so tempting. A few yards of colon, some nice bits of membrane, an eye (but where could he put it? Even Davey would look rather odd with three)—finally he picked on a kidney. He's been after a suitable one for ages—he's having it grafted. It's to give the others a chance. Now who else would have thought of that? Wonderful fella—and all for nothing, don't you know? We pay—health service.'

'It sounds rather terrific—how did he seem?'

'Strong as a bull and having the time of his life. Doctors and nurses so proud of him—exhibit A. I asked if they couldn't give me a new lung but they wouldn't touch it. Kill me stone dead they said, with my heart in the state it is. You want to be in the pink, like Davey, to have these graftings.'

'Delicious girdle cake.'

'Comes from the Shelter—they've got a Scotch cook there now. Davey's been telling me about your mother's new husband. You know how he likes to be in on things—he went to the wedding.'

'No—how he could! Weren't the papers awful?'

'I thought so too, but he says not nearly as bad as they might have been. It seems to have been a thick week, luckily for us, with all these heiresses running to leper colonies and the Dockers docking at Monte Carlo. What they did put in they got wrong, of course. Have you seen him, Fanny?'

'Who? Oh, my mother's husband? Well, no she has rather stopped asking Alfred and me to meet her fiancés. They've gone abroad now, haven't they?'

'To Paris, I believe. He's only twenty-two, did you know?'

'Oh dear, I can easily believe it.'

'She's as pleased as Punch, Davey says. He says you must hand it to her, she didn't look a day over forty. It seems your boy Basil was at the wedding—he introduced them in the first place.'

'Goodness! Did he really?'

'They both belong to the same gang,' said Uncle Matthew, adding rather wistfully, 'we didn't have these gangs when I was young. Never mind, though, we had wars. I liked the Boer War very much, when I was Basil's age. If you won't have wars you must expect gangs, no doubt.'

'Does my stepfather, aged twenty-two (oh really, Uncle Matthew, it is past a joke. Why, he is the boys' step-grandfather, you realize?), does he do any work or is he just a criminal?'

'Davey said something about him being a travel agent. That's why they've gone abroad, most likely.'

The words of that Teddy boy came back to me. 'Old Baz is a travel agent . . . he's joined up with his Grandad.' I became very thoughtful. What was I going to tell Alfred when I got home?

I said: 'At least that sounds fairly respectable?'

'Don't you believe it. A chap in the House was telling me about these travel agents. Bandits, he said. Take people's money and give them ten days of hell. Of course, going abroad in itself would be hell to me. Now how many would you say that makes, Fanny?'

'What, Uncle Matthew?'

'How many husbands has the Bolter had now?'

'The papers said six——'

'Yes, but that's absurd. They left out the African ones—it's eight or nine at least. Davey and I were trying to count up. Your father and his best man and the best man's best friend, three. That takes us to Kenya and all the hot stuff there—the horsewhipping and the aeroplane and the Frenchman who won her in a lottery. Davey's not sure she ever married him, but give her the benefit of the doubt: four. Rawl and Plugge five and six, Gewan seven, the young man who writes books on Greece—relatively young—old enough to be the father of this one—eight and the new boy nine. I can't think of another, can you?'

At this point the telephone bell rang and my uncle picked up the receiver. 'That you, Payne? Where are you now—East India Docks? I'd like the *Evening Standard*, please. Thank you, Payne.' He rang off. 'He can take you to the station, Fanny. I suppose you're catching the 6.5? If you wouldn't mind being a bit on the early side so that he can be back here in good time for the cocktail party.'

'Cocktail party?' I said. I was stunned. Uncle Matthew loathed parties, execrated strangers and never drank anything, not even a glass of wine with his meals.

'It's a new idea—don't you have them at Oxford? You will soon, mark my words. I rather like them. You're not obliged to talk to anybody and when you get home, it's bedtime.'

Timidly, without much conviction, but feeling it my duty to do so, I now broached the subject which was the reason for my visit. I asked him if he would like to see Fabrice, Linda's child whom Alfred and I had adopted. He was at school with our Charlie; they had been born on the same day and in the same nursing home; Linda had died; I had survived and left the home with two babies instead of one. Aunt Sadie went to Eton sometimes and took the boys out but Uncle Matthew had not set eyes on his grandson since he was a baby, during the war.

'Oh, no, my dear Fanny, thank you very much,' he muttered, embarrassed, when he understood what I was trying to say. 'I don't set great store by other people's children, you know. Give him this and tell him to keep away, will you?' A pocket book lay beside him—he took out a fiver. This unlucky idea of mine was a cold spoon in the soufflé; the conversation lapsed and I was thankful when Payne arrived with the *Evening Standard*.

'Eighteen and six on the clock, m'lord.'

My uncle gave him a pound and two half-crowns. 'Thank you, Payne.'

'Thank you—much obliged, m'lord.'

'Now, Payne, you'll take Miss Fanny to Paddington—no scorching, I beg, we don't want her in the ditch, we are all very fond of Miss Fanny. While you are there, would you go to Wyman's, present my compliments to Mr. Barker of the book-stall and see if he could oblige me with a ball of string? Come straight back, will you?—we are going to Lord Fortinbras in Groom Place. I am invited for six-thirty—it wouldn't do to miss the beginning.'

When I arrived at Oxford I was startled to see Alfred waiting for me on the platform. He never came to meet me as a rule—I had not even said what train I would take. 'Nothing wrong?' I said. 'The boys——?'

'The boys? Oh dearest, I'm sorry if I frightened you.' He then told me that he had been appointed Ambassador to Paris.

CHAPTER II

IT may be imagined that I got little sleep that night. My thoughts whizzed about, to begin with quite rational; more and more fantastic as the hours went on; finally between sleeping and waking, of a night-mare quality. In the first place, of course, I was happy to think that my dear Alfred's merits should have been publicly recognized at last, that he should receive a dazzling prize (as it seemed to me) to reward him for being so good and clever. Surely he was wasted in a chair of Pastoral Theology, even though his lectures on the pastoral theme made a lasting impression on those who heard them. During the war he had filled a post of national importance; after that I had quite expected to see him take his place in the arena. But (whether from lack of ambition or lack of opportunity I never really knew) he had returned quietly to Oxford when his war-work came to an end and seemed fated to remain there for the rest of his days. For my part, I have already told[1] how, as an eager young bride, I had found University life disappointing; I never reversed that opinion. I was used to being a don's wife, I knew exactly what it involved and felt myself adequate; that was all. The years rolled by with nothing to distinguish them; generations of boys came and went; like the years I found that they resembled each other. As I got older I lost my taste for the company of adolescents. My own children were all away now: the two youngest at Eton; Basil—oh where was he and when should I confide my fears about him to Alfred? Bearded David, the eldest, was a don at a red-brick university, living with the times, or so he informed me. In moments of introspection I often thought that a woman's need for children is almost entirely physical. When they are babies one cuddles and kisses and slaps them and has a highly satisfying animal relationship with them. But when they grow up and leave the nest they hardly seem to belong any more. Was I much use to the boys now? As for Alfred, detached from all human emotions, I thought it more than likely that if I were to disappear he would go and live in college, as happy as he had ever been with me. What was I doing on earth at all and how was I going to fill in the thirty-odd years which might lie ahead before the grave?

Of course I knew that this state of mind is common among middle-aged, middle-class women whose children have gone into the world. Its causes, both psychological and physiological, are clearly understood nowadays and so is the fact that there is no remedy. What can't be cured must be endured. But Alfred's miraculous appointment might effect a miraculous cure. I had often longed to leave behind me a token of my existence, a shell on the seashore of eternity. Here was my chance; Alfred might become one of those plenipotentiaries whose names are ever remembered with gratitude and respect, and some of the credit might be mine. At the very least I would now have a little tiny place in history as one of the occupants of a famous house.

All this was rather cheerful, if high-falutin', midnight stuff. But by the early hours doubts and terrors were crowding in. I knew little enough about Paris or diplomatic life, but I did know, like everybody

---

[1] In *Love in a Cold Climate.*

else, that Sir Louis and Lady Leone, whom we were to replace, held a
glittering court there, reminiscent of the great embassies of olden days.
Lady Leone was universally admitted to be more beautiful, charming
and witty than any other woman in public life. Absurd to think that I
could compete with her—how could I fill her place even adequately?
Not only had I no training, not the very slightest knowledge of
diplomacy, but I had certain decided disabilities. I can never remember people, for instance, either their names or their faces or anything at all about them. I am a poor housekeeper. When I first arrived
in Oxford as a young bride I had resolved not to be as other dons'
wives in this respect; to begin with my dinners were decidedly better
than theirs. However, my dear Mrs. Heathery never improved beyond
a certain point, I had four hungry boys to shovel down the vitamins
and a husband who never noticed what he ate. After the end of
coupons, other people's food improved, mine did not. I had never
presided over a large household or had more than three servants (one
of them a daily) in my life. What would the domestic side of the
Embassy be like, mismanaged by me? Visiting Ministers, or worse,
visiting Royalty, would complain and this would be bad for Alfred.
My clothes—better to draw a veil. So, with my absent-mindedness and
ghastly food and ghastly clothes I should become the Aunt Sally of
diplomatic life, a butt and a joke.

I only wished I could go to sleep for a bit and forget the whole
thing. Yes, a joke. I began to see myself in farcical situations. This silly
habit of kissing everybody—quite new since the war. My ex-under-
graduates and other men friends kiss when they see me; it has become
an automatic gesture. Mental picture: a party in some official building,
very pompous and grand. Out of pure distraction I kiss the President
of the Republic.

I suffer from weak ankles and sometimes topple over unexpectedly.
When this happens in the Turl nobody minds; I am picked up by some
friendly young chap, go home and change my stockings. Mental
picture: The Arc de Triomphe, military music, wreaths, television
cameras. Flop, down I come, extinguishing the Eternal Flame. Now I
really must wake myself up properly from these half-nightmares, undermining my morale. I stood at the window and, watching the sun's first
rays as they fell upon Christ Church, I let myself get very cold. Then I
went back to my warm bed, and fell into a dreamless sleep.

In the morning when I told Alfred some of these unnerving thoughts
(not the kissing and falling-down ones however) he said, 'I specially
didn't want you to lie in bed working yourself up, that's why I never
mentioned your side of the business last night. I'm glad to say Philip is
in England and I've told him to come and have luncheon with you
today. You'll be able to talk it all over with him and get these worries
out of your system. I must go to London for a few hours.'

'Oh, of course we shall find Philip in Paris—I'd quite forgotten he was there. I say, what a comfort!'

'Yes, and a great comfort to me, too. Meanwhile do remember that the social side is quite unimportant. As I told you last night mine is intended to be a serious mission—sobriety, security the keynotes. The ci-devants have had their day with the Leones, I intend to concentrate on the politicians and people of real importance. And by the way, dearest, perhaps your—shall I say—flightier relations could be discouraged from paying us too many visits?'

'Yes, darling, I quite agree. But the boys——'

'The boys! Why of course it will be their home whenever they want to come. Nice to have a healthy youthful element, which has been lacking there of late.'

This was clearly not the moment to mention my worries about Basil. Anyhow, the holidays were about to begin, when he was supposed to be leaving the crammer to work on his own in some quiet place. I decided to wait and see what happened.

Philip Cliffe-Musgrave sauntered in at one o'clock. Ten years younger than me, he was by far my favourite of all the undergraduates who had passed through our hands, so to speak. Owing to the war, he had come late to Oxford, a man, not a boy. He had, I thought, been slightly in love with me and I might easily have returned this slight love had not the example of my mother, the Bolter, for ever discouraged me from such adventures which begin so cheerfully and finish so shoddily, I had noticed. However, we had trodden the pleasant path of a loving friendship and I had remained extremely fond of him. He was an elegant creature, the best-dressed man I have ever seen, and one of those people who seem to have been born with a knowledge of the world. Alfred thought him very brilliant.

'Well,' we said now, looking at each other and laughing.

'Madame l'Ambassadrice. Too interesting for words. There have been the wildest rumours about Sir Louis' successor, but truth is certainly stranger than fiction. The dinners I shall be asked to when it gets out that I actually know you!'

'Philip, I'm terrified!'

'No wonder. They'll gobble you up, all those smart women. At first, that is. I think you'll defend yourself in the long run.'

'You are horrid—Alfred said you would reassure me.'

'Yes, yes, I'm only teasing.'

'Be careful—I'm in a delicate state. Such a lot of things I want to ask; where to begin? Do the Leones know?'

'That they are leaving? Oh yes.'

'I mean about us?'

'When I came away, three days ago, he had been told it was a possibility. They'll be pleased, I think. That is, it will kill her to leave the Embassy but if she has to hand it over she'd rather it were to someone like you.'

'Oh. Dreary, d'you mean?'

'Different. And above all not the wife of a colleague. You don't know what the jealousy between wives is like, in that service. As for Sir Louis he is a typical career diplomat. He despises the amateur and is certain that Alfred will make an unholy mess of the job. This, of course, will soften the blow of leaving quite considerably.'

'Philip, do tell me—why have they chosen Alfred?'

'Up to their clever tricks, you know.'

'Now what's coming?' I said, uneasily.

'Don't be so nervous. I only mean that when the war was comfortably over, the Entente doing all right, the allies in love with each other—not the rulers but the people—everybody busy with their own internal affairs, they sent Sir Louis to captivate the French. And oh, how he succeeded—they eat out of his hand. Now that we are running into choppy seas they send Alfred to puzzle them.'

'And will he puzzle them?'

'As he does everybody. His whole career has been one long mystery if you come to consider it. What was he doing with Ernie Bevin during the war? Have you ever understood? Nobody else has. Did you know that he lunches at No. 10, alone with the P.M., at least once a week? Bet you didn't. Or that the well-informed regard him as one of those people who really govern the country?'

'Alfred is very secret,' I said reflectively. 'I often think that's why I'm so happy with him. Plate glass is such a bore.'

'I shall be very much interested to see him at work. No doubt he will keep Bouche-Bontemps and his merry men in a state of chronic perplexity which may be very useful.'

'Who is Bouche-Bontemps?'

'My poor Fanny, you'll have to mug up the political situation a bit. Surely you must have heard of him—he's the French foreign minister.'

'They change so often.'

'Yes, but there are a few old faithfuls who reappear like the soldiers in *Faust* and he is one.'

'I know about M. Mendès-France.'

'Only because he's called France. Everybody in England has heard of him because the *Daily Post* goes on about Mr. France, which makes it nice and easy.'

'I know about General de Gaulle.'

'Yes, well you can forget him, for the moment at any rate.'

'To go back to the Leones. She minds leaving dreadfully?'

'All Ambassadresses mind. They are generally carried screaming from the house—"encore un instant, M. le Bourreau"—poor Pauline, yes, she is in despair.'

'And you'll hate to lose her?'

'Yes. I adore her. At the same time, Fanny, as it's you, I shall be on your side.'

'Need there be sides? Must we be enemies?'

'It is never otherwise. You'd better know the form. By the time you arrive she'll have had an enormous send-off at the Gare du Nord—the whole of Paris—flashlights, flowers, speeches, tears. All her world will have heard—not directly from her but by a sort of bush telegraph—what brutes you and Alfred are. I suppose I shall swim against the tide, but I shan't exhaust myself—a few languid strokes—because it will turn so quickly. The point is that, until you arrive, Parisian society will curse upon your name and wish you dead, but from the moment you set foot in the Embassy you will become entirely delightful. Soon we shall hear that the Leones never really quite *did*, in Paris.'

'How cynical you are.'

'That's life, I guess. Mind you their friends will continue to love them, give dinners for them when they go back and so on. But people are always attracted by power and high office; a house like the Embassy, to which the rulers of the earth gravitate, is worth more to its occupant than the prettiest face, the kindest heart, the oldest friendship. Come now, Fanny, you know enough of the world to know that, I suppose. In this case you are the beneficiary. Soon it will be as though Pauline had never been there—Pauline Leone. Pauline Borghese never leaves and she is on the side of the sitting tenant.'

'Why Pauline Borghese?'

'It was her house, you know. We bought it from her, furniture and all, after Waterloo.'

'Oh, dear. You haven't really reassured me very much. There's another thing, Philip—clothes. Of course there's always Elliston's Petite Boutique but it's so expensive.'

'I shouldn't worry. As soon as you arrive, you'll make an arrangement with one of the dressmakers there. Aren't you rather rich now, Fanny?'

'Richer, yes we are. My father left me quite a lot—I was surprised. But what with the boys and so on I never feel I ought to spend much on myself.'

He then told me about the running of an embassy and calmed my fears in that direction. According to him, the comptroller and the housekeeper do the work. 'You will only need a social secretary—some nice quiet girl who won't get married at once.'

'I'd thought of that. My cousin Louisa Fort William has got the very one, Jean Mackintosh.'

'Yes, I know her. Not a ball of fire, is she? By the way, whom d'you think I saw at a cocktail party last night? Lord Alconleigh.'

'No! Do tell me what he was doing?'

'He was standing with his back to the wall, a large glass of water in his hand, glaring furiously into space. The rest of the company was huddled together, rather like a herd of deer with an old lion in the offing. It was impressive—not altogether cosy, you know.'

Alfred's appointment was well received by the responsible newspapers, partly no doubt because many of their employees had been at Oxford and known him there. It was violently opposed by the *Daily Post*. This little paper, once considered suitable for schoolroom reading, had been bought by a press peer known to the world as Old Grumpy and now reflected his jaundiced view of life. It fed on scandal, grief and all forms of human misery, exposing them with a sort of spiteful glee which the public evidently relished, since the more cruelly the *Daily Post* tortured its victims the higher the circulation rose. Its policy, if it could be said to have one, was to be against foreign countries, cultural bodies, and the existing government, whether Conservative or Labour. Above all, it abominated the Foreign Office. The burden of its song on this occasion was, what is the point of maintaining an expensive foreign service which cannot produce a trained man to be Ambassador in Paris but has to fall back on a Professor of Pastoral Theology.

The French papers were perfectly friendly, if puzzled. The *Figaro* produced a leading article by a member of the Académie Française in which the word pastoral was wilfully misunderstood and theology left out altogether. The Knight on horseback (Alfred) coming to the Shepherdess in her orchard (Marianne) was the theme. No mention of the Knight's wife and boys (Alfred was a Knight now; he had been to London and seen the Queen).

I received many letters of congratulation, praising Alfred, praising me, saying how well we were suited to the work we should have to do and then going on to speak of some child or friend or protégé of the writer's who would like to join our establishment in almost any capacity. Louisa Fort William, ever practical, cut out the praise and offered me Jean. Alfred knew this Jean, who had been up at Oxford, and did not include her among my flightier relations. With his approval I wrote and engaged her to be our social secretary.

At Oxford, Alfred's colleagues and their wives took but little account of our news. This was no surprise to me. Nobody who has not lived in a university town can have any idea of its remoteness from the world. The dons live like monks in a cloister, outside time and space, occupied only with the daily round; ambassadors to Paris do not enter their ken or interest them in the very least. To be Warden or Dean would seem to them a far greater thing. At this time, it is true, there were some rich, worldly dons whose wives dressed at Dior, and who knew about Paris and embassies, a tiny minority on the fringe of the University—in every way; they did not even live in the town itself as we did. They regarded Alfred as a bore; he disregarded them; their wives disregarded me. These Dior dons were not pleased by our appointment; they laughed long and loud, as kind friends informed us, at the idea of it and made witty jokes at our expense. No doubt they thought the honour would sit better upon them; how I agreed with them, really!

After twenty-five years of university life my outlook was more akin to that of the monkish than to the Dior type of don, but, though I had little first-hand experience of the world, I did know what it was. My cousin Linda had been in contact with it and my mother had always been of it, even during her wildest vagaries. Lady Montdore, though she saw real life through distorting glasses, had had the world and its usage at her fingertips; I had not been a sort of lady-in-waiting to her for nothing. How I wished she were still alive to see what fate had brought to me—like the Dior dons she would have mocked and disapproved but unlike them she would have been rather impressed, no doubt.

Our summer holidays passed as usual. Alfred and I went to stay with Davey Warbeck, in Kent, and paid one or two other visits. Our youngest boys, Charlie and Fabrice, were hardly with us at all. They were invited by a boy called Sigismond de Valhubert, who was at their house at Eton, to stay in Provence, after which all three went shooting in Scotland. Bearded David sent postcards from the Lakes—he was on a walking tour. As for Basil, he might have been dead for all I knew; I weakly told Alfred that he had gone to Barcelona to rub up his Spanish. Very soon we came to the last days of August and of our monotonous but familiar Oxford life.

CHAPTER III

I SHALL never forget my first impression of the Embassy. After the hurly-burly of our reception at the Gare du Nord, after the drive through Paris traffic which always unnerves those not accustomed to it, the large, beautiful, honey-coloured house, in its quiet courtyard, seemed a haven of delight. It has more the atmosphere of a country than a town house. For one thing, no town noises can be heard, only the rustle of leaves, the twittering of birds, an occasional mowing-machine, an owl. The french windows on the garden side fill the rooms with sunshine and air in amazing quantities. They open to a vista of trees; the only solid edifice in sight is the dome of the Invalides, a purple shadow on the horizon, hardly visible through summer leaves. Except for that and the Eiffel Tower, on the extreme right hand of this prospect, there is nothing to show that the house is situated in the centre of the most prosperous and busy capital on the continent of Europe. Philip took us straight up to the first floor. At the top of the fine staircase there is an antichamber leading to the yellow drawing-room, the white and gold drawing-room, the green drawing-room (to be our private sitting-room) and Pauline Borghese's bedroom, so recently vacated by the other Pauline. These rooms all face south and open into each other. Behind them, looking north over the courtyard, are the Ambassador's dressing-room and library and the social secretary's office. Well-wishers had filled the house with flowers; they made it look very beautiful, glowing in the evening light, and also reassured me. Many people seemed prepared, at any rate, to like us.

I believe it would have been normal for me to have paid a visit to the outgoing ambassadress soon after our appointment was announced. However, the said ambassadress had set up such an uninhibited wail when she knew she was to leave, proclaiming her misery to all and sundry and refusing so furiously to look on the bright side (a happy and respected old age in a Kensington flat), that it was felt she might not be very nice to me. Her attitude seemed rather exaggerated until I saw what it was that we were usurping; then I understood. Lady Leone had reigned in this palace—the word reign is not too much, with her beauty, elegance and great funniness she had been like a Queen here—for five whole years; no wonder she left it all with death in her heart.

As for me, my fears fell away and so did my middle-aged gloom. The house seemed to be on my side; from the very first moment I set foot in it I was stimulated, interested, amused and ready for anything. When I woke up next morning to find myself in Pauline's bed, the bed of both the Paulines, opening my eyes on the dark red walls and mahogany furniture, a curious contrast to the light gaiety of the rest of the house, I thought, 'This is the first day, the beginning.' Then I wondered how I should feel on the last day, the end. I was deeply sorry for Lady Leone.

Alfred appeared, in high spirits. He was going to have breakfast in his library. 'Philip will come and talk to you while you have yours. He says you must never get up too early. You'll have a tiring life here; try and be quiet in the morning.' He dumped a lot of papers on my bed and went off. There was nothing much about us in them—a small flashlight photograph in the *Figaro*—an announcement in *The Times* that we had arrived—until, at the bottom of the heap, I came to the *Daily Post*. The whole of the front page was covered with an enormous photograph of Alfred, mouth idiotically open, apparently giving the Hitler salute. My heart sank; horrified I read:

The mission of the former Pastoral Theologian, Sir Alfred Wincham, to Paris has begun with an unfortunate incident. As M. Bouche-Bontemps, who had interrupted his holiday to meet Sir Alfred at the Gare du Nord, came forward with a gesture of welcome, our envoy rudely brushed him aside and confabulated, at length, IN GERMAN, with a tall fair young man in the crowd. . . .

I looked up from the paper. Philip was standing by my bed, laughing.

'Is this all right? One always used to see Pauline before she got up—it seemed a good moment.'

'Oh dear,' I said, 'you'll miss that lovely face under the baldaquin.'

'This is different,' he sat down on the end of the bed, 'and in some ways nicer. So, I see you've got to the incident.'

'Philip!'

'Don't say it has upset you. It's nothing to what there will be—the *Daily Post* man here, Amyas Mockbar (you mustn't forget that name), is preparing the full treatment for you; you're on Old Grumpy's black list.'

'But why are we?'

'The English Ambassador here always is; besides, Lord Grumpy personally dislikes Alfred, who seems unaware of his existence.'

'He is unaware. There's one blessing, Alfred only reads *The Times* and I shan't mind what the *Daily Post* says.'

'Don't you be too sure. Mockbar has a wonderful knack of making people mind. I've had to give up seeing him and I mind that—he's such a jolly old bird, there's nothing more enjoyable than drinking whisky with old Amyas at the Pont Royal bar.'

'But this incident,' I said.

'You see, you are minding already.'

'Yes, because it's entirely invented.'

'Not entirely—he never entirely invents, that's where he's so devilish.'

'Alfred talked to a German at the Gare du Nord?'

'While you were being introduced to Mme Hué, Alfred spied poor old Dr. Wolff of Trinity peering at him under the arc lights. Of course, being Alfred, he darted off—then he came straight back and explained the whole thing to Bouche-Bontemps. The incident was of no consequence, but it wasn't entirely invented.'

'But Dr. Wolff isn't a tall, fair, young German—he's a tiny little old dark one.'

'Mockbar never sees things quite like other people, his style is strictly subjective; you'll have to get used to it.'

'Yes, I see.'

'There are a lot of things you'll have to get used to here, but I think he is the worst. What have you done about a social secretary?'

'I've got Jean Mackintosh coming next week. I wanted to settle myself in first and Alfred thought you'd lend me a hand until then, though I know you are far too important.'

'Certainly I will. It amuses me and I can help you as I know the form. There's no other work at present—total lull on the international front and all the ministers are away. Bouche-Bontemps is off again to-morrow. So let's get down to it. First, here's a list of the people who have sent flowers; you'll want to thank them yourself. Then Alfred thought you had better see the arrangements for this week—rather hectic, I'm afraid. You have to polish off the colleagues—visit them, you know—and there are eighty embassies here so it takes a bit of doing.'

'Are there so many countries in the world?'

'Of course not—the whole thing is great nonsense—but we have to keep up the fiction to please the Americans. There's nothing the millionaires like so much as being ambassadors; at present there are eighty of them, keenly subscribing to party funds. We have to tag along. In small countries like the Channel Islands practically all the male adults are ambassadors, nowadays.'

I was looking at the list of names he had given me. 'I only know one of the people who have sent flowers—Grace de Valhubert.'

'She's still away,' said Philip. 'How do you know her?'

'Her boy and my two are friends at school. They've just been staying down in Provence with her. If they have kindly said they will come here for Christmas it's chiefly on account of Sigismond.'

'Sweet Sigi, fascinating child,' said Philip with a good deal of feeling. 'I may as well tell you, Fanny, since we are such old friends and anyhow you're sure to find out, that I'm in love with Grace.' I felt a small, stupid pang when he said this. No doubt I would selfishly have preferred him to concentrate on me, as he used to when he was at Oxford.

'With what result?'

He said bitterly, 'Oh, she keeps me hanging about. She probably rather likes to show her husband, whom she is madly in love with, that somebody is madly in love with her.'

'Silly old love,' I said, 'bother it. Let's go on with the list. Who is Mrs. Jungfleisch?'

'Mildred *Youngfleesh*. The Americans have begun to copy our tiresome habit of not pronouncing names as they are spelt. She says you know her.'

'Really? But I never remember——'

'Nor you do. She's always going to Oxford so I expect you have met her.'

'With the Dior dons probably, though I hardly ever see them—not their cup of tea at all,'

'I suppose not.'

'There, you see yourself how I'm not. So how shall I manage here where people are twice as frightening?'

'Now—now!'

'Mrs. Jungfleisch is a *femme du monde*, I suppose?'

'Yes, indeed. I've known her for years—we went to the same charm school in New York when I was with U.N.O.'

'You went to a charm school? I always thought you were charm personified!'

'Thank you. Mildred and I went to see if we couldn't pick up a little extra warmth of manner, but as you so kindly suggest we found we were too advanced for the course.'

'The person who needs it is me.'

'Wouldn't be any good to you, because of not remembering who people are. A memory for names and faces is the A.B.C. of charm, it's all built up on the pleased-to-see-you formula, but you must show that you know who it is you're being pleased to see.'

'I know so few Americans,' I said. 'Do you like them, Philip?'

'Yes, I'm paid to.'

'In your heart of hearts?'

'Oh, poor things, you can't dislike them. I feel intensely sorry for them, especially the ones in America—they are so mad and ill and frightened.'

'Shall we see a lot of them here?—I suppose so. Alfred has been told he must collaborate.'

'You can't avoid it, the place teems with them.'

'Any friendly ones?'

'Friendly? They make you long for an enemy. You'll like some of them though. They fall into three categories, the ones here. There are the business men trying to make a better position for themselves at home as experts on Yurrup. They are afraid there may be a boom in Yurrup. Of course they don't want to miss anything if there is. For instance, there's the art market—all these old antique objects to marry up to the dollar. (Art is booming so they love it, they even call their children it.) There are dollars in music too—Schu and Schu can be quite as profitable as Tel and Tel. Art and music are only to be found in Yurrup; they come over prospecting for them—at the same time they don't want to be left out of things at home, so they play an uneasy game of musical chairs between Yurrup and the States, hurtling to and fro in rockets, getting iller and madder and more frightened than ever.'

'Frightened of what?'

'Oh, somebody else being in on something first; falling down dead; a recession—I don't know, dreadfully fidgety. Then there are literally thousands of officials who are paid to be here. One never sees them, except for a few diplomatic colleagues. They are dreadfully unhappy;

they huddle together in a sort of ghetto—terrified of losing their American accent.'

'What a funny thing to mind losing.'

'It would be ghastly for them if they did. They'd be branded for ever as un-American. Finally we have the Henry James type of expatriates who live here because they can't stick it at home—perfect dears. A bit on the serious side perhaps, but at least they don't jabber on about art and dollars—it's the future of mankind with them. Mildred is in that camp—camp commandant you might say.'

'Shall I like her?'

'You won't get the chance. She adores Pauline and is preparing to be very cold and correct with you.'

'Then why does she send me flowers?'

'It's an American tic. They can't help doing it—they send them to friend and foe alike. Whenever they pass a flower shop their fingers itch for a pen to write down somebody's name and address.'

'I'm all for it,' I said, looking at the Jungfleisch sweet-peas on my dressing table. 'Lovely, they are——'

After a few days in the Embassy I began to suspect that something was afoot. Of course in a new house one cannot account for every sight and sound; even allowing for this I sensed a mystery. From my bedroom I distinctly heard a gathering of people making merry, some sort of party which went on every evening until the early hours; I would wake up in the night to shriek upon shriek of laughter. I thought the noise must come from the next house until I discovered that this is a block of offices belonging to the American government. Surely their employees did not laugh all night? By my bed there was a telephone with a line direct to the public exchange, not through the Embassy, and a discreet little buzzing bell. This sometimes rang and when I answered it I would hear confused phrases like 'Oh Lord—I forgot', 'C'est toi, chérie? Oh pardon, Madame, il y a erreur'—or merely 'Aïe!' before the line went dead. Twice Alfred's *Times* arrived late with the cross-word puzzle already done.

The courtyard always seemed to be full of elegantly dressed people. I presumed they had come to write their names in our book (whose pages, according to Alfred, read like a dramatis personae of the whole history of France). Why, then, were they so often grouped on the little outside staircase in the south-west corner of the courtyard? I could have sworn that I saw the same ones over and over again, people with famous faces known even to me; a bejewelled dressmaker like a puppet in a film cartoon, face composed of brown golf balls; a Field-Marshal; a pianist with a guilty look; an ex-king. A pretty young woman, vaguely familiar to me, seemed to live in the courtyard, constantly up and down the little staircase with flowers, books, or gramophone records; sometimes she was carrying a huge picnic basket. Catching my eye one day she blushed and looked away. Mockbar, whom I had now met, was often in the Faubourg peering through our gateway. No mistaking him; he had the bucolic appearance of some little old groom, weather-beaten face, curved back, stiff bandy legs, wildly flailing elbows and an aureole of fuzzy grey hair.

'I wonder if you would like to make a statement?' he said, rolling towards me as I was walking home from the dressmaker one afternoon.

'Statement?'

'On the situation in your house.'

'Oh you are kind, but no, thank you very much, you must ask my husband.' I went indoors and sent for Philip.

'Philip,' I said, 'I'm a paper. Would you like to make a statement?'

'Statement?'

'On the situation in my house.'

He gave me a whimsical look, half-amused, half-worried.

'Who has the rooms on the right-hand side of the courtyard—did I see them when you showed me round?'

'Yes, it's time you knew,' he said. 'The fact is, Pauline has dug herself in there and we can't get her to leave.'

'Lady Leone? But she did leave. I saw her on a newsreel, in floods. How can she still be here?'

'She left the Gare du Nord all right, but she had the train stopped at Orry-la-Ville and came straight back, still holding Bouche-Bontemps' roses. She said she was very ill, possibly dying, and forced Mrs. Trott to make the bed in the entr'sol for her. There's a sort of little flat where the social secretary used to live. Naturally she's not ill in the least. She has the whole of Paris in there day and night—I wonder you haven't heard them.'

'I have. I thought it was the Americans next door.'

'Americans never shriek like that.'

'Now I understand everything. But Philip, this is very bad for Alfred. Such an absurd situation, at the beginning of his mission.'

'That's what the F.O. thinks. They tell us to get her out—yes, but how? I've just been on to Ashley again. You see, at the beginning one thought it was a lark—that in a day or two she'd get tired of it. So the idea was not to bother you. But now the Parisians have joined in the joke and it's the fashion to go and see her there. People are pouring back from their holidays so as not to be left out. The smart resorts are in despair—nobody left to be photographed on the beaches. So, of course, she's having the time of her life and quite honestly I don't see how we shall ever induce her to go. We're all at our wits' end.'

'Can't we tell the servants not to feed her?'

'They don't. Mildred brings her food, like a raven.'

'The one with picnic basket? We could stop her coming—tell the concierge not to let her in?'

'Very difficult—it would be awfully embarrassing for him to have to bar the way. He's known her for years.'

'Yes, I see, and of course we can't very well kidnap her. Then could we bribe her? What does she like best in the world?'

'English top policy makers.'

'What, M.P.s and things?'

'Ministers, bankers, the Archbishop, Master of the Belvoir, editor of *The Times* and so on. She likes to think she is seeing history on the boil.'

'Well, that's rather splendid. Surely these policy makers must be on our side? Why don't they lure her to England—luncheon at Downing Street or a place for the big debate on Thursday?'

'I see you don't understand the point of Mildred. They worship her in the House—they can hardly bear to have a debate at all until she's in her place there. She's the best audience they've ever had. As for luncheon at Downing Street, why, she stays there when she's in London.'

'Oh, bother——!'

'And now I come to think of it, she isn't really the clue to our problem.'

'You said she brought the food.'

'I know. Food means nothing to Pauline.'

'Still, she can't live without it.'

'The point is, she can. She's for ever going off to Tring for the starvation cure. It's a mystery to me, this starving. People on rafts begin eating each other after a week; Pauline and Mildred are sometimes at Tring for a whole month—not a nibble out of each other's shoulders.'

'Oh dear, we don't want her here for another month. Surely the policy makers must stand by their employees, Philip, and lend a hand? Have you spoken to any of them?'

'They are doing what they can. The P.M. had a word with Sir Louis at Brooks's last night. No good at all. Sir Louis just sat with his hand over his nose heaving with giggles in that endearing way he has,' said Philip, affectionately. 'But after all what can he do? Apart from the fact that it amuses him to death——'

'Some important person ought to come over and see her—tell her she's being unpatriotic and so on. She is, too.'

'We've tried that. Moley came between two aeroplanes. He arrived very strict, but he didn't keep it up. He said she lay there like a beautiful stag dying in the forest, and he hadn't the heart to be cross.'

'Why do you think she's doing it?'

'Oh, I don't think there's any very profound reason—it amuses her—

she's got nothing else to do—and if it teases you she can easily bear that. She thinks Alfred got the job by plotting against Sir Louis.'

'You know he didn't.'

'Didn't he? In any case, Sir Louis wouldn't have stayed on—it was time for a change.'

'I saw Mockbar in the street.'

'He'll go to town on it all right.'

'Has he seen Lady Leone?'

'Certainly not. Even Pauline draws the line somewhere.'

'We shall have to tell Alfred before Mockbar's piece appears.'

'He knows. It's he who has been saying don't tell Fanny.'

Distant, derisive laughter assailed my ear. The evening was drawing on; the entr'sol was waking up. I felt quite furious.

'How is the Quai d'Orsay taking it?'

'Thrilled. Hughie has given out that no wives are to join in, but I'm not sure I didn't see——'

'Who is Hughie?'

'Jacques-Olivier Hué, head of the protocol. Always known as Hughie.'

I was getting more irritated every minute. I have a sense of humour, I hope; this situation was clearly very funny; it was maddening not to be able to join in such a good joke, to be on the stuffy, official side against all these jolly bandits. I said, spitefully, 'As far as Alfred can make out, your friend Sir Louis simply lived for pleasure when he was here.'

'Ambassadors always go on like that about each other,' said Philip. 'One's predecessor is idle and one's successor is an intriguer. It's a classic of the service. But Sir Louis was an excellent ambassador, make no mistake about it.'

'Oh all right,' I said. 'Let's try and keep our tempers. If we think it over calmly there must be a solution.'

A long silence fell between us. At last I said, 'I'm going to speak to Mrs. Jungfleisch.'

'You can now if you want to—she's sitting in her car in the court-yard, reading the New Deal.'

'Why isn't she in there shrieking with the others?'

'I tell you, she's a very serious girl—she puts aside certain hours every day for historical study. Besides she says the room is too hot—twenty people in that tiny room on a day like this—it must be the Black Hole of Calcutta.'

'Then why not go home and read the New Deal there?'

'She likes to be in on things.'

'The cheek of it!' I said.

I stumped out into the courtyard, opened the door of Mrs. Jung-fleisch's Buick and boldly got in beside her. She was very fair and pretty with a choir-boy look, accentuated by the big, white, pleated collar she wore and straight hair done with a fringe. She turned her calm, intelligent blue eyes upon me, put down a document she was reading and said, 'How d'you do? I am Mildred Jungfleisch. We did meet, ages ago, at Oxford.'

I was agreeably surprised by her voice which was not very American, rather more like that of an Englishwoman who has once lived in the United States. Although I knew about the charm school prospectus being too elementary for her and guessed that this was the fully qualified charmer's voice, specially warm, for soothing an irate ambassadress in the grounds of her own embassy, it worked. Feeling decidedly soothed, I said: 'Please excuse me for getting into your motor without an invitation.'

'Please excuse me for sitting in your courtyard without an invitation.'

'I want to talk to you.'

'I'm sure you must, Lady Wincham. It's about Pauline, of course?'

'Yes—how long do you think she intends to stay?'

'Pauline is utterly unpredictable. She will leave when she feels inclined to. Knowing her as I do, I guess she'll still be here at Christmas.'

'With you still feeding her?'

'I'm afraid so.'

'If my husband were a private person, none of this would matter. As things are, I intend to get rid of Lady Leone.'

'How?'

'I don't know.'

'In my experience of Pauline it is impossible to deflect her from her purpose.'

'Aha! She has a purpose?'

'Please do not misunderstand me, Lady Wincham. Her purpose is a simple one, she wants to have a good time. She has no desire to upset you, still less to damage the embassy or embarrass the Foreign Office. It all began because she had a sudden impulse to stop the train at Orry-la-Ville and spend one last night in this house which she worships —you can have no idea what she feels about it.'

'I quite understand, on the contrary. People do get like that about houses and this one is so very extraordinary.'

'You are under the spell already! Then she found she was having fun. She rang up a few friends, for a joke; they came around. It started to be the thing to do; one signs your book and then one goes in to see Pauline. Excuse me, please, there's the Nuncio—I think he's looking for her door.'

She got out of the motor, put the prelate on his way and came back again.

'Philip tells me that you are a very responsible person,' I said. 'Couldn't you explain to her that if she goes on like this she will undo all the good she and Sir Louis have done during their brilliant embassy?'

The honest choir-boy eyes opened wide. 'Indeed, Lady Wincham, I have told her. I've even pointed out that only one person, in the end, can reap an advantage from her action.'

'And who is that?'

'Why, Mr. Khrushchev.'

I felt this was going rather far; still it was all on the right side.

'Unfortunately Pauline has no public conscience whatever. I find many European women are like that. They do not give a thought to the great issues of our time, such as the delicate balance of East and West—they will not raise a finger to ease the path of N.A.T.O., U.N.E.S.C.O., O.E.E.C. or the World Bank. Pauline is frankly not interested.'

'So there's nothing you can do?'

'Regretfully, no.'

'All right,' I said, 'I may look rather mousy but I must tell you that I very often get my own way. Goodbye.'

'Goodbye, Lady Wincham. Awfully nice to have seen you.'

CHAPTER IV

'WE must send for Davey,' I said.

This uncle of mine by marriage had long filled the same role in our family as the Duke of Wellington in that of Queen Victoria. Whenever some apparently insuperable difficulty of a worldly nature arose, one consulted him. While Alfred and I had been staying with him, we had of course talked of little else than our appointment and Davey had urged me not to forget that he understood the French. He had once lived in Paris (some forty years ago), had frequented salons and been the darling of the hostesses. He understood them. He had never liked them much, 'cross, clever things', and indeed, before the Nazis had taken over, during the decadent days of the Weimar Republic, he had greatly preferred the Germans. It was a question of shared interests; his two chief ones, health and music, were catered for better in Germany. As soon as the healthy, musical race began to show other preoccupations, Davey left Berlin and all the delightful Bads he was so fond of and which did him so much good, never to return. He always said thereafter that he did not understand the Germans. But he continued to understand the French.

I don't know what magic wand I expected him to wave, since Lady Leone and Mrs. Jungfleisch were not French and he had never claimed to understand them. True, he was a childhood friend of Lady Leone's but that was no reason why he should prove more persuasive than the head of the Foreign Office. It would, however, be a comfort to have him with me as I felt sure he would be on my side, more sure than I was about Philip whose loyalties must, in the nature of things, be rather divided. After my talk with Mrs. Jungfleisch I had a long discussion with Alfred as a result of which I telephoned there and then to Davey.

'It's an S.O.S.,' I said. 'I'll explain when I see you.'

'You have run into storms,' said Davey, hardly bothering to conceal his glee, 'even sooner than I had expected. I'll let you know as soon as I've got a place on an aeroplane.'

The next morning, one read in Mockbar's page:

DUKES

Four French Dukes, three ex-Ministers, nine Rothschilds and countless Countesses crossed the courtyard of the British Embassy yesterday evening. Were they going to pay their respects to our envoy, Sir Alfred Wincham? They were not.

ALONE

The former Pastoral Theologian and Lady Wincham sat alone in the great suite of reception rooms on the first floor, waiting for callers who never came. The cream of Parisian society, meanwhile, was packed into a tiny room off their back staircase.

TWO AMBASSADRESSES

It is no secret to anybody here that an unexpected and awkward situation exists at the Embassy where we now seem to have one ambassador and two ambassadresses. Lady Leone, wife of the last envoy, is still living there. Lady Wincham, though a woman of charm, cannot compete with her brilliant predecessor; she is left out in the cold. The Corps Diplomatique is wondering what the upshot will be.

I went to Orly to meet Davey. Although he was now past the middle sixties, his appearance had hardly changed since the day, nearly thirty years ago, when I first saw him with my sharp little girl's eyes at Alconleigh looking, as I thought, unlike a captain and unlike a husband. (On the second count, at any rate, I had been completely wrong. Nobody ever had a happier marriage than my dear Aunt Emily.) If his face had become rather like a portrait by Soutine of that other younger face, his figure was perfect. Elegant and supple, waving the *Daily Post*, he darted out of the group of arrivals from London. 'A pretty kettle of fish !' he cried cheerfully. 'Must see my luggage through the customs—wait for me in the motor.'

Then, getting in beside me, he said, 'Mind you, it's not a new situation, far from it. Lady Pickle kept the key of the Embassy garden in Rome and gave a garden party there weeks after the Betteridges had arrived. Sir George looked out of the window and saw her receiving the whole of the Embassy black list. Lady Praed opened a junk shop in the Faubourg here and nabbed people as they were going into the Embassy. Lady Pike went back to Vienna and then I seem to think she lived in a tree like a bird. English ambassadresses are usually on the dotty side and leaving their embassies drives them completely off their rockers. Alfred's statement is out in the evening papers—perfect, very dignified.' Alfred had said that Lady Leone not being well enough to travel, he was, of course, delighted to lend her the secretary's flat until she was better. 'You needn't worry, Fanny, the sitting ambassador holds all the cards—he can't help winning in the end.'

'If he doesn't win soon it may be the end,' I said.

'Yes, it's time she went. I lunched at Boodle's just now—Alfred's enemies are beginning to crow—you may imagine. *Daily Post* in great demand there.'

'We utterly count on you, Davey.'

'Quite right. As soon as we get back I must have a very strong cocktail and then I'll go straight to Pauline.'

'Good,' I said. 'I've got an ambassadress from some invented country (the real ones are all away still) coming to call on me at six. That fits in very well and we'll see you at dinner.'

As I sat with a little rat of a woman in black velvet with jet sleeves (dressed for the thé dansant I thought until I remembered what an old-fashioned notion that was), I heard the usual irritating sounds of distant laughter, punctuated now by Davey's well-known and rather specially piercing shriek. He was evidently enjoying himself. I found it even more difficult than usual to concentrate on the thé dansant lady's domestic problems. 'The Americans get them all because they don't mind what they pay.'

Davey reappeared in a black tie, at dinner-time.

'Nobody to meet me?' he said, seeing three cocktail glasses only.

'I thought you would be tired after the journey.'

'Now that I've got this extra kidney I'm never tired. No matter.'

'Whom would you like to see—anybody special? A lot of people are still away but Philip could find somebody for tomorrow, I expect, and of course, Davey, you must ask your own friends, while you're here.'

'Well, tomorrow——' a little shade of embarrassment perhaps—'I said I'd take pot luck with Pauline.'

'Don't tell me poor Mrs. Jungfleisch has got to stagger here with a pot for a whole dinner party now?'

'Only for Pauline and me. The others will dine at home and look in after.'

'Perhaps you'd like my chef to send something up?' I said, sarcastically.

'Now, Fanny, don't be cross and suspicious. This is only a little exploratory operation—if I'm to effect a cure I must know all about the case, mustn't I?'

'Mm. Who was there?'

'They came and went—awfully elegant and pretty and funny, one must hand them that. I'd forgotten about French clothes being so different. They think it was very brave of you to beard Mrs. Jungfleisch in her own motor.'

'She was in my own courtyard. Do they talk about me?' I said, not best pleased.

'My dear, you are topic A. They know absolutely everything you do, which dressmaker you've got an arrangement with, what the arrangement is, what clothes you have ordered ("ça, alors!"), what impression Alfred makes at the Quai ("évidemment ce n'est pas Sire Louis") and so on. When they heard I was your uncle they were all over me. Thought to be a new feather in Pauline's cap, getting somebody who is actually staying with you and a relation to boot. By the way, Philip Cliffe-Musgrave—I suppose he is on your side? If you ask me he has been in communication with the enemy.'

'That's inevitable under the circumstances.' Alfred now appeared and we went in to dinner.

The next morning was spent trying to get in touch with Davey's Paris friends of olden times. He had lost his foreign address book, it seemed. I sent for Philip to assist; he looked carefully at the names but said he had never heard of any of them in spite of having had four years in intensive social life all over France. None of them were in the telephone book. 'That doesn't mean anything,' said Philip, 'you wouldn't believe how many people here aren't. There is the pneumatique, you see, for urgent messages.'

He and Davey sat on my bed surrounded by books of reference. 'To begin with,' said Philip, 'we'd better consult Katie.' Katie was Miss Freeman of the Embassy telephone exchange, a great dear, soon to become a key figure in our lives. He took my telephone and said, 'Have a look at your list, Katie, will you, see if you've got any of these people and ring me back.' He read out the names of Davey's friends. A few minutes later the bell rang and Philip answered. 'None? Not even on G.P.O.? Thanks, Katie.'

'What is G.P.O.?' I asked.

'Garden Party Only. It runs into thousands. If they're not on that it means they've never set foot here. Now we must start on these directories.'

At this point Davey took his list back and jettisoned several mysterious figures, saying he had not really known them so very well or even liked them so very much. He could die happy without having seen them again. But he absolutely clung to three who must be found at all costs. They were a Marquis, an Academician and a doctor. We began with the Marquis who was neither in the Bottin Mondain nor the Cahiers Noirs de la Fausse Noblesse nor the Dictionnaire des Contemporains. Two fellow Marquises whom Philip rang up had never heard of him (though they said of course the name was that of a famous family) nor had George at the Ritz bar.

'What are his hobbies?' said Philip.

'He used to be the greatest living expert on Russian genealogies.'

'Try Père Lachaise,' said Philip.

'Not at all, he's quite alive, he sent me a faire part of his grand-daughter's marriage just the other day.'

'What address on the faire part?'

'I lost it. I can only remember the church—St. François Xavier.'

Philip rang up the Curé of St. François who gave him an address in Picardy. A telegram was duly dispatched there.

'That's one,' said Philip. 'Now, what about this alleged Academician?'

'Do you mean to say his name means nothing to you?'

'No, and furthermore I'll take a huge bet he's not in the Académie Française. I know those old Forty by heart and oh how I despise them. There they are, supposed to be looking after the language, do they ever raise a finger to check ghastly misuses of it? The French wireless has started talking about Bourguiba Junior—Junior—I ask you—why not Bourguiba Fils?'

'That's awful, but what could the Forty do?'

'Make a fuss. Their prestige is enormous. But they don't care a bit. Anyway, as I was saying——'

'But I've got a photograph of him in his uniform—I sent a pound to help buy his sword—I know he is a member.'

'What's his subject?'

'He's the greatest living expert on Mauretanian script.'

'Aha!' said Philip. 'Then he'll be of the Académie des Inscriptions. English people always forget there are five academies under the same cupola and mix them up.'

Davey was displeased at being thus lumped together with ignorant English people but Philip was quite right. A pneumatique was sent off to the Institut de France.

As for the doctor, he seemed to have found the perfect hideout. 'Docteur Lecœur,' said Davey impatiently, 'the greatest living expert on the vésicule bilière.'

I asked what that was. 'It's a French disease we don't have in England,' said Philip, rather too spry.

Davey shot him a look of great dislike. 'It's not a disease at all, it's a part of the body. We all have it. You ought to see the stones that came out of mine.'

Philip giggled annoyingly. He then rang up several famous doctors and the Ecole de Médecine; nobody had ever heard of this greatest living expert.

'He used to live in the rue Neuve des Petits Champs.'

'Doesn't exist any more.'

'Pulled down? Those lovely houses?'

'Not yet, thank goodness. Only rechristened.'

'Oh, it is too bad. What about the "Ballad of Bouillabaisse"?

> "A street there is in Paris famous,
>   For which no rhyme our language yields,
>   Rue Neuve des Petits Champs its name is,
>   The New Street of the Little Fields."

How cruel to give it a new name. The Academicians might well have protested about that.'

'Not they!'

'I wonder if Docteur Lecœur isn't still there? D'you know, I think I'll go round and see—I must have a little walk anyhow. Where is the best chemist?'

He went off in slight dudgeon. Philip said, 'The English so often have these unknown French friends, I've noticed. Collaborators one and all, mark my words. And talking of that, has it occurred to you that your uncle isn't perfectly sound? He seems to be keenly fratting with Pauline in her entr'sol.'

'The only person in Paris who isn't is me,' I said. 'I'm feeling thoroughly out of it.'

Philip looked guilty. 'Oh well,' he said, 'that's the whole morning wasted. How thankful I shall be when Miss Mackintosh arrives.'

I was sorry that he and Davey were not quite hitting it off. I never saw my uncle again all day. Alfred and I had to lunch with the American Ambassador, who was passing through Paris between two holidays, and my evening was again taken up with ambassadresses from improbable lands which I could certainly not have pin-pointed on a globe; as I discussed the disappearance of the genus footman with them I again heard those shrieks which undoubtedly meant that Davey was keenly fratting in the entr'sol. I began to be very downhearted indeed.

To add to my trials, the morning post brought news that good, clever plain Jean Mackintosh, not attractive to men, unlikely to get married, whose sensible support was going to facilitate my task in such a variety of ways, was now not coming. She had married, suddenly, not sensibly at all, a member of the Chelsea Set; Louisa wrote to tell me this news, evidently thinking herself more to be pitied than I was.

'Her godmother left her £4,000 and a tiara. It seems this Chelsea setter is always marrying or deed-polling people for little things like that. Oh Fanny!'

Jean, I knew, was her favourite child. She ended up a perfect wail of despair: 'PS. I am sending you Northey instead but it won't be the same.'

I had a feeling it would not be at all the same. I racked my brains to remember what I could about Northey, whom I had not seen since the early days of the war when Louisa and I were living at Alconleigh with our babies. A flaxen-haired toddler, she used to be brought to the drawing-room at tea-time and made to sing loud, tuneless songs, 'S'all I be p'etty, s'all I be rit?' We all thought her tremendously sweet. Louisa once told me that she was conceived in the Great Northern Hotel—hence her curious name. My children knew her well as they often stayed with the Fort Williams in Scotland; I seemed to have noticed that their verdict was rather scornful. 'Northey is old-fashioned.' 'Northey, brimming as usual.'

'Brimming?'

'Yes, her eyes are always brimming over with tears.'

'What about?'

'Everything.'

Basil could have given me an account of her, he was good at describing people. Naughty Baz, in Spain, in Spain. I had at last received a sheet of paper from him, dirty and crumpled, having spent many a week in a trouser pocket, with a Barcelona postmark, on which was written, 'I shan't be able to lunch Saturday, all news when we meet. Love from Baz.'

I wondered if I should not do well to put off this Northey, in spite of the fact that I had no other candidate and was beginning to feel the need of a secretary. Then my eye fell on the envelope of Louisa's letter and I saw that she had scribbled something almost illegible on the back of it, by which I understood that the child was already on her way, in a cattle boat going from Glasgow via I couldn't read what.

'Good luck to her,' said Philip, when I told him this. 'What time do you think your uncle left the entr'sol last night?' he added sourly.

'About half past three,' I said. 'I heard them. Mrs. Jungfleisch brought champagne, by the sound of it.'

'I've been talking to Mildred, she says it was absolutely hilarious— Pauline and Mr. Warbeck are wonderful together, telling tales of the 1920's. If I were you I should put a stop to all this, it's only prolonging the agony. Mildred says Pauline, who had been getting rather bored, has taken on a new lease of life.'

'We must give him time, Philip. He's only been here two days—I'm sure he'll fix it in the end, he is so clever.'

'Hm—I feel very doubtful.'

So, in my heart of hearts, did I.

Davey now appeared, bright and bustling, not at all like a man in the late sixties who had been up until half past three. 'Sorry I'm late. Docteur Lecœur has just been round to give me an injection of bull's brains.'

'Oh, so you found him then.'

'He's dead. But his son carries on in the same old house, with the same concierge. Paris is extraordinary the way nothing changes. If I hadn't lost that address book I would have found all those nice friends of mine, or at least their children.'

'And what about the Marquis and the Academician?'

'Both away. Hope to see me next time I come. Anyhow, Lecœur was the important one—goodness, I felt exhausted this morning—the lives you lead here—I wasn't in bed till four!'

'I heard you shrieking,' I said, reproachfully.

'I wish you'd popped down. Pauline was at the peak of her form. We had the life cycle of the Bolter, among other things, and now of course they are all longing to meet you.'

Philip looked at me significantly.

I said, 'I hope you had a good dinner?' Davey was fussy about food.

'Not very. Coarsely mashed potatoes—there's no excuse for that, nowadays. However, enough of this frivolity, agreeable as it has been. I was quite right to go into the thing thoroughly and in fact I only thought of the solution to our problem late at night after several glasses of wine.'

'You have thought of a solution?'

'Yes. It's very simple but none the worse for that, I hope. As Philip so truly says, one can't starve Pauline out and one certainly can't lecture her out. We must bore her out. The problem is how to stop all these Dukes and Rothschilds and countless Countesses from going to visit her. Now I suppose the social life here is built up on "extras", those men in white coats who go from party to party handing things round?'

'Indeed it is,' said Philip, 'more so every day.'

'You must get hold of one who is seen at all the big receptions. Is SEEN are the operative words. He must know everybody by sight, but above all they must be well aware he does. Post him at the steps to the entr'sol, paper and pencil in hand, and tell him to write down the names of Pauline's visitors—he might ask them as they go in—it must be very much underlined, what he is up to. At the same time, Philip, you must put it about on the grape vine that those who are found frequenting the entr'sol will not be invited to anything here during The Visit. I think you'll find that will do the trick all right.'

Philip gave a great shout of laughter—Davey joined in and they rocked to and fro. 'Wonderful,' Philip said.

'I think it's rather neat myself.'

'But what Visit?' I was considerably unnerved.

'Not necessary to specify,' said Philip, who now showed the true nice-ness of his character by accepting Davey's scheme with whole-hearted appreciation, 'the word Visit, with a capital V, is magical in Paris. To the gens du monde it is as the din of battle to the warrior. They will never risk missing it, like brave Crillon, simply in order to have a few more jolly evenings with Pauline. Hitherto it has been a sign of social failure not to be seen in the entr'sol—from now on it will be social death to go there. I'd have given anything to have thought of your scheme myself—what a genius you are. The decks will be cleared in half an hour.'

'It must be properly organized,' said Davey.

'Yes, indeed. We won't allow it to go off at half-cock, that would never do. First I'll ring up the greatest gossips I know. Then I'll go and engage M'sieur Clément. He's our boy, he rules the concierges of the Avenue du Bois with a rod of iron and is the king-pin of that neigh-bourhood. All Paris knows him by heart. So I've got a busy day, better get on with it. I congratulate you keenly,' he said to Davey and went off.

Davey said complacently, 'I hope now you are sorry that you suspected me of changing sides.'

'Davey—I humbly apologize.'

'Not that I mind. But you realize how it was. I had to find out what sort of people she was seeing. There are many amusing and delightful people here who wouldn't care a rap about a Visit or even expect to be invited if there is one. Docteur Lecœur, for instance. Those friends of hers, however, would. As I told you before, I understand the French.'

CHAPTER V

DAVEY's plan could not be put into operation for a day or two. When M'sieur Clément understood what he was being hired to do he de-manded an enormous bribe. He pointed out that Lady Leone's acquaintances all employed him in one capacity or another; if they suspected him of betraying them to *les Anglais* he might lose the many lucrative engagements and transactions on which his living depended. Philip, after a long session with him, came back to report and explained this to Davey and me but said that in fact no Parisian, especially not those who lived in M'sieur Clément's district, would dare get on the wrong side of him. He had been king of the black market during the war and was now indispensable for things like difficult railway and theatre tickets and for his ability to produce any requirement, from unlimited whisky to a trained nurse, not to speak of other, more sinister commodities, at a moment's notice. Undoubtedly very thick with the police, he knew all about the private lives of a vast section of the community. Philip had suggested to him that he would not really be risking very much by undertaking our assignment and had said that we, for our part, were obliged to take into account the remuneration he would receive from people wanting him to keep dark the fact that they had been about to visit Lady Leone. After long, hard bargaining and double bluffing on both sides, Philip got him down to £500. They shook hands on this. M'sieur Clément, wreathed now in smiles, said it might seem rather expensive but he guaranteed that the work would be impeccable. Philip then flew to London and, with some difficulty, persuaded the powers that be to disburse this amount from the secret funds. All these negotiations had to take place without the knowledge of Alfred who would certainly never have allowed them for a single minute.

At last the stage was set. Davey, Philip and I were the audience, established behind muslin curtains at Philip's bedroom window. His flat, which was over one of our lodges, had good views both of the courtyard and the street and was therefore in a commanding position. One could see and not be seen.

'I haven't been so excited since chub-fuddling days with Uncle Matthew,' I said to Davey.

M'sieur Clément, a lugubrious individual with bottle nose, had posted himself by the staircase of the entr'sol. For some reason he was not only dressed in inky black from head to foot but the sheets of paper which he held ready for the guilty names were black-edged like those put out, for the congregation to sign, at a French funeral. No doubt, in fact, pinched from one, according to Philip, since M'sieur Clément was, of course, a beadle. (Another of his part-time jobs was that of executioner's assistant.)

Presently a group of Lady Leone's gossips sauntered elegantly into the courtyard. There were five or six of them, all seemed to have arrived together and they were deep in talk. A tall, commanding man began to recount something, the others clustered round him, savouring his words. Two more people came in from the street; they joined the group, shook hands and were evidently put into the picture, after which the teller continued his tale. Suddenly, looking round as if to illustrate some point, his eye fell on M'sieur Clément. He stopped short, clutched the arm of a young woman and pointed; they all turned and looked. Consternation. Hesitation. Confabulation. Flight. Never had chub been more thoroughly fuddled; they flapped off, mouths open, and disappeared into the main stream of the Faubourg.

After this, incidents succeeded each other. A well-known pederast fainted dead away on seeing M'sieur Clément and was heaved, like

Antony to the Monument, into the entr'sol. Women screamed; very few kept their heads and demanded to sign our book. Nobody else went near Lady Leone. Gradually, the intervals between visitors became longer; at eight o'clock, when the entr'sol was usually at its liveliest, a whole hour had gone by without a single soul coming through our gate.

'It's done the trick,' Philip said, 'all the telephones in Paris must be engaged. I'd better go and give the old fiend his ill-gotten gains and then we can dine. Good work!' he said to Davey.

'I must say I never saw £500 so easily earned.'

'M'sieur Clément would reply, like Whistler, that we are paying for the knowledge of a lifetime.'

Lady Leone was now deserted by her friends, except for faithful Mrs. Jungfleisch, but greatly to my disappointment she showed no signs of leaving us. She lay on in her bed, perfectly contented, according to Davey, with her embroidery, the crossword puzzle and a very loud gramophone. When I suggested that we might take the gramophone away, since it did not belong to her at all but had been presented to the Embassy by a visiting rajah long ago, Davey and Philip made me feel like some cruel gaoler trying to remove the last solace of a lovely, unfortunate, incarcerated princess. It was less irritating, certainly, for me to hear strains of Mozart or the war speeches of Sir Winston Churchill, which she was inordinately fond of and which she played at full blast, than shrieks of laughter; at least Lady Leone could not be discussing me and my mother with a gramophone. The sting of her presence had been drawn by Davey's clever manœuvre—now that nobody went near her any more the fiction of illness could be maintained. Alfred's face was saved. All the same it annoyed me that she should still be under my roof and so did the fact that Davey was in the habit of slipping downstairs for a game of scrabble before dinner. However, both he and Philip were rather reassuring. They said she was bored and restless; furthermore Mrs. Jungfleisch was anxious to go to London for a debate at Chatham House. Their view was that Lady Leone would not be with us much longer, that she was merely biding her time in order to make a suitable exit. 'Pauline won't sneak out unobserved, you can be very sure. I expect she is hiring the Garde Républicaine to conduct her with trumpets and drums.'

I had various preoccupations at this time, still without a secretary, Philip much busier than he had been at the beginning. The days seemed too short for the hundred and one things which I must see to, among others our first entertainment, a cocktail party for the Dominions' Ambassadors. I was terrified at the thought of it, nightmares crowding in. I had not felt so nervous since the first dinner party I gave at Oxford, many years ago, for Alfred's professor. This was rather unreasonable since I had very little to do with the organization. Philip made out the lists and Major Jarvis, our comptroller, saw to the drink and the food of which there was to be a mountain. 'How can people eat anything at all between an enormous luncheon and an even more terribly stuffing dinner?' I asked.

'You'll see how they can. Are you going to do the flowers, Lady Wincham?'

The day came. I bought a lot of pink carnations (my favourite flowers) and stuck them into silver bowls. They looked so pretty, I was quite amazed at my own cleverness. Then I went upstairs and put on my cocktail dress. Nobody could have said that it looked pretty; hideous it was and very strange. My maid, Claire, pronounced it to be 'chic', but without much conviction. I had never liked it, even when worn by a wonderfully elegant Indo-Chinese mannequin, and had only been persuaded into ordering it because my vendeuse, in urging it on me, seemed to have the backing of a prominent English writer on fashion.

'Make no mistake,' asserted this pundit (photograph appended), with her usual downright authority, 'waists have gone for good.'

Having no wish to make a mistake over a dress which cost what had formerly been my allowance for a whole year, I had plumped for this waistless creation and oh! how I loathed it. However, there was nothing to be done; I was in it now, I must hope for the best and only try not to see myself in a glass.

The party was to take place in the state rooms on the ground floor. I went down and found Philip and Davey in hilarious mood, having had, I thought, good strong cocktails. I hurried towards them. They were kind enough not to remark on my dress but began making silly criticisms of the flowers.

'So like you, Fanny—why didn't you ask us first?'

'Carnations dumped in vases simply don't do any more. Haven't you ever heard of Arrangements? Don't you know about the modern hostess and her clever ways? Still-lifes—imaginative—not only flowers but yards of red velvet, dead hares, pumpkins, wrack from the seashore, common grasses from the hedgerow and the Lord knows what rubbish! Or else Japanesey, one reed by itself cunningly placed is worth five dozen roses, nowadays.'

I did know what they meant. Once, asked to the house of a Dior don, with other wives (women in Oxford have no identity, they are lumped together as wives), I had noticed a lot of top-heavy old-man's-beard in an urn surrounded by cabbages on the floor, and thought it all looked like a harvest home. People were saying, 'Utterly divine, your Arrangements.'

'Did Lady Leone go in for them?'

'Yes, indeed. Her feeling for colour and sense of form were the despair of all the hostesses here.'

'Shall I tell you something?—I intend to stick to pink carnations.'

Alfred joined us, saying, 'What's that dress, Fanny?' in a falsetto voice he sometimes used to denote that he was being quizzical.

'It's the fashion.'

'We are not here to be fashionable, you know.'

There were voices in the hall now, our guests were beginning to arrive; Alfred and I stood by the fireplace waiting to come forward effusively when they were announced. Philip had suggested that warm American rather than cold English manners might be adopted on this occasion and that we must do our best to look as if we were pleased to see the people.

'I can't say it, it wouldn't seem a bit real.'

'Don't force yourself then, but do just bare the gums.'

So there we were, preparing to simper, under the eyes of King George and Queen Mary, bad copies of bad portraits. I felt them disapproving of the fashionable dress, of the grins and of the whole notion of a cocktail party but approving of the carnations. Nobody came into the room. I felt perfectly idiotic planted there like a waxwork, horrible dress and artificial smile. There were clearly a lot of people in the hall; a curious silence had fallen on them. Davey and Philip went over to the door; when they got there they looked left towards the entrance and then, as though following the gaze of others, they sharply turned their heads to the staircase. They remained quite still, looking up it, with a stupefied expression.

'What is this all about?' said Alfred, going over to join them. He too stood eyes to heaven, with his mouth slightly open. I followed him. The hall presented a scene like a picture of the Assumption: a mass of up-turned faces goggling at the stairs down which, so slowly that she hardly seemed to be moving, came the most beautiful woman in the world. She was dressed in great folds of white satin; she sparkled with jewels; her huge pale eyes were fixed, as though upon some distant view, over the heads of the crowd. Following her, two of my footmen were carrying a large gramophone; then came Mrs. Jungfleisch, elegant in white linen, a basket on her arm. All the time, more guests were arriving. When Lady Leone got to the bottom of the stairs they divided into two lanes; she shook hands, like a royal person, with one here and there as she sailed out of the house for ever.

CHAPTER VI

CHARMING Northey, how to describe her? Can this creature of Commedia dell' Arte really have resulted from the copulation on a hard, brass, hotel bed, trains rumbling below, of dear old Louisa and terribly dull John Fort William? Some pretend that the place of conception, that of birth, and also the Christian name have a bearing on personality. Northey, product of King's Cross and Hill View Clinic, Oban, and with that name, must be a living refutation of this theory. Nothing of the northerner about her, no vague mistiness, no moments of absence; she was not romantic nor did she yearn after the unknown. She was the typical product, one would have said, of an ancient civilization beneath cerulean skies. Impossible to believe that she had a Scotch father, old enough to be her grandfather, and Pictish ancestors; yet surely good Louisa—oh no, perish the thought! She was incapable of inventing such a wealth of detail to cover up a sin. I incline to think that Northey must have been a changeling; that carelessness occurred in Hill View Clinic, Oban, by which the child of some noble Roman lady and a strolling player was exchanged for Louisa's brat. Physically she bore no resemblance whatever to the other Mackintoshes who all had solid frames, ginger heads and freckles. She was like a small exquisite figure in enamelled glass, with hair the colour of a guinea; her eyes the liveliest and most expressive I ever saw, not very large, brilliantly blue. In moments of excitement or distress they became diamond-shaped. When she talked she used her whole body in the concentrated effort of expressing herself, gesticulating, wriggling, as babies and puppies do. Her little thin hands never lay still in her lap. Furthermore, there was something indescribably lovable about her, she radiated affection, happiness, goodwill towards men. From the first moment we set eyes on her Alfred and I were her slaves.

She exploded into our household as we were dining alone together, tired and depressed, after the Dominions party. Davey had gone off saying that his friend the Marquis was now in Paris; it seemed that Philip was obliged to dine with his London stockbroker; both, I suspected, had really joined Lady Leone at Mrs. Jungfleisch's. I thought the party had been a total flop, though I heard afterwards that it was the most successful ever given at the Embassy in the sense that those who had missed it were wild with fury while those who had been present were sought after by the whole of Paris and supplied with free meals for weeks. But as Alfred and I could not discuss the great topic of the evening with our guests we were naturally the last people they wanted to talk to. They were longing to compare notes with others who had witnessed Lady Leone's exit, to buttonhole newcomers who had not and tell them about it, above all to leave as soon as they decently could and get on to the telephone. Everybody was very polite; indeed I was finding out that diplomats are diplomatic, it is one thing you can say for them. After the frank and outspoken rudeness I was accustomed to in Oxford this made a pleasant change. There were, too, moments of encouragement as when somebody said, 'Ah! The Irish Ambassador! That is a feather in Sir Alfred's cap—he never came to the Leones.'

The Ambassador of the Channel Islands praised my carnations, a major export, so he told me, of his country. A marvellous-looking Othello of a man gorgeously draped in pale blue taffeta (slightly marred by boots sticking out below, as my walking shoes had stuck out from beneath the Chinese robe) had invited me to go lion shooting in his. But the party had had a restless undercurrent and was certainly not much fun for the hosts.

So now it was over and we were dining. All of a sudden Northey was there, in the doorway, an inquiring look on her face. 'It's me,' she said.

'Darling!'

'I'm so sorry, I had to ask them to pay the taxi. No money at all. The station-master had to lend me a ticket. Yes I did, but I lost it.'

'Nothing matters now you're here. You must have had a beastly journey.'

'Oh Cousin Fanny (oh, you are kind, may I really), oh Fanny——' the soft skin of her forehead crumpled like tissue paper, her eyes took on a diamond-shaped, tormented expression which was to become very familiar to me and they brimmed. I saw exactly what Basil had meant about the brimming. 'You can't, you can't imagine. There were sweet bullocks on board. You don't know the sadness—the things they do to them. Their poor horns had been cut off—imagine the pain—and all because they get a pound more for them without horns and that's because then they can pack them tighter. I'd like to drop a hydrogen bomb on Ireland.'

'And kill millions of cows and all the birds and animals and the Irish also who are so charming?' Alfred said, gently.

'Charming!'

'Oh yes, they are. They have to export these bullocks in order to live. They have no industries, you see.'

'I hate and loathe and execrate them.'

'Darling, you mustn't be so worked up.'

'But I must be. These little creatures are put in the world for us to look after them. We are responsible. How do we treat them? They don't sleep you know, cows, they never have a moment of forgetting. Their comfort is to chew the cud—nobody feeds them properly on the journey—not enough water—fourteen hours in the train after the boat, with no water in this weather. And when they get to the—you know— dreadful place, does anybody give them water there?'

These things have worried me all my life; as I despise myself for not having the strength of character to do more than give an occasional pound to the R.S.P.C.A., I try to put them out of my mind.

'Come and have your dinner, dearest.'

'No, I couldn't,' she said, when the butler put a plate of con-sommé before her, 'nothing made of meat—I won't prey on them— never again.'

Alfred said, 'But if nobody ate meat the whole race of cows and sheep and pigs would become extinct. They have happy little lives you know and death is never agreeable, it won't be for us, either. It's the price we all have to pay.'

'Yes, but not torture. That's too much. Fanny, do promise you'll never have cruel food here.'

'What is cruel food?'

'For instance, lobsters and Irish horses and foie gras. A Frenchman on board told me what they do to sweet geese for pâté de foie gras.'

'Very wrong and stupid of him.'

'He told to make me care less about the bullocks.'

'This journey has been a nightmare. Now you must forget it.'

'But if people always forget these things they go on and on. All right, I suppose I'm boring you.'

'You're not boring us,' said Alfred, looking at her with love, 'but we don't like to see you so upset.'

'But you understand why, don't you? There we were, all travelling together—I used to go and chat to them, they looked so sad and good, poor little creatures—then I come to this lovely house and you, while they——' she was eating the remains of a cheese soufflé now, evidently very hungry. 'The captain of the *Esmeralda*,' she said, with her mouth full, 'was a most unpleasant person. He was ghastly to the bullocks and he offered to—you know—to hug me. But the sweet Frenchman who was there got me off.'

'Weren't there any women on board?'

'Only me.'

'And this Frenchman—he didn't want to hug you himself?'

'M. Cruas? He might have liked to but he didn't offer. He *is* kind. So is the station-master. When we got on shore and I looked for my ticket, quelle horrible surprise—there it wasn't. M. Cruas is poor, you know, so he couldn't buy me one, he could only carry my luggage to save porters. So the station-master lent. Can we pay him back at once, Sir Alfred—oh you are kind, may I really? Alfred? He knows about us because Lady Leone never has a ticket, or any money, or a passport—just a basket he says. Sacrée Lady Leone. Why sacred I wonder?'

'It only means that blooming Lady Leone,' said Alfred, in his falsetto. 'How's your French, Northey?'

'Very nice. M. Cruas is a teacher, so he taught me.'

'Did you not learn it at school?' An embarrassed, pouting wriggle was the answer to this. 'You went to school, I suppose?'

'I went. Only I didn't stay.'

'Why not?'

'It was too dread.'

'You'll have to learn quickly you know or you won't be any good to Fanny.'

'Yes. I've thought of that. So M. Cruas will come here and go on with the lessons.'

Alfred said to me afterwards, 'Your cousin Louisa is a fool. Imagine letting that child go alone on a cattle boat and sending her to a school where she was so unhappy she had to leave. I've no patience with such people. The poor little thing seems to have been utterly mismanaged.'

Implacable where his own contemporaries were concerned, Alfred had infinite indulgence for the young; in fact I sometimes thought he was too much on their side—hoodwinked by them. It was plain to see that Northey would twist him round her little finger.

Presently Philip came in. Perhaps he felt sorry for us, all alone as he thought, dwelling on that horrid party. When he saw Northey, he said, 'Don't tell me, I'm going to guess. I suppose this must be the wonderfully efficient young lady who is going to make life easier for all of us? Northey, in fact. How d'you do? How was the cattle boat?'

Alfred and I began talking simultaneously to change the subject. Northey made a sad little noise like a kitten but went on eating; the food, and the sight of Philip (that, perhaps most of all, she was gazing at him as if she had never seen a young man before) seemed to be taking the edge off her sorrow.

'This is Philip,' I said, 'he is busy, he mustn't be put upon, but in real emergency you'll find that he will come to the rescue.'

'Each for each is what we teach,' said Northey, looking at him from under her eyelashes. Oh bother, I thought, silly old love, again. Why does he have to be in it already, with Grace? Like all happily married people I am inclined to make matches; Philip and Northey seemed, on the face of it, such an ideal couple.

'What would a real emergency be?' she asked him.

'Let me think. Well, if you invited the Tournons to the same dinner party as les faux Tournons, that would be a pretty kettle of fish.'

'Please explain.'

'There is a couple here called M. et Mme de Tournon—social butterflies, pretty, delightful, perfectly useless. They are the real Tournons. Then there are M. et Mme Tournon. He is a deputy, a brilliant young man who specializes in finance, hard-working, ambitious, a parliamentary under-secretary. His wife is a prominent physicist. In spite of the fact that he is almost bound to become Prime Minister, while she may well end up with the Nobel prize, they are known to the whole of Paris as the false Tournons. Now if you had the two couples here together, protocol would demand that the false Tournons, elected by the people, should take precedence of the others. Thereupon the real Tournons would turn their plates upside down and say, "il y a erreur". I suppose you have understood every word? What a look! Never mind, in six months' time all this will be second nature to you.'

'You know, Philip,' said Alfred, 'I don't wish to fill this house with the ornaments of society.'

'No, Sir. If I may be allowed to make an observation, all ambassadors begin by saying that. The fact is, however, that if you don't have a sprinkling of them the others don't care to come. By the way, I really looked in to tell you that Bouche-Bontemps has just telephoned. He wants to know if he can see you tomorrow.'

I liked M. Bouche-Bontemps very much, felt natural and at my ease with him. 'He's a dear,' I said.

'Yes. The old-fashioned kind—a jolly Roman Catholic. All the up-and-coming young men seem to be Protestants—makes them so priggish.'

'I thought the old ones were free-thinkers?'

'It's the same as far as jollity goes.'

'Let's ask him to luncheon, shall we?' I said.

'Tomorrow? I don't know if he could with this crisis impending.'

'Of course, there's a crisis. I've been too much occupied with our own to take much notice.'

'All the same it might just suit him. I'll go and see.'

'What crisis?' said Northey, following him out of the room with her eyes.

'One of your duties here will be to read the papers,' said Alfred. 'You can read, I suppose?'

'I can read and I have a certain native intelligence. Don't be sarcastic with me, I beg.'

'Well, then, there's a parliamentary crisis going on and it looks as if this government may fall.'

'Then there'll be a general election? You see, I know about politics.'

'The point is that there will not. Fanny must give you some books to read about the state of France.'

Philip came back and said the Foreign Minister would be very much pleased to lunch, but he had business to do with the Ambassador and must see him alone.

'Northey and I can eat in the Salon Vert,' I said, 'and you can have your secrets in the upstairs dining-room. But do bring him in for a cocktail first, if you think he has time.'

'They always have time in the middle of the day,' said Philip. 'They can be up all night and start intriguing again before breakfast but the hours between one and three are sacred. That's why they are all so well—one never hears of a French politician dying—they live for ever, haven't you noticed?'

'I've come to say goodbye,' said Davey, arriving with my tray in the morning.

'Davey, don't go. It's so comfortable to feel you're here. Why don't you stay on in some capacity—comptroller? I think Major Jarvis is leaving us. Take his place—oh do!'

'Sweet of you, Fanny, but I couldn't live with the French. I understand them too well. Besides, I have fish to fry at home. New curtains for the drawing-room. And I can't live for ever without Mrs. Dale. Tea-time at home is delightful—blinds are drawn at the witching hour of 4.30 and I have her on the wireless.'

'We've got a wireless; you can have her here.'

'I've tried. She doesn't sound the same.'

'I wanted you to see Northey.'

'I have. We had our breakfast together just now. Rocks ahead there. So, I'm off. When you're next in trouble send for me, won't you? See you very soon in that case.'

When the Foreign Minister saw Northey he said we must all lunch together. He could do his business with Alfred in two minutes on his way out—he had never meant that the charming Ambassadress should be excluded from their talk. Mees Nortee was no doubt aware that her job demanded enormous discretion and indeed he could see by her face that she was a serious woman. During luncheon he addressed himself to her in a tender, avuncular, bantering tone of voice.

'So you are studying French. But why? Everybody here speaks English. And reading books on the state of France by English experts? I know these experts. They are all in love with Arabs.'

'No,' said Alfred firmly, 'respectable, married men.'

'The English who specialize in French affairs fill me with misgivings. Why are there so many of them and why must they concentrate on my poor country—are there no others in the world whose state is worth considering? Why not the state of Denmark for a change?'

'You ought to be flattered,' said Alfred. 'The publishers know they can sell any amount of books about France—in fact France, like Love, is a certain winner on a title-page.'

'Ah! So Mees Nortee is to learn about France and Love. I shall teach her, I know more than the English experts.'

'You are kind,' said Northey, 'because I can see that these books are a bore. No pictures, no talk and such terribly long sentences.'

'You told me you could read,' said Alfred.

'Like all of us she can read what interests her. When you have been here for a year, Mees, you will probably find yourself enjoying books about the state of France—though what this state will be by then, who can say?' He sighed deeply. 'Now, we will begin our lesson. Your uncle, the Ambassador here, has two bones to pick over with the French government, whenever there is a government. There are Les Iles Minquiers, a very nice point. You will hear more of them in due course—hats off to the Intelligence Service! And there is the European

Army, known as C.E.D. or E.D.C., nobody can ever remember why. One of your uncle's assignments is to persuade us to merge our army, which is overseas, fighting, with that of the Germans which is non-existent. This merging is desired by the Americans who see everything in black and white—with a strong preference for black.'

'M. le Ministre——' said Alfred sharply.

'Your protest is registered, M. l'Ambassadeur. The English are really indifferent, they don't care, but whenever they can please the Americans without it costing anything they like to do so. Armies have never meant much to them in times of peace—one army—another army—zero they think, anyhow, in the face of the Bomb. At the same time they have never been averse from weakening the Continental powers. All their Generals and Field-Marshals tell them that a European force would be quite unworkable so they say come on, the Americans want it, it rather suits us, let's have it. Now, if it were a question of commerce, M. l'Ambassadeur, I believe the nation of shop-keepers would sing a very different song? Suppose we wanted a European market, Excellency, what would you say to that?'

This lesson seemed to be more for the benefit of Alfred than of Northey who, crumpled forehead, looked extremely puzzled.

Alfred said, 'My American colleague tells me that you are going to accept the European Army, however.'

'Your American colleague has a beautiful wife whom everybody wants to please. No Frenchman can bear to see somebody so exquisite looking sad for a single moment. So wherever she goes, in Paris or the provinces, the deputies and mayors and ministers and igames say "of course" to whatever she tells them. And she tells them, most beguilingly, that they are going to accept the European Army. We shall never accept. This government, as you see, is tottering. It will fall during the night, no doubt. But no French government could pass such a measure. We may be weak—nobody can say we are very strong at present—but we have an instinct for self-preservation. We shall appear to be about to give way, over and over again, but in the end we shall resist.'

'And over the Minquiers,' said Alfred, 'you will appear to resist, but in the end you will give way?'

'You have said it, M. l'Ambassadeur, not I.'

'And then what about Europe? If the C.E.D. fails?'

'It will be built up on a more peaceful and workable foundation. My great hope is, that when the time comes, you will not oppose it.'

After luncheon M. Bouche-Bontemps said, 'Shall I take Mees to the Chambre? She could then see the state of France in action.'

'Oh, you are kind. The only thing is, M. Cruas said he would come at five.'

'Who is M. Cruas?'

'He teaches me French.'

'Ring him up. Say you have another lesson today.'

'He's poor. He hasn't got a telephone.'

'Send a pneumatique,' said the Minister, impatiently.

He had a word on the staircase with Alfred and then left the house accompanied by Northey, who hopped, skipped and jumped across the marble paving of the hall, Alfred said, like a child going to a pantomime. I saw no more of her that day. Philip, in and out of the Chambre, reported during the evening that she seemed perfectly entranced, determined to stay to the end. The government fell in the early hours and Northey slept until luncheon-time.

'So what was it like?' I said, when she finally appeared.

'Terribly like that dread school I went to. Desks with inkpots and a locker. From where I sat you could see there are lollipops in the lockers and when they are pretending to listen to the lecturer or read lesson books they are really having a go at the illustrated mags. All the same they do half-listen because suddenly all the Madames get up and stamp and roar and shout and the master has to ring a bell and shout back at them.'

I had a vision of ghastly women, Erinyes, tricoteuses, obstructing the business of the Chambre. 'Madames? Women deputies?'

'No, Fanny,' said Northey as one explaining a well-known fact to a child. 'Madames are the Social Republicans, so called because their party headquarters are in the rue Madame. The Republican Socialists, whose H.Q. is in the rue Monsieur, are called les Monsieurs. They are each other's worst enemies. You see how sweet M. Bouche-Bontemps was quite right and going is better than reading.'

'What was the debate about?'

'Really, Fanny, I'm surprised that you should ask me that. Have you not seen your *Figaro* this morning? I hear that it is very well reported. Pensions for remarried war widows, of course.'

'Are you sure?'

'Quite sure. There was a nice person in the box called Mrs. Jung-fleisch who told me all about it. And an Englishwoman married to one of the deputies—a marquis I suppose because when he got up to speak the Communists chanted "imbécile de Marquis" and he became quite giggly and lost his place.'

'That must be Grace de Valhubert,' I said, pleased to think that she was back in Paris.

'Yes. She knows Fabrice and Charlie and she sent you her love. She talks with such a pretty French accent and Fanny! her clothes! Sweet M. Bouche-Bontemps came and took me out to dinner. He said if he fell he would be able to devote himself to my education. Well, he has fallen, so—— Philip brought me home,' she added, nonchalantly.

I thought I understood now why she had stayed so late.

CHAPTER VII

Now that the French were comfortably without a government, Alfred received instructions from the Foreign Office to make strong representations at the Quai d'Orsay about Les Iles Minquiers. These islands, which were to occupy his waking thoughts for many a long month to come, are described in Larousse as dangerous rocks near St. Malo and given no independent notice in the *Encyclopaedia Britannica*. There are three of them and at high tide they are completely submerged. During the liberation of France, General de Gaulle found time to have a tricolor run up, at low tide, on the Ile Maîtresse or middle island. Never has the adage 'let sleeping dogs lie' been more justified. This flag was immediately spotted by the Argus-eyed Intelligence Service and the Admiralty found time to send a frogman, at high tide, to haul it down again. Now that the attention of Whitehall was drawn to the existence of the Minquiers, some busybody with a turn for international law began to study the complicated question of their ownership. It transpired that the Traité de Brétigny (1360) which gave Normandy to the Kings of France, and Calais, le Quercy, le Ponthieu, Gascony, etc., to the English crown, made no allocation of the Minquiers. They were not covered by the various Channel Island treaties and have existed throughout history as a no-man's land. As they are within sight, when they can be seen at all, of the French coast, no doubt they were always assumed to be part of France, but nobody seems to have minded one way or the other. It was bad luck for Alfred that the government which appointed him to Paris should be determined to paint the Minquiers pink on the map; nothing could have been more calculated to annoy the French at that particular juncture.

'But what is the point of these islands?' I asked as Alfred was about to leave for the Quai d'Orsay.

'Islands are always rather desirable—the Royal Yacht Squadron would like them to be English; our fishermen could use them, I suppose. The Foreign Secretary says the question must be settled now in the interests of Western solidarity. I must say, I'm not delighted to have to make a nuisance of myself at such a time.'

The President of the Republic, M. Béguin the outgoing Prime Minister, and the heads of the parties, one of whom was M. Bouche-Bontemps, had been up for several nights trying to resolve the crisis; tempers were beginning to be frayed. The English newspapers were pointing out the impossibility of relying on an ally who never seems to have a government. In decidedly gloating tones they inquired: will France be represented at the Foreign Ministers' Conference next week or shall we, as usual, see an empty seat? Can the Western Alliance afford these continual tergiversations? The people of England look on with dismay, they have but one desire, to see our French friends strong, prosperous and united.

The French papers urged the political parties to settle their differences with the least possible delay since 'nos amis Britanniques' were clearly about to make use of the situation to further their own sinister schemes. The two old neighbours are not always displeased by each other's misfortunes, nor do they trust each other not to take advantage of them.

'And you will notice when you have lived here for a bit,' said Grace de Valhubert, 'that it is the English who are the more annoying. The French never sent arms to the Mau-Mau, that I heard of.'

Grace counted herself as a sort of supernumerary English ambassadress; like most people who have been accredited for years to a foreign country she could only see one side of every question and that not the side of her own, her native land. Everything French was considered by her superior to its English equivalent. She was inclined to talk a sort of pidgin English, larded with French words; she slightly rolled her r's; at the same time her compatriots in Paris noted with glee that her French was by no means perfect. She was a bit of a goose, but so good-natured, pretty, and elegant that one could not help liking her. It was the fashion to say that she had a terrible time with her husband but when I saw them together they always seemed to be on very comfortable terms. She was evidently quite uninterested in Philip.

She had come to call on me, sweet and affectionate, bringing me flowers. 'So sorry not to have been here when you arrived but I always stay at Bellendargues as long as I can. It's what I like best in the world. Anyway, who knows that I would have resisted the entr'sol? Too awful if you hadn't been able to ask me when next there is a Visit!'

'Oh Grace, the rules would be quite different for you!'

I took her to my room to see the fashionable dress I hated so much. She transformed it instantly by putting a belt on it, after which it became the prettiest I had ever had. 'Never believe that we have seen the last of the waist—the English have been saying it ever since the New Look went out—wishful thinking I suppose. An Englishwoman's one idea is to get into something perfectly shapeless and leave it at that.'

I thought of the Chinese robe.

'As a matter of fact,' she went on, 'if you're like me and get fond of your clothes and want to wear them for years the first rule is to stick to the female form. Everything that doesn't is dated after one season. Perhaps I'd better take you to my dressmaker—he's in the Faubourg— very nice and convenient for you—his clothes are more ordinary and far more wearable. I always think Dolcevita really wants to make one look a figure of fun.'

I thanked her for this advice, on all of which I acted. 'Come back to the Salon Vert and we'll have some tea.'

'You've moved the furniture about—it's better like this,' said Grace, looking round the room. 'It never seemed very much lived in. Pauline used that gloomy bedroom more.'

I poured out the tea and said I hoped the boys had behaved themselves at Bellendargues.

'We never saw them except at meals. They were very polite. Do you know about Yanky Fonzy?'

'I don't think so—is he at school with them?'

'He's a jazz biggy,' said Grace, 'he sends them. All that lovely weather they were shut up with a gramophone in Sigi's room being sent by Yanky. Haven't you seen their shirts with Yank's the Boy for Me printed on them? It's a transfer from Disc.'

'What does that mean?'

'I don't know, I'm quoting.'

'How did your husband take it?'

'Don't ask,' said Grace, shutting her eyes. 'However, it's entirely Charles-Edouard's own fault for insisting on Eton instead of letting the child go to Louis-le-Grand like everybody else. Then he'd never have heard of this ghastly Yanky.'

'Any news of him since they all arrived in Scotland?'

'Silence de glace. But as a matter of fact I have never received a letter from Sigismond in my life—I wouldn't know his writing on an envelope if I saw it. I pity the women who fall in love with him. When he first went to Eton I gave him those printed postcards: I am well, I am not well—you know, rayer la mention inutile. Of course he never put one in the box. Steamed off the stamps, no doubt. Afterwards he said the only thing he wanted to tell me was that his fag-master had stolen £5 from him and he couldn't find that on the list. They went back yesterday, didn't they?'

'Day before, I think.'

'I rang up my father in London this morning—thick fog over there, needless to say—look at the glorious sun here, it's always the same story —yes, so I begged him to go down and see them. No good worrying, is it? Charles-Edouard doesn't in the least. He says if Sigi is ill they'll have to let one know and when he's expelled he'll come home. He'll be obliged to, if only to worm some money out of us.'

'I suppose so, at that age. Later on they don't seem to need money and then they vanish completely.' I was thinking of Basil.

'What d'you hear of the crisis?' said Grace.

'Can you explain why the government fell at all? It seems so infinitely mysterious to me. War widows or something?'

'They were already bled to death on foreign affairs. The pensions for remarried war widows only finished them off. It's always the same here, they never actually fall on a big issue—school meals, subsidies for beet-root, private distilling, things of that sort bring them down. It's more popular with the electorate (they like to feel the minorities are being looked after) and then the deputies don't absolutely commit themselves to any major policy. C'est plus prudent.'

'Does your husband like being in the Chambre?'

'He gets dreadfully irritated. You see he's a Gaullist; he can't bear to think of all these precious years being wasted while the General is at Colombey.'

'Nobody seems to think he'll come back.'

'Charles-Edouard does, but nobody else. I don't think so, though I wouldn't say it, except to you. Meanwhile all these wretched men are doing their best, one supposes. M. Queuille has failed—did you know? —it was on the luncheon-time news. Charles-Edouard thinks the President will send for M. Bouche-Bontemps now.'

The telephone bell rang and Katie Freeman said, rather flustered, 'I've got M. Bouche-Bontemps on the line.'

'But the Ambassador is in the Chancery.'

'Yes, I know that. It's Northey he wants and I can't find her—she's not in her office and not in her room. He's getting very impatient—he's speaking from the Elysée.'

'Let me think—Oh I know, I believe she's trying on something in my dressing-room.' She had borrowed two months' wages from me, bought a lot of stuff and had turned my maid, Claire, into her private dress-maker. 'Just a moment,' I said to Grace, 'it's M. Bouche-Bontemps.' I went to look and sure enough, there was Northey being pinned into a large green velvet skirt. 'Come quickly, you're wanted on the telephone.'

She gathered up the skirt and ran into the Salon Vert. 'Hullo, oh, B.B.?' she said. 'Yes, I was working—not in my office—my work takes many different forms. That would be lovely. Ten o'clock would be best —I'm dining with Phyllis McFee but then I'll say I must go to bed early. Ten, and you'll pick me up? Oh, poor you, must you really? Never mind, soon be over.' She rang off.

Grace looked very much surprised at this conversation.

'B.B. has to see the President now, which is a bore he says. But when that's over he'll take me to Marilyn Monroe.'

'That means he's going to refuse,' said Grace. 'The crisis will go on and the English will bag the Iles Minquiers, you mark my words. It's intolerable.' She said to Northey, 'You must come and dine one evening and we'll go dancing. I'll arrange something as soon as the household is a bit organized.'

'The utter kindness of you,' said Northey and trotted back to Claire. 'What a darling!'

'Oh, isn't she! You can't imagine how much I love her—so does Alfred.'

'And Bouche-Bontemps, it seems.'

'He's very kind to her. Don't look like that, Grace, he's a grand-father.'

'Mm,' said Grace.

'And she's as good as gold.'

'All right, I believe you.'

'Yes, you must. I sometimes think I would swop all my naughty boys for one daughter like Northey.'

'I've got three little girls, you know, but they are babies. The eldest is only six. I wonder—they are heavenly now, but people say girls can be so difficult.'

These words of Grace's soon came true. Adorable as she was, Northey was by no means an easy proposition. She was now in love, for the first time (or so she said, but is it not always the first time and, for that matter, the last?) and complained about it with the squeaks and yelps of a thwarted puppy. Her lack of reticence astounded me. When dealing with the children, I always tried to think back to when my cousins and I were little; any of us would have died sooner than admit to unrequited love, even in a whisper to each other, in the Hons' cup-board, while the grown-ups never had the smallest idea of what went on in our hearts. But with Northey there was no question of concealing the worm, the canker and the grief; she displayed them. The loved one himself was not spared.

'Oh, Philip, I worship you.'

'Yes, I know.'

'Shall I chuck B.B. and dine with you instead?'

'No, thank you. I'm dining out.'

'Chuck!'

'No fear. It's a most amusing dinner.'

'The pathos! Well, if you won't take me out to dinner you might throw me a civil word.'

'If you go on like this, I'll throw something blunt and heavy. I must explain, m'lord, that my life had been made a purgatory. My work was suffering, I gave way to an uncontrollable impulse—it may have been wrong; it was inevitable. Fanny will be a witness for the defence, won't you?'

The fact that every Frenchman who saw her fell in love made her no easier to deal with and considerably complicated my task as am-bassadress. Instead of a nice, sensible, methodical secretary ever at my elbow to help and support me I had this violent little fascinator flitting about the house, bewailing her lovelorn condition to anybody who would listen, or paralysing Alfred's private line as she wailed down it to one of her new friends. They were not spared the desperate state of her heart any more than we were. How could sobriety and security, the keynotes of our mission, be maintained under these circumstances? Northey created a circumambience of insobriety and doubtful security. Nothing could have been more unfortunate than her choice of followers. Such personages as the first Vice-President of the Chambre, the Secretary-General of the Elysée, an ex-Minister of Justice, the Ambassador of the Channel Islands, the Governor of the Bank of France, the Prefect of the Seine, not to speak of the outgoing Foreign Secretary who looked like being the next Prime Minister, could hardly be treated as ordinary young dancing partners. Difficult for Alfred to insist that they must not come to the house until they were invited or that they should at least limit themselves to the usual hours for calling on young ladies. They were all busy with the crisis, so they came when they could or else lengthily telephoned.

Perhaps unwisely, we had given Northey the entr'sol recently vacated by Lady Leone, with its own entrance to the courtyard. At all hours of the day and night one was apt to see French government or C.D. motors there whose owners were not transacting business with Alfred, while motor-bicyclists dressed like Martians continually roared up the Faubourg to stop at our concierge's lodge with notes or flowers or chocolates for Northey. She had taken to the social and political life of Paris with an ease more often exhibited nowadays by pretty boys than by pretty girls. Philip, who knew that esoteric world better than anybody else in the Embassy, said it was almost incredible how quickly she was picking up its jargon and manners. While I was still feeling my way through a thick fog, not knowing who anybody was, summoning small talk with the greatest difficulty, Northey seemed completely at home with the different groups which make up French society.

In one respect, however, she remained the same little Scotch girl who had arrived on the cattle boat. Her passion for animals was in no way modified and, as might have been foreseen, she began to accumulate pets which she had rescued from some misfortune.

'Yes, I saw this group of children in the Tuileries. Now I've always noticed that if you see children clustered round something and looking down at it fixedly it's going to be a creature and they are going to be cruel to it. Sure enough, they had got hold of this sweet torty. They kept picking her up and waving her about and putting her down again. You know how it's dread for a tortoise to be waved because she naturally thinks she is in the clutches of an eagle. So cruel, to bring them here from Greece—thousands of them—and wave them about all the summer and then leave them to die in the winter. Ninety per cent die, I read. Oh Fanny, the world! Anyway I bought her from those ghastly children for 1,000 francs, which I luckily had on me (we must have a little talk about money) and now she can be happy until the cold weather. Just look at the way she walks though, anybody can see her nerves are in ribbons.

'Would you like to see my cat? She's old. She's bandaged up like this because her abscesses keep breaking out. The Duke's vet comes every morning when he has finished with the pugs and gives her penicillin. How d'you mean, kinder? Can't you see she's enjoying her life? She lies there purring, quite happy. Could I borrow a little money? Yes, well, penicillin is expensive, you know. You are kind—I'm keeping a strict account.'

Then she went for a walk on the quays and saw a badger asleep in a cage on the pavement outside an animal shop. 'The cruelty—they hate daylight—they live all day in a sett and only come out when it's dark. Imagine keeping it like that—why bring it here from its wood, poor little creature? So I came back for Jérôme and the Rolls Royce and borrowed some money from Mrs. Trott (darling, could you pay her for me if I promise to keep a strict account?) and together we lugged Mr. Brock into the motor, huge and heavy he is, and brought him to the Avenue Gabriel, through that gate, and he's in the garden now. Do come and look——'

'Oh Northey, was that a good idea? As it's broad daylight in the garden—I don't see much difference.'

'Oh, the dear fellow will manage somehow.'

He did. The next morning there was an enormous, banked-up hole like an air-raid shelter in the middle of the lawn.

She was wildly unrealistic about money; each for each, her favourite adage, was evidently the keynote of her faith in such matters. She borrowed from any and everybody out of whom she could wheedle the stuff and then made Alfred or me pay them back, saying, 'I'm keeping a strict account. I've had my wages now until June of next year.'

'Dearest,' I said one day, 'what about M. Cruas? Ought we not to pay him for his lessons?' He came every afternoon for at least an hour, so Northey told me; he was evidently a good teacher as her French progressed amazingly.

'No, Fanny, it's not necessary, he comes for love. But if you have got a few thousand francs to spare, Phyllis McFee and me did a little recce in Main Street and saw un cocktail, prix shock, which is just my affair. Sharpen your wits, darling, it's French for a cheap afternoon dress.'

This Phyllis McFee was a Scotch friend of Northey's, from Argyll-shire, who also had a job in Paris. So far I had not met her. I was glad that Northey had somebody to run round with, other than elderly cabinet ministers.

'Oh you are kind, now I can go and buy it. So I've had my wages until August I think—anyway, I keep a strict account you know, it's all written carefully down.'

It could not exactly be said that Northey's work suffered from all these distractions, she had such a genius for delegating it. 'Each for each is what we teach' meant that Alfred and I, Mrs. Trott the house-keeper, Jérôme the chauffeur, Major Jarvis and Philip did practically all her various jobs for her. Our reward was 'You are kind, oh the kind-ness of you.' But quite apart from extraneous calls on her time and attention, she was not cut out to be a secretary, nobody has ever been less of a career woman. She lived, quite frankly, for pleasure.

'I see what my boys mean when they say she is old-fashioned,' I observed to Philip, 'she is as frivolous as a figure of the twenties.'

'Thank goodness for that anyway. These new ones make me despair of the female sex. I belong to the old world, that's what it is, I talk its language—I'd sooner marry a Zulu woman of my own age than one of these gloomy beauties in red stockings.'

Quite good, I thought, as far as it went, but I was sorry to see that Philip showed no sign of falling in love with Northey. He burned for Grace and I feared that when that flame died down for want of fuel it would never be relit by Northey whom he regarded as a charming, funny little sister. I told her so. She had discovered that Grace was his love (enlightened, probably, by one of the followers, hoping to further his own suit) and came, eyes like diamonds, to communicate her dismay.

'Horrible, horrible Grace, how could he?'

I thought it better to be astringent, not too sympathetic. 'Last time we talked about her you said she was so fascinating.'

'Never! Idiot, rolling her *r*'s and dressing up French. Besides, she's as old as Time.'

'As old as Philip.'

'It's different for a man as you know very well. Fanny, I can't understand it.'

'I'm afraid we never understand that others may be preferred to ourselves.'

'Has Alfred ever preferred anyone to you?'

'Yes, and very boring it was.'

'But you managed?'

'As you see. I think it's a good thing, really, that you know about Philip and Grace.'

'Why is it? I was much happier before.'

'Because now you won't go on harbouring dangerous illusions.'

'More dangerous for me to despair.'

'Don't despair, but don't be too hopeful, either. Remember that it would be a miracle if Philip fell in love with you, under the circum-stances.'

'Well, there are miracles. Why shouldn't God do something for me?'

'Yes, I only say don't count on it.'

Philip, overhearing these words as he came into the Salon Vert, said, 'If you're after a miracle, St. Expédite is your boy. He's a dear little

Roman saint who deals with lost causes and he hangs out at St. Roch. Only he doesn't like it if you begin asking before the cause is really lost; you must be quite sure before you bother him. I thought we might get him on to the European Army soon. What do you want a miracle for, Mees?'

'It was love and love alone that made King Edward leave his throne.'

'Oh, love! Don't tell me you're keenly running after Bouche-Bontemps?'

'You know I'm not, you brute.' Brimming. 'You know quite well who it is.'

'By the way, I'd forgotten! That is a lost cause, I can tell you and I should know. There, there, mop them up. Are you going to the Chambre to see the old boy present his ministry?'

'Of course. I'm his Egeria.'

'Don't be up until five again,' I said.

'No. He's going to make one of his nutshell speeches—not more than two hours—he says they'll have thrown him out by midnight.'

'Oh, that's how it is?' said Philip. 'I wasn't sure. Excellent. Then we can get on with the Iles Minquiers.'

'I wish I understood about these islands,' said Northey.

'So do I,' said Philip.

'Why do our papers keep saying the French should be urged to give them up for their own sake?'

'Because we want them.'

'If it's good for us to have them, why is it good for the French to get rid of them?'

'In the first place they almost certainly belong to us. Then there's our altruism. In our great, true, sincere love for the French, knowing they will be better without the islands (and a great many other places as well) we are willing to take the responsibility for them off their shoulders. Now, put that in your pipe and stop asking questions. I'm a civil servant, policy is nothing to do with me, I am there to obey orders. I may add that I wish to heaven the bloody thing could be settled and forgotten—it's poisoning my existence.'

The telephone bell rang. 'Answer,' I said to Northey, 'and ask who it is.'

'Hullo—oh—yes, he's here—who is it? Quelle horrible surprise! It's for you, an affected foreign voice,' she said loudly, handing the receiver to Philip.

'Grace? Oh, don't pay any attention, she's not quite all there, you know. The Times? No, I haven't. There's a leader? Well, it won't be the last, they've got to fill that space every day—ghastly for them. And a letter from Spears? Not a bit surprised. But, Grace, I've told you it's nothing to do with me. I don't approve or disapprove, I'm not meant to have an opinion. No, I won't resign, it never does any good and then one is unemployed. Do you want me to leave Paris? And all because of a few rocks which honestly don't matter either way. We'll talk about it presently. Yes, of course I will, I'd love to.' He rang off and said to me, 'We're both dining there, aren't we, Fanny? She wants me to take her to the Chambre later on.'

'You said you'd pick me up and take me,' Northey brimmed.

'But we will. Grace won't mind a bit.'

'I mind.'

'Ah! Then you'd better tell them to send the Presidential motor, with its moon, for you.'

'Very funny and witty.'

'Jérôme can take you, darling. Send him on to the Valhuberts', that's all.'

'It's because—I don't like going in there alone. I know.' She took the telephone and said, 'Katie, love, put me through to the Bureau of the Assemblée, will you? I'll speak in my own room.'

CHAPTER VIII

ALFRED had gone to London for a day or two, so Philip took me to the Valhubert dinner. I was beginning to lose my fear of such social occasions now that I knew some of the people likely to be present. They were all very nice to me. I was dazzled by the French mode of life; they keep up a state in Paris which we English only compete with in country houses. A Paris dinner party, both from a material point of view and as regards conversation, is certainly the most civilized gathering that our age can produce, and while it may not be as brilliant as in the great days of the salons, it is unrivalled in the modern world.

The Hôtel de Valhubert, like the Hôtel de Charost (the English Embassy), lies between a courtyard and a garden. It is built of the same sandy-coloured stone and, though smaller and of a later date, its ground plan is very similar. There the resemblance ends. The Embassy, having been bought lock, stock and barrel from Napoleon's sister, is decorated and furnished throughout in a fine, pompous, Empire style very suitable to its present use. The Hôtel de Valhubert is a family house. The rooms still have their old panelling and are crammed with the acquisitions of successive Valhuberts since the French revolution (when the house was sacked and the original furnishings dispersed). Beautiful and ugly objects are jumbled up together, and fit in very well. Grace's flowers were perfection; no yards of velvet, no dead hares, not a hint of harvest home, pretty bouquets in Sèvres vases.

After praising my dress, which was, I thought myself, quite lovely and which came from her dressmaker, Grace introduced me to various people I did not know already. 'It's pouring in London tonight,' she said, 'I've just had a word with Papa. He'd been to Eton and taken the boys out—you'll be glad to hear they are all three alive. He says he never saw such rain!'

Mrs. Jungfleisch said the weather had been perfect when she was in London, much better than in Paris.

'Come off it, Mildred. You see London through rose-coloured specs, though I notice you don't go and live there.'

I had not met Mrs. Jungfleisch since she came down my staircase, in white linen, actively participating in the rapine of the gramophone. She showed no signs of embarrassment but said, 'Nice to see you again.' I felt as if I had behaved badly in some way and had now been forgiven.

At dinner I sat next to Valhubert and we talked about the children, a ready-made topic whenever he and I saw each other.

'Poor Fabrice,' he said, speaking of my Fabrice's father. 'He was my hero when I was a little boy and as soon as I grew up we were more like brothers than cousins. I must say the child has a great look of him. I was telling my aunt—naturally she is anxious to see him—will you allow me to take him down there when he comes for Christmas? It could be to his advantage, she is rich and there is nobody left of the Sauveterre family. She might adopt him—no—you wouldn't care for that?'

'I don't think I would mind. After all, she is his grandmother. In another five years I suppose he will have gone out of my life. These boys seem to vanish away as soon as they are grown up.'

'And then what do they do?'

'I wish I knew. Alfred and I have always acted on the principle with them of never asking questions.'

'Like the Foreign Legion?'

'Exactly. Now I sometimes wonder if it has been a good plan. We have no idea what goes on; the two elder ones might be dead for all we see or hear of them.'

'Where are they—in diplomacy?'

I began telling him about Beard and Ted, but I could see that he was not listening. He was interested in his own Sigi and in his cousin's Fabrice while accepting our Charlie as inseparable from the others. Bearded professors, whiskered travel agents (if that was what Basil had become) were out of his ken. I knew that my encounter in the street with Basil's accomplice would have seemed strange and dreadful to any man of my own generation; I had never told Alfred of it.

'Aren't you going down to the House?' I said, to change the subject. I knew that the session began at nine o'clock.

'My father-in-law always says down to the House—I like it very much. Yes, presently I will. There's no hurry, we know to a minute what is happening. Jules Bouche-Bontemps at this moment is launching a pathetic appeal—no, pathetic is not the translation, it is one of those trap words which mean different things in the two languages. Rousing, perhaps, a rousing call, or a moving speech. (Nobody will be roused or moved by it, but let that pass.) I could make this speech for him if he fell ill in the middle. I know it as well as he does and so does the whole of his audience. He will begin by saying that our divisions suit nobody except certain allies who had better be nameless. Here we shall have a long digression on Les Iles Minquiers, their history and moral attachment to France. (Those islands are a bore, I can't listen to anything which concerns them, it is too dull.) This will be put in so that if we lose them—and who, except, of course, Grace, cares if we do?—he will be able to say that it is the fault of my party and les Madames who are all preparing, as he very well knows, to vote against him. He will pretend to be deeply shocked by the unholy alliance between les Madames and the Gaullists, all playing London's game. Well, that's a change from Moscow's game, isn't it, which he generally accuses us of playing? Then he will move on to next week's railway strike. The rotting vegetables and stranded tourists will also be the fault of ourselves and Mesdames. Of course all these gloomy prophecies and reproaches and upbraidings will have not the slightest effect and he knows it. He knows to a vote where he will be at the end of the session, that is to say out, not in, so he really might save himself the trouble of making this speech. But he is fond of speaking, it amuses him, and above all it amuses him to publish the iniquities of his fellow-countrymen. Do you like him?'

'Oh yes—very much.'

'I love him—I really love old Bouche-Bontemps.'

Philip leant across the table and said to me, 'All French politicians love each other, or so they say. You see, they never know when they may want to join each other's governments.'

Everybody laughed. Conversation became general, people shouting remarks at each other in all directions. I like this lively habit which enables one to listen without the effort of joining in, unless one has something to say. When the babel died down again I asked M. Hué, my other neighbour, what would happen if the crisis went on.

'René Pléven, Jules Moch and Georges Bidault, in that order, will try and form governments and they will fail. Anglo-French relations will deteriorate; social troubles will multiply; North Africa will boil. In the end even the deputies will notice that what we chiefly need is a government. They will probably come back to Bouche-Bontemps who will get in with the same ministers and the same programme they will have rejected tonight. Is it true that Sir Harald Hardrada is coming over to give a lecture?'

'So Alfred tells me.'

'That's bad.'

'Oh—I was looking forward——'

'I don't mean the lecture. There is nothing on earth more enjoyable than listening to Sir Harald. But it is a storm signal—the first in a sequence of events only too well known to us at the Quai d'Orsay. Whenever your government is planning some nasty surprise they send over Sir Harald to lull our suspicions and put us in a good humour.'

'What's the subject of the lecture?' Valhubert asked me.

'I think I heard it was to be Lord Kitchener.'

The two Frenchmen looked at each other.

'Nom de nom——!'

'We always think we can tell what is coming by the subject, you see. How well I remember "A Study in Allied Solidarity". It was intensely brilliant—delivered in Algiers just before the Syrian affair. "Lord Kitchener" can only mean goodbye to Les Iles Minquiers. Well, if it's that, it's no great surprise. Let's hope the Intelligence Service is not preparing something much worse.'

'Talking of the Service,' said Valhubert, 'when do I meet the irresistible Mees Nortee?'

'Oh, poor Northey, so she's a spy, is she?'

'Of course. And such a successful one. It was devilish work sending her.'

'Well, you'll be able to see for yourself at our dinner party next week.'

'Good. Can I sit next to her?'

'Certainly you can't,' said Philip.

'Why not? If it's an official dinner, I get the bout de table anyway.'

'No—we have other candidates—me for one—it's a big dinner and you'll be well above the salt.'

'I thought the English never bothered about protocol?'

'When in Rome, however, we do as the Romans do—eh, Hughie?'

'Put me next to Mees——'

'After dinner,' said Philip, 'you may have a tête-à-tête with her on a sofa. It's as far as I can go.'

As we left the dining-room Valhubert and two or three other deputies took themselves off, leaving a preponderance of Anglo-Saxons. Philip looked sadly across the room at Grace. I noticed that when she was present Philip became unsure of himself in his anxiety to please her and, as a result, lost much of the charm which lay in his lounging, bantering, casual, take-it-or-leave-it manner. It was rather pathetic to see him sitting bolt upright, hands folded on his knees like a small boy. Presently Mrs. Jungfleisch moved over to join him. She began questioning him about what all the Americans in Paris seemed to call the Eels. I listened with half an ear. I had got M. Hué again and he was telling a long, probably funny story about Queen Marie of Roumania. It was the kind of thing I often have trouble in listening to; this time, I had a feeling he had told it to me before and that I had not listened then, either.

Mrs. Jungfleisch was saying, 'This parochial squabble over a few small rocks hardly seems to fit into the new concept of a free and balanced world community, does it?'

'Does it?' Philip spoke mechanically, his eyes on Grace.

'A certain absence of rationalism here?'

'To say the least of it.'

'If there are no inhabitants, how does auto-determination apply?'

'It can't.'

'But the modern concept of sovereignty is built up, surely, on auto-determination?'

'That's what we are told.'

'Another query which comes to mind. Where there are no inhabitants how can one know whether the Eels are French- or English-speaking?'

'One can't.'

'And yet language is a powerful determinant of the concept of sovereignty?'

'It's a question of law, not of language.'

'The French say they will soon have a Bomb.'

'Makes no odds. They won't drop it on London because of the Iles Minquiers.'

'I don't believe I have a perfectly comprehensive grasp of this problem from the point of view of you Britishers. Could you brief me?'

'I could. It would take hours. The whole thing is very complicated.'

I saw that Philip was longing for the party to break up so that he could drive Grace to the Chambre, have her alone with him for a few minutes in his motor. I was dying to go to bed. Although it was rather early I put on my gloves and said good night.

CHAPTER IX

BOUCHE-BONTEMPS' ministry was rejected by the Assembly. 'L'homme des Hautes-Pyrénées', as the French papers often called him, as if he were some abominable snowman lurking in those remote highlands, made his pathetic or rousing or moving oration to about three hundred and fifty pairs of dry eyes and flinty hearts. The two hundred and fifty who were sufficiently moved to vote for him were not enough to carry him to office. It was rather annoying for Alfred and me, because, shortly before M. Béguin fell, we had invited him and most of the members of his cabinet to a dinner party. Now it looked as if our first big dinner would be given to a lot of disgruntled ex-ministers.

The railway strike duly occurred. As always in France, the human and regional element played a part here. The northern workers came out to a man; their meridional colleagues, more whimsical, less disciplined, by no means as serious, brought quite a lot of trains into Paris. This caused a bottleneck; tourists on their way home from late holidays got as far as the capital and could get no further. Amyas Mockbar said:

STRANDED

Thousands of Britons are stranded in strike-torn Paris. They are camping round the idle stations, foodless, comfortless, hopeless. What is the British Embassy doing to alleviate their great distress? Organizing a lorry service to take them to the coast where British ships could rescue them? Arranging accommodation? Lending them francs with which to buy themselves food? Nothing whatever.

Miss Northey Mackintosh, niece and social secretary to Ambassadress Lady Wincham, told me today: 'My aunt is far too busy arranging a big dinner party to bother about the tourists.' N.B. Estimated cost of such ambassadorial entertainment, £10 a head.

'Did you tell him?' I asked, handing her the *Daily Post*. I was having my breakfast and she was perched on the end of my bed. She came every morning at this time for orders—those orders which were carried out by anybody but herself.

'Quelle horrible surprise! Of course I didn't tell him—would I have said my aunt when you are my first cousin once removed?'

'But do you see him, darling?' I knew that she did. Philip had met them walking up the Faubourg hand in hand looking, he said, like Red Riding Hood and the grandmother.

'Poor little Amy, he's a good soul,' said Northey, 'you'd love him, Fanny.'

'I doubt it.'

'Can I bring him here one day?'

'Certainly you can't. Whenever he sees Alfred or me he writes something utterly vile about us. You ought to be furious with him for this horrible invention. And now I must scold you, Northey. It's partly your fault for mentioning a dinner party at all, though of course I know quite well you didn't say those words. When one sees inverted commas in the paper these days it means speech invented by the writer. If you must go out with him, which I greatly deprecate, please remember never to tell him anything at all about what goes on here.'

'Oh the pathos! It's Lord Grumpy who forces the poor soul to write gossip. What interests him is political philosophy—he says he wants to concentrate on the Chambre but Lord Grumpy drags him back to the Chambre à coucher. You see, he's a witty soul!'

'I wonder if he's really such a good political journalist? It's rather a different talent from gossip writing, you know.'

'Oh, don't tell poor little Amy that—he might commit——'

'I only wish he would commit——'

'He's a father, Fanny.'

'Many revolting people are.'

'And he has to feed his babies.'

'So do tigers. One doesn't want to be their dinner, all the same.'

'Fanny,' wheedling voice.

'Mm?'

'He wants to do a piece on Auntie Bolter. He says when she got married he had a thick week with the Dockers and the Duke of Something and couldn't do her justice. He'd like to know when she's coming to stay here so that he can link her up with you and Alfred.'

'Yes, I expect he would love that. Just the very thing for a political philosopher to get his teeth into—now, Northey, please listen to me,' I said, in a voice to which she was quite unaccustomed. 'If we have trouble with Mockbar and if it turns out to be your fault I shall be obliged to send you back to Scotland. I am here to protect Alfred from this sort of indiscretion.'

Northey looked mutinous, her eyes brimmed and her mouth went down at the corners.

The door now burst open and a strange figure loomed into the room. Side whiskers, heavy fringe, trousers, apparently moulded to the legs, surmounted by a garment for which I find no word but which covered the torso, performing the function both of coat and of shirt, such was the accoutrement of an enormous boy (I could not regard him as a man), my long-lost Basil.

'Quelle horrible surprise!' said Northey, not at all displeased at this diversion from her own indiscretions, past and future.

Basil looked from one to the other. When he realized that we were both delighted to see him, the scowl which he had arranged on his face gave way to a particularly winning smile.

'Well, Ma,' he said, 'here I am. Hullo, Northey!'

'This is very exciting. I thought I'd lost you for ever.'

'Yes, I expect you did. What about breakfast—I could press down some bacon and eggs—in short I am starving. I say, this is all very posh, isn't it! Cagey lot of servants here, Ma—I had to show them my passport before they would let me in.'

'Have you caught sight of yourself in a glass lately?' said Northey, taking the telephone to order his breakfast.

'They must have seen a Ted before—how about les blousons noirs?'

'Not in embassies, darling, it's another world.'

'And what's this?' said Northey, fingering an armband he wore inscribed with the words: 'Grandad's Tours'.

'That's magic. Open sesame to the whole world of travel.'

'Where have you come from, Baz?'

'This minute, from the Gare d'Austerlitz. Actually from the Costa Brava.'

'Begin at the beginning, miserable boy. Do remember I've seen and heard nothing of you for three whole months.'

'Why, that's right, nor you have.'

'Not since you cut our luncheon that day.'

'But I wrote and put you off.'

'Six weeks later.'

'I wrote at once—I'm afraid there was posting trouble. Well, it's like this. You know old Grandad? Yes, Ma, of course you do, Granny Bolter's new old man.'

'I've never seen him.'

'Still, you know he exists. Actually, Granny met him with me—old Grandad and me have been matey for an age—he was the brains of our gang. I can tell you, Granny's got a good husband this time, just what she deserves. You can't think how well they get on.'

I had always noticed that, while my children regarded everybody over the age of thirty as old sordids, old weirdies, ruins, hardly human at all, the Bolter, at sixty-five, was accepted as a contemporary. She had an astonishing gift of youth due, perhaps, to a combination of silliness with infinite good nature and capacity for enjoyment. Physically she was amazing for her age; it was easy to see that her heart had never been involved in any of her countless love affairs.

Basil went on in his curious idiom, which consisted in superimposing, whenever he remembered to do so, cockney or American slang on the ordinary speech of an educated person, 'Old Grandad found that Granny's money is earning a paltry four or five per cent on which she pays taxes into the bargain. Now that's not good enough for him, so 'e scouts round, see, and finds out about this travel racket—oh boy, and is racket the word? 'E lays down a bit of Granny's lolly for premises and propaganda and now he's all set for the upper-income group—tax free of course—and I'm on the bandwagon with him and soon I'll be about to give you and Father the whizz of an old age. Grandad's the brainy boss and I'm the brawny executive; the perfect combination. So you see now why I couldn't lunch that day—I had just embarked on my career.'

'Which is?'

'I'm the boy wot packs in the meat.'

'Here's your breakfast.'

'Thanks very much. It's many a day since proper food crossed my palate. Ever been to Spain? Don't! Well, to go on with my exposey—Grandad assembles the cattle and I herd it to and fro. In plain English, Grandad, with many a specious promise and hopeful slogan—"No hurry, no worry if you travel the Grandad way" and so on—gets together parties of tourists, takes their cash off them and leaves me to

conduct them to their doom. Ghastly it is—fifteen to a carriage across
France and worse when we change for the peninsula. Then, when they
finally disembark, more dead than alive after days without food or
sleep, they have to face up to the accommodation. "Let Grandad rent
you a fisherman's cottage" says the prospectus. So he does. The beds
are still hot from the honest fisher folk prized out of them by yours
truly! That's when the ruminants begin collapsing—disappointment
finishes them off. Anyhow the old cows drop like flies when the
temperature is over a hundred—Britons always think they are going to
love the heat but in fact it kills them—we usually plant one or two in
the bone-orchard before we start for home. I keep a top hat over there
now, for the funerals, it looks better. Lucky I'm tough, you need to be
for this work, I can tell you!'

'I wonder they don't complain?'

'Complain! But what's the good, they've got to go through with it
once they are caught up in the machine. There's no escape.'

'How I should hate you!' said Northey.

'They hate all right—the point is they utterly depend. They can't
speak any language bar a little basic British and they've got no money
because Grandad bags whatever they can afford for the trip before they
leave. So they are at my mercy. You should see the letters they write
when they get home about "your tall, dark courier", threatening my
life and everything. Bit too late then of course, I'm far away, packing in
the next lot.'

'Whatever induces them to go in the first place, without making a
few inquiries? It seems perfectly mad!'

'Ah! There you have the extraordinary genius of me Grandad. He
literally mesmerizes them with his propaganda. All built up on smooth-
ing the path of sex. "Let Grandad take you to the Land of Romance,
Leisure and Pleasure." "Will you hear a Spanish lady, how she wooed
an Englishman?" See the sort of thing? We've got a plate-glass window
at the office, with life-sized dummies of a señorita riding behind a
caballero. Inside it's lined with wedding snaps of people who have
married Spanish grandees during Grandad tours (no funeral snaps of
course). There's something in it, mind you, some of the girls do sleep
with customs officers.'

'On those horrid tables?' said Northey, interested.

'But how do they have time?' I asked. 'I always seem to be in too
much of a hurry to sleep with people at the customs.'

'Next time you must try Grandad's way—*no hurry*. The trouble is you
travel soft. You don't know what a journey can be like when you go cheap
—it beats imagination. The Leisure, the Pleasure! The waits are endless, whole days sometimes—hours to spare at every frontier you come
to. Of course the douaniers, being in uniform, get the pick. The older
ladies are obliged to pay waiters and beach attendants and such like.'

'I thought they had no money?'

'They tear off their jewels.'

'Well then, just tell the programme. You go sight-seeing or what?'

'Nothing whatever. The British female goes abroad for romance and that's that.'

'Ay de mi!' said Northey, 'how true!'

'And the men? Aren't Spanish women very much guarded?'

'The men usually arrive dead beat. They take the journey worse than the women do and fury tires their hearts. They just have the energy to strip and peel, I don't think they would ever manage—you know, in the state they are in. Besides, their emotions and energies, if any, are concentrated on revenge.'

'And how do you spend your time?' I vaguely hoped for an account of advanced lessons in Spanish.

'Me? I lie on my face on the beach. It's safer. Once we've arrived at the place and they've seen where they've got to doss down and when they've smelt the food, redolent of rancidol, which they are expected to press down, the younger male Britons only have one idea. Señoritas be blowed—they just want to kick my lemon—give me a fat lip, see? So I lie there, camouflaged by protective colouring. My back is black, but my face is white; they don't connect the two and I am perfectly all right providing I never turn over. When the day comes for going home they need me too much to injure me.'

'Goodness, Basil!'

'You may well say so. Where's Father?'

'He's been in London—back any time now. Look, darling, I haven't told him about your summer—I didn't know anything for certain—so I let him think, what I rather hoped myself, that you were polishing up your pure Castilian. He might not like the idea of you—well——'

'Carting out the rubbish?'

'Oh dear, no, he wouldn't like it. But I don't think we need tell him. Now the holidays are over and you'll be going back to your crammer I think we might, without being deceitful, forget the whole thing?'

'Only I'm not going back to the crammer. That wasn't a holiday, Ma—funny sort of hol that would be—no, it's my career, my work, my future.'

'Lying on your face in the sand is?'

'Yeah.'

'You're giving up the Foreign Service?'

'You bet.'

'Basil!'

'Now listen, Mother dear, the Foreign Service has had its day—enjoyable while it lasted no doubt, but over now. The privileged being of the future is the travel agent. He lives free, travels soft—don't think he shares the sufferings of his people, he has a first-class sleeper, the best room in the hotel. Look at me now, washed, shaved, relaxed and rested. I only wish you could see my victims at this moment! Haven't taken their clothes off for days. Some of them stood the whole way last night while I lay at my ease. Even during a railway strike you've only got to exhibit the armband and the officials will do anything for you. You see we hold the national tourist industries in the hollow of our hands. There's nothing they dread more than a lot of unorganized travellers wandering about their countries exhibiting individualism. They'd never force a tourist on his own into those trains and hotels—he'd go home sooner. But you can do anything with a herd and the herd must have its drover. As he keeps the tickets and the money and the passports (no worry) even the most recalcitrant of the cattle are obliged to follow him. No good jibbing when the conditions are ghastly because what is the alternative? To be stranded without hope of succour. So the authorities need us; the tourists need us; we are paramount. Oh, it's a wonderful profession and I'm lucky to have the family backing which got me into it.'

My blood ran cold at these words. I have seen the promise of too many young men fade away as the result of taking a wrong step after leaving their university not to feel appalled at the prospect of this brilliant boy, easily my favourite child, thus jeopardizing his future. There is no sadder spectacle than that of a lettered beachcomber, a pass to which Basil seemed to have come in three short months.

'And your first in history,' I said, 'your gift for languages—all to be wasted?'

'It's no good, Ma, you'll have to be realistic about this. The world isn't like it was when you were young. There's more opportunity, more openings for a chap than there were then. You can't really expect me to swot away and get into the Foreign Service and put up with an aeon of boredom simply to end my days in a ghastly great dump like this? I love Father, you know I do, and I don't want to hurt your feelings, but I've no intention of wasting the best years of my life like he has and nothing you can say will persuade me to. So now, having partaken of this smashing breakfast, for which I'm truly very grateful, I must wend my way back to the hungry sheep who will look up, poor brutes, and not be fed.'

'They must be fed. Where are they?'

'Sitting on bursting canvas bags at the Gare du Nord—at least I hope so. I put them into the metro, before taking a cab myself, and told them where to get out and that I'd be along. I said to meet at the bus stop of the 48 because I believe the crowds at the station are terrific and one sheep looks very much like another. I expect they'll be there now for days—only hope this fine weather will go on.'

'You horrify me. Can't we do something for them?'

'They're all right. Singing "Roll out the Barrel" like Britons always do at waits—wish they'd learn a new tune.'

'How many are there?'

'In my party? About twenty-five. You don't need to bother about them, Ma, honest.'

'Please go straight to the Gare du Nord and bring them here. I'll have breakfast for them in the garden, ready by the time they arrive.'

A wail from Northey. 'No, Fanny, you're not to—they'll petrify my badger.'

'Surely he's blacked out in his air-raid shelter?'

'He'll smell them down there and tremble. A badger's sense of smell is highly developed—people don't understand about creatures.'

'Don't you take on,' said Basil, 'they smell like badgers themselves. He'll be thrilled—he'll think his mates have arrived.'

'Go at once, Baz,' I said.

'But, Ma, this strike will probably last for days. You'll get awfully tired of "Roll out the Barrel".'

'Yes. As soon as you've brought them there you must see about a lorry to take them to the coast.'

'No fear. All our profit would melt away—Grandad would kill me.'

'I'll pay.'

'You're soft. Another thing—have I got to face all those posh butlers with that lot in tow?'

'Northey can go with you and bring you in through the Avenue Gabriel. It's nearer for the metro. Get the key of the garden, dearest, from Mrs. Trott as you go out and tell Jérôme to be ready to help Baz find a lorry. Go on, Basil, twitch your mantle blue.'

I was not at all surprised when Basil's Britons turned out to be entirely delightful, very different indeed from the furious, filthy, haggard, exhausted, sex-starved mob which anybody not knowing Basil and not knowing England might have expected from his description. They were, in fact, sensible, tidy and nicely dressed, covered with smiles and evidently enjoying this adventure in a foreign land. There were rather more women than men, but it was unimaginable that any of them could have gone to bed with customs officers or waiters or indeed that they should commit fornication or adultery under any circumstances whatever. They looked more than respectable. I was glad to be confirmed in my suspicion that Basil's account of his own tough and unmerciful behaviour was an invention, to startle Northey and me. The Britons were full of his praises and when he explained that I was his mother they crowded round to tell me what a wonder boy or miracle child I had produced. They had no idea that they were in an embassy—not that they would have been impressed had they known it, since the English are less conscious than any other race of diplomatic status; they evidently thought I kept an hotel in Paris. 'Nice here,' they said, 'we must tell our friends.' Any strangeness in their situation they would put down to being abroad. 'Very nice,' they said of the breakfast, which they ate with the relish of extreme hunger.

When they had finished they told me, in detail, how splendid Basil had been. Hundreds of Britons, it seemed, many of whom had paid much more for the trip than they had, were left behind at Port-Vendres; Basil had literally forged a way through the mob, and, using his gigantic strength in conjunction with his mastery of languages, had lifted and pushed and shoved and lugged and somehow inserted every single member of his party on to a train already full to suffocation.

'Now all the others who were on it are stifling at that horrid Gare du Nord while here we are in these nice grounds.'

'Masterly organization,' said an elderly man of military aspect. 'He'll do well in the next war—a genius for improvisation—marvellous linguist—I think you should be proud of him. I could have done with more like him in the Western Desert. Now he's gone off to get a lorry to take us to the coast. What initiative! We are all going to subscribe for a memento when we get home.'

I said: 'You must be so tired.'

'Oh no.' A cheerful woman like a W.V.S. worker spoke up. 'After the holiday we've had, a night or two in the train seems nothing. Yes, forty-eight hours we've been since leaving. Quite an adventure!'

'And I suppose it wasn't too comfortable in Spain?'

'You don't go abroad for comfort exactly, do you? I always say, plenty of that at home. One likes to see how the foreigners live, for a change. There's no end to what they'll put up with. The toilet arrangements! You'd never believe!'

'Excuse me, but is that a badger's sett?'

'You are clever!' said Northey, twinkling and sparkling at the poor man whose head was turned there and then.

'Are there many badgers in this part of Paris?'

'I've never seen another but there may be. Do you have them where you live?'

'Oh no, not in the Cromwell Road. I knew what it was from the TV. I see you have a redstart, now that's a delightful bird.'

'Yes, and an owl at night. But we haven't got a TV.'

'Shame,' said the Briton. 'They don't seem to go in for them abroad we've noticed. Still, with so much nature about you hardly need one. That's what I have mine for, the nature. I didn't know Paris was like this, wouldn't mind living here myself.'

As Northey and I went back to the house we met Alfred. 'I was looking for you. Who are all these people?'

'Sweet Britons,' said Northey.

'Stranded by the railway strike,' I added. He seemed satisfied with this explanation. 'How was London?'

'Worrying. I'll tell you later—I must go to the Chancery now. Are we lunching in? Oh, thank goodness——'

I told Northey to see that the Britons got off all right, to have some sandwiches made up for them and to say goodbye to Basil for me. My business now was to protect Alfred, tired and preoccupied as he seemed, from the sight of his son in such a garb.

The Britons had a little nap on the grass. Then they began a sing-song. We had 'Lily Marlene', 'Colonel Bogey' (whistling only) and 'Nearer my God to Thee'. The noise was not disagreeable, thinly floating on a warm breeze. Just before luncheon-time I heard female voices sounding a cheer in the Avenue Gabriel.

Northey came running, to announce that they had gone, in a car.

'What, all twenty-five in one motor?'

'Car is French for charabang. Basil sends his love and he'll probably be back next week. He seems to think the Embassy can be his Paris H.Q. in future, if you're lucky. He's cooking a lot of schemes, I note. Then faithful Amy turned up.'

'You don't mean Mockbar?' I was horrified.

'Good little soul, indeed I do. But don't worry. I told Baz you wouldn't like to have him hanging about in the garden and he got rid of him in a tick.'

'How did he? That's a formula worth knowing.'

'It's not one you can use very often though. He pretended the Britons were all radioactive. Amy buggered off before you could say canif.'

'I absolutely forbid you to say that word, Northey. No, not canif, you know quite well. Wherever did you pick it up?'

'The Captain of the *Esmeralda*. He was a most unpleasant person, but I rather liked some of his expressions.'

'Well, I beg you won't use that one again.'

'All the same, do you admit it's perfect for describing the exits of Amy?'

I dreaded the *Daily Post* after that. Sure enough:

RADIOACTIVE

Some two score radioactive Britons sought the protection of our Embassy in Paris yesterday. Did Sir Alfred Wincham send for scientific aid? Are they now receiving treatment at a clinic?

DUMPED

No British officials went near them. They were hustled into a lorry by our amateur envoy's son Mr. Basil Wincham and dumped at the coast. All efforts to get in touch with them subsequently have been fruitless. Where is this dangerous lorryload now? Have the sanitary authorities been informed? If they went home on a British ship were the necessary precautions taken to see that their fellow-travellers were not contaminated? This whole incident seems to typify the slack and unprofessional outlook which permeates our Paris mission today.

I was quite terrified, envisaging awful developments. After a consultation with Philip we decided not to tell Alfred until something happened, knowing that he would never look at the *Daily Post* of his own accord. Nothing happened at all. The powers that be in England knew better than to believe an unsupported statement by Mockbar; the French were unaware of his existence and of that of the *Daily Post*. Philip said that even if their sanitary authorities should raise the question he could easily deal with them. 'You know what the French are, they don't quite believe in modern magic. They all go to fortune-tellers (M. de Saint-Germain is booked up for months), they read the stars every day and make full use of spells. But they don't get into a state about things like radioactivity.'

Old Grumpy, having failed to make any mischief for us, had to drop the story because Basil and his Britons, merged among thousands struggling home on Channel steamers, were never identified and therefore could not be interviewed.

In London, Alfred had submitted his own views on the likelihood of the French ever accepting the European Army; they were in direct contradiction to those of his American colleague. The Cabinet would naturally have preferred to be told what they wanted to hear and Alfred's prognostications were not well received. He was merely instructed to stiffen his attitude and informed that London regarded the C.E.D. as inevitable and essential. He was also informed that our government were going full steam ahead over the Minquiers and that he must make this perfectly clear in Paris. The Foreign Secretary announced that he would be coming over to see his opposite number, as soon as he had one. I believe that Alfred heartily wished himself back in Oxford, though he did not say so to me.

CHAPTER X

M. MOCH, M. Pléven and M. Bidault all tried to form governments and all duly failed. Then Bouche-Bontemps tried again and was accepted by the Chambre the very day before our dinner party. Alfred and I were delighted. For one thing, he had become a friend and it was most fortunate for us to have him to help and even sometimes guide us while we were still finding our feet; besides which our dinner was, we thought, saved. Bouche-Bontemps was taking the direction of foreign affairs himself, anyhow for a while, so that the government was virtually the same as that which had been in power before this long crisis. M. Béguin was now Vice-Président instead of Président du Conseil, and one or two minor ministries were given to new men, belonging to groups hitherto in opposition. This procedure, known as *dosage* and frequently resorted to during the Fourth Republic, had ensured the extra votes necessary to put Bouche-Bontemps in.

I told Northey and requested Philip to come to my bedroom early on the morning of the dinner in order to talk over dispositions. Philip appeared, punctual as always. 'Isn't this a mercy!' I said. The morning papers hailed the end of the crisis, giving Bouche-Bontemps a friendly reception. In fact a naif and optimistic reader, like myself, would suppose that a long term of stable government lay ahead. *The Times*, in a leading article, compared Bouche-Bontemps to Raymond Poincaré; the *Daily Telegraph* said he was the strongest man thrown up by the Fourth Republic so far and shared many characteristics with Clémenceau.

Philip looked sceptically at the headlines. 'You can thank the General for this. If he were not sitting like the rock of ages at Colombey we should never have a government here at all. As it is they are obliged to come to these little temporary arrangements simply in order to keep King Charles in exile. This ministry won't last six weeks. Hullo—have you seen Mockbar?'

'No—don't tell me—better not shake my nerve———!'

'Not too bad. It's headed: Paris Dinner Muddle. "Confusion—bungling—secrecy—lack of organization are casting a shadow over our amateur envoy's first official dinner." And so on. Zero, in fact. The old boy's losing his grip—he'll get the sack if he can't do better than that. Where's Mees—I thought she was to come for orders?'

'Naughty girl. I suppose she's overslept as usual.'

'She's not in her room—I banged as I came up the back stairs—nor in the bath, I banged there, too.'

'Are you sure? How very odd. I wonder if Katie knows anything?'

Katie knew everything, as she always did, in her cage and told what she knew with evident enjoyment. Philip listened in to her account with the earphone. It seemed that while Alfred and I had been out the evening before, rushing from the National Day of Iceland to a party for the Foreign Minister of Bali, ending up at a concert at the Costa Rican embassy, a hamper of live lobsters had arrived for me. They were a present from M. Busson, a deputy with a seaside constituency, one of the people invited to our dinner. The chef, overjoyed, unable to get hold of me, had informed Northey, saying that the menu would now have to be altered. It would then have been Northey's plain duty to send interim acknowledgment and thanks to M. Busson. No such thing. On seeing the dear lobsters, which were lurching about on the kitchen floor, she flew into a fantigue. She made Katie put her through to the Ministère de la Marine where, strange to say, she had no friend, and asked to speak to the Chef de Cabinet. Presenting Alfred's compliments she inquired at what point the Seine became salt. The answer was Rouen. She then ordered Jérôme for 8.30 a.m. When the time came she forced the furious chef to cram the lobsters back into their hamper, and made the footmen load them on to the Rolls Royce (not in the boot, for fear of smothering the darlings, but inside, on the pretty carpet). By now she was well on the way to Normandy where the sweet creatures would duly be put back in their native element.

'Thank you, Katie.' I rang off and looked at Philip, suppressing a giggle as best I could. He shook his head, not very much amused.

'This Northey!' he said. 'In the first place the French navy, a thoroughly Anglophobe institution, will immediately assume that we are up to some monkey work. Why should Alfred want to know where the Seine becomes tidal, all of a sudden? In the second place Busson, who is the new Minister of Atomic Energy, is the leader of a small but powerful group in the Chambre. He is also a famous gourmet. He will be angry and disappointed when his lobsters fail to appear this evening—he may never forgive. In the third place, I think it's too irresponsible of Mees to go off like this on the one day when she might be some slight use to you!'

The telephone bell rang: Katie again. 'I forgot to say, she took a follower. At least I expect he is one by now——'

'Who?'

'The Chef de Cabinet. She arranged to pick him up at the side door of the Ministry in the rue St. Florentin.'

'That's quite a good thing,' I said to Philip, 'at least he'll see for himself she's not spying.'

'My dear, they are madly suspicious of Mees—all the ones who aren't in love with her, that is. The sweet lobsters won't reassure them, I can tell you.'

'What time should you say she'll be back?'

'Who knows? Rouen is nearly 100 miles, I think. The Chef de Cabinet will spin it out as long as he can, no doubt. Oh well—it's not as if she'd be much use here, one can't trust her even to put cards round the table, let alone work out the seating. I should have had to do it for you in any case. I'll get on to old Hughie, presently.'

'Let's put M. Busson next to Northey so that she can explain about the lobsters in her own words——?'

'And make an enemy for life? He has never been a minister before, he wouldn't at all relish sitting next to your social secretary. We must make her apologize to him before dinner—lucky she's so irresistible to French politicians. Now—business. Let's see who we've got. I suppose I shall have to have Mees—no hope of Grace for me, eh? Talking of

Grace, why not ask her to come and give you a hand with the flowers and things? I know she'd love to.'

'Philip, what a good idea!'

'Yes, I'm going to telephone now—she'll turn up trumps, you'll see.'

He was quite right. Grace came for me in her motor after luncheon and took me to St. Cloud to pick flowers for the party. Valhubert had a property there, just outside the park, an ancient garden on the site of a hunting-lodge which the Germans had destroyed in 1870. Here he grew flowers and fruit for his own use. It was a melancholy, romantic spot, especially in the autumn when the dark green leaves of the adjacent woodlands were flecked with yellow and the old fruit trees covered with apples and pears and peaches. Impossible to imagine that one was only ten minutes away from Paris. The flowers that were visible all grew in tubs and stone vases, while those for cutting were planted in regular rows, like vegetables, behind a hornbeam hedge. 'Charles-Edouard hates to see flowers growing in the earth,' Grace explained. 'Look how the hot summer has brought out the orange blossom and even ripened a few oranges; very rare, in this climate.' Wearing a dark grey linen dress with broderie anglaise collar and cuffs she looked exactly right there, as she always did whatever the circumstances. She gave me a pair of sécateurs with which to cut the old-fashioned roses, lilies, hollyhocks, tuberoses, carnations, fuchsias and geraniums. 'We'll make a lovely mixture,' she said. 'Don't they smell better than those you buy in shops?'

'And no nursing-home flowers,' I said. 'That's rare at this time of year.'

'Those horrible gladioli, we don't dream of allowing them. Aren't English autumn flowers too loathsome!'

'Nursing homes here have them too.'

'Not quite such brutes. The English are for ever building themselves up as being so good at growing flowers, best gardeners in the world and all that, and what does it boil down to en fin de compte? Michaelmas daisies and chrysanths, sentant le cimetière.' Grace was off on her hobby-horse now. 'Have you ever noticed it's just those very things the English pride themselves on most which are better here? Trains: more punctual; tweeds: more pretty; football: the French always win. Doctors: can't be compared, nobody ever dies here until they are a hundred. Horses, we've got M. Boussac. The post, the roads, the police —France is far better administered——'

I felt quite furious. 'Well, come on, Fanny,' she said, 'I'm waiting for the answer—you're the Ambassadress, you're meant to know it——'

'It isn't fair. You've got these things all ready to trot out, and I suppose facts and figures to bolster them up if I begin to query them. Before I see you next I shall do a bit of prep, but for the moment my mind is a blank. Oh! I know—justice. Better and much quicker at home—admit?'

'We hurry people to the gallows all right. Fluster them up in the witness box and then swing them. Give me a dear old juge d'instruction, plodding away, when I'm in trouble——'

'No, Grace, we don't hang them any more.'

'Not even murderers?'

'Specially not them.'

'What are you telling me? I don't care for this news at all! Do you mean people can murder one as much as they like and nothing happen to them?'

'Yes. Unless you're a policewoman. I'm not sure they are meant to poison one either or perhaps it's shooting that's not allowed. I can never remember. But don't worry. If they know nothing will happen they don't murder so much.'

'Are you sure?'

'Yes, it was all in the papers. I say—I've thought of something else—the papers are better at home——'

'Are they? I can't say I ever see them except when Mockbar has a go at us, then some kind friend cuts it out and sends it. He's a delightful writer, such polish, such accuracy!'

'You take in *The Times*,' I said. 'I know you do. Try and be more truthful, Grace——'

'My father sends it, but we hardly ever open it. I keep it for covering the furniture in the summer.'

'I've thought of something else—digestives.'

'All right, I'll give you digestives and I'll give you Cooper's Oxford and if you're very good potted shrimps as well. Now that's rather typical. The only subject we agree on is food, which is not supposed to be an English talent at all. It's the things they pretend to be good at which are such flops.'

'It's THEY now, is it!' I said.

'Don't be angry, Fanny. After all, Charles-Edouard and the children are French——'

'That's no reason for downing the English.'

'I don't down them—not really, but they annoy me with their pretended superiority. And oh, how they chill me! Not only the climate——'

'Same as here.'

'Nonsense, darling, there's no comparison—but also the hearts. I was noticing that yesterday. I had to go to a wedding at the Consulate —cold as charity it was. Gabble gabble gabble—gabble gabble gabble —may I give you my best wishes? Over. Think of the difference between that and a wedding in a mairie! When the bride and bride-groom come in, M. le Maire, in his sash of office, throws up his arms like General de Gaulle: "Mes enfants! Voici la plus belle journée de votre vie——" '

'Yes, Grace. I daresay, but people must be themselves you know. Can you imagine poor Mr. Stock throwing up his arms like General de Gaulle and saying "My children, this is the most beautiful day of your lives"? It would be simply ridiculous if he did.'

'Ridiculous, because he hasn't got a heart. That's what I complain of.'

'Anyhow it wouldn't have sounded very convincing at yesterday's wedding when you think that the Chaddesley-Corbetts are both nearly seventy and have been divorced I don't know how many times.'

We snipped away in silence. Presently Grace asked how the Minquiers were getting on.

'Nothing new, I think. Mr. Gravely comes here next week to see M. Bouche-Bontemps. Partly about the Eels, I suppose.'

'Oh, does he? Bringing Angela?'

'No. Wives mustn't come too often because of foreign currency. It seems she was here in the summer.'

'So she was. Isn't it mad of the Treasury the way they drive these important politicians to the brothels just for the sake of the few pounds it would cost to bring their wives with them!'

'Darling! He's sixty, looks like an empty banana skin and is only coming for the inside of a week——'

'Some chaps can't stand more than twenty-four hours, you know.'

The Chef de Cabinet did indeed spin it out. Grace and I had done the flowers and done the table and she had gone home to dress when Northey reappeared. She seemed quite unaware of having done wrong and I saw no point in scolding as that particular misdeed was unlikely to recur. Besides, I was longing to hear about her day as much as she was longing to tell. The sweet lobsters having been returned to their native element the Chef de Cabinet had told Jérôme to make a little détour of about fifty miles which took them to a three-star restaurant. Here they ordered luncheon and then went for a walk in beautiful woods. The Chef de Cabinet, no doubt in an emotional state, had lost his head and ordered homard a l'armoricaine. When Northey discovered that this was French for lobster, and the cruellest sort at that, she was furious; she cried and sent him to Coventry for half an hour. They made it up again, ordered a different luncheon and got rather tipsy while it was being cooked. Back in Paris at last, the Chef de Cabinet, unable to endure the parting, put it off by taking her to see Notre Dame. 'Though really,' said Northey, 'when you know the outside you can guess what the inside is going to be like and he made me miss my fitting at Lanvin——'

'Fitting at Lanvin?'

'Didn't I tell you? M. Castillo has offered me Cecil Beaton. Oh, sharpen your wits, Fanny—Cecil Beaton, that heavenly dress with the bobbles——'

CHAPTER XI

OUR guests assembled under the gaze of King George and Queen Mary. When there is a large dinner at the Embassy it takes place in a banqueting-hall added on to the ground floor by Pauline Borghese. Though by no means beautiful, it is of an earlier date and therefore less catastrophically hideous than its equivalent at the Elysée which so torments the ghost of poor little Mme de Pompadour. The eighteenth-century dining-room on the first floor, with Flemish tapestries painful to a French eye, where we usually had our meals, only holds about twenty people.

When M. Busson arrived, Philip grabbed Northey by the shoulder and steered her towards him, saying that she had something to explain. She took him into a corner and I could see her launching into a pantomime, partly French, partly English, mostly dumb show, tortured expression and flying hands. He looked puzzled, though fascinated, and then amused. Finally, to my relief, he burst out laughing. He gathered his colleagues round him and gave a rapid résumé of Northey's statement. 'And now,' he ended up in English, 'these succulent crustaceans are no doubt swimming away to Les Iles Minquiers.'

'Swimming!' said Northey, scornfully. 'I have yet to see a lobster with fins.'

M. Béguin, who was always rather grumpy and more so now that he was no longer Président du Conseil, remarked sourly that these succulent crustaceans were more likely to be boiling away, at this very moment, in peasant cottages. Far better for them, he explained in his cold, clipped voice, had they been cooked at the Embassy, because the cottage saucepans would be smaller, the cottage fires weaker and the agony more prolonged.

Northey was unmoved by this argument. 'I could see on their sweet faces when they were bug—I mean making off—that they would never let themselves be caught again,' she said, comfortably.

Bouche-Bontemps said, 'Perhaps Mees is quite right, who knows? The Holy Office forbade the boiling alive of heretics—they tried it once, in Spain, and even Spanish nerves gave way at the sight. Ought we really to subject living creatures to such terrible cruelty in order to have one or two delicious mouthfuls?'

'M. le Président,' said Northey, 'je vous aime.'

'It is reciprocal.'

M. Béguin looked like a Nanny whose charges have gone too far in silliness. He said something to M. Hué about the frivolity of les Britanniques being beyond endurance. M. Hué, a good-natured fellow, replied that while naturally deploring the waste of delicious lobsters, he found the whole thing funny, touching and plutôt sympathique. M. Béguin raised his eyes to heaven. His shoulders, too, went up until it seemed as if they would never come down again. He looked round for a partisan, saw that Mme Hué's gaze was also fixed to the ceiling and that she was clearly on his side. They went off together to a sofa where they sat talking very fast, throwing malignant glances in the direction of Northey.

The Valhuberts now arrived, raising the level of looks and elegance. I introduced him to Northey and had the satisfaction of seeing that this well-known ravager of the female heart fell there and then victim to the charm of Mees. The evening seemed to have begun extremely well; most of the guests, if not all, were there and were getting on famously. I am always struck by how easily a French party slides down the slip-way and floats off to the open sea. People arrive determined to enjoy themselves instead of, as at Oxford, determined (apparently) to be awkward. There are no pools of silence, all the guests find congenial souls, or at least somebody with whom to argue. Even M. Béguin's dis-approval had that positive quality which facilitates the task of a hostess; it led to lively talk and a reshuffling of the company.

At this point, Northey was supposed to count the guests and let me know if they were all there. However she was so completely sur-rounded by ministers that I could not catch her eye to remind her of her duty. Philip, with a resigned wink in my direction, performed it for her. 'That's it,' he said, presently.

The door opened. I supposed that dinner was going to be announced and vaguely wondered why by that door and not the one which led to the dining-room. For a moment nothing happened. Then my bearded son David came crab-wise into the room, pulling after him a blue plastic cradle and a girl attached to its other handle. He was dressed in corduroy trousers, a duffle coat, a tartan shirt and sandals over thick, dirty, yellow woollen socks. The girl was tiny, very fair with a head like a silk-worm's cocoon, short white skirt (filthy) swinging over a plastic petticoat, a black belt, red stockings and high-heeled, pointed, golden shoes.

In the silence which fell as this curious group came into the room I heard a voice (M. Béguin's I expect) saying something about 'cet individu de mine patibulaire' and another (Charles-Edouard de Valhubert probably) 'pas mal, la petite'.

I am always pleased when my children turn up. The sight of them rejoices me, I rush forward, I smile and I embrace. I did so now. David and the girl dumped the cradle on a precious piece by Weisweiller. He kissed me warmly (oh horrid, scrubbing-brush beard) and said, 'Ma, this is Dawn.'

Alfred's reactions were not as immediately enthusiastic as mine. With him it is not so much a physical instinct as a matter of principle that makes him welcome the boys whatever the circumstances of their arrival. Our house is their home, their shelter from the stormy blast. If they are naked they must be clothed; if hungry, fed; if the police of five nations are hot on their heels they must be hidden. No questions must ever be asked. Now he came forward and shook hands with his son, giving him a stern, grave, penetrating look. 'This is Dawn, Father.'

'How do you do?'

Alfred led Dawn and David round the room, introducing them, while I held a hurried consultation with Philip about fitting them in to our dinner.

He said, 'Do you really think it's a good idea? They are so travel-stained——'

Unfortunately I knew my David far too well to think that the stains had anything to do with travel.

'We can't possibly send them out when they have just arrived,' I said. 'Alfred wouldn't hear of it.'

'There's no room for them here. The table only holds fifty—it would take at least an hour to put in another leaf and re-do it.'

'Oh dear, oh dear,' I considered a moment. 'In that case, Philip, I'm most dreadfully afraid, and too sorry, that you'll have to take Northey out to dinner. Go to the Crémaillère—on the house of course. Do you mind?'

'Yes,' said Philip, displeased at this turn of affairs. Though we had not been able to arrange the seating so that he would be next to Grace (he was between Northey and Mrs. Jungfleisch) he had been placed exactly opposite her so that he would be able to look at her all the time and occasionally lean over and exchange a remark. 'I mind but I bow to the inevitable.'

'What a funny little person,' I said, 'who do you imagine she is?'

'An heiress, by the look of her.'

'How too splendid that would be. Northey—come here—Philip is going to take you to dine at the Crémaillère to make room for David and the young lady.'

'Oh goody gum trees!' said Northey, eyes shooting out electricity.

'Yes, darling. And before you go, will you give that baby to Mrs. Trott and ask her to keep an eye on it and also say I want two bedrooms got ready. Then come straight back after dinner, won't you?'

'We will,' said Philip.

Northey picked up the cradle, swung it round her, performed a pirouette and said, 'Come on, worshipful, let's bugger——'

The spontaneous sound of discontent rising from a dozen French throats as Northey left the room was silenced by the announcement of dinner. When at last I had got the women through the dining-room doors—all holding back politely and saying 'passez—passez' to each other—I led David and the young lady to the places designed for Philip and Northey.

'Why do you put me next my wife?' he said angrily. 'This seems most unusual.'

'But, dear duck, I'm not a fortune teller. How am I expected to know that she is your wife?' I said to Dawn: 'Please forgive me, but we can't do the table all over again. You must simply try and imagine that you are at a city banquet.'

She looked at me with huge, terrified, grey eyes, and I saw, what the extraordinary clothes had hitherto prevented me from realizing, that she was very pretty. I also noticed that she was pregnant.

I went to my place between Bouche-Bontemps and Béguin. They were already plunged in a violent political discussion; seeing that I was not really present in the spirit they continued it across me. David had Mrs. Jungfleisch on his right. We had asked her because Philip had asserted that it was impossible to give a dinner party in Paris without her; how thankful I felt now that she had accepted. With a lack of inhibition which no European woman would have exhibited under the circumstances, she went straight to the point. I strained my ears and listened as hard as I could; this was made possible by the fact that except for my two neighbours, everybody else was doing likewise.

'Your wife is quite beautiful,' she said, 'is she a model?'

'No. She's a student.'

'Indeed. And what does she study?'

'Modern languages.'

'How old is the baby?'

'I'm not sure. Not old at all.'

'Are you staying here long?' I held my breath at this.

'No. We are on our way to the East.'

'I envy you that. Provins and Nancy are at their best in the fall. Such interesting towns. Try and go to Cirey, it's well worth it, and just outside Paris don't forget to stop your car at Grosbois——'

'We haven't got a car. We are walking.'

'Walking to Provins? With the baby?'

'The baby? Oh yes, he's coming too. Not to Provins, to China.'

'My! That's quite some walk. China—let me see now—after Provins and Nancy—don't miss the Place Stanislas—you can take in Munich and Nuremberg and Prague. I envy you that. Lemberg, they say, has charm. After Moscow there is the holy city of Zagorsk, the tomb of

St. Serge in solid silver. Are you looking for a special school of architecture or just going haphazard? By the way, I suppose you have your
visas for China. I heard it was none too easy——'

David said they had no visas for anywhere. They were looking for
Truth, he added.

'Aren't you afraid you may end up in gaol?'

He said, loftily, that Truth flourished in gaols, specially in Eastern
ones.

'We are the bridge,' he added, 'between pre-war humanity with its
selfishness and materialistic barriers against reality and the new race of
World Citizens. We are trying to indoctrinate ourselves with wider
concepts and for this we realize that we need the purely contemplative
wisdom which comes from following the Road.'

Mildred Jungfleisch now had her clue. As soon as she realized that
David was not on an ordinary House and Gardens honeymoon, but was
in search of Truth, she knew exactly where she was and how to cope.
She dropped the Place Stanislas and Grosbois and brought out such
phrases as 'Mind-stretching interpretation of the Cosmos', 'Interchange
of ideas between sentient contemporary human creatures', 'Explode the
forms and habits of thought imposed by authority', 'I once took a
course in illogism and I fully realize the place it should hold in contemporary thought', 'Atmosphere of positive thinking—change is life'.

One saw why she was such an asset in society; she could produce the
right line of talk in its correct jargon for every occasion. She never put
a foot wrong. David was clearly both delighted and amazed to find
so kindred a spirit at his parents' table; they talked deeply until the
end of dinner. Their neighbours lost interest in the conversation as
soon as it moved from personal to eternal issues (the highlight having
been the disclosure that David did not know the age of his own baby)
and the usual parrot-house noise of a French dinner party broke out.
As for the student of modern languages, she never opened her mouth.
M. Hué, who was next her, tried all sorts of gambits in French, English,
German, Portuguese and Norwegian. She merely looked as if she
thought he was about to strike her and held her peace.

I now tried to put these children out of my mind for the present and
do my duty as a hostess.

'What does patibulaire mean?' I asked M. Bouche-Bontemps. I
thought M. Béguin had the grace to look embarrassed; he turned
hurriedly to his neighbour.

'Patibulum is Latin for a gibbet.'

'I see exactly.'

M. Bouche-Bontemps was very kind and tactful. Instead of abruptly
wrenching the conversation in an obvious manner from the subject
which was clearly preoccupying me, he began talking about difficult
young persons of former days. In seventeenth-century England there

were the Ti Tyre Tu, educated gangsters who called themselves after the first line of Virgil's first eclogue. In the 1830s, 'the same length of time from Waterloo as we are from Dunkirk', young Frenchmen called Bousingos, like the Ti Tyre Tu, wore strange clothes and committed lurid crimes. I could have wished he had left out the lurid crimes, but I saw the connection.

'I don't know about England,' he said, 'but in France mothers are frightened of making their children frown. They love them so much that they cannot bear to see a shadow on their happiness; they never scold or thwart them in any way. I see my daughter-in-law allowing everything, there's no authority outside school and the children do exactly as they like in their spare time. I am horrified when I see what it is that they do like. They never open a book, the girls don't do embroidery, the boy, though he is rather musical, doesn't learn the piano. They play stupid games with a great ball and go to the cinema. We used to be taken to the Matinée Classique at the Français and dream of Le Cid—that's quite old fashioned—it's The Kid now. How will it end?'

'I think you'll find they will grow out of it and become like everybody else.'

'Who is everybody else, though—you and me and the Ambassador or some American film actor?'

'You and me,' I said firmly. 'To our own children we must be the norm, surely. They may react from our values for a while but in the end they will come back to them.'

'But these grandchildren of mine are getting so big—they don't seem to change. They still throw that idiotic football at each other as soon as their lessons are over.'

'Good for the health, that's one thing.'

'I don't care. I don't want them to win the Olympic Games. Furthermore healthy children are generally stupid. Those wise old monks knew what they were doing when they founded the universities in unhealthy places. I hate health—the more over-populated the world becomes the more people bother about it. Hünde, wollt ihr ewig leben? says I!'

'To your own grandchildren?'

'Specially to them!'

'I don't believe you.'

'I am very serious, however. This is a moment in the history of the world when brains are needed more than anything else. If we don't produce them in Western Europe where will they come from? Not from America where a school is a large, light building with a swimming-pool. Nor from Russia where they are too earnest to see the wood for the trees. As for all the rest, they may have clever thoughts about Karl Marx and so on, but they are not adult. If the children of our old civilization don't develop as they ought to, the world will indeed become a dangerous playground.'

I said, 'My two grown-up boys were perfect when they were little, very, very brilliant, longing to learn, all for Le Cid as opposed to The Kid. They both did well at Oxford. Now look at them. Bearded David there, with a first in Greats if you please, is walking to China in search of Truth. In other words he has given way to complete mental laziness. The other one, Basil, even cleverer, my pride and joy, lies on his face all day on a Spanish beach. How do you explain that?'

'I think they've got a better chance than my poor grandchildren because at least they have some furniture in their heads already.'

'If you ask me they'll all come out of these silly phases. They are nothing new—my cousins and I were quite idiotic when we were young. The only difference is that in those days the grown-ups paid no attention, while we concentrate (too much probably) on these children and their misdoings. How old are yours, by the way?'

'They must be quite seven, eight and nine by now.'

He was very much surprised when I laughed.

'At their age,' he said, 'I was reading the great classics in my spare time.'

'We all think that about ourselves, but it isn't always quite true!'

As soon as we left the dining-room, David took his wife away. He explained that they had an important rendezvous at the Alma. 'We are several days late—we must go at once.'

'But you'll come back for the night?'

'Possibly, or we may sleep there.'

'Where?'

'Under the bridge, where we are meeting our friend.'

'Oh, don't do that. You must be tired.'

'The great Zen Master, Po Chang, said when you are tired, sleep. We can sleep anywhere.'

'And the baby?'

'He'll come too. He sleeps all the time. Good night, Ma.'

'Shall we see you tomorrow?'

'Possibly. Good night.'

Philip and Northey reappeared. Valhubert sprang from his chair beside Mme Hué and in a rapid and skilful manœuvre he whisked Northey to an unoccupied sofa. They sat there for the rest of the evening, laughing very much. Grace, half-listening to Philip who had made a bee-line for her, looked at them imperturbably, quizzically, even, I thought. At the usual time and in the correct precedence, the guests came and thanked us for a delightful evening and went their way. I have seldom felt so exhausted.

CHAPTER XII

I SAT on my bed, looking at Alfred.

'Do we laugh or cry?' he said. 'Did you see the baby?'

'Not really. It seemed to be asleep. I saw the cradle all right.'

'Whose do you think it is?'

'Oh, surely theirs?'

'It's yellow.'

'Babies often are.'

'No, darling. I mean it's an Asiatic baby.'

'Heavens! Are you quite sure? I thought it was our grandchild.'

'It may be. A throw-back. Had you a Chinese ancestor of any sort, Fanny?'

'Certainly not. Perhaps you had?'

'I doubt it. The Winchams, as you know, were yeomen in Hereford-shire, in the same village since the Middle Ages. If one of our ancestors had gone to the East and brought back an exotic wife it would have become a thrilling legend of the family—don't you think? That little young lady didn't look Mongolian, did she?'

'Not a bit. How very mysterious. Well, if they're taking it to China that will be coals to Newcastle, won't it?'

For two days we saw nothing of David, Dawn or the cradle; on the third day they turned up again. Alfred and I were having our tea in the Salon Vert. 'It looks as if they've gone for good,' I was saying. 'Weren't we nice enough to them?'

'I don't see what more we could have done.'

'I suppose not. I have this guilty feeling about David, as I've often told you, because of loving him less than the others.'

'One must see things realistically, my darling. You love him less because he is less lovable—it's as easy as that.'

'But may it not be because I loved him less from the beginning—I lie awake, trying to remember——'

'He has always been exactly the same,' said Alfred, 'he was born so——'

Then they sidled, crabwise, cradle between them, through the door.

'Oh good, oh good,' I said, 'there you are. We were beginning to be afraid you had gone East.'

David pressed his beard into my face and said, 'On the contrary we went back a little—West—to Issy-les-Moulineaux. But now we are really on the road. We've just called in to say good-bye.'

I rang for more tea cups and said to Dawn, hoping to bring her into the conversation, 'Issy-les-Moulineaux is such a pretty name. What's it like when you get there?'

She turned her headlamps on to me, dumb, while David scowled. He despised small talk and civilized manners.

'It's just a working-class suburb,' he said. 'Nothing to interest anybody like you. We went to see a practising Zen Buddhist who's got a room there.'

'And where did you stay?'

'In his room.'

'For three whole days?'

'Was it three days? How do I know? It might have been three hours or three weeks. Dawn and I don't use watches and calendars since we have no [voice of withering scorn] "social engagements"!'

'I thought you said he lived under a bridge.'

'He used to, but they have turned the embankment into a road. Imagine motor-cars speeding through your bedroom all night. He says the French are becoming simply impossible——'

The baby now began to scream. 'I expect he wants changing,' said David.

Dawn got up and bent over the cradle as if to do so there and then. 'Come upstairs,' I said. We each took a handle and went to the lift. 'I got this room ready for you hoping you would stay for a night or two. It's called the Violet Room. Mrs. Hammersley and Mr. Somerset Maugham were born here, imagine——'

She smiled. She was a duck, I thought—I did so wish she could speak. When she picked up the baby I saw that Alfred was quite right, it was as yellow as a buttercup, with black hair and slit black eyes, certainly not European : a darling little papoose of a baby.

'The pet,' I said. 'What's its name?'

At last the pretty mouth opened. ' 'Chang.'

I saw that a canvas bag with a broken zip fastener had been deposited on a folding table meant for luggage. 'I'll send my maid, Claire, to unpack for you.' She shook her head vehemently.

'She's not frightening a bit and she'd love the baby—very well, if you'd rather not. Have you got what you need, dearest?' She nodded. 'Come down again when you are ready.'

I went back to the Salon Vert. David was saying, 'Zen forbids thought' and Alfred was looking sad, no wonder, at these words which were the negation of his whole life's work. 'It does not attempt to be intelligible or capable of being understood by the intellect, therefore it is difficult to explain.'

'It must be.' (Falsetto.)

'The moment you try to realize it as a concept, it takes flight.'

'Mm.' (On a very high note.)

'Its aim is to irritate, provoke and exhaust the emotions.'

To my utter amazement, Alfred now lost his temper. During twenty-six years of married life I had never seen that before. He said, furiously, 'You have succeeded in irritating, provoking and exhausting my emotions to a point at which I must tell you that, in my view, most Asiatics are incapable of thought. Zen must be simply perfect for them. But you are not an Asiatic; you have studied the great philosophies——'

'Please, Father, say Asian.' David had not even noticed the effect he was having on Alfred.

'I suppose, alone with you and your mother, I may be allowed to use the correct——'

'Not if it hurts my feelings. You see, our baby is one——'

'Adorable!' I said.

'Oh my dear boy, I beg your pardon a thousand times. Well, I've got some papers to read so perhaps I'll go back to the Chancery. Good-bye for the present.'

'He's called 'Chang, Dawn told me,' I said as the door shut on Alfred.

'We named him after the great Zen Master Po Chang. We dropped the Po. You have heard of him?'

'I seem to know the name—I'm awfully ignorant though, about all that.'

'It was Po Chang who placed a pitcher before his followers and asked them "What is this object?" They made various suggestions. Then one of the followers went up to it and kicked it over. Him Po Chang appointed to be his successor.'

'Oh of course! Well, anyhow, I thought the baby a perfect angel.'

'He's everything to us.'

This rule about never asking questions, though I knew it to be sound and would never break it, sometimes made life rather difficult. I was dying to know the origins of baby 'Chang but how could I find out?

'You must have one of your own,' I hazarded.

'We are going to—that's why we got married.'

'When you've got two babies, which makes a family, will you not settle down?'

'The wheel of birth and death, in the face of eternity, is of no more importance than sleeping or waking. Do you not know that new bodies are only created so that we can work out our own Karma?'

'Oh, do shut up and talk sensibly,' I said.

'To talk in terms that you would understand, Ma, I can't approve, I never have, of your way of life. I hate the bourgeoisie. In Zen I find the antithesis of what you and Father have always stood for. So I embrace Zen with all my heart. Do you see?'

'Yes. I wonder why you feel like that?'

'It seems almost incredible that people like you should still be living in the 1950s.'

'You can't expect us to commit suicide in order to fall in with your theories.'

'Oh, I don't mind you being alive, it's the way you live. Basil feels as I do. I've implored him for years to cut the umbilical cord and now at last he has.'

'That's your doing, is it? Thanks very much. He lies on his face on hot sand, instead of reading for his exam. It seems appalling waste of time to me.'

'Time does not exist. People who have clocks and watches are like bodies squashed into stays. Anything would be better than to find oneself in your and Dad's stays when one is old. Dawn and I are looking for an untrammelled future. Where is she?'

'If you go to the room above this one you'll find her.'

He went. Presently I heard his heavy footfall over my head. When David was a child Uncle Matthew used to say he walked like two men carrying a ladder. Greatly relieved, I telephoned to the Chancery. I got Philip. 'Just tell Alfred,' I said, 'that old Zennikins has gone and he can come back and finish his tea.'

Alfred kissed the top of my head. 'To think he took a first in Greats!'

'Let me pour you out another cup—that's cold. I remember, when the boys were little, you used to say if they don't revolt against all our values we shall know they are not much good.'

'That was not very clever, was it?'

'You were very clever—you took a first in Greats yourself. Another thing was: "I hope when they see me coming into a room they will look at each other as much as to say: here comes the old fool. That is how children ought to regard their father." '

'How very odd of me. I've quite forgotten.'

'Yes, one forgets——'

'Hot news,' Northey said, next day. 'David and Dawn are drinking whisky with sweet Amy in the Pont Royal bar. 'Chang has been dumped with the men's coats.'

'How do you know?'

'I've just seen them.'

'And what were you doing at the Pont Royal bar?'

'I was meeting Phyllis McFee, the friend of my far-distant youth in Caledonia stern and wild.'

'Northey, it's not a suitable place for young girls. Please find somewhere else to meet her—why not here? What's the good of giving you that pretty room——?'

'You're saying all this because you don't like clever little Amy.'

'No, I do not.'

The answers to all the questions we had so discreetly not asked now became available to us in the *Daily Post*.

ZEN BUDDHISTS AT PARIS EMBASSY

Bearded, sandalled, corduroyed and piped, accompanied by wife Dawn and baby 'Chang, David Wincham, the eldest son of our envoy to France (former Professor of Pastoral Theology, Sir Alfred Wincham), is staying with his parents on his way East, where he plans to join a Zen community. During a Parisian tea-ceremony yesterday David outlined his projects.

EXPECTING

'Dawn and I were married last week. We are expecting our first baby in two months. Dawn's father, the Bishop of Bury, disapproves. He wanted her to finish her studies and he was against our adopting little 'Chang, the child of our Zen Master.'

WORLD CITIZEN

'Yes, 'Chang is a Chinese name; our child is a World Citizen. Dawn's father is against World Government. He does not understand Zen nor does he realize the importance of the empty or no-abiding mind. He thinks that people ought to work; Dawn and I know that it is sufficient to exist.'

SEVEN

So David, Dawn and 'Chang are existing very comfortably at the expense of the taxpayer. I asked when they expect to leave for the East. 'In seven hours, seven days, seven weeks or seven years. It's all the same to us.'

'If it's seven years,' said Philip, 'your successor will have to give them the entr'sol.'

As a matter of fact, we heard no more about going East; they settled quite contentedly into the best spare room over the Salon Vert. It seemed that the long maturing of the Sacred Unsubstantiality could come to pass quite as well in the Hôtel de Charost as in a Siberian gaol —better, perhaps, because they were not certain to find a Zen Master in the gaol whereas there was this excellent one at Issy-les-Moulineaux. Dawn felt tired and was not anxious to recontemplate the wisdom of the road. David told Mildred Jungfleisch all this and she kindly passed it on. No explanations were vouchsafed to me or Alfred, but the portents seemed to indicate a good long stay. I bought an Empire cradle which I set up in the Salon Vert and banned the blue plastic one from any of the rooms inhabited by us. This was the only step I took to assert my personality.

CHAPTER XIII

VALHUBERT joined the throng of Northey's suitors. No doubt this
was inevitable, but it worried me since he was in quite a different
category from the others: a man of the world, experienced seducer,
with time on his hands; I thought he would make mincemeat of the
poor child. Besides I was very fond of Grace, my most intimate friend
in Paris. She was obviously changing her mind about Northey; I never
seemed to hear her say 'What a darling' any more. The other followers
were rather a nuisance; they took up far too much of Northey's time
and attention and doubled the work of our telephone exchange but I
did not think them dangerous. I used to have long confabulations on
the subject with Katie, who, fond of Northey and in a commanding
position, was invaluable to me. She was sensible in a particularly
English way in spite of having lived abroad for years. She had been at
the Embassy longer than anybody else, since before the war, during
which she had worked with the Free French.

'Of course, I don't listen,' she said, 'but sometimes I can't help
hearing.'

'Do listen as hard as you can, Katie. It's so important for me to
know what she's up to. I'm responsible for her, don't forget.'

'You needn't worry—she doesn't care a pin for any of them; she
drags in the name of Philip whenever possible. They must be sick of
being told that she worships him, poor things. Of course, the ones who
can use the secret line, but I feel it's exactly the same. She's so trans-
parent, isn't she!'

'What do the French think of it all, I wonder?'

'The worst, of course, but then they always do. If she had no followers at all they would say she's a Lesbian or has got a lover in the
Embassy. You can't count what they think.'

'Tell me something, Katie. Does she often speak to Phyllis McFee?'

'Who?'

'A Scotch girl who is working here in Paris——'

'Never, as far as I know.'

'That's funny. When she doesn't want to do anything she always
drags in Phyllis McFee as an excuse.'

'She's probably shut up in some office where she can't use the
telephone.'

'Well——' I said, 'I wonder!'

I did not ask Katie about M. de Valhubert but I knew that he was
constantly on the line. I also noticed that Phyllis McFee, whose name

had hitherto cropped up at regular but reasonable intervals, now seemed to be Northey's inseparable companion.

'Northey, aren't you rather behind-hand with my letters?'

'Not bad—about twelve, I think.'

'Why don't you sit down and finish them after dinner, then they would be off your mind?'

'Because tonight, actually, Phyllis McFee and me are going to Catch.'

'Catch?'

'That's French for all-in wrestling.'

'Darling, it's really not suitable for two girls to go alone to all-in wrestling.'

'We shan't be alone. Phyllis McFee and me have got admirers. We shall be escorted.'

'How can you bear to watch it?'

'I adore it. I love to see horrible humans torturing each other for a change instead of sweet animals. L'Ange Blanc, the champion, has got the fingers of a doctor, he knows just where it hurts the most——'

'Funny sort of doctor. But there's still the question of the letters. They can't be put off indefinitely.'

'I say, Fan, you know how you're not dining out?'

'You want me to do them? But what do I pay you for?'

'You won't be paying me anything at all until November 28th next year. I've borrowed until then. Fanny—each for each?'

'Oh, very well. Bring me your little typewriter and I'll do them in bed.' Only young once; we did not have these boring jobs at that age. Indeed when we were that age, Polly Hampton, my cousins and I, it was as much our duty to go out with young men and enjoy ourselves as now it was Northey's to write twelve letters. I only wished I could be certain that Phyllis McFee was really going to be of the party and that the escort was not Valhubert. As I wrote my letters I resolved that I would have to speak to Northey; the Foreign Legion policy of no questions may be quite all right with boys; girls are a very different proposition, giddy, poor things, hopelessly frivolous, wayward and shortsighted. Although I hate all forms of interference between human beings I felt, nevertheless, that I had a duty to carry out.

I was busy just then. Mr. Gravely, the Foreign Minister, came and went. I saw little of him as the dinner which Alfred gave in his honour was for men only. He seemed a dry old stick. I said to Philip, 'I do love Grace's idea of him being driven to the brothels because his wife didn't come!'

'She's not far wrong. All English politicians want to do dirty things as soon as they get to Paris. Only of course they don't want to be seen by Mockbar. It's a nuisance that the only night club which is fairly respectable should happen to be called Le Sexy. La Tomate sounds quite all right but we really could not let them go there—no, I couldn't possibly tell you. Ask Mees——'

Contrary to all known precedent, Mr. Gravely did not fall in love with Northey, in fact he hardly noticed her. He gave her various odd jobs to do for him, speaking in a dry, official, impersonal voice which so took her by surprise that she actually did them all herself, quite efficiently.

The night he left we dined at home. Alfred seemed tired and depressed; the visit had probably added to his difficulties. I had not yet had an account of it. David and Dawn had gone to share a bowl of rice with a friend—they never could say they were dining out, like anybody else. However, when we got to the dining-room we found that my social secretary was honouring us, a very unusual occurrence.

'Your cows, Northey,' said Alfred, 'are a nuisance.'

'I know—isn't it splendid! B.B. has stopped them, Fanny, I quite forgot to tell you. You see what can be done, by making a fuss!'

'Again I say, they are a nuisance. The Irish Ambassador was so friendly to me, everything seemed perfect between us. Now he has been called home by his government for consultation. It's very serious for the Irish—one of their main exports has vanished overnight. They all think it's due to the devilish machinations of the English.'

'So it is and serves them right for being so cruel!'

'All poor peasant communities are cruel to animals, I'm afraid—and not only the Irish. If they can't export cattle to France they'll be even poorer. It's not the way to make them kinder. The result will probably be that they will send the unhappy beasts to other countries where the journey will be longer and the slaughterhouses more primitive.'

'B.B. doesn't think so. He says there are no other practicable markets.'

'You know you should use your, apparently absolute, power to make the French eat frozen food. If they would do that these journeys could all be stopped and the beasts could be killed at home.'

'They won't,' said Northey, 'they call it frigo and they loathe it. B.B. says they are quite right—it's disgusting.'

'All very well—they'll have to come to it in the end.'

After dinner she said she was simply exhausted. 'I must dree my weird to bed—oh the pathos of the loneliness!' She trotted off to her entr'sol. We too went early to our rooms. Before I went to bed I heard a little cheeping noise, very far off, rather like a nest of baby birds, which meant that Northey was on the telephone. I could just hear her when all was quiet in the house. As I went to sleep she was still at it. I woke up again at three in the morning; she was still piping away.

When she came for her orders next day I said, 'Northey, I don't want to be indiscreet, but were you telephoning practically half the night?'

'The agony of clutching the receiver all those hours! My arm is still aching!'

'Who was it? M. Bouche-Bontemps?' She looked surprised that I should ask but replied, nonchalantly, 'No, poor duck, he is too busy nowadays. It was Charles-Edouard.'

Just as I thought. It was evidently time that I should intervene, unless I were going weakly to let things take their course. I went on, very much against my own inclination, 'Whatever was it all about?'

'My investments.'

'Indeed! Have you investments——?'

'Yes. He has forwarded me my wages until Alfred's sixtieth birthday by which time you will retire and I shall be out of a job. Now he is advising me how to place the money. He says it's very important because nobody else will ever employ me and I am facing a penurious old age. So I have bought Coffirep, Finarep and Rep France. You can't imagine how they whizz. Les reps sont en pleine euphorie, the *Figaro* said, yesterday.'

'I don't think you ought to let M. de Valhubert talk to you all night. Grace might not like it.'

Northey's face closed up in a mutinous expression. 'Who cares?'

'I do, for one. But it's not that, darling, I worry about you. I'm so dreadfully afraid you will fall in love with Charles-Edouard.'

'Fanny! Hoar antiquity!'

'No hoarier than most of your followers—they all seem to be over forty and Bouche-Bontemps——'

'But I'm not in love with any of them. Is this a talking-to?'

'I suppose it is a sort of one.'

'Quelle horrible surprise! You never scold me. What's come over you?'

'I'm not scolding, I'm trying to advise. There are sometimes moments in people's lives when they take a wrong direction. I feel that both Basil and David have—but men can more easily get back to the right path than women. You ought to reflect upon what you want, eventually, and steer towards that. Now, as M. de Valhubert has noticed, you don't seem to have professional ambitions, so I suppose you are after marriage?'

'Perhaps I would prefer to be a concubine——'

'Very well. In that case the first rule is don't enter a seraglio where there is a head wife already.'

'I see your mind is still running on Charles-Edouard.'

'All this midnight telephoning makes it run.'

'But Fanny, if I wanted to hug Charles-Edouard I would do it in bed, not on the end of a telephone line.'

'I don't say you do want to hug, yet. I'm simply afraid that presently you may.'

'I've often told you I'm in love with Worshipful.'

'Yes, often, indeed! Do you think it's true?'

'St. Expédite is covered with candles—why do you ask me that?'

'If you want to marry Philip you're setting about it in a very funny way.'

'I never said I wanted to marry him. Why shouldn't I be his concubine?'

'Philip isn't a Pasha, he's an ambitious English civil servant. The last thing he would do would be to saddle himself with a concubine—drag her round after him from post to post, can you imagine it! He'd very soon get the sack if he did. The only thing he might do would be to marry you.'

'Fanny—you said it was hopeless——'

'You are making it quite hopeless by your behaviour.'

'How ought I to behave?'

'Be more serious. Show that you are the sort of person who would make a splendid Ambassadress—pay more attention to your work——'

'Now I see exactly what you are getting at——'

'Our interests happen to coincide. And go slow with the followers.'

'I don't understand why, as I don't hug——'

'I might believe that but nobody else will. With Frenchmen love leads to hugs.'

'They're not in love.'

'What makes you think so?'

'They wouldn't mind a hug or two, I must admit, and they do sometimes very kindly offer, but they're not in love. I know, because as soon as somebody is I can't bear him. There was somebody at home—oh, Fanny, the horror of it!'

'Dear me, this is very inconvenient. How are we ever going to get you settled?'

'With Worshipful of course, who you say never will be——'

Alfred came in. 'Bouche-Bontemps seems to be on the telephone for you,' he said to Northey, 'in the library. They made a mistake (Katie's day off) and put the call through to me—his secretary was very much embarrassed.' As Northey skipped away, delighted, no doubt, at being delivered from a tiresome lecture, he shouted after her, 'Ask him if his government will survive the debate on the national parks, will you?'

'No. I'm not the Intelligence Service! Ask your spies——!'

'Is that rather cheeky! Never mind. I say, Fanny, our son Basil has appeared. He is dressed [falsetto] like "O Richard, O mon Roi!" What do you think this portends?'

'I hardly care to tell you. He has left the crammer, given up all idea of the Foreign Service and has become a travel agent.'

'Good God,' said Alfred, 'Basil too?'

'But he's not quite as bad as poor darling David,' I hastened to say, 'because there is no bogus philosophy, no wife, no adopted baby involved and at least he has work and prospects of a sort. He doesn't do nothing all the time. Oh, how I wish I knew where we went wrong with those boys——!'

'Perhaps it's the modern trend and not exactly our fault.'

'Where is he now?' I asked.

'Having breakfast with the Zen family in the dining-room. David has come down in his dressing-gown today—he looks ghastly. They started nagging away at each other—I couldn't stand it, I took my coffee to the library.'

'Nagging about what?'

'It seems [falsetto] that Beards never get on with Teds. Well, I must go, I'm due at the Affaires Etrangères.'

'The Eels?'

'Oh yes indeed—the Eels, the European Army, Guinea, Arms to Arabs—I've got a horrible morning ahead.'

'And the young man who pirated Dior's designs?'

'No, Mr. Stock copes with that, thank goodness. See you presently.'

My next visitor was Basil. I saw what Alfred meant: with his loose garment, tight trousers and hair curling under at the back he had the silhouette of a troubadour. Although I vastly preferred his appearance to that of David (he was quite clean, almost soigné in fact) I wished so much that they could both be ordinary, well-dressed Englishmen. I felt thankful that we had been able to send the two youngest to Eton; presumably they at least, when grown up, would look like everybody else.

Basil plumped on to my bed. 'I say, old David's gone to seed, hasn't he? Of course one knows he's holy and all that—still——!'

'How long since you saw him?'

'About a year, I should think.'

'He told me it was he who advised you to take to the road, or whatever it is you have taken to?'

'The coffee-and-jump, did he just? What a build-up! It's true, he used to bang out long saintly letters in that weird old Bible script of his but naturally I never read them.'

'I worry about you boys. What are you up to, Baz?'

'Well, it's like this. The Spanish season is over, thanks be. I've brought over a flock of the bovines on the hoof—turned them out to graze in the Louvre this morning—this afternoon I shall be flogging them down to Versailles. But these little tours are peanuts; we want to keep the racket going until Grandad can get the hustle on his new phenangles. And oh boy! Is he cooking up some sleigh-rides!'

My heart sank. If I did not quite understand what Basil was saying I felt instinctively against phenangles and sleigh-rides. They were not likely to denote a kind of work that Alfred would approve of. 'Could you talk English, darling?'

'Yes, Mother dear, I will. I gets carried away when I thinks of me ole Grandad. Well then, with Granny Bolter's capital (she sends her love incidentally) he is building a fleet of telly-rest coaches. Get the idea? The occupational disease of the British tourist is foot and mouth. Their feet are terrible, it makes even my hard heart bleed when I see what they suffer after an hour or two in a museum. By the evening several of them will be in tears. There are always some old bags who flatly refuse to get out of the bus towards the end of a day; they just sit in the car-park while their mates trail round the gilded saloons to see where the sneering aristocrats of olden times used to hit it up. Sometimes gangrene sets in—we had two amputations at Port Bou—very bad for trade—just the sort of thing that puts people off lovely holidays in Latin lands. The other trouble, mouth, is worse. Britons literally cannot digest Continental provender—it brings on diarrhoea and black vomit as surely as hemlock would. The heads I've held—I ought to know. After a bit they collapse and die in agony—no more foreign travel for them. So I reports all this to ole Grandad and 'e strikes 'is forehead and says, "Now I've got a wizard wheeze" and just like that, in a flash, this man of genius has invented the telly-rest coach. When they gets to the place they've come to see—the Prado, say, or some old-world hill town in Tuscany, they just sits on the coach and views the 'ole thing comfortable on TV while eating honest grub, frozen up in Britain, and drinking wholesome Kia-ora, all off plastic trays like in aeroplanes. If they wants a bit of local atmosphere, the driver can spray about with a garlic gun. You wait, Ma, this is going to revolutionize the tourist trade. Grandad has got a board of experts working out the technical details and we hope to have the first coaches ready by next summer. We reckon it will save many a British life—mine among others, because they will no longer need a courier.'

'Ah! So then what will you do?'

'Specials. Millionaires and things like that. We've got an interesting special coming off next month which I'm partly here to see about. Grandad wants to capture the do-gooders market, he thinks it has enormous possibilities for the future—you know, all those leisured oldsters who sign letters to *The Times* in favour of vice. Now they and their stooges are for ever going abroad, to build up schools the French have bombed, or rescue animals drowning in dams, or help people to escape from Franco gaols. They've got pots of money and Grandad thinks no harm in extracting a percentage.'

'I don't think it's right to cash in on people's ideals, Basil, even if you haven't got any yourself.'

'Somebody's got to organize their expeditions for them. Now me Grandad has thought of a particularly tempting line-up, see—an atom march. These do-gooders are not like ordinary Britons, they have feet of sheer cast iron and they love a good long walk. But they've had Britain. They've done John o'Groat's and all that and they know every inch of the way to Aldermaston. So me Grandad thinks they might like to walk to Saclay, where the French atom scientists hang out—make a change. If that's a success they can go on to the great atom town in the Sahara. We call it A.S.S.—they start at Aldermaston as usual—Saclay–Sahara. Well, Ma, I wish you could see the provisional bookings. It is a smashing pisseroo old Grandad's got there. He's busy now, working out the cost. He'll make them pay a sum down, quite substantial—you see it's a different public from our Spanish lot, ever so much richer. Then the idea is to have some treats on the side which they'll pay extra for—interviews with atom ministers and such like. I thought Father would come in useful there?'

'I wouldn't count on it.'

'Oh well then, Northey can——'

'What can I do?' She reappeared, with Philip. 'Hot news,' she said. 'Bigman's going to fall again (that's French for Président du Conseil)—not national parks, Sunday speed limit—so we shall see more of him. Goody gum-trees.'

'It's gum drops, not gum trees,' Basil said, scornfully.

'Oh Lord,' said Philip, 'not another chap in fancy dress? What have you come as, may one ask? Really, Fanny, your children! Do you know, the Ambassador has just been obliged to go to the Quai in a taxi because David sent Jérôme with the Rolls Royce to fetch his Zen Master?'

'No! It's too bad of David—I can't have him doing that sort of thing. Go upstairs, Northey, and tell him to come here at once, will you?'

'Wouldn't be any use—they'll be Zenning away with the door locked by now. They go back to bed after breakfast to empty their minds again. Suzanne can never get in to do the room until luncheon-time. The mess is not to be believed. Have you been up there, Fanny?'

'I had a feeling I'd better not.'

'I went to have a chat with Dawnie yesterday when David was out. It's rather fascinating. You'd never think so much deep litter could come out of one canvas bag. Then they've stuck up mottoes everywhere: "How miraculous this is: I draw water and I carry fuel" (it would be, if they did) and a picture of a hoop saying "The man and his rice bowl have gone out of sight".'

'When you chat with Dawn what does she talk about?'

'I do the talking. She looks sweet and says nothing. She can explain about the ten stages of spiritual dish-washing but she hasn't much ordinary conversation. I love her and adorable 'Chang. If only old David would bugger off and leave them both behind——'

'Northey, if you say that word again I shall send you straight back to Fort William.'

'Northey,' said Basil, 'do you know any atom-ministers?'

'Yes, there's a dear one called Busson in the rue de Varennes, terribly excited about his old bomb. He's going to poop it off in 1960.'

'Is he indeed?' said Philip. 'Thanks for the tip, Mees. At last you've produced the solid fruit of all that spying you do.'

'I read it in *Aux Ecoutes*, to tell you the truth.'

Basil said, 'Could you get permission for a few people to see him?'

'What sort of people?'

'Britons.'

'Rather,' said Philip. 'He simply dotes on Britons, he's always hanging about here, under the Union Jack, keenly waiting for one.'

'Witty,' said Northey. 'Yes, Baz, I expect so. You must put it in writing. You can get permission for anything in France if you send up a written request. Come to my office and I'll type it out for you.' She gave Philip a long look under her eyelashes which would have transported any of the followers and left the room with Basil.

When they had gone, I said to Philip, 'Oh! the children! What a worry they are. Basil has got some horrible new scheme on foot. Never mind. Meanwhile I've decided that somehow or other I must get rid of the Davids.'

'Now you've mentioned it—I didn't like to—but how?'

'So far I haven't thought of a way. After all, our house is their home. We can't turn them out if they don't want to go, Dawn so pregnant and that darling 'Chang, and let David drag them off to China. Then it's no good arguing with him, he has studied philosophy and knows all the answers.'

'Besides, he's such a humbug. All that rot about time meaning nothing—turns up sharp enough for meals, I notice, and the Guru is on the dot when Jérôme goes for him—won't miss a lift if he can help it.'

'Yes—yes,' I said rather impatiently. Poor David, it was too easy to criticise and laugh at him and really got us no further.

'Need your house be his home now that he is married?'

'I suppose the boys never seem grown up to me. Yes, I like them to feel that it is. Nothing would matter if it didn't upset Alfred, but he has got such a lot of worries now and I can see that David is fearfully on his nerves. I must protect him—I must try and get them to go back to England. David can always earn a living there with his qualifications.'

'What are they using for money?'

'A tiny little pittance I give him.'

'Can't you cut it off and say he must find work?'

'His pathetic allowance? No, really, I don't think I could.'

'One doesn't have to be a fortune-teller to see they'll be here the full seven years.'

'I'm not sure, Philip. I often get my own way—Lady Leone left quite quickly, did you notice? Oh!' I said, sitting up in bed and seizing the telephone. 'Davey! We must get him over—I'll ring him up now this very minute!'

CHAPTER XIV

DAVEY arrived post-haste, in the early afternoon of the following day. 'Quite right to send for me. Oh—this room?' he said displeased, when I had taken him upstairs. He had had the Violet Room before but it was now occupied by David and Dawn and I had been obliged to change him over. I sat on his bed. 'I'll tell you the reason. It's all to do with why I asked you to come.'

'Don't begin yet. I must go for a walk. The thing about having three kidneys is that you need a great deal of exercise. Until you have had it you are apt to see things out of proportion.'

'That won't do. We are all trying to keep a sense of proportion. Can I come with you? I'd love a walk. Is there anywhere special you'd like to go to?'

'Yes, there is.' He opened his medicine chest and took out a piece of glass. I looked at it, fascinated, wondering what part of his anatomy it could be destined for.

'My housemaid broke this off a candelabra I'm fond of. I want to see if the man in the rue de Saintonge who used to blow glass is still there. I last saw him forty years ago—Paris being what it is I'm quite sure we shall find him.'

'Where is the rue de Saintonge?'

'I'll take you. It's a beautiful walk from here.'

It was indeed a beautiful walk. Across the Tuileries, through the Cour Carré, and the Palais Royal and then past acres of houses exactly as Voltaire, as Balzac, must have seen them, of that colour between beige and grey so characteristic of the Ile de France, with high slate roofs and lacy ironwork balconies. Though the outsides of these houses have a homogeneity which makes an architectural unit of each street, a glimpse through their great decorated doorways into the court-yards reveals a wealth of difference within. Some are planned on a large and airy scale and have fine staircases and windows surmounted by smiling masks, some are so narrow and dark and mysterious, so over-built through the centuries with such ancient, sinister rabbit-runs lead-ing out of them, that it is hard to imagine a citizen of the modern world inhabiting them. Indeed, witch-like old women, gnome-like old men do emerge but so, also, do healthy laughing children, pretty girls in stiletto heels and their prosperous fathers, Legion of Honour in buttonhole. Most of the courtyards contain one or two motor-cars—quite often D.S. or Jaguars—mixed up with ancient handcarts and pedal bicycles. The ground floors are put to many different uses, shops, workshops, garages, cafés; this architecture has been so well planned in the first place that it can still serve almost any purpose.

Davey and I walked happily, peering and exclaiming and calling to each other to come and look. I said, 'Bouche-Bontemps and the other Frenchmen I see always talk as if old Paris has completely gone; Théophile Gautier died of grief because of what Haussmann did here; a book I've got, written in 1911, says that Paris has become an American city. Even so, it must have far more beautiful old houses left than any other capital in the world. We have walked for half an hour and not seen one ugly street.'

'What I think sad about modern buildings,' Davey said, 'is that when you've seen the outside you know exactly what the inside will be like.'

'Northey said that, about Notre Dame. But I must admit she was in a hurry to get to Lanvin.'

The rue de Saintonge itself is inhabited by artisans. Its seventeenth-century houses, built originally for aristocrats and well-to-do burgesses, have not been pulled down (except for one block where the Département de la Seine has perpetrated a horror) but they have been pulled about, chopped and rechopped, parcelled and reparcelled by the people who have lived and worked in them during the last two hundred years. Here are the trades which flourish in this street:

Workers in morocco, fur, indiarubber, gold, silver and jewels; makers of buttons, keys, ribbons, watches, wigs, shoes, artificial flowers and glass domes; importer of sponges; repairer of sewing-machines; great printer of letters; mender of motor-cars; printer; midwife. There may be many more hidden away; these put out signs for the passer-by to read.

At the end of the street we came to Davey's glassblower, still there, covered with smiles. He and Davey greeted each other as if it were only a week instead of forty years since they last met. The piece of glass, produced from Davey's pocket, was examined. It could be copied, quite easily, but there would be a delay of perhaps two months.

'That has no importance,' said Davey, in his perfect, literary French, 'my niece here is our Ambassadress—when it's ready you will send it round to her.'

More smiles, compliments, protestations of love: 'How we thought of you, when London was bombed.'

'And how we thought of you, during the Occupation. Thousands of times worse to have them marching about the streets than flying about overhead.'

'Yes, perhaps. My son deported—my son-in-law murdered—c'est la vie——!'

Back in the Tuileries gardens we sat down in order to begin our, what statesmen call, discussions about David. I described the arrival of the Holy Family and their subsequent behaviour. Davey was very much interested. 'My dear! The unkind French! So how did they take it?'

'Sweet and polite as they always are, to me anyhow.'

'I wish I could have heard what they said to each other, afterwards. Of course I saw Mockbar's account of the Zen Buddhists and paid no attention, but for once there seems to have been a grain of truth in his ravings. I say, look at that statue of an ancient Gaul. What can he be doing?'

'He seems to be eating a Pekinese—or perhaps he's kissing it?'

'No—it's his own beard, but why is he holding it up like that with both hands?'

'Most peculiar.'

'You might have let me know that my godson was married.'

'Nobody let anybody know. The Bishop of Bury saw it in the paper— Alfred rang him up and they mourned together. Oh, Dave, isn't the modern world difficult!'

'Ghastly. No standards of behaviour any more.'

We sat sadly looking at the Gaul.

Presently Davey said, 'I expect I know what we shall have to do for David. It must be the old, old pattern of emotional unstability and absence of rationalism plus a serious defection of the glands. He will almost certainly have to have a series of injections and a course of psychotherapy. I count on the Jungfleisches to find us a good man— where there are Americans there are couches galore. Madness is their national industry. What's the joke?'

'In other words, send for the doctor. Davey, how like you——!'

'No, Fanny. Did I order doctors for Pauline? Did I get rid of her?'

'All right, I admit. And there may be something in what you say. But I'm wondering if he will co-operate. He's become so difficult.'

'He'll be delighted to. He is evidently an exhibitionist—that is shown by the beard, the pipe, the strange clothes and Chinese baby. The more attention paid to him the better pleased he'll be. Say what you like about the modern world, we must give three cheers for science. Look at me! If I'd been born fifty years sooner I'd have been pushing up the daisies by now.'

'Very likely, since you would have been a hundred and sixteen. Uncle Matthew always says you are the strongest man he has ever met.'

'It is too bad of Matthew when he knows quite well how delicate I am.' Davey was seriously annoyed. He rose to his feet and said he must go home and have a rest before dinner.

'We've asked some people to meet you.'

'Oh dear! You always seem to dine alone, so I made a little plan with Mildred. One can count on interesting conversation there.'

As Davey and I came to the Place de la Concorde we saw that there was something going on. A mob of men in mackintoshes, armed with cameras, were jostling each other on the roadway outside the Hôtel Crillon. Mockbar leant against the wall by the revolving door of the hotel. I never can resist a crowd. 'Do let's find out who it is they are waiting for,' I said.

'It can only be some dreary film star. Nothing else attracts any interest nowadays.'

'I know. Only, if we don't wait we shall hear afterwards that something thrilling occurred and we shall be cross.' I showed him Mockbar. 'There's the enemy. He looks more like a farmer than a gossip writer.'

'Lady Wincham—how are you?' It was *The Times* correspondent. There was a moment of agony when I could remember neither his name nor Davey's. I feebly said, 'Do you know each other?' However my embarrassment was covered by the noisy arrival of policemen on motor-bicycles.

'Who is it?' I shouted to *The Times* man.

'Hector Dexter. He has chosen Freedom. He and his wife are expected here from Orly any minute now.'

'Remind me——' I shouted.

'That American who went to Russia just before Burgess and Maclean did.'

I vaguely remembered. As everybody seemed so excited I could see that he must be very important. The noise abated when the policemen got off their bicycles. Davey said: 'You must remember, Fanny—there was a huge fuss at the time. His wife is English—your Aunt Emily knew her mother.'

More police dashed up, clearing the way for a motor. It stopped before the hotel; the journalists were held back; a policeman opened the door of the car and out of it struggled a large Teddy-bear of an American in a crumpled beige suit, a coat over his arm, holding a brief-case. He stood on the pavement, blinking and swallowing, green in the face; I felt sorry for him, he looked so ill. Some of the journalists shouted questions while others flashed and snapped away with their cameras. 'So what was it like, Heck?' 'Come on, Heck, how was the Soviet Union?' 'Why did you leave, Heck? Let's have a statement.'

Mr. Dexter stood there, silent, swaying on his feet. A man pushed a microphone under his nose. 'Give us your impressions, Heck, what's the life like, out there?'

At last he opened his mouth. 'Fierce!' he said. Then he added, in a rush, 'Pardon me, gentlemen, I am still suffering from motion dis-comfort.' He hurried into the hotel.

'Suffering from what?' said Davey, interested.

'It means air sickness,' said *The Times* man. 'I wonder when we shall get a statement. Dexter used to be a tremendous chatterbox—he must be feeling very sick indeed to be so taciturn all of a sudden.'

A large pink knee loomed in the doorway of the motor. It was followed by a woman as unmistakably English as Dexter was American. She merely said 'Shits' to the snapping and flashing photographers. Using the *New Statesman* as a screen she ran after her husband. Her place was taken by a fat, pudding-faced lad who stood posing and grinning and chewing gum until everybody lost interest in him. I saw that Mockbar's elbows were getting into motion, followed by the rheumaticky superannuated stable-boy action of his lower limbs, the whole directed at me. 'Come on,' I said to Davey, 'we must get out of this, quick——'

Philip was invited to the Jungfleisch dinner as well as Davey and next morning he came to report. The return of the Dexters had been, of course, the sole topic of conversation. When it transpired that Davey had actually witnessed it he became the hero of the evening.

'They are puzzled, poor dears,' said Philip.

'Who—the Jungfleisches?'

'All the Americans here. Don't know how to take the news. Is it Good or Bad? What does it mean? How does Mr. Khrushchev evaluate it? What will the State Department say? The agony for our friends is should they send flowers or not? You know how they can't bear not to be loved, even by Dexter—it's ghastly for them to feel they are not welcoming old Heck as they ought to—at the same time it was very, very wrong of him to leave the Western Camp and it wouldn't do for them to appear to condone. The magic, meaningless word Solidarity is one of their runes; old Heck has not been solid and that's dreadfully un-American of him. But one must remember old Heck has now chosen Freedom, he has come back to the Western Camp of his own accord and they would like to reward him for that. So they are in an utter fix. In the end it was decided that Mildred must have a dinner party for policy makers; Jo Alsop, Elsa Maxwell, Mr. Gallagher and Mr. Shean are all flying over for it—but most of them can't get here before the end of the week. We shan't know any more until they have been consulted. Meanwhile there's the question of the flowers. Either you send at once or not at all; what are they to do? Davey suggested sending bunches with no cards, so that presently, if they want to, they can say, "Did you get my roses all right, Heck?"'

'Isn't Davey wonderful?'

'It went down very badly. They were sharked.'

Davey got to work on his godson. Dr. Lecœur came and took many tests, David co-operating quite satisfactorily. The Americans at Mrs. Jungfleisch's dinner had been unanimous in recommending Dr. Jore, head psychoanalyst to Nato. Davey brought him to the Salon Vert to have a word with me before taking him up to see his patient. He wanted to get the background first. He was a gangling young man, perhaps really much older than he looked. Davey seemed to like him; I tried to put prejudice out of my mind and do the same. When I had told him all I knew about my son, going back to babyhood, even trying to remember how I had taught him to use a pot ('I suppose I smacked him'), Dr. Jore cleared his throat.

'As I see it then, Mrs. Ambassadress, though of course I may be wrong since no system of psychiatry is as yet I believe infallible, the human element playing, as it must play in all human affairs, its part, since we are only endeavouring towards daylight and though I think I may say that the system by which I personally am guided is now very largely perfectioned, the foregoing reservation must be very distinctly borne in mind. With this reservation, then, very distinctly borne in mind, what I am about to say may be deemed to approximate the facts as they most probably are. Your son, Mrs. Ambassadress, in addition to a condition of aboulia which is probably due to oily terlet training, and which may be possible to combat but which is likely to be difficult, stubborn and lengthy, in short not easy, to overcome, your son has an anoetic Pull to the East. Period.'

'A Pull to the East?' I said.

'Please let Dr. Jore speak,' Davey said, sternly.

Dr. Jore slightly bowed and went on. 'Perhaps I could put this matter rather more succinctly by stating a paradigm which I believe to be unconfutable. Human beings, in my view and in the view of others more qualified than I, are roughly divided (in respect of what I am about to enucleate, to the best of my endeavour and without having had access to my case), human beings, then, fall into two roughly definable categoremia: those who are subject and liable to a Pull to the East and others, I am happy to say an appreciably larger grouping, who are subject and liable to a Pull to the West. Perhaps I could explain this matter more readily comprehensibly if I were to state that those on the continent of Europe who feel a very compelling wish and desire to visit England, Ireland and the Americas feel little wish or desire to go to Russia, China and the Indias, whereas those forcibly attracted to China, Russia and the Indias——'

'Don't want to go to America.'

'Please let Dr. Jore finish what he is saying,' Davey said peevishly. 'It's so interesting, Fanny——'

'Of course,' I said. 'If you go far enough East you come to the West. If you could manage to push my son a little further we might get him to Hollywood. Then he could join up with Auden and everybody,' I said to Davey, 'and Jassy could keep an eye on him. That might be a solution?'

Davey sighed deeply. 'And now, perhaps, we could be allowed to hear what the doctor has to say?'

Dr. Jore had shut his eyes while I spoke. He opened them again. 'Mrs. Ambassadress, ma'am, you have put your finger on the very heart of the matter.'

I looked triumphantly at Davey who said 'Ssh'.

'This is a point which has by no means escaped the learned professor who was the first to proclaim this doctrine of Oriental versus Occidental attraction. Now this attraction (whether towards the Orient or East or towards the Occident or West) occurs in the persons subjected to its magnetism in greater or lesser degrees and we practising psychiatrists find it possible to cure or check it according to its strength. May I explain myself? If the pull, whether to the East or to the West (a pull to the West, of course, is very much more desirable than its converse, and rarely needs to be cured, though in a few, very extreme, cases it should be checked), if the pull, then, is very strong it is comparatively easy to cure. If it is overwhelmingly strong the patient has only to be encouraged to follow it and in these days of jet travel he will find himself back where he started in a surprisingly short time. Period. In the case, however, Mrs. Ambassadress, of your son, the pull, by all the evidence which I have been able to garner, is weak. It has pulled him over the English Channel and across Normandy as far as Paris. Here it seems to have left him. Where there is so little for me to combat, the case is difficult. Therefore when your uncle suggested that I should work in collaboration with a physician I gladly agreed to do so. I feel that by super-adding the action of certain glands it should be possible to augment the will-power of your son, thus giving myself a basis on which to proceed. I must now touch upon another and more serious aspect of the Pull. Should the patient yearn towards the manners, customs and ways of thought of the Eastern Lands—should he sit on the floor eating rice; should the muezzin call for him in the Champs Elysées; should he dream of military deploys in the Red Square and think the bronzes of Démé-Jioman superior to those of Michelangelo—then, what I might call the jet treatment will not be sufficient. Then we must wean him back to the manners, customs and ways of Western Civilization and this we must do by means of his subconscious. Here the silent, long-playing gramophone record during sleep has its role, super-added to a daily personal collocution with myself or one of my assistants. Period.'

Dr. Jore shut his eyes again and there was silence. I did not dare to break it. At last Davey said, 'Excellent. That is precisely the conclusion I had come to myself. Now I think you should see your patient in his own surroundings—I'll take you up to his room.'

Dr. Jore was with David for about an hour, after which he went to Davey's room for an uninterrupted consultation. David came rocketing down to me.

'I see that you and Uncle Davey think I'm mad.'

'Oh, no, darling—whatever makes you say that?'

'Then why have you called in this ghastly Yank?'

'Davey—you know what it is—thought you weren't looking very well.'

'He's quite right there. I don't feel a hundred per cent. But isn't Dr. Lecœur coping with that? Why should I need an alienist?'

'You must ask Davey,' I said weakly. 'He's your godfather, he has taken you on, it's nothing to do with me.'

'You told this doctor about teaching me to pee into a pot, didn't you?'

'He asked.'

'Yes, well, another time please let him ask. After all this was most private between you and me, I call it wildly indiscreet of you to discuss it with a stranger. Another thing, Ma, if Dr. Jore comes here every day like he says he's going to he will drive me mad. Really, properly barking. I am quite serious.'

'I must say I see your point.'

'I heard him telling Davey he's going to empty my mind and re-furnish it with contemporary Western ideas. Now my Zen Master empties my mind and fills it with the ancient unlearning of the East. It can't be right for them to go on emptying and filling it in competition with each other?'

'I must say it doesn't sound right. You wouldn't think of giving up the Zen Master?'

'I don't like talking to you about Zen—I know you think it's funny—you're laughing now, Ma, aren't you? That's what makes it difficult to confide in you, you laugh at everything.'

'Darling, never at you,' I said, guiltily.

'In that case I'm the only one. You're nothing but a mocking materialist, like all your generation. If your children are not well-balanced you have only yourself to blame.'

'Oh dear. Do you think that you and Basil are different from other people because I mocked?' I was very much disturbed at this notion.

'Different from other people—different from whom? You go about the world with your eyes shut. If you opened them you would see thousands of people exactly like me and Basil—Beards and Teds abounding in every direction. Next time you go driving in that awful great hearse of yours, just look out of the window. You'll see that we're not as different from other people as all that——'

'Then in what way do you think you are unbalanced?'

'I lack self-confidence and will-power. That's what Dr. Jore thought.'

'And you don't feel that he can help you?'

'I've told you, Dr. Jore would drive me into a bin Only two people can help me. Dawn is one and the Zen Master is the other. They understand. I could never give them up, either of them.'

'No, darling, you shan't. I absolutely agree about Dr. Jore—he's a bore.'

'There you are, with your scale of false values! You divide human souls into bores and non-bores, don't you? I'm a bore and Basil isn't, that I've always known. You ought to be considering where everybody stands in the universal scheme instead of laughing at them and saying they are bores.'

'Anyway, in this case our different methods bring us to the same conclusion. I say Jore is a bore; you say Jore's standing in the universal scheme is low: we both say Jore must go.'

At this David became more agreeable. He kindly admitted that though I was regrettably frivolous I was not without a certain comprehension. He harrowed my face with his beard and we parted on the best of terms.

Davey was more hurt than surprised when I told him that he must get rid of Jore. In my view, I explained, he was calculated to give anybody who had to see much of him a nervous breakdown and I refused to have one of my own children handed over to him. 'David can't bear him,' I said, 'so I'm sure he wouldn't be much good.'

'He's far better than the Zen Master,' said Davey, who, unlike me, had been allowed to meet this legendary figure.

'That I can easily believe. However, David doesn't think so; people must be allowed to go to hell their own way.'

'It's the greatest pity he has taken against Jore. I thought his diagnosis quite amazing—he hit the nail on the head in one. Mildred says he is intensely brilliant; the Supreme Commander has him every afternoon.'

'How can he bear the dissertation?'

'You must remember, with Americans, that they are fighting to express themselves in a language they've never properly learnt. They need the dissertation; the kind of shorthand that we talk would be useless to them.'

The next evening, Davey was good enough to dine in. We were waiting for Alfred and sipping cocktails.

'Why does one never see Northey?' Davey was asking, upon which the door opened and the pretty face looked round it.

'I say, what's happened to David? He fell on me like a stallion just now, in my office.'

'Oh good,' said Davey. 'Dr. Lecœur's super-adding gland injection must have begun to work.'

'Really, Davey, I call that rather inconvenient!' I said. 'What about all the young women in the Chancery? I'm supposed to be responsible for their morals, you know.'

'This is Paris. They must be used to dealing with satyrs.'

'In the Bois, perhaps, but not in the Embassy. Is it necessary to turn the poor fellow into a satyr?'

'Please, Fanny, I must ask you not to interfere any more with my treatment of David.'

'Oh, very well. Do you dine with us, darling?'

'Not really. I'm after *France Soir*. Goody gum-trees, the Bourse has found her vigour again—but Ay de mi, the Reps have reacted unfavourably to M. Bourguiba's speech. Now there will be a pause for introspection, mark my words. The worry of it!'

'Where's Baz?' I said.

'Buggered. He'll be coming back next week.'

'Buggered!' said Davey, faintly.

'Now, Davey, you tell her she mustn't.'

'It's all right, I know I mustn't and I'm trying desperately hard not to.'

'Is he bringing the atom marchers next week?'

'No, ruminants until the end of the month. He's been very busy organizing the march—he spent hours yesterday with precious Amy, seeing about the publicity. Anything for me to do, Fanny? Don't say yes, there's a darling, but lend me your little mink jacket, I'm so tired of my bunny.'

'Very well, on condition you reform your language. What are you up to?'

'Phyllis McFee and me are going to the Return of the Cinders with M. Cruas. He's poor, he can't take us to a proper theatre. Le Retour des Cendres, Fanny, sharpen your wits—the body of Napoleon coming back to the Invalides. So I go and get the jacket—you are lucky to be so kind—good night——'

'They were talking about her at Mildred's,' Davey said. 'It seems she is in full fling with Valhubert.'

I could not help remarking, 'One can always be sure of some good conversation there——'

'Fanny, be serious. Aren't you worried about it?'

'More worried about Valhubert than the others certainly—but no, you know, not really. Northey is a good little child.'

'There are certain women who go through life in a cloud of apparent innocence under cover of which they are extremely unchaste.'

'Yes. My mother for one. But if Northey's like that I don't see what we can do about it. I did scold her for talking half the night to Valhubert on the telephone—she replied that if there was anything wrong between them she would have been in bed with him, not just chatting. Very true I should think.'

'Yes, there's something in that. How much does she remind you of Linda?'

'On the face of it, very much indeed. But there are differences. She's not nearly so concentrated. When Linda was in love she never bothered about followers—they only cropped up when she was out of love with one man and not yet in with another.'

'But is Northey in love?'

'Oh yes, hasn't she told you? She's meant to be madly in love with Philip—I suppose she is, but sometimes I can't help wondering. She never moons about as Linda used to (do you remember the games of patience, the long staring out of the window, the total distraction from real life?). Northey lives in an absolute rush, with at least twenty different admirers. When she has half an hour to spare I think she does go and have a word with St. Expédite about Philip.'

'St. Expédite,' said Davey, 'how that takes me back! He's a good saint, if ever there was one—I must go and see him again, but only for old sake's sake, alas! At my age one doesn't have these desperately hopeless desires. So she's in love with Philip—how perfect that would be. Doesn't he fancy her—why not?'

'He adores Grace, unfortunately. But I've begun to think, just lately, that he's getting fonder than he knows of Northey and that finally it may all come right.'

'That makes it important to scotch the Valhubert business now at once. Remember, being in love with Prince André didn't stop Natasha from making a fool of herself.'

'I know. Cressida too. Young women are very silly.'

'I think you ought to have a word with him.'

'What, with Valhubert? Davey, the terror! I really don't think you can ask me to do that!'

'Alfred then? It might be easier for him?'

'Oh, no, no! Don't tell Alfred—he has enough to worry him. The children are my affair—I never allow him to be bothered by them if I can possibly help it. How late he is, by the way. What can he be doing?'

'Philip told me he had gone to a football match, but surely that must be over by now?'

When at last Alfred appeared he seemed quite worn out. 'I'm sorry to be late—I had to get quickly into a bath—I was simply soaked with rotten eggs at the France versus England. Lord, how I do hate sport. Then I had an endless visit from the Irish Ambassador about those wretched cows.'

CHAPTER XV

FOR a long time now Charles-Edouard de Valhubert had been urging me to go with him and visit the old Duchesse de Sauveterre at her country house, the Château de Boisdormant. He said she wanted to talk about her grandchild, little Fabrice. We had twice made plans to do this; for one reason or another they had come to nothing; at last a day was fixed which suited all of us. Grace, who was expecting a baby and felt rather sick, decided to stay at home. I had always felt nervous at the idea of a long motor drive alone with Valhubert, who intimidated me, but since my talk with Davey I positively dreaded it. If it was really my duty to speak about Northey, now would be the time. However, sitting in the front seat of a new Jaguar, with Valhubert at the wheel, I soon found that the physical terror far outweighed the moral.

'Have I not a style of my own, in driving?' he said, weaving up the rue Lafayette. 'I don't take the outer boulevards, they are too ugly.'

The style consisted in never slowing down. I began to pray for the traffic lights to go red and stop him; my foot was clamped to an imaginary brake until the muscles hurt. The terror increased when he began to imitate the style of other drivers: the young chauffeur of a Marshal of France, the old chauffeur of an American hostess, the driver of a police car (hands never on the wheel) and M. Bouche-Bontemps. He kept looking at me to see if I were laughing, which, indeed, I was; finally his eyes never seemed to be on the road at all. 'Oh please, do be yourself!' I said, and wished I had not as he spurted forward.

Once outside Paris and past Le Bourget I calmed down. He was in full control of the machine, though he went much too fast. We chatted away enjoyably and I realized that he was not at all frightening, much less than he seemed to be when one met him at a Parisian party. When we passed the cross-roads at Gonesse he recited the names of all the people he knew who had been killed there in motor-car accidents, after which silence fell, because of my inability, since I had not known any of them, to aliment the conversation. Thinking that now was my chance, I bravely forced myself to say, 'I worry about Northey.'

'I love this little girl.'

'Yes. That's exactly why I worry.' I was astounded at my own courage.

'Ah—no!' He looked vastly amused and not at all embarrassed. 'I don't love her—I mean I like her very much.'

'It's not you I worry about. She might love. She tells me she thinks of being a concubine.'

He roared with laughter. 'Not in my harem, I can assure you. Why, she is only two years older than Sigi—and half his mental age.'

'That's no protection, surely?'

'With me it is. I don't happen to be attracted by children—not yet—no doubt that will come, one of the horrors of senility. And I dislike the sensation of doing wrong.'

'I thought it added to the amusement?'

'Greatly, if one is cocufying some old prig one was at school with. But to seduce Northey would do her harm and also lead to trouble. I love Mees and I hate trouble. No, we must marry her to Philip—I'm working for that. If he thinks I am courting her and if she seems to cool off him, that, human nature being what it is, may do the trick. He has sighed after Grace quite long enough, it's a bore. Like this I hope to kill two birds with one stone.'

I was not completely reassured but there was nothing more I could say. It was another beautiful day. (When I look back on our first months in France we seem to have enjoyed an uninterrupted Indian summer.) Valhubert and I were now crossing the Seine-et-Marne country where everything is on an enormous scale. Avenues of poplar trees rush over vast horizons and seem to encircle the globe; down the roads bordered by them the largest, whitest of horses draw ancient wagons loaded with beetroots the size of footballs; each farm with its basse-cour, kennels, cow-byres, stables, barns and sheds occupies enough space for a whole village. The land breathes of prosperity; the predominating colour at that time of year is gold.

'This is the battlefield of the Marne,' he told me, 'where thousands of young men were killed in 1914, on days like this, almost before they could have realized they were at war. The Uhlans, mounted, with their lances, the Cuirassiers glittering in polished armour, went into action on horseback. Those battles were more like a military tournament than modern warfare—to read of them now is reminiscent of Agincourt or Crécy. One can't believe they happened in living memory and that there are still many people we know who took part in them.'

We came to a village of whitewashed houses clustered round a twelfth-century church. 'I have an uncle who was wounded here at St. Soupplets. When he came to, in hospital, they said, "You were in the Battle of the Marne." He was perfectly amazed. He remembered seeing a few Germans round that inn across the road there—and then he was knocked down by a bullet, but he had no idea he had been in anything as important as a battle.'

'Stendhal's description of Waterloo is rather like that—casual and unfrightening.'

'I love this country so much but now it makes me feel sad to come here. We must look at it with all our eyes because in ten years' time it will be utterly different. No more stooks of corn or heaps of manure to dot the stubble with light and shade, no more peasants in blue overalls, no more horses and carts, nothing but mechanicians driving tractors and lorries. The trees are going at a fearful rate. Last time I came along this road it was bordered by apple trees—look, you can see the stumps. Some admirer of Bernard Buffet has put up these telegraph poles instead.'

'It is still very beautiful,' I said, 'I never saw the apple trees so I don't grieve for them as you do. When I go to the country I always wonder how any of us can bear to live in towns—it seems perfect madness.'

'I'm sure you didn't feel like that when you were Northey's age.'

'Now I come to think of it, when I was Northey's age I did live in the country and my only idea was how to get to London.'

'Of course it was. Young people need urban life, to exchange thoughts and see what goes on in the world—it's quite right and natural. By degrees the tempo slows down and we take to peaceful pleasures like gardening or just sitting in the sun. Very few young people are sensitive to beauty, that's why there are so few poets.'

'Yes. But now it seems almost unbearable to think what one is missing by being in a town as the days and months go by. So dreadful only to know the seasons by the flower and vegetable shops.'

'I call that rather ungrateful. Your embassy is in a forest.'

'I know. Our Oxford house is not, however.'

'When were you born?'

'In 1911.'

'And I the year after. So we remember the old world as it had been for a thousand years, so beautiful and diverse, and which, in only thirty years, has crumbled away. When we were young every country still had its own architecture and customs and food. Can you ever forget the first sight of Italy? Those ochre houses, all different, each with such character, with their trompe-l'œil paintings on the stucco? Queer and fascinating and strange even to a Provençal like me. Now, the dreariness! The suburbs of every town uniform all over the world, while perhaps in the very centre a few old monuments sadly survive as though in a glass case. Venice is still wonderful, though the approach to it makes me shudder, but most of the other Italian towns are engulfed in sky-scrapers and tangles of wire. Even Rome has this American rind! "Roma senza speranza", I saw in an Italian paper; all is said.' He sighed deeply. 'But like you with the apple trees, our children never saw that world so they cannot share our sadness. One more of the many things that divide us. There is an immense gap between us and them, caused by unshared experience. Never in history has the past and the present been so different; never have the generations been divided as they are now.'

'If they are happy and good in the new world it doesn't much matter,' I said.

'Will they be happy? I think modern architecture is the greatest anti-happiness there has ever been. Nobody can live in those shelves, they can't do more than eat and sleep there; for their hours of leisure and their weeks of holiday they are driven on to the roads. That is why a young couple would rather have a motor-car than anything else—it's not in order to go to special places but a means of getting away from the machine where they exist. The Americans have lived like that, between earth and sky, for a generation now and we are beginning to see the result. Gloom, hysteria, madness, suicide. If all human beings must come to this, is it worth struggling on with the world? So,' he said, narrowly missed by a D.S. which, at a hundred miles an hour and the law on its side, hurtled at us from a right-hand turning, 'shall we put an end to it all?'

'No,' I said hurriedly, 'we must wait and see. I have a few things to leave in order when I go—Northey—the boys. It may not be as bad as we fear. There may be less happiness than when we were young—there is probably less unhappiness. I expect it all evens out. When would you have liked to be born?'

'Any time between the Renaissance and the Second Empire.'

I trotted out the platitude, 'But only if you were a privileged person?'

He said, simply, 'If I were not, I wouldn't be me.'

Very true. Such men as Valhubert, my father, Uncle Matthew would not have been themselves had they not always been kings in their own little castles. Their kind is vanishing as surely as the peasants, the horses and the avenues, to be replaced, like them, by something less picturesque, more utilitarian.

I said, 'Perhaps the Russians will explore some nice empty planet and allow people like us to go and live on it.'

'No good to me,' said Valhubert, 'I wouldn't care a bit for oceans on which Ulysses never sailed, mountains uncrossed by Hannibal and Napoleon. I must live and die a European.'

We whizzed down the ancient roads leading to the Holy Roman Empire in silence now, each thinking his own thoughts. I was no longer frightened by the speed, but exhilarated, enjoying myself. Up in the sky two parallel white lines drawn by two tiny black crosses showed that young men in aeroplanes were also enjoying themselves on this perfect day. At last a signpost marked Boisdormant showed that we were nearing our destination.

'Madame de Sauveterre——?' I said. 'Just tell me——'

'You have never seen her?'

'Such years ago. I used to stay with an old woman called Lady Montdore——'

'The famous one?'

'Yes, I suppose she was. When I was about eighteen I met Sauveterre and his mother there. It's the only time I ever saw him.'

'Poor Fabrice! He was the most charming person I have known, by very far.'

'So was my cousin Linda.'

'Le coquin! You say he hid her in Paris for months and nobody had any idea of it.'

'She wasn't divorced. Besides, she was terrified that her parents would find out.'

'Yes. And the war had only just begun and didn't seem serious, then. Life appeared to be endless in front of one. Also I think Fabrice had somebody else—another reason for secrecy. Always these complications!'

'Were you very intimate?'

'Oh, very. His mother is my great-aunt—Fabrice was much older than me, twelve years at least—but as soon as I was grown up we became bosom friends. It was an adoration on my side. Hard to think of him as dead, even now.'

'His mother——' I said, coming back to the point.

'She's a worldly old woman as you will see. Fabrice was the only meaning to her existence. Now that he has gone she lives for money and food, torn between miserliness and greed. Enormously rich, no family, no heir. That's why it's important that she should see the boy.'

'Good of you to take so much trouble. You must remember he may not play up. Children are unpredictable—at his age old people are a bore and money hardly seems to exist.'

'He has good manners and he looks like his father. I'll be very much surprised if he doesn't win her over.'

We were now on a little white, untarred country lane winding between rank hedgerows. The crop of berries that year was rich and glistening; I thought I had not seen so white a road and such scarlet berries since I was a child. Presently we came to a park wall of stones covered with peeling plaster—perched up in one corner of it like a bird's nest there was a little round thatched summer-house.

'Is it not typically French, all this?' said Valhubert. 'What makes it so, I wonder? The colour of that wall, perhaps?'

'And that ruin on the hill, with a walnut tree growing out of it; and the trees in the park, so tall and thin and regular——'

An avenue of chestnuts led from the lodge gates to the house, their leaves lay in the drive, unswept. A flock of sheep, watched by a shepherd with a crook, were cropping away at long dark green grass. The house, an old fortress built round three sides of a square, was surrounded by a moat, the turrets at its corners were entirely covered, even to their pointed roofs, with ancient ivy so that they looked like four huge mysterious trees. Valhubert stopped the engine, saying, 'I don't trust that drawbridge. I think we'll walk from here.'

The oldest butler in the world opened the front door long before we reached it. He greeted Valhubert in the way of a servant with some-body he has known and loved from childhood, hurried us upstairs into a round white drawing-room, inside one of the ivy trees, sunny and cheerful, and vanished at the double.

'She'll be down in exactly a quarter of an hour,' said Valhubert. 'Grace thinks she can't bear to begin painting her face until she actually sees us arriving for fear we should have an accident on the road and then all the powder and paint and eye black would be wasted. She and Oudineau are hard at it now. He's her lady's maid as well as butler, caretaker, woodman, chauffeur, gardener and game-keeper. Nobody has ever been so much à tout faire. The exquisite luncheon we are about to eat (you'll see how it's worth the journey for that alone) will have been fished, shot and grown by Oudineau and cooked by his son. This Jacques has an enormous situation in Paris, but he is obliged to drive down here and do the cooking when my aunt has guests. I must say it only happens once in a blue moon.'

'Is he a chef, in Paris?'

'By no means! He directs an enormous electrical concern—Jacques Oudineau will produce all the atomic plant of the future. He's im-mensely powerful and very attractive, one meets him dining out everywhere—that's his Mercedes, parked by the kitchen garden.'

'What a charming room this is!'

'Yes—there's nothing so pretty as a château-fort—redecorated in the eighteenth century. This panelling is by Pineau. Look at those heaps of illustrated papers—they go back fifty years and more. One day Grace and I were waiting for her to come down and we began looking at them (I am particularly fond of Matania—orgies—galley-slaves—jousting and so on). Literally showers of banknotes came tumbling out of them, all obsolete. Yes, she's a miser in the true sense of the word.'

Presently our hostess appeared looking, I thought, exactly the same as she had some twenty-seven years ago, at Hampton. She had then been in her fifties; she was now in her eighties; she had seemed old then and not a day older now. She must once have been pretty, with little turned-up nose and black eyes, but almost before middle age, probably, she had become stout; there was something porcine in her look. It was hard to imagine that she could have given birth to the irresistible Fabrice. Almost on her heels, Oudineau reappeared and in a voice of thunder announced, ' 'chesse est servie.'

We lunched, in a narrow room with windows on both sides, off Sèvres plates which must literally have been worth their weight in gold. 'They belonged to Bauffremont—you know them very well, my dear Charles-Edouard. I never allow Jacques Oudineau to wash them up; he is quite a good cook, but a most unreliable boy in other ways.'

The luncheon was indeed worth the journey. We began with brochet. Why is brochet so good and pike so nasty, since the dictionary affirms that they are one and the same? Then partridges, followed by thick juicy French cutlets quite unlike the penny on the end of a brittle bone which is the English butcher's presentation of that piece of meat. They were burnt on the outside, inside almost raw. Boiled eggs suddenly appeared, with fingers of buttered toast, in case anybody should still be famished. Then a whole brie on bed of straw; then chocolate profiterolles. I was beginning to get used to such meals, but they always made me feel rather drunk and stupid for an hour or two afterwards.

When she tasted the salad, Mme de Sauveterre said 'Vinegar!'

'Jacques is in despair, Mme la Duchesse, he forgot to bring a lemon.'

'It's inadmissible. This boy always forgets something. Last time it was the truffles. He has no head. Thank goodness I haven't got shares in his concern.'

'Thank goodness I have,' said Valhubert, 'since they double every year.'

The Duchess asked a hundred questions about the Embassy, specially wanting to know what had become of all the English people she had known there in the past.

'Et cette adorable Ava—et la belle Peggy—et ce vieux type si agréable du Service, Sir Charles?'

When she saw how little I could tell her about any of them she put me down for what I am, provincial. Valhubert, however, knew all the answers. He told her that she had met me already, at Hampton, after which she got on to Lady Montdore and her circle. Here I did better.

'Yes, she died before the war, of heart failure while having an operation in Switzerland.'

I did not add that it was an operation for leg-lifting which Cedric, the present Lord Montdore, had persuaded her to undergo against a great deal of medical advice. He said that he utterly refused to be seen with her at the Lido again until it had been done. Her heart, worn out by dieting and excessive social life, had stopped under the anaesthetic. As this happened at a very convenient moment for him, the whole affair seemed fishy and many people openly said that he had murdered her. Soon afterwards the war broke out and he fled to America. 'Darling, you can't really imagine ONE going over the top?'

Indeed it was an unlikely conception. However, having killed Lady Montdore and failed to kill Germans, he was badly received in England when he returned there after the war. He had very soon gone back and settled in his native continent.

'The present Montdore? Yes, he lives in the West Indies. I miss him very much. Polly? She is happy, has thousands of children and has completely lost her looks.'

'Fabrice always said she would. And Lady Montdore's lover—ce vieux raseur—I forget his name?'

'Boy Dougdale? He has become one of our foremost biographers.'

'Now tell me about yourself, charmante Ambassadrice. I hear you have two boys at school with that little monster of Charles-Edouard's? I don't know much about young people as I never see any, but one hears such tales——'

'Does one?' said Charles-Edouard, amused. 'What sort of tales penetrate to Boisdormant, ma tante?'

'You would know how true it is,' she said to me, 'but I am told the boys and girls nowadays are against birth?'

'Against birth?'

'Against being born.'

'My aunt means they don't care whether they belong to good families or not, any more.'

'Oh, I see.' I had supposed she meant something to do with birth control. 'But do you think young people ever cared about such things?'

'When I was young we did. In any case it is shocking to be against. The grandchildren of a friend of mine actually started a newspaper against birth—horrible, I find, and so of course one of the girls married somebody who wasn't born——'

'Yes,' said Valhubert, with a quizzical look in my direction, 'it won't do. We can't have these goings-on in society, though I must say the unborn young man is rather solid for a disembodied spirit.'

'You laugh now, Charles-Edouard, but when your daughters are grown up you will see these things in a very different light. Tell me more about your boys, Mme l'Ambassadrice, I hear that one of them is called Fabrice?'

'He is the child of my cousin, who is dead. I have adopted him.'

Suddenly we both found that we could not go on with this conversation. We looked at Valhubert who came to the rescue. 'When all three of them come over for the Christmas holidays I'll bring them here for a few days.'

'Yes, you must. Old Oudineau can teach them to ride bicycles—children like that very much, I find. Do you heat the Embassy with coal or mazout?'

CHAPTER XVI

When we got back to the Embassy Philip was crossing the courtyard. Charles-Edouard refused a cup of tea; he said Grace would be longing to hear about our day and he thought he had better get back. He drove straight off. Philip came into the house with me. I said, 'I like Valhubert very much.'

'The thing about lady-killers is that they kill ladies,' he replied, grumpily. 'That ass of a Northey is dining with him again tonight.'

'Oh, Philip—alone?'

'I've no idea. Did you see the papers this morning?'

'Hardly. I was in a rush.'

'Didn't see Mockbar?'

I stood still. We were halfway up the stairs. 'Now what?'

'He has found out that the famous Frenchman who won your mother in a lottery is none other than poor old Bouche-Bontemps. He says he is able to reveal that the French premier is one of the ex-stepfathers of Ambassadress Lady Wincham.' Philip pulled a newspaper cutting from his pocket. 'Here we are—able to reveal, yes—Her sixty-three-year-old mother, he goes on—yes, listen to this, it's stirring stuff—ex-Lady Logan, ex-Mrs. Chaddesley-Corbett, ex-Viscountess Tring, ex-Madame Bouche-Bontemps, ex-Mrs. Rawle, ex-Mrs. Plugge, ex-Señora Lopez, ex-Mrs. Chrisolithe, is now married to Pimlico man "Grandad" Markson, 22, organizer of Grandad's Tours. Interviewed in London, Mrs. Markson said she had lost touch with husband number four. "We were madly in love," she said. Asked if it was true that M. Bouche-Bontemps won her in a lottery, she said, "I think it was a tombola." '

'Now what?'

'Bouche-Bontemps is frantic, I've had him on the telephone a dozen times. He says he remembers keenly living with this lady, out of her head, but pretty and funny, and he thinks they were together for two or three months but he certainly never married her.'

'Goodness!' I said, 'that seems to put him in an awkward position, doesn't it? Like when are you going to stop beating your wife? If he married the Bolter it's bad but if he didn't marry her it's worse?'

'No, no. You don't understand the French, as Davey would say. If he married her that's the end of his career but if he only lived with her nobody here would think anything of it. Can't you ring her up and find out?'

'Dear me! But I'm afraid she says [I was looking at Mockbar's piece] husband number four. Come on, we'll put a call through now.'

It was not necessary, however. In the Salon Vert there was a telegram on top of my afternoon letters. 'Never married him darling it was deed-pollers gave no interview have taken it up with Grumpy who promises denial tomorrow in Daily Post Bolter.'

'Oh well,' said Philip when I handed him this. 'That will make it much better. If they really deny it in the Daily Post the French papers won't copy it. They are far keener on accuracy than ours.'

'Don't you think Mockbar has gone too far? Might he not get the sack?'

'Not he! Much more likely to get a rise so that he can fatten his brats until the next jump in the cost of living forces him to make another scoop.' He lifted up the receiver. 'Katie, get the Président du Conseil for Lady Wincham, will you?'

'Is that my stepfather?' I said and was nearly blown over by a burst of laughter. 'Listen—I've had a telegram from my mother which Philip thinks will make everything all right. She says the paper is denying a marriage. It was only deed-poll she says.'

'Deed-poll,' said Bouche-Bontemps suspiciously, 'what is this?'

'What's deed-poll in French?' I asked Philip and repeated after him. 'Acte unilatéral but you don't have it here like we do. You know—it means she took your name.'

'Did she? There was certainly no acte. But why should she take my name?'

'For the neighbours I expect.'

'But, chère Mme l'Ambassadrice, it was at Harrar! The neighbours were Abyssinians—never mind, go on.'

'Anyhow, the point is there will be a denial tomorrow. Oh dear, I'm so sorry—though it's not exactly my fault.'

'But nothing matters as long as I am not supposed to be bigame—what is it in English?—bigamous. That would be very annoying—the Hautes Pyrénées would not like it and nor would my late wife's family les Pucelards (textiles Pucelard) from Lille. The only person who would be delighted is my daughter-in-law who hates me, it would quite compensate her for being married to a bastard. Now, of course, I shall be labelled Intelligence Service but as the only Frenchman of whom that is never said is General de Gaulle I suppose I can bear it. Sacrée Dorothée—is she really your mother? How strange! No women could be less alike—though I now see a striking resemblance between her and Mees.'

'Oh don't! I always try not to!'

When I had finished talking to Bouche-Bontemps I went to find Northey. Her room was full of newborn wails. 'Mélusine has had six lovely babies, clever girl.'

'I thought you said she was old?'

'Yes. They are miracle-children.'

'So now what? Hadn't somebody better bucket them at once? Before she has got fond of them?'

'Fanny!'

'I know. But darling duck, we can't keep them here.'

'In this enormous house? I saw a dear rat in the courtyard only yesterday.'

'It was a visiting rat then. There aren't any in the house and we've got a perfectly good cat in the kitchen.'

'Sweet Minet. Very well, if you are so unwelcoming I shall give them away.'

'Yes. You must. Did you enjoy the Return of the Cinders?'

'It was lovely. We all shouted Vive l'Empereur—a bit late, but never mind.'

'I hear you are going out with M. de Valhubert again?'

'On business, Fanny. I must have a long serious talk about the porte-feuille. If the assainissement de notre place goes on like this all my profits will disappear and then what will my old age be like? Can you afford to pension me off? I'm getting seriously annoyed about it.'

'You talk worse pidgin than Grace. Do try to keep to one language at a time. I suppose you read Mockbar this morning?'

'Clever little soul. By the way, Davey asked me to say goodbye.'

'Davey has buggered off?'

'Fanny! Never mind, I won't tell Alfred. Yes. He says he can feel himself getting cancer of the lungs at every breath he takes in Paris.'

'What nonsense! Among all these trees! There's no smell of petrol here.'

'He says it's the scentless fumes, heavier than air, which do all the damage.'

'I must say that's a bit too much. He turns David into a sex-maniac and then leaves us to bear the brunt.'

'He'll bravely come back when he's decarbonized, to see about David. Meanwhile Docteur Lecœur has given him a calming injection so the idea is that all our virtues are saved for the present. Katie had a ghastly time with him last night—she says it was the nearest thing— That beard and those feet, how can poor Dawnie? Why are Zen-men's feet always so awful?' She shuddered.

'I wish Docteur Lecœur would give Mockbar a calming injection.'

'No, Fanny, he's courting. It would be too unfair.'

'Courting whom?'

'Phyllis McFee, for one.'

'Tell me something, Northey. Does Phyllis McFee really exist?'

Wide-eyed, injured look. 'How d'you mean, does she really exist?'

'You haven't invented her, by any chance?'

'She's my old friend of for ever. (The poor make no new friends—oh don't! That wretched Bourse!) Surely I'm allowed the one?'

'Then I can't understand why you never bring her to see me?'

'She works.'

'What at?'

'World Something.'

'Not in the evening surely?'

'Specially then because, you know, the World is round so it's later in America. When that great throbbing, teeming, bustling heart of little old New York begins to beat, Phyllis McFee, relaxed, efficient, smiling (not to grin is a sin), suitably dressed in her latest Mainbocher, immaculate hair-do, neat ankles and red nails, must be on the Trans-atlantic line. She has no time to waste on people like you.'

'Bring her to luncheon one day?'

'She's far too busy. She can't do more than un queek dans un drog which is French for luncheon in a chemist's shop. Just imagine, scrumptious grub all among the cotton wool—takes thinking of—admit——'

'All right then, don't bring her. I don't mind. She seems to work a good deal harder than some people we know.'

'Is that a hint? Not very kind, Fanny. As a matter of fact, Phyllis McFee has ambitions, she wants to hug her boss (which would be French for employer if it didn't happen to mean bruise). I don't.'

'Another person I never see, while we are on the subject of invisible beings, is M. Craus.'

'He's timid. He wouldn't like to be seen by you. And speaking as your secretary, quite as much up to date, thorough and efficient as Phyllis, may I remind you that you and Alfred have got the National Day of the North Koreans, after which you dine early with the Italians to go to a lovely play, at the Théâtre des Nations, about refrigerators. Some people have all the luck——!'

Feeling myself dismissed, I went up to my bedroom and tried to forget my manifold worries in a long, hot, scented bath.

It took us some time to get from the North Korean to the Italian Embassy. Between the hours of seven and eight all the Americans who live in Paris bring out motor-cars the size of lorries, shiny, showy and horribly cheap-looking, and sally forth to meet each other, drink whisky and rub up their accents. This also happens to be the time when the Parisians are on the move from work-place to home; the streets become almost impassable.

As we drove towards the Alma, at about one mile an hour, Alfred said, 'You seem preoccupied, darling. Is there something on your mind?'

'Something! About a ton of different things——'

'Such as?'

'Mockbar, to begin with. I suppose you didn't see it——'

'Yes, I did. Philip put it under my eyes. Anything sillier I have seldom read. Bouche-Bontemps says it's quite untrue and he must know. Really—if that's all——'

'Oh, how I wish it were. Northey worries me dreadfully.'

'Northey? Why?'

'Any little girl as attractive as she is must be a worry until one has married her off. The followers——'

'Safety in numbers, surely.'

'There are one or two whom I don't think safe.' I did not want to specify Valhubert to Alfred without more proof than I had that he was really a danger.

'Can you wonder they follow? The other day—it was after your luncheon party—she took Mme Meistersinger downstairs. I'd just been seeing off the Burmese and then had gone into Mrs. Trott's room to telephone. When I came out the hall was empty—the footman was putting the old woman into her motor and behind their backs, at the top of the steps, Northey was going through a sort of pantomime of ironical reverences. Oh I can't describe how funny it was! Of course she had no idea anybody was watching. It made me realize that one might be terribly in love with that little creature.'

'We all are,' I said, 'except Philip. One does so long for her to have a happy life, not like the Bolter.'

Alfred now said something extraordinary: 'Deeply as I disapprove of your mother and her activities I don't think she could be described as unhappy.'

I looked at him in amazement. We were all so much accustomed in my family to deploring the Bolter's conduct that one took for granted the great unhappiness to which it must have, if only because it ought to have, led.

'You should try and see things as they are, Fanny. Whether her behaviour has been desirable or not is a different proposition from whether it has made her unhappy. I don't think it has; I think she is perfectly happy and always was.'

'Perhaps. Still, you wouldn't want that sort of happiness for Northey, I suppose. My prayer is that she will marry Philip and settle down.'

'I agree. I don't want it for her. But neither do I want her to marry him because, if she does, mark my words, she won't settle down. She will bolt.'

'Alfred, why do you say that?'

'Philip wouldn't hold her. Not enough fantasy, no roughage. Although vastly superior in every way to Tony Kroesig he is in some sort not the contrary of him. Just as Tony didn't do for Linda, so Philip wouldn't for Northey.'

'I see in a way what you mean—they are both rich, conventional Englishmen—but really it's very unfair to Philip.'

'I'm extremely fond of him, I only say he's not the husband for her.'

'I wonder! Luckily it's out of our hands—something they must settle for themselves. Are you beginning to be interested in people in your old age, darling?'

'Old age?' Falsetto.

'Well, I really think it must be that. You used utterly to despise me when I made these sort of speculations.'

'I'm interested in the children and I count Northey as one.'

'I sometimes wish she was our one and only—no, of course I don't mean that, but I could wish that David and Baz hadn't reached these difficult stages just when you and I have our hands full. We can be of so little use to them, under the circumstances.'

'I don't know. We seem to be lodging David and his family, providing medical attention and everything. Basil comes and goes as he likes—what more could we do? I think it's just as well we are busy; it takes our minds off them. Useless for us to worry and we have no cause to reproach ourselves. They are only suffering from growing pains I think—nothing very serious.'

'I do reproach myself for not having sent them to Eton. If we had they might have turned out so differently.'

'I don't agree. Eton produces quite as large a percentage of oddities as other schools. In any case we weren't rich enough, then. We did our best for them, and that's that.'

'We must count our blessings. How I'm looking forward to going over on St. Andrew's Day and taking out the little boys. They are perfect.'

'Perfect?' Falsetto again.

'I mean like other people.'

'Oh. So it's perfect to be like other people, is it? Grace tells me they think of nothing but jazz.'

'That's a phase.'

'So are the eccentricities of Basil and David, no doubt . . .'

'My point is that going to Eton will have minimized the danger of such extreme phases in the case of Charlie and Fabrice.'

'Unberufen,' said Alfred, as we drove into the courtyard of the Hôtel de Doudeauville.

CHAPTER XVII

THE word 'unberufen' rang so unaccustomed on the lips of Alfred that it stuck in my mind. Whether it was the result of old age or of having a new position in the world, he seemed to be mellowing; the Alfred of a year ago would have conducted our conversation in the motor on different, sterner lines and would not have said 'unberufen'. However, when, the next day before luncheon, Katie told me that there was a personal call for him from Windsor, I knew that he must have unberufened in vain. He had gone to the railway carriage in the forest of Compiègne to celebrate the Armistice; I said that I would take the call. No doubt some sort of worst had occurred; I prayed, wrongly, weakmindedly, that it would prove to be a moral and not a physical worst. For a few seconds there was a muddle on the line: ' 'allo Weendzor—parlez Weendzor,' during which time an amazing amount of horrible speculations managed to pass through my head. The moment I heard the housemaster's voice, decidedly peevish but not sad, I was reassured: Charlie and Fabrice were obviously still with us on this earth. He did not beat about the bush or try to prepare me for bad news; he told me that the boys had left.

'Run away?' I said, perhaps too cheerfully, in my relief.

'People don't exactly run away any more. The snivelling boy dragged off the stagecoach by an usher is a thing of the past.'

I laughed hysterically at this piece of light relief, put in perhaps to steady my nerves.

'No, you could hardly call it that. In any case, running away is a spontaneous action with which one can have a certain sympathy. This was a premeditated, indeed an organized, departure. They asked to speak to me after early school and announced it, quite politely I must say. Then all three got into a Rolls Royce, apparently hired for the purpose, and drove off——'

'All three?'

'Valhubert was with them.'

'Oh, he was, was he! And did they give a reason?'

'The excuse was the food—in other words, no excuse at all because I think I may say the food in my house is excellent. I eat it myself. They pretended that poor little Billy last half—you remember the tragedy—threw himself into the weir on purpose because of it. Nothing could be more far-fetched. They said the choice was between a suicide pact and immediate departure.'

'Naughty!' I stifled a giggle.

'I need hardly tell you that I shall be unable to take them back again after this. The drama was played out in public—half the school saw them go. It seems they stopped in Slough for Fabrice to say goodbye to his mistress and three children.'

'Rubbish,' I said irritably. 'I've heard about this mistress in Slough all my life—ever since my cousins were at school. And the King of Siam's seven wives living over the post-office. Typical Eton tales.'

'That may be. I'm only telling you to show the effect of all this on the other boys and the impossibility of my overlooking their conduct.'

'Oh yes, I see, and I quite realize. Does M. de Valhubert know?'

'Not yet. I shall ring him up now.'

'Just tell me where they've gone, will you?'

'I have no idea.'

'No idea! Didn't you ask them?'

'Certainly I did not.'

My irritation turned to fury. What did we pay the wretched man for? With incredible frivolity he had allowed these children we had put in his care, while we were serving our country overseas, to vanish into the blue. All very well for him to be so lighthearted about it; he had got rid of them for good. My troubles were just beginning, but that evidently left him cold.

'Then there's nothing more to say?'

'Nothing, I'm afraid.' We rang off.

I told Katie to keep the line clear until Mme de Valhubert should ring up. Presently I asked her, 'What's become of Northey? I haven't seen her this morning.'

'She was up all night with the kittens. Mélusine doesn't seem to have any milk—too old probably—so it's the fountain-pen filler. Poor Northey's trying to get some sleep; I've taken over for her. Every two hours, and one of them isn't sucking properly. I think this is Mme de Valhubert now—that was her butler's voice——'

'Fanny—you are au courant?'

'Yes, indeed. That idiot rang us up first. I'm simply furious——'

'Old Tartuffe! Did you ever hear anything so shameful!'

'It's a disgrace, Grace. I shall tell Alfred he's not to pay a penny for this half.'

'No, don't let's. The boys have never cost him much at any time— Sigi lived on mercy parcels I had to send from Hédiard. The wretch! Calmly telephoning to say he let the boys leave without even having taken the trouble to find out where they were going! I expect they are all being murdered by a sex maniac in the fog at this very minute, poor little things——'

'Oh well, I expect not——'

'You know what England is, darling. I was wondering if we couldn't porter plainte against the school?'

'What does Charles-Edouard say?'

'He's down in his circonscription for the Armistice—and I suppose Alfred has gone to Compiègne? What ought we to do? So dreadful to think of those children all alone in London.'

'We aren't even sure they've gone to London.'

'Knowing Sigi I think they have. Who will feed them?'

'I've a good mind to go over now and see what they are up to,' I said.

'You can't. There's a fog as usual. Didn't you notice, no English papers? Look at it here, such a heavenly day——'

'In any case it wouldn't be much good for me to wander round London looking for them like Thomas à Becket's mother, without a clue as to where they are. I suppose we must wait and consult with our husbands when they get back. We'll keep in touch, but let's anyhow meet tomorrow and talk it over. I should think we'll know more by then.'

'You're an optimist!' said Grace. 'A demain then, unless there's any news before.'

However, at tea-time she rang up again. 'Almost too irritating,' she said, 'I've just telephoned to my father on the chance he might know something and sure enough he gave them all luncheon at Wilton's. Of course the wicked old man is on their side—he would be. Like all Englishmen he's a schoolboy himself really. What a race! He says they ate everything within sight. They showed him menus of all the meals they've had this half which they kept as pièces justificatives and he says he can't think how they stuck it as long as they did. Naturally no mention of the mercy parcels. Clever of Sigi, that was, the way to my father's heart has always been through his stomach.'

'Little brutes!' I said. I had transferred some of my rage with the housemaster to the boys, as, I noticed, had Grace.

'The maddening thing is,' she went on, 'he admits he gave them money.'

'How much?'

'He pretends he can't remember—a few pounds he says. If I know Papa, he'll have had at least £50 on him and if I know Sigi, he'll have wheedled it all. So now goodness alone knows when we shall hear any more of them. They were still alive at luncheon-time, apart from that the situation is worse than if he hadn't seen them.'

'Didn't you ask where they were staying?'

'Naturally I did. He only said not with him. Trust him not to make himself uncomfortable in any way!'

At this point Katie cut in, saying, 'Do we take a reversed charge call from London?'

'Oh yes,' I said, 'that's always one of the boys. I'll ring you up presently, Grace.'

'Ma?' It was Basil. 'Look, Ma, it's like this. Old Charles and Fabrice and Sigi are here.'

'Basil, you are a faithful boy. I've been so worried!'

'Oh, so you knew they'd left the booby-hatch, did you?'

'Yes, their tutor rang up this morning and of course Sigi's mother and I have been in the most fearful state wondering what had happened to them.'

'I suppose you thought the robins had covered them with leaves! Your capacity for worry beats anything I ever heard of. Anyway, knowing you, I thought I'd better ease your mind. They are quite alive and nobody has interfered with them, not yet.'

'So what are they going to do?'

'Live it up here. They've gone to a pop show now this minute to see their idol, Yanky Fonzy.'

'Have they got much money?'

'There you are, being your old bourgeoise self. Money! Didn't you know it doesn't count in the modern world? Everybody's got the stuff nowadays. As a matter of fact, they seem to be quite specially well fixed for it—they've pooled Charles's savings, Fabrice's camera and what Sigi's old ancestor gave them just now.'

'Where are they living?'

'Me Grandad has set them up in a shack he happened to own.'

'Then quickly give me the address—I've got a pencil. Good. Any telephone number?'

'I'm not allowed to give it. They don't want the O.C.s beefing down the line—specially Sigi doesn't.'

The O.C.s, I knew, meant the old couples, in other words us and the Valhuberts. 'Aren't they afraid the O.C.s may arrive and beef in person?'

'Not really. They reckon Father's too busy—Sigi's mother is pregnant—Sigi's father wouldn't demean himself and if you come over they can cope.'

'Oh indeed! Let me tell you, Baz, I've seldom been so furious.'

'That's not reasonable of you, Ma. I don't see 'ow you could expect them kids to go on wasting the best years of their lives in that ole cackle factory.'

'Anyway, darling, it was awfully good of you to telephone——'

Alfred surprised me by taking the news very badly indeed. I said, 'I don't know why you should mind this more than you did about David and Baz. After all, they are intellectuals, far more brilliant than the little boys, it is dreadfully sad that they should have become so peculiar. But yesterday you said it was only a phase, growing pains. So it is with the others, probably.'

'I mind less about David and Basil precisely because they are cleverer. They have got their degrees. When they see the futility of their present state they can return to more rewarding occupations. Also there is something in their heads. We may feel annoyed with them for not following the path we had hoped they would, but as human beings they are perfectly entitled to decide for themselves what they wish to do. These boys are only in the middle of their lessons—I don't see how the gap in their education is ever to be filled. There is no philosophical basis for their conduct; it comes from sheer irresponsibility. You know what I feel about education.'

I could see that Alfred, whatever he might say, had counted as much as I had on magic Eton to produce two ordinary, worthy, if not specially bookish young men and was disappointed as well as disturbed by this new outbreak of non-conformism.

The Valhuberts came round and the two stricken families held a conference. Charles-Edouard was in a rage, with Grace crowing over him annoyingly, I thought.

'Of course, poor Charles-Edouard is angry with me for being right all along. Such a pity to send the child to Eton, when we could have kept him here and fed him up and had him taught by the Jesuits at Sainte Geneviève.'

'My dear Grace, they would never have taken Sigi at Sainte Geneviève. That's a school for clever boys. Franklin, perhaps—not sure. No. I sent him to Eton for the education, not for the instruction, Sigi has the brain of a bird, as even you must admit. I wanted him to be at least a well-dressed bird with good manners. Besides, I can only stand a limited amount of his company. Now he'll be back on our hands all the year round unless I can persuade them to take him at Les Roches.'

'If he runs away from Eton he would never stay at Les Roches. It will have to be the Jesuits—you must go and see the Superior at Franklin.'

'When you do, will you be so good as to ask him to recommend a tutor for our two?' said Alfred. 'I suppose we shall have to have them here where we can keep an eye on them; they can at least get a proper grounding in French before they cram for Oxford.'

'Have them here?' I said, quite as much dismayed at the prospect as Valhubert was. It seemed to me we had enough on our hands already, what with the holy Zen family, Northey's caravan of followers and Basil's Cheshire-cat appearances and wild-cat schemes.

'What else can we do?' said Alfred. 'That school they call the Borstal Boys' Eton might take them—think of the friends they would pick up there!'

'Gabbitas and Thring?'

Alfred buried his head in his hands.

Grace now said, with perfect truth, that we were looking too far ahead. We must get them away from London and the shack found for them by my stepfather, under our own influence again, before making these elaborate plans. It was decided that we had better wait until it was reasonable to suppose that they would have run out of cash and that then one of us should go over and bring them back.

'But what about your father, Grace? If he goes on supplying them they won't ever run out.'

'I'm thankful to say he has now left London for a round of shoots and he'll be away at least a month.'

It then became evident, just as the little brutes had foreseen, that I should be the one deputed to go after them. The only alternative was Valhubert and he said himself that he was too angry and would be sure to lose his temper at the mere sight of them. The words 'if you do, they can cope' rang a mocking chime in my ears, but I had no choice; I accepted the mission.

So we planned for our sons, hoping to undo the harm they had done themselves. It never occurred to us that they would refuse to co-operate. We were soon to learn our mistake.

We let the rest of November go by; then I sent them a telegram, reply paid, asking them to dine with me at the Ritz the following day. They were kind enough to accept the invitation quite promptly. Alfred said this showed they were starving and should easily be caught, like animals in the snow.

'The gilt will be off the gingerbread by now—they'll have begun to see what it's like to be alone in London with no money. It was far better not to go at once.'

On St. Andrew's Day I arrived at the Ritz. When I had unpacked and had a bath I was still about half an hour too early for our appointment; there was nothing else to do so I went downstairs, sat on one of those little sofas below the alcove, where I have perched at intervals all my life, and ordered a glass of sherry. Never possessing a London house of my own I have always found the Ritz useful when up for the day or a couple of nights; a place where one could meet people, leave parcels, write letters, or run into out of the rain. It now remains one of the few London interiors which have never changed a scrap; the lace antimacassars are still attached to the armchairs with giant hairpins; the fountain tinkles as it has for fifty years; there is the same sound of confident footfall on thick carpet and the same delicious smell of rich women and promising food. As in the Paris Ritz, the management has been clever enough not to touch the decoration designed by M. Meuwes, the excellent architect employed by M. Ritz, though I have been told that the late Lady Colefax once refused a commission to redecorate the ground floor, saying that it would be wrong to alter any of it.

I sipped my sherry and reflected on the enormous length of human life and the curious turns it takes, a train of thought always set off by a place with which I have been familiar at irregular intervals for many years. Some people, I know, feel aggrieved at the shortness of life; I, on the contrary, am amazed at how long it seems to go on. The longer the better. Paris had cured me of my middle-aged blight exactly as I had hoped it would; if I was sometimes worried there I never felt depressed, bored and useless, as at Oxford. I managed the work far better than I had expected to. I had neither kissed the President nor extinguished the Eternal Flame nor indeed, as far as I knew, committed any major gaffe. As I am not shy, and most of the people I met were engaged in responsible, therefore interesting, work I found no difficulty in conversing with them. Philip had provided me with one or two useful gambits. ('I suppose you are very tired, M. le Ministre' would unloose floodgates.)

Alfred was an undoubted success with the French, whatever Mockbar might say. He was more like their idea of an Englishman, slow, serious, rather taciturn, than the brilliant Sir Louis, who had been too much inclined to floor them on their own ground. Such worries as I had all came from the children; Alfred's were more serious. He was obliged to

press the European Army upon the French although personally convinced by now of its unacceptability. The Iles Minquiers, too, were still
giving him a lot of uncongenial work. However, Mr. Gravely seemed
quite satisfied with the way these things were shaping. The Americans
had assured him that the European Army was almost in the bag. He
thought he had himself persuaded M. Bouche-Bontemps to give up the
Minquiers and that it was only, now, a matter of time before they
became British Isles.

Two men coming out of the alcove and passing my sofa roused me
from these thoughts. 'When I got to the factory,' one of them said, 'they
told me that seven of the girls were knocked up—well, pregnant in
fact. It's the new German machine.'

'You don't surprise me at all,' said his friend, 'these new German
machines are the devil.'

I have overheard many a casual remark in my life; none has ever
puzzled me more. As I pondered over it I saw three figures ambling
towards me from the Arlington Street entrance. They were dressed as
Teddy-boys, but there was no mistaking the species. With their slouch-
ing, insouciant gait, dead-fish hands depending from, rather than
forming part of, long loose-jointed arms, slightly open mouths and
appearance of shivering as if their clothes, rather too small in every
dimension, had no warmth in them, they would have been immediately recognizable, however disguised, on the mountains of the
Moon, as Etonians. Here were the chrysalises of the elegant, urbane
Englishmen I so much longed for my sons to be; this was the look
which, since I was familiar with it from early youth, I found so right,
and which I had missed from the tough premature manliness of the
other two boys. Charlie and Fabrice had changed their clothes but not
yet their personalities; what a relief!

CHAPTER XVIII

'WE didn't think we were late?'

'You're not. I was early.'

'Pretty dress, Mum. We've brought you some flowers.'

'Oh, you are nice. Thanks so much—roses!' (But this was rather
sinister. Roses are expensive on St. Andrew's Day; they must still have
got some money.) 'My favourites! Give them to the porter, Charlie, will
you, and ask him to have them put in a vase for me. There—let's go
and dine.'

I thought the boys were feeling quite as much embarrassed as I was
and I counted on food to unbutton us all. They ordered, as I knew they

would, smoked salmon and roast chicken and then politely tried to put me at my ease.

'Did you have a good journey?'

'Was it a Viscount?'

'Have you seen the new Anouilh in Paris?'

'Have you read *Pinfold*?'

I said yes to everything but was too much preoccupied to enlarge on these topics. General conversation was really not possible under the circumstances; I ordered a bottle of wine and bravely plunged. 'Perhaps you'll tell me now what this is all about?'

Charlie and Sigi looked at Fabrice who was evidently the spokesman. 'Are you furious with us?' he said.

'I'm more worried than furious. Your fathers are very angry indeed. But why did you do it?'

'The ghoulishness of the food——' Sigi said, in a high wail.

'It's no good telling me about the food,' I said firmly, 'because I know perfectly well that had nothing to do with it. I'd like the real reason, please.'

'You must try and put yourself in our place,' said Fabrice, 'wasting the best years of our lives (only three more as teenagers—every day so precious, when we ought to be hitting it up as never again), wasting them in that dark creepy one-horse place with Son et Lumière (the head beak) and all the other old weirdies yattering at us morning and night and those ghoulish kids mouldering in the same grave with us. It's a living death, Mum; we've been cheesed off for months. In the end it became more than flesh and blood could stand. Do you blame us?'

I was uncertain how to say what must be said. 'What's that you've got on your jersey, Charles?'

'Yank's the Boy for Me. Do you like it?'

'Only rather. Who is Yank?'

'Who is Yank? Yanky Fonzy of course, the Birmingham-born Bomb. I should have thought even you would have heard of Yank—that lanky Yank from Brum,—the toughest guy that breathes. He's a disc star.'

'And he's the boy for you?'

'Oh definitely. Of course he's a man's man, you might not dig him like we do, lots of girls don't and hardly any oldsters. But we're his fans, the screamin' kids who follow him around the Beat Shows. Boy! does he wow us!'

'Oh,' I said, flummoxed.

'You ought to come and see for yourself,' said Sigi. 'Tout comprendre c'est tout pardonner!'

'Do you think I would understand though?'

'If you saw you would,' said Fabrice. 'Yank, coming right into the attack—treating the kids like a man squeezing an orange. That ole mike is putty in his hands; he rolls on the floor with it—uses it as a gun

—throws it around, spins it, snarls into it. Then, sudden, dramatic, he quiets down into a *religioso*: "I count them over, every one apart, my Rosary." From that it's Schehera-jazz: "Pale hands I loved beside the Shalimar." "Oh Shenandoah, I long to hear you." Ending up with the patriotic stuff: "Shoot if you must this old grey head but spare my country's Flag, she said." Something for everybody, see?'

'Oh Mum, do try and realize how it makes jolly boating weather seem like a rice pudding.'

'Perhaps I do. But all this has no connection with real life, which is very long, very serious and for which, at your age, you ought to be preparing.'

'No. The whole point is that we are too old, now, to be preparing. This is life, it has begun, we want to be living.'

'Dearest, that's for your parents to decide. As we support you we must be allowed to have a say in your activities, I suppose?'

'Ah! But I'm just coming to that. Teenagers are definitely commercial nowadays. It's not like we were back in history—David Copperfield. The modern Copperfield doesn't have to tramp to Dover and find Aunt Betsy—no—he is rich—he earns £9 a week. That's what we are making; not bad for a start?'

'£9 a week?' I was very much taken aback. Starving animals in the snow, indeed! This was going to make my task difficult if not impossible. 'For doing what, may I inquire?'

'Packing.'

'That's nearly £500 a year!'

'Definitely.'

'What do you pack?'

'Shavers—you know, razors.'

'Do you like it?'

'Does anybody like work?'

I snatched at this opening.

'Oh, indeed they do, when it's interesting. That's the whole point of lessons, so that one can finally have work which is more enjoyable than packing.'

'Yes, that's what we've heard. We don't believe it. We think all work is the same and it's during the time off that you live your life. No use wasting these precious years preparing for jobs that may be far worse than packing when we shall be old and anyway not able to feel anything, good or bad. As it is we get two days off and our evenings. In between we are inspired by Yank.'

'But my dear children, you can't go on packing for the rest of your lives. You must think of the future.'

'Why must we? All you oldies thought and thought of the future and slaved and saved for the future, and where did it get you?'

'It got your father to Paris.'

'And what good does that do him? How many days off does he get? How does he spend his evenings? Who is his idol?'

'In any case it's now we want to be enjoying ourselves, not when we are rotting from the feet up at thirty or something ghoulish.'

'Just tell me,' I said, 'were you unhappy at Eton? People hardly ever are, in my experience.'

They looked at each other. 'No—not exactly unhappy. It was this feeling of waste we had.'

'It wasn't the Perthshire Set?' I knew that when they first arrived they had been teased (according to their own statements, discounted by me, positively martyrized) by Scotch boys larger and older than they, one of whom was Sigi's fag-master, who were alleged to have stolen their money and borrowed and broken such treasures as cameras, besides inflicting dire physical torments on them.

'Ay, the gret black monolisks fra' Pitlochry,' said Fabrice, 'a' change heer for Ballachulish.' The others were shaking with laughter at what was evidently an ancient and well-loved joke. 'Nu—now we are na' longer wee bairnies they canna scaith us.'

'You didn't leave because of them?'

'They are still ghoulish (in Pop now) but no, definitely not.'

'And you haven't been beaten this half?'

'Oh definitely. I was beaten for covering a boy with baby-powder and Sigi was for holding a boy's head under the bath-water.'

'Sigi!' There was such horror in my voice that he looked quite startled and quickly said, 'But I didn't hold it for as long as they thought.'

'Mum—nobody minds being beaten, you know.'

'Speak for yourself, Charlie,' said Fabrice, making a face.

'Of course it's rather ghoulish pacing up and down one's room before. But not nearly enough for running away. Our reasons were positive, not negative.'

The others agreed. 'Definitely. It was the feeling that life was passing us by and we weren't getting the best out of it.'

'Packing and rocking and rolling aren't the best, either. They will stop wowing you very soon and then where will you be?'

'By then nothing will matter any more. Our teens will have gone and we shall be old and we shall die. Isn't it sad!'

'Very sad but not quite true. You will get old and die, but after the end of your teens until your deathbeds there will be endless years to fill in somehow. Are you going to spend them all, all those thousands of days, packing shavers? Is it for this that you were created?'

'You see, you haven't understood, just like we were so afraid you wouldn't.'

'Why don't you come back with me to Paris in the morning?'

They looked at each other uncomfortably. 'You see, we think

London is a better town to live in at our age. Paris isn't much good for teenagers.'

'Definitely less commercial.'

'So you won't come?'

'You see, we've signed on for our work.'

It was evidently no good pursuing the subject so we spoke of other things. They asked how Northey was. 'By the way,' I said, 'she's a teenager but she's perfectly happy in Paris; she loves it.'

They said, scornfully but quite affectionately, that she had never acted like a teenager.

'Act is the word,' I said, beginning to lose my temper, 'acting and showing off. If you had to leave Eton why couldn't you have gone at the end of the half instead of having a scene with your tutor and hiring a Rolls Royce to take you, in full view of everybody? So vulgar, I'm ashamed of you. And how I wish you knew how babyish you look in that silly fancy dress.'

'This dinner party is going downhill,' said Fabrice.

'Definitely,' said Sigi.

'Ghoulish,' said Charlie.

'Yes. I think I'm tired after the journey.' I looked at my children and thought how little I knew them. I felt much more familiar with David and Baz. No doubt it was because these boys had always been inseparable. As with dogs, so with children, one on its own is a more intimate pet than two or three. The death of my second baby had made a gap between David and Basil; I had had each of them in the nursery by himself. I suppose I had hardly ever been alone with either of the other two in my life; I was not at all sure what they were really like.

'Don't be tired,' said Fabrice. 'We thought we'd take you to the Finsbury Empire. It's not Yank unfortunately (he's in Liverpool) but quite a good pop show.'

'Darling—no, I can't anyhow. I promised I'd ring up Sigi's mother and tell the news. She's expecting a baby, Sigi.'

If I'd hoped to soften him with this statement I was disappointed. 'I know!' he said furiously. 'It really is too bad of her. What about the unearned income? There'll be nothing for any of us if she goes on like this.'

'Lucky you're so good at packing.' I felt I had scored a point.

As soon as the children had finished their pudding I paid the bill and said goodbye to them. There seemed to be no point in prolonging the interview only to hear, as I was already sick of hearing from David and Baz, what a ghastly (or ghoulish) failure Alfred and I had made of our lives; how we had wasted our youth and to what purpose? It was true that I was tired and, in fact, deeply depressed and upset. I had been unable to touch my dinner; I longed to be alone and lie down in the dark. First, however, I telephoned to Grace. (Alfred I knew was dining out, I would speak to him in the morning.) She was not surprised to hear about the crooner.

'It went on the whole summer at Bellandargues—lanky Yank the Boy from Brum, till I could have killed them. You didn't quite take it in when I told you. It's an absolute mania. But then, Fanny, aren't they getting hard up?'

'I'm coming to that,' I said, just as Fabrice had, 'hold everything, it's far the worst part. They've got a job—they're quite all right for money and I'd just like you to guess what they are earning.'

'Perhaps—I don't know—they couldn't be worth £3 a week?'

'Nine.'

'Pounds a week? Each? But it's perfectly insane! We shall never get them back now.'

'Exactly.'

'But what do they get it for?'

'Packing, Grace. They pack all day, five days a week, in order to have their evenings free for the Birmingham-born Bomb.'

There was a long pause while she digested this fact. Then she said, 'My dear, the person who gives Sigismond £9 a week to pack for him must be out of his mind. I only wish you could see his box when he comes back from school!'

The next day at Orly the lively face of Northey was in the crowd waiting for friends by the entrance. There was something about the mere sight of that child which made my spirits rise, as that of my own boys, alas, no longer did. She had hopped into the Rolls Royce when she saw it leaving the Embassy. 'Anything to down tools for an hour or two,' she said, frankly, adding, 'hot news!'

'Don't, Northey!'

'Good news I mean—Coffirep has had children. Oh dear, I'm so over-excited——!'

'Dearest—is that the badger?'

'Fanny, do sharpen your wits and concentrate on my life. Coffirep is my shares—so I'm rich, my old age will be nice, oh do be pleased!'

'I can't tell you how delighted I am, specially about it not being the badger.'

'As if he could all alone, poor duck. In the spring I'll get him a sweet little wife—I'm sure he's made a breeding chamber down there, we don't want him to feel disappointed. Oh, I was dying to tell somebody. Alfred didn't properly listen (he's in a do about the boys); Philip only said he wished he knew if there really is any marketable oil in the Sahara; the holies don't care about money, or so they say. (I note they always make me pay the cab if we go in one.) And Charles-Edouard is shooting, which he calls hunting, in Champagne. It's very dull having nobody to take an interest—thank goodness you are back.'

Not another word about the boys; she was either being tactful or was too much occupied with her own affairs—the latter I suspected. She babbled on until we got home. When we drove into the courtyard I saw a group of people, who were obviously not followers, waiting by Northey's entrance.

'Mr. Ward,' she explained, 'has very kindly allowed me to put up a notice in W. H. Smith offering my kittens to good homes. It gives me a lot of extra work, taking up references and so on; they have to be rather special people as you may imagine. They must promise not to— you know—castrate; they must live on the ground floor with a garden (I go myself and see), and above all they must not be related to any scientist, chemist or furrier. The kits aren't ready to leave me and Katie yet; this is only for when they are.'

Of course Mockbar duly informed the world that Envoy's Sons had left Eton because the headmaster had threatened to thrash them and were now employed by the London firm of such and such in their packing department. Mockbar hardly annoyed me any more nor even extracted a wry laugh; I was getting used to his style and the ob- servations which punctuated all our doings. His paragraphs no longer made me tremble for Alfred's career. Six million people read them, so one was told, and evidently regarded them as enjoyable fiction. He was too often obliged, by the solicitors of some victim, to withdraw a statement for the public to place much reliance in his word.

A few days later Charles-Edouard left hurriedly for London. To my secret rage and disgust he returned that same evening with Master Sigismond in tow. Grace informed me of this, adding, 'He cracked the whip, darling. Thank God I married a Frenchman. Whatever you may say, they do have some authority in the family!'

'The thing is, Alfred can't go over just now; I don't feel I ought to worry him by suggesting that he should. He's having a difficult time, he's busy.'

'He must be. The English! Words can't express what I feel! They are being quite simply too awful. I'm sure Sir Alfred can't approve. Having that Niam on an official visit! Fanny, it's the limit. He has eaten simply hundreds of Frenchmen and now he's got a loan from Stalin—yes, I know, but they're all Stalin to me, I can't keep learning their new names—so that he can catch and eat hundreds more.'

'Nonsense, Grace. In a profile of Dr. Niam I read somewhere, they said he is a vegetarian and very pro-French at heart.'

'At stomach they mean. Oh good, I've made a joke, I must tell Charles-Edouard. I've been too pregnant, lately.'

'They say he's firmly attached to the Western World and has a great sense of humour.'

'Oh, do shut up. Are the English our allies or are they not?'

How I wished I knew what whip, cracked by his father, had brought
Sigismond to heel. Cracking whips seemed to be something of which
neither Alfred nor I was capable. When our boys refused to listen to
reason we were done for. It was beginning to be borne in on me that as
parents we were a resounding failure. While all three boys had been in
full revolt I could just bear it; now that Sigi had returned to parental
authority, the evil conduct of our two was stressed. Surely we, too,
ought to be able to find some way of mastering them?

'Hot news!' said Northey. 'Guess why Sigi is here?'

'I thought M. de Valhubert went over and cracked a whip?'

'Yes, well, if you really want to know, he went over because Sigi was
in bad with the police. He was caught nicking shavers.'

'Doing what, dearest?'

'They were packing shavers—you knew that, didn't you? And were
getting £9 a week, which, incidentally, makes skilled secretarial work
in embassies seem rather underpaid but let that pass. Clever Sigi discovered that if you nick a few every day (no, Fanny, *don't* keep asking
what things mean, sharpen your wits and listen) you can bump up the
screw to quite a pound a day more. But as he's not used to stealing, so
far, he was caught and there was a fearful rumpus. Charles-Edouard
had to go and buy him off or he'd have gone to a remand home or
something. Can you beat it!'

I felt a glow of superiority. 'Poor Grace,' I said, 'how dreadful.'

'By the way, the old foreign lady is not to be told.'

'Ah! Quite right—of course she mustn't be. So is Charles-Edouard
furious?'

'Not a bit. He thinks it's most frightfully funny and he's delighted to
have Sigi delivered into his hands. Now he'll be obliged to go to the
strict Jesuits after all!'

'I shouldn't think even the strictest Jesuits will do that boy much
good—he'll come to a bad end all right.'

Northey bashed me out of my complacency with: 'Charlie and
Fabrice have got the knack of it now.'

'The knack of nicking?'

'Yes. Sigi says he invented a foolproof method on the way over and
rang them up to tell, very kindly. They'll get lovely and rich, he says,
in no time.'

CHAPTER XIX

HOLY David had been looking decidedly better since Docteur Lecœur took him in hand, even slightly cleaner. His interest in secular or non-Zen affairs seemed to be reviving; he came with me to the Louvre one day and saw one or two plays with Dawn. I had become devoted to her, which shows that speech is not an essential factor in human understanding. (Northey said who ever thought it was? Think of creatures and how well we get on with them in silence.) I was very hopeful that if the improvement in David continued at this rate he would go back to his university and resume his career.

Then he told me, casually, one day, that he and Dawn were about to resume their journey to the East. I was sorry, indeed, that it should be East rather than West but to tell the truth I felt such a surge of relief that at first I hardly cared which direction they were taking. David's presence in the house was not convenient. The servants and the whole of Alfred's staff disliked him. English statesmen and important officials who came and went in a fairly steady stream cannot have relished the sight of his gowned form and naked feet at breakfast. He was on his father's nerves. Whenever Mockbar was short of a story he fell back on Envoy's Son for some spiteful little paragraph. How heavenly to think that the Zen family was on the move at last! Concealing joy, I said, 'You'll tell me when you would like Jérôme to take you to the station?'

'Not the station, the road. Send us to Provins; after that we will fend for ourselves.'

'With Dawn in her present condition? Oh no, David, that's not possible.'

'Pregnant women have astonishing powers of survival. That has been proved in every great exodus of history. All the same, I think I will leave little 'Chang here.'

The surge of relief subsided, the joy was extinguished. I might have guessed there would be a snag somewhere. 'No, you can't,' I said, putting up what I really knew would be a perfectly ineffectual resistance. 'Who's going to look after him?'

'Mrs. Trott and Katie simply love him.'

'We all simply love him; that's not the point. Neither Mrs. Trott nor anybody else here has time to nurse little 'Chang. He's your responsibility; you adopted him; nobody asked you to! Why did you, anyway?'

'We wanted a brother for our baby so that they can be brought up together. It was very bad for my young psychology to be three years older than Basil; Dawn and I don't intend to repeat that mistake of yours.'

'But if he's here and your baby is in the East?'

'As soon as our baby is born it must join little 'Chang. I shall send it to you at once so that they can unfold their consciousness together.'

'So I've got to bring up your family?'

'It will be a boon to you. Middle-aged women with nothing to do are one of the worst problems that face the modern psychologist.'

'But I've got far, far more to do than I can manage already.'

'Cocktail parties—trying on clothes—nothing to get your teeth into. You must try not to be so selfish. Think of poor Dawn, you really can't ask her to carry half the cradle like she used to. 'Chang has put on pounds and pounds and she doesn't feel very well.'

'Leave her here. I'd love to keep her. Then she can have her baby under proper conditions, comfortably, poor duck.'

'I didn't marry Dawn in order to leave her. I need her company all the time.'

She now appeared with the World Citizen, making furious Chinese noises, in her arms. I thought she looked very frail.

'Dawnie, David has just told me he is on the move again. Why don't you stay comfortably here with little 'Chang and all of us, at any rate until after the baby?'

I had forgotten about the dumbness; her huge eyes projected their gaze on her husband's face and he spoke for her. 'You see she has no desire whatever to stay comfortably here. Dawn has never had such a bourgeois reaction in her life.'

I went to my bedroom and rang up Davey. I begged him to come and save the situation. He was unco-operative and unsympathetic; said that it was impossible for him to move for the present. 'My drawing-room curtains have gone wrong—much too short and skimpy. They must all be made again and I must be here to see to it. That's the sort of thing your Aunt Emily used to do—everything in the house was perfect when she was alive. I do hate being a widower; it really was too bad of her to die.'

'Davey, you haven't understood how serious it is about David.'

'My dear Fanny, I think you are being rather ungrateful to me. You asked me to get rid of him; he is going, is he not?'

'I know—but——'

'If he is going East and not West that is entirely your own fault for not insisting on Dr. Jore. I told you that a psychiatrist was needed in conjunction with a physician. Docteur Lecœur strengthened his will-power by working on his glands and correcting his inertia. Dr. Jore would have altered the trend of his thought. By rejecting Jore you abandoned him to the Zen Master—the Temple Bells are calling and the flying-fishes play. Another time perhaps you will allow me to know best.'

'I wouldn't mind so much if it weren't for Dawnie. I think he'll kill her, poor little thing.'

'Oh no he won't. Women are practically indestructible, you know.'

'Then think of Alfred and me beginning nurseries all over again. Chinese ones at that.'

'Very tiring for you,' said Davey. 'I must go now or I shall miss the Archers.' He rang off.

David and Dawn left that afternoon. The Rolls Royce took them to Bar-le-Duc and only returned the next day. David had borrowed money from every single person in the Embassy; all, pitying the plight of Dawn and probably confident of being paid back by me (as of course they were), had produced as much as they had available. It amounted to quite a tidy sum. Mrs. Trott found a solid peasant girl from Brittany to look after 'Chang.

'Hot news!' Northey said to Alfred. 'Faithful Amy has had orders from Lord Grumpy to give you treatment number one.'

'Oh, indeed?' Falsetto. 'And how does this differ from that which I have been receiving?'

'Differ? So far you have only had number three, watered down at that by precious Amy on account of loving us all so much.'

'He loves me?'

'Oh yes—he's always saying I like that man. He reveres you. It's very distressing for him to be obliged to write all these horrid and not quite true things about us here when he would give his eyes to be part of the family.'

'Part of the family? In what capacity, may I ask?'

'Perhaps you could adopt him?'

'Thank you. We've got 'Chang and the badger, I don't think we want any more pets.'

'Poor soul.'

FAILURE

It is no secret that Sir Alfred Wincham has proved a failure in Paris and that Whitehall now wishes to replace him with a more dynamic personality. Sir Alfred's well-known aptitude for university intrigue has not carried him very far along the twisting paths of French foreign policy. More professional talent, it is felt, is needed at a time when Anglo-French relations have never been worse.

FRIENDSHIP

In view of M. Bouche-Bontemps' old friendship with Lady Wincham's mother (first revealed in this column) French political circles feel that the Embassy has an unfortunate preference for his party, the L.U.N.A.I.R. Members of opposition parties are never received there any more. Sir Alfred is out of touch with French public opinion.

RANGOON

Well-informed circles are speculating on Sir Alfred's future and rumour has it that he may shortly be posted to Rangoon.

Northey and Philip raced each other to my bedroom the morning these delightful paragraphs appeared. She dumped 'Chang on my bed. I always had him for a bit after breakfast and found him delightful company; a contented, healthy baby, easily amused and anxious to please. I thought, when I was with him, that his generation may be on the way to rejecting the anticharm which is the fashion now, may even develop a sense of humour and seek to attract rather than repel. If my grandchild turned out to be half as nice as the World Citizen I would not be at all sorry to have the two of them for keeps.

'At last Mockbar has overreached himself,' Philip said. 'I think it's actionable; Alfred must speak to his lawyer and we might even get rid of him, who knows?'

'Then the poor little soul will starve,' said Northey.

'No matter.'

'Fanny, you brute. What about his babies?'

'They'll survive,' I said. 'Are Anglo-French relations really so bad, Philip?'

'That part I'm afraid is true. Not Alfred's fault (quite the contrary) but boiling up for a first-class crisis. We are determined to get those bloody islands and to help the Americans rearm the Germans.'

'Seems mad, doesn't it?'

'Not if we really need them as allies.'

Northey said, 'I wish I knew why people want the Germans on their side. I have yet to hear of them winning a war.'

'They'd be all right with French generals.'

'I wish the whole thing could be settled. The Bourse is strongly disconcerted by all these elements.'

'You can't wish it more than I do,' said Philip.

'I must dree my weird. Shall I leave 'Chang? I've got a lot of work.'

'Yes, leave him. Your work has been very satisfactory of late; you're a good girl and I'm pleased with you.'

'It's the well-known cure for a broken heart,' she said with a tragic look at Philip.

'Go on,' he said, 'I like it.'

I asked her, 'Darling, what are you up to tonight?'

'Docteur Lecœur.'

'Lecœur soupire la nuit le jour, qui peut me dire si c'est l'amour?' said Philip.

'Yes, it is.'

'And I suppose,' he went on, 'that every time you pass the Palais Bourbon, the statues of Sully and l'Hôpital get up and bow to you?'

'Yes, they do. It's the English who don't appreciate me. Good-bye, all.'

We looked at each other when she had gone, laughing. 'Northey!'

He said, 'The diplomatic hostesses here are furious with Mees because she has got Tony de Lambesc in tow—yes, Fanny—that small, fair chap one sees everywhere. They regard him and me as the only sortable bachelors in this town—we have to do all their dinner parties. There are hundreds of unattached Frenchmen who would like to be asked but you know what those women are, too timid to try anybody new. They might have to deal with unexpected dialogue and that would never do. The conversation must run on familiar lines, according to some well-worn old formula. Suppose somebody mentions Prince Pierre—of course the correct move is, he simply worships his daughter-in-law! Now a stranger might say do you mean the explorer? or worse still, Prince Pierre in *War and Peace*? and the whole party would feel a wrong turn had been taken—they might even have to begin using their brains. That would never do. They like a gentle game of pat-ball and have no desire for clever young polytechnicians hitting boundaries. Lambesc and I know the right answers in our sleep. But now he's always either taking Mees out or hoping to. He waits till the last moment, praying she'll be chucked; it's no use asking him a week ahead. The only hope is to ring him up at half past eight and get him to come round, disgruntled, there and then. It has upset social life dreadfully. Time Mees got married, that's what it is.'

'Yes, but to whom?'

'Who is there? Bouche-Bontemps is a bit old— that Chef de Cabinet (always forget his name) is too ugly—Cruas is said to be poor——'

'Would that matter?'

'With Mees? She would ruin a poor man in no time.'

'Does Cruas exist? I've still never seen him, have you?'

'Somebody has taught her French; she rattles away at a hundred miles an hour. Then Lecœur is too busy—Charles-Edouard too much married (worse luck)—the Ambassador to the Channel Islands has a fort des halles he adores—Amyas now, what about him? An eligible widower——'

'I'm against,' I said, 'though I may be prejudiced.'

'Then there's Lambesc, but he has his scutcheon to gild.'

I said boldly, 'Why don't you marry her?'

'Well, you know, I might. In spite of the carry-on, I can't imagine life without Mees, now I'm used to her. I suppose she is the last of the charmers. The horsetail girls don't seem to be interested in any of the things I like, least of all sex. They join up with the Teds and the Beats and wander about Europe with them, sharing beds if it happens to suit; three in a bed if it's cheaper like that (shades of Sir Charles Dilke) and probably nothing happens! Sex is quite accidental. Is there a baby on the way or isn't there? They hardly seem to notice. Now Northey is a wicked little thing but at least she is out to please and my word how she succeeds!'

'She's not wicked at all. I even think she is virtuous.'

'Anyway, she's a human being. Very likely I shall end by proposing to her.'

'Only, Philip, don't leave it too long or she'll fall in love with somebody else, you know!'

CHAPTER XX

SIR HARALD HARDRADA now came to give his lecture. It was very brilliant and a great success, Sir Harald being one of the few living Englishmen who, even the French allow, has a perfect mastery of their language. As they detest hearing it massacred and really do not like listening to any other, foreign lecturers are more often flattered than praised at the end of their performance (not that they know the difference). We all went to the Sorbonne where the lecture took place and then Mildred Jungfleisch gave a dinner party. The company was: Sir Harald, M. Bouche-Bontemps, the Valhuberts, the Hector Dexters, an American couple called Jorgmann, Philip and Northey, Alfred and me. The Dexters had been given a clean bill by the State Department, to the enormous relief of their compatriots in Paris. Having had enough, it seemed, of political activities, Mr. Dexter was now acting as liaison between leading French and American art dealers.

Mrs. Jungfleisch lived in a cheery modernish (1920) house near the Bois de Boulogne. Its drawing-room, painted shiny white and without ornament of any sort, had an unnaturally high ceiling and stairs leading to a gallery; the effect was that of a swimming-bath. One felt that somebody might dive in at any moment, the Prime Minister of England, perhaps, or some smiling young candidate for the American throne. Almost the only piece of furniture was an enormous pouf in the middle of the room on which people had to sit with their backs to each other. As Americans do, she left a good hour between the arrival of the guests and the announcement of dinner, during which time Bourbon (a kind of whisky) could be imbibed.

Bouche-Bontemps had come to the lecture. He and Sir Harald were old friends. They now sat on the pouf, craning round to talk to each other.

'Excellent, my dear Harald! Nothing could have been more fiendishly clever than your account of Fashoda—you haven't got the K.C.V.O. for nothing! I very much liked the meeting between Kitchener and Marchand on the Argonne front—some time you must read the page from Kipling where he describes the naif joy of the French poilus as they witnessed it. They thought the hatchet had been buried for ever and that if we won that war, les Anglais would become real friends and leave us our few remaining possessions. Never mind——'

'Like all the French,' Sir Harald said urbanely, to the company at large, who were twisting their necks to be in on this conversation, 'M. le Président has the work of our great Imperial protagonist by heart.'

'We defend ourselves as best we can,' said Bouche-Bontemps, 'poor Marchand, I knew him well.'

'Were you already living at Fashoda with the Bolter when he arrived?'

'No. Precocious as I may have been, at six months old I was still living with my parents.'

'You can't imagine how fascinated we all were to learn that the famous Frenchman in her life was none other than yourself. I had always pictured an old douanier with a beard and a wooden leg.'

'Not at all. A jolly young ethnographer. Dorothée—tellement gentille——'

'I'd no idea you had this African past, Jules. Whatever were you doing there?'

'In those days I was passionately fond of ethnography. I managed to get on to the Djibouti–Dakar mission.'

'Oh! You rogue! Everything is becoming as clear as daylight. So it was you who took away the Harar frescoes?'

'Took away? We exchanged them.'

'Yes. Kindly tell Mrs. Jungfleisch here and her guests what it was you exchanged them for?'

'A good exchange is no robbery, I believe? Harar acquired some delightful wall-paintings in the early manner of your humble servant and the gifted mother of your ambassadress. Oh! How we were happy and busy, painting those enormous frescoes—perhaps the happiest days of my life. Everybody was so pleased—the Fuzzie-wuzzies greatly preferred our bright and lively work to the musty old things we took away with us.'

'We don't say Fuzzie-wuzzies,' said Sir Harald.

'Indeed?'

'No. Like your foreign policy, all this is old-fashioned.'

'Hélas! I am old-fashioned, and old as well. C'est la vie, n'est-ce pas, Mees?'

'When are you going to fall again?' said Northey. '(Golly, my neck is aching!) We never see you, it's a bore.'

'With the assistance of the present company it should be any day. What are you preparing for us, Harald?'

Sir Harald became rather pink and looked guilty.

Hector Dexter, who had pricked up his ears at the word frescoes, said, 'And where are the Harar paintings now, M. le Président?'

'Safe in the cellars of the Louvre, thanks to me, where no human eye will ever behold them.'

'I have a client in the States who is interested in African art of unimpeachable provenance. Are there no more ancient frescoes at Harar or in its environs?'

'No,' said Sir Harald, 'the frogs swiped the lot.'

'We don't say frogs any more,' said Bouche-Bontemps, 'it's old-fashioned, like taking away other people's islands.'

There was a little silence. Ice clicked in the glasses, people swallowed, Mrs. Jungfleisch handed round caviar. Sir Harald turned from Bouche-Bontemps to the opposite side of the pouf and said, 'Now, Geck, we want to hear all about Russia.'

Hector Dexter cleared his throat and intoned: 'My day-to-day experiences in the Union of Soviet Socialist Russia have been registered on a long-playing gramophone record to be issued free to all the members of the North Atlantic Treaty. This you will be able to obtain by indenting for a copy to your own ambassador to Nato. I was there, as you may know, for between nine and eight years, but after the very first week I came to the conclusion that the way of life of the Socialist Soviet citizen is not and never could be acceptable to one who has had cognizance of the American way of life. Then it took me between nine and eight years to find some way of leaving the country by which I could safely bring Carolyn here and young Foster with me. It became all the more important for me to get out because my son Foster, aged now fifteen, is only ten points below genius and this genius would have been unavailing and supervacaneous, in other words wasted, behind the iron curtain.'

'Why? There can't be so many geniuses there?'

'There is this out-of-date, non-forward-looking view of life. They have not realized the vast potentialities, the enormous untapped wealth of the world of Art. They have this fixation on literature; they do not seem to realize that the written word has had its day—books are a completely outworn concept. We in America, one step ahead of you in Western Europe, have given up buying them altogether. You would never see a woman, or a man, reading a book in the New York subway. Now in the Moscow subway every person is doing so.'

'That's bad, Heck,' said Mr. Jorgmann, heavily.

'Why is it bad?' I asked.

'Because books do not carry advertisements. The public of a great modern industrial state ought to be reading magazines or watching television. The Russians are not contemporary; they are not realist; they exude a fusty aroma of the past.'

'So young Foster is going into Art?'

'Yes, Sir. By the time my boy is twenty-one, I intend he shall recognize with unerring certainty the attribution of any paint on any canvas (or wood or plaster), the marks of every known make of porcelain and every known maker of silver, the factory from which every carpet and every tapestry——'

'In short,' said Sir Harald, 'he'll be able to tell the difference between Rouault and Ford Madox Brown.'

'Not only that. I wish him to learn the art trade from the beginning to the end; he must learn to clean and crate and pack the object as well as to discover it and purchase it and resell it. From flea-market to Jayne Wrightsman's boudoir, if I may so express myself.'

'I should have thought that sort of talent could have been used in the Winter Palace?'

'There is too much prejudice against the West. The Russians do not possess correct attitudes. It was an unpleasant experience to discuss with individuals whose thinking is so lacking in objectivity that one was aware it was emotively determined and could be changed only by change of attitude. Besides, hypotheses, theories, ideas, generalizations, awareness of the existence of unanswered and/or unanswerable queries do not form part of their equipment. So such mental relationships as Carolyn here and I and young Foster Dexter were able to entertain with the citizens of Soviet Socialist Russia were very, very highly unsatisfactory.'

'But, Geck,' said naughty Sir Harald (I remembered that the Russian alphabet has no H), 'one doesn't want to say I told you so—not that I did, only any of us could have if you'd asked our advice—why on earth did you go?'

'When I first got back here some four or three weeks since, I could have found that question difficult, if not impossible, to answer. However, as soon as I arrived here in Paris I put myself in the hands of a brilliant young doctor, recommended to me by Mildred: Dr. Jore. I go to him every evening when he has finished with the Supreme Commander. Now Dr. Jore very, very swiftly diagnosed my disorder. It seems that at the time when I left this country some nine or eight years ago I was suffering from a Pull to the East which, in my case, was so overwhelmingly powerful that no human person could have resisted it. As soon as Dr. Jore sent his report to the State Department they entirely exonerated me from any suspicion of anti-American procedure, deviation from rectitude, improbity, trimming or what have you and recognized that I was, at the time when I turned my back on the West, a very, very sick man.'

'Poor old Heck,' said the Jorgmanns.

'Another Bourbon?' said Mrs. Jungfleisch.

'Thank you. On the rocks.'

Sir Harald asked, 'And how does he set about curing a Pull to the East?'

'In my case, of course, I have already undergone the most efficacious cure, which is a long sojourn there. But we must prevent any recurrence of the disease. Well, the doc's treatment is this. I lie on his couch and I shut my eyes and I force myself to see New York Harbour, the Empire State building, Wall Street, Fifth Avenue and Bonwit Teller. Then very, very slowly I swivel my mental gaze until it alights on the Statue of Liberty. All this time Dr. Jore and I, very, very softly, in unison, recite the Gettysburg Address. "Four score and seven years ago our fathers——"'

'Yes, yes,' said Sir Harald, almost rudely, I thought, breaking in on Mr. Dexter's fervent interpretation. 'Very fine, but we all know it. It's in the *Oxford Book of Quotations*.'

Mr. Dexter looked hurt; there was a little silence. Philip said, 'Did you see anything of Guy and Donald?'

'When Guy Burgess and Donald Maclean first arrived we all shared a dacha. I cannot say it was a very happy association. They did not behave as courteously to me as they ought to have. The looked-for Anglo-Saxon solidarity was not in evidence. They hardly listened to the analysis of the situation, as noted and recounted by me, in Socialist Soviet Russia; they laughed where no laughter was called for; they even seemed to shun my company. Now I am not very conversant with the circumstances of their departure from the Western camp, but I am inclined to think it was motivated by pure treachery. I am not overfond of traitors.'

'And how did you get away?'

'In the end very easily. After nine or eight years in the U.S.S.R., the Presidium having acquired a perfect confidence in my integrity, I was able to induce them to send me on a fact-finding mission. On arrival here, as I explained to them, the accompaniment of wife and son lending a permanent appearance to my reintegration in the Western Camp, I would easily persuade my compatriots that I had abandoned all tendency to communism. When their trust in me was completely re-established, I would be in a position to send back a great deal of information, of the kind I knew they wanted, to the Kremlin.'

'Nom de nom!' said Valhubert.

Bouche-Bontemps shook with laughter: 'C'est excellent!'

Alfred and Philip exchanged looks.

The Jorgmanns exclaimed, 'That was smart of you, Heck!' Mrs. Jungfleisch said, 'And now let's go and dine.'

We all stood up and, like so many geese, stretched our necks. That hour on the pouf had been absolute agony.

The day after Sir Harald's lecture, Alfred had to communicate a very stiff note indeed to the Quai d'Orsay on the subject of the Iles Minquiers. The French were invited immediately to abandon their claim to these islands which, said the Note, was quite untenable, against their own interests, and was undermining the Western Alliance. Simultaneously an anti-French campaign of unprecedented violence was launched in London. Bludgeon and pin were brought into play. Dr. Niam duly paid his official visit which was reported in a manner calculated to infuriate the French. Bouche-Bontemps was rudely taken to task in Parliament and the newspapers for the criminal obstinacy with which he was refusing to make a united Europe. At U.N.O. the English voted against the French on an important issue. After these bludgeonings came the pinpricks. The newspapers said that Spanish champagne was better than the real sort. Tourists were advised to go to Germany or Greece and to miss out expensive France. Women were urged to buy their clothes in Dublin or Rome. Several leading critics discovered that Françoise Sagan had less talent than one had thought.

When some softening up on these lines had been delivered the campaign settled down to its real objective, the Iles Minquiers. Facts and figures were trotted out, heads were shaken over them and judgement severely passed. It transpired, that after a thousand years of French administration, the islands had no roads, no post-office, no public services. They sent no representative to Paris; there was no insurance against old age; the children were not given vitamins or immunized against diphtheria; there was no cultural life. The fact that there were no inhabitants either was, of course, never stated. The kind-hearted English public was distressed by all these disclosures. As a gesture of solidarity with the islands, an expedition was organized to go and build a health centre on the Ile Maîtresse (Grandad cashed in on this). The Ambulating Raiments were immediately dispatched there. These baleful bales are full of ghastly old clothes collected at the time of the Dutch floods. Since then they have been round the world over and over again, bringing comfort to the tornadoed, the scorched, the shaken, the stateless, the volcanoed, the interned, the famished, the parched, the tidal-waved; any communities suffering from extreme bad luck or bad management are eligible for the Raiments, which are so excellently organized that they arrive on the scene almost before the disaster has occurred. There is a tacit understanding that they are never to be undone, indeed nobody, however great their want, would dare to risk the vermin and disease which must fly out from them as from Pandora's Box. The recipients take their presence as a sort of lucky sign or sympathetic visiting card. (It is only fair to say that in cases of great distress the Raiments are often followed up by a gift of money.) There was just time to have the bundles photographed, at low tide, on the rocks of the Ile Maîtresse before they had to be dispatched to Oakland, California, where a gigantic fire had wiped out acres of skyscrapers.

The French sharply resented all these insults. Their press and wireless, which are at least as clever as ours when it comes to throwing vitriol, now revealed terrifying depths of hatred for their old crony over the way. M. Bouche-Bontemps' government, given up for lost, came unscathed through a debate on vegetables out of season which in normal times would have annihilated it. None of the opposition parties wanted to take over in the middle of such a crisis. When the full perfidy of Albion had been exposed for a few days, French opinion was stirred, flickered, then blazed into fury. Individual citizens began to give expression to the public feeling. The shop called Old England was re-christened New England. The windows of W. H. Smith were smashed. English decorations and medals, signed photographs of King Edward VII and Northey's kittens were deposited at the Embassy accompanied by disagreeable messages. Anglo-French sporting events were called off. Import licences for Christmas puddings were withheld. Grace was beside herself, of course. She announced that she was going to empty the English blood from her veins and have them refilled from the blood bank of the VIIIth arrondissement.

Alfred sent an alarmed report to the Foreign Office but was told that these waves of ill feeling come and go and are not to be taken seriously. Philip, however, said that he had never seen the two old ladies so cross with each other.

CHAPTER XXI

At no season does Paris look more beautiful than early in December. There is a curious light, particular to the Ile de France and faithfully interpreted by the painter Michel, which brings out all shades, from primrose to navy blue, implicit in the beige and grey of the landscape and buildings. The river becomes a steely flood which matches the huge clouds rolling overhead. As this is not, like harvest time or the first warm days of spring, one of those seasons that induce an almost animal craving for field and forest, you can sit by the fire, look out of the window and peacefully enjoy the prospect. I was doing exactly this in the Salon Vert one afternoon, reflecting with satisfaction that for the rest of that week we had no social engagements (they had fallen off notably of late). I had been writing to Aunt Sadie, to give her news of us all, specially of her granddaughter Northey, my pen was poised while I searched for some little titbit to end up with.

I became conscious of a clamour outside, an unidentified noise which had perhaps been going on for some time, heard by my ears but not realized by my brain. I went over to the window, looked down at the garden and was very much startled by what I saw there. A large crowd was stamping about on the lawn, pushed forward by an ever-increasing multitude milling in from the Avenue Gabriel; between it and the house, like idle maids flicking dusters, a few policemen were half-heartedly manipulating their capes. For the moment they were holding the crowd in check; one felt that a really determined push would easily submerge them. When the fishwives surged into Versailles, the Queen's first instinct was to find her husband; so, now, was mine. Like Louis XVI on the same occasion, Alfred was frantically looking for me. We wasted several minutes missing each other in the huge house; I ran through to the Chancery—he had left it; he found the Salon Vert empty; finally we met in Northey's office off the ante-room at the top of the stairs.

'Go to the nursery, darling,' I was telling her, 'and fetch 'Chang. There's a riot or something in the garden. We'd better all stay together.'

Alfred said, 'The French have had enough and I don't altogether blame them. I wrote in my last dispatch that it would end like this; now it has. Not a bad thing perhaps, it will shake both the governments into seeing sense. Meanwhile I hope these hooligans will bear in mind that the person of an Ambassador is sacred and the territory of an Embassy inviolable.'

'They haven't remembered about the territory. They are completely ruining all our nice new shrubs—just come and see.'

We went back to the Salon Vert and looked out at the rioters.

'I shall lodge a complaint. The police force is inadequate, in my view. What are they shouting? It sounds like a slogan.'

'Listen—no, I can't make it out.' They seemed to be shouting two words and stamping in unison.

Philip ran in, breathless, having come from his own flat. 'The Faubourg is full of demonstrators,' he said. 'Good Lord—the garden too! We are completely surrounded in other words. They are shouting "Minquiers Français", do you hear?'

'That's it, of course,' said Alfred. 'Minquiers Français, Minquiers Français. I only hope this will show the Foreign Office there are limits of ineptitude beyond which they should not go. Another time perhaps they will listen to the man on the spot.'

I said, 'They are nearly up to the veranda now—ought you not to let Bouche-Bontemps know?'

'All in good time,' said Alfred, 'no need to panic. We are his responsibility.'

Northey appeared, 'Chang in her arms, grumbling about her badger.

'Pity we can't all be safely down there with him,' I said.

'I've just had a word with B.B.,' said Northey, 'he is the absolute, utter limit. Shrieking with laughter if you please. He says we may have to stand a long siege and he hopes we've got plenty of Spanish champagne. He can't get the police to do much, he says, it's only a crowd of children.'

'Yes, they do look young—I was thinking that. Why should these boys and girls mind about the Iles Minquiers?'

'Agitators. You can work up a crowd on any subject.'

'B.B. is delighted. He says the teenagers here are supposed to think of nothing but jazz—look at them now! Riddled with patriotism.'

'So he's not going to rescue us?'

'Not he!'

'Then who will? What about Nato?'

'We only know one thing for certain about Nato—it can't get a force into the field in less than six weeks.'

'Anyhow,' said Philip, 'this is the Supreme Commander's time for Dr. Jore—nobody's allowed to interrupt them, they'll be in full flood of Gettysburg at this very minute—can't you hear it? "Foor-scoor and savan eers ago oor faethers brourt fourth——" '

'Don't tell me the Supreme Commander has a Pull to the East?'

'Of course. All Dr. Jore's patients have.'

Alfred said, 'You must try and check this latent anti-Americanism, Philip—I've already spoken to you about it.'

'Yes, Sir.'

'Now I'm going to the Chancery to do some telephoning. You take Northey and Fanny to your flat, will you? The rioters can come through the veranda any minute, those feeble policemen aren't going to stop them.'

'Minquiers Français—Minquiers Français——' rose ever more insistent from the garden.

'I do wish they would leave off stamping, they are ruining the lawn.'

'The French government will be obliged to make good any damage.'

'Come on,' said Philip. 'Alfred's quite right, you'll be better over there. Besides, I want to see what's happening in the Faubourg.'

We crossed the courtyard, went into Philip's flat and looked out of his dining-room window at the street which was jammed as far as the eye could see with young people stamping and shouting 'Minquiers Français'. I was glad to notice quite a large force of policemen looking, I thought, very much amused, but keeping the crowd away from our gate and exhibiting more authority than those in the garden.

'Oh do look!' said Northey. 'There's good little Amy—the brave soul.'

'I don't see him?'

'Yes, in the ancient bibelot shop, pretending to be a Dresden figure.' She leant out of the window and waved at Mockbar who looked

sheepish and seemed not to see her. Then she shouted 'Aimee!' whereupon he began scribbling in his notebook.

'He's ashamed of you,' said Philip. 'Anyway I'm glad to see he's on
the job all right. For once we need all the publicity we can get; it's the
only way to stop this silly bickering—give Bouche-Bontemps and our
Foreign Minister a bit of a jolt. They don't want actual war, one
supposes.'

'Can't see that it's B.B.'s fault.'

'He'd much better let the thing go to The Hague and be settled once
for all.'

Suddenly the shouting and stamping and clapping subsided and a
rather sinister silence fell on the crowd. Philip said, anxiously, 'Don't
like this much, I hope they're not waiting for a signal.'

Almost as he spoke, the crowd came violently, terrifyingly to life. It
surged in the narrow street as if it must burst apart the houses; the
slogan took on a blood-curdling note. 'Chang began to scream at the
top of his voice; the din was deafening. The police now joined hands
and forced the rioters away from the entrance to our courtyard; to my
horror I saw that the huge wooden gates were slowly opening.

'Look,' said Northey, 'the gates—a traitor——!'

'Good Lord,' said Philip and made as though to go downstairs.

'Don't leave us——' I was frightened for the baby who might so
easily be hurt if the mob poured in and overwhelmed us. I looked out
again. The police seemed to be in control. In the middle of the screaming crowd a London taxi, escorted by policemen, was crawling up the
street. It was driven by Payne; Uncle Matthew, deeply interested,
craned from the window; on its roof, dressed from head to foot in shiny
black plastic material, were our boys, Fabrice and Charlie, with
another boy, a stranger to me, dressed in shiny white. This child was
waving a guitar at the crowd as though he thought the screams and
shrieks were meant for him. The more the people cried Minquiers
Français the more he grinned and waved in acknowledgement. With a
superhuman effort, the police cleared a passage for the taxi, got it into
the courtyard and shut the gates behind it. We all ran downstairs.

Uncle Matthew was being helped out of the cab by Charlie and
Fabrice. The other boy was fidgeting about, snapping his fingers. He
looked cross and impatient.

'Excitable lot, these foreigners,' said my uncle, 'how are you, Fanny?
Here are your spawn, safe and sound thanks to Payne. We found them
in the aeroplane or at least they found me, I didn't know them from
Adam of course. They recognized me and hopped into the cab. Do you
know, we flew it over—now your stepfather thought of that, very
competent fellow.'

'This is Yanky Fonzy, Mum,' said Fabrice, indicating the third lad.
He was an unprepossessing hobbledehoy, with pasty face, sloppy look

about the mouth and hair done like Queen Alexandra's after the typhoid. 'Didn't the kids give him a wonderful reception—you heard them screaming, "Yanky Fonzy, Yanky Fonzy"? It's never been like this in London.'

'D'you mean that terrifying riot was all about him?' I said.

'It only was a riot of enthusiasm,' said the youth. 'The kids are never nasty or out for manslaughter. They buy my discs and support me. Why are they shut away from here? Where can I go and wave to them? Why are the arrangements breaking down? Where's my French agent?' He fired these questions at each of us in turn, snapping his fingers. He seemed in a thoroughly bad humour.

This curious new light having been thrown on the situation, Philip burst into a loud laugh and went into the house, no doubt, I supposed, to find Alfred.

'He's not much to look at,' said Uncle Matthew, indicating Mr. Fonzy, 'and his clothes would frighten the birds, but I'm bound to tell you he whacks merry hell out of that guitar. We had tunes the whole way here.'

I took Charles by the arm and led him out of earshot of the others. 'Just tell me what this means? Your packing job—have you left it?'

'Definitely. Chucked it.'

'Tell me truthfully, Charlie, you haven't been nicking shavers?'

'Oh no, Mum, hardly at all. But even you wouldn't want us to go on packing for the rest of our lives? It turned out to be rather ghoulish and there's no future in it whatever. No, we've moved on. We're in the Showbiz now where there are fortunes to be picked up. Actually we are Yanky's publicity agents. Grandad arranged it for us—he's a smashing old forebear! It was he who thought of arriving like that with the weirdie in the taxi—oh boy, what a gimmick! Yank's Continental debew has started with a real explosion, hasn't it?—there must be thousands of kids round this dump.'

Fabrice came over to us. 'I say, Mum, the kiddos are yearning for Yank, you know. They may easily turn ghoulish if you keep him shut up in this yard for ever.'

'Definitely,' said Charles.

'But how did they know he was coming?'

'That's all done by Sigi, our Paris agent. First-class organization!'

The hobbledehoy was now behaving like a prima donna. 'Where can I go and be with my fans? What's happening here? They'll turn dangerous if they don't see me soon. I say, you kids, something has gone wrong. Please send me my Paris agent at once.'

'Here I am.' Sigi appeared out of the blue.

'Well done, Sigi,' said Fabrice, 'jolly spiffing show.'

'So far,' said Yanky, 'but we must keep up the tempo. Where are the kids now? I want to be with them.'

'They've all gone round to the other side of the house,' said Sigi. 'There's a huge garden and a balcony where you can do your act. I've just been rigging up the mike. Come on, no time to waste. Excuse us,' he said to me, ever polite, kissing my hand, 'but if they don't see him soon they will rush the place.' He ran into the house, followed by the other boys.

I turned to Uncle Matthew, feeling I had not made enough fuss of him in all the commotion. 'How d'you do, Payne?'

'Payne's just had a word with your porter,' said Uncle Matthew, 'it seems the street is clear now so I think we'll be on our way. I never meant to bother you at all—Paris isn't on our itinerary—we came here to oblige those boys.'

'Now you are here, do stay. Where are you off to, anyhow?'

'Ypres,' said my uncle. 'Payne and I thought we'd like to see old Wipers again. A fellow in the House told me there's a sector they're preserved exactly as it was. We had the time of our lives in those trenches when we were young, didn't we, Payne?'

'To tell the truth, m'lord, I'd just as soon see them in present circumstances.'

'Nonsense! It will all seem very dull, though better than nothing no doubt.'

'But there's no hurry, is there? Don't go yet. Now you are here, stay for a few days.'

'Oh my dear child, but where?'

'Here, with us, of course.'

'You haven't got room?'

'Darling Uncle Matthew—in that enormous house? Jérôme, our chauffeur, will show Payne where to put the cab and fill it up and everything.'

'Well, that's very civil of you, Fanny. I do feel rather tired. Will there be a cocktail party?'

'Yes, indeed, nearly every evening. I know we've got some people coming presently.'

Uncle Matthew gave me a superior look, saying, 'I thought you'd find out about them sooner or later. Well, that's splendid. If I could see my room I'll go and sit down for a few minutes, then I'll be ready for anything.'

'Take your grandfather up in the lift,' I said to Northey. 'I think we'll give him the Violet room. Then will you send Jérôme out to look after Payne, please? I must go and see what those boys are up to.'

On the stairs I was overtaken by Philip. 'That unspeakable Sigi,' he said.

'Where's Alfred?'

'He's gone to the Quai to complain—he went out by the Chancery as soon as the street began to clear. Now listen, Fanny——'

'Yes, but hurry. I must go and stop it all——'

'This is very important though. Don't tell Alfred. I don't believe those journalists in the Faubourg have understood—I hope that at this very moment they are whizzing back stories of a riot about the Minquiers. Alfred has already informed the F.O. If we can keep up the fiction, this so-called riot will have a splendid effect. Both sides will feel they have gone too far and there'll be a beautiful reconciliation.'

'That would be perfect but I'm afraid it's too good to be likely. They are all in the garden still, according to Sigi.'

'Yes, they are, I've just been through to have a look. The boy is crooning and the fans are swooning and so on. But the only people there who look like journalists all belong to jazz papers—they won't get anything into the general news and they don't even know that they are in the Embassy garden. Now I'm off to the Crillon to see the press boys there. So sealed lips, eh?—and shoo Yanky off, that's your job.'

'Yes, indeed. But Philip—you'll have to square Mees or good little Amy will know all. She's taken 'Chang to the nursery I think.'

'Right, I'll do that first.'

I ran on up to the yellow drawing-room where I found the boys making a perfect exhibition of themselves. The french windows were wide open; on the little balcony Yank Fonzy was bellowing into a microphone; behind him on the parquet my boys and Sigi were stamping and clapping while the huge crowd of children in the garden had lost all control. The scene was vividly evoked afterwards in *Le Discophile* and I cannot do better than to quote: 'L'atmosphère fut indescriptible. Ce jazz-man chanta avec une passion qui n'appartient qu'aux grands prédicateurs. On dansait, on entrait en transes, on se roulait au sol tout comme les convulsionaires de Saint Médard. Le gazon était lacéré, les arbustes déchiquetés—affligeant spectacle.'

I pounced forward and very crossly dragged Master Yanky back into the room, then I disconnected the microphone and slammed the windows on the afflicting spectacle. He was so much surprised at this unaccustomed behaviour that he put up no resistance; in any case his body felt as if it were made of dough. Sigi opened the windows again, went on to the balcony and shouted, 'Tous au Vel d'Hiv': a cry which was taken up by the crowd and had the effect of clearing the garden. Chanting 'Yanky Fonzy—Yanky Fonzy' the fans made off in the direction of the river.

'I'm sorry, Mme l'Ambassadrice,' ever polite, 'but it was the best way to get rid of them.'

'And what next?' I said. I was almost too angry with Sigismond to be able to speak to him, but it must be said that he was the only one of the boys in control of himself. The others were still rolling and stamping about like poor mad things, well and truly sent.

'Please don't worry at all, we are going now. I'll take Yanky,

Charlie and Fabrice to the Club to meet the Duke. After that we're joining up with the kids at the Vélodrome d'Hiver, where there is the great Yanky Fonzy Pop Session you have no doubt seen advertised on all the kiosks.'

'The Club? The Duke?' I had a horrid vision of Yanky in white leather and my boys in black leather bursting in on the Duc de Romanville at the Jockey Club.

'Le Pop Club de France. We've got a rendezvous with Duke Ellington there.'

'Now listen to me, Sigi, I'm not going to have that boy to stay.'

'No, no.' Sigi laughed inwardly, reminding me of his father. 'He has got the honeymoon suite at the George V. I went there to see that everything was all right, which is why I was a bit late. You can't imagine what the flowers and chocolates are like. I managed to nick some and gave them to the concierge for you.'

'Too good of you. And now be off, I beg, and don't use this house any more for your disreputable activities.'

'Count on me, Mme l'Ambassadrice,' he said, with his annoying politeness.

CHAPTER XXII

As six o'clock struck, a remarkable demonstration of English punctuality occurred in the Salon Vert. Uncle Matthew stood at the ready by the fireplace, while a procession, of a sort very familiar to me by now, came across the Salon Jaune. Few days ever passed without this sort of influx. First there was Brown, the butler. Two fine, upstanding men, older than they looked, as could be seen by grey flecks in the hair, but without a line on their faces or, obviously, a care in the world, marched close on his heels. Conservatives I knew they were, from one or other of the Houses of Parliament. Two elderly wives panted and limped after them in an effort to keep up, one arm weighed down by those heavy bags which Conservative women affect and in which they conserve an extraordinary accumulation of rubbish and an extraordinarily small amount of cash. Two or three boys of a demeanour already described, which proclaimed that they had but recently left Eton, trailed along behind them, then two or three pretty, cheerful, elegant schoolgirls who seemed to view their relations rather objectively. They were probably about to be confided to 'families' and I would be asked to keep an eye on them. They looked, and no doubt were, ready for anything and I only hoped that I should not be held responsible when anything overtook them.

Simultaneously Alfred, whom I had not seen since the riot, came through the door which led to his own room and library. I had just time to say, 'Alfred, here's Uncle Matthew who has come for a few days. Imagine, he has brought our two little boys—they all arrived in the middle of the excitement!' when the Conservative wives, breaking into a rapid hobble, managed to catch up with Brown and precede their husbands through the double doors.

'We've brought the whole family!' Loud English voices, familiar since all time. 'Thought you wouldn't mind! Let me see now, I don't think you know my sister-in-law, do you?'

I didn't think I knew any of them, though on the telephone, when they had asked to come, there had been something about having met at Montdore House in the old days; I tried to look welcoming but I was dying for a word with Alfred. 'What would you like to drink?'

'My dear! Liquid fire if you've got it! Vodka—just the very thing! We are utterly, completely and absolutely whacked! Well, the shops all the morning, only to have a look of course—the prices! Then luncheon, that set us back considerably. Then we went to see Myrtle's Madarm—now here's the name (you know, I couldn't remember it yesterday on the telephone).' Delving among the alluvial deposits in the bag and bringing out a crumpled piece of paper. 'Comtesse de Langalluire—that's a tongue-twister if ever there was one! You've never heard of her? I say, I only hope there's nothing fishy. The flat (Boulevard Haussmann) is none too clean and when we arrived Madarm had gone to the police; one of the girls had escaped.'

'No, Mum, she hadn't escaped at all in the end. You know quite well, she'd only gone out to lunch and forgotten to say.'

'So we saw the Monsewer—a sinister little hunchback.'

'The concierge was sweet.' Myrtle was evidently determined to be confided to Madarm whatever happened.

'There was a son who looked quite idiotic and rather frightening.'

'Yes, but I shan't see anything of him as I'll be out all day at the Sorbonne.'

'However, when Madarm herself arrived we thought she seemed rather nice.'

'She had a crew cut,' said one of the boys.

'Her face was sensible, I thought.'

While all this was going on, the Conservative husbands were expressing amazement at finding Uncle Matthew, whom they knew quite well but who clearly did not know them from Adam.

'This is Lord Alconleigh, Peggy.'

'How d'you do? I'm a great friend of Jennifer's.'

'For pity's sake! What on earth do you see in her?'

'It seems you had a spot of trouble here this afternoon?' the other M.P. was saying to Alfred.

'No harm was done; personally I think it will have a good result.

Both sides will have to be more conciliatory—both have been to blame. This may clear the air.'

'Can't see the point of making bad blood over those islands, myself. Massigli tells me they are submerged most of the time.'

'There has never been a more pointless quarrel,' said Alfred, firmly. 'Now I hope the question will be sent up to The Hague and that we shall hear no more about it.'

When everybody was happily chattering, Alfred murmured to me, 'Did you say Charlie and Fabrice are here?'

'Uncle Matthew brought them.'

'How splendid of the old boy. Where are they now?'

'Gone to a concert, with Sigi.'

'Good. That's very good news. Now we must take serious steps—get them into a lycée if we can——'

Brown reappeared, announcing 'Madame la Duchesse de Sauveterre and Monsieur le Marquis de Valhubert.'

'We've just heard about your riot,' said Charles-Edouard, 'we called to see if you were alive. When the concierge said you were at home we came up. Tante Odile is in Paris for a few days.'

'How kind you are.' I was frantic inside because of not knowing what names to put to the loud Conservative voices. To my relief, Alfred did the introducing. When he got to Uncle Matthew, I said, 'My uncle saw more of the riot than any of us because he arrived when it was at its worst and drove through the thick of it, escorted by policemen——'

'I call that very brave,' said an M.P.

'My dear fellow, they were a perfectly harmless lot—just a pack of children. I didn't think much of it—if that's the best they can put on——'

'Never underestimate a French crowd,' said the Duchess. 'I speak with knowledge. Three of my grandmothers perished in the Terror.'

'Three!' said Uncle Matthew, much interested. 'Did you have three grandfathers as well? What happened to them?'

'We say grandmothers when we mean ancestresses,' Charles-Edouard explained.

The Duchess said, 'Oh, various things. One of them was murdered in the Jacquerie and the best housemaid I ever had was shot dead in the Stavisky riots. So don't talk to me of a French crowd being harmless.'

Uncle Matthew seemed to be struggling to remember something and came out with, 'Joan of Arc—didn't she have a sticky end? I suppose she was a relation of yours?'

'Certainly, if she was a d'Orléans, as most people think nowadays.'

'Really?' said Charles-Edouard, with his inward laugh. 'Why do they?'

'Voyons, mon cher! La Pucelle d'Orléans! Did she not sit at the King's table? That simple fact alone is all the proof I need. For a woman who was not born to sit at the table of a King of France would be a greater miracle than any voices, let me tell you.'

'My aunt takes no account of historical characters unless they happen to be relations of hers. Luckily they nearly all are. Charles X was a great-grandfather so that arranges the legitimate royal lines of every country except Russia, while her Murat grandmother brings in Napoleon and the Marshals.'

Mme de Sauveterre asked Alfred to show her his library which had been redecorated during the time of Sir Louis Leone. She said she had seen coloured photographs of it in a magazine which Jacques Oudineau had brought down to Boisdormant. 'He knows I like picture papers so he brings me all the ones he has finished with when he comes to see his father. You wouldn't believe how extravagant he is—abonné to everything under the sun and you know the price they are nowadays. People are getting much too rich, it can't be a good thing.'

'I want to see Jacques Oudineau,' said Charles-Edouard. 'I hear he has got a Moreau l'aîné he wouldn't mind selling——'

Uncle Matthew began telling the Conservatives about Yanky. 'Teenage Beats,' I heard him say. 'You must remember the name, Yanky Fonzy, and ask for his records because he gets money for every one they sell. Of course, I'm not saying he's Galli-Curci——'

I took Valhubert by the arm. 'I must have a word with you.' In a loud voice I added, 'Come in here, the National Gallery has sent us a large, dull picture and I want you to advise me where to hang it.' We went into the yellow drawing-room. 'Have you seen Grace this evening?'

'Not yet. When we got back from the country my concierge said there had been this riot so I drove straight on here to see what it was all about.'

I told him everything. He shook with laughter, especially when I got to the Club and the Duke. 'But my dear Fanny, what now? What does Alfred say?'

'You do realize we must never tell him about the riot not being real. He would look the most awful fool if it got out—I haven't told Grace by the way——'

'No, better not. Pity to spoil her fun—an anti-English riot is just her affair—she must be thrilled!'

'She is naughty! Philip says if we can keep up the fiction there's some hope of making them all see sense. As for the boys, Alfred doesn't know the full horror. When these people have gone I shall have to explain about Yanky and the Showbiz. Oh, Charles-Edouard, *children*!'

'Don't worry. They'll soon be off our hands, in prison.'

'Here's Philip, oh good. So what's up?'

'It's wonderful. I've been with the press boys ever since I saw you. The best hoax of all time. Simply nobody has twigged. The stories will be amazing, you'll see.'

The newspapers played up exactly as Philip had hoped they would. The reputable ones stated, quite soberly, correctly as far as it went, that several hundred students had gathered outside the British Embassy shouting slogans and that after about half an hour they had dispersed of their own accord. These reports were accompanied by editorial comment to the effect that if there was a serious misunderstanding between France and England it was time that it should be cleared up. Perhaps the English had not used the most tactful of methods in pressing their rightful claim to the Minquiers Islands. No doubt it had been necessary to entertain Dr. Niam (now in Pekin) but the timing of his visit had been unfortunate. As for the European Army, while we in England realized its desirability and inevitability, we had not shown much comprehension of French difficulties in this respect. All in all, we should do well to keep in with our friends since our enemies were legion. The French papers were even more conciliatory, digging into the history of the Entente and saying that so solid an edifice was not to be shaken by a few students exhibiting bad manners.

The Grumpy group reported the affair in their own inimitable style:

'POST' MAN IN PARIS RIOTS
I WALK WITH THE SCREAMING TEN THOUSAND

According to Mockbar, a fearful mob, baying for British blood, had milled in the Faubourg utterly uncontrolled by the police who looked as if they would join in for tuppence. It reminded him of the worst days of the Commune. No mention of sheltering among the ancient bibelots; heroic Mockbar had swayed to and fro in the thick of young devils who, had they guessed he was a Briton, would have scuppered him then and there. While, inside the Embassy, women wailed and babies wept ('That's you and 'Chang, Northey,' I said), the Ambassador had escaped by a back door and taken shelter at the Quai d'Orsay. His First Secretary was drinking at the bar of a nearby hotel.

Lord Grumpy's editorial said: British lives are threatened, British property is menaced. Where? Behind the Iron Curtain? In barbarous lands across the seas? Not at all. These things occurred in Paris. How did our Ambassador the Pastoral Theologian respond to the outrage? Was he at his post? We think there should be a full inquiry into the events of this black day in the history of British diplomacy. If Sir Alfred Wincham has failed to do his duty, he should go.

Lord Grumpy's remarks, as usual, gave much pleasure. They were read with delight and absolutely unheeded by several million Englishmen. Later in the week, Alfred went home to report on the, now vastly improved, situation and to see, with the Foreign Office experts, what could be done to re-establish the Entente. This was made easier by the fact that Junior across the Atlantic was annoying Mother and Auntie with behaviour learnt, it must be said, at their knees. Under a cunning pretext of anti-colonialism, the Americans were scooping up trade in a part of the world where hitherto French and English interests had been paramount. The quarrel over the Eels began to look silly; as soon as the newspapers had lost interest in them and gone on to more important subjects, the dispute was quietly submitted to The Hague Court where the islands were judged to belong to England. In harmony with the spirit of the age, we then granted them full independence.

During the Anglo-French honeymoon which now began, Basil disembarked his atom marchers at Calais. They were all in fancy dress, the men in kilts, the women in trousers; the weather was clear and sparkling and not too cold; the whole expedition was permeated from the start with a holiday atmosphere. Since atom objectors do not exist in France, literally the only public matter on which all Frenchmen are united being the desirability of a Bomb of one's own, the French immediately assumed that the march was a congratulatory gesture to unite Aldermaston with Saclay. The word *jumelage* was freely used by the newspapers; the two establishments were henceforward twin sisters, friends for ever. When the Britons got off their boat they were met with flowers, flags, speeches and wine; from the moment they landed they hardly drew a sober breath. None of them knew any French so, cleverly prompted by Basil, they concluded that the reception meant that the whole population felt as they did; in a joyful Kermesse they danced rather than marched across Normandy. They were not allowed to pay for a meal, a drink or a bed; Basil and his Grandad, who had extorted huge sums for the all-in trip, garnered a rich profit. At Saclay the Atom Minister himself, sent by Northey, was there to greet them. There were more flowers, more flags, stronger wine and longer speeches. The Britons were cordially invited to go to the Sahara and witness the first French atomic explosion whenever it should take place. In a happy haze of drunken misapprehension, they were then driven in official motors, with a circus turn of motorbicyclists escorting them, to Orly and sent home free by Air France.

'Never, since the war, have Anglo-French relations been so cloudless,' said The Times. The Daily Telegraph said, 'Sir Alfred Wincham's wise and subtle manœuvring in a difficult situation has been triumphantly successful.' Lord Grumpy said the cunning French had twisted the lion's tail once more and that their valet, Wincham, ought to be sent, forthwith, to Rangoon. Plans and projects for The Visit were now put into operation.

CHAPTER XXIII

'I WOULDN'T mind the boys calling me Dad,' said Alfred (who did mind, however, and had made great efforts, successful with David and Baz, to be called Father), 'if only they wouldn't pronounce it Dud.'

It was the morning after the riot; Grace and Charles-Edouard had come round for another conference on what could be done with the children. Our two had had breakfast with Alfred; there had been a long, perfectly fruitless argument on lines which were becoming all too familiar. In a sincere effort to use language that Alfred could understand they explained that members of the Showbiz were the aristocracy of the modern world; that Yanky was its King and that as Yanky's gentlemen-in-waiting they had the most covetable position of any living teenagers. Alfred asked what their plans were for the immediate future. 'Driftin' with Yank to Russia,' was the reply. (Driftin', it seems, is Showbiz for touring.) They were to drift through France, Switzerland and Czechoslovakia, possibly taking in the Balkans; their final objective was Moscow. 'So lucky we all opted to learn Russian at school.'

'And wherever we appear,' Fabrice said, 'the kids will go screaming, raving mad because in those countries everybody has Yanky's discs which they buy on the black market. You should see the fan-mail he gets from iron teenagers.'

Alfred then spoke, in the tongue of our ancestors. He summoned up all his wisdom, all his eloquence, he drew tears from his own eyes as he argued his case for civilization. They listened politely for an hour. When they were quite sure he had finished and that they were in no way interrupting him they replied that his fate had been an example to them. They couldn't help noticing that he had led a sorrowful existence year after year, growing old without having known any pleasure, fun or enjoyment and that as a result he had landed up in this deplorable, antiquated giggle-academy, the English Embassy at Paris.

'When I left the room,' he said, after telling us all this, 'I heard Charlie say to Fabrice "Poor Dud, he's had it!" I think that pretty well sums up their attitude. We are duds, Valhubert, and we've had it. Yes, even you.'

'I don't know why you should say even me. Specially me, I should have thought.'

'You are a man of action and as such they might have had a certain respect for you. Of course they know quite well that you had a good war, but I'm afraid that means nothing to them because what were you fighting for? They don't care a fig for liberty, equality, fraternity or any of our values—still less for their King and Country. The be-all and end-all of their existence is to have a good time. They think they could have rocked and rolled quite well under Hitler and no doubt so they could.' Alfred buried his face in his hands and said despairingly, 'The black men affirm that we are in full decadence. Nothing could be truer, if these boys are typical of their generation and if they really mean all the things they told me just now. The barbarians had better take over without more ado. We made the last stand against them. At least we have that to be proud of. But you have fought in vain, my life's work has come to nothing—this job the most pointless part of it, very likely.'

'My dear Ambassador,' said Valhubert, 'you take it all too tragically. Young persons in prosperous circumstances live for pleasure. They always have and no doubt they always will. When I think what Fabrice and I were like, right up to the war! Between women and hunting, we never had a serious thought. Of course when we were Sigi's age, our noses were pressed in the direction of a grindstone by force of economic sanctions. If we could have earned £9 a week packing shavers do you really think we would have stayed at the lycée another hour? And I bet we'd have found some watertight method of nicking, by the way.'

'I'm sorry, Valhubert, but I cannot agree with you. Many adolescents, even rich ones, have a love of learning for its own sake. I know, because as a don I have had hundreds of civilized rich young men through my hands.'

'But with these boys you must face the fact that they are not, and never will be, intellectuals. Hard for you, I know—still two out of four in your family took firsts, quite an honourable percentage. The other two never will, in a hundred years. In the end they will probably be the most conformist all the same.'

'But nowadays no respectable career is open to people without degrees.'

'To speak practically. Sigi will be very rich—I have never had to work so I can't exactly blame him if he doesn't, can I? Little Fabrice only has to play his cards well enough to refrain from throwing them in Tante Odile's face to be in the same circumstances.'

'But Charlie must earn his living.'

'Don't you see, darling,' I intervened, 'the point is that he can. He was making this huge amount in London, and now, at sixteen, he is one of the kings of Showbiz!' I trust that a note of pride could not be detected as I said these words.

'You torture me. Have we brought a human soul to this stage of development only to see him promoting pop sessions?'

'But, dearest, how can we prevent it? Charles-Edouard is quite right. We can't do more for the boys now (any of them) than look on at their vagaries with tolerance and provide a background when they need one.' Twinge of conscience here. Had I been nice enough to David?

Valhubert said, 'Exactly. They are grown up. Each man in the last resort is responsible for himself. Let them be—let them go. Sigi tells me they are drifting off tomorrow with Yanky Fonzy, taking 20 per cent of his earnings, plus their expenses and anything else they can nick. All right. Count it as the Grand Tour; they'll see the world; it's better than packing. When they come back, if they are eighteen by then, they can go to the wars like everybody else. Only do send Charlie this afternoon to see Tante Odile.'

'How French you are, Charles-Edouard,' said Grace, laughing.

'Hot news!' This was Northey, coming in with my breakfast. 'The Bomb from Brum has buggered!'

'Already? And the boys never came to say goodbye?'

'The point is, he has left them behind. There was the most terrific bust up yesterday at Le Pop Club and he has gone.'

'Can it be true? What happened?'

'It was all about the publicity. You see when Yank saw those kids in Main Street—biggest outdoor reception even he has dreamed of—he thought he'd never had it so good. He expected to hit the headlines on the front pages. Grandfather in the taxi, he thought, gave that little extra something that journalists love, then the crowds, the police, Alfred going to the Quai (I must say it wrung my withers not telling the dear little soul about it).'

'If you had, Northey——'

'Yes, well, I didn't, did I? So Yank thought the boys were geniuses and honestly, Fanny, in a way they were. You've got to hand it to Sigi —he mobilized that enormous crowd—then the Vel d'Hiv was a whizz, every teenager in Paris must have been there and the receipts broke all records. At the Club they were congratulating Yank on his wonderful agents and he was so pleased he kept signing travellers' cheques, giving them to the boys. Of course he could hardly wait to see the papers. Came the Dawn—quelle horrible surprise! As you know, sweet Amy and the rest of them barked up the wrong tree—Yank might have stayed in London for all they knew and the bitter thing was his wonderful riot was put down to those silly old islands. His name wasn't mentioned in the news at all—no photographs of him with the screaming kids—taxi gimmick thrown away. A few paragraphs in the entertainment pages saying that he had arrived in Paris and sang from a balcony in the Avenue Gabriel. There'll be a story in the jazz papers of course, but he always has them on his side and this time he'd counted on the dailies. In short, Sigi did marvels, but he only warned the jazz journalists and he got all of them in the garden. He never thought of telling the others—he had no idea, of course, that there would be such a mob of kids in Main Street. So the whole thing has fallen as flat as a pancake. Yank says that's what comes of dealing with bloody amateurs; he telephoned to London for his old agent he's always had and as soon as he arrived they drifted off——'

'Northey! It's too interesting and unexpected! So how are the boys taking it?'

'If you ask me, they are relieved. They had begun to see that Yanky is a most unpleasant person. And Fanny, it's my opinion they've had about enough of earning their own livings. They admit now that the shavers were a tremendous bore—it seems you are shut up in a horrible sort of place which brings on headaches. Driftin' would have been rather fun, but not with Yank. He has put them right off the Showbiz— and they didn't much care for the people at the Club (except for the Duke, who is heaven). They were all on Yanky's side and made the boys feel inferior. Then one of their friends at Eton has asked them to a boys' shoot in Jan which they long to accept. Apparently it's a spiffing house to stay in, where the oldies know their place. They'd like to become ordinary again, you know—they'd really give anything to go back to Eton.'

'Well, that's out of the question—silly little fools. We shall have to see what can be done with them—Condorcet probably, before they cram for Oxford. Meanwhile it's almost the Christmas holidays and they can go to their old shoot. Oh, darling, you don't know what a weight off my mind this is!'

At dinner that evening the boys were studiously normal. They wore dinner jackets, their hair, which had been standing on end, was now watered and brushed in the usual way; they were clean. They gave us looks which I well remembered from their early nursery days and which I could remember bestowing, myself, on the grown-ups; looks which said if all can be forgotten and forgiven we will be good again. They called Alfred Father, and asked him to explain about the C.E.D. They asked me what books I had been reading—I quite expected them to say 'Have you been abroad lately?' a favourite gambit with people they hardly knew. They were sweet and attentive to Uncle Matthew and told him about the shoot they were going to. His old face lit up because it had once belonged to a relation of his and he had shot there many a time in the past.

'Who has got it now?'

'The father of our friend Beagle. He has made nine (you know, the big ones, millions, I mean), since the war.'

'Like blissful Jacques Oudineau,' said Northey, half to herself.

'Has he indeed? You want to look out, in the Sally Beds, not to shoot up the hill. Feller peppered me there once good and proper. Where's young Fonzy this evening?'

Sheepish looks. 'Gone to Moscow,' said Northey.

'What's he want to do that for? Payne and I had our luncheon at a place where the cabmen eat. They haven't got proper shelters; this is a restaurant. Dangerous good snack. We got talking with a Russian there who seemed heartily dissatisfied with his government—you'd hardly believe the things he told us. Now young Fonzy is a very civil chap. He gave me a lot of his records, signed. Of course the signature doesn't make the smallest difference—I mean you can't hear it—but he meant it kindly no doubt.'

'What have you been doing all day, Uncle Matthew?'

'After luncheon we went to the museum. Saw old Foch's coat and a lot of dummy horses and some pictures of battles we liked very much. Then I came back to see if there would be a cocktail party but you were out.'

'Oh bother, yes—it was a National Day we had to go to.'

'It didn't matter. I was rather tired you know, really.'

After dinner he said it was bedtime and he'd better say goodbye. 'We have an early start—I shan't come and disturb you in the morning, Fanny—I know you've never been much use before seven and I want to be off at half past five. Many thanks. Payne and I have enjoyed ourselves.'

'Come again,' I said.

All three boys were invited to stay at Boisdormant. Before they left I screwed up my courage to have a long-postponed talk with Fabrice. This was a moment I had always dreaded, when I must tell him who his father was. He knew that my cousin Linda was his mother and presumably thought that her husband, Christian Talbot, whose surname he bore, was his father. He had never seen Christian or exhibited any interest whatever in him and since he had asked no questions I had not raised the subject. I found it, for some reason, deeply embarrassing to do so.

'Fabrice, darling, you're sixteen now——'

'Definitely.'

'Which is really grown up. In fact you have taken charge of your own life; you're not a child any more. So I suppose I can talk frankly to you——'

'If this is a pi-jaw hadn't I better fetch Charlie?'

'No, it isn't. One doesn't pi-jaw with one's fellow grown-ups. I simply want to talk about your parents. Now I've always told you that my darling cousin Linda was your mother.'

'Definitely. And my father was the son of this old woman we are going to stay with.'

'Yes, but how did you know?'

'Mum, you are a scream! Of course I've known since I was nine—from the very first moment I saw Sigi at Easterfields. He had heard the Nannies telling each other when he was meant to be asleep.'

I suppose my feelings on hearing this must have been the same as those of a mother who finds that her girl has been conversant with the facts of life since childhood. Thankful, really, not to have to enter into difficult explanations, I felt slightly aggrieved to think that Fabrice had kept such important knowledge from me all these years and not best pleased at the way in which he had found it out.

'Everything's always arranged by Sigi,' I said, crossly. 'Never mind. So, darling, be very nice to your grandmother, won't you?'

'Then she might adopt me and leave me a lot of money?'

'Oh dear! How cold-blooded you are——'

But I knew that at sixteen people put on a cold-blooded air partly because they are terrified of betraying sentiments which might embarrass them. Fabrice would be incapable now of saying that Alfred and I were his heart's father and mother; that would come much later, if at all.

He went on, 'Sigi thinks we might make a syndicate for getting what we can out of her. She can take the place of Yanky in our lives.'

'Good luck to you!' I said. 'I expect that Duchess is capable of looking after herself—just like Yanky. You boys aren't quite as clever as you think you are——'

'Don't be ghoulish, Mum.'

They stayed a week at Boisdormant and came back in tearing spirits, having greatly enjoyed themselves. Oudineau had taken them out shooting every day and Jacques Oudineau, who kept a little aeroplane at a nearby aero-club, had allowed them to flop out of it in parachutes to their hearts' content. In the evenings they had listened with real, not simulated, interest to the Duchess's endless tales of her family and the history of Boisdormant. They were taking notes of episodes suitable to be incorporated in the Son et Lumière and other attractions for tourists which they planned to produce there the following summer. Jacques Oudineau would see to the technical details, Sigi was to be publicity agent in Paris while our boys, collaborating with Basil and Grandad, would supply an endless stream of Britons. Beautiful Boisdormant was clearly destined to wake up one day and find itself the French Woburn. As these activities were not likely to get the boys into much trouble and could easily be combined with their lessons, I could only feel thankful at the turn their lives had taken. Jacques Oudineau, young and dynamic, seemed to have gained a far more complete ascendancy over them in one week than Alfred and I during their whole lives; they could only talk of him. He had decreed that they must now work very hard and pass all the exams with which the modern child is plagued; then he would take them into his business and they would be happy ever after. As for the Duchess, according to Valhubert she found that Fabrice more than came up to her expectations. As soon as she saw Uncle Matthew, she said, she realized that the family was bien. Fabrice himself then won her heart by looking like her late son and exhibiting perfect manners. Her will, it seemed, had already been altered in his favour.

CHAPTER XXIV

AFTER Christmas, Philip was posted to Moscow. It seemed to me that everybody had either gone or was going there. M. Bouche-Bontemps, in a fur hat, was conferring with Mr. K. at the Kremlin; the French papers were full of lines and sidelines on Russia, no photograph without its onion dome. On Boxing Day, David and Dawn had their baby in a snowstorm between Omsk and Tomsk, causing the maximum amount of trouble to Alfred's colleague in Moscow; telegrams flew back and forth. They were illegally on Soviet territory; it was not easy to get permission for them to stay there until David should be out of danger. (The other two had risen above the experience but it had nearly killed him.) However, the kind Ambassadress took them all in; knowing by experience how difficult it would be to budge them again, I felt sorry for the Ambassador. Yanky Fonzy was enjoying a triumphant season at the Bolshoi. Basil and Grandad had just got their visas and were going to Moscow to negotiate a long-term exchange of tourists.

It was more of a blow than a surprise to learn that we were to lose Philip. We had always known that he was due for a move and that he had only been left at Paris long enough to see us comfortably into the Embassy before becoming Counsellor somewhere else. When he came to tell me his news I said, 'Talk about a Pull to the East—I feel as if I were living in the last act of *The Three Sisters*. All we get back from Moscow is Hector Dexter, a very poor exchange for you and Northey.'

'How d'you mean, me and Northey?'

'I naturally suppose you'll be taking her. You're not going to leave her here with a broken heart, Philip—don't tell me that?'

'Oh, dearest Fanny, do I really want the whole of the Praesidium milling round my dacha? Not to speak of faithful wolves and sweet Siberian crows in one's bedroom?'

'As soon as she's married, with a baby, all that will stop, I've seen it so often. How is your love for Grace?'

'Very hopeless, what with one thing and another. My own fault for telling Mees about St. Expédite. Every time I go to St. Roch, there she is keenly putting up candles. It's quite ridiculous—the saint doesn't know which way to turn, as Mees said herself, last time we met there.'

'Chuck the whole thing and marry her.'

'What a matchmaker you are.'

'It's time the poor duck was settled. Besides, think how lonely you'd be in Moscow, without any of us.'

'Good for trade,' said Philip, 'promotion, important post and so forth, but I can't say I greatly look forward to it. I would certainly find it much jollier if I had Mees there. But what would you do without her yourself?'

'It won't be the same, but I can have sister Jean now. The Chelsea setter has already found another girl with more money and a larger tiara, and Jean is looking for a job.'

'Oh dear—how I hate taking irrevocable decisions!'

'Go on, Philip. No time like the present. She's in her office—go and propose to her this very minute.'

'All right. So long as you realize that it's entirely your responsibility.' He kissed me on both cheeks and went off.

I was now seized by misgivings. Left to himself, would not Philip have havered and wavered and in the end gone away without coming to a decision? I had induced him to propose, deliberately ignoring the wise reflections of Alfred, although I knew that there was a great deal of truth in them. On the face of it, Philip had the makings of an excellent husband. Attractive, kind, clever, gay and amusing, never boring, he was also very rich. Nevertheless something was missing, some sort of intensity or ardent flame which, had it existed, might well have won over Grace, or, in the old Oxford days, me myself. Furthermore, he had been in love with us as he was not with Northey. She had fallen in love at first sight, so she loved an image which she had invented and which might easily be rubbed away in daily wear and tear. On the other hand, I told myself, there are no rules for successful marriage. Northey and Philip seemed rather suited, she so lively, he so orthodox; her superabundant vitality, the maternal instinct she lavished on creatures, would turn into their proper channel when she had babies; she was accustomed, now, to Embassy life.

Another factor, I must say, weighed with me. Mockbar had, of late, taken Northey as the heroine of his page. It was no secret now to the readers of the *Daily Post* that the Marquis de Valhubert, who had escorted the world's most beautiful women, was her 'friend'. His British-born wife was expecting her fifth child in March; Mockbar gave the impression that, after this happy event, Valhubert would announce his engagement to Northey.

'Really, darling,' Grace said, 'I shall have to find out what sort of thing the bridegroom's wife is expected to wear at a wedding.'

'Poor soul,' was Northey's reflection, 'he has found out the truth about the riots and he is minding. Hard put to it to mollify Lord

Grumpy, just as the children are getting to the age of a glass of wine with their food, you know. However, there's hot news today. M. Cruas is engaged to Phyllis McFee!'

I wondered why these characters were suddenly being liquidated. M. Cruas may have been based on fact; Phyllis McFee was certainly a figment of Northey's imagination; both played a useful part in what Philip called 'the carry-on'. During the last week or two they had been unusually busy—hardly a day without one or other being invoked. It seemed rash of her to make such a clean sweep; I felt a little uneasy. 'Is it wise to get rid of them both at a blow?' I asked.

'Much as I shall miss the beloveds, I have their happiness to consider. Each for each is what we teach. They are buggering off on a long, long honeymoon in Asia Minor.'

Everything considered, was it not my duty to Louisa to get this wayward creature married if I could?

Northey stood in the doorway. Her eyes were like blue brilliants; she radiated happiness. She stood quite still and said, 'It's me, Fanny! I'm engaged!'

'Darling—yes, I know. I can't tell you how delighted I am!'

'You know?'

'Philip told me.'

'But I've only just told him.'

I saw that I had been tactless, of course she would not like the idea of Philip having discussed the matter beforehand.

'He was looking everywhere for you and I suppose he felt so happy that he couldn't resist telling me.'

'Oh yes, I see—he did very kindly offer. Only think, Fanny, two short weeks ago I would have accepted.' She shuddered.

'But, darling, I don't quite understand. I thought you said you were engaged?'

'Yes. I'm engaged to Jacques Oudineau.'

PENGUIN OMNIBUSES

☐ **_Victorian Villainies_**

Fraud, murder, political intrigue and horror are the ingredients of these four Victorian thrillers, selected by Hugh Greene and Graham Greene.

☐ **_The Balkan Trilogy_ Olivia Manning**

This acclaimed trilogy – _The Great Fortune, The Spoilt City_ and _Friends and Heroes_ – is the portrait of a marriage, and an exciting recreation of civilian life in the Second World War. 'It amuses, it diverts, and it informs' – Frederick Raphael

☐ **_The Penguin Collected Stories of Isaac Bashevis Singer_**

Forty-seven marvellous tales of Jewish magic, faith and exile. 'Never was the Nobel Prize more deserved . . . He belongs with the giants' – _Sunday Times_

☐ **_The Penguin Essays of George Orwell_**

Famous pieces on 'The Decline of the English Murder', 'Shooting an Elephant', political issues and P. G. Wodehouse feature in this edition of forty-one essays, criticism and sketches – all classics of English prose.

☐ **_Further Chronicles of Fairacre_ 'Miss Read'**

Full of humour, warmth and charm, these four novels – _Miss Clare Remembers, Over the Gate, The Fairacre Festival_ and _Emily Davis_ – make up an unforgettable picture of English village life.

☐ **_The Penguin Complete Sherlock Holmes_ Sir Arthur Conan Doyle**

With the fifty-six classic short stories, plus _A Study in Scarlet, The Sign of Four, The Hound of the Baskervilles_ and _The Valley of Fear_, this volume contains the remarkable career of Baker Street's most famous resident.

PENGUIN OMNIBUSES

☐ *Life with Jeeves* **P. G. Wodehouse**

Containing *Right Ho, Jeeves, The Inimitable Jeeves* and *Very Good, Jeeves!* in which Wodehouse lures us, once again, into the ever-green world of Bertie Wooster, his terrifying Aunt Agatha, his man Jeeves and other eggs, good and bad.

☐ *The Penguin Book of Ghost Stories*

An anthology to set the spine tingling, including stories by Zola, Kleist, Sir Walter Scott, M. R. James, Elizabeth Bowen and A. S. Byatt.

☐ *The Penguin Book of Horror Stories*

Including stories by Maupassant, Poe, Gautier, Conan Doyle, L. P. Hartley and Ray Bradbury, in a selection of the most horrifying horror from the eighteenth century to the present day.

☐ *The Penguin Complete Novels of Jane Austen*

Containing the seven great novels: *Sense and Sensibility, Pride and Prejudice, Mansfield Park, Emma, Northanger Abbey, Persuasion* and *Lady Susan*.

☐ *Perfick, Perfick!* **H. E. Bates**

The adventures of the irrepressible Larkin family, in four novels: *The Darling Buds of May, A Breath of French Air, When the Green Woods Laugh* and *Oh! To Be in England*.

☐ *Famous Trials*
Harry Hodge and James H. Hodge

From Madeleine Smith to Dr Crippen and Lord Haw-Haw, this volume contains the most sensational murder and treason trials, selected by John Mortimer from the classic Penguin Famous Trials series.

A CHOICE OF PENGUINS

☐ **Small World** David Lodge

A jet-propelled academic romance, sequel to *Changing Places*. 'A new comic débâcle on every page' – *The Times*. 'Here is everything one expects from Lodge but three times as entertaining as anything he has written before' – *Sunday Telegraph*

☐ **The Neverending Story** Michael Ende

The international bestseller, now a major film: 'A tale of magical adventure, pursuit and delay, danger, suspense, triumph' – *The Times Literary Supplement*

☐ **The Sword of Honour Trilogy** Evelyn Waugh

Containing *Men at Arms, Officers and Gentlemen* and *Unconditional Surrender*, the trilogy described by Cyril Connolly as 'unquestionably the finest novels to have come out of the war'.

☐ **The Honorary Consul** Graham Greene

In a provincial Argentinian town, a group of revolutionaries kidnap the wrong man . . . 'The tension never relaxes and one reads hungrily from page to page, dreading the moment it will all end' – Auberon Waugh in the *Evening Standard*

☐ **The First Rumpole Omnibus** John Mortimer

Containing *Rumpole of the Bailey*, *The Trials of Rumpole* and *Rumpole's Return*. 'A fruity, foxy masterpiece, defender of our wilting faith in mankind' – *Sunday Times*

☐ **Scandal** A. N. Wilson

Sexual peccadillos, treason and blackmail are all ingredients on the boil in A. N. Wilson's new, *cordon noir* comedy. 'Drily witty, deliciously nasty' – *Sunday Telegraph*

A CHOICE OF PENGUINS

☐ *Stanley and the Women* **Kingsley Amis**

'Very good, very powerful . . . beautifully written . . . This is Amis *père* at his best' – Anthony Burgess in the *Observer*. 'Everybody should read it' – *Daily Mail*

☐ *The Mysterious Mr Ripley* **Patricia Highsmith**

Containing *The Talented Mr Ripley, Ripley Underground* and *Ripley's Game*. 'Patricia Highsmith is the poet of apprehension' – Graham Greene. 'The Ripley books are marvellously, insanely readable' – *The Times*

☐ *Earthly Powers* **Anthony Burgess**

'Crowded, crammed, bursting with manic erudition, garlicky puns, omnilingual jokes . . . (a novel) which meshes the real and personalized history of the twentieth century' – Martin Amis

☐ *Life & Times of Michael K* **J. M. Coetzee**

The Booker Prize-winning novel: 'It is hard to convey . . . just what Coetzee's special quality is. His writing gives off whiffs of Conrad, of Nabokov, of Golding, of the Paul Theroux of *The Mosquito Coast*. But he is none of these, he is a harsh, compelling new voice' – Victoria Glendinning

☐ *The Stories of William Trevor*

'Trevor packs into each separate five or six thousand words more richness, more laughter, more ache, more multifarious human-ness than many good writers manage to get into a whole novel' – *Punch*

☐ *The Book of Laughter and Forgetting*
Milan Kundera

'A whirling dance of a book . . . a masterpiece full of angels, terror, ostriches and love . . . No question about it. The most important novel published in Britain this year' – Salman Rushdie

A CHOICE OF PENGUINS

☐ **Further Chronicles of Fairacre** **'Miss Read'**

Full of humour, warmth and charm, these four novels – *Miss Clare Remembers, Over the Gate, The Fairacre Festival* and *Emily Davis* – make up an unforgettable picture of English village life.

☐ **Callanish** **William Horwood**

From the acclaimed author of *Duncton Wood*, this is the haunting story of Creggan, the captured golden eagle, and his struggle to be free.

☐ **Act of Darkness** **Francis King**

Anglo-India in the 1930s, where a peculiarly vicious murder triggers 'A terrific mystery story . . . a darkly luminous parable about innocence and evil' – *The New York Times*. 'Brilliantly successful' – *Daily Mail*. 'Unputdownable' – *Standard*

☐ **Death in Cyprus** **M. M. Kaye**

Holidaying on Aphrodite's beautiful island, Amanda finds herself caught up in a murder mystery in which no one, not even the attractive painter Steven Howard, is quite what they seem . . .

☐ **Lace** **Shirley Conran**

Lace is, quite simply, a publishing sensation: the story of Judy, Kate, Pagan and Maxine; the bestselling novel that teaches men about women, and women about themselves. 'Riches, bitches, sex and jetsetters' locations – they're all there' – *Sunday Express*

A CHOICE OF PENGUINS

☐ **West of Sunset Dirk Bogarde**

'His virtues as a writer are precisely those which make him the most compelling screen actor of his generation,' is what *The Times* said about Bogarde's savage, funny, romantic novel set in the gaudy wastes of Los Angeles.

☐ **The Riverside Villas Murder Kingsley Amis**

Marital duplicity, sexual discovery and murder with a thirties back-cloth: 'Amis in top form' – *The Times*. 'Delectable from page to page . . . effortlessly witty' – C. P. Snow in the *Financial Times*

☐ **A Dark and Distant Shore Reay Tannahill**

Vilia is the unforgettable heroine, Kinveil Castle is her destiny, in this full-blooded saga spanning a century of Victoriana, empire, hatreds and love affairs. 'A marvellous blend of *Gone with the Wind* and *The Thorn Birds*. You will enjoy every page' – *Daily Mirror*

☐ **Kingsley's Touch John Collee**

'Gripping . . . I recommend this chilling and elegantly written medical thriller' – *Daily Express*. 'An absolutely outstanding storyteller' – *Daily Telegraph*

☐ **The Far Pavilions M. M. Kaye**

Holding all the romance and high adventure of nineteenth-century India, M. M. Kaye's magnificent, now famous, novel has at its heart the passionate love of an Englishman for Juli, his Indian princess. 'Wildly exciting' – *Daily Telegraph*

A CHOICE OF PENGUINS

☐ *Man and the Natural World* **Keith Thomas**

Changing attitudes in England, 1500–1800. 'An encyclopedic study of man's relationship to animals and plants . . . a book to read again and again' – Paul Theroux, *Sunday Times* Books of the Year

☐ *Jean Rhys: Letters 1931–66*
Edited by Francis Wyndham and Diana Melly

'Eloquent and invaluable . . . her life emerges, and with it a portrait of an unexpectedly indomitable figure' – Marina Warner in the *Sunday Times*

☐ *The French Revolution* **Christopher Hibbert**

'One of the best accounts of the Revolution that I know . . . Mr Hibbert is outstanding' – J. H. Plumb in the *Sunday Telegraph*

☐ *Isak Dinesen* **Judith Thurman**

The acclaimed life of Karen Blixen, 'beautiful bride, disappointed wife, radiant lover, bereft and widowed woman, writer, sibyl, Scheherazade, child of Lucifer, Baroness; always a unique human being . . . an assiduously researched and finely narrated biography' – *Books & Bookmen*

☐ *The Amateur Naturalist*
Gerald Durrell with Lee Durrell

'Delight . . . on every page . . . packed with authoritative writing, learning without pomposity . . . it represents a real bargain' – *The Times Educational Supplement*. 'What treats are in store for the average British household' – *Daily Express*

☐ *When the Wind Blows* **Raymond Briggs**

'A visual parable against nuclear war: all the more chilling for being in the form of a strip cartoon' – *Sunday Times*. 'The most eloquent anti-Bomb statement you are likely to read' – *Daily Mail*